PETER STRAUB

The Throat

HarperCollins*Publishers*

HarperCollins*Publishers*
77–85 Fulham Palace Road,
Hammersmith, London W6 8JB

Special overseas edition 1993
1 3 5 7 9 8 6 4 2

First published in Great Britain by
HarperCollins*Publishers* 1993

Copyright © Seafront Corporation 1993

ISBN 0 586 21849 1

Set in Times

Printed in Great Britain by
Clays Ltd, St Ives plc

PETER STRAUB

Peter Straub was born in Milwaukee, Wisconsin, in 1943, and was educated at the University of Wisconsin, Columbia University and University College, Dublin. His bestselling books include *Ghost Story*, *Shadowland*, *Floating Dragon* (winner of the 1983 British Fantasy Award), *The Talisman* (with Stephen King), *Koko* (winner of the 1989 World Fantasy Award), *Mystery* and *Houses Without Doors*. Peter Straub has spent ten years in Britain and Ireland, and now lives in Connecticut and New York.

By Peter Straub

Novels

Marriages
Under Venus
Julia
If You Could See Me Now
Ghost Story
Shadowland
Floating Dragon
The Talisman (with Stephen King)
Koko
Mystery
The Throat

Poetry

Open Air
Leeson Park & Belsize Square

Collections

Wild Animals
Houses Without Doors

For
Ann Lauterbach
and
Susan Straub

A being can only be touched where it yields. For a woman, this is under her dress; and for a god it's on the throat of the animal being sacrificed.
　　　　　　　　　　　　　　　– GEORGE BATAILLE, *Guilty*

I see again my schoolroom in Vyra, the blue roses of the wallpaper, the open window. . . . Everything is as it should be, nothing will ever change, nobody will ever die.
　　　　　　　　　　　　　– VLADIMIR NABOKOV, *Speak, Memory*

Contents

Acknowledgments

I owe thanks to all who helped by contributing their insight, intelligence, advice, stories, and support: Charles Bernstein; Tom Noli; Hap Beasley; Scott Hamilton; Warren Vaché; Lila Kalinich; Joe Haldeman; Eda Rak; my brother, John Straub; and my wondrous editor, Laurie Bernstein.

PART ONE

Tim Underhill

1

An alcoholic homicide detective in my hometown of Millhaven, Illinois, William Damrosch, died to ensure, you might say, that this book would never be written. But you write what comes back to you, and then afterward it comes back to you all over again.

I once wrote a novel called *The Divided Man* about the Blue Rose murders, and in that book I called Damrosch Hal Esterhaz. I never alluded to my own connections to the Blue Rose murders, but those connections were why I wrote the book. (There was one other reason, too.) I wanted to explain things to myself – to see if I could slice through to the truth with that old, old weapon, the battered old sword, of story telling.

I wrote *The Divided Man* after I was processed out of the army and had settled into a little room near Bang Luk, the central flower market in Bangkok. In Vietnam I had killed several people at long distance and one close up, so close that his face was right before me. In Bangkok, that face kept coming back to me while I was writing. And with it came, attached like an enormous barnacle to a tiny boat, the other Vietnam, the Vietnam before Vietnam, of childhood. When my childhood began coming back to me, I went off the rails for a bit. I became what you could charitably call 'colorful.' After a year or so of disgrace, I remembered that I was thirty-odd years old, no longer a child, that I had a calling of a kind, and I began to heal. Either childhood is a lot more painful the second time around, or it's just less bearable. None of us are as strong or as brave as the children we used to be.

About a year after I straightened out, I came back to America and wound up writing a couple of books with a novelist named Peter Straub. These were called *Koko* and *Mystery*, and maybe you read them. It's okay if you didn't. Peter's a nice enough kind of guy, and he lives in a big gray Victorian house in Connecticut, just off Long Island Sound. He has a wife and two kids, and he doesn't get out much. Peter's office on the third floor of his house was the size of my whole loft on Grand Street, and his air conditioning and his sound system always worked.

Peter liked listening to my descriptions of Millhaven. He was fascinated with the place. He understood exactly how I felt about it. 'In Millhaven, snow falls in the middle of summer,' I'd say, 'sometimes in Millhaven, flights of angels blot out the whole sky,' and he'd beam at me for about a minute and a half. Here are some other things I told him about Millhaven: once, on the near south side of town, a band of children killed a stranger, dismembered him, and buried the pieces of his body beneath a juniper tree, and later the divided and buried parts of the body began to call out to each other; once a rich old man raped his daughter and kept her imprisoned in a room where she raved and drank, raved and drank, without ever remembering what had happened to her; once the pieces of the murdered man buried beneath the juniper tree called out and caused the children to bring them together; once a dead man was wrongly accused of terrible crimes. And once, when the parts of the dismembered man were brought together at the foot of the tree, the whole man rose and spoke, alive again, restored.

For we were writing about a mistake committed by the Millhaven police and endorsed by everyone else in town. The more I learned, the worse it got: along with everyone else, I had assumed that William Damrosch had finally

16

killed himself to stop himself from murdering people, or had committed suicide out of guilt and terror over the murders he had already done. Damrosch had left a note with the words BLUE ROSE on the desk in front of him.

But this was an error of interpretation – of imagination. What most of us call intelligence is really imagination – sympathetic imagination. The Millhaven police were wrong, and I was wrong. For obvious reasons, the police wanted to put the case to rest; I wanted to put it to rest for reasons of my own.

I've been living in New York for six years now. Every couple of months I take the New Haven Line from Grand Central, get off at the Greens Farms stop, and stay up late at night drinking and talking with Peter. He drinks twenty-five-year-old malt whiskey, because he's that kind of guy, and I drink club soda. His wife and his kids are asleep and the house is quiet. I can see stars through his office skylight, and I'm aware of the black bowl of night over our heads, the huge darkness that covers half the planet. Now and then a car swishes down the street, going to Burying Hill Beach and Southport.

Koko described certain things that happened to members of my old platoon in and after the war, and *Mystery* was about the long-delayed aftermath of an old murder in a Wisconsin resort. Because we liked the idea, we set the novel on a Caribbean island, but the main character, Tom Pasmore – who will turn up later in these pages – was someone I knew back in Millhaven. He was intimately connected with the Blue Rose murders blamed on William Damrosch, and a big part of *Mystery* is his discovery of this connection.

After *Mystery* I thought I was done with Damrosch, with Millhaven, and with the Blue Rose murders. Then I got a call from John Ransom, another old Millhaven acquaintance, and because much in his life had changed, my life changed too. John Ransom still lived in Millhaven. His wife had been attacked and beaten into a coma, and her attacker had scrawled the words BLUE ROSE on the wall above her body.

2

I never knew John Ransom very well. He lived in a big house on the east side and he went to Brooks-Lowood School. I lived in Pigtown, on the fringes of the Valley, south of downtown Millhaven and a block from the St Alwyn Hotel, and I went to Holy Sepulchre. Yet I knew him slightly because we were both tackles, and our football teams played each other twice a year. Neither team was very good. Holy Sepulchre was not a very big school, and Brooks-Lowood was tiny. We had about one hundred students in each grade. Brooks-Lowood had about thirty.

John Ransom said, 'Hi,' the first time we faced each other in a game. These preppies are a bunch of cupcakes, I thought. When play started, he hit me like a bulldozer and pushed me back at least a foot. The Brooks-Lowood quarterback, a flashy bit of blond arrogance named Teddy Heppenstall, danced right past me. When we lined up for the next play, I said, 'Well, hi to you, too,' and we butted shoulders and forearms, utterly motionless, while Teddy Heppenstall romped down the other side of the field. I was sore for a whole week after the game.

Every November, Holy Sepulchre sponsored a Christian Athletes' Fellowship Dinner, which we called 'the football supper.' It was a fundraiser held in the church basement. The administration invited athletes from high schools all over Millhaven to spend ten dollars on hamburgers, potato chips, baked beans, macaroni salad, Hawaiian Punch, and a speech about Christ the Quarter-back from Mr Schoonhaven, our football coach. Mr Schoonhaven believed in what used to be called muscular Christianity. He knew that if Jesus had ever been handed a football, He would have demolished anyone who dared to get between Him and the endzone. This Jesus bore very little resemblance to Teddy Heppenstall, and none at all to the soulful, rather stricken person who cupped His hands beneath His own incandescent heart in the garish portrait that hung just inside the church's heavy front doors.

Few athletes from other schools ever attended the football suppers, although we were always joined by a handful of big crew-cut Polish boys from St Ignatius. The St Ignatius boys ate hunched over their plates as if they knew they had to hold in check until next football season their collective need to beat up on someone. They liked to communicate *threat*, and they seemed perfectly attuned to Mr Schoonhaven's pugnacious Jesus.

At the close of the season in which John Ransom had greeted me and then flicked me out of Teddy Heppenstall's way, a tall, solidly built boy came into the church basement near the end of the first, informal part of the football supper. In a couple of seconds we would have to snap into our seats and look reverential. The new boy was wearing a tweed sports jacket, khaki pants, a white button-down shirt, and a striped necktie. He collected a hamburger, shook his head at the beans and macaroni salad, took a paper cup of punch, and slid into the seat beside mine before I could recognize him.

Mr Schoonhaven stood up to the microphone and coughed into his fist. A report like a gunshot resounded through the basement. Even the St Ignatius delinquents sat up straight. 'What is a Gospel?' Mr Schoonhaven bellowed, beginning as usual without preamble. 'A

Gospel is something that may be believed.' He glared at us and yelled, 'And what is football? It too is something that can be believed.'

'Spoken like a true coach,' the stranger whispered to me, and at last I recognized John Ransom.

Father Vitale, our trigonometry teacher, frowned down the table. He was merely distributing the frown he wished to bestow on Mr Schoonhaven, who was a Protestant and could not keep from sounding like one on these occasions. 'What are the Gospels about? Salvation. Football is about salvation, too,' said the coach. 'Jesus never dropped the ball. He won the big game. Each of us, in our own way, is asked to do the same. What do we do when we're facing the goalposts?'

I took my pen out of my shirt pocket and wrote on a creased napkin, *What are you doing here?* Ransom read my question, turned over the paper, and wrote, *I thought it would be interesting*. I raised my eyebrows.

Yes, it's interesting, John Ransom wrote on the napkin.

I felt a flash of anger at the thought that he was slumming. To all the rest of us, even the St Ignatius hoodlums, the cinder-block church basement was as familiar as the cafeteria. In fact, our cafeteria was almost identical to the church basement. I had heard that waiters and waitresses served the Brooks-Lowood students at tables set with linen tablecloths and silverware. Actual waiters. Actual silverware, made of silver. Then something else occurred to me. I wrote, *Are you Catholic?* and nudged John Ransom's elbow. He looked down, smiled, and shook his head.

Of course. He was a Protestant.

Well? I wrote.

I'm waiting to find out, he wrote.

I stared at him, but he returned to Mr Schoonhaven, who was telling the multitude that the Christian athlete had a duty to go out there and *kill* for Jesus. *Stomp!*

Batter! Because that was what He wanted you to do. Take no prisoners!

John Ransom leaned toward me and whispered, 'I like this guy.'

Again I felt a chill of indignation. John Ransom imagined that he was better than us.

Of course, I thought that I was better than Mr Schoonhaven, too. I thought I was better than the church basement, not to mention Holy Sepulchre and, by extension, the eight intersecting streets that constituted our neighborhood. Most of my classmates would end up working in the tanneries, can factories, breweries, and tire recapping outfits that formed the boundary between ourselves and downtown Millhaven. I knew that if I could get a scholarship I was going to college; I planned to get out of our neighborhood as soon as possible. I liked the place I came from, but a lot of what I liked about it was that I had come from there.

That John Ransom had trespassed into my neighborhood and overheard Mr Schoonhaven's platitudes irritated me, and I was about to snarl something at him when I noticed Father Vitale. He was getting ready to push himself off his chair and smack me on the back of my head. Father Vitale knew that man was sinful from the mother's womb and that 'Nature, which the first human being harmed, is miserable,' as St Augustine says. I faced forward and clasped my hands in front of my plate. John Ransom had also noticed the surly old priest gathering himself to strike, and he too clasped his hands on the table. Father Vitale settled back down.

There must have been some envy in my irritation. John Ransom was a fairly good-looking boy, as good looks were defined in the days when John Wayne was considered handsome, and he wore expensive clothes with unself-conscious ease. One look at John Ransom told me that he owned closets full of good jackets and expensive

21

suits, that his drawers were stuffed with oxford-cloth shirts, that he owned his own *tie rack*.

Mr Schoonhaven sat down, the parish priest stood to give a prayer, and the dinner was over. All the football and baseball players from St Ignatius and Holy Sepulchre began to move toward the steps up to the nave.

John Ransom asked me if we were supposed to take our plates into the kitchen.

'No, they'll do it.' I nodded toward the weary-looking women, church volunteers, who were now standing in front of the serving tables. They had cooked for us, and most of them had brought beans and macaroni in covered dishes from their own kitchens. 'How did you hear about this, anyhow?'

'I saw an announcement on our notice board.'

'This can't be much like Brooks-Lowood,' I said.

He smiled. 'It was okay. I liked it. I liked it fine.'

We started moving toward the stairs behind the other boys, some of whom were looking suspiciously at him over their shoulders.

'You know, Tim, I enjoyed playing against you,' John Ransom said. He was smiling at me and holding out his hand.

I stared stupidly at his hand for a couple of beats before I took it. At Holy Sepulchre boys never shook hands. Nobody I knew shook hands in this way, socially, unless they were closing a deal on a used car.

'Don't you love being a lineman?' he asked.

I laughed and looked up from the spectacle of our joined hands to observe the expressions on the faces of Father Vitale and a few of the women volunteers. It took me a moment to figure out this expression. They were looking at me with interest and respect, a combination so unusual in my experience as to be rare. I understood that neither Father Vitale nor the volunteers had ever had much contact with someone like John Ransom; to them it looked as if he had come all the way from the east side just to shake my hand.

No, I wanted to protest, *it's not me*. Because I finally understood: every year, Holy Sepulchre sent out flyers about the Christian Athletes' Fellowship Dinner to every high school in the city, and not only was John Ransom the first Brooks-Lowood student who had ever come, he was the only student from the entire east side who had ever been interested enough to attend the football supper. That was the point: he was interested.

The other boys were already up in the church vestibule by the time John Ransom and I reached the bottom of the stairs. I could hear them laughing about Mr Schoonhaven. Then I heard the voice of Bill Byrne, who weighed nearly three hundred pounds and was the Bluebirds' center, saying something about a 'dork tourist,' and then, even more horribly, 'some east side fag who showed up to suck Underhill's dick.' There was a burst of dirty laughter. It was just aimless, all-purpose hostility, but I almost literally prayed that John Ransom had not heard it. I didn't think a well-dressed hand-shaking boy like John Ransom would enjoy being called a pervert – a fairy, a queer, a *cocksucker*!

But because I had heard it, he had too, and from the hiss of indrawn breath behind me, so had Father Vitale. John Ransom surprised me by laughing out loud.

'Byrne!' shouted Father Vitale. 'You, Byrne!' He put one hand on my right shoulder and the other on John Ransom's left and shoved us apart so that he could push between us. My classmates opened the creaking side door onto Vestry Street as Father Vitale squeezed into the space between John Ransom and myself. He had forgotten we were there, I think, and his big swarthy face moved past mine without a glance. I could see enormous black open pores on his nose, as if even his skin was breathing hard, stoking in air like a furnace. He was panting by the

23

time he got to the top of the stairs. The stench of cigarettes followed him like a wake.

'That priest smokes too much,' John Ransom said.

We reached the top of the steps just as the door slammed shut again, and we walked through the vestibule, hearing running footsteps on Vestry Street and the priest's yells of *Boys! Boys!*

'Maybe we should give him a minute,' John Ransom said. He put his hands in his pockets and ambled off toward the arched entrance to the interior of the church.

'Give him a minute?' I asked.

'Let him catch his breath. He certainly isn't going to catch *them*.' John Ransom was gazing appreciatively into the long, dim length of Holy Sepulchre. He might have been in a museum. I saw him take in the font of holy water and the ranks of flickering intermittent candles, some new, some guttering nubs. Ransom looked into the depths of our church as if he were memorizing it: he wasn't smiling anymore, but his evident pleasure was not in any way diminished by the reappearance of Father Vitale, who came back in through the Vestry Street door and huffed and puffed like a tugboat through the gray air. He did not speak to either of us. As he moved down the aisle, Father Vitale almost instantly lost his individuality and became a scenic element of the church itself, like a castle on a German cliff or a donkey on a dusty Italian road. I was seeing Father Vitale as John Ransom saw him.

He turned around and inspected the vestibule in the same way, as if *seeing* it was *understanding* it. He was not the supercilious tourist for whom I had mistaken him. He wanted to *take it in*, to experience it in a way that would probably not have occurred to any other Brooks-Lowood boy. I thought that John Ransom would have taken that same attitude to the bottom of the world.

Later, John Ransom and I both went to the bottom of the world.

When I was seven years old, my sister April was killed – murdered. She was nine. I saw it happen. I thought I saw *something* happen. I tried to help her. I tried to stop whatever it was from happening, and then I was killed too, but not as permanently as April.

I guess I think the bottom of the world is the *center* of the world; and that sooner or later we all see it, all of us, according to our capacities.

The next time I saw John Ransom was in Vietnam.

3

Ten months after I graduated from Berkeley, I was drafted – I let it happen to me, not out of any sense that I owed my country a year of military service. Since graduating I had been working in a bookstore on Telegraph Avenue and writing short stories at night. These invariably came back in the stamped, self-addressed manila envelopes I had folded inside my own envelopes to the *New Yorker* and *Atlantic Monthly* and *Harpers* – not to mention *Prairie Schooner*, *The Kenyon Review*, *Antaeus*, *The Massachusetts Review*, and *Ploughshares*. At least I think it was *Ploughshares*. I knew that I did not want to teach, and I had no faith that teaching deferments would hold (they didn't). The more that my stillborn stories came back to me, the more discouraging it became to spend forty hours a week surrounded by other people's books. When my 2-S classification was adjusted to 1-A, I felt that I might have been given a way out of my impasse.

I flew to Vietnam on a commercial airline. About

three-fourths of the passengers in tourist class were green-horns like me, and the stewardesses had trouble looking at us directly. The only really relaxed passengers in our section of the plane were the weather-beaten lifers at the back of the cabin, noncoms, who were as loose and clubby as golfers on a weekend flight to Myrtle Beach.

In the first-class cabin at the front of the plane sat men in dark suits, State Department functionaries and businessmen making a good thing for as long as they could out of cement or building supplies in Vietnam. When they looked at us, they smiled – we were their soldiers, after all, protecting their ideals and their money.

But between the patriots at the front and the relaxed, disillusioned lifers at the rear, in two rows just aft of first class, was another group I could not figure out at all. As a group, they were lean, muscular, short-haired, like soldiers, but they wore Hawaiian shirts and khaki pants, or blue button-down shirts with crisp blue jeans. They looked like a college football team at a tenth-year reunion. These men took no notice of us at all. What language I overheard was bright, hard-edged military jargon.

When one of the lifers walked past my seat, stretching his legs before going to sleep, I touched his wrist and asked him about the men at the front of the cabin.

He bent low and squeezed out a single word.

Greenies?

We landed at Tan Son Nhut in sunlight that seemed almost visibly *dense*. When the stewardess swung open the jet's door and the astonishing heat rolled in, I felt that my old life had gone forever. I thought I could smell the polish melting off my buttons. In that moment I decided not to be afraid of anything until I really had to be – I felt that it was possible to step away from my childhood. This was the first of the queer exaltations – the sudden sense of a new freedom – that sometimes visited me in Vietnam, and which I have never felt elsewhere.

My orders sent me to Camp White Star, a base in II Corps located outside of Nha Trang. There I was supposed to join other new members of my regiment for transport north to Camp Crandall in I Corps. One of the unexplained glitches not unusual in army life occurred, and the men I was supposed to join had been sent on ahead of me. I was left awaiting orders for eight days.

Every day I reported to a cynical captain named McCue, Hamilton McCue, who rubbed his square fingers over his babyish pink cheeks and assigned me to whatever task took his momentary fancy. I moved barrels from beneath the latrine and poured kerosene into them so old Vietnamese women could incinerate our shit; I cannibalized broken-down jeeps for distributor caps, alternators, and working fuel pumps; I raked stones out of the fifteen square yards of dust in front of the officers' club. Eventually McCue decided that I was having an unseemly amount of fun and assigned me to the body squad. The body squad unloaded corpses from the incoming helicopters, transferred them to the 'morgue' while the paperwork was done, and then loaded them into the holds of planes going to Tan Son Nhut, where they were flown back to the States.

The other seven members of the body squad were serving out their remaining time in Vietnam. All of them had once been in regular units, and most of them had re-upped so that they could spend another year in the field. They were not ordinary people – the regiment had slam-dunked them into the body squad to get them out of their units.

Their names were Scoot, Hollyday, di Maestro, Picklock, Ratman, Attica, and Pirate. They had a generic likeness, being unshaven, hairy – even Ratman, who was prematurely bald, was hairy – unclean, missing a crucial tooth or two. Scoot, Pirate, and di Maestro wore tattoos

27

(BORN TO DIE, DEALERS IN DEATH, and a death's head suspended over an umber pyramid, respectively). None of them ever wore an entire uniform. For the whole of my first day, they did not speak to me, and went about the business of carrying the heavy body bags from the helicopter to the truck and from the truck to the 'morgue' in a frosty, insulted silence.

The next day, after Captain McCue told me that my orders still had not come through and that I should return to the body squad, he asked me how I was getting on with my fellow workers. That was what he called them, my 'fellow workers.'

'They're full of stories,' I said.

'That's not all they're full of, the way I hear it,' he said, showing two rows of square brown teeth that made his big cheeks look as if his character were being eroded from within. He must have seen that I had just decided I preferred the company of Ratman, Attica, and the rest to his own, because he told me that I would be working with the body squad until my orders came through.

On the second day, the intensity of my new comrades' disdain had relaxed, and they resumed the unfinishable dialogue I had interrupted.

Their stories were always about death.

'We're pounding the boonies,' Ratman said, shoving another wrapped corpse into the back of our truck. 'Twenty days. You listening, Underdog?'

I had a new name.

'Twenty days. You know what that's like out there, Underdog?'

Pirate spat a thick yellow curd onto the ground.

'Like forty days in hell. In hell you're already dead, but out in the boonies everybody's trying to kill you. Means you never sleep right. Means you *see* things.'

Pirate snorted and tossed another body onto the truck. 'Fuckin' right.'

28

'You see your old girlfriend fuckin' some numbnuts *fuck*, you see your fuckin' friends get *killed*, you see the fuckin' *trees* move, you see stuff that never happened and never will, man.'

''Cept here,' Pirate said.

'Twenty days,' Ratman said. The back of the truck was now filled with bodies in bags, and Ratman swung up and locked the rear panel. He leaned against it on stiff arms, shaking his drooping head. His fingertips were bulbous, the size of golf balls, and each came to a pointed tip at the spot where his fingerprints would have been centered. I found out later that he had earned his name by eating two live rats in a tunnel where his platoon had found a thousand kilos of rice. 'Too fat for speed,' he was supposed to have said.

'Every sense you got is *out* there, man, you hear a mouse move – '

'Hear rats move,' di Maestro said, slapping the side of the truck as if to wake up the bodies in the green bags.

' – hear the dew jumpin' out of the leaves, hear the insects moving in the *bark*. Hear your own fingernails grow. Hear that thing in the ground, man.'

'Thing in the ground?' Pirate asked.

'Shit,' said Ratman. 'You don't know? You know how when you lie down on the trail you hear all kinds of shit, all them damn bugs and monkeys, the birds, the people moving way up ahead of you – '

'Better be sure they're not coming your direction,' di Maestro said from the front of the truck. 'You takin' notes, Underdog?'

' – *all* kinds of shit, right? But then you hear the *rest*. You hear like a humming noise underneath all them other noises. Like some big generator's running way far away *underneath* you.'

'Oh, that thing in the ground,' Pirate said.

'It *is* the ground,' said Ratman. He stepped back from

the truck and gave Pirate a fierce, wild-eyed glare. 'Fuckin' ground makes the fuckin' noise by *itself*. You hear me? An' that engine's always on. It never sleeps.'

'Okay, let's move,' di Maestro said. He climbed up behind the wheel. Hollyday, Scoot, and Attica crowded into the seat beside him. Ratman scrambled up behind the cab, and Picklock and Pirate and I followed him. The truck jolted down the field toward the main body of the camp, and the helicopter pilot and some of the ground crew turned to watch us go. We were like garbagemen, I thought. It was like working on a garbage truck.

'On top of which,' Ratman said, 'people are seriously trying to interfere with your existence.'

Picklock laughed, but instantly composed himself again. So far, neither he nor Pirate had actually looked at me.

'Which can fuck you up all by itself, at least until you get used to it,' Ratman said. 'Twenty-day mission. I been on longer, but I never went on any worse. The lieutenant went down. The radio man, he went down. My best friends at that time, they went down.'

'Where is this?' Pirate asked.

'This is Darlac Province,' said Ratman. 'Not too damn far away.'

'Right next door,' said Pirate.

'Twentieth day,' said Pirate. 'We're out there. We're after some damn cadre. Hardly any food left, and our pickup is in forty-eight hours. This target keeps *moving*, they go from ville to ville, they're your basic Robin Hood-type cadre.' Ratman shook his head. The truck hit a low point in the road on the outskirts of the base, and one of the bags slithered down the pile and landed softly at Ratman's feet. He kicked it almost gently.

'This guy, this friend of mine, name of Bobby Swett, he was right ahead of me, five feet ahead of me. We hear some kind of crazy whoop, and then this big red-and-yellow bird flashes past us, big as a turkey, man, wings like fuckin' *propellers*, man, and I'm thinkin', okay, what woke this mother *up*? And Bobby Swett turns around to look at me, and he's grinnin'. His grin is the last thing I see for about ten minutes. When I come to I remember seeing Bobby Swett come apart all at once, like something inside him exploded, but – you get it? – I'm remembering something I didn't really see. I think I'm dead. I fucking *know* I'm dead. I've covered in blood and this brownskin little girl is bending over me. Black hair and black eyes. So now I know. There are angels, and angels got black hair and black eyes, hot shit.'

A brown wooden fence hid the long low shed we called the morgue, and when we had passed the stenciled GRAVES REGISTRATION sign, Ratman vaulted off the back of the truck and opened the storage bay. We had four hours turnaround time, and today there were a lot of bodies.

Di Maestro backed the truck up into the bay, and we started hauling the long bags into the interior of the shed.

'Long nose?' asked Pirate.

'Long nose, shit yes.'

'A Yard.'

'Sure, but what did I know? She was a Rhade – most of the Yards in Darlac Province, of which they got about two thousand, are Rhade. "I died," I say to this girl, still figuring she's a angel, and she coos something back at me. It seems to me that I can remember this big flash of light – I mean, that was something I actually *saw*.'

'Good ol' Bobby Swett tripped a mine,' said Pirate.

I was getting to like Pirate. Pirate knew I was the real subject of this story, and he was selfless enough to keep things rolling with little interjections and explanations. Pirate was slightly less contemptuous of me than the rest of the body squad. I also liked the way he looked, raffish without being as *ratlike* as Ratman. Like me, Pirate tended toward the hulking. He seldom wore a shirt in the daytime, and always had a bandanna tied around his head or his neck. When I had been out in the field for a time, I found myself imitating these mannerisms, except for when the mosquitos got bad.

'You think I don't know that? What I'm saying is' – Ratman shoved another dead soldier in a zippered bag into the darkness of the shed – 'What I'm *sayin'* is, I was dead too. For a minute, maybe longer.'

'Of what?'

'Shock,' Ratman said simply. 'That's the reason I never saw Bobby Swett get blown apart. Didn't you ever hear about this? I heard about it. Lotsa guys I met, it happened to them or someone they knew. You die, you come back.'

'Is that true?' I asked.

For a second, Ratman looked wrathful. I had challenged his system of belief, and I was a person who knew nothing.

Pirate came to my rescue. 'How come you could remember seeing this guy get wasted, if you didn't see it in the first place?'

'I was out of my body.'

'Goddamn it, Underdog,' said Picklock, and grabbed the handle of the heavy bag I had nearly dropped. 'What the fuck is the matter with you?' Single-handedly, he tossed the bag into the shed behind us.

'Underdog, never drop the fucking bags,' said di Maestro, and deliberately dropped a bag onto the concrete. Whatever was inside it gurgled and splatted.

For a moment or two we continued to unload the bodies into the shed.

Then Ratman said, 'Anyhow, about a second later I found out I was still alive.'

'What makes you think you're alive?' asked Attica.

'On top of everything else, this guy shoves his face into mine, and for sure he ain't no angel. I can see the goddamn canopy above his head. The birds start screeching

32

again. The first thing I know for sure is Bobby Swett is gone, man – I'm *wearing* whatever's left of him. And this guy says to me, "Get on your feet, soldier." I can just about make out what he's saying through the ringing in my ears, but you know this asshole is used to obedience. I let out a groan when I try to move, because, man, every square inch of me feels like hamburger.'

'Ah,' said Picklock and Attica, nearly in unison. Then Attica said, 'You're a lucky son of a bitch.'

'Bobby Swett didn't even make it into one of these bags,' said Ratman. 'That fucker turned into *vapour*.' He sullenly grabbed the handles of another bag, inspected it for a second, said, 'No tag,' and shoved it on top of the others in the shed.

'Oh, goody,' said Attica. Attica had a smooth brown head, and his biceps jumped in his arms when he lifted the bags. He pulled a marker from his fatigues and made a neat check on the end of the bag. As he turned back to the truck, he grinned at me, stretching his lips without opening his mouth, and I wondered what was coming.

'Finally I got up, like in a kinda daze,' Ratman said. 'I still couldn't hear hardly nothing. This guy is standing in front of me, and I see he's totally crazy, but not like *we* go crazy. This mother's crazy in some absolutely new kinda way. I'm still so fucked up I can't tell what's so different about him, but he's got these eyes which they are not human eyes.' He paused, remembering. 'Everybody else in my platoon is sort of standing around watching. There's the little Yard mascot in these real loose fatigues, and there's this big guy in front of me on the trail with the sun behind his head. I mean this dude is in command. He *is* the show. Even the lieutenant, who is a fucking ramrod, is just standing there. Well, shit, I think, he just saw this guy raise me from the dead, what else is he gonna do? The big guy is still checking me out – he's scoping me. He's got these eyes, like some animal in a pit that just killed all the animals that were down there with him.'

'He looked like Attica,' said di Maestro.

'Damn straight he did,' Attica said. 'I'm a warrior, I ain't like you losers, I'm a fucking god of war.'

'And then I see what's really funny about this guy,' said Ratman. 'He's got this open khaki shirt and tan pants and there's a little black briefcase on the ground next to him.'

'Uh oh,' said di Maestro.

'Plus which, there's scars all over his chest – punji stick scars. The bastard fell on punji sticks and he lived.'

'Him,' said di Maestro.

'Yeah, him. Bachelor.'

'This is after *twenty days*. Bobby Swett gets turned into – into *red fog* right in front of me. I get killed or *something* like that, and nobody's moving because of this guy with the briefcase. "I am Captain Franklin Bachelor, and I've been hearing about you," this guy says to me. Like I didn't know. But he's really talking to all of us, he's just checking me out to see how bad I got hurt.

'And then I look down at my hands and I see they're this funny color – sort of purple. Even under Bobby's blood, I can see my skin is turning this purple color. And I push up my sleeve and my whole damn *arm* is purple. And it's swelling up, fast.

'"This fool's a walking bruise," says Captain Bachelor. He gives the whole platoon a disgusted look. We're in his part of the world now, by God, and we better know it. For two weeks we been getting in his way, and he wants us out. He's asking us politely, and we're on the same side, after all, which is worth remembering, but if we don't get outa his share of the countryside, our luck might take a turn for the worse. He just kind of smiles at us, and the Montagnard girl is standing right up next to him, and she's got an M-16, and *he's* got some kind of fancy machine I never saw before or since but I think was some

34

kind of *Swedish* piece, and I got to thinkin' about what's in the briefcase, and then I got it. All at once.'

'Got what?' I asked, and everyone in the body squad looked down, or at the stack of bodies in the shed, and then they unloaded the last two bodies. We went into the shed to begin the next part of the job. Nobody spoke until di Maestro looked at the tag taped to the bag closest to him and started checking the names.

'So you got out of there,' he said.

'The lieutenant used Bachelor's radio, and even before the argument was over, we was on our way toward the LZ. When we got back to the base, we got our showers, we got real food, we got blasted every possible way, but afterward I never felt the same. Those scars. That fuckin' briefcase, man. And the little Yard chick. You know what? He was havin' a ball. He was throwin' a party.'

'They more or less got their own war,' said Scoot. He was a short skinny man with deep-set eyes, a ponytail, and a huge knife that dangled from his waistband on a dried, crinkly leather thong that looked like a body part. He could lift twice his own weight, and like a weight lifter he existed in some densely private space of his own.

'Green Berets are cool with me,' said Attica, and then I understood part of it.

'Some of them were on my flight,' I said. 'They – '

'Can't we get some work done around here?' asked di Maestro, and for a time we checked the dog tags against our lists.

Then Pirate said, 'Ratman, what was the payoff?'

Ratman looked up from beside a body bag and said, 'Five days after we got back to camp, we heard about a couple dozen Rhade Yards took out about a *thousand* VC. They went through all these hamlets in the middle of the night. 'Course, the way I heard it, some of those thousand VC were little babies and such, but CIDG did itself a power of good that night.'

'CIDG?' I asked.

'I heard of fifty–sixty guys, First Air Cav, offed by friendly fire,' Scoot said. 'Shit happens.'

'Friendly fire?' I said.

'Comes in all shapes and sizes,' Scoot said, smiling in a way I did not understand until later.

Ratman uttered a sound halfway between a snarl and a laugh. 'And the rest was, I puffed up about two times my size. Felt like a goddamn football. Even my *eyelids* were swole up, man. They finally put me in the base hospital and packed me in ice – but not a bone broken, man. Not a bone broken.'

'Now, I wonder what shape this boy is in,' said Attica, patting the body without a tag. Nearly all the bags had been named by the time they got to us, and it was our task to ensure that all had names by the time they left. We had to unzip the bags and compare the name on the tag taped to the body bag with the name on the tag either inserted into the dead man's mouth or taped to his body. From Vietnam the bodies went back to America, where the army decanted them into wooden coffins and sent them home.

'Your turn, Underdog,' said Attica. 'Your hands ain't dirty yet, are they? You check this unit out.'

'You puke on it, I'll stomp your guts out,' said di Maestro, and surprised me by laughing. I had not heard di Maestro laugh before. It was a creaky, humorless bray that might have come from one of the bags lined up before us.

'Yeah, don't puke on the unit,' said Pirate. 'That really messes 'em up.'

Attica had intended me to open the bag and find the dead soldier's tag from the moment he had noticed that the matching tag was missing. 'You're new boy,' he said. 'This the new boy's job.'

I moved toward Attica and the bag with the check. For

a moment I suspected that when I unzipped the bag, some hideous creature would jump out at me, drenched in blood like Ratman after Bobby Swett had disintegrated in front of him. *Because that was why he told the story!* They wanted me to scream, they wanted my hair to turn white. After I vomited, they'd take turns stomping my guts out. It was their version of friendly fire.

I had not entirely left my old self behind on the tarmac at Tan Son Nhut, after all.

Scoot was regarding me with real curiosity. 'It's the new boy's *job*,' Attica repeated, and I guessed that although the term was ridiculous when applied to him, he had been the new boy before me.

I bent over the long black bag. There were fabric handles on each end, and the zipper ran from one to the other.

I grasped the zipper and promised myself that I would not close my eyes. Behind me, the men took a collective breath. I pulled the zipper across the bag.

And I almost did vomit, not because of what I saw but because of the dead boy's stench, which moved like a huge black dog out of the opening in the bag. For a second I did have to close my eyes. A greasy web had fastened itself over my face. The gray ruined face inside the bag stared upward with open eyes. My stomach lurched. This was what they had been waiting for, I knew, and I held my breath and yanked the zipper another twelve inches down the bag.

The dead boy's mud-colored face was shot away from his left cheek down. His upper teeth closed on nothing. A few loose teeth had lodged in the back of his neck. The other tag was not in the cavity. The uniform shirt was stiff and black with blood, and the blast that had taken away the boy's lower jaw had also removed his throat. The small, delicate bones of the top vertebrae were fouled with blood.

37

'There's no tag on this guy,' I said, though what I wanted to do was scream.

Di Maestro said, 'You ain't finished yet.'

I looked up at him. A big fuzzy belly drooped over his pants, and four or five days' growth of beard began just under his rapacious eyes. He looked like a fat goat.

'Who cleans these people up?' I asked before I realized that the answer might be that the new guy does.

'They make 'em presentable at the other end.' Di Maestro grinned and crossed his arms over his chest. The tattoo of a grinning skull floated over a brown pyramid on his right forearm. Millhaven, *my* Millhaven, was now present all about me, the frame houses with peeling brickface crowded together, the vacant lots and the St Alwyn Hotel. I saw my sister's face.

'If you can't find the tag inside the shirt, sometimes they put 'em in the pockets or the boots.' Di Maestro turned away. The others had already lost interest.

I struggled with the top button of the stiffened shirt, trying not to touch the jagged edges of flesh around the collar. The odor poured up at me. My eyes misted.

The button finally squeezed through the hole, but the collar refused to separate. I pulled it open. Dried blood crackled like breakfast cereal. His throat had been opened like a surgical diagram. A few more teeth were embedded in the softening flesh. I knew that what I was seeing I would see for the rest of my life – the ropes of flesh, the open cavity that should have been filled with speech. Lost teeth.

The tag was nowhere inside his neck.

I unbuttoned the next two buttons and found only a pale bloodied chest.

Then I had to turn away to breathe and saw the rest of the body squad going efficiently down the rows of bodies, dipping into the unzipped bags, making sure the names matched. I turned back to my anonymous corpse and began fighting with a shirt pocket.

The button finally passed through the buttonhole, and I pushed my fingers into the opening, cracking it open like the pocket of a stiffly starched shirt. A thin hard edge of metal caught beneath my fingernail. The tag came away from the cloth with a series of dry little pops. 'Okay,' I said.

Di Maestro said, 'Attica used to shake down these units in five seconds flat.'

'Two seconds,' Attica said, not bothering to look up.

I got away from the gaping body in the bag and held out the unreadable tag.

'Underdog's a pearl diver,' di Maestro announced. 'Now wash it off.'

The stained, crusty sink stood beside a spattered toilet. I held the tab beneath a trickle of hot water. The stench of the body still clung to me, as gummy on my hands and face as the film of fat from ham hocks. Flakes of blood fell off the tag and dissolved to red in the water. I dropped the tag and scrubbed my hands and face with PhisoHex until the greasy feeling was gone. The body squad was cracking up behind me. I rubbed my face with the limp musty rag that hung between the sink and the toilet.

'Looking forward to the field?' Ratman said.

'The unit's name,' I said, picking the tag out of the pink water at the bottom of the sink, 'is Andrew T. Majors.'

'That's right,' said di Maestro. 'Now tape it to the bag and help us with the rest of them.'

'You knew his name?' I was too startled to be angry. Then I remembered that he had the field officer's list, and Andrew T. Majors was the only name on it not also found on a tag.

'You'll get used to it,' di Maestro said, not unkindly.

I had not even understood what the rest of the body squad had seen at once, that Bobby Swett had been killed

39

by an American explosive; and that Captain Franklin Bachelor, the Green Beret with the briefcase and the Rhade mistress, had scared Ratman's lieutenant right back to camp because he was leading the 'cadre' the lieutenant had spent two weeks chasing.

When I turned up at the shed the next day, Attica actually greeted me. I jolted along in the back of the truck with Attica and Pirate and felt a naive pride in myself and what I was doing.

Five units tagged with the right names waited on the tarmac. All five had died of concussion in a field. (Walking across anything that resembles a field still makes me nervous.) Apart from killing them, the shell did no damage at all. Three of them were eighteen-year-olds who looked like wax dummies, one was a heavyset baby-faced lieutenant, and the fifth man was a captain in his mid-thirties. It was all over in about five minutes.

'Shall we pop over to the country club, play a round a golf?' Attica asked in a surprisingly passable British accent.

'I fancy a fucking tea dance,' Scoot said. His slow-moving drawl made the sentence sound so odd that no one laughed.

'Well, there is one thing we could do,' said Pirate.

Again I felt a comprehensive understanding from which I was excluded.

'I guess there is,' said di Maestro. He stood up. 'How much money you got on you, Underdog?'

I was tempted to lie, but I took what I had out of my pocket and showed it to him.

'That'll do,' he said. 'You ever been in the village?' When I looked blank he said, 'Outside the gate. The other part of the camp.'

I shook my head. When I got to White Star, I had been still so turned around that I had noticed only a transition from an Asian turmoil to the more orderly disorder of an army base. I had the vague impression of having gone through a small town.

'Never?' He had trouble believing it. 'Well, it's about time you got wet.'

'Get wet time,' Pirate said.

'You walk through the gate. As long as you're on foot, they don't bullshit you. They're supposed to keep the gooks out, not keep us in. They know where you're going. You turn into the first lane and keep going until the second turn –'

'By the bubble,' Attica said.

'You see a sign says BUBBLE in big letters. Turn right there and go under the sign. Go six doors down. Knock on the green door that says LY.'

'Lee?'

He spelled it. 'Li Ly. Say you want six one hundreds. It'll be about thirty bucks. You get 'em in a plastic bag, which you put into your shirt and forget you have. You don't want to look too fuckin' sneaky coming back through.'

'Some Jack,' Scoot said.

'Why not? Across from BUBBLE, go into this little shack, pick up two fifths, Jack Daniels. Shouldn't cost more than ten bucks.'

'New guy buys a round,' said Attica.

Without confessing that I had no idea what one hundreds were, I nodded and stood up.

'Lock and load,' said Scoot.

I walked out of the shed into the amazing noontime heat. When I went around the fence that isolated us, I saw soldiers lining up at the distant mess hall, the dusty walkways and the rows of wooden buildings, the two ballroom-sized tents, the flags. A jeep was rolling toward the gate.

By the time I reached the gate, I was sweating hard.

There was no guardhouse or checkpoint, only a lone soldier beside the dirt road.

The road out of the main part of the camp extended straight through a warren of ramshackle buildings and zigzag streets – the military road was the only straight thing in sight. Two hundred yards away, in harsh brilliant light, I saw a real checkpoint with a flag and a guardhouse and a striped metal gate. The jeep was just beginning to approach the checkpoint, and a guard stood in front of the gate to meet it. I was aware of being watched as soon as I passed through the gate – it was like stepping out of the elevator into a men's suit department.

Beside a hand-painted sign reading HEINECKEN COLD BEER ROCK a Vietnamese boy in a white shirt lounged in a narrow doorway. An old woman carried a full basket of laundry down a steep flight of stairs. Vietnamese voices floated down from upper rooms. Two nearly naked children, one of them different from the other in a way I did not take the time to figure out, appeared at my legs and began whining for *dollah, dollah*.

By the time I reached the BUBBLE sign, five or six children had attached themselves to me, some of them still begging for *dollah*, others drilling questions at me in an incomprehensible mixture of English and Vietnamese. Two girls leaned out the windows of BUBBLE and watched me pass beneath the sign.

I turned right and heard the girls taunting me. Now I could smell wood smoke and hot oil. The shock of this unexpected world so close to the camp, and an equal, matching shock of pleasure almost made me forget that I had a purpose.

But I remembered the green door, and saw the name Ly picked out in sharp businesslike black letters above the knocker. The children keened and tugged at my clothes. I knocked softly at the door. The children became frantic. I dug in my pockets and threw a handful of coins into the street. The children rushed away and began fighting for the coins. My entire body was drenched in sweat.

The door cracked open, and a white-haired old woman with a plump, unsmiling face frowned out at me. Certain information was communicated instantly and wordlessly: I was too early. Customers kept her up half the night. She was doing me a favor by opening the door at all. She looked hard at my face, then looked me up and down. I pulled the bills from my pocket, and she quickly opened the door and motioned me inside, protecting me from the children, who had seen the bills and were running toward me, squeaking like bats. She slammed the door behind me. The children did not thump into the door, as I expected, but seemed to evaporate.

The old woman took a step away from me and wrinkled her nose in distaste, as if I were a skunk. 'Name.'

'Underhill.'

'Nevah heah. You go way.'

She was still sniffing and frowning, as if to place me by odor.

'I'm supposed to buy something.'

'Nevah heah. Go way.' Li Ly snapped her fingers at the door, as if to open it by magic. She was still inspecting me, frowning, as if her memory had failed her. Then she found what she had been looking for. 'Dimstro,' she said, and almost smiled.

'Di Maestro.'

'Da dett man.'

The dead man? The death man?

She lowered her arm and gestured me toward a camp table and a wooden chair with a rush seat. 'What you want?'

I told her.

'Sis?' Again the narrow half-smile. Six was more than di Maestro's usual order: she knew I was being diddled.

43

She padded into a back room and opened and closed a series of drawers. In the enclosed front room, I began to smell myself. Da dett man, that was me too.

Li Ly came out of the back room carrying a rolled cellophane parcel of handmade cigarettes. *Ah*, I thought, *pot*. We were back to the recreations of Berkeley. I gave Li Ly twenty-five dollars. She shook her head. I gave her another dollar. She shook her head again. I gave her another two dollars, and she nodded. She tugged at the front of her loose garment, telling me what to do with the parcel, and watched me place the wrapped cigarettes inside my shirt. Then she opened the door to the sun and the smells and the heat.

The children materialized around me again. I looked again at the smallest, the filthy child of two I had noticed earlier. His eyes were round, and his skin was a smooth shade darker than the dusty gold of the others. His hair was screwed up into tight rabbinical curls. Whenever the old children bothered to notice him, they gave him a blow. I sprinted across the street to another open-fronted shop and bought Jack Daniels from a bowing skeleton. The children followed me almost to the gate, where the soldier on duty scattered them with a wave of his M-16.

In the shed di Maestro unrolled the cellophane package and inspected each tight white tube. 'Li Ly loves your little educated ass,' he said.

Scoot had produced a bag of ice cubes from the enlisted man's club and dropped some of them into plastic glasses. Then he cracked open the first bottle and poured for himself. 'Life on the front,' he said. He drank the entire contents of his glass in one swallow. 'Outstanding.' He poured himself another glass.

'Take this slow,' di Maestro said to me. 'You won't be used to this stuff. In fact, you might wanna sit down.'

'What do you think we did at Berkeley?' I said, and

several of my colleagues called me a sorry-ass shit.

'This is a little different,' di Maestro said. 'It ain't just grass.'

'Give him some and shut him the fuck up,' said Attica.

'What is it?' I asked.

'You'll like it,' di Maestro said. He placed a cigarette in my mouth and lit it with his Zippo.

I drew in a mouthful of harsh, perfumed smoke, and Scoot sang, '*Hoo-ray and hallelujah, you had it comin' to ya, Goody for her, goody goody for me, I hope you're satisfied, you rascal you.*'

Holding the smoke as di Maestro inhaled and passed the long cigarette to Ratman, I scooped ice cubes into a plastic glass. Di Maestro winked at me, and Ratman took two deep drags before passing the cigarette to Scoot. I poured whiskey over the ice and walked away from the table.

'*Hoo-ray and hallelujah,*' Scoot rasped, holding the smoke in his lungs.

My knees felt oddly numb, almost rubbery. Something in the center of my body felt warm, probably the Jack Daniels. Picklock lit up the second cigarette, and it came around to me by the time I had taken a couple of sips of my drink.

I sat down with my back against the wall.

'*Goody goody for it, goody goody for shit, goody goody for war, goody goody for whores . . .*'

'We oughta have music,' Ratman said.

'We have Scoot,' said di Maestro.

Then the world abruptly went away and I was alone in a black void. A laughing void lay on either side of me, a world without time or space or meaning.

For a moment I was back in the shed, and Scoot was saying, 'Damn right.'

Then I was not in the shed with the body squad and the five units, but in a familiar world full of noise and color. I

45

saw the peeling paint on the side of the Idle Hour Tavern. A neon beer sign glowed in the window. The paint had once been white, but the decay of things was as beautiful as their birth. Elm leaves heaped up in the gutter brown and red, and through them cool water sluiced toward the drain. Experience itself was sacred. Details were sacred. I was a new person in a world just being made.

I felt safe and whole – the child within me was also safe and whole. He set down his rage and his misery and looked at the world with eyes refreshed. For the second time that day I knew I wanted more of something: a taste of it was not enough. I knew what I needed.

This was the beginning of my drug addiction, which lasted, off and on, for a little more than a decade. I told myself that I wanted more, more of that bliss, but I think I really wanted to recapture this first experience and have it back entire, for nothing in that decade-and-a-bit ever surpassed it.

During that decade, a Millhaven boy who has much more to do with this story than I do began his odd divided life. He lost his mother at the age of five; he had been taught to hate, love, and fear a punishing deity and a sinful world. The boy's name was Fielding Bandolier, but he was known as Fee until he was eighteen; after that he had many names, at least one for each town where he lived. Under one of these names, he has already appeared in this story.

I was in Singapore and Bangkok, and Fee Bandolier's various lives were connected to mine only by the name of a record, *Blue Rose*, recorded by the tenor saxophonist Glenroy Breakstone in 1955 as a memorial to his pianist, James Treadwell, who had been murdered. Glenroy Breakstone was Millhaven's only great jazz musician, the only one worthy of being mentioned with Lester Young and Wardell Gray and Ben Webster. Glenroy Breakstone could make you see musical phrases turning over in the air. Passionate radiance illuminated those phrases, and as they revolved they endured in the air, like architecture.

I could remember *Blue Rose* note for note from my boyhood, as I demonstrated to myself when I found a copy in Bangkok in 1981, and listened to it again after twenty-one years in my room upstairs over the flower market. It was on the Prestige label. Tommy Flanagan replaced James Treadwell, the murdered piano player. Side One: 'These Foolish Things'; 'But Not for Me'; 'Someone to Watch Over Me'; 'Star Dust.' Side Two: 'It's You or No One'; 'Skylark'; 'My Ideal'; ''Tis Autumn'; 'My Romance'; 'Blues for James.'

4

When I emerged from the trance induced by Li Ly's cigarettes, I found myself seated on the floor of the shed beside the desk, facing the open loading bay. Di Maestro was standing in the middle of the room, staring with great concentration at nothing at all, like a cat. His right index finger was upraised, as if he were listening to a complicated bit of music. Pirate was seated against the opposite wall, holding another 100 in one hand and a dark brown drink in the other.

'Enjoy the trip?'

'What's in there besides grass?' My mouth was full of glue.

'Opium.'

'Aha,' I said. 'Any left?'

He inhaled and nodded toward the desk. I craned my neck and saw two long cigarettes lying loose between the typewriter and the bottle. I took them from the desk and put them in my shirt pocket.

Pirate made a *tsk, tsk* sound against his teeth with his tongue.

I squinted into the sunlight on the other side of the bay and saw Picklock lying in the bed of the truck, either asleep or in a daze. He looked like an oversized dog. If you got too close he would bristle and woof. Di Maestro attended to his imperious music. Scoot was ranging back and forth over the body bags, humming to himself as he looked at the tags. Attica was gone. Ratman, at first glance also missing, finally appeared as a pair of boots protruding from beneath the body of the truck. One of the bottles of Jack Daniels had disappeared, probably with Attica, and the other was three-fourths empty.

I discovered the glass in my hand. All the ice had melted. I drank some of the warm watery liquid, and it cut through the glue in my mouth.

'Who lives outside the camp?' I asked.

'Where you were? That's *inside* the camp.'

'But who are they?'

'We have won their hearts and minds,' Pirate said.

'Where do the kids come from?'

'Benny's from heaven,' Pirate said, obscurely.

Di Maestro lowered his finger. 'I believe I'd accept another cocktail.'

To my surprise, Pirate got to his feet, walked in my direction across the shed, and put his hand around a glass left on the desk. He poured an inch of whiskey into it and gave the glass to di Maestro. Then he went back to his old place.

'When I first came to this fucking paradise,' di Maestro said, still carefully regarding his invisible point in space, 'there must have been no more than two–three kids out there. Now there's almost ten.' He drank about half of what was in his glass. 'I think all of 'em kinda look like Red Dog Atwater.' This was the name of our CO.

Scoot stopped humming. 'Oh, shit,' he said. 'Oh, sweet Jesus on a pole.'

'Listen to that hillbilly,' di Maestro said.

Scoot was so excited that he was pulling on his ponytail. 'They finally got him. He's here. The goddamn son of a bitch is dead.'

'It's a friend of Scoot's,' Pirate said.

Scoot was kneeling beside one of the body bags, running his hands over it and laughing.

'Close friend,' said Pirate.

'He nearly got in and out before I could pay my respects,' said Scoot. He unzipped the bag in one quick movement and looked up, challenging di Maestro to stop him. That smell that set us apart came from the bag.

Di Maestro leaned over and peered down into the bag. 'So that's him.'

Scoot laughed like a happy baby. 'This makes my fuckin' *month*. And I almost missed him. I knew he'd get wasted some day, so I kept checkin' the names, but today's the day he comes in.'

'He's got that pricky little nose,' di Maestro said. 'He's got those pricky little eyes.'

Picklock stirred in the truck bed, sat up, rubbed his eyes, and grinned. Like Scoot, Picklock was generally cheered by fresh reminders that he was in Vietnam. The door at the far end of the shed opened, and I turned around to see Attica saunter in. He was wearing sunglasses and a clean shirt, and he brought with him a sharp clean smell of soap.

'Chest wound,' di Maestro said.

'He died slow, at least,' said Scoot.

'That Havens?' Attica's saunter picked up a little speed. He tilted his head and tipped an imaginary hat as he passed me.

'I found Havens,' Scoot said. There was awe in his

49

voice. 'He almost got through.'

'Who checked his tag?' Attica asked, and stopped moving for an instant.

Di Maestro slowly turned toward me. 'On your feet, Underdog.'

I picked myself up. A fragment of that peace that had altered my life had returned.

'Did you check the tags on Captain Havens?'

It was a long time ago, but I could dimly remember checking a captain's tags.

Attica's rich dark laugh sounded like music – like Glenroy Breakstone, in fact. 'The professor didn't know shit about Havens.'

'Uh huh.' Scoot was gloating down into the bag in a way that made me uneasy.

I asked who Havens was.

Scoot tugged his ponytail again. 'Why do you think I wear this fuckin' thing? Havens. This is my *protest*.' The word struck him. 'I'm a protestor, di Maestro.' He stuck up two fingers in the peace symbol.

'Baby,' di Maestro said. 'Bomb Hanoi.'

'Fuck that, bomb Saigon.' He leveled an index finger at me. His eyes burned far back in his head, and his cheeks seemed sunken. Scoot was always balanced on an edge between concentration and violence, and all the drugs did was to make this more apparent. 'I never told you about Havens? Didn't I give you the Havens speech?'

'You didn't get around to it yet,' di Maestro said.

'Fuck the Havens speech,' said Scoot. His sunken, intent look was frightening exactly to the extent that it showed he was thinking. 'You know what's wrong with this shit, Underdog?' He gave the peace symbol again and looked at his own hand as if seeing the gesture for the first time. 'All the wrong people do this. People who think there are rules behind the rules. That's *wrong*. You fight for your life till death do you part, and then you got it

50

made. Peace is the fight, man. You don't know that, you're fucked *up*.'

'Peace is the fight,' I said.

'Because there ain't no rules behind the rules.'

That I nearly understood what he was saying scared me – I did not want to know whatever Scoot knew. It cost too much.

Havens must have been the reason Scoot was on the body squad instead of out in the field where he belonged. I had been wondering what someone like Scoot could do that would be bad enough to banish him from his regular unit, and it occurred to me that now I was about to find out.

Scoot stared at di Maestro. 'You know what's gonna happen here.'

'We'll send him home,' di Maestro said.

'Gimme a drink,' Scoot said. I poured the rest of the Jack Daniels into my glass and walked across the shed to get a look at Captain Havens. I gave Scoot the glass and looked down at a brown-haired American man. His jaw was square, and so was his forehead. He had that pricky little nose and those pricky little eyes. A transparent sheet of adhesive plastic covered the hole in his chest. Scoot tossed the glass back to me and detached his knife from its peculiar thong, which looked more than ever like a body part. Then I saw what it was.

Scoot noticed my quiver of revulsion, and he turned his crazy glance on me again. 'You think this is about revenge. You're wrong. It's proof.'

Proof that he was right and Captain Havens had been wrong – wrong from the start. No matter what he said, I still thought it was revenge.

Attica took an interested step forward. Picklock sat up straight in the back of the truck.

Scoot leaned over Captain Havens's body and began sawing off his left ear. It took more effort than I had imagined it would, and the long cords of muscle stood out in his arm. At length the white-gray bit of flesh stretched and came away, looking smaller than it had on Captain Havens's head.

'Dry it out, be fine in a week or two,' Scoot said. He placed the ear beside him on the concrete and bent over Captain Havens like a surgeon in midoperation. He was smiling with concentration. Scoot pushed the double-edged point beneath the hair just beside the wound he had made and began running the blade upward along the hairline.

I turned away, and someone handed me the last of the hundred that had been circulating. I took another hit, handed back the roach, and walked past Attica toward the door. 'Make a nice wall mount,' Attica said.

As soon as I got outside, the sunlight poured into my eyes and the ground swung up toward me. I staggered for a moment. The sound of distant shelling came to me, and I turned away from the main part of the camp, irrationally afraid that body parts were going to fall out of the sky.

I moved aimlessly along a dirt track that led through a stand of weedy trees – spindly trunks with a scattering of leaves and branches at their tops, like afterthoughts. It came to me that the army had chosen to let these miserable trees stand. Normally they leveled every tree in sight. Therefore, they wanted to hide whatever was behind the trees. I felt like a genius for having worked this out.

An empty village had been erected on the far side of the growth of trees. One-story wooden structures marched up both sides of two intersecting streets. There were no gates and no guards. Before me in the center of the suburb, on a little green at the intersection of the two streets, an unfamiliar military flag hung limply beside the Stars and Stripes.

It looked like a ghost town.

A man in black sunglasses and a neat gray suit walked out of one of the little frame buildings and looked at me. He crossed over the rough grass in front of the next two structures, glancing at me now and then. When he reached the third building he jumped up the steps and disappeared inside. He had looked as out of place as Magritte's locomotive coming out of a fireplace.

The instant the door closed behind Magritte, another opened and a tall soldier in green fatigues emerged. It was like a farce: a clockwork village where one door opened as soon as another closed. The tall soldier glanced at me, seemed to hesitate, and began moving toward me.

Fuck you, I thought, I have a right to be here. I do the dirty work for you assholes.

He kicked up dust as he walked. He was carrying a .45 in a black leather holster hung from his web belt, and two ballpoint pens jutted out of the slanted, blousy pocket of his shirt. There were two crossed rifles on his collar, and a captain's star on his epaulets. He carried something soft in one hand, and a wristwatch with a steel band hung upside down from a slot in his collar.

Too late, I remembered to salute. When my hand was still at my forehead, I saw that the man coming toward me had the face I had just seen in a body bag. It was Captain Havens. My eyes dropped to the name tag stitched to his shirt. The steel watch covered the first two or three letters, and all I could read was SOM.

Good trick, I thought. First I see him being scalped, then I see him coming at me.

I thought of wet elm leaves in a gutter.

The ghost of Captain Havens smiled at me. The ghost called me by name and asked, 'How'd you find out I was here?' When he came closer I saw that the ghost was John Ransom.

5

'Just a guess,' I said, and when his smile turned quizzical, 'I was just following the road to see where it went.'

'That's pretty much how I got here, too,' Ransom said. He was close enough to shake my hand, and as he reached out he must have caught the stench of the shed, and maybe the smells of whiskey and the one hundreds too. His eyebrows moved together. 'What have you been doing?'

'I'm on the body squad. Over there.' I nodded toward the road. 'What do you do? What is this place?'

He had grasped my hand, but instead of shaking it, he spun me around and marched me away from the empty-looking camp and into the spindly trees. 'You better stay out of sight until you straighten up,' he said.

'You should see what the rest of them are doing,' I said, but sat down at the base of one of the trees and leaned against the slick, spongy bark. The man in the gray suit and sunglasses came out of the building he had entered earlier and strode back across the grass to the building he had left. He jumped up onto the stoop and touched his breast pocket before he went in.

'Johnny got his gun,' I said.

'That's Francis Pinkel, Senator Burrman's aide. Pinkel thinks he's James Bond. That's a Walther PPK in his shoulder holster. We're giving the senator a briefing, and then we'll take him up in a helicopter and show him one of our projects.'

'You in some kind of private army?'

He showed me the soft green cap in his hand.

'You're one of those guys in Harry Truman shirts who carry briefcases and live out in Darlac Province, messing around with the Rhades.' I laughed.

'Sometimes we're asked to fly in wearing civvies,' he said. He placed the beret on his head. It was a dark forest green with a leather roll around its bottom seam, and it had a patch with two arrows crossing a sword above the words *De Oppresso Liber*. It looked good on him. 'How'd a lousy grunt like you learn so much?'

'You learn a lot, working on the body squad. What is this place here?'

'Special Operations Group. We ride piggyback on White Star when we're not in Darlac Province, messing around with the Rhade.'

'You really do that?'

John Ransom explained that the CIDG program in Darlac Province had been going since the early sixties, but that he had been assigned to border surveillance in the highlands near the Laotian border, in Khan Duc. Last year, they had parachuted in a bulldozer and carved a landing strip out of a jungle ridge line. While they looked for the Khatu tribesmen he was supposed to be working with, his actual troops were press-ganged teenagers from Danang and Hue. The teenagers were a little hairy, Ransom said. They weren't much like the Rhade Montagnards. He sounded frustrated when he told me about his troops, and angry with himself for letting me see his frustration – the teenagers played transistors on patrol, he said. 'But they kill everything that moves. Including monkeys.'

'How long have you been here?'

'Five months, but I've been in the service three years. Did the Special Forces training at Bragg, got here just in time to help set up Khan Duc. It's not like the regular army.' He had begun to sound oddly defensive to me.

'We actually get out and do things. We get into parts of the country the army never sees, and our A teams do a lot of damage to the VC.'

'I wondered who was doing all that damage,' I said.

'These days people don't believe in an elite, even the army has problems with that, but that's what we are. You ever hear of Sully Fontaine? Ever hear of Franklin Bachelor?'

I shook my head. 'We're a pretty elite group in the body squad, too. Ever hear of di Maestro? Picklock? Scoot?'

He nearly shuddered. 'I'm talking about heroes. We have guys who fought the Russians with *Germany* – we have guys who fought the Russians in Czechoslovakia.'

'I didn't know we were fighting the Russkies yet,' I said.

'We're fighting communism,' he said simply. 'That's what it's all about. Stopping the spread of communism.'

He had maintained his faith even during five months of shepherding teenage hoodlums through the highlands, and I thought I could see how he had done it. He was staring forward to see something like pure experience.

I wished that he could meet Scoot and Ratman. I thought Senator Burrman should meet them, too. They could have an exchange of views.

'How did you get on the body squad?' Ransom asked me.

Francis Pinkel popped out of a building and scouted the ghost town for marauding VC. A burly gray-haired man who must have been the senator came out after him, followed by a Special Forces colonel. The colonel was short and solid and walked as if he were trying to drive his feet into the ground by the sheer force of his personality.

'Captain McCue thought I'd enjoy the work.'

I saw Ransom memorizing the name. He asked me

where I was supposed to join my unit, and I told him.

He flipped up the watch hanging from his collar. 'About time for my dog and pony show. Can't you get a shower and drink a lot of coffee or something?'

'You don't understand the body squad,' I said. 'We work better this way.'

'I'm going to take care of you,' he said, and began to trot out of the woods toward the senator's building. Then he turned around and waved. 'Maybe we'll run into each other at Camp Crandall.' It was clear he thought that we never would.

I met John Ransom twice at Camp Crandall. Everything about him had changed by the first time we met again, and by the second time he had changed even more. He'd had a narrow scrape at a fortified Montagnard village called Lang Vei. Most of his Bru tribesmen had been killed, and so had most of the Green Berets there. After a week, Ransom escaped from an underground bunker filled with the bodies of his friends. When the surviving Bru finally made it to Khe Sanh, the marines took away their rifles and ordered them back into the jungle. By this time a prominent marine officer had publicly ridiculed what he called the Green Berets' 'anthropological' warfare.

6

I have used the phrase 'the bottom of the world' twice, and that is two times too often. Neither I, nor John Ransom, nor any other person who returned ever saw the real bottom of the world. Those who did can never speak. Elie Wiesel uses the expression 'children of the night' to describe Holocaust survivors: some children came out of that night and others did not, but the ones who did were changed forever. Against a background of night and darkness stands a child. The child, whose hand is extended toward you, who is smiling enigmatically, has come straight out of that dark background. The child can speak or must be silent forever, as the case may be.

7

My sister April's death – her murder – happened like this. She was nine, I was seven. She had gone out after school to play with her friend Margaret Rasmussen. Dad was where he always was around six o'clock in the evening, at the end of South Sixth Street, our street, in the Idle Hour. Mom was taking a nap. Margaret Rasmussen's house was five blocks away, on the other side of Livermore Avenue. It was only two blocks away if you crossed Livermore and went straight through the arched tunnel like a viaduct that connected the St Alwyn Hotel to its annex. Bums and winos, of which our neighborhood had a share, sometimes gathered in this tunnel. My sister, April, knew she was supposed to go the three blocks around the front of the St Alwyn and then back down Pulaski Street, but she was always impatient to get to Margaret Rasmussen's house, and I knew that she usually went straight through the tunnel.

This was a secret. It was one of our secrets.

I was listening to the radio alone in our living room. I want to remember, I sometimes think I really do remember, a sense of dread directly related to the St Alwyn's tunnel. If this memory is correct, I knew that April was going to have crossed Livermore Street in no more than a minute, that she was going to ignore the safety of the detour and walk into that tunnel, and that something bad waited for her in there.

I was listening to 'The Shadow,' the only radio program that actually scared me. *Who knows what evil lurks in the hearts of men? The Shadow knows.* After this came a sinister, even a frightening, laugh. Not long before, Dad had shown me a *Ledger* article claiming that the real Shadow, the one the radio series was based on, was an old man who lived in Millhaven. His name was Lamont von Heilitz, and a long time ago he called himself 'an amateur of crime.'

I turned off the radio and then, sneakily, switched it back on again in case Mom woke up and wondered what I was doing. I walked out of the front door and jogged down the path to the sidewalk, where I began to run toward Livermore Street. April was not waiting on the corner for the light to change, which meant that she had already crossed Livermore and would be in the tunnel. All I wanted was to get past the Idle Hour unnoticed and to see April's slight blond figure emerging into the sunlight on the far side of the tunnel. Then I could turn around and go home.

I don't believe in premonitions, not personally. I believe that other people have them, not me.

A stalled truck kept me from seeing across Livermore Avenue. The truck was long and shiny, with some big name painted on its side, ALLERTON maybe, or ALLINGHAM. Elms still lined Millhaven's streets, and their leaves were strewn thickly in the gutter, where clear water from a broken hydrant gurgled over and through them and carried a few, like toast-colored rafts, to the drain down the street. A folded newspaper lay half in, half out of the water; I remember a photograph of one boxer hitting another in a spray of sweat and saliva.

At last the truck began to move forward, ALLERTON or ALLINGHAM with it.

The truck moved past the front of the arched little bridge to the St Alwyn annex, and I leaned forward to see through the trafic. Cars slid by and interrupted my view. April's pale blue dress was moving safely through the tunnel. She was about half of the way down its length, and had perhaps four feet to go before coming out into the disappearing daylight. The flow of cars cut her off from me again, then allowed me another flash of blue.

An adult-sized shadow moved away from the darkness of the wall and moved toward April. The traffic blocked my view again.

It was just someone coming home through the tunnel – someone on his way to the Idle Hour. But the big shadow had been moving *toward* April, not past her. I imagined that I had seen something in the big shadow's hand.

Through the sound of horns and engines, I thought I heard a voice rising to a scream, but another blast of horns cut it off. Or something else cut it off. The horns stopped blaring when the traffic moved – homeward traffic at six-fifteen on an autumn night, moving beneath the elms that arched over Livermore and South Sixth Street. I peered through the cars, nearly hopping with anxiety, and saw April's oddly limp back. Her hair fell back past her shoulders, and the whole streak of blond and pale blue that was her back went *up*. The man's arm moved. Dread froze me to the sidewalk.

For a moment it seemed that everything on the street, maybe everything in Millhaven, had stopped, including me. The thought of what was happening across the street pushed me forward over the leaves packed into the gutter and down into the roadbed. There was no traffic anymore, only an opening between cars through which I saw April's dress floating in midair. I moved into the opening, and only then became aware that cars were flowing past on both sides of me and that most of them were blowing their horns. For a moment, nearly my last moment, I knew that all movement had ceased in the tunnel. The man stopped moving. He turned toward the noise in the street, and I saw the shape of his head, the set of his shoulders.

At that point, though I was unaware of it, my father came out of the Idle Hour. Several other men came with him, but Dad was the first one through the door.

A car horn blasted in my ear, and I turned my head. The grille of an automobile was coming toward me with what seemed terrific slowness. I was absolutely unable to move. I knew that the car was going to hit me. This certainty existed entirely apart from my terror. It was like knowing the answer to the most important question on a test. The car was going to hit me, and I was going to die.

Writing about this in the third person, in *Mystery*, was easier.

My vision of things ceases with the car coming toward me with terrific unstoppable slowness, frame by frame, as a car would advance through a series of photographs. Dad and his friends saw the car hit me; they saw me adhere to the grille, then slip down to be caught on a bumper ornament and dragged thirty feet before the car jolted to a halt and threw me off.

At that moment I died – the boy named Timothy Underhill, the seven-year-old me, died of shock and injury. He had a fractured skull, his pelvis and his right leg were shattered, and he died. Such a moment is not visible from a sidewalk. I have the memory of sensation, of being torn from my body by a giant, irresistible force and being accelerated into another, utterly different dimension. Of blazing light. What remains is the sense of leaving the self behind, all personality and character, everything merely personal. All of that was gone, and something else was left. I want to think that I was aware of April far ahead of me, sailing like a leaf through some vast dark cloudgate. There was an enormous, annihilating light, a bliss, an ecstasy you have to die to earn. Unreasoning terror surrounds and engulfs this memory, if that's what it is. I dream about it two or three times a week, a little more frequently than I dream about the man I killed face-to-face. The experience was entirely nonverbal and, in some basic way, profoundly *inhuman*. One of my clearest and strongest impressions is that living people are *not supposed to know*.

I woke up encased in plaster, a rag, a scrap, in a hospital room. There followed a year of wretchedness, of wheelchairs and useless anger – all this is in *Mystery*. Not in that book is my parents' endless and tongue-tied misery. My own problems were eclipsed, put utterly into shadow by April's death. And because I see her benevolent ghost from time to time, particularly on airplanes, I guess that I have never really recovered either.

On October fifteenth, while I was still in the hospital, the first of the Blue Rose murders took place on almost exactly the same place where April died. The victim was a prostitute named Arlette Monaghan, street name Fancy. She was twenty-six. Above her body on the brick wall of the St Alwyn, the murderer had written the words BLUE ROSE.

Early in the morning of October twentieth, James Treadwell's corpse was found in bed in room 218 of the St Alwyn. He too had been murdered by someone who had written the words BLUE ROSE on the wall above the body.

On the twenty-fifth of October, another young man, Monty Leland, was murdered late at night on the corner of South Sixth and Livermore, the act sheltered from the sparse traffic down Livermore at that hour by the corner of the Idle Hour. The usual words, left behind by the tavern's front door, were painted over as soon as the police allowed by the Idle Hour's owner, Roman Majestyk.

On November third, a young doctor named Charles 'Buzz' Laing managed to survive wounds given him by an unseen assailant who had left him for dead in his house on Millhaven's east side. His throat had been slashed from behind, and his attacker had written BLUE ROSE on his bedroom wall.

The final Blue Rose murder, or what seemed for forty-one years to be the final Blue Rose murder, was that of Heinz Stenmitz, a butcher who lived on Muffin Street with his wife and a succession of foster children, all boys. Four days after the attack on the doctor, Stenmitz was killed outside his shop, next door to his house. I have no difficulty remembering Mr Stenmitz. He was an unsettling man, and when I saw his name in the *Ledger*'s subhead (the headline was BLUE ROSE KILLER CLAIMS FOURTH VICTIM), I experienced an ungenerous satisfaction that would have shocked my parents.

I knew, as my parents did not – as they refused to believe, despite a considerable scandal the year before – that there were two Mr Stenmitzes. One was the humorless, Teutonic, but efficient butcher who sold them their chops and sausages. Tall, blond, bearded, blue-eyed, he carried himself with an aggressive rectitude deeply admired by both my parents. His attitude was military, in the sense that the character played over and over by C. Aubrey Smith in Hollywood films of the thirties and forties was military.

The other Mr Stenmitz was the one I saw when my parents put two dollars in my hand and sent me to the butcher shop for hamburger. My parents did not believe in the existence of this other man within Mr Stenmitz. If I had insisted on his presence, their disbelief would have turned into anger.

The Mr Stenmitz I saw when I was alone always came out from behind the counter. He would stoop down and rub my head, my arms, my chest. His huge blond bearded head was far too close. The smells of raw meat and blood, always prominent in the shop, seemed to intensify, as if they were what the butcher ate and drank. 'You came to see your friend Heinz?' A pat on the cheek. 'You can't stay away from your friend Heinz, can you?' A sharp, almost painful pat on the buttocks. His thick red fingers found my pockets and began to insinuate themselves. His eyes were the lightest, palest blue eyes I've ever seen, the eyes of a Finnish sled dog. 'You have two dollars? What are these two dollars for? So your friend Heinz will show you a nice surprise, maybe?'

'Hamburger,' I would say.

The fingers were pinching and roaming through my pocket. 'Any love letters in there? Any pictures of pretty girls?'

Sometimes I saw the miserable child who had been sent to his house, a child for whom Mr and Mrs Stenmitz were paid to care, and the sight of that hopeless Billy or Joey made me want to run away. Something had *happened* to these children: they had been squeezed dry and ironed flat. They were slightly dirty, and their clothes always looked too big or too small, but what was scary about them was that they had no humanity, no light – it had been drained right out of them.

When I saw Mr Stenmitz's name under the terrible headline I felt amazed and fascinated, but mainly I felt relief. I would not have to go into his shop alone anymore; and I would not have to endure the awful anxiety of going there with my parents and seeing what *they* saw, C. Aubrey Smith in a butcher's apron, while also seeing the other, terrible Heinz Stenmitz winking and capering beneath the mask.

I was glad he was dead. He couldn't have been dead enough, to suit me.

8

Then there were no more of the murders. The last place someone wrote BLUE ROSE on a wall was outside Stenmitz's Quality Meats and Home-Made Sausages. The man who wrote those mysterious words near his victims' bodies had called it quits. His plan, whatever it was, had been fulfilled, or his rage had satisfied itself. Millhaven waited for something to happen; Millhaven wanted the second shoe to drop.

After another month, in a great fire of publicity, the second shoe did drop. One of the clearest memories of the beginning of my year of convalescence is of the *Ledger*'s revelations about the secret history of the murders. The *Ledger* found a hidden coherence in the Blue Rose murders and was delighted, with the sort of delight that masquerades as shock, by the twist at the story's end. I read a tremendous amount during that year, but I read nothing as avidly as I did the *Ledger*. It was terrible, it was tragic, but it was all such a tremendous *story*. It became my story, the story that most opened up the world for me.

As each installment of William Damrosch's story appeared in the *Ledger*, I cut it out and pasted it into an already bulging scrapbook. When discovered, this scrapbook caused some excitement. Mom thought that a seven-year-old so interested in awfulness must be awful himself; Dad thought the whole thing was a damn shame. It was over his head, out of his hands. He gave up on everything, including us. He lost his elevator job at the St Alwyn and moved out. Even before he was fired from the St Alwyn, he had given indications of turning into one of the winos who hung out in Dead Man's Tunnel, and after he had been fired and moved into a tenement on Oldtown Way, he slipped among them for a time. Dad did not drink in Dead Man's Tunnel. He carried his pint bottle wrapped in a brown paper bag to other places around the Valley and the near south side, but his clothes grew dirty and sour, he seldom shaved, he began to look old and hesitant.

The front pages of the *Ledger* that I pasted into my Blue Rose scrapbook described how the homicide detective in charge of the murder investigation had been found seated at his desk in his shabby basement apartment with a bullet hole in his right temple. It was the day before Christmas. The *Ledger* being what it was, the blood and other matter on the wall beside the body was not unrecorded. Detective Damrosch's service revolver, a Smith & Wesson .38 from which a single shot had been fired, was dangling from his right hand. On the desk in front of the detective was a bottle of Three Feathers bourbon, all but empty, an empty glass, a pen and a rectangular sheet of paper torn from a notebook, also on the desk. The words BLUE ROSE had been printed on the paper in block capitals. Sometime between three and five o'clock in the morning, Detective Damrosch had finished his whiskey, written two words on a sheet of notebook paper, and by committing suicide confessed to the murders he had been supposed to solve.

Sometimes life is like a book.

The headlines that followed traced out Detective William Damrosch's extraordinary background. His real name was Carlos Rosario, not William Damrosch, and he had been

66

not so much born as propelled into the world on a freezing January wind – some anonymous citizen had seen the half-dead child on the frozen bank of the Millhaven River. The citizen called the police from the telephone booth in the Green Woman Taproom. When the police scrambled down from the bridge to rescue the baby, they found his mother, Carmen Rosario, stabbed to death beneath the bridge. The crime was never solved: Carmen Rosario was an illegal immigrant from Santo Domingo and a prostitute, and the police made only perfunctory efforts to find her killer. The nameless child, who was called Billy by the social worker who had taken him from the police, was placed into a series of foster homes. He grew up to be a violent, sexually uncertain teenager whose intelligence served mainly to get him into trouble. Given the choice of prison or the army, he chose the army; and his life changed. By now he was Billy Damrosch, having taken the name of his last foster mother, and Billy Damrosch could use his intelligence to save his life. He came out of the army with a box full of medals, a scattering of scars, and the intention of becoming a policeman in Millhaven. Now, with the prescience of hindsight, I think he wanted to come back to Millhaven to find out who had killed his mother.

According to the police, he could not have killed April, because Bill Damrosch only killed people he knew.

Monty Leland, who had been killed in front of the Idle Hour, was a small-time criminal, one of Damrosch's informants. Early in his career, before his transfer from the vice squad, Damrosch had many times arrested Arlette Monaghan, the prostitute slashed to death behind the St Alwyn, a tenuous link considering that other vice squad officers past and present had arrested her as often. It was assumed that James Treadwell, the piano player in Glenroy Breakstone's band, had been murdered because he had seen Damrosch kill Arlette.

The most telling connections between Detective Damrosch and the people he murdered entered with the remaining two victims.

Five years before the murders began, Buzz Laing had lived for a year with William Damrosch. This information came from a housekeeper Dr Laing had fired. They was more than friends, the housekeeper declared, because I never had to change more than one set of sheets, and I can tell you they fought like cats and dogs. Or dogs and dogs. Millhaven is a conservative place, and Buzz Laing lost half of his patients. Fortunately, he had private money – the same money that had paid for the disgruntled housekeeper and the big house on the lake – and after a while, most of his patients came back to him. For the record, Laing always insisted that it was not William Damrosch who had tried to kill him. He had been attacked from behind in the dark, and he had passed out before he was able to turn around, but he was certain that his attacker had been larger than himself. Buzz Laing was six feet two, and Damrosch was some three inches shorter.

But it was the detective's relationship with the last victim of the Blue Rose murderer that spoke loudest. You will already have guessed that Billy Damrosch was one of the wretched boys who passed through the ungentle hands of Heinz Stenmitz. By now, Stenmitz was a disgraced man. He had been sent to the state penitentiary for child molestation after a suspicious social worker named Dorothy Greenglass had finally discovered what he had been doing to the children in his care. During his year in jail, his wife continued to work in the butcher shop while broadcasting her grievances – her husband, a God-fearing hardworking Christian man, had been railroaded by liars and cheats. Some of her customers believed her. After Stenmitz came home, he went back behind the counter as if nothing had happened. Other people remembered the testimony of the social worker and the few grown boys who had agreed to speak for the prosecution.

It was what you would expect – one of those tormented boys had come back to exact justice. He had wanted to forget what he had done – he hated the kind of man Stenmitz had turned him into. It was tragic. Decent people would put all this behind them and go back to normal life.

But I turned the pages of my scrapbook over and over, trying to find a phrase, a look in the eye, a curl of the mouth, that would tell me if William Damrosch was the man I had seen in the tunnel with my sister.

When I tried to think about it, I heard great wings beating in my head.

I thought of April sailing on before me into that world of annihilating light, the world no living person is supposed to know. William Damrosch had killed Heinz Stenmitz, but I did not know if he had killed my sister. And that meant that April was sailing forever into that realm I had glimpsed.

So of course I saw her ghost sometimes. When I was eight I turned around on a bus seat and saw April four rows back, her pale face turned toward the window. Unable to breathe, I faced forward again. When I turned back around, she was gone. When I was eleven I saw her standing on the lower deck of the double-decker ferry that was taking my mother and myself across Lake Michigan. I saw her carrying a single loaf of French bread to a car in the parking lot of a Berkeley grocery store. She appeared among a truckful of army nurses at Camp Crandall in Vietnam – a nine-year-old blond girl in the midst of the uniformed nurses, looking at me with an unsmiling face. I have seen her twice, riding by in passing taxis, in New York City. Last year, I was flying to London on British Airways, and I turned around in my seat to look for the stewardess and saw April seated in the last seat of the last row in first class, looking out of the window with her chin on her fist. I faced forward and held my breath. When I looked around again, the seat was empty.

9

This is where I dip my buckets, where I fill my pen.

10

My first book, *A Beast in View*, was about a false identity, and it turned out that *The Divided Man* was also about a mistaken identity. I was haunted by William Damrosch, a true child of the night, who intrigued me because he seemed to be both a decent man and a murderer. Along with Millhaven, I assumed that he was guilty. *Koko* was essentially about a mistaken identity and *Mystery* was about the greatest mistake ever made by Lamont von Heilitz, Millhaven's famous private detective. He thought he had identified a murderer, and that the murderer had then committed suicide. These books are about the way the known story is not the right or the real story. I saw April because I missed her and *wanted* to see her, also because she wanted me to know that the real story had been abandoned with the past. Which is to say that part of me had been waiting for John Ransom's phone call ever since I read and reread the *Ledger*'s description of William Damrosch's body seated dead before his desk. The empty bottle and the empty glass, the dangling gun, the words printed on the piece of notebook paper. The block letters.

The man I killed face-to-face jumped up in front of me on a trail called Striker Tiger. He wore glasses and had a round, pleasant face momentarily rigid with amazement. He was a bad soldier, worse even than me. He was carrying a long wooden rifle that looked like an antique. I shot him and he fell straight down, like a puppet, and disappeared into the tall grass. My heart banged. I stepped forward to look at him and imagined him raising a knife or lifting that antique rifle where he lay hidden in the grass. Yet I had seen him fall the way dead birds fall out of the sky, and I knew he was not lifting that rifle. Behind me a soldier named Linklater was whooping, 'Did you see that? Did you see Underdown nail that gook?' Automatically I said, 'Underhill.' Conor Linklater had some minor mental disorder that caused him to jumble words and phrases. He once said, 'The truth is in the pudding.' Here is the pudding. I felt a strange, violent sense of triumph, of having *won*, like a blood-soaked gladiator in an arena. I went forward through the grass and saw a leg in the black trousers, then another leg opened beside it, then his narrow chest and outflung arms, finally his head. The bullet had entered his throat and torn out the back of his neck. He was like the mirror image of Andrew T. Majors, over whose corpse I had become a pearl diver for the body squad. 'You got him, boy,' said Conor Linklater. 'You got him real good.' The savage sense of victory was gone. I felt empty. Below his thin ankles, his feet were as bony as fish. From the chin up he looked as if he were working out one of those algebra problems about where two trains would meet if they were traveling at different speeds. It was clear to me that this man had a mother, a father, a sister, a girlfriend.

I thought of putting the barrel of my M-16 in the wound in his throat and shooting him all over again. People who would never know my name, whose names I would never know, would hate me. (This thought came later.) 'Hey, it's okay,' Conor said. 'It's okay, Tim.' The lieutenant told him to button his lip, and we moved ahead on Striker Tiger. While knowing I would not, I almost expected to hear the man I had killed crawling away through the grass.

11

On the morning of the day that John Ransom called me, I shuddered awake all at once. A terrible dream clung to me. I jumped out of bed to shake it off, and as soon as I was on my feet I realized that I had only been dreaming. It was just past six. Early June light burned around the edges of the curtain near my bed. I looked down from my platform over the loft and saw the books stacked on my coffee table, the couches with their rumpled covers, the stack of papers that was one-third of the first draft of a novel on my desk, the blank screen and keyboard of the computer, the laser printer on its stand. Three empty Perrier bottles stood on the desk. My kingdom was in order, but I needed more Perrier. And I was still shaken by the dream.

I was seated in a clean, high-tech restaurant very different from Saigon, the Vietnamese restaurant two floors beneath my loft on Grand Street. (Two friends, Maggie Lah and Michael Poole, live in the loft between my place and the restaurant.) Bare white walls instead of painted palm fronds, pink linen tablecloths with laundry creases. The waiter handed me a long stiff folded white menu printed with the restaurant's name, *L'Imprime*. I opened the menu and saw Human Hand listed among *Les Viandes*. Human hand, I thought, that'll be interesting, and when the waiter returned, I ordered it. It came almost immediately, two large, red, neatly severed hands covered with what looked more like the rind of a ham than skin. Nothing else was on the white disc of the plate. I cut a section from the base of the left hand's thumb and put it in my mouth. It seemed a little undercooked. Then the sickening realization that I was chewing a piece of a hand struck me, and I gagged and spat it out into my pink napkin. I shoved the plate across the table and hoped that the waiter would not notice that I did not have the stomach for this meal. At that moment I woke up shuddering and jumped out of bed.

From the light that gathered and burned around the edge of the curtain, I knew that the day would be hot. We were going to have one of those unbearable New York summers when the dog shit steams like dumplings on the sidewalks. By August the entire city would be wrapped in a hot wet towel. I lay back down on the bed and tried to stop shaking. Outside, in the sunny space between buildings, I heard the cooing of a bird and thought it was a white dove. The dove made a morning sound, and my mind stalled for a moment on the question of whether the bird was a morning or a mourning dove. It had a soft, questioning cry, and when the sound came again, I heard what the cry was. *Oh*, it drew in its breath, *who? Oh* (indrawn breath), *who, who? Oh, who?* It seemed a question I had been hearing all my life.

I got up and took a shower. In the way that some people sing, I said, *Oh, who?* After I dried myself I remembered the two red hands on the white plate, and wrote this memory down in a notebook. The dream was a message, and even if I was never able to decode it, I might be able to use it in a book. Then I wrote down what the dove had said, thinking that the question must be related to the dream.

My work went slowly, as it had for four or five mornings in a row. I had reached an impasse in my book – I had to solve a problem my story had given me. I wrote a few delaying sentences, made a few notes, and decided to take a long walk. Walking gives the mind a clean white page. I got up, put a pen in my shirt pocket and my notebook in the back pocket of my trousers, and let myself out of the loft.

When I walk I cover great distances, both distracted and lulled by what happens on the street. In theory, the buckets go down into the well and bring up messages from my notebook while my attention is elsewhere. I don't get in my own way; I think about other things. The blocks go by, and words and sentences begin to fill the clean white page. But the page stayed empty through Soho, and by the time I was halfway across Washington Square, I still had not taken my notebook out of my pocket. I watched a teenage boy twirl a skateboard past the drug dealers with their knapsacks and briefcases and saw a motorboat clipping over blue water. One of my characters was steering it. He was squinting into the sun, and now and then he raised his hand to shield his eyes. It was very early morning, just past sunrise, and he was speeding across a lake. He was wearing a gray suit. I knew where he was going, and took out my notebook and wrote: *Charlie – speedboat – suit – sunrise – docks at Lily's house – hides boat in reeds*. I saw fine drops of mist on the lapels of Charlie's nice gray suit.

So that was what Charlie Carpenter was up to.

I began walking up Fifth Avenue, looking at all the people going to work, and saw Charlie concealing his motorboat behind the tall reeds at the edge of Lily Sheehan's property. He jumped out onto damp ground,

74

letting the boat drift back out into the lake. He moved through the reeds and wiped his face and hands with his handkerchief. Then he dabbed at the damp places on his suit. He stopped a moment to comb his hair and straighten his necktie. No lights showed in Lily's windows. He moved quickly across the long lawn toward her porch.

At Fourteenth Street I stopped for a cup of coffee. At Twenty-fourth Street Lily came out of her kitchen and found Charlie Carpenter standing inside her front door. *Decided to stop off on your way to work, Charlie?* She was wearing a long white cotton robe printed with little blue flowers, and her hair was shapeless. I saw that Lily had recently applied eggplant-coloured polish to her toenails. *You're full of surprises*.

Then it stopped moving, at least until it would start again. At Fifty-second Street, I went into the big B. Dalton to look for some books. In the religion section downstairs I bought *Gnosticism*, by Benjamin Walker, *The Nag Hammadi Library*, and *The Gospel According to Thomas*. I took the books outside and decided to walk to Central Park.

When I got past the zoo I sat on a bench, took out my notebook, and looked for Charlie Carpenter and Lily Sheehan. They had not moved. Lily was still saying *You're full of surprises*, and Charlie Carpenter was still standing inside her front door with his hands in his pockets, smiling at her like a little boy. They both looked very fine, but I was not thinking about them now. I was thinking about the body squad and Captain Havens. I remembered the strange, disordered men with whom I spent that time and saw them before me, in our shed. I remembered my first body, and Ratman's story about Bobby Swett, who had disappeared into a red mist. Mostly, I could see Ratman as he was telling the story, his eyes angry and sparkling, his finger jabbing, his whole being coming to life as he talked about the noise the earth made by itself. Ratman seemed astonishingly young now – skinny, with a boy's unfinished skinniness.

Then, without wanting to, I remembered some of what happened later, as I occasionally do when a nightmare wakes me up. I had to get up off the bench, and I shoved my notebook in my pocket and started walking aimlessly through the park. I knew from experience that it would be hours before I could work or even speak normally to anyone. I felt as though I were walking over graves – as though a lot of people like Ratman and di Maestro, both of whom had only been boys too young to vote or drink, lay a few feet beneath the grass. I tensed up when I heard someone coming up behind me. It was time to go home. I turned around and went toward what I hoped was Fifth Avenue. A pigeon beat its wings and jumped into the air, and a circle of grass beneath it flattened out in the pattern made by an ascending helicopter.

It is as though some old part of yourself wakes up in you, terrified, useless in the life you have, its skills and habits destructive but intact, and what is left of the present you, the person you have become, wilts and shrivels in sadness or despair: the person you have become is only a thin shell over this other, more electric and endangered self. The strongest, the least digested parts of your experience can rise up and put you back where you were when they occurred; all the rest of you stands back and weeps.

I saw the face of the man I had killed on a Chinese man carrying his daughter on his shoulders. He jumped up on an almost invisible trail. His face looked frozen – it was almost funny, all that amazement. I watched the Chinese man carry his daughter toward a Sabrett's hot dog cart. The girl's round face filled like a glass with serious, gleeful concentration. Her father held a folded dollar in his hand. He was carrying a ridiculous old rifle that was probably

76

less accurate than a BB gun. He got a hot dog wrapped in white tissue and handed it up to his daughter. No ketchup, no mustard, no sauerkraut. Just your basic hot dog experience. I raised my M-16 and I shot him in the throat and he fell straight down. It looked like a trick.

Charlie Carpenter and Lily Sheehan had turned away from me, they were grinding their teeth and wailing.

I sat down on a bench in the sun. I was sweating. I was not sure if I had been going east toward Fifth Avenue, or west, deeper into the park. I slowly inhaled and exhaled, trying to control the sudden panic. It was just a bad one. It was just a little worse than normal. It was nothing too serious. I grabbed one of the books I had bought and opened it at random. It was *The Gospel According to Thomas*, and here is what I read:

> The Kingdom of Heaven
> Is like a woman carrying a jug
> Full of meal on a long journey.
> When the handle broke,
> The meal streamed out behind her, so that
> She never noticed anything was wrong, until
> Arriving home, she set the jug down
> And found that it was empty.
> The Kingdom of Heaven
> Is like a man who wished to assassinate a noble.
> He drew his sword at home, and struck it
> against the wall,
> To test whether his hand were strong enough.
> Then he went out, and killed the noble.

I thought of my father drinking in the alley behind the St Alwyn Hotel. Hard Millhaven sunlight bounced and dazzled from the red bricks and the oil-stained concrete. Drenched in dazzling light, my father raised his pint and drank.

I stood up and found that my legs were still shaking. I sat down again before anyone could notice. Two young women on the next bench laughed at something, and I glanced over at them. One of them said, 'You are sworn to secrecy. Let us begin at the beginning.'

Back on Grand Street I typed my notes into the computer and printed them out. I saw that I had mapped out the next few days' work. I thought of going downstairs for lunch so I could show Maggie Lah those enigmatic, barbaric verses from the gnostic gospel, but remembered it was Friday, one of the days she worked on her philosophy MA at NYU. I went into my own kitchen and opened the refrigerator. Fastened to the door is a photograph I cut out of the *New York Times* the day after Ted Bundy was executed. It shows his mother holding a telephone receiver to her ear while she plugs her other ear with an index finger. She has bangs and big glasses and concentration has pulled her thick eyebrows together. The caption is *Louise Bundy, of Tacoma, Wash., saying goodbye by telephone to her son, Theodore Bundy, the serial killer who was executed for murder yesterday morning in Florida.*

Whenever I see this terrible photograph, I think about taking it down. I try to remember why I cut it out in the first place. Then I open the refrigerator door.

The telephone rang as soon as I pulled the handle, and I closed the door and went into the loft's main room to answer it.

I said, 'Hello,' and the voice on the other end said the same thing and then paused. 'Am I speaking to Timothy Underhill? Timothy Underhill, the writer?'

When I admitted to my identity, my called said, 'Well, it's been a long sime since we've met. Tim, this is John Ransom.'

And then I felt an *of course*: as if I had known he would call, that predetermined events were about to unfold, and that I had been waiting for this for days.

'I was just thinking about you,' I said, because in Central Park I had remembered the last time I had seen him – he had been nothing like the friendly, self-justifying captain I had met on the edge of Camp White Star, parroting slogans about stopping communism. He had reminded me of Scoot. Around his neck had been a necklace of dried blackened little things I'd taken for ears before I saw that they were tongues. I had not seen him since, but I never forgot certain things he had said on that day.

'Well, I've been thinking about you, too,' he said. Now he sounded a long way from the man who had worn the necklace of tongues. 'I've been reading *The Divided Man*.'

'Thanks,' I said, and wondered if that was what he was calling about. He sounded tired and slow.

'That's not what I mean. I thought you'd like to know something. Maybe you'll even want to come out here.'

'Out where?'

'Millhaven,' he said. Then he laughed, and I thought that he might be drunk. 'I guess you don't know I came back here. I'm a professor here, at Arkham College.'

That was a surprise. Arkham, a group of redbrick buildings around a trampled little common, was a gloomy institution just west of Millhaven's downtown. The bricks had long ago turned sooty and brown, and the windows never looked clean. It had never been a particularly good school, and I knew of no reason why it should have improved.

'I teach religion,' he said. 'We have a small department.'

'It's nice to hear from you again,' I said, beginning to disengage myself from the conversation and him.

'No, listen. You might be interested in something that happened. I want, I'd like to talk to you about it.'

'What happened?' I asked.

79

'Someone attacked two people and wrote BLUE ROSE near their bodies. The first person died, but the second one is in a coma. She's still alive.'

'Oh.' I couldn't say any more. 'Is that really true?'

'The second one was April,' he said.

My blood stopped moving.

'My wife, April. She's still in a coma.'

'My God,' I said. 'I'm sorry, John. What happened?'

He gave me a sketchy version of the attack on his wife. 'I just wanted to ask you a question. If you have an answer, that's great. And if you can't answer, that's okay too.'

I asked him what the question was, but I thought I already knew what he was going to ask.

'Do you still think that detective Damrosch, the one you called Esterhaz in the book, killed those people?'

'No,' I said – almost sighed, because I half suspected what a truthful answer to that question would mean. 'I learned some things since I wrote that book.'

'About the Blue Rose murderer?'

'You don't think it's the same person, do you?' I asked.

'Well, I do, yes.' John Ransom hesitated. 'After all, if Damrosch wasn't the murderer, then nobody ever caught the guy. He just walked away.'

'This must be very hard on you.'

He hesitated. 'I just wanted to talk to you about it. I'm – I'm – I'm not in great shape, I guess, but I don't want to intrude on you anymore. You told me more than enough already. I'm not even sure what I'm asking.'

'Yes, you are,' I said.

'I guess I was wondering if you might want to come out to talk about it. I guess I was thinking I could use some help.'

You are sworn to secrecy.

Let us begin at the beginning.

PART TWO

Franklin Bachelor

1

My second encounter with John Ransom in Vietnam took place while I was trying to readjust myself after an odd and unsettling four-day patrol. I did not understand what had happened – I didn't understand something I'd seen. Actually, two inexplicable things had happened on the last day of the patrol, and when I came across John Ransom, he explained both of them to me.

We were camped in a stand of trees at the edge of a paddy. That day we had lost two men so new that I had already forgotten their names. Damp gray twilight settled around us. We couldn't smoke, and we were not supposed to talk. A black, six-six, two-hundred-and-fifty-pound grunt named Leonard Hamnet fingered a letter he had received months before out of his pocket and squinted at it, trying to read it for the thousandth time while spooning canned peaches into his mouth. By now, the precious letter was a rag held together with tape.

At that moment someone started shooting at us, and the lieutenant yelled, '*Shit!*' and we dropped our food and returned fire at the invisible people trying to kill us. When they kept shooting back, we had to go through the paddy.

The warm water came up to our chests. At the dikes, we scrambled over and splashed down into the muck on the other side. A boy from Santa Cruz, California, named Thomas Blevins got a round in the back of his neck and dropped dead into the water just short of the first dike, and another boy, named Tyrell Budd, coughed and dropped down right beside him. The FO called in an artillery strike. We leaned against the backs of the last two dikes when the big shells came thudding in. The ground shook and the water rippled, and the edge of the forest went up in a series of fireballs. We could hear the monkeys screaming.

One by one we crawled over the last dike onto the solid ground on the other side of the paddy. A little group of thatched huts was visible through the sparse trees. Then the two things I did not understand happened, one after the other. Someone off in the forest fired a mortar round at us – just one. One mortar, one round. I fell down and shoved my face in the muck, and everybody around me did the same. I considered that this might be my last second on earth and greedily inhaled whatever life might be left to me. I experienced that endless moment of pure helplessness in which the soul simultaneously clings to the body and readies itself to leave it. The shell landed on top of the last dike and blew it to bits. Dirt, mud, and water slopped down around us. A shell fragment whizzed overhead, sliced a hamburger-sized wad of bark and wood from a tree, and clanged into Spanky Burrage's helmet with a sound like a brick hitting a garbage can. The fragment fell to the ground. A little smoke drifted up from it.

We picked ourselves up. Spanky looked dead, but he was breathing. Leonard Hamnet picked up Spanky and slung him over his shoulder.

When we walked into the little village in the woods on the other side of the rice paddy, I experienced a kind of foretaste of the misery we were to encounter later in a place called Ia Thuc. If I can say this without setting off all the Gothic bells, the place seemed intrinsically, inherently wrong – it was too quiet, too still, completely without noise or movement. There were no chickens, dogs, or pigs; no old women came out to look us over, no old men toffered conciliatory smiles. The huts were empty – something I had never seen before in Vietnam, and never saw again.

Michael Poole's map said that the place was named Bong To.

Hamnet lowered Spanky into the long grass as soon as we reached the center of the empty village. I bawled out a few words in my poor Vietnamese.

Spanky groaned. He gently touched the sides of his helmet. 'I caught a head wound,' he said.

'You wouldn't have a head at all, you was only wearing your liner,' Hamnet said.

Spanky bit his lips and pushed the helmet up off his head. He groaned. A finger of blood ran down beside his ear. Finally the helmet passed over a lump the size of an apple that rose up from under his hair. Wincing, Spanky fingered this enormous knot. 'I see double,' he said. 'I'll never get that helmet back on.'

The medic said, 'Take it easy, we'll get you out of here.'

'Out of *here*?' Spanky brightened up.

'Back to Crandall,' the medic said.

A nasty little wretch named Spitalny sidled up, and Spanky frowned at him. 'There ain't nobody here,' Spitalny said. 'What the fuck is going on?' He took the emptiness of the village as a personal affront.

Leonard Hamnet turned his back and spat.

'Spitalny, Tiano,' the lieutenant said. 'Go into the paddy and get Tyrell and Blevins. Now.'

Tattoo Tiano, who was due to die six and a half months later and was Spitalny's only friend, said, 'You do it this time, Lieutenant.'

Hamnet turned around and began moving toward Tiano and Spitalny. He looked as if he had grown two sizes larger, as if his hands could pick up boulders. I had forgotten how big he was. His head was lowered, and a rim of clear white showed above the irises. I wouldn't have been surprised if he had blown smoke from his nostrils.

'Hey, I'm gone, I'm already there,' Tiano said. He and Spitalny began moving quickly through the sparse trees. Whoever had fired the mortar had packed up and gone. By now it was nearly dark, and the mosquitoes had found us.

Hamnet sat down heavily enough for me to feel the shock in my boots.

Poole, Hamnet, and I looked around the village.

'Maybe I better take a look,' the lieutenant said. He flicked his lighter a couple of times and walked off toward the nearest hut. The rest of us stood around like fools, listening to the mosquitoes and the sounds of Tiano and Spitalny pulling the dead men up over the dikes. Every now and then Spanky groaned and shook his head. Too much time passed.

The lieutenant came hurrying back out of the hut.

'Underhill, Poole,' he said, 'I want you to see this.'

Poole and I glanced at each other. Poole seemed a couple of psychic inches from either taking a poke at the lieutenant or exploding altogether. In his muddy face his eyes were the size of hen's eggs. He was wound up like a cheap watch. I thought that I probably looked pretty much the same.

'What is it, Lieutenant?' he asked.

The lieutenant gestured for us to follow him into the hut and went back inside. Poole looked as if he felt like shooting the lieutenant in the back. *I* felt like shooting the lieutenant in the back, I realized a second later. I grumbled something and moved toward the hut. Poole followed.

The lieutenant was fingering his sidearm just inside the hut. He frowned at us to let us know we had been slow to obey him, then flicked on his lighter.

'You tell me what it is, Poole.'

He marched into the hut, holding up the lighter like a torch.

Inside, he stooped down and tugged at the edges of a wooden panel in the floor. I caught the smell of blood. The Zippo died, and darkness closed down on us. The lieutenant yanked the panel back on its hinges. The smell floated up from whatever was beneath the floor. The lieutenant flicked the Zippo, and his face jumped out of the darkness. 'Now. Tell me what this is.'

'It's where they hide the kids when people like us show up,' I said. 'Did you take a look?'

I saw in his tight cheeks and almost lipless mouth that he had not. He wasn't about to go down there and get killed by the Minotaur while his platoon stood around outside.

'Taking a look is your job, Underhill,' he said.

For a second we both looked at the ladder, made of peeled branches lashed together with rags, that led down into the pit.

'Give me the lighter,' Poole said, and grabbed it away from the lieutenant. He sat on the edge of the hole and leaned over, bringing the flame beneath the level of the floor. He grunted at whatever he saw, and surprised both the lieutenant and me by pushing himself off the ledge into the opening. The light went out. The lieutenant and I looked down into the dark open rectangle in the floor.

The lighter flared again. I could see Poole's extended arm, the jittering little flame, a packed-earth floor. The top of the concealed room was less than an inch above the top of Poole's head. He moved away from the opening.

'What is it? Are there any' – the lieutenant's voice made a creaky sound – 'any bodies?'

'Come down here, Tim,' Poole called up.

I sat on the floor and swung my legs into the pit. Then I jumped down.

Beneath the floor, the smell of blood was sickeningly strong.

'What do you see?' the lieutenant shouted. He was trying to sound like a leader, and his voice squeaked on the last word.

I saw an empty room shaped like a giant grave. The walls were covered by some kind of thick paper held in place by wooden struts sunk into the earth. Both the thick brown paper and two of the struts showed old bloodstains.

'Hot,' Poole said, and closed the lighter.

'Come *on*, damn it,' came the lieutenant's voice. 'Get out of there.'

'Yes, sir,' Poole said. He flicked the lighter back on. Many layers of thick paper formed an absorbent pad between the earth and the room. The topmost, thinnest layer had been covered with vertical lines of Vietnamese writing. The writing looked like the left-hand pages of Kenneth Rexroth's translation of Tu Fu and Li Po.

'Well, well,' Poole said, and I turned to see him point at what first looked like intricately woven strands of rope fixed to the bloodstained wooden uprights. Poole stepped forward and the weave jumped into sharp relief. About four feet off the ground, iron chains had been screwed to the uprights. The thick pad between the two lengths of chain had been soaked with blood. The three feet of ground between the posts looked rusty. Poole moved the lighter closer to the chains, and we saw dried blood on the metal links.

'I want you guys out of there, and I mean *now*,' whined the lieutenant.

Poole snapped the lighter shut, and we moved back toward the opening. I felt as if I had seen a shrine to an obscene deity. The lieutenant leaned over and stuck out his hand, but of course he did not bend down far enough for us to reach him. We stiff-armed ourselves up out of the hole. The lieutenant stepped back. He had a thin face and a thick, fleshy nose, and his adam's apple danced around in his neck like a jumping bean. 'Well, how many?'

'How many what?' I asked.

'How many are there?' He wanted to go back to Camp Crandall with a good body count.

'There weren't exactly any bodies, Lieutenant,' said Poole, trying to let him down easily. He described what we had seen.

'Well, what's that good for?' He meant, *How is that going to help me?*

'Interrogations, probably,' Poole said. 'If you questioned someone down there, no one outside the hut would hear anything. At night, you could just drag the body into the woods.'

'Field Interrogation Post,' said the lieutenant, trying out the phrase. 'Torture, Use Of, highly indicated.' He nodded again. 'Right?'

'Highly,' Poole said.

'Shows you what kind of enemy we're dealing with in this conflict.'

I could no longer stand being in the same three square feet of space with the lieutenant, and I took a step toward the door of the hut. I did not know what Poole and I had seen, but I knew it was not a Field Interrogation Post, Torture, Use Of, highly indicated, unless the Vietnamese had begun to interrogate monkeys. It occurred to me that the writing on the wall might have been names instead of poetry – I thought that we had stumbled into a mystery that had nothing to do with the war, a Vietnamese mystery.

For a second, music from my old life, music too beautiful to be endurable, started playing in my head. Finally I recognized it: 'The Walk to the Paradise Gardens,' from *A Village Romeo and Juliet* by Frederick Delius. Back in Berkeley, I had listened to it hundreds of times.

If nothing else had happened, I think I could have replayed the whole piece in my head. Tears filled my eyes, and I stepped toward the door of the hut. Then I stopped moving. A boy of seven or eight was regarding me with great seriousness from the far corner of the hut. I knew he was not there – I knew he was a spirit. I had no belief in spirits, but that's what he was. Some part of my mind as detached as a crime reporter reminded me that 'The Walk to the Paradise Gardens' was about two children who were about to die and that in a sense the music *was* their death. I wiped my eyes with my hand, and when I lowered my arm, the boy was still there. I took in his fair hair and round dark eyes, the worn plaid shirt and dungarees that made him look like someone I might have known in my childhood in Pigtown. Then he vanished all at once, like the flickering light of the Zippo. I nearly groaned aloud.

I said something to the other two men and went through the door into the growing darkness. I was very dimly aware of the lieutenant asking Poole to repeat his description of the uprights and the bloody chain. Hamnet and Burrage and Calvin Hill were sitting down and leaning against a tree. Victor Spitalny was wiping his hands on his filthy shirt. White smoke curled up from Hill's cigarette, and Tina Pumo exhaled a long white stream of vapour. The unhinged thought came to me with absolute conviction that *this* was the Paradise Gardens. The men lounging in the darkness; the pattern of the cigarette smoke, and the patterns they made, sitting or standing; the in-drawing darkness, as physical as a blanket; the frame of the trees and the flat gray-green background of the paddy.

My soul had come back to life.

Then I became aware of something wrong about the men arranged before me, and again it took a moment for my intelligence to catch up to my intuition. I had registered that two men too many were in front of me. Instead of seven, there were nine, and the two men that made up the nine of us left were still behind me in the hut. A wonderful soldier named M. O. Dengler was looking at me with growing curiosity, and I thought he knew exactly what I was thinking. A sick chill went through me. I saw Tom Blevins and Tyrell Budd standing together at the far right of the platoon, a little muddier than the others but otherwise different from the rest only in that, like Dengler, they were looking directly at me.

Hill tossed his cigarette away in an arc of light, Poole and Lieutenant Joys came out of the hut behind me. Leonard Hamnet patted his pocket to reassure himself that he still had his mysterious letter. I looked back at the right of the group, and the two dead men were gone.

'Let's saddle up,' the lieutenant said. 'We aren't doing jack shit around here.'

'Tim?' Dengler asked. He had not taken his eyes off me since I had come out of the hut. I shook my head.

'Well, what was it?' asked Tina Pumo. 'Was it juicy?'

Spanky and Calvin Hill laughed and slapped hands.

'Aren't we gonna torch this place?' asked Spitalny.

The lieutenant ignored him. 'Juicy enough, Pumo. Interrogation Post. Field Interrogation Post.'

'No shit,' said Pumo.

'These people are into torture, Pumo. It's just another indication.'

'Gotcha.' Pumo glanced at me and his eyes grew curious. Dengler moved closer.

'I was just remembering something,' I said. 'Something from the world.'

'You better forget about the world while you're over here, Underhill,' the lieutenant told me. 'I'm trying to keep you alive, in case you hadn't noticed, but you have to cooperate with me.' His adam's apple jumped like a begging puppy.

The next night we had showers, real food, cots to sleep

in. Sheets and pillows. Two new guys replaced Tyrell Budd and Thomas Blevins, whose names were never mentioned again, at least by me, until long after the war was over and Poole, Linklater, Pumo, and I looked them up, along with the rest of our dead, on the Wall in Washington. I wanted to forget the patrol, especially what I had seen and experienced inside the hut.

I remember that it was raining. I remember the steam lifting off the ground, and the condensation dripping down the metal poles in the tents. Moisture shone on the faces around me. I was sitting in the brothers' tent, listening to the music Spanky Burrage played on the big reel-to-reel recorder he had bought on R&R in Taipei. Spanky Burrage never played Delius, but what he played was paradisical: great jazz from Armstrong to Coltrane, on reels recorded for him by his friend back in Little Rock and which he knew so well he could find individual tracks and performances without bothering to look at the counter. Spanky liked to play disc jockey during these long sessions, changing reels and speeding past thousands of feet of tape to play the same songs by different musicians, even the same song hiding under different names – 'Cherokee' and 'KoKo,' 'Indiana' and 'Donna Lee' – or long series of songs connected by titles that used the same words – 'I Thought About You' (Art Tatum), 'You and the Night and the Music' (Sonny Rollins), 'I Love You' (Bill Evans), 'If I Could Be with You' (Ike Quebec), 'You Leave Me Breathless' (Milt Jackson), even, for the sake of the joke, 'Thou Swell,' by Glenroy Breakstone. In his single-artist mode on this day, Spanky was ranging through the work of a great trumpet player named Clifford Brown.

On this sweltering, rainy day, Clifford Brown was walking to the Paradise Gardens. Listening to him was like watching a smiling man shouldering open an enormous door to let in great dazzling rays of light. The world we were in transcended pain and loss, and imagination had banished fear. Even SP4 Cotton and Calvin Hill, who preferred James Brown to Clifford Brown, lay on their bunks listening as Spanky followed his instincts from one track to another.

After he had played disc jockey for something like two hours, Spanky rewound the long tape and said, 'Enough.' The end of the tape slapped against the reel. I looked at Dengler, who seemed dazed, as if awakening from a long sleep. The memory of the music was still all around us: light still poured in through the crack in the great door.

'I'm gonna have a smoke *and* a drink,' Cotton announced, and pushed himself up off his cot. He walked to the door of the tent and pulled the flap aside to expose the green wet drizzle. That dazzling light, the light from another world, began to fade. Cotton sighed, plopped a wide-brimmed hat on his head, and slipped outside. Before the stiff flap fell shut, I saw him jumping through the puddles on the way to Wilson Manly's shack. I felt as though I had returned from a long journey.

Spanky finished putting the Clifford Brown reel back into its cardboard box. Someone in the rear of the tent switched on Armed Forces radio. Spanky looked at me and shrugged. Leonard Hamnet took his letter out of his pocket, unfolded it, and read it through very slowly.

Dengler looked at me and smiled. 'What do you think is going to happen? To us, I mean. Do you think it'll just go on like this day after day, or do you think it's going to get stranger and stranger?' He did not wait for me to answer. 'I think it'll always sort of look the same, but it won't be – I think the edges are starting to melt. I think that's what happens when you're out here long enough. The edges melt.'

'Your edges melted a long time ago, Dengler,' Spanky said, and applauded his own joke.

Dengler was still staring at me. He always resembled a

serious, dark-haired child, he never looked as though he belonged in uniform. 'Here's what I mean, kind of,' he said. 'When we were listening to that trumpet player – '

'*Brownie*, Clifford *Brown*,' Spanky whispered.

' – I could see the notes in the air. Like they were written out on a long scroll. And after he played them, they stayed in the air for a long time.'

'Sweetie-*pie*,' Spanky said softly. 'You pretty hip, for a little ofay square.'

'When we were back in that village,' Dengler said. 'Tell me about that.'

I said that he had been there too.

'But something happened to you. Something special.'

I shook my head.

'All right,' Dengler said. 'But it's happening, isn't it? Things are changing.'

I could not speak. I could not tell Dengler in front of Spanky Burrage that I had imagined seeing the ghosts of Blevins, Budd, and an American child. I smiled and shook my head. It came to me with a great and secret thrill that someday I would be able to write about all this, and that the child had come searching for me out of a book I had yet to write.

2

I left the tent with a vague notion of getting outside into the slight coolness that followed the rain. The sun, visible again, was a deep orange ball far to the west. A packet of white powder rested at the bottom of my right front pocket, which was so deep that my fingers just brushed its top. I decided that what I needed was a beer.

The shack where an enterprising weasel named Wilson

Manly sold contraband beer and liquor was all the way on the other side of camp. The enlisted men's club was rumored to serve cheap Vietnamese '33' beer in American bottles.

One other place remained, farther away than the enlisted men's club but closer than Manly's shack and somewhere between them in official status. About twenty minutes away, at the curve in the steeply descending road to the airfield and the motor pool, stood an isolated wooden structure called Billy's. Billy had gone home long ago, but his club, supposedly an old French command post, had endured. When it was open, a succession of slender Montagnard boys who slept in the nearly empty upstairs rooms served drinks. I visited these rooms two or three times, but I never learned where the boys went when Billy's was closed. Billy's did not look anything like a French command post: it looked like a roadhouse.

A long time ago, the building had been painted brown. Someone had once boarded up the two front windows on the lower floor, and someone else had torn off a narrow band of boards across each of the windows, so that light entered in two flat white bands that traveled across the floor during the day. There was no electricity and no ice. When you needed a toilet, you went to a cubicle with inverted metal bootprints on either side of a hole in the floor.

The building stood in a grove of trees in the curve of the road, and as I walked downhill toward it in the sunset, a muddy camouflaged jeep gradually emerged from invisibility on the right side of the bar, floating out of the trees like an optical illusion.

Low male voices stopped when I stepped onto the rotting porch. I looked for insignia on the jeep, but mud caked the door panels. Some white object gleamed dully from the backseat. When I looked more closely, I saw in a coil of rope an oval of bone that it took me a moment to recognize as the top of a painstakingly cleaned and bleached human skull.

The door opened before I could reach the handle. A boy called Mike stood before me in loose khaki shorts and a dirty white shirt too large for him. Then he saw who I was. 'Oh,' he said. 'Yes. Tim. Okay. You can come in.' He carried himself with an odd defensive alertness, and he shot me an uncomfortable smile.

'It's okay?' I asked, because everything about him told me that it wasn't.

'*Yesss*.' He stepped back to let me in.

The bar looked empty, and the band of light coming in through the opening over the windows had already reached the long mirror, creating a bright dazzle, a white fire. Pungent cordite hung in the air. I took a couple of steps inside, and Mike moved around me to return to his post.

'Oh, hell,' someone said from off to my left. 'We have to put up with *this*?'

I turned my head and saw three men sitting against the wall at a round table. None of the kerosene lamps had been lighted yet, and the dazzle from the mirror made the far reaches of the bar even murkier.

'Is okay, is okay,' said Mike. 'Old customer. Old friend.'

'I bet he is,' the voice said. 'Just don't let any women in here.'

'No women,' Mike said. 'No problem.'

I went through the tables to the furthest one on the right.

'You want whiskey, Tim?' Mike asked.

'Tim?' the man said. '*Tim?*'

'Beer,' I said, and sat down.

A nearly empty bottle of Johnny Walker Black, three glasses, and about a dozen cans of beer covered the table before them. The soldier with his back against the wall

96

shoved aside some of the beer cans so that I could see the .45 next to the Johnny Walker bottle. He leaned forward with a drunk's well-guarded coordination. The sleeves had been ripped off his shirt, and dirt darkened his skin as if he had not bathed in years. His hair had been cut with a knife.

'I just want to make sure about this,' he said. 'You're not a woman, right? You swear to that?'

'Anything you say,' I said.

He put his hand on the gun.

'Got it,' I said. Mike hurried around the bar with my beer.

'Tim. Funny name. Sounds like a little guy – like him.' He pointed at Mike with his left hand, the whole hand and not merely the index finger, while his right still rested on the .45. 'Little fucker ought to be wearing a dress. Hell, he practically *is* wearing a dress.'

'Don't you like women?' I asked. Mike put a can of Budweiser on my table and shook his head rapidly, twice. He had wanted me in the club because he was afraid the drunken soldier was going to shoot him, and now I was just making things worse.

I looked at the two men with the drunken officer. They were dirty and exhausted – whatever had happened to the drunk had also happened to them. The difference was that they were not drunk yet.

'This rear-echelon dipshit is personally interfering with my state of mind,' the drunk said to the burly man on his right. 'Tell him to get out of here, or a certain degree of unpleasantness will ensue.'

'Leave him alone,' the other man said. Stripes of dried mud lay across his lean, haggard face.

The drunken officer startled me by leaning toward the other man and speaking in a clear, carrying Vietnamese. It was an old-fashioned, almost literary Vietnamese, and he must have thought and dreamed in it to speak it so well. He assumed that neither I nor the Montagnard boy would understand him.

This is serious, he said. *Most of the people in the world I do not despise are already dead, or should be.*

There was more, and I cannot swear that this was exactly what he said, but it's pretty close.

Then he said, in that same flowing Vietnamese that even to my ears sounded as stilted as the language of a third-rate Victorian novel: *You should remember what we have brought with us.*

It takes a long time and a lot of patience to clean and bleach bone. A skull would be more difficult than most of a skeleton.

Your prisoner requires more drink, he said, and rolled back in his chair, looking at me with his hand on his gun.

'Whiskey,' said the burly soldier. Mike was already pulling the bottle off the shelf. He understood that the officer was trying to knock himself out before he would find it necessary to shoot someone.

For a moment I thought that the burly soldier to his right looked familiar. His head had been shaved so close he looked bald, and his eyes were enormous above the streaks of dirt. A stainless-steel watch hung from a slot in his collar. He extended a muscular arm for the bottle Mike passed him while keeping as far from the table as he could. The soldier twisted off the cap and poured into all three glasses. The man in the center immediately drank all the whiskey in his glass and banged the glass down on the table for a refill.

The haggard soldier, who had been silent until now, said, 'Something is gonna happen here.' He looked straight at me. 'Pal?'

'That man is nobody's pal,' the drunk said. Before anyone could stop him, he snatched up the gun, pointed it across the room, and fired. There was a flash of fire, a huge explosion, and the reek of cordite. The bullet went straight through the soft wooden wall, about eight feet to my left. A stray bit of light slanted through the hole it made.

For a moment I was deaf. I swallowed the last of my beer and stood up. My head was ringing.

'Is it clear that I hate the necessity for this kind of shit?' said the drunk. 'Is that much understood?'

The soldier who had called me 'pal' laughed, and the burly soldier poured more whiskey into the drunk's glass. Then he stood up and started coming toward me. Beneath the exhaustion and the stripes of dirt, his face was taut with anxiety. He put himself between me and the man with the gun.

The captain began pulling me toward the door, keeping his body between me and the other table. He gave me an impatient glance because I had refused to move at his pace. Then I saw him notice my pupils. 'Goddamn,' he said, and then he stopped moving altogether and said, 'Goddamn' again, but in a different tone of voice.

I started laughing.

'Oh, this is – ' He shook his head. 'This is really – '

'Where have you *been*?' I asked him.

John Ransom turned to the table. 'Hey, I know this guy. He's an old football friend of mine.'

The drunken major shrugged and put the .45 back on the table. His eyelids had nearly closed. 'I don't care about football,' he said, but he kept his hand off the weapon.

'Buy the sergeant a drink,' said the haggard officer.

John Ransom quickly moved to the bar and reached for a glass, which the confused Mike put into his hand. Ransom went through the tables, filled his glass and mine, and carried both back to join me.

We watched the major's head slip down by notches toward his chest. When his chin finally reached his shirt,

Ransom said, 'All right, Jed,' and the other man slid the .45 out from under the major's hand. He pushed it beneath his belt.

'The man is out,' Jed told us.

Ransom turned back to me. 'He was up three days straight with us, God knows how long before that.' Ransom did not have to specify who *he* was. 'Jed and I got some sleep, trading off, but he just kept on talking.' He fell into one of the chairs at my table and tilted his glass to his mouth. I sat down beside him.

For a moment no one spoke. The line of light from the open space across the windows had already left the mirror and was not approaching the place on the wall that meant it was going to disappear. Mike lifted the cover from one of the lamps and began trimming the wick.

'How come you're always fucked up when I see you?'

'You have to ask?'

He smiled. He looked very different from when I had seen him preparing to give a sales pitch to Senator Burrman at Camp White Star. This man had taken in more of the war, and that much more of the war was inside him now.

'I got you off graves registration at White Star, didn't I?'

I agreed that he had.

'What did you call it, the body squad? It wasn't even a real graves registration unit, was it?' He smiled and shook his head. 'The only one with any training was that sergeant, what's his name. Italian.'

'Di Maestro.'

Ransom nodded. 'The whole operation was going off the rails.' Mike lit a big kitchen match and touched it to the wick of the kerosene lamp. 'I heard some things – ' He slumped against the wall and swallowed whiskey. I wondered if he had heard about Captain Havens. He closed his eyes.

100

I asked if he were still stationed in the highlands up around the Laotian border. He almost sighed when he shook his head.

'You're not with the tribesmen anymore? What were they, Khatu?'

He opened his eyes. 'You have a good memory. No, I'm not there anymore.' He considered saying more, but decided not to. He had failed himself. 'I'm kind of on hold until they send me up around Khe Sanh. It'll be better up there – the Bru are tremendous. But right now, all I want to do is take a bath and get into bed. Any bed. I'd settle for a dry place on level ground.'

'Where did you come from now?'

'Incountry.' His face creased and he showed his teeth. The effect was so unsettling that I did not immediately realize that he was smiling. 'Way incountry. We had to get the major out.'

'Looks like you had to pull him out, like a tooth.'

My ignorance made him sit up straight. 'You mean you never heard of him? Franklin Bachelor?'

And then I thought I had, that someone had mentioned him to me a long time ago.

'In the bush for years. Bachelor did stuff that ordinary people don't even *dream* of – he's a legend. The Last Irregular. He fell on punji sticks and lived – he's still got the scars.'

A legend, I thought. He was one of the Green Berets Ransom had mentioned a lifetime ago at White Star.

'Ran what amounted to a private army, did a lot of good work in Darlac Province. He was out there on his own. The man was a hero. That's straight.'

Franklin Bachelor had been a captain when Ratman and his platoon had run into him after a private named Bobby Swett had been blown to pieces on a trail in Darlac Province. Ratman had thought his wife was a black-haired angel.

101

And then I knew whose skull lay wound in rope in the back seat of the jeep.

'I did hear of him,' I said. 'I knew someone who met him. The Rhade woman, too.'

'His *wife*,' Ransom said.

I asked him where they were taking Bachelor.

'We're stopping overnight at Crandall for some rest. Then we hop to Tan Son Nhut and bring him back to the States – Langley. I thought we might have to strap him down, but I guess we'll just keep pouring whiskey into him.'

'He's going to want his gun back.'

'Maybe I'll give it to him.' His glance told me what he thought Major Bachelor would do with his .45, if he was left alone with it long enough. 'He's in for a rough time at Langley. There'll be some heat.'

'Why Langley?'

'Don't ask. But don't be naive, either. Don't you think they're . . .' He would not finish that sentence. 'Why do you think we had to bring him out in the first place?'

'I suppose something went wrong.'

'The man stepped over some boundaries, maybe a lot of boundaries – but tell me that you can do what we're supposed to do without stepping over boundaries.'

For a second, I wished that I could see the sober shadowy gentlemen of Langley, Virginia, the gentlemen with slicked-back hair and pinstriped suits, questioning Major Bachelor. They thought *they* were serious men.

'It was like this place called Bong To, in a funny way.' Ransom waited for me to ask. When I did not, he said, 'A ghost town, I mean. I don't suppose you've ever heard of Bong To.'

'My unit was just there.' His head jerked up. 'A mortar round scared us into the village.'

'You saw the place?'

I nodded.

'Funny story.' Now he was sorry he had ever mentioned it.

I said that I wasn't asking him to tell me any secrets.

'It's not a secret. It's not even military.'

'It's just a ghost town.'

Ransom was still uncomfortable. He turned his glass around and around in his hands before he drank.

'Complete with ghosts.'

'I honestly wouldn't be surprised.' He drank what was left in his glass and stood up. 'Let's take care of Major Bachelor, Jed,' he said.

'Right.'

Ransom carried our bottle to the bar.

Ransom and Jed picked up the major between them. They were strong enough to lift him easily. Bachelor's greasy head rolled forward. Jed put the .45 into his pocket, and Ransom put the bottle into his own pocket. Together they carried the major to the door.

I followed them outside. Artillery pounded hills a long way off. It was dark now, and lantern light spilled through the gaps in the windows.

All of us went down the rotting steps, the major bobbing between the other two.

Ransom opened the jeep, and they took a while to maneuver the major into the backseat. Jed squeezed in beside him and pulled him upright.

John Ransom got in behind the wheel and sighed. He had no taste for the next part of his job.

'I'll give you a ride back to camp,' he said.

I took the seat beside him. Ransom started the engine and turned on the lights. He jerked the gearshift into reverse and rolled backward. 'You know why that mortar round came in, don't you?' he asked. He grinned at me, and we bounced onto the road back to the main part of camp. 'He was trying to chase you away from Bong To, and your fool of a lieutenant went straight for the place

103

instead.' He was still grinning. 'It must have steamed him, seeing a bunch of roundeyes going in there.'

'He didn't send in any more fire.'

'No. He didn't want to damage the place. It's supposed to stay the way it is. I don't think they'd use the word, but that village is like a kind of monument.' He glanced at me again.

Ransom paused and then asked, 'Did you go into any of the huts? Did you see anything unusual there?'

'I went into a hut. I saw something unusual.'

'A list of names?'

'I thought that's what they were.'

'Okay,' Ransom said. 'There's a difference between private and public shame. Between what's acknowledged and what is not acknowledged. Some things are acceptable, as long as you don't talk about them.' He looked sideways at me as we began to approach the northern end of the camp proper. He wiped his face, and flakes of dried mud fell off his cheek. The exposed skin looked red, and so did his eyes. 'I've been learning things,' Ransom said.

I remembered thinking that the arrangement in the hut's basement had been a shrine to an obscene deity.

'One day in Bong To, a little boy disappeared.'

My heart gave a thud.

'Say, three. Old enough to talk and get into trouble, but too young to take care of himself. He's just gone – *poof*. A couple of months later, it happened again. Mom turns her back, where the hell did Junior go? This time they scour the village. The *villagers* scour the village, every square foot of that place, and then they do the same to the rice paddy, and then they look through the forest.

'What happens next is the interesting part. An old woman goes out one morning to fetch water from the well, and she sees the ghost of a disreputable old man from another village, a local no-good, in fact. He's just standing near the well with his hands together. He's hungry – that's what these people know about ghosts. The skinny old bastard wants *more*. He wants to be *fed*. The old lady gives a squawk and passes out. When she comes to again, the ghost is gone.

'Well, the old lady tells everybody what she saw, and the whole village gets in a panic. Next thing you know, two thirteen-year-old girls are working in the paddy, they look up and see an old woman who died when they were ten – she's about six feet away from them. Her hair is stringy and gray and her fingernails are about a foot long. They start screaming and crying, but no one else can see her, and she comes closer and closer, and they try to get away but one of them falls down, and the old woman is on her like a cat. And do you know what she does? She rubs her filthy hands over the screaming girl's face and licks the tears and slobber off her fingers.

'The next night, two men go looking around the village latrine behind the houses, and they see two ghosts down in the pit, shoving excrement into their mouths. They rush back into the village, and then they both see half a dozen ghosts around the chief's hut. They want to eat. One of the men screeches, because not only did he see his dead wife, he saw her pass into the chief's hut without the benefit of the door.

'The dead wife comes back out through the wall of the chief's hut. She's licking blood off her hands.

'The former husband stands there pointing and jabbering, and the mothers and grandmothers of the missing boys come out of their huts. All these women go howling up to the chief's door. When the chief comes out, they push past him and take the hut apart. And you know what they find.'

Ransom had parked the jeep near my battalion headquarters five minutes before, and now he smiled as if he had explained everything.

'But what *happened*?' I asked. 'How did you hear about it?'

He shrugged. 'I probably heard that story half a dozen times, but Bachelor knew more about it than anyone I ever met before. They probably carried out the pieces of the chief's body and threw them into the excrement pit. And over months, bit by bit, everybody in the village crossed a kind of border. By that time, they were seeing ghosts all the time. Bachelor says they turned into ghosts.'

'Do you think they turned into ghosts?'

'I think Major Bachelor turned into a ghost, if you ask me. Let me tell you something. The world is full of ghosts, and some of them are still people.'

I got out of the jeep and closed the door.

Ransom peered at me through the jeep's window. 'Take better care of yourself.'

'Good luck with your Bru.'

'The Bru are fantastic.' He slammed the jeep into gear and shot away, cranking the wheel to turn the jeep around in a giant circle in front of the battalion headquarters before he jammed it into second and took off to wherever he was going.

PART THREE

John Ransom

1

Once I had started remembering John Ransom, I couldn't stop. I tried to write, but my book had flattened out into a movie starring Kent Smith and Gloria Grahame. I called a travel agent and booked a ticket to Millhaven for Wednesday morning.

The imagination sometimes makes demands the rest of the mind resists, and Tuesday night I dreamed that the body Scoot was busily dismembering was my own.

I jerked awake into suffocating darkness.

The sheet beneath me was cold and greasy with sweat. In the morning the blurry yellow pattern of my body would be printed on the cotton. My heart thundered. I turned over the pillow and shifted to a dry place on the bed.

2

I realized at last that the thought of seeing Millhaven again filled me with dread. Millhaven and Vietnam were oddly interchangeable, fragments of some greater whole, some larger story – a lost story that preceded the fables of Orpheus and Lot's wife and said, *You will lose everything if you turn around and look back.* You turn around, you look back. Are you destroyed? Or is it that you see the missing, unifying section of the puzzle, the secret, filled with archaic and godlike terror, you have kept from yourself?

Early Wednesday morning, I showered and packed and went out onto the street to get a cab.

3

I got to the gate, boarded the plane, took my seat, buckled myself in, and it hit me that, at nearly fifty years of age, I was traveling halfway across the continent to help someone look for a madman.

Yet my motives had been clear from the moment that John Ransom had told me his wife's name. I was going to Millhaven because I thought that I might finally learn who had killed my sister.

The stewardess appeared in front of me to ask what I wanted to drink. My brain said the words, 'Club soda, please,' but what came out of my mouth was 'Vodka on the rocks.' She smiled and handed me the little airline bottle and a plastic glass full of ice cubes. I had not had a drink in eight years. I twisted off the cap of the little bottle and poured vodka over the ice cubes, hardly believing I was doing it. The stewardess moved on to the next row. The sharp, bitter smell of alcohol rose up from the glass. If I had wanted to, I could have stood up, walked to the toilet, and poured the stuff into the sink. Death was leaning against the bulkhead at the front of the plane, smiling at me. I smiled back and raised the glass and gave myself a good cold mouthful of vodka. It tasted like flowers. An unheeded little voice within me shouted no no no, o god no, this is not what you want, but I swallowed the mouthful of vodka and immediately took another, because it was exactly what I wanted. Now it tasted like a frozen cloud – the most delicious frozen cloud in the history of the world. Death, who was a dark-haired, ironic-looking man in a gray double-breasted suit, nodded and smiled. I remembered everything I used to like about drinking. When I thought about it, eight years of abstinence really deserved a celebratory drink or two. When the stewardess came back, I smiled nicely at her, waggled my glass, and asked for another. And she gave it to me, just like that.

I idly turned around to see who else was on the plane, and the alcohol in my system instantly turned to ice: two rows behind me, at the window seat in the last row of the first-class section, was my sister April. For a moment our eyes met, and then she turned away toward the gray nothingness beyond the window, her chin propped on her nine-year-old palm. I had not seen her for so long that I had managed to forget the conflicting, violent sensations her appearances caused in me. I experienced a rush of love, mixed as always with grief and sadness, also with anger. I took her in, her hair, her bored, slightly discontented face. She was still wearing the blue dress in which she had died. Her eyes shifted toward me again, and I nearly stood up and stepped out into the aisle. Before I had time to move, I found myself staring at the covered buttons on the uniform of the stewardess who had placed herself between April and myself. I looked up into her face, and she took a step back.

'Can I help you with anything?' she asked. 'Another vodka, sir?'

I nodded, and she moved up the aisle to fetch the drink. April's seat was empty.

111

4

After I sauntered dreamily out into the clean, reverberant spaces of Millhaven's airport, looking for another upright gray wraith like myself, I didn't recognize the overweight balding executive in the handsome gray suit who had been inspecting my fellow passengers until he finally stepped right in front of me. He said, 'Tim!' and burst out laughing. Finally I saw John Ransom's familiar face in the face of the man before me, and I smiled. He had put on a lot of pounds and lost a lot of hair since Camp Crandall. Except for an enigmatic, almost restless quality in the cast of his features, the man pronouncing my name before me might have been the president of an insurance company. He put his arms around me, and for a second everything we had seen of our generation's war came to life around us, distanced now, a part of our lives we had survived.

'Why are you always wrecked whenever I see you?' he asked.

'Because when I see you I never know what I'm getting into,' I told him. 'But this is just a temporary lapse.'

'I don't mind if you drink.'

'Don't be rash,' I said. 'I think the whole idea of coming out here must have spooked me a little.'

Of course Ransom knew nothing of my early life – I still had to tell him why I had been so fascinated by William Damrosch and the murders he was supposed to have committed – and he let his arms drop and stepped back. 'Well, that makes two of us. Let's go down and get your bags.'

When John Ransom left the freeway to drive through downtown Millhaven on the way to the near east side, I saw a city that was only half-familiar. Whole rows of old brick buildings turned brown by grime had been replaced by bright new structures that gleamed in the afternoon light; a parking lot had been transformed into a sparkling little park; on the site of the gloomy old auditorium was a complex of attractive concert halls and theaters that Ransom identified as the Center for the Performing Arts.

It was like driving through the back lot of a movie studio – the new hotels and office buildings that reshaped the skyline seemed illusory, like film sets built over the actual face of the past. After New York, the city seemed unbelievably clean and quiet. I wondered if the troubling, disorderly city I remembered had disappeared behind a thousand face-lifts.

'I suppose Arkham College looks like Stanford these days,' I said.

He grunted. 'No, Arkham's the same old rock pile it always was. We get by. Barely.'

'How did you wind up there in the first place?'

'Come to think of it, which I seldom do, that must seem a little strange.'

I waited for the story.

'I went there because of a specific man, Alan Brookner, who was the head of the religion department. He was famous in my field, I mean *really* famous, one of the three or four most significant people in the field. When I was in graduate school, I hunted down everything he'd ever written. He was the only real scholar at Arkham, of course. I think they gave him his first job, and he never even thought about leaving for a more glamorous position. That kind of prestige never meant anything to him. Once the school realized what they had, they let him write his own ticket, because they thought he'd attract other people of his stature.'

'Well, he attracted you.'

'Ah, but I'm not even close to Alan's stature. He was

113

one of a kind. And when other famous religious scholars came out here, they generally took one look at Arkham and went back to the schools they came from. He did bring in a lot of good graduate students, but even that's fallen off a bit lately. Well, considerably, to tell you the truth.' John Ransom shook his head and fell silent for a moment.

Now we were driving past Goethe Avenue's sprawling stone mansions, long ago broken up into offices and apartment houses. The great elms that had lined these streets had all died, but Goethe Avenue seemed almost unchanged.

'I gather that you became quite close to this professor,' I said, having forgotten his name.

'You could say that,' Ransom said. 'I married his daughter.'

'Ah,' I said. 'Tell me about that.'

After Vietnam, he had gone to India, and in India he had turned back toward life. He had studied, meditated, studied, meditated, courted calm and won it: he would always be the person who had burrowed through a mountain of dead bodies, but he was also the person who had crawled out on the other side and survived. In all of this, he had a Master, and the Master had helped him see over the horrors he had endured. His Master, the leader of a small following containing only a few non-Indians like Ransom, was a young woman of great simplicity and beauty named Mina.

After a year in the ashram, his nightmares and sudden attacks of panic had left him. He had seen the other side of the absolute darkness into which Vietnam had drawn him. Mina had sent him intact out into the world again, and he had spent three years studying in England and then another three at Harvard without telling more than half a dozen people that he had once been a Green Beret in

Vietnam. Then Alan Brookner had brought him back to Millhaven.

A month after he began working at Arkham under Brookner, he had met Brookner's daughter, April.

John thought that he might have fallen in love with April Brookner the first time he had seen her. She had wandered into the study to borrow a book while he was helping her father organize a collection of essays for publication. A tall blond athletic-looking girl in her early twenties, April had shaken his hand with surprising firmness and smiled into his eyes. 'I'm glad you're helping him with this muddle,' she had said. 'Left to his own devices, he'd still be getting mixed up between *Vorstellung* and *vijnapti*, not that he isn't anyhow.' The incongruity between her tennis-player looks and allusions to Brentano and Sanskrit philosophy surprised him, and he grinned. She and her father had exchanged a few good-natured insults, and then April wandered off toward her father's fiction shelves. She stretched up to take down a book. Ransom had not been able to take his eyes off her. 'I'm looking for a work of radically impure consciousness,' she said. 'What do you think, Raymond Chandler or William Burroughs?' The title of Ransom's dissertation had been *The Concept of Pure Consciousness*, and his grin grew wider. '*The Long Goodbye*,' he said. 'Oh, I don't think that's impure enough,' she said. She turned over the book in her hands and cocked her head. 'But I guess I'll settle for it.' She showed him the title of the book she had already selected: it was *The Long Goodbye*. Then she dazzled him with a smile and left the room. 'Impure consciousness?' Ransom had asked the old man. 'Watch out for that one,' said the old man. 'I think her first word was *virtuoso*.' Ransom asked if she really knew the difference between *Vorstellung* and *vijnapti*. 'Not as well as I do,' Brookner had grumped. 'Why don't you come

115

for dinner next Friday?' On Friday, Ransom had shown up embarrassingly overdressed in his best suit. He had still enjoyed dinner, yet April was so much younger than he that he could not imagine actually taking her out on a date. And he was not sure he actually knew what a 'date' was anymore, if he ever had. He didn't think it could mean the same thing to April Brookner that it did to him – she'd want to play tennis, or spend half the night dancing. She looked as if she relished *exertion*. Ransom was stronger than he appeared to be (especially when he was wearing a banker's suit). He jogged, he swam in the college pool, but he did not dance or play tennis. His idea of a night out involved an interesting meal and a good bottle of wine: April looked as if she would follow a couple of hours of archery with a good fast run up one of the minor Alps. He asked her if she had liked the Chandler novel. 'What a poignant book,' she said. 'The hero makes one friend, and by the end he can't stand him. The loneliness is so brutal that the most emotional passages are either about violence or bars.' 'Deliver me from this young woman, Ransom,' Brookner said. 'She frightens me.' Ransom asked, 'Was *virtuoso* really her first word?' 'No,' April said. 'My first words were *senile dementia*.'

About a year ago, the memory of this remark had ceased to be funny.

There had been a courtship unlike any Ransom had ever experienced. April Brookner seemed to be constantly assessing him according to some impenetrably private standard. April was very sane, but her sanity transcended normal definitions. Ransom later learned that two years earlier she had backed out of marriage with a boy who had graduated from the University of Chicago with her because – in her words – 'I realized that I hated all his metaphors. I couldn't live with someone who would never understand that metaphors are *real*.' She had

116

recognized the loneliness in the Chandler novel because it echoed her own.

Her mother had died in April's fourth year, and she had grown up the brilliant daughter of a brilliant man. After graduating Phi Beta Kappa and *summa cum laude* from Chicago, she moved back to Millhaven to do graduate work at the Millhaven branch of the University of Illinois. April never had any intention of teaching, but she wanted to be near her father. Ransom sometimes felt that she had married him because she couldn't think of anything else to do.

– Why me?, Ransom had asked her once.

– Oh, you were obviously the most interesting man around, she said. You didn't act like a jerk just because you thought I was beautiful. You always ordered just the right thing in Chinese restaurants, you were kind of experimental, and my jokes didn't make you mad. You didn't act like your mission in life was to *correct* me.

After they married, April left graduate school and took a job in a brokerage house. Ransom had thought she would quit within six months, but April astounded him by the speed and pleasure with which she had learned the business. Within eighteen months, she knew minute details of hundreds of companies – companies of all sizes. She knew how the division presidents got on with their boards; she knew which factories were falling apart; she knew about new patents and old grudges and unhappy stockholders. 'Really it isn't any harder than learning everything there is to know about sixteenth-century English poetry,' she said. 'These guys come in drooling with greed, and all I have to do is show them how they can make a little more money. When I do that, they give me a chunk of their pension funds. And when that does well, they fall down and kiss my feet.'

'You have corrupted my daughter,' Brookner said to him once. 'Now she is a money machine. The only consolation is that I will not have to spend my declining years in a room with a neon sign flashing outside the window.'

'It's just a game to April,' Ransom had said to him. 'She says her real master is Jacques Derrida.'

'I spawned a postmodern capitalist,' Brookner said. 'You understand, at Arkham it is an embarrassment suddenly to possess a great deal of money.'

The marriage settled into a busy but peaceful partnership. April told him that she was the world's only ironic Yuppie – when she was thirty-five, she was going to quit to have a baby, manage their own investments, learn to be a great cook, and keep up her elaborate research projects into local history. Ransom had wondered if April would ever really leave her job, baby or not. Certainly none of her customers wanted her to abandon them. The Millhaven financial community had given her their annual Association Award at a dinner April had privately ridiculed, and the *Ledger* had run a photograph of the two of them smiling a little shamefacedly as April cradled the huge cup on which her name was to be inscribed.

Ransom would never know if April would have left her job. Five days after April had won the hideous cup, someone had stabbed her, beaten her, and left her for dead.

He still lived in the duplex he and April had rented when they were first married. Twenty-one Ely Place was three blocks north of Berlin Avenue, a long walk from Shady Mount, but close to the UI-M campus, where April had once been enrolled, and only a ten-minute drive to Millhaven's downtown, where he and April had both had their offices. April's money had allowed them to buy the building and convert it into a single-family house. Now Ransom had a book-lined office on the third floor, April an office filled with glittering computers, stacks of annual reports, and a fax machine that continued to disgorge papers; the second floor had been converted into a giant master bedroom and a smaller guest room, both with bathrooms; the ground floor contained the living room, dining room, and kitchen.

5

'How is your father-in-law handling all this?'

'Alan doesn't really know what happened to April.' Ransom hesitated. 'He, ah, he's changed quite a bit over the past year or so.' He paused again and frowned at the stack of books on his coffee table. All of them were about Vietnam – *Fields of Fire*, *The Thirteenth Valley*, *365 Days*, *The Short Timers*, *The Things They Carried*. 'I'll make some coffee,' he said.

He went into the kitchen, and I began to take in, with admiration and even a little envy, the house Ransom and his wife had made together. Extraordinary paintings, paintings I could not quite place, covered the wall opposite the long couch that was my vantage point. I closed my eyes. A few minutes later, the clatter of the tray against the table awakened me. Ransom did not notice that I had dozed off.

'I want an *explanation*,' he said. 'I want to know what happened to my wife.'

'And you don't trust the police,' I said.

'I wonder if the police think *I* did it.' He threw out his arms, lifted them, then poured coffee into pottery mugs. 'Maybe they think I'm trying to mislead them by bringing up all the old Blue Rose business.' He took his own mug to a tufted leather chair.

'But you haven't been charged with anything.'

'I get the feeling that the homicide detective, Fontaine, is just waiting to pounce.'

'I don't understand why a homicide detective is involved in the first place – your wife is in the hospital.'

'My wife is dying in the hospital.'

'You can't really be sure of that,' I said.

He started shaking his head, misery and conflict printed clearly on his face, and I said, 'I guess I'm confused. How can a homicide detective investigate a death that hasn't happened?'

He looked up, startled. 'Oh. I see what you mean. The reason for that is the other victim.'

I had completely forgotten the other victim.

'The assault on April falls into an ongoing homicide investigation. When and if she dies, of course, Fontaine will be in charge of that investigation, too.'

'Did April know this guy?'

Ransom shook his head again. 'Nobody knows who he is.'

'He was never identified?'

'He had no identification of any kind, nothing at all, and nobody ever reported him missing. I think he must have been a vagrant, a homeless person, something like that.'

I asked if he had seen the man's body.

He shifted in his chair. 'I gather the killer scattered pieces of the guy all over Livermore Avenue.'

Before I could respond, Ransom went on. 'The guy who's doing this doesn't care who he kills. I don't even think he needed an actual *reason*. It was just time to get to work again.'

One reason John Ransom had wanted me to come back to Millhaven was that he had been talking nonstop to himself inside his head for weeks, and now he had to let some of these arguments out.

'Tell me about the person who did this,' I said. 'Tell me who you think he is – the kind of person you see when you think of him.'

Ransom looked relieved.

'Well, I *have* been thinking about that, of course. I've been trying to work out what kind of person would be capable of doing these things.' He leaned toward me, ready, even eager, to share his speculations.

I settled back in my own chair, all too conscious of the disparity between what Ransom and I were discussing and our setting. It was one of the most beautiful private rooms I had ever seen, beautiful in a restrained way centered in the paintings that filled the room. I thought that one of these must be a Vuillard, and the others seemed oddly familiar. The soft colors and flowing shapes of the paintings carried themselves right through the room, into the furniture and the few pieces of sculpture visible on low tables.

'I think he's about sixty. He might have had an alcoholic parent, and he was probably an abused child. You might find some kind of head injury in his history – that turns up surprisingly often, with these people. He is very, very controlled. I bet he has a kind of inflexible inner schedule. Every day, he does the same things at the same time. He's still strong, so he might even exercise regularly. He would probably seem to be the last person you'd suspect of these crimes. And he is intelligent.'

'What does he look like? What did he do for a living? How does he relax?'

'I think the only thing that distinguishes him physically, apart from his being in excellent condition for his age, is that he looks very respectable. And I think he might live down in that area where the murders took place, because with one exception, he stuck with it.'

'You mean, he lives in my old neighborhood?' The exception he had mentioned must have been his wife.

'I think so. People see him, but they don't really notice him. As for relaxing, I don't think he really can relax, so he wouldn't take vacations or anything – probably couldn't really afford that, anyhow – but I bet he was a gardener.'

'And the phrase *Blue Rose* is related to his gardening?'

Ransom shrugged. 'It's a funny choice of words – it's his way of identifying himself. And I think gardening would suit this guy very well – he could work out some of his tensions, he could indulge his compulsion for order, and he can do it alone.'

'So if we go down to the near south side and find a healthy-looking but boring sixty-year-old man who has a neat flower garden in back of his house, we'll have our man.'

Ransom smiled. 'That'll be him. Handle with care.'

'After being Blue Rose for a couple of months forty years ago, he managed to control himself until this year, when he snapped again.'

Ransom leaned forward again, excited to have reached the core of all his theorizing. 'Maybe he wasn't in Millhaven during those years. Maybe he had some job that took him here and there – maybe he sold ladies' stockings or shoelaces or men's shirts.' Ransom straightened up, and his eyes burned into me. 'But I think he was in the military. I think he joined up to escape the possibility of arrest and spent all the time between then and now in army bases all over the country and Europe. He would have been in Korea, he might even have been in Vietnam. He probably spent some time in Germany. He *undoubtedly* lived on a lot of those bases set outside small towns all over the South and Midwest. And every now and then, I bet he went out and killed somebody. I don't think he ever stopped. I think he was a serial killer before we even knew such things existed. Nobody ever connected his crimes, nobody ever matched the data – Tim, they only

122

began to think about doing that five or six years ago. The FBI had never heard of this guy because nothing he ever did was reported to them. He'd get off the base, persuade some civilian to follow him into an alley or a hotel – he's a very persuasive guy – and then he'd kill them.'

6

As I listened to John Ransom, my eyes kept returning to the painting I thought was a Vuillard. A middle-class family that seemed to consist entirely of women, children, and servants moved through a luxuriant back garden and sat beneath the spreading branches of an enormous tree. Brilliant molten lemon yellow light streamed down through the intense electric green of the thick leaves.

Ransom took off his glasses and polished them on his shirt. 'You seem fascinated by this room, especially the paintings.' He was smiling again. 'April would be pleased. She picked most of them out. She pretended that I helped her, but she did all the work.'

'I am fascinated,' I said. 'Isn't that a Vuillard? It's a beautiful painting.' The other paintings and little sculptures in the room seemed related to the Vuillard in some fashion, though they were clearly by several different artists. Some were landscapes with figures, some had religious themes, others were almost abstract. Most of them had a flat, delicate, decorative quality that had been influenced, like Van Gogh and Gauguin, but after them, by Japanese prints. Then I recognized that a small painting of the descent from the Cross was by Maurice Denis, and then I understood what April Ransom had done and was struck by its sheer intelligence.

She had collected the work of the group called the

Nabis, the 'prophets' – she had found paintings by Séru-sier, K.-X. Roussel, and Paul Ranson, as well as Denis and Vuillard. Everything she had bought was good, and all of it was related: it had a significant place in art history, and because most of these artists were not well known in America, their work would not have cost a great deal. As a collection, it had a greater value than the pieces would have had individually, and the pieces them-selves would already be worth a good deal more than the Ransoms had paid for them. And they were pleasing paintings – they aestheticized pain and joy, grief and wonder, and made them graceful.

'There must be more Nabis paintings in this room than anywhere else in the country,' I said. 'How did you find them all?'

'April was good at things like that,' Ransom said, suddenly looking very tired again. 'She went to a lot of the families, and most of them were willing to part with a couple of pieces. It's nice that you like the Vuillard – that was our favorite, too.'

It was the centerpiece of their collection: the most important painting they owned, and also the most pro-found, the most mysterious and radiant. It was an outright celebration of sunlight on leaves, of the interaction of people in families and of people with the natural world.

'Does it have a name?' I stood up to get a closer look.

'I think it's called *The Juniper Tree*.'

I looked at him over my shoulder, but he gave no indication of knowing that there was a famous Brothers Grimm story with that name, nor that the name might have meant anything to me. He nodded, confirming that I had heard him right. The coincidence of the painting's name affected me as I went toward the canvas. The people beneath the great tree seemed lonely and isolated, trapped in their private thoughts and passions; the occasion that had brought them together was a sham, no more than a formal exercise. They paid no attention to the radiant light and the vibrant leaves, nor to the shimmer of color which surrounded them, of which they themselves were a part.

'I can see April when I look at that,' Ransom said behind me.

'It's a wonderful painting,' I said. It was full of heartbreak and anger, and these feelings magically increased its radiance – because the painting itself was a consolation for them.

He stood up and came toward me, his eyes on the painting. 'There's so much happiness in that canvas.'

He was thinking of his wife. I nodded.

'You can help me, can't you?' Ransom asked. 'We might be able to help the police put a name to this man. By looking into the old murders, I mean.'

'That's why I'm here.'

Ransom clamped his fist around my arm. 'But I have to tell you, if I find out who attacked my wife, I'll try to kill him – if I get anywhere near him, I'll give him what he gave April.'

'I can understand how you'd feel that way,' I said.

'No, you can't.' He dropped his hand and stepped closer to the painting, gave it a quick, cursory glance, and began wandering back to his chair. He put his hand on the stack of Vietnam novels. 'Because you never had the chance to know April. I'll take you to the hospital with me tomorrow, but you won't really – you know, the person lying there in that bed isn't – '

Ransom raised a hand to cover his eyes. 'Excuse me. I'll get you some more coffee.'

He took my cup back to the table, and I took in the room again. The marble fireplace matched the pinks and grays in the paintings on the long walls, and one vivid slash of red was the same shade as the sky in the Maurice Denis painting of the descent from the Cross. A pale,

125

enormous Paul Ranson painting of a kneeling woman holding up her hands in what looked like prayer or supplication hung above the fireplace. Then I noticed something else, the flat edge of a bronze plaque laid flat on the marble.

I walked around the furniture to take a look at it, and John Ransom came toward me with the mug as soon as I stood the plaque upright. 'Oh, you found that.'

I read the raised letters on the surface of the bronze. 'The Association Award of the Financial Professionals of the City of Millhaven is hereby given to April Ransom on the Occasion of the Annual Dinner, 1991.'

John Ransom sat down and held out his hand for the plaque. I exchanged it for the coffee, and he stared at it for a second before sliding it back onto the mantel. 'The plaque is just a sort of token – the real award is having your name engraved on a big cup in a glass case in the Founder's Club.'

Ransom raised his eyes to mine and blinked. 'Why don't I show you the picture that was taken the night she won that silly award? At least you can see what she looked like. You'll come to the hospital with me, too, of course, but in a way there's more of the real April in the picture.' He jumped up and went out into the hallway to go upstairs.

I walked over to the Vuillard painting again. I could hear John Ransom opening drawers in his bedroom upstairs.

A few minutes later, he came back into the living room with a folded section of the *Ledger* in one hand. 'Took me a while to find it – been intending to cut out the photograph and stick it in an album, but these days I can hardly get anything done.' He gave me the newspaper.

The photograph took up the top right corner of the first page of the financial section. John Ransom was wearing a tuxedo, and his wife was in a white silk outfit with an oversized jacket over a low-cut top. She was gleaming into the camera with her arms around a big engraved cup like a tennis trophy, and he was nearly in profile, looking at her. April Ransom was nearly as tall as her husband, and her hair had been cropped to a fluffy blond helmet that made you notice the length of her neck. She had a wide mouth and a small, straight nose, and her eyes seemed very bright. She looked smart and tough and triumphant. She was a surprise. April Ransom looked much more like what she was, a shrewd and aggressive financial expert, than like the woman her husband had described to me during the ride to Ely Place from the airport. The woman in the photograph did not suffer from uselessly complicated moral sensitivities: she bought paintings because she knew they would look good on her walls while they quadrupled in value, she would never quit her job to have a child, she was hardworking and a little merciless and she would not be kind to fools.

'Isn't she beautiful?' Ransom asked.

I looked at the date on the top of the page, Monday, the third of June. 'How long after this came out was she attacked?'

Ransom raised his eyebrows. 'The police found April something like ten days after the awards dinner – that was on Friday, the thirty-first of May. That unknown man was killed the next Wednesday. On Monday night April never came home from the office. I went crazy, waiting for her. Around two in the morning I finally called the police. They told me to wait another twenty-four hours, and that she would probably come home before that. I got a call the next afternoon, saying that they had found her, and that she was unconscious but still alive.'

'They found her in a parking lot, or something like that?'

Ransom placed the folded section of the newspaper on the coffee table next to the stack of books. He sighed. 'I guess I thought I must have told you. A maid at the St Alwyn found her when she went to check on the condition of a room.' There was something like defiance in his eyes and his posture, in the way he straightened his back, when he told me this.

'April was in a room at the St Alwyn Hotel?'

Ransom jerked down the front of his suit jacket and smoothed his tie. 'The room where the maid found her had been empty all day, and someone was due to take it on that night. April got up to that room, or was *brought* up to that room, conscious or not, without anyone seeing her go into the hotel.'

'So how did she get there?' I asked. I felt sorry for John Ransom and asked my stupid question to buy time while I absorbed this information.

'She flew. I don't have any idea how she got into the hotel, Tim. All I know is that April would never have met any kind of *boyfriend* at the St Alwyn, because even if she had a boyfriend, which she did not, the St Alwyn is too seedy. She'd never go inside that place.'

I thought: not unless she wanted a little seediness.

'I know her – you never met her. I've been married to her for fourteen years, and you've only seen a picture of her. She would never have gone into that place.'

Of course, John was right. He did know her, and I had been merely drawing inferences from a newspaper photograph and what had seemed to me the striking degree of calculation that had created her art collection.

'Wait a second,' I said. 'What was the room number?'

'The maid found April in room 218. Room 218 of the St Alwyn Hotel.' He smiled at me. 'I wondered when you were going to get around to asking that question.'

It was the same room in which James Treadwell had been murdered, also by someone who had signed the wall with the words BLUE ROSE.

'And your detective doesn't think that's significant?'

Ransom threw up his hands. 'As far as the police are concerned, nothing that happened back in 1950 has any connection to what happened to my wife. William Damrosch got them all off the hook. He killed himself, the murders ended, that's it.'

'You said the first victim was found on Livermore Avenue.'

Ransom nodded, fiercely.

'Where on Livermore Avenue?'

'You tell me. You know where it was.'

'In that little tunnel behind the St Alwyn?'

Ransom smiled at me. 'Well, that's where I'd bet they found the body. The newspaper wasn't specific – they just said "in the vicinity of the St Alwyn Hotel." It never occurred to me that it might be the same place where the first victim was found in the fifties until April, until they found, um, until they found her. You know. In that room.' His smile had become ghastly – I think he had lost control over his face. 'And I couldn't be sure about anything, because all I had to go on was your book, *The Divided Man*. I didn't know if you'd changed any of the places . . .'

'No,' I said. 'I didn't.'

'So then I read your book and thought I might call just to see – '

'If I still thought Damrosch was the man you call Blue Rose.'

He nodded. That dead smile was fading, but he still looked as if a fishhook had caught in his mouth. 'And you said no.'

'And so – ' I paused, stunned by what I had just learned. 'And so, what it looks like is that Blue Rose is not only killing people in Millhaven again, but killing them in the same places he used forty years ago.'

'That's the way it looks to me,' Ransom said. 'The question is, can we get anyone else to believe it?'

7

'They'll believe it in hurry after one more murder,' I said.

'The third one was the exception I mentioned before – the doctor,' said Ransom.

'I thought you were talking about your wife.'

He frowned at me. 'Well, in the book, the third one was the doctor. Big house on the east side.'

'There won't be one on the east side,' I said.

'Look at what's *happening*,' Ransom said. 'It'll be at the same address. Where the doctor died.'

'The doctor didn't die. That was one of the things I changed when I wrote the book. Whoever tried to kill Buzz Laing, Dr Laing, cut his throat and wrote BLUE ROSE on his bedroom wall, but ran away without noticing that he wasn't dead yet. Laing came to in time and managed to stop the bleeding and get himself to a hospital.'

'What do you mean, "whoever tried to kill him"? It was Blue Rose.'

I shook my head.

'Are you sure about this?'

'As sure as I can be without evidence,' I said. 'In fact, I think the same person who cut Buzz Laing's throat also killed Damrosch and set it up to look like suicide.'

Ransom opened his mouth and then closed it again. 'Killed Damrosch?'

I smiled at him – Ransom looked a little punchy. 'Some information about the Blue Rose case turned up a couple of years ago when I was working on a book about Tom Pasmore and Lamont von Heilitz.' He started to say something, and I held up my hand. 'You probably remember

130

hearing about von Heilitz, and I guess you went to school with Tom.'

'I was a year behind him at Brooks-Lowood. What in the world could *he* have to do with the Blue Rose murders?'

'He didn't have anything to do with them, but he knows who tried to kill Buzz Laing. And who murdered William Damrosch.'

'Who is this?' Ransom seemed furious with excitement. 'Is he still alive?'

'No, he's not. And I think it would be better for Tom to tell you the story. It's really his story, for one thing.'

'Will he be willing to tell it to me?'

'I called him before I left New York. He'll tell you what he thinks happened to Buzz Laing and Detective Damrosch.'

'Okay.' Ransom nodded. He considered this. 'When do I get to talk to him?'

'He'd probably be willing to see us tonight, if you like.'

'Could I hire him?'

Almost every resident of Millhaven over the age of thirty would probably have known that Tom Pasmore had worked for a time as a private investigator. Twenty years ago, even the Bangkok papers had run the story of how an independent investigator, a self-styled 'amateur of crime' living in the obscure city of Millhaven, Illinois, had brilliantly reinterpreted all the evidence and records in the case of Whitney Walsh, the president of TransWorld Insurance, who had been shot to death near the ninth hole of his country club in Harrison, New York. A groundskeeper with a longstanding grudge against Walsh had been tried, found guilty, and sentenced to life imprisonment. Working on his own and without ever leaving Millhaven, Tom Pasmore had succeeded in identifying and locating the essential piece of evidence necessary to arrest and convict the real murderer, a former employee.

The innocent man had been freed, and after he had told his story to a number of newspapers and national magazines, it was learned that Tom Pasmore had done essentially the same thing in perhaps a dozen cases: he had used public information and trial records to get innocent men out of jail and guilty ones in. The Walsh case had merely been the most prominent. There followed, in the same newspapers and magazines, a number of lurid stories about 'The Real-Life Sherlock Holmes,' each containing the titillating information that the wizard habitually refused payment for his investigations, that he had a fortune of something between ten and twenty million dollars, that he lived alone in a house he seldom left, that he dressed with an odd, old-fashioned formality. These revelations came to a climax with the information that Tom Pasmore was the natural son of Lamont von Heilitz, the man who had been the inspiration for the radio character Lamont Cranston – 'The Shadow.' By the time all of this had emerged, Tom ceased to work – scorched into retirement by unwelcome publicity. The press never unearthed another incident in which Tom Pasmore of Millhaven, Illinois, intervened from afar to free an innocent man and jail a guilty one for murder. Yet from my contact with him, I thought it was almost certain that he continued this work anonymously, and that he had created the illusion of retirement to maintain in absolute darkness the secret the press had not discovered, that he had long been the lover of a woman married into one of Millhaven's wealthiest families.

Tom would never consent to being hired by John Ransom, and I told him so.

'Why not, if he's willing to come over?'

'In the first place, he was never for hire. And ever since the Walsh case, he's wanted people to think that he doesn't even work. And secondly, Tom is not willing to "come over." If you want to see him, we'll have to go to his house.'

'But I went to school with him!'

'Were you friends?'

'Pasmore didn't have friends. He didn't want any.' This suggested another thought, and he turned his head from the study of his interlaced hands to revolve his suspicious face toward mine. 'Since he's so insistent on keeping out of sight, why is he willing to talk to me now?'

'He'd rather explain to you himself what happened to Buzz Laing and Detective Damrosch. You'll see why.'

Ransom shrugged and looked at his watch. 'I'm usually back at the hospital by now. Maybe Pasmore could join us for dinner?'

'We have to go to his house,' I said.

He thought about it for a while. 'So maybe we could have an audience with His Holiness between visiting April and going for dinner? Or is there something else about the sacred schedule of Thomas Pasmore that you haven't told me yet?'

'Well, his day generally starts pretty late,' I said. 'But if you point me toward the telephone, I'll give him some advance warning.'

Ransom waved his hand toward the front of the room, and I remembered passing a high telephone table in the entrance hall. I stood up and left the room. Through the arch, I saw Ransom get up and walk toward the paintings. He stood in front of the Vuillard with his hands in his pockets, frowning at the lonely figures beneath the tree. Tom Pasmore would still be asleep, I knew, but he kept his answering machine switched on to take messages during the day. Tom's dry, light voice told me to leave a message, and I said that Ransom and I would like to see him around seven – I'd call him from the hospital to see if that was all right.

Ransom spun around as I came back into the room. 'Well, did Sherlock agree to meet me before midnight?'

'I left a message on his machine. When we're ready to leave the hospital, I'll try him again. It'll probably be all right.'

'I suppose I ought to be grateful he's willing to see me at all, right?' He looked angrily at me, then down at his watch. He jammed his hands into his trousers pockets and glared at me, waiting for the answer to a rhetorical question.

'He'll probably be grateful to see you, too,' I said.

He jerked a hand from his pocket and ran it over his thinning hair. 'Okay, okay,' he said. 'I'm sorry.' He motioned me back toward the entrance hall and the front door.

8

Once we were outside and on the sidewalk, I waited for John Ransom to move toward his car. He turned left toward Berlin Avenue and kept walking without pausing at any of the cars parked along the curb. I hurried to catch up with him.

'I hope you don't mind walking. It's humid, but this is about the only exercise I get. And the hospital isn't really very far.'

'I walk all over New York. It's fine with me.'

'If it's all right with you, we could even walk to Tom Pasmore's house after we leave the hospital. He still lives on Eastern Shore Road?'

I nodded. 'Across the street from where he grew up.'

Ransom gave me a curious look, and I explained that Tom had moved long ago into the old von Heilitz house.

'So he's still right there on Eastern Shore Road. Lucky guy. I wish I could have taken over my family's old house. But my parents moved to Arizona when my father sold his properties in town.'

We turned north to walk down Berlin Avenue, and traffic noises, the sound of horns and the hiss of tires on asphalt, took shape in the air. Summer school students from the college moved up the block in twos and threes, heading toward afternoon classes. Ransom gave me a wry glance. 'He did all right on the deal, of course, but I wish he'd held onto those properties. The St Alwyn alone went for about eight hundred thousand, and today it would be worth something like three million. We get a lot more conventions in town than we used to, and a decent hotel has a lot of potential.'

'Your father owned the St Alwyn?'

'And the rest of that block.' He shook his head slowly and smiled when he saw my expression. 'I guess I assumed you knew that. It adds a little irony to the situation. The place was run much better when my father owned it, let me tell you. It was as good as any hotel anywhere. But I don't think the fact that my father owned the place twenty years ago has anything to do with April winding up in room 218, do you?'

'Probably not.' Not unless his father's ownership of the hotel had something to do with the first Blue Rose murders, I thought, and dismissed the idea.

'I still wish the old man had held out until the city turned around,' said Ransom. 'An academic salary doesn't go very far. Especially an Arkham College salary.'

'April must have more than compensated for that,' I said.

He shook his head. 'April's money is hers, not mine. I never wanted to have the feeling that I could just dip into the money she made on her own.'

Ransom smiled at some memory, and the sunlight

softened the unhappiness in his face.

'I have an old Pontiac I bought secondhand for when I have to drive somewhere. April's car is a Mercedes 500SL. She worked hard – spent all night in her office sometimes. It was her money, all right.'

'Is there a lot of it?'

He gave me a grim look. 'If she dies, I'll be a well-off widower. But the money didn't have anything to do with who she really was.'

'It could look like a motive to people who don't understand your marriage.'

'Like the wonderful Millhaven police department?' He laughed – a short, ugly bark. 'That's just another reason for us to learn Blue Rose's name. As if we needed one.'

9

We came around the bend past the third-floor patients' lounge, and a short, aggressive-looking policeman in his twenties lounged out of one of the doorways. His name tag read MANGELOTTI. He checked his watch, then gave Ransom what he thought was a hard look. I got a hard look, too.

'Did she say anything, officer?' Ransom asked.

'Who's this?' The little policeman moved in front of me, as if to keep me from entering the room. The top of his uniform hat came up to my chin.

'I'm just a friend,' I said.

Ransom had already stepped into the room, and the policeman turned his head to follow him. Then he tilted his head and gave me another glare. Both of us heard a woman inside the hospital room say that Mrs Ransom had not spoken yet.

136

The cop backed away and turned around and went into the room to make sure he didn't miss anything. I followed him into the sunny white room. Sprays of flowers in vases covered every flat surface – vases filled with lilies and roses and peonies crowded the long windowsill. The odor of the lilies filled the room. John Ransom and an efficient-looking woman in a white uniform stood on the far side of the bed. The curtains around the bed had been pushed back and were bunched against the wall on both sides of the patient's head. April Ransom lay in a complex tangle of wires, tubes, and cords that stretched from the bed to a bank of machines and monitors. A clear bag on a pole dripped glucose into her veins. Thin white tubes had been fed into her nose, and electrodes were fastened to her neck and the sides of her head with white stars of tape. The sheet over her body covered a catheter and other tubes. Her head lay flat on the bed, and her eyes were closed. The left side of her face was a single enormous blue-purple bruise, and another long blue bruise covered her right jaw. Wedges of hair had been shaved back from her forehead, making it look even broader and whiter. Fine lines lay across it, and two nearly invisible lines bracketed her wide mouth. Her lips had no color. She looked as if several layers of skin had been peeled from the sections of her face left unbruised. She had only the smallest resemblance to the woman in the newspaper photograph.

'You brought company today,' said the nurse.

John Ransom spoke our names, Eliza Morgan, Tim Underhill, and we nodded at each other across the bed. The policeman walked to the back of the room and sat down beneath the rows of windows. 'Tim is going to stay with me for a while, Eliza,' John said.

'It'll be nice for you to have some company,' said the nurse. She looked at me from the other side of the bed, letting me adjust to the sight of April Ransom.

137

Ransom said, 'You've heard me speak about Tim Underhill, April. He's here to visit you, too. Are you feeling any better today?' He moved a section of the sheet aside and closed his hand around hers. I saw a flash of white bandage pads and even whiter tape around her upper arm. 'Pretty soon you'll be strong enough to come home again.'

He looked up at me. 'She looked a lot worse last Wednesday, when they finally let me see her. I really thought she was going to die that day, but she pulled through, didn't she, Eliza?'

'Sure she did,' the nurse said. 'Been fighting ever since.'

Ransom leaned over the bed and began speaking to his wife in a steady, comforting voice. I moved away from the bed. The policeman seated beneath the row of bright windows straightened up in his chair and looked at me brightly and aggressively. His left hand wandered toward the bulge of the notebook in his shirt pocket.

'The patients' lounge is usually empty around this time,' the nurse said, and smiled at me.

I walked down the curving hallway to the entrance of a large room lined with green couches and chairs, some of them arranged around plain polished wooden tables. Two overweight women in T-shirts that adhered to their bodies smoked and played cards in a litter of splayed magazines and paper bags at a table in the far corner. They had pulled one of the curtains across the nearest window. An elderly woman in a gray suit occupied a chair eight feet from them with her back to an uncovered window, reading a Barbara Pym novel as if her life depended on it. I moved toward the windows in the left-hand corner of the room, and the old woman glanced up from her book and stabbed me with a look fiercer than anything Officer Mangelotti could have produced.

I heard footsteps behind me and turned around to see April Ransom's private duty nurse carrying a pouchy

138

black handbag into the lounge. The old woman glared at her, too. Eliza Morgan plopped her bag onto one of the tables near the entrance and motioned me toward her. She fished around in the big handbag and pulled out a pack of cigarettes and looked at me apologetically. 'This is the only place in this whole wing of the hospital where smoking is allowed,' she said in a voice not far above a whisper. She lit the cigarette with a match, tossed the match into a blackened copper ashtray, blew out a white feather of smoke, and sat down. 'I know it's a filthy habit, but I'm cutting way down. I have one an hour during my shift here, and one after dinner, and that's it. Well, that's *almost* the truth. Right at the start of my shift, I sit in here and smoke three or four of the darned things; otherwise I'd never make it through the first hour.' She leaned forward and lowered her voice again. 'If Mrs Rollins gave you a dirty look when you came in, it's because she was afraid you were going to start polluting the place. I distress her no end, because she doesn't think nurses should smoke at all – probably they shouldn't!'

I smiled at her – she was a nice-looking woman a few years older than I was. Her short black hair looked clean and silky, and her brisk friendliness stopped far short of being intrusive.

'I suppose you've been here ever since Mrs Ransom was put into the hospital,' I said.

She nodded, exhaling another vigorous plume of smoke. 'Mr Ransom hired me as soon as he heard.'

She put her hand on her bag. 'You're staying with him?'

I nodded.

'Just get him to talk – he's an interesting man, but he doesn't know half of what's going on inside him. It'd be terrible if he started to fall apart.'

'Tell me,' I said. 'Does his wife have a chance? Do you think she'll come out of her coma?'

She leaned across the table. 'You just be there to help him, if you're a friend of his.' She made sure that I had heard this and then straightened her back and snubbed out the cigarette, having said all she intended to say.

'I guess that's an answer,' I said, and we both stood up.

'Who ever said there were answers?'

Then she came toward me, and her dark eyes looked huge in her small, competent face. She put the flat of her hand on my chest. 'I shouldn't be saying any of this, but if Mrs Ransom dies, you should go through his medicine chest and hide any prescription tranquilizers. And you shouldn't let him drink too much. He's had a good marriage for a long time, and if he loses it, he's going to become someone he wouldn't even recognize now.'

She gave my chest a single, admonitory pat, dropped her hand, and turned around again without saying another word. I followed her back into April Ransom's room. John was leaning over the side of the bed, saying things too soft to be overheard. April looked like a white husk.

It was past five, and Tom Pasmore was probably out of bed. I asked Eliza where to find a pay telephone, and she sent me around the nurses' station and down a hallway to another bank of elevators. A row of six telephones hung opposite the elevators, none of them in use. Swinging doors opened to wide corridors on both sides. Green, red, and blue arrows streaked up and down the floor in lines, indicating the way to various departments.

Tom Pasmore answered after five or six rings. Yes, it would be fine if we came around seven-thirty. I could tell that he was disappointed – on the few occasions Tom welcomed company, he liked it to arrive late and stay until dawn. He seemed intrigued that we would be on foot.

'Does Ransom walk everywhere? Would he walk downtown, say, from Ely Place?'

'He drove me to his house from the airport,' I said.

'In his or his wife's car?'

'His. His wife has a Mercedes, I guess.'

'Is it parked in front of their house?'

'I didn't notice. Why?'

He laughed. 'He has two cars and he's marching you all over the east side.'

'I walk everywhere, too. I don't mind.'

'Well, I'll have some cold towels and iced lemonade ready for you when you trudge up the driveway at the break of dawn. In the meantime, see if you can find out what happened to his wife's car.'

I promised to try. Then I hung up and turned around to find myself facing a huge broad-shouldered guy with a gray ponytail and beard, the gold dot of an earring in one ear, and a four-button double-breasted Armani suit. He sneered at me as he moved toward the phone. I sneered back. I felt like Philip Marlowe.

10

At seven John Ransom and I walked out of the hospital and went down the hedge-lined path to Berlin Avenue. He moved quickly but heedlessly, as if he were all by himself in an empty landscape. The air could have been squeezed like a sponge, and the temperature had cooled off to something like eighty-five. There was still at least an hour and a half of sunlight. Ransom hesitated when we reached the sidewalk. For a second I thought he might wade out into the crowded avenue – I didn't think he could see anything but the room he had just left. Instead of stepping off the curb, he let his head drop so that his chin pressed into the layer of fat beneath it. He wiped his face with his hands. 'Okay,' he said, more to himself than to me. Then he looked at me. 'Well, now you've seen her. What do you think?'

'You must be doing her some good, coming every day,' I said.

'I hope so.' Ransom shoved his hands into his pockets. For a moment he looked like a balding, overweight version of the Brooks-Lowood student he had been. 'I think she's lost some weight in the past few days. And that big bruise seems to have stopped fading. Wouldn't you think that's a bad sign, when a bruise won't fade?'

I asked him what her doctor had said.

'As usual, nothing at all.'

'Well, Eliza Morgan will do everything possible for April,' I said. 'At least you know she's getting good care.'

He looked at me sharply. 'She sneaks away to smoke cigarettes in the lounge, did you notice? I don't think nurses should smoke, and I don't think April should be left alone.'

'Isn't that cop always there?'

Ransom shrugged and began walking back down the way we had come. 'He spends most of his time staring out of the window.' His hands were still stuffed into his trousers pockets, and he hunched over a little as he walked. He looked over at me and shook his head.

I said, 'It can't be easy to see April like that.'

He sighed – sighed up from his heels. 'Tim, she's dying right in front of me.'

We both stopped walking. Ransom covered his face with his hands for a moment. A few people walking past us stared at the unusual sight of a grown man in a handsome gray suit crying in public. When he lowered his hands, moisture shone on his red face. 'Now I'm a public embarrassment.' He pulled a handkerchief from his pocket and wiped his face.

'Do you still want to see Tom Pasmore? Would you rather just go home?'

142

'Are you kidding?'

He straightened his spine and began moving down the sidewalk again, past the card shop and the grocery store and the florist with its striped awning and its sidewalk display of flowers. 'Whatever happened to April's Mercedes? I don't think I saw it when we left the house.'

Ransom frowned at me. 'You hardly could have. It's gone. I suppose it'll turn up eventually – I've had other things to think about.'

'Where do you think it is?'

'To tell you the truth, I don't *care* what happened to the car. It was insured. It's just a car.'

We walked several more blocks through the heat, not talking. Now and then John Ransom pulled his handkerchief from his pocket and blotted his forehead. We were getting close to the UI campus, and bookstores and little restaurants had replaced the grocery stores and florists. The Royal, Millhaven's only art film house, was showing a season of thrillers from the forties and fifties – the marquee showed a complicated schedule beginning with a double feature of *Double Indemnity* and *Kiss Me Deadly* and ending, sometime in August, with *Pickup on South Street* and *Strangers on a Train*. In between they were running *From Dangerous Depths*, *The Big Combo*, *the Asphalt Jungle*, *Chicago Deadline*, *DOA*, *The Hitchhiker*, *Laura*, *Out of the Past*, *Notorious*. These were the movies of my youth, and I remembered the pleasure of slipping into the cool of the Beldame Oriental on a hot day, of buying popcorn and watching a doom-laden film noir in the nearly empty theater.

Suddenly I remembered the nightmare I'd had on the morning of the day John Ransom had called me – the thick hands on the big white plate. Cutting off human flesh, chewing it, spitting it out in revulsion. The heat made me feel dizzy, and the memory of the dream brought with it the gritty taste of depression. I stopped moving and looked up at the marquee.

'You okay?' Ransom said, turning around just ahead of me.

The title of one of the films seemed to float out an inch or two from the others – a trick of vision, or of the light. 'Have you ever heard of a movie called *From Dangerous Depths*?' I asked. 'I don't know anything about it.'

Ransom walked back to join me. He looked up at the crowded marquee. 'Cornball title, isn't it?'

Ransom plunged acoss Berlin Avenue and walked east on a block lined with three-story frame and redbrick houses separated by thick low hedges. Some of the tiny front lawns were littered with bicycles and children's toys, and all of them bore brown streaks like burn scars. Rock and roll drifted down from an upstairs window, tinny and lifeless.

'I remember Tom Pasmore,' Ransom said. 'The guy was an absolute loner. He didn't really have any friends. The money was his grandfather's, wasn't it? His father didn't amount to much – I think he ran out on them in Tom's senior year.'

That was the sort of detail everyone at Brook-Lowood would have known.

'And his mother was an alcoholic,' Ransom said. 'Pretty lady, though. Is she still alive?'

'She died about ten years ago.'

'And now he's retired? He doesn't do anything at all?'

'I suppose just looking after his money is a full-time job.'

'April could have done that for him,' Ransom said.

We crossed Waterloo Parade and walked another block in silence while Ransom thought about his wife.

After we crossed Balaclava Lane, the houses began to be slightly larger, set farther apart on larger lots. Between Berlin Avenue and Eastern Shore Drive, the value of property increases with every block – walking eastward, we were moving toward John Ransom's childhood neighborhood.

Ransom's silence continued across Omdurman Road, Victoria Terrace, Salisbury Road. We reached the long street called The Sevens, where sprawling houses on vast lawns silently asserted that they were just as good as the houses one block farther east, on Eastern Shore Road. He stopped walking and wiped his forehead again. 'When I was a kid, I walked all over this neighborhood. Now it seems so foreign to me. It's as if I never lived here at all.'

'Aren't the same people basically still here?'

'Nope – my parents' generation died or moved to the west coast of Florida, and people my age all moved out to Riverwood. Even Brooks-Lowood moved, did you know that? Four years ago, they sold the plant and built a big Georgian campus out in Riverwood.'

He looked around, and for a moment he seemed to be considering buying one of the big showy houses. 'Most people like April, people with new money, they bought places out in Riverwood. She wouldn't hear of it. April liked being in the city – she liked being able to walk. She liked that little house of ours, and she liked it just where it is.'

He was using the past tense, I noticed, and I felt a wave of pity for all he was going through.

'Sometimes,' he said, 'I get so discouraged.'

We walked up the rest of the block and turned right onto Eastern Shore Drive. Mansions of every conceivable style lined both sides of the wide road. Huge brick piles with turrets and towers, half-timbered Tudor structures, Moorish fantasies, giant stone palaces with stained-glass windows – money expressing itself unself-consciously and unfettered by taste. Competing with one another, the people who built these enormous structures had bought grandeur by the yard.

Eventually, I pointed out Tom Pasmore's house. It was on the west side of the drive, not the lake side, and dark green vines grew up the gray stone of its façade. As always in Lamont Von Heilitz's day, the curtains were closed against the light.

We went up the walk to the front door, and I rang the bell. We waited for what seemed a long time. John Ransom gave me the look he'd give a student who did not hand in a paper on time. I pressed the bell again. Maybe twenty seconds passed.

'Are you sure His Lordship is up?'

'Hold on,' I said. Inside the house, footsteps came toward the door.

After shooting me another critical glance, John pulled his damp handkerchief from his pocket and wiped the back of his neck and his forehead. The lock clicked. He squared his shoulders and worked his face into a pretty good imitation of a smile. The door swung open, and Tom Pasmore stood on the other side of the screen, blinking and smiling back. He was wearing a pale blue suit with a double-breasted vest still partially unbuttoned over a snowy white shirt and dark blue silk tie. Comb marks separated his damp hair. He looked tired and a little out of focus.

11

Ransom said, 'Hey, big fella!' His voice was too loud. 'You had us worried!'

'Tim and John, what a pleasure,' said Tom. He was fumbling with the buttons of the vest as his eyes traveled back and forth between us. 'Isn't this something?' He pushed the screen door open, and John Ransom had to

146

step backward to move round it. Still moving around the screen door on the expanse of the front step, Ransom stuck out his right hand. Tom took it and said, 'Well, just imagine.'

'It's been a long time,' John Ransom said. 'Too long.'

'Come on in,' Tom said, and dropped backward into the relative darkness of the house. I could smell traces of the soap and shampoo from his shower as I stepped into the house. Low lamps glowed here and there, on tables and on the walls. The familiar clutter filled the enormous room. I moved away from the door to let John Ransom come in.

'You're very good to agree to – ' Ransom stopped talking as he finally saw what the ground floor of Tom Pasmore's house really looked like. He stood with his mouth open for a moment, then recovered himself. 'To agree to see me. It means a lot to me, all the more since I gather from Tim that what you can tell me is, ah, rather on the personal side – '

He was still taking in the interior, which would have matched none of his expectations. Lamont von Heilitz, the previous owner of Tom's house, had turned most of the ground floor into a single enormous room filled with file cases, stacks of books and newspapers, tables strewn with the details of whatever murder was on his mind at the moment, and couches and chairs that seemed randomly placed. Tom Pasmore had changed the room very little. The curtains were still always drawn; old-fashioned upright lamps and green-shaded library lamps still burned here and there around the room, shedding warm illumination on the thousands of books ranged in dark wooden cases along the walls and on the dining table at the rear of the room. Tall stereo speakers stood against the walls, connected to shelves of complicated audio equipment. compact discs leaned against one another like dominoes on half a dozen bookshelves, and hundreds of others had been stacked into tilting piles on the floor.

Tom said, 'I know this place looks awfully confusing at first glance, but there *is*, I promise you, a comfortable place to sit down at the other end of the room.' He gestured toward the confusion. 'Shall we?'

John Ransom was still taking in the profusion of filing cabinets and office furniture. Tom struck off through the maze.

'Say, I know I haven't seen you since school,' said John Ransom, 'but I've been reading about you in the papers, and that was an amazing job you did on Whitney Walsh's murder. Amazing. You put it together from here, huh?'

'Right in this house,' Tom said. He motioned for us to sit on two couches placed at right angles to a glass coffee table stacked with books. An ice bucket, three glasses, a jug of water, and various bottles stood in the middle of the table. 'Everything was right there in the newspapers. Anyone could have seen it, and sooner or later someone else would have.'

'Yeah, but haven't you done the same thing lots of times?' John Ransom sat facing a paneled wall on which hung half a dozen paintings, and I took the couch on the left side of the table. Ransom was eyeing the bottles. Tom seated himself in a matching chair across the table from me.

'Now and then, I manage to point out something other people missed.' Tom looked extremely uncomfortable. 'John, I'm very sorry about what happened to your wife. What a terrible business. Have the police made any progress?'

'I wish I could say yes.'

'How is your wife doing? Do you see signs of improvement?'

'No,' Ransom said, staring at the ice bucket and the bottles.

'I'm so sorry.' Tom paused. 'You must be in the mood

for a drink. Can I get anything for you?'

Ransom said he would take vodka on the rocks, and Tom leaned over the table and used silver tongs to drop ice cubes into a thick low glass before filling the glass nearly to the top with vodka. I was watching him act as if there was no more on his mind than making John Ransom comfortable, and I wondered if he would make a drink for himself. I knew, as Ransom did not, that Tom had been out of bed for no more than half an hour.

During the course of telephone conversations in the middle of the night that sometimes lasted for two and three hours, I had sometimes imagined that Tom Pasmore started drinking when he got out of bed and stopped only when he managed to get back into it. He was the loneliest person I had ever met.

Tom's mother had been a weepy drunk all during his childhood, and his father – Victor Pasmore, the man he had thought was his father – had been distant and short-tempered. Tom had known Lamont von Heilitz, his biological father, only a short time before von Heilitz was murdered as a result of the only investigation the two of them had conducted together. Tom had found his father's body upstairs in this house. That investigation had made Tom Pasmore famous at the age of seventeen and left him with two fortunes, but it froze him into the life he still had. He lived in his father's house, he wore his father's clothes, he continued his father's work. He had drifted through the local branch of the University of Illinois, where he wrote a couple of monographs – one about the death of the eighteenth-century poet-forger Thomas Chatterton, the other about the Lindbergh kidnapping – that caused a stir in academic circles. He began law school at Harvard in the year that an English graduate student there was arrested for murder after being found unconscious in a Cambridge motel bedroom with the corpse of his girlfriend. Tom talked to people, thought about things, and presented the police with evidence that led to the freeing of the student and the arrest of a famous English professor. He refused the offer from the parents of the freed student to pay his tuition through the rest of law school. When reporters began following him to his classes, he dropped out and fled back home. He could only be what he was – he was too good at it to be anything else.

I think that was when he started drinking.

Given this history, he still looked surprisingly like the young man he had been: he had all his hair, and, unlike John Ransom, he had not put on a great deal of weight. Despite the old-fashioned, dandyish elegance of his clothes, Tom Pasmore looked more like a college professor than Ransom did. The badges of his drinking, the bags under his eyes, the slight puffiness of his cheeks, and his pallor might have been the result of nothing more than a few too many late nights in a library carrel.

He paused with his hands on the vodka bottle and a new glass, regarding me with his exhausted blue eyes, and I knew that he had seen exactly what was going through my mind.

'Feel like a drink?' He knew all about my history.

John Ransom looked at me speculatively.

'Any soft drink,' I said.

'Ah,' Tom said. 'We'll have to go into the kitchen for that. Why don't you come with me, so you can see what I've got in the fridge?'

I followed him to the back of the room and the kitchen door.

The kitchen too had been left as it had been in Lamont von Heilitz's time, with high wooden cupboards, double copper sinks, wainscoting and weak, inadequate lighting. The only modern addition was a gleaming white refrigerator nearly the size of a grand piano. A long length of open cupboards had been cut away to make room for it. Tom swung open the wide door of this object – it was like opening the door of a carriage.

The bottom shelf of the otherwise nearly empty refrigerator held at least a dozen cans each of Coke and Pepsi and a six-pack of club soda in bottles. I chose club soda. Tom dropped ice into a tall glass and poured in the club soda.

'Did you ask him about his wife's car?'

'He said he supposes that it'll turn up.'

'What does he think happened to it?'

'It might have been stolen from in front of the St Alwyn.'

Tom pursed his lips together. 'Sounds plausible.'

'Did you know that his father owned the St Alwyn?' I asked.

Tom raised his eyes to mine, and I saw the glimmer of something like a sparkle in them. 'Did he, now?' he said, in such a way that I could not tell whether or not he had already known it. Before I was able to ask, a yelp of pain or astonishment came from the other room, accompanied by a thud and another yelp, this time clearly one of pain.

I laughed, for I suddenly knew exactly what had happened. 'John finally saw your paintings,' I said.

Tom lifted his eyebrows. He gestured ironically toward the door.

When we came out of the kitchen, John Ransom was standing on the other side of the table, looking at the paintings that hung on that wall. Ransom was bending down to rub his knee, and his mouth was open.

He turned to stare at us.

'Did you hurt yourself?' Tom asked.

'You own a Maurice Denis,' John Ransom said, straightening up. 'You own a Paul Ranson, for God's sakes!'

'You're interested in their work?'

'My God, that's a beautiful Bonnard up there,' John said. He shook his head. 'I'm just astounded. Yes, well,

151

my wife and I own a lot of work by the Nabis, but we don't – ' *But we don't have anything as good as that*, he had been going to say.

'I'm particularly fond of that one,' said Tom. 'You collect the Nabis?'

'It's so rare to see them in other people's houses . . .' For a moment Ransom gaped at the painting. The Bonnard was a small oil painting of a nude woman drying her hair in a shaft of sunlight.

'I don't go into other people's houses very much,' Tom said. He moved around to his chair, sat down, regarded the bottles and the ice bucket for a moment, and then poured himself a drink of another, less expensive brand of vodka than the one he had given John Ransom. His hand was completely steady. He took a small, businesslike sip. Then he smiled at me. I sat down across from him. A small spot of color like rouge appeared in both of his cheeks.

'I wonder if you've ever thought about selling anything,' John said, and turned expectantly around.

'No, I've never thought about that,' Tom said.

'Would you mind if I asked where you found some of this work?'

'I found them exactly where you found them,' Tom said. 'On the back wall of this room.'

'How could you – ?'

'I inherited them when Lamont von Heilitz left me this house in his will. I suppose he bought them in Paris, sometime in the twenties.' For a second more he indulged John Ransom, who looked as if he wanted to pull out a magnifying glass and scrutinize the brush strokes on a four-foot-square Maurice Denis, and then he said, 'I gathered you were interested in talking about the Blue Rose murders.'

Ransom's head snapped around.

'I read what the *Ledger* had to say about the assault on

your wife. You must want to learn whatever you can about the earlier cases.'

'Yes, absolutely,' Ransom said, finally leaving the painting and walking a little tentatively back to his seat.

'Now that Lamont von Heilitz's name has come up, it may be as well to go into it.'

Ransom slid onto the other couch. He cleared his throat, and when Tom said nothing, swallowed some of his vodka before beginning. 'Did Mr von Heilitz ever do any work on the Blue Rose murders?'

'It was a matter of timing,' Tom said. He glanced at the glass he had set on the table, but did not reach for it. 'He was busy with cases all over the country. And then, it seemed to come to a neat conclusion. I think it bothered him, though. Some of the pieces didn't seem to fit, and by the time I got to know him, he was just beginning to think about it again. And then I met someone at Eagle Lake who had been connected to the case.'

He bent forward, lifted his glass and took another measured sip. I had never had the good luck to meet Lamont von Heilitz, but as I looked at Tom Pasmore, I had the uncanny feeling that I was seeing the old detective before me. John Ransom might have been seeing him, too, from the sudden tension in his posture.

'Who did you meet at Eagle Lake?' John asked. This was the privately owned resort in northern Wisconsin to which a select portion of Millhaven's society families went every summer.

'In order to tell you about this,' Tom said, 'I have to explain some private things about my family. I want to ask you not to repeat what I have to say.'

John promised.

'Then let me tell you a story,' Tom said.

12

'You probably remember meeting my mother now and then, at school functions.'

'I remember your mother,' Ransom said. 'She was a beautiful woman.'

'And fragile. I'm sure you remember that, too. My mother would spend whole days in her bedroom. Sometimes she'd cry for hours, and even she didn't know why, she'd just stay up there and weep. I used to get so angry with her for not being like anyone else's mother . . . Well, instead of getting angry, I should have been thinking about what could have made her be so helpless.' Tom let that sink in for a moment, then reached for his glass again. His pale lips made a round aperture for the slightly larger sip of vodka. He hated having to tell this story, I saw. He was telling it because he would have hated my telling it even more, and because he thought that John Ransom ought to know it. He set the glass down and said, 'I suppose you knew something about my grandfather.'

John blinked. 'Glendenning Upshaw? Of course. A powerful man.' He hesitated. 'Passed away in your senior year. Suicide, I remember.'

Tom glanced at me, for we both knew the real circumstances of his grandfather's death. Then he looked back at John. 'Yes, he was powerful. He made a fortune in Millhaven, and he had some political influence. He was a terrible man in almost every way, and he had a lot of secrets. But there was one secret he had to protect above all the others, because he would have been ruined if it ever came out. He killed three people to protect this secret, and he nearly succeeded in killing a fourth. His wife learned about it in 1923, and she drowned herself in Eagle Lake – it destroyed her.'

Tom looked down at his hands in his lap. He raised his eyes to mine, briefly, and then looked at John Ransom. 'My grandfather fired all his servants when my mother was about two. He never hired any more, even after his wife died. He couldn't afford to have anyone discover that he was raping his daughter.'

'Raping?' Ransom sounded incredulous.

'Maybe he didn't have to use force, but he forced or coerced my mother into having sex with him from the time she was about two until she was fourteen.'

'And in all that time, no one found out?'

Tom took another swallow, I think from relief that he had finally said it. 'He went to great lengths to make sure that would never happen. For obvious reasons, my mother went to the doctor he had always used. In the early fifties, this doctor took on a young partner. Needless to say, the young doctor, Buzz Laing, did not get my mother as one of his patients.'

'Okay, Buzz Laing,' Ransom said. 'Everybody always thought he was the fourth Blue Rose victim, but Tim told me that he was attacked by someone else. What did he do, find out about your mother?'

'Buzz took the office records home at night to build up backgrounds on his patients. One night he just grabbed the wrong file. What he saw there disturbed him, and he went back to his partner to discuss it. Years before, the older doctor had recorded all the classic signs of sexual abuse – vaginal bleeding, vaginal warts, change in personality, nightmares. Et cetera, et cetera. It was all there in the records.'

When Tom set his glass down, it was empty. Ransom pushed his own glass toward him, and Tom added ice and vodka to it.

'So the older doctor called your grandfather,' John

Ransom said when Tom had taken his seat again.

'One night Buzz Laing came home and went upstairs, and a big man grabbed him from behind and almost cut his head off. He was left for dead, but he managed to stop the bleeding and call for help. The man who had tried to kill him had written BLUE ROSE on his bedroom wall, and everyone assumed that Laing was the fourth victim.'

'But what about William Damrosch? He had been Laing's lover. That butcher, Stenmitz, had abused *him*. And the case ended when he killed himself.'

'If the case ended, why are you sitting here listening to ancient history?'

'But how could your grandfather know about some detective's private life?'

'He had a close friend in the police department. A sort of protégé – they did each other a lot of good, over the years. This character made sure he knew everything that might be useful to him, and he shared whatever he found out with my grandfather. That was one of his functions.'

'So this cop – '

'Told my grandfather about Damrosch's history. My grandfather, good old Glendenning Upshaw, saw how he could wrap everything up into one neat little package.'

'He killed Damrosch, too?'

'I think he followed him home one night, waited three or four hours or however long he thought it would take Damrosch to get too drunk to fight back, and then just knocked on his door. Damrosch let him in, and my grandfather got his gun away from him and shot him in the head. Then he printed BLUE ROSE on a piece of paper and let himself out. Case closed.'

Tom leaned back in the chair.

'And after that, the murders stopped.'

'They stopped with the murder of Heinz Stenmitz.'

Ransom considered this. 'Why do you think Blue Rose

stopped killing people for forty years? Or do you even think it's the same person who attacked my wife?'

'That's a possibility.'

'Have you noticed that the new attacks took place on the same sites as the old ones?'

Tom nodded.

'So he's repeating himself, isn't he?'

'If it's the same man,' Tom said.

'Why do you say that? What are you thinking?'

Tom Pasmore looked as if he were thinking about nothing but getting us out of his house. His head lolled back against the back of the chair. I thought he wanted us to leave so that he could get to work. His day was just beginning. He surprised me by answering Ransom's question. 'Well, I always thought it might have something to do with place.'

'It has something to do with place, all right,' Ransom said. He set down his empty glass. There was a band of red across his cheekbones. 'It's his neighborhood. He kills where he lives.'

'No one knows the identity of the man on Livermore Avenue, is that right?'

'Some homeless guy who thought he was going to get a handful of change.'

Tom nodded in acknowledgment rather than agreement. 'That's a possibility, too.'

'Well, sure,' John Ransom said.

Tom nodded absentmindedly.

'I mean, who goes unidentified these days? Everybody carries credit cards, cards for automatic teller machines, driver's licenses . . .'

'Yes, it makes sense, it makes sense,' Tom said. He was still staring at some indeterminate point in the middle of the room.

Ransom shifted forward on the couch. He rocked his empty glass back and forth on the table for a moment. He

157

raised his eyes to the paintings Lamont von Heilitz had bought in Paris sixty years ago. 'You're not really retired, are you, Tom? Don't you still do a little work here and there, without telling anybody about it?'

Tom smiled – slowly, almost luxuriantly.

'You do,' Ransom said, though that was not what I thought the strange inward smile meant.

'I don't know if you would call it work,' Tom said. 'Sometimes something catches my attention. I hear a little music.'

'Don't you hear it now?'

Tom focused on him. 'What are you asking me?'

'We've known each other a long time. When my wife is beaten and stabbed by a man who committed Millhaven's most notable unsolved murders, I would think you couldn't help but be interested.'

'I was interested enough to invite you here.'

'I'm asking you to work for me.'

'I don't take clients,' Tom said. 'Sorry.'

'I need your help.' John Ransom leaned toward Tom with his hands out, separated by a distance roughly the length of a football. 'You have a wonderful gift, and I want that gift working for me.' Tom seemed hardly to be listening. 'On top of everything else, I'm giving you the chance to learn the name of the Blue Rose murderer.'

Tom slumped down in his chair so that his knees jutted out and his chin rested on his chest. He brought his joined hands beneath his lower lip and regarded Ransom with a steady speculation. He seemed more comfortable, more actually present than at any other time during the evening.

'Were you considering offering me some payment for this assistance?'

'Absolutely,' John Ransom said. 'If that's what you want.'

'What sort of payment?'

Ransom looked flustered. He glanced at me as if asking

for help and raised his hands. 'Well, that's difficult to answer. Ten thousand dollars?'

'Ten thousand. For identifying the man who attacked your wife. For getting the man you call Blue Rose behind bars.'

'It could be twenty thousand,' John said. 'It could even be thirty.'

'I see.' Tom pushed himself back into an upright position, placed his hands on the arms of his chair, and pushed himself up. 'Well, I hope that what I told you will be of some help to you. It's been good to see you again, John.'

I stood up, too. John Ransom stayed seated on the couch, looking back and forth between Tom and me. 'That's it? Tom, we were talking about an offer. Please tell me you'll consider it.'

'I'm afraid I'm not for hire,' Tom said. 'Not even for the splendid sum of thirty thousand dollars.'

Ransom looked completely baffled. Reluctantly, he pushed himself up from the couch. 'If thirty thousand isn't enough, tell me how much you want. I want you on my team.'

'I'll do what I can,' Tom said. He moved toward the maze of files and the front door.

Ransom stood his ground. 'What does that mean?'

'I'll check in from time to time,' Tom said.

Ransom shrugged and shoved his hands in his pockets. He and I went around opposite sides of the glass table toward Tom. For the first time I looked down at the stacks of books beside the bottles and the ice bucket and was surprised to see that, like the books on John Ransom's table, nearly all of them were about Vietnam. But they were not novels – most of the books on the table seemed to be military histories, written by retired officers. *The US Infantry in Vietnam. Small Unit Actions in Vietnam, 1965–66. History of the Green Berets.*

'I wanted you to know how I felt,' Ransom was saying. 'I had to give it a try.'

'It was very flattering,' Tom said. They were both working their way toward the door.

I caught up with them just as Ransom looked back over his shoulder to see the paintings on the long back wall. 'And if you're ever interested in selling some of your art, I hope you'll speak to me first.'

'Well,' Tom said. He opened the door to scorching heat and the end of daylight. Above the roofs of the lakefront houses, the moon had already risen into a darkening sky in which a few shadowy clouds drifted in a wind too far up to do us any good.

'Thanks for your help,' said John Ransom, holding out his hand. Tom took it, and Ransom raised one shoulder and grimaced, squeezing hard to show his gratitude.

'By the way,' Tom said, and Ransom relaxed his grip. Tom pulled back his hand. 'I wonder if you've been thinking about the possibility that the attack on your wife was actually directed at you?'

'I don't see what you mean.' John Ransom probed me with a look, trying to see if I had made sense of this question. 'You mean Blue Rose thought April might be *me*?'

'No.' Tom smiled and leaned against the door frame. 'Of course not.' He looked across the street, then up and down, and finally at the sky. Outside, in the natural light, his skin looked like paper that had been crumpled, then smoothed out. 'I just wondered if you could think of someone who might want to get at you through your wife. Someone who wanted to hurt you very badly.'

'There isn't anyone like that,' Ransom said.

Down the block, a small car turned the corner onto Eastern Shore Road, came some twenty feet in our direction, then swung over to the side of the road and parked. The driver did not leave the car.

'I don't think Blue Rose could know anything about April or me,' said Ransom. 'That's not how these guys work.'

'I'm sure that's right,' Tom said. 'I hope everything turns out well for you, John. Good-bye, Tim.' He gave me a little wave and waited for us to move down onto the walk. He waved again, smiling, and closed his door. It was like seeing him disappear into a fortress.

'What was that about?' Ransom asked.

'Let's get some dinner,' I said.

13

John Ransom spent most of dinner complaining. Tom Pasmore was one of those geniuses who didn't seem too perceptive. Tom was a drunk who acted like the pope. Sat all day in that closed-up house and pounded down the vodka. Even back in school, Pasmore had been like the Invisible Man, never played football, hardly had any friends – this pretty girl, this knockout, Sarah Spence, long long legs, great body, turned out she had a kind of a *thing* for old Tom Pasmore, always wondered how the hell old Tom managed that . . .

I didn't tell Ransom that I thought Sarah Spence, now Sarah Youngblood, had been the driver of the car that had turned the corner and pulled discreetly up to the curb thirty feet from Tom Pasmore's house as we were leaving. I knew that she visited Tom, and I knew that he wished to keep her visits secret, but I knew nothing else about their relationship. I had the impression that they spent a lot of time talking to each other – Sarah Spence Youngblood was the only person in the whole of Millhaven who had free access to Tom Pasmore's house, and in those long evenings and nights after she slipped through his front door, after the bottles were opened and while the ice cubes settled in the brass bucket, I think he talked to her – I think she had become the person he most needed, maybe the only person he needed, because she was the person who knew most about him.

John Ransom and I were in Jimmy's, an old east-side restaurant on Berlin Avenue. Jimmy's was a nice wood-paneled place with comfortable banquettes and low lights and a long bar. It could have been a restaurant anywhere in Manhattan, where all of its tables would have been filled; because we were in Millhaven and it was nearly nine o'clock, we were nearly the only customers.

John Ransom ordered a Far Niente cabernet and made a ceremonial little fuss over tasting it.

Our food came, a sirloin for Ransom, shrimp scampi for me. He forgot Tom Pasmore and started talking about India and Mina's ashram. 'This wonderful being was beautiful, eighteen years old, very modest, and she spoke in short plain sentences. Sometimes she cooked breakfast, and she cleaned her little rooms by herself, like a servant. But everyone around her realized that she had this extraordinary power – she had great wisdom. Mina put her hands on my soul and opened me up. I'll never stop being grateful, and I'll never forget what I learned from her.' He chewed for a bit, swallowed, took a mouthful of wine. 'By the time I was in graduate school, Mina had become well known. People began to understand that she represented one very pure version of mystic experience. Because I had studied with her, I had a certain authority. Everything unfolded from her – it was like having studied with a great scholar. And in fact, it *was* like that, but more profound.'

'Haven't you ever been tempted to go back and see her again?'

162

'I can't,' he said. 'She was absolutely firm about that. I had to move on.'

'How does it affect your life now?' I asked, really curious about what he would say.

'It's helping me make it through,' he said.

He finished off the food on his plate, then looked at his watch. 'Would you mind if I called the hospital? I ought to check in.'

He signaled the waiter for the check, drank the last of the wine, and stood up. He pulled a handful of change from his pocket and went toward the pay telephone in a corridor at the back of the restaurant.

The waiter brought the check on a saucer, and I turned it over and read the amount and gave the waiter a credit card. Before the waiter returned with the charge slip, Ransom came charging back toward the table. He grabbed my arm. 'This is – this is unbelievable. They think she might be coming out of her coma. Where's the check?'

'I gave him a card.'

'You can't do that,' he said. 'Don't be crazy. I want to pay the thing and get over there.'

'Go to the hospital, John. I'll walk back to your house and wait for you.'

'Well, how much was it?' He dug in his trousers pockets for something, then rummaged in the pockets of his suit jacket.

'I already paid. Take off.'

He gave me a look of real exasperation and fished a key from his jacket pocket and held it out without giving it to me. 'That was an expensive bottle of wine. And my entree cost twice as much as yours.' He looked at the key as if he had forgotten it, then handed it to me. 'I still say you can't pay for this dinner.'

'You get the next one,' I said.

He was almost hopping in his eagerness to get to the hospital, but he saw the waiter coming toward us with the credit card slip and leaned over my shoulder to see the amount while I figured out the tip and signed. 'You tip too much,' he said. 'That's on your head.'

'Will you get away?' I said, and pushed him toward the door.

14

Apart from two UI students in T-shirts and shorts walking into a bar called Axel's Tuxedo, the sidewalks outside Jimmy's were empty. John Ransom was moving quickly away from me, swinging his arms and going north along Berlin Avenue to Shady Mount, and as he went from relative darkness into the bright lights beneath the Royal's marquee, his lightweight suit changed color, like a chameleon's hide.

In two or three seconds Ransom passed back into the darkness on the other side of the marquee. A car started up on the opposite side of the street. Ransom was about fifty feet away, still clearly in sight, moving quickly and steadily through the pools of yellow light cast by the street lamps.

I turned around to go up the block and saw a blue car move away from the curb across the street. For a second I stopped moving, aware that something had caught in my memory. Just before the car slid into the light spilling out from the Royal's marquee, I had it: the same car had pulled over to the curb on Eastern Shore Drive so that we would be out of sight when Sarah Spence Youngblood drove into Tom Pasmore's driveway. Then light from the movie theater fell on the car, and instead of Sarah

Youngblood, a man with big shoulders and long gray hair pulled back into a ponytail sat behind the wheel. The light caught the dot of a gold earring in his left ear. It was the man I had almost bumped into at the hospital pay phones. He had followed us to Tom Pasmore's house, then to Jimmy's, and now he was following John to the hospital.

And since I had seen him first at the hospital, he must have followed us there, too. I turned to watch the blue car creep down the street.

The driver bumped along behind John. Whenever his target got too far in front of him, he nudged the car out into the left lane and slowly rolled forward another twenty or thirty feet before cutting back into the curb. If there had been much other traffic, he would not have been noticeable in any way.

I walked along behind him, stopping when he stopped. I could hear the soles of Ransom's shoes ticking against the sidewalks. The man in the blue car swung away from the curb and purred along the nearly empty street, tracking him like a predator.

Still hurrying along, Ransom was now only a block from the hospital, moving in and out of the circles of light on the sidewalk. The man in the blue car pulled out of an unlighted spot and rolled down the street. He surprised me by going right past Ransom. I thought he had seen me in his rearview mirror and swore at myself for not even getting his license number. Then he surprised me again and swung into the curb across the street from the hospital. I saw his head move as he found John Ransom in his side mirror.

I started walking faster.

Ransom turned into the narrow path between tall hedges that led up to the visitors' entrance at Shady Mount. The door of the blue car opened, and the driver got out. He pushed the door shut behind him and began to amble across the street. He was about my height, and he walked with a slightly tilted-back swagger. The apostrophe of gray hair jutted out from his head and fell against his back. His big shoulders swung, and the loose jacket of the suit billowed a little. I saw that his hips were surprisingly wide and that his belly was heavy and soft. The way he moved, his hips floating, made him look like he was swimming through the humid air.

I got my notebook out of my pocket and wrote down the number of his license plate. The blue car was a Lexus. He stepped up onto the sidewalk and turned into the path. He had given John Ransom enough time to get into an elevator. I walked down the block as quickly as I could, and by the time I turned into the path, he was just letting the visitors' door close behind him. I jogged up the path and came through the door while he was still floating along toward the elevator. I went across the nearly empty lobby and touched him on the shoulder.

He looked over his shoulder to see who had touched him. His face twitched with irritation, and he turned round to face me. 'Something I can help you with?' he said. His voice was unadulterated Millhaven, flat, choppy, and slightly nasal.

'Why are you following John Ransom?' I asked.

He sneered at me – only half of his face moved. 'You must be outa your mind.'

He started to turn away, but I caught his arm. 'Who told you to follow Ransom?'

'And who the hell are you?'

I told him my name.

He looked around the lobby. Two of the clerks behind the long desk sat unnaturally still at their computer keyboards, pretending not to be eavesdropping. The man frowned and led me away from the elevators, toward the far side of the lobby and a row of empty chairs. Then he squared off in front of me and looked me up and down.

166

He was trying to decide how to handle me.

'If you really want to help this guy Ransom, I think you should go back to wherever you came from,' he said finally.

'Is that a threat?'

'You really don't understand,' he said. 'I got nothing to do with you.' He wheeled round and started moving fast toward the visitors' entrance.

'Maybe one of these nervous clerks should call the police.'

He whirled to confront me. His face was an unhealthy red. 'You want police? Listen, you asshole, I'm the police.'

He reached into his back pocket and came out with a fat black wallet. He flipped it open to show me one of the little gold badges given to officers' wives and contributors to police causes.

'That's impressive,' I said.

He stuck his broad forefinger into my chest, hard, and pushed his big face toward me. 'You don't know what you're messing with, you stupid fuck.'

Then he marched past me and out the door. I walked after him and watched him jam the wallet back into his pants on the way down the walk between the hedges. He moved across the street without bothering to look for other cars. He pulled open the door of the Lexus, bent down, and squeezed himself in. He slammed the door, started the car, and looked out of the open window to see me watching him. His face seemed to fill the entire space of the window. He twitched the car out into Berlin Avenue and roared off.

I walked off the sidewalk and watched his taillights diminish as he moved away. The brake lights flashed as he stopped at a traffic light two blocks down. The Lexus went another block north on Berlin Avenue and then turned left without bothering to signal. There was no other car on the street, and the night seemed huge and black.

I went back up between the hedges and into the hospital.

15

Before I got to the elevator, a police car pulled up into the ambulance bay outside the Emergency Room. Dazzling red and blue lights flashed like Morse code through the corridor. A few clerks leaned over the partition. A short balding man with an oversized nose got out of the car. The detective charged through the parting glass doors. A nurse skittered toward him, grinning and holding her hands clasped beneath her chin. The detective said something I couldn't hear, picked her up, and carried her along a few steps before whispering something into her ear and depositing her on the ground again just at the beginning of the corridor. Bent double, the nurse gasped and waved at his back before straightening up and smoothing out her uniform.

The detective held me with his eyes as he moved toward me.

I stopped and waited. As soon as he got into the lobby, he said, 'Go on, get the elevator, don't just stand there.' He waved me toward the buttons. The clerks who had been leaning over the partition to see what was going on smiled at him and then at each other. 'You were going to call the elevator, weren't you?'

I nodded and went to the closed doors and pushed the UP button.

The detective nodded at the clerks. His heavy face seemed immobile, but his eyes gleamed.

'You didn't call us, did you?'

'No,' I said.

'We're all right, then.'

I smiled, and the gleam died theatrically from his eyes. He was a real comedian, with his saggy face and his unpressed suit. 'Police should never go to hospitals.' He had the kind of face that could express subtleties of feeling without seeming to move in any way. 'Will you get inside that thing, please?' The elevator had opened up before us.

I got in and he followed me. I pushed the third floor button. The elevator ascended and stopped. He left the elevator, taking the turns that would lead him to April Ransom's room. I followed. We went past the nurses' station and rounded the bend of the circular corridor. A young uniformed officer came out of April's room.

'Well?' the detective said.

'This could actually happen,' said the uniformed policeman. His nameplate read THOMPSON. 'Who is this, sir?'

The detective looked back at me. 'Who's this? I don't know who this is. Who are you?'

'I'm a friend of John Ransom's,' I said.

'News gets around fast,' the detective said. He led the way into April's room.

John Ransom and a doctor who looked like a college freshman were standing on the far side of the bed. Ransom looked slightly stunned. He looked up when he saw me – his eyes moved to the unkempt detective, then back to me. 'Tim? What's going on?'

'What *is* going on?' asked the detective. 'We got more people in here than the Marx Brothers. Didn't you call this guy?'

'No, I didn't call him,' John said. 'We had dinner together.'

'I see,' said the detective. 'How is Mrs Ransom doing, then?'

John looked vague and uncertain. 'Ah, well . . .'

'Good, incisive,' said the detective. 'Doctor?'

'Mrs Ransom is showing definite signs of improvement,' said the doctor. His voice was a thick plank of dark brown wood.

'Does it look like the lady might actually be able to say something, or are we standing in the line at Lourdes here?'

'There are definite indications,' said the doctor. The heavy wooden voice sounded as if it were coming from a much larger and older person who was standing behind him.

John looked wildly at me across the bed. 'Tim, she might actually come out of it.'

The detective came up behind him and insinuated himself at the bedside. 'I'm Paul Fontaine, and the assault on your friend's wife is related to a homicide case I'm handling.'

'Tim Underhill,' I said.

He cocked his big oval head. 'Well, Tim Underhill. I read one of your books. *The Divided Man*. It was crappy. It was ridiculous. I liked it.'

'Thanks,' I said.

'Now, what was it you came here to tell Mr Ransom, unless it is something you would prefer to conceal from our efficient police department?'

I looked at him. 'Will you write down a license number for me?'

'Thompson,' he said, and the young policeman took out his pad.

I read the license number of the man's car from the page in my notebook. 'It's a blue Lexus. The owner followed John and me all day long. When I stopped him in the lobby downstairs, he flashed a toy badge and said

170

he was a policeman. He ran away just before you got here.'

'Uh, huh,' said Fontaine. 'That's interesting. I'll do something about that. Do you remember anything about this man? Anything distinguishing?'

'He's a gray-haired guy with a ponytail. Gold post earring in his left ear. About six-two and probably two hundred and thirty pounds. Big belly and wide hips, like a woman's hips. I think he was wearing an Armani suit.'

'Oh, one of the Armani gang.' He permitted himself to smile. He took the paper with the license number from Thompson and put it in his jacket pocket.

'*Following me?*' John asked.

'I saw him here this afternoon. He trailed us to Eastern Shore Drive, then down to Jimmy's. He was going to come up to this floor, but I stopped him in the lobby.'

'That was a pity,' Fontaine said. 'Did this character really say that he was a policeman?'

I tried to remember. 'I think he said that he was with the police.'

Fontaine pursed his mouth. 'Sort of like saying you're with the band.'

'He showed me one of those little gold badges.'

'I'll look into it.' He turned away from me. 'Thompson, visiting hours are over. We are going to wait around to see if Mrs Ransom comes out of her coma and says anything useful. Mr Underhill can wait in the lounge, if he likes.'

Thompson gave me a sharp look and stepped back from the bed.

'John, I'll wait for you at home,' I said.

He smiled weakly and pressed his wife's hand. Thompson came around the end of the bed and gestured almost apologetically toward the door.

Thompson followed me out of the door. We went past the nurses' station in silence. The two women behind the counter pretended unsuccessfully not to stare.

Thompson did not speak until we had almost reached the elevators. 'I just wanted to say,' he began, then looked around to make sure that nobody was listening. 'Don't get Detective Fontaine wrong. He's crazy, that's all, but he's a great detective. In interrogation rooms, he's like a genius.'

'A crazy genius,' I said, and pushed the button.

'Yeah.' Officer Thompson looked a bit embarrassed. He put his hands behind his back. 'You know what we call him? He's called Fantastic Paul Fontaine. That's how good he is.'

'Then he ought to be able to find out who owns that blue Lexus,' I said.

'He'll find out,' Thompson said. 'But he might not tell you he found out.'

16

I let myself into the house and groped for a light switch. A hot red dot on the answering machine blinked on and off from the telephone stand, signaling that calls had been recorded. The rest of the downstairs was a deep, velvet black. Central air conditioning made the interior of Ransom's house feel like a refrigerator. I found a switch just beside the frame and turned on a glass-and-bronze overhead lamp that looked as if it had been made to hold a candle. Then I closed the door. A switch next to the entrance to the living room turned on most of the lamps inside the room. I went in and collapsed onto a sofa.

Eventually I went up to the guest room. It looked like a room in a forty-dollar-a-night hotel. I hung my clothes in the closet beside the door. Then I brought two books back downstairs, *The Nag Hammadi Library* and a paperback Sue Grafton novel. I picked a chair facing the fireplace and opened the book of gnostic texts and read for a long time, waiting for John Ransom to bring good news home from the hospital.

Around eleven I decided to call New York and see if I could talk to a man named An Vinh, whom I had first met in Vietnam.

Six years ago, when my old friend Tina Pumo was killed, he left Saigon, his restaurant, to Vinh, who had been both chef and assistant manager. Vinh eventually *gave* half of the restaurant to Maggie Lah, Tina's old girlfriend, who had taken over its management while she began work on her Philosophy MA at NYU. We all lived above the restaurant, in various lofts.

I hadn't seen Vinh for two or three days, and I missed his cool unsentimental common sense.

It was eleven o'clock in Millhaven, midnight in New York. With any luck Vinh would have turned the restaurant over to the staff and gone upstairs for an hour or so, until it was time to close up and balance the day's receipts. I went into the foyer and dialed Vinh's number on the telephone next to the blinking answering machine. After two rings, I got the clunk of another machine picking up and heard Vinh's terse message: *Not home.* Buzzing silence, and the chime of the tone. 'Me,' I said. 'Having wonderful time, wish you were here. I'll try you downstairs.'

Maggie Lah answered the telephone in the restaurant office and burst into laughter at the sound of my voice. 'You couldn't take your hometown for even half a day? Why don't you come back here, where you belong?'

'I'll probably come back soon.'

'You found everything out in one day?' Maggie laughed again. 'You're better than Tom Pasmore, you're better than *Lamont von Heilitz*!'

173

'I didn't find anything out,' I said. 'But April Ransom seems to be getting better.'

'You can't come home until you find *something* out,' she said. 'Too humiliating. I suppose you want Vinh. He's standing right here, hold on.'

In a second I heard Vinh's voice saying my name, and at once I felt more at peace with myself and the world I was in. I began telling him what had happened during the day, leaving nothing out – someone like Vinh is not upset by the appearance of a familiar ghost.

'Your sister is hungry,' he said. 'That's why she shows herself to you. Hungry. Bring her to the restaurant, we take care of that.'

'I know what she wants, and it isn't food,' I said, but his words had suddenly reminded me of John Ransom seated in the front seat of a muddy jeep.

'You in a circus,' Vinh said. 'Too old for the circus. When you were twenty-one, twenty-two, you *love* circuses. Now you completely different, you know. Better.'

'You think so?' I asked, a little startled.

'Totally,' Vinh said, using the approximate English that served him so well. 'You don't need the circus anymore.' He laughed. 'I think you should go away from Millhaven. Nothing there for you anymore, that's for sure.'

'What brought all this on?' I asked.

'Remember how you used to be? Loud and rough. Now you don't puff your chest out. Don't get high, go crazy, either.'

I had that twinge of pain you feel when someone confronts you with the young idiot you used to be. 'Well, I was a soldier then.'

'You were a circus bear,' Vinh said, and laughed. '*Now* you a soldier.'

After a little more conversation, Vinh gave the phone to Maggie, and she gave me a little more trouble, and then we hung up. It was nearly twelve. I left one of the

174

lights burning and took the Sue Grafton novel upstairs with me.

17

The front door slammed shut and woke me up. I sat up in an unfamiliar bed. What hotel was this, in what city? I could hear someone climbing the stairs. The sneering face of the gray-haired man with the ponytail swam onto my inner screen. I could identify him, and he was going to try to kill me as he had tried to kill April Ransom. The heavy footsteps reached the landing. I rolled off the bed. My mouth was dry and my head pounded. Adrenaline sparkled through my body. I stationed myself behind the door and braced myself.

The footsteps thudded toward my door and went past it without even hesitating. A second later, another door opened and closed.

And then I remembered where I was. I heard John Ransom groan as he fell onto his bed. I unpeeled myself from the wall.

It was a few minutes past eight o'clock in the morning.

I knocked on Ransom's bedroom door. A barely audible voice told me to come in.

I pushed open the door and stepped inside the dark room. It was more than three times the size of the guest room. Beyond the bed, on the opposite side of the room, a wall of mirrors on closet doors dimly reflected the opening door and my shadowy face. His suit jacket lay crumpled on the floor next to the bed. Ransom lay face-down across the mattress. Garish suspenders made a bright Y across his back.

'How is she doing?' I asked. 'Is she out of the coma?'

Ransom rolled onto his side and blinked at me as if he were not quite sure who I was. He pursed his lips and exhaled, then pushed himself upright. 'God, what a night.' He bent forward and pulled off his soft brown wingtips. He tossed them toward the closet, and they thudded onto the carpet. 'April's doing a lot better, but she's not out of the woods yet.' He shrugged his shoulders from beneath his suspenders and let them droop to his sides.

Ransom smiled up at me, and I realized how tired he looked when he was not smiling. 'But things look good, according to the doctor.' He untied his tie and threw it toward a sofa. The tie fell short and fluttered onto the rose-colored carpet. 'I'm going to get a few hours' sleep and then go back to Shady Mount.' He grunted and pushed himself to the bottom end of the bed.

Two enormous paintings hung on facing walls, a male nude lying on lush grass, a female nude leaning forward against a tree on outstretched arms, both figures outlined in the Nabis manner. They were the most sensual Nabis paintings I had ever seen. John Ransom saw me looking back and forth from one to the other, and he cleared his throat as he unbuttoned his shirt.

'You like those?'

I nodded.

'April bought them from a local kid last year. I thought he was kind of a hustler.' He threw his shirt onto the floor, dropped his keys, change, and bills onto an end table, unbuckled his belt, undid his trousers and pushed them down. He pulled his legs out of them, yanked off his socks, and half-scooted, half-crawled up the bed. A sour, sweaty odor came from his body. 'I'm sorry, but I'm really out.'

He began to scoot under the light blanket and the top sheet. Then he stopped moving, kneeling on the bed and holding up the covers. His belly bulged over the top of his boxer shorts. 'You want to use the car? You could look around in Pigtown, see if it looks any – '

He flopped onto his sheets and smacked his hand on his forehead. 'I'm sorry, Tim. I'm even more tired than I thought.'

'It's okay,' I said. 'Even the people who live there call it Pigtown.'

This was not strictly true – the people who lived in my old neighborhood had always resented the name – but it seemed to help him. 'Good for them,' he said. He groped for the pulled-back sheet and tugged it up. Then he rolled his head on the pillow and looked at me with bloodshot eyes. 'White Pontiac.'

'I guess I will take a look around,' I said.

Ransom closed his eyes, shuddered, and fell asleep.

PART FOUR

Walter Dragonette

1

On the way to my old neighborhood, I realized that I wanted to go somewhere else first and turned Ransom's white Pontiac onto Redwing Avenue and drove past traces of the old Millhaven – neighborhood bars in places that were not real neighborhoods anymore. Blistering morning sun seemed to wish to push the low wood and stone buildings down into the baking sidewalks. Millhaven, my Millhaven, was thinning out all around me, disappearing into a generic midwestern cityscape.

I would have been less convinced of the disappearance of the old Millhaven if I had turned on the radio and heard Paul Fontaine and Detective Sergeant Michael Hogan announcing the arrest of the soon-to-be-notorious serial killer Walter Dragonette, the Meat Man, but I left the radio off and remained ignorant of his name for another few hours.

Two or three miles went by in a blur of traffic and concrete on the east-west expressway. Ahead of me, the enormous wedding cake of the baseball stadium grew larger and larger, and I turned off on the exit just before it. This early in the morning, only the groundskeepers' cars stood in the vast parking lot. Two blocks past the stadium, I turned in through the open gates of Pine Knoll Cemetery and parked near the gray stone guardhouse. When I got out, the heat struck me like a lion's breath. Rows of differently sized headstones stretched off behind the guard's office like a messy Arlington. Furry hemlock trees ranged along the far end. White gravel paths divided the perfect grass. Sprinklers whirled glittering sprays of water in the distance. Thirty feet away, an angular old man in a white shirt, black tie, black trousers, and black military hat puttered through the rows of headstones, picking up beer cans and candy wrappers left behind by teenagers who had climbed into the cemetery after the baseball game last night.

The graves I wanted lay in the older section of Pine Knoll, near the high stone wall that borders the left side of the cemetery. The three headstones stood in a row: Albert Hoover Underhill, Louise Shade Underhill, April Shade Underhill. The first two headstones, newer than April's, still looked new, bone-dry in the drenching sun. All three would have been warm to the touch. The grass was kept very short and individual green blades glistened in the sun.

If I had anything to say to these graves, or they to me, now was the time to say it. I waited, standing in the sun, holding my hands before me. A few bright moments came forward from a swirling darkness: sitting safe and warm on the davenport with my mother, watching drivers wading through waist-high snow after abandoning their cars; April skipping rope on the sidewalk; lying in bed with a fever on St Patrick's Day while my mother cleaned the house, singing along with the Irish songs on the radio. Even these were tinged with regret, pain, sorrow.

It was as if some terrible secret lay buried beneath the headstones, in the way a more vibrant, more real Millhaven burned and glowed beneath the surface of everything I saw.

2

Twenty minutes later, I turned south off the expressway at Goethals Street and continued south in the shadows of the cloverleaf overpasses. The seedy photography studios and failing dress shops gave way to the high blank walls of the tanneries and breweries. I caught the odor of hops and the other, darker odor that came from whatever the tanners did in their tanneries. Dented, hard-worked vans lined the street, and men on their breaks leaned against the dingy walls, smoking. In the partial light, their faces were the color of metal shavings.

Goethals Street reverted to the jarring old cobblestones, and I turned right at a corner where a topless bar was selling shots of brandy and beer chasers to a boisterous night-shift crowd. A block south I turned onto Livermore Avenue. The great concrete shadow of the viaduct floated away overhead, and the big corporate prisons vanished behind me. I was back in Pigtown.

The places where the big interlocking elms once stood had been filled with cement slabs. The sun fell flat and hard on the few people, most of them in their sixties and seventies, who toiled past the empty barber shops and barred liquor stores. My breath caught in my throat, and I slowed down to twenty-five, the speed limit. The avenue was almost as empty as the sidewalks, and so few cars had parked at the curb that the meter stands cast straight parallel shadows.

Everything seemed familiar and unfamiliar at once, as if I had often dreamed of but never seen this section of Livermore Avenue. Little frame houses like those on the side streets stood alongside tarpaper taverns and gas stations and diners. Once every couple of blocks, a big new grocery store or a bank with a drive-through window had replaced the old structures, but most of the buildings I had seen as a child wandering far from home still stood. For a moment, I felt like that child again, and each half-remembered building that I passed shone out at me. These buildings seemed uncomplicatedly beautiful, with their chipped paint and dirty brick, the unlighted neon signs in their streaky windows. I felt stripped of layers of skin. My hands began to tremble. I pulled over to the empty curb and waited for it to pass.

The sight of my family's graves had cracked my shell. The world trembled around me, about to blaze. The archaic story preserved in fragments about Orpheus and Lot's wife says – look back, lose everything.

3

The yellow crime scene ribbons closing off the end of the brick passage behind the St Alwyn drooped as though melted by the sun. I leaned as far inside the little tunnel as I could without touching the tape. The place where my sister had been murdered was larger than I remembered it, about ten feet long and nine feet high at the top of the rounded arch. Wind, humidity, or the feet of policemen had gradually erased the chalked outline from the gritty concrete floor of the passage.

Then I looked up and saw the words. I stopped breathing. They had been printed across a row of bricks five feet above the ground in letters about a foot high. The words slanted slightly upward, as if the man writing them had been tilting to one side. The letters were black and thin, inky, and imperfections in the bricks made them look chewed. BLUE ROSE, another time capsule.

I back away from the crime scene tape and turned around to face Livermore Avenue. Imaginary pain began to sing in my right leg. Fire traveled lightly through my bones, concentrating on all the little cracks and welds.

Then the child I had been, who lived within me and saw through my eyes, spoke the truth with wordless eloquence, as he always does.

A madman from my own childhood, a creature of darkness I had once glimpsed in the narrow alley at my back, had returned to take more lives. The man with the ponytail might have assaulted April Ransom and imitated his method, but the real Blue Rose was walking through the streets of Millhaven like a man inhabited by an awakened demon. John Ransom was right. The man who called himself Blue Rose was sitting over a bowl of cereal and a cup of coffee in his kitchen, he was switching on his television to see if we were in for cooler weather, he was closing his front door to take a stroll through the sunlight.

Tom Pasmore had said something about place being the factor that linked the victims. Like his mentor, Tom Pasmore never told you everything he knew; he waited for you to catch up. I went up to the corner and crossed when the light changed, thinking about the places where Blue Rose had killed people forty years ago.

One outside the St Alwyn, one inside. One across the street, outside the Idle Hour, the small white frame building directly in front of me. One, the butcher, two blocks away outside his shop. These four were the genuine Blue Rose murders. Standing at the side of the Idle Hour, I turned around to look across the street.

Three of the four original murders had happened on the doorstep of the St Alwyn Hotel, if not inside.

I looked past the street at the old hotel, trying to put

185

myself in the past. The St Alwyn had been built at the beginning of the century, when the south side had thrived, and it still had traces of its original elegance. At the entrance on Widow Street, around the corner, broad marble steps led up to a huge wooden door with brass fittings. The name of the hotel was carved into a stone arch over the front door. From where I stood, I could see only the side of the hotel. Over the years it had darkened to a dirty gray. Nine rows of windows, most of them covered on the inside by brown shades, punctuated the stone. The St Alwyn looked defeated, worn out by time. It had not looked very different forty years ago.

4

Our old house stood four doors up the block, a foursquare rectangular wooden building with two concrete steps up to the front door, windows on both sides of the door, two windows in line with these on the second floor, and a small patchy front lawn. It looked like a child's drawing. During my childhood, the top floor had been painted brown and the bottom one yellow. Later my father had painted the entire house a sad, terrible shade of green, but the new owners had restored it to the original colors.

The old house hardly affected me. It was like a shell I had grown out of and left behind. I'd been more moved at Pine Knoll Cemetery – just driving into Pigtown on Livermore Avenue had affected me more deeply. I tried to let the deep currents, the currents that connect you to the rest of life, run through me, but I felt like a stone. What I remembered about the old house had to do with an old Underwood upright on a pine desk in a bedroom where blue roses climbed up the wallpaper, with onionskin paper and typewriter ribbons, and with telling stories to charm the darkness: a memory of frustration and concentration, and of time disappearing into a bright elastic eternity.

Then there was one more place I had to see, and I walked back down South Sixth, crossed Livermore, and turned south.

From two blocks away I saw the marquee sagging toward the sidewalk, and my heart moved in my chest. The Beldame Oriental had not survived the last three decades as well as the Royal. Sliding glass panels crusty with stains had once protected the letters that spelled out the titles of the films. Nothing remained of the ornate detail I thought I remembered.

Two narrow glass doors opened off the sidewalk. Behind them, before a set of black lacquered doors, the glass cubicle of the ticket booth was only dimly visible through the smudgy glass. Jagged pieces of cement and smoke-colored grit littered the black-and-white tile floor between the two sets of doors. The paltriness, the meanness of this distance – the stingy littleness of the entire theater – gave me a shock so deep that at the moment I was scarcely aware of it.

I stepped back and looked down the street for the real Beldame Oriental. Then I went up to the two narrow glass doors and tried either to push myself inside the old theater or simply to see better – I didn't know which. My reflection moved forward to meet me, and we touched.

An enormous block of feeling loosed itself from its secret moorings and moved up into my chest. My throat tightened and my breathing stopped. My eyes sparkled. I drew in a ragged breath, for a moment uncertain if I were going to stay on my feet. I could not even tell if it were joy or anguish. It was just naked feeling, straight from the heart of my childhood. It even tasted like childhood. I pushed myself away from the old theater and wobbled over the sidewalk to lean on a parking meter.

Warmth on my head and shoulders brought me a little way back to myself, and I blew my nose into my handkerchief and straightened up. I stuffed the handkerchief back into my pocket. I moved away from the parking meter and pressed my hands over my eyes.

Across the street, a little old man in a baggy double-breasted suit and a white T-shirt was staring at me. He turned to look at some friends inside a diner and made a circular motion at his temple with his forefinger.

I uttered some noise halfway between a sigh and a groan. It was no wonder that I had been afraid to come back to Millhaven, if things like this were going to happen to me. All that saved me from another spell was the sudden memory of what I'd read in the gnostic gospel while I waited for John to come back from the hospital: *If you bring forth what is within you, what you bring forth will save you; if you do not bring forth what is within you, what you do not bring forth will destroy you.*

I was trying to bring it forth – had been trying to bring it forth since I stood in front of the graves in Pine Knoll cemetery – but what in the world was it?

5

I nearly went straight back to the Pontiac and returned to John Ransom's house. At the back of my mind was the idea of booking a seat back to New York on the evening flight. I was no longer so sure I cared about what had happened more than forty years ago in, near, or because of the St Alwyn's Hotel. I had already written that book.

Either in spite of or because of the experience I'd just had, I suddenly felt hungry. Whatever I was going to do would have to wait until I ate some sort of breakfast. The neon scimitar in the restaurant window had not been turned on yet, but an OPEN sign hung from the inside doorknob. I went into the hotel for a morning paper at the desk.

What I saw when I came into the lobby must have been almost exactly what Glenroy Breakstone and his piano player, the murdered James Treadwell, had known forty years ago; and what my father had seen, walking across the lobby to his elevator. Worn leather furniture, and squat brass spittoons stood on an enormous, threadbare oriental rug. One low-wattage bulb burned behind a green glass shade next to a couch.

A small stack of the morning's *Ledger* lay on the desk. I picked one up and slid thirty-five cents toward the clerk. He was sitting down behind the desk with his chin in his hand, concentrating on the newspaper folded over his knees. He heard the sound of the coins and looked up at me. The whites of his eyes flared. 'Oh! Sorry!' He glanced at the three copies that remained on the desk. 'Got to get up early to get a paper today,' he said, and reached for the coins. I looked at my watch. It was nine-thirty: the St Alwyn got up late.

I carried the paper into Sinbad's Cavern. A few silent men ate their breakfasts at the bar, and two couples had taken the tables at the front of the room. A waitress in a dark blue dress that looked too sophisticated for early morning was standing at the end of the bar, talking with the young woman in the white shirt and black bow tie working behind it. The place was quiet as a library. I sat down in an empty booth and waved at the waitress until she grabbed a menu off the bar and hurried over. She was wearing high heels, and she looked a little flushed, but it might have been her makeup.

She put the menu before me. 'I'm sorry, but it's been so hard to *concentrate* today. I'll get you some coffee and be right back.'

I opened the menu. The waitress went to a serving

stand on the near side of the bar and came back with a glass pot of cofee. She filled my cup. 'Nobody around here can believe it,' she said. 'Nobody.'

'I'll believe anything today,' I said.

She stared at me. She was about twenty-two, and all the makeup made her look like a startled clown. Then her face hardened, and she took her pad from a side pocket of her sleek blue suit. 'Are you ready to order, sir?'

'One poached egg and whole wheat toast, please.' She wrote it down wordlessly and walked back through the empty tables and brushed through the aluminum door to the kitchen.

I looked at the blond girl in the bow tie at the end of the bar and at the couples seated at the far tables. All of them had sections of the morning newspaper opened before them. Even the men eating on stools at the bar were reading the *Ledger*. The waitress emerged from the kitchen, stabbed me with a glance, and whispered something to the girl behind the bar.

The only customers not engrossed in their morning papers were four silent men arranged around a table across the room. The two men in suits affected an elaborate disengagement from the others, who might have been truck drivers, and from each other. All four ignored the cups before them. The sense of mutual distrust was so strong that I wondered what had brought them together. One of the men in suits saw me looking at them and snapped his head sideways, his face stiff with discomfort.

My copy of the *Ledger* lay folded on the table in front of me. I pulled it toward me, turned it over, and momentarily forgot the men across the room and everything I had thought and experienced that morning as I took in the big banner headline. Beneath it was a color photograph of dozens of uniformed and plainclothes policemen standing on the front lawn of a small white frame house. One of the detectives was the joker I had met at the

190

hospital the previous night, Paul Fontaine. Another, a tall commanding-looking man with an indented hairline, deep lines in his face, and a William Powell mustache, was identified as Fontaine's immediate superior, Detective Sergeant Michael Hogan. Almost as soon as I began to read the article to the left of the photograph, I saw that, among at least a dozen other unsuspected killings, the murder of the unknown man in the passage behind the St Alwyn and the attack on April Ransom had been solved. A twenty-six-year-old clerk in the Glax Corporation's accounts department named Walter Dragonette had confessed. In fact, he had confessed to everything under the sun. If he had thought of it, he would have confessed to strangling the little princes in the tower.

The big headline read: HORROR IN NORTH SIDE HOME.

The story all but obliterated the rest of the news. Five million dollars' worth of cocaine had been seized from a fishing boat, an unnamed woman claimed that a Kennedy nephew had raped her in New York three years before being charged with rape in Palm Beach, and a state representative had been using military planes for personal trips: the rest of the paper, like every issue of the *Ledger* to come out for a week, dealt almost exclusively with the young man who, when surrounded and asked, 'Is your name Walter Dragonette?' by a squad of policemen, had said, 'Well, I guess you know.' 'What do we know?' asked a policeman pointing a gun at his chest. 'That I'm the Meat Man,' answered Dragonette. He smiled a charming, self-deprecating smile. 'Otherwise, I must have a lot of unpaid parking tickets.'

The *Ledger* reporters had done an astonishing amount of work. They had managed to get the beginning of the saga of Walter Dragonette, his history and deeds, out onto the street only a couple of hours after they were discovered. The reporters had been busy, but so had Walter Dragonette.

Dragonette's little white house on North Twentieth Street, only a block south of the Arkham College campus, was in the midst of a 'transitional' area, meaning that it had once been entirely white and was now 60 to 70 percent black. In this lay the roots of much of the troubles that came later. Dragonette's black neighbors claimed that when they had called the police to complain of the sounds of struggle, the thudding blows and late-night screaming they had heard coming from the little white house, the officers had never done anything more than drive down the street – sometimes they ridiculed the caller, saying that these sounds were hardly rare in their neighborhood, now, were they? If the caller wanted peace, why didn't she try moving out to Riverwood – it was always nice and quiet, out in Riverwood. When one male caller had persisted, the policeman who had answered the telephone delivered a long comic monologue which ended, 'And how about you, Rastus, when you hit your old lady upside the head, do you want us charging there and giving you heat? And if we did, do you actually think she'd swear out a complaint?' Rastus, in this case a forty-five-year-old English teacher named Kenneth Johnson, heard cackling laughter in the background.

After someone was missing for three or four days, the police took notes and filled out forms, but generally declined to take matters further – the missing son or brother, the missing husband (especially the missing husband) would turn up sooner or later. Or they would not. What were the police supposed to do, make a house-to-house search for a dude who had decided to get a divorce without paperwork?

Under these circumstances, the neighborhood people had not even thought of calling the police to complain about the sounds of electrical saws and drills they had sometimes heard coming from the little white house, nor about the odor of rotting meat, sometimes of excrement, that drifted through its walls and windows.

They knew little of the presentable-looking young man who had lived in the house with his mother and now lived there alone. He was friendly. He looked intelligent and he wore suits to work. He had a shy little smile, and he was friendly in a distant way with everybody in the neighborhood. The older residents had known and respected his mother, Florence Dragonette, who had worked at Shady Mount Hospital for better than forty years.

Mrs Dragonette, a widow in her early thirties with an ironbound reputation and a tiny baby, had moved into the little white house when North Twentieth Street had been nearly as respectable as she was herself. She had raised that child by herself. She put the boy through school. Florence and her son had been a quiet, decent pair. Walter had never needed many friends – oh, he got into a little trouble now and them, but nothing like the other boys. He was shy and sensitive; he pretty much kept to himself. When you saw them eating dinner together on their regular Saturday nights at Huff's restaurant, you saw how polite he was to his mother, how friendly but not familiar to the waiters, just a perfect little gentleman. Florence Dragonette had died in her sleep three years ago, and Walter took care of all the details by himself: doctor, casket, cemetery plot, funeral service. You'd think he'd have been all broken up, but instead he kept his grief and sorrow on the inside and made sure everything was done just the way she would have wanted it. Some of the neighbors had come to the funeral, it was a neighborly thing to do, you didn't need an invitation, and there was Walter in a nice gray suit shaking hands and smiling his little smile, holding all that grief inside him.

After that, Walter had come out of himself a little bit more. He went out at night and he brought people home with him. Sometimes the neighbors heard loud music coming from the house late at night, loud music and laughter, shouting, screaming – things they had never heard while his mother was alive.

'Oh, I'm really sorry,' Walter would say the next day, standing next to the little blue Reliant his mother had driven, anxious to get to work, polite and charming and slightly shamefaced. 'I didn't know it got so noisy in there. You know. I certainly don't want to disturb anybody.'

Every now and then, late at night, he played his records and his television a little too loud. The neighbors smelled rotting meat and came up to him as he was watering his lawn and said – You put out rat poison, Walter? Seems like a rat or two musta died underneath your floorboards. And Walter held the hose carefully away from his neighbor and said, Oh, gosh, I'm really sorry about that smell. Every now and then that old freezer of ours just ups and dies and then everything in it goes off. I'd buy a new one in a minute, but I can't afford a new freezer right now.

6

Walter Dragonette's curtains had been open only two or three inches, a narrow gap, ordinarily nothing but entirely wide enough for two small boys, Akeem and Kwanza Johnson, to look through, giggling and jostling each other out of the way, fighting to press their faces up against the glass.

Akeem and Kwanza, nine and seven, lived across the street from Walter Dragonette. Their father was Kenneth Johnson, the English teacher who had been addressed as 'Rastus' by a Millhaven policeman eighteen months before. The Johnson house had four bedrooms and a porch and a second floor, and Mr Johnson had himself installed in his living room floor-to-ceiling oak book-shelves, every spacious shelf of which was packed with books. Subsidiary piles of books stood on the coffee table, on the nightstands and end tables, on the floor, and even on top of the twelve-inch black-and-white television that was the only set Mr Johnson had in his house.

Akeem and Kwanza Johnson were much more interested in television than in books. They *hated* the old black-and-white set in their kitchen. They wanted to watch TV in the living room, the way their friends did and they wanted to watch it in color on a big screen. Akeem and Kwanza would have settled for a twenty-one-inch set, as long as it was color, but what they really wanted, what they dreamed of persuading their father to buy, was something roughly the size of the oak book-shelves. And they knew that their neighbor across the street owned such a television set. They had been hearing him watch late-night horror movies for years, and they knew Walter's TV had to be *dope*. Walter's TV set was so great their father called up the police twice to *complain* about it. Walter's TV set was so bad that you could hear it *all the way across the street*.

On the night before the morning when Walter Drago-nette greeted fifteen armed policemen by telling them that he was the Meat Man, nine-year-old Akeem Johnson had come awake to hear the faint but unmistakable sounds of a grade-A horror movie coming from the speakers of the wonderful television set across the street. His father never let him go to horror movies and did not permit them on the television set at home, but a friend of Akeem's had shown him videotapes of Jason in his hockey mask and Freddy Krueger in his hat, and he knew what horror movies sounded like. What he was listening to, faint as it was, made Jason and Freddy sound like wimps. It had to be one of those movies he had heard about but never seen, like *The Evil Dead* or *Texas Chainsaw Massacre*, where

195

folks got hunted down and cut up, man, right there in your face. Akeem heard a man howling like a dog, sobbing like a woman, roaring, screeching, wailing . . .

He got out of bed and walked to his window and looked across the street. Instead of meeting as they usually did, Walter's curtains showed a narrow gap filled with yellow light. Akeem realized that if he got out of bed and sneaked out of the house, he could hide beneath the window, peek in, and actually watch the movie playing on Walter's big television. He also realized that he was not going to do that. What he could do, however, was wait for Walter to leave his house in the morning, and then just walk across the street and take a look inside that window and at least see if Walter's TV was the beast it sounded like.

The faint sounds from across the street came to an end as the movie shifted to one of the boring parts that always followed the excitement.

In the morning, Akeem went down to the kitchen and poured milk over his Cocoa Puffs and parked himself at the kitchen table where he could watch Walter's house through the window. About ten minutes later, his little brother dragged in, rubbing his eyes and complaining about a bad dream. After Akeem told him what he was doing, Kwanza got his own bowl of cereal and sat beside him at the table, and the two of them watched the house across the street like a pair of burglars.

Walter burst through his front door just after seven. He was wearing a white T-shirt and jeans, so wherever he was going, he would have to come back to change clothes before he went to work. Walter hustled down his walk, looked over both his shoulders as he unlocked his car, got in, and zoomed off.

'Okay?' Akeem asked.

'Yo,' said his brother.

They slid out of their chairs and went to the front door. Akeem quietly unlocked and opened it. They stepped outside, and Akeem gently let the door slide back into the frame without quite closing. The brothers walked over their front lawn. The dew pasted grass shavings to their bare feet. They felt funny and exposed when they stepped onto Walter's front yard and ran up to the window hunched over. Akeem reached the window first, but Kwanza butted him sideways, like a little goat, before he got a good look in through the curtains.

'You take your turn,' Akeem said. 'Yo, this was my idea.'

'Me too, I wanna look too,' Kwanza complained, and slipped in front of him when he bent his face again to the uncovered stripe of glass. Both boys peered in to see the enormous television set.

At first it looked as though Walter had been painting his living room. Most of the furniture had been pushed against the far wall, and newspapers were covering the floor. 'Akeem,' Kwanza said.

'Where is that thing?' Akeem said. 'I know it's here, no way it ain't here.'

'Akeem,' his brother said again, in exactly the same tone of voice.

Akeem looked down at the floor where his brother was pointing, and he too saw the corpse of a large, heavy black man stretched out in a swamp of bloody newspapers. The man's head lay some feet away, rolled on its side so that it seemed to be contemplating the broken hacksaw blade stuck halfway through what had been its left shoulder. The broad back, about the color of the Cocoa Puffs dissolving into mush back on the Johnsons' kitchen table, stared up at them. Deep cuts punctured it, and sections of skin had been sliced off leaving red horizontal gashes.

A few houses away, a car started up, and both boys screamed, thinking that Walter had come back and caught them. Akeem was the first to be able to move, and he stepped back and put his right arm around his brother's waist and pulled him away from Walter's house.

'Akeem, it wasn't no *movie*,' Kwanza said.

Too shocked and frightened to speak, Akeem grimaced at him, frantically gesturing that Kwanza should start running for home right *now*. 'Damn,' Kwanza said, and sprinted away like a jack-rabbit. In seconds they were pounding up their own lawn toward the front door.

Akeem yanked the door open, and the boys tumbled inside.

'It wasn't no *movie*,' Kwanza said. 'It wasn't – '

Akeem ran up the stairs toward his parents' bedroom.

He woke up his father, shaking his shoulder and babbling about a dead man with his head cut off across the street, this guy was all dead, his head was all cut off, blood was all around . . .

Kenneth Johnson told his wife to stop screaming at the kid. 'You saw a dead man in the house across the street? Mr Dragonette's house?'

Akeem nodded. He had begun to cry, and his brother sidled into the bedroom to witness this astonishing spectacle.

'And you saw it, too?'

Kwanza nodded. 'It wasn't no movie.'

His wife sat up straight and grabbed Akeem and pulled him into her chest. She gave her husband a warning look.

'Don't worry, I'm not going over there,' he said. 'I'm calling the police. We'll see what happens this time.'

Two policemen pulled up in a black-and-white about ten minutes later. One of them marched up to the Johnson house and rang the bell, and the other sauntered across the lawn and peered through the gap in the curtains. Just as Kenneth Johnson opened the door, the second policeman stepped away from the window with a stunned expression on his face. 'I think your friend would like you to join him,' Johnson said to the man on his doorstep.

Before another twenty minutes had passed, six

unmarked police cars had been installed up and down the street. The original black-and-white and one other stood parked around the corners at both ends of the block. While they all waited, a young policewoman with a soothing voice talked to Kwanza and Akeem in the living room. Kenneth Johnson sat on one side of the boys, his wife on the other.

'You've heard loud noises from the Dragonette house on other occasions in the past?'

Kwanza and Akeem nodded, and their father said, 'We all heard those noises, and a couple of times, I called to complain. Don't you keep a record of complaints down at the station?'

She smiled at him and said in her soothing voice, 'In all justice, Mr Johnson, the situation we have now is a good deal more serious than a loud argument.'

Johnson frowned until the smile wilted. 'I don't know for sure, but I'm willing to bet that Walter over there seldom stopped at the argument stage.'

It took the policewoman a moment to understand this remark. When she did understand it, she shook her head. 'This is Millhaven, Mr Johnson.'

'Apparently it is.' He paused to consider something. 'You know, I wonder if that fellow over there even owns a freezer.'

This irrelevance was too much for the young woman. She stood up from where she had been kneeling in front of the two boys and patted Kwanza's head before closing her notebook and tucking her pen into her pocket.

Johnson said, 'I can't help it, I'm sorry for you people.'

'This is *Millhaven*,' the policewoman repeated. 'If you'll permit me, I want to suggest that your boys have already been through enough for one day. In situations of this kind, counseling is always recommended, and I can provide you with the names of – '

'My God,' Johnson said. 'You still don't get it.'

The policewoman said, 'Thank you for your cooperation,' and walked away to stand in front of the Johnsons'
living room window and wait for Walter Dragonette to
come back home.

7

An hour and a half before Walter Dragonette was due at
his desk in the accounts department, the old blue Reliant
appeared at the end of the block. Other cars up and down
the street began backing out of driveways and easing away
from the curb. The lurking patrol cars swung into the
street at either end and slowly moved toward the white
house in the middle of the block. Walter Dragonette
drove blithely down the street and pulled up in front of
his house. He opened his door and put a foot on the
concrete.

The two squad cars sped forward and spun sideways,
their tires squealing, to block the ends of the street. The
unmarked cars raced up to the Reliant, and in an instant
the street was filled with policemen pointing guns at the
young man getting out of his car.

Kenneth Johnson, who described all of this to me,
including what his children had done to bring such envel-
oping turmoil upon the Millhaven police department, told
me later that when Walter Dragonette got out of his car
and faced all those cops and guns, he gave them his secret
smile.

The police ordered him away from his car, and he
cheerfully moved. They spoke, and Walter told them that
he was the Meat Man. Yes, of course he would come
down to the station with them. Well, certainly he would
put down the paper bag in his hand. What was in the

bag? Well, the only thing in the bag was the hacksaw blade he had just purchased. That was why he had left the house – to get a new hacksaw blade. Paul Fontaine, who still knew nothing about what had happened to April Ransom since he and John Ransom had left her bedside that morning, took a card from his jacket pocket and read Dragonette his rights under the Miranda decision. Walter Dragonette eagerly nodded that yes, he understood all of that. He'd want a lawyer, that was for sure, but he didn't mind talking now. It was time to talk, wouldn't the detective agree?

Detective Fontaine certainly did think that it was time to talk. And would Mr Dragonette permit the police to search his house?

The Meat Man took his eyes from Detective Fontaine's interesting face to smile and nod at Akeem and Kwanza, who were looking at him through their living room window. 'Oh by all means – I mean, they really *should* look through the place, really they *should*.' Then he looked back at Detective Fontaine. 'Are they prepared for what they're going to find?'

'What are they going to find, Mr Dragonette?' asked Sergeant Hogan.

'My people,' the Meat Man said. 'Why else would you be here?'

Hogan asked. 'Which people are we talking about, Walter?'

'If you don't know about my people – ' He licked his lips, and twisted his head to look over his shoulder to see his little white house. 'If you don't know about them, what made you come here?' His eyes moved from Fontaine to Hogan and back again. They did not answer him. He put his hand over his mouth and giggled. 'Well, whoever goes into my house *is* in for a little surprise.'

8

I never heard the waitress put the plate on the table. Eventually I realized that I could smell toast, looked up, and saw breakfast steaming beside my right elbow. I moved the plate in front of me and ate while I read about what the first policemen inside Walter Dragonette's house had found there.

First, of course, had been Alfonzo Dakins, whose shoulder joint had broken Dragonette's hacksaw blade and forced him into an early morning trip to the hardware store. Alfonzo Dakins had met Walter Dragonette in a gay bar called The Roost, accompanied him home, accepted a beer treated with a substantial quantity of Halcion, posed for a nude Polaroid photograph, and passed out. He had partially reawakened to find Walter's hands around his neck. The struggle that followed this discovery had awakened Akeem Johnson. If Dakins had not been woozy with Halcion and alcohol, he would easily have killed Dragonette, but the smaller man managed to hit him with a beer bottle and to snap handcuffs on him while he recovered.

Roaring, Dakins had gotten back on his feet with his hands cuffed in front of him, and Dragonette stabbed him in the back a couple of times to slow him down. Then he stabbed him in the neck. Dakins had chased him into the kitchen, and Walter banged him on the head with a cast-iron frying pan. Dakins dropped to his knees, and Walter slammed the heavy pan against the side of his head and knocked him out more successfully than the first time.

He covered the living room floor with old newspapers and dragged Dakins out of the kitchen. Three more layers of papers went around and beneath his body. Then Walter had removed the trousers, underwear, and socks he had been wearing, mounted Dakins's huge chest, and finished the job of strangling him.

He had photographed Dakins once more.

Then he had 'punished' Dakins for giving him so much unnecessary trouble and stabbed him half a dozen times in the back. When he felt that Dakins had been punished enough, he had anal intercourse with his dead body. Afterward, he went into the kitchen for his hacksaw and cut off Dakins's big bowling-ball head. Then the blade had broken.

On the top shelf of Dragonette's refrigerator, the police discovered four other severed heads, two of black males, one of a white male, and one of a white female who appeared to be in her early teens. The second shelf contained an unopened loaf of Branola bread, half a pound of ground chuck in a supermarket wrapper, a squeezable plastic container of French's mustard, and a six-pack of Pforzheimer beer. On the third shelf down stood two large sealed jugs each containing two severed penises, a human heart on a white china plate, and a human liver wrapped in Clingfilm. In the vegetable crisper on the right side of the refrigerator were a moldering head of iceberg lettuce, an opened bag of carrots, and three withered tomatoes. In the left crisper, police found two human hands, one partially stripped of its flesh.

Human Hand, on the list of *Les Viandes*.

On a shelf in the hall closet, in a row with two felt hats, one gray, one brown, were three skulls that had been completely cleaned of flesh. Two topcoats, brown and gray, a red-and-blue down jacket, and a brown leather jacket, hung from hangers; beneath the two jackets was a sixty-seven-gallon metal drum with three headless torsos floating in a dark liquid at first thought to be acid but later identified as tap water. Beside the drum was a spray can of Lysol disinfectant and two bottles of liquid bleach. When the big drum had been removed from the closet, a smaller drum was discovered behind it. Inside the second drum, two penises, five hands, and one foot had been kept in a liquid later determined to be tap water, vodka, rubbing alcohol, and pickle juice.

A row of skulls stood as bookends and decorations on a long shelf in the living room – they had been meticulously cleaned and painted with a gray lacquer that made them look artificial, like Halloween jokes. (The books that separated the skulls, chiefly cookbooks and manuals of etiquette, had belonged to Florence Dragonette.)

A long freezer in excellent working condition stood against one wall of the living room. When the policemen opened the freezer, they discovered six more heads, three male and three female, each of these encased in a large food-storage bag, two pairs of male human legs without feet, a freezer bag of entrails labeled STUDY, a large quantity of pickles that had been drained and dumped into a brown paper bag, two pounds of ground round, and the hand of a preteen female, minus three fingers. To the left of the freezer were an electric drill, an electrical saw, a box of baking soda, and a stainless-steel carving knife.

A manila envelope on top of a dresser in the bedroom contained hundreds of Polaroid photographs of bodies before death, after death, and after dismemberment. Behind the house, police found a number of black plastic garbage sacks filled with bones and rotting flesh. One policeman described Dragonette's backyard as a 'trash dump.' Bones and bone fragments littered the uncut grass, along with ripped clothes, old magazines, some discarded eyeglasses and one partial upper plate, and broken pieces of electrical equipment.

The initial assessment of the investigating officers was that the remains of at least nineteen people, and possibly as many as another five, had been located in Dragonette's house. An Associated Press reporter made the obvious point that this made the Dragonette case – the 'Meat Man' case – among the worst instances of multiple murder in American history, and, to prove the point, listed some of the competition:

1980s: about fifty murdered women, most of them prostitutes, found near the Green River in the Seattle-Tacoma area
1978: the bodies of thirty-three young men and boys found at John Wayne Gacy's house in suburban Chicago
1970s: twenty-six tortured and murdered youths discovered in the Houston area, and Elmer Wayne Henley convicted in six of the deaths
1971: the bodies of twenty-five farmworkers killed by Juan Corona discovered in California

The reporter went on to list James Huberty, who killed twenty-one people in a McDonald's; Charles Whitman, who killed sixteen people by sniping from a tower in Texas; George Banks, the murderer of twelve people in Pennsylvania; and several others, including Howard Unruh of Camden, New Jersey, who in 1948 shot and killed thirteen people in the space of twelve minutes and said, 'I'd have killed a thousand if I'd had enough bullets.' In the heat of his research, the AP reporter forgot to mention Ted Bundy and Henry Lee Lucas, both of whom were responsible for more deaths than any of these; and it is possible that he had never heard of Ed Gein, with whom Walter Dragonette had several things in common, although Walter Dragonette had certainly never heard of him.

A college professor in Boston who had written a book about mass murderers and serial killers said – presumably via telephone to the offices of the *Ledger* – that serial killers 'tended to be either of the disorganized or the organized type,' and that Walter Dragonette seemed to him 'a perfect example of the disorganized type.' Disorganized serial killers, said the professor, acted on impulse, were usually white male loners in their thirties with blue-collar jobs and a history of failed relationships. (Walter Dragonette, in spite of the professor's confidence, had a white-collar job, and had known exactly one supremely successful relationship in all his life, that with his mother.) Disorganized serial killers liked to keep the evidence around the house. They were easier to catch than the organized killers, who chose their victims carefully and covered their tracks.

And how, the *Ledger* asked, could anyone do what Walter Dragonette had done? How could Lizzie Borden had done it? How could Jack the Ripper have done it? And how, for the *Ledger* writers did remember this name, could Ed Gein have dug those women out of their graves and skinned their bodies? If the professor in Boston could not answer this question – for wasn't this question the essential question? – then the *Ledger* needed more experts. It had no trouble finding them.

A psychologist at a state mental hospital in Chicago offered the suggestion that 'none of these people will win any mental health awards,' and that they cut up their victims' bodies to conceal what they had done. He blamed 'violent pornography' for their actions.

A criminologist in San Francisco who had written a 'true crime' book about a serial killer in California blamed the anonymity of modern life. A Millhaven priest blamed the loss of traditional religious values. A University of Chicago sociologist blamed the disappearance of the traditional family. The clinical director of the Lakeshore Psychiatric Hospital told the *Ledger* that serial killers 'confused sex and aggression.' The head of a crime task force in New York blamed the relaxation of sexual mores which had made homosexuality and 'perversion in general' more acceptable. Someone blamed sunspots, and someone else blamed the 'climate of economic despair that is all around us now.'

A woman holding her two-year-old daughter on her shoulders in the crowd that had already collected in front of the white house on North Twentieth Street thought that Walter Dragonette did it because he wanted to be famous, and that the plan was going to work out just fine: 'Well, take me, I came down here, didn't I? This is history, right here. In six months, everything you see in front of you is going to be a miniseries on Channel Two.'

These were the *Ledger*'s answers to the question of how anyone could do the things Walter Dragonette had confessed to doing.

One article claimed that 'the eyes of the world, from Akron to Australia, from Boise to Britain, from Cleveland to Canton' had 'turned toward a white, one-story house in Millhaven.' Neighbors were talking to reporters from the BBC and news teams from three networks. One Philadelphia reporter was heard asking a resident of North Twentieth Street to describe what he called 'the stench of death.' And here came the answer, written down by two reporters: 'A real bad stink, real bad.'

Another article reported that 961 men, women, and children were missing in the state of Illinois. A spokesman for the FBI said that if you were over twenty-one, you had the right to be missing.

Arkham College officials warned their students to be careful about crime on campus, although students interviewed felt little concern for their own safety. 'It's just too strange to worry about,' said Shelley Manigault of Ladysmith, Wisconsin. 'To me, it's a lot more frightening to think about the position of women in society than about what one twisted white guy does when he's inside his house.'

The *Ledger* reported that Walter Dragonette had been

friendless in high school, where his grades had varied from A to F. Classmates recalled that his sense of humor had been 'weird.' He had been fascinated with the Blue Rose murders and had once run for class treasurer under the name Blue Rose, earning a schoolwide total of two votes. In the sixth grade, he had collected the corpses of small animals from the streets and empty lots and experimented with ways of cleaning their skeletons. In the eighth grade, he had privately exhibited in a plush-lined cigar box an object he had claimed to be the skeletal hand of a five-year-old boy. Those who had seen the object declared that it had been a monkey's paw. For several days on end, he had pretended to be blind, coming to school with dark glasses and a white cane, and once he had nearly managed to persuade his homeroom teacher that he had amnesia. Twice during the time that he attended Carl Sandburg High School, Dragonette had used chalk to draw the outlines of bodies on the floor of the gymnasium. He told Detective Fontaine and Sergeant Hogan that the outlines were of the bodies of people he had actually killed – killed while he was in high school.

For Dragonette claimed to have killed a small child named Wesley Drum in 1979, after having sex with him in a vacant lot. He said that when he was a sophomore at Carl Sandburg, the year he ran for class treasurer under the name of Blue Rose, he had killed a woman who picked him up while he was hitchhiking – stabbed her with an army surplus knife while she stopped at a red light. He could not remember her name, but he knew that he had stuck her right in the chest, and then stuck her a couple more times while she was still getting used to the idea. He grabbed her purse and jumped out of the car a couple of seconds after the light changed. He was sorry that he had stolen the lady's purse, and he wanted it known that he would be happy to return the $14.78 it had contained to her family, if someone would give him the right name and address.

Both of these stories matched unsolved murders in Millhaven. Five-year-old Wesley Drum had been found dead and mutilated (though still in possession of both hands) in an empty lot behind Arkham College in 1979, and in 1980, Walter Dragonette's fifteenth year, Annette Bulmer, a thirty-four-year-old mother of two dying from numerous deep stab wounds, had been pulled from a stalled car at the intersection of Twelfth Street and Arkham Boulevard.

Walter readily gave the police what the *Ledger* called 'assistance' on 'several prominent recent cases.'

I continued to leaf through the paper as I finished my breakfast, realizing that now I was free to do whatever I liked. April Ransom was recovering, and her confessed attacker had been arrested. A sick little monster who called himself the Meat Man had diverted himself from his amusements (or whatever it was when you killed people and had sex with their corpses) long enough to reenact the Blue Rose murders. No retired soldier in the sixties, back from Korea and Germany, patrolled Livermore Avenue in search of fresh victims: no murderer's rose garden grew in the backyard of a well-kept little house in Pigtown. The past was still buried with the rest of my family in Pine Knoll.

I folded the paper and waved to the waitress. When she came over to my booth, I told her that I could see why she'd been having trouble concentrating on her work this morning.

'Well, yeah,' she said, warming up. 'Things like that don't happen in Millhaven – they're not *supposed* to.'

9

The machine answered when I called Ransom from the St Alwyn's lobby, so he was either still asleep or already back at the hospital.

I walked back to the Pontiac, made a U-turn on Livermore Avenue, and drove back beneath the viaduct toward Shady Mount.

Because I didn't want to be bothered with a meter, I turned into one of the side streets on the other side of Berlin Avenue and parked in front of a small redbrick house. A big flag hung from an upstairs window and a yellow ribbon had been tied into a grandiose bow on the front door. I walked across the empty street in the middle of the block, wondering if April Ransom had already opened her eyes and asked what had happened to her.

It was my last afternoon in Millhaven, I realized.

For a moment, opening the visitors' door, I wondered what name I would give to my unfinished book; and then, for the first time in a long dry time, the book jumped into life within me – I wanted to write a chapter about Charlie Carpenter's childhood. It would be a lengthy tour of hell. For the first time in months, I saw my characters in color and three dimensions, breathing city-flavored air and scheming for the things they thought they needed.

These fantasies occupied me pleasantly as I waited for, and then rode up in, the elevator. I barely noticed the two policemen who stepped inside the elevator behind me. The radios on their belts crackled as we ascended and stepped out of the elevator on the third floor. It was like having an escort. As burly and contained as a pair of Clydesdales, the two policemen moved around me and then turned the corner toward the nurses' station.

I rounded the corner a few seconds behind them. The policemen turned right at the nurses' station and went toward April Ransom's room through a surprising number of people. Uniformed police, plainclothes detectives, and what looked like a few civilians formed a disorganized crowd that extended from the station all the way around the curve to Mrs Ransom's room. The scene reminded me uncomfortably of the photograph of Walter Dragonette's front lawn. All these men seemed to be talking to one another in little groups. An air of exhaustion and frustration, distinct as cigar smoke, hung over all of them.

One or two cops glanced at me as I came nearer to the nurses' station. Officer Mangelotti was seated in a wheelchair before the counter. A white bandage stained red over his ear wrapped around his head, leaving his face so exposed it looked peeled. A man with a monkish hairline knelt in front of the wheelchair, speaking quietly. Mangelotti looked up and saw me. The man in front of him stood up and turned around to show me his saggy clown's face and drooping nose. It was Detective Fontaine.

His face twitched in a sorrowful smile. 'Someone I know wants to meet you,' he said. Plummy pouches hung underneath his eyes.

A uniformed policeman nearly seven feet tall moved toward me out of the corridor leading to April Ransom's room. 'Sir, unless you are on the medical staff of this hospital you will have to vacate this area.' He began shooing me away, blocking me from seeing whatever was going on behind him. 'Immediately, sir.'

'Leave him be, Sonny,' Fontaine said.

The enormous cop turned to make sure he had heard correctly. It was like watching the movement of a large blue tree. Behind him two men pushed a gurney out of one of the rooms along the curve of the corridor. A body covered with a white sheet lay on the gurney. Three other policemen, two men in white coats, and a mustached man in a lightweight blue pinstriped suit followed the gurney out of the room. The last man looked familiar. Before the blue tree cut off my view, I caught a glimpse of Eliza Morgan leaning against the inner wall of the circular corridor. She moved away from the wall as the men pushed the gurney past her.

Paul Fontaine came up beside the big officer. He looked like the other man's monkey. 'Leave us alone, Sonny.'

The big cop cleared his throat with a noise that sounded like a drain unblocking. He said, 'Yes, sir,' and walked away.

'I told you police should never go to hospitals, didn't I?' His eyes looked poached above the purple bags, and I remembered that he had been up all night long, first here, then at North Twentieth Street, and then back here again. 'Do you know what happened?' A kind of animation moved in his face, but at a level beneath the skin, so that whatever he was feeling showed only as a momentary flash in his sagging eyes.

'I thought I'd find John Ransom here.'

'We got him at home. I thought you were staying with him.'

'My God,' I said. 'Tell me what happened.'

His eyes widened, and his face went still. 'You don't know?' The men in white coats pushed the gurney past us, and three policemen came along behind them. Fontaine and I looked down at the small covered body. I remembered Eliza Morgan leaning against the wall, and suddenly I understood whose body it was. For a moment my stomach turned *gray* – it felt as though everything from the bottom of my rib cage to my bowels had gone flat and dead, mushy.

'Somebody – ?' I tried again. 'Somebody killed April Ransom?'

Fontaine nodded. 'Have you seen the newspaper this

morning? Watch any morning news? Listen to the radio?'

'I read the paper,' I said. 'I know about that man, ah, Walter Dragonette. You arrested him.'

'We arrested him,' Fontaine said. He made it sound like a sad joke. 'We did. We just didn't do it soon enough.'

'But he confessed to attacking Mrs Ransom. In the *Ledger* – '

'He didn't confess to attacking her,' Fontaine said. 'He confessed to killing her.'

'But Mangelotti and Eliza Morgan were in that room.'

'The nurse went for a cigarette right after she came on duty.'

'What happened to Mangelotti?'

'While Mrs Morgan was out of the room, our friend Walter sauntered past the nurses' station without anybody seeing him, ducked into the room, and clobbered Mangelotti on the side of the head with a hammer. Or something resembling a hammer. Our stalwart officer was seated beside the bed at the time, reading entries in his notebook. Then our friend beat Mrs Ransom to death with the same hammer.' He looked up at me and then over at Mangelotti. He looked as if he had bitten into something sour. 'This time, he didn't bother signing the wall. And then he walked away past the patients' lounge and went downstairs and got into his car to go to the hardware store for a hacksaw blade.' He looked at me again. Anger and disgust burned in his tired eyes. '*He* had to wait for the hardware store to open, so *we* had to wait. In the meantime, the nurse left the patients' lounge and found the body. She yelled for the doctors but it was too late.'

'So Dragonette knew that she was about to come out of her coma?'

He nodded. 'Walter called to ask about her condition this morning. It must have been the last thing he did before he left home. Doesn't that make you feel all warm and happy on the inside?' His eyes had gotten a little wild, and red lines threaded through the whites. He mimed picking up a telephone. 'Hello, I just wanted to see how my dear lovely friend April Ransom is getting along, yes yes . . . Oh, you don't say, really, well, isn't that sweet? In that case, I'll be popping in to pay her a little social call, oh my yes indeedy, as soon, that is, as I cut the head off the guy on my living room floor, so you go ahead and make sure she'll be alone, and if you can't arrange that, please see that nobody but Officer Mangelotti is alone in the room with her, yes, that's M-A-N-G-E-L-O-DOUBLE T-I – '

He did not stop so much as strangle on his own emotions. The other policemen watched him surreptitiously. In his wheelchair, Mangelotti heard every word, and flinched at the spelling of his name. He looked like a slaughterhouse cow.

'I don't get it,' I said. 'He went to all that trouble to protect himself, and the second you guys get out of your cars and wave your guns at him, he says, Well, I didn't just kill everybody inside there, I also knifed those Blue Rose people. And then he was so lucky – to get here exactly when the nurse went out of the room. It seems a little unlikely.'

Fontaine reared back and widened his bloodshot eyes. 'You want to talk about unlikely? *Unlikely* doesn't count anymore.'

'No, but it confuses the civilians,' said a voice behind me. I turned around to see the man in the pinstriped suit who had followed April Ransom's body out of her room. Deep vertical lines cut down his face on either side of his thin forties mustache. His light brown hair was combed straight back, exposing deep indentations in his hairline. He had looked familiar to me earlier because I had seen his picture in the paper that morning. He was Detective Sergeant Michael Hogan, Fontaine's superior.

Hogan put his hand on Fontaine's elbow.

'This is the guy who wanted to meet you,' Fontaine said.

I sensed immediately that I was in the presence of a real detective, someone even Tom Pasmore would respect. Michael Hogan possessed a powerful personal authority. Hogan had the uncomplicated masculinity of old movie stars like Clark Gable or William Holden, both of whom he resembled in a generalized, real-world fashion. You could see Hogan commanding a three-masted schooner through a heavy storm or sentencing mutineers to death on the yardarm. His offhand remark about 'civilians' seemed perfectly in character.

What I was most conscious of at the moment when Michael Hogan shook my hand was that I wanted his approval – that most abject, adolescent desire.

And then, in the midst of the crowd of policemen and hospital staff, he did an astonishing thing. He gave me his approval.

'Didn't you write *The Divided Man*?' I barely had time to nod before he said, 'That was a very perceptive book. Ever read it, Paul?'

As amazed as myself, Fontaine said, 'Read it?'

'About the last word on the Blue Rose business.'

'Oh, yes,' said Fontaine. 'Yes.'

'It was the last word before Walter Dragonette came along,' I said.

Hogan smiled at me as if I had said something clever. 'Nobody is very happy about Mr Dragonette,' Hogan said, and changed the subject without losing any of his remarkable civility. 'I suppose you came here to find your friend Ransom.'

'I did, yes,' I said. 'I tried calling him, but all I got was the machine. Does he know – he does know what happened, doesn't he?'

'Yes, yes, yes,' Hogan said, sounding like an ancient

215

uncle rocking in front of a fire. 'After Paul and I got the call about his wife, we got him at home.'

'You heard April had been killed before Dragonette confessed to doing it?' I asked. I didn't quite know why, but this seemed important.

'That's probably enough,' said Paul Fontaine. Before I saw the implications of my question, he sensed an implied criticism. 'We've got work to do, Mr Underhill. If you'd like to see your friend – '

Hogan had immediately understood the nature of this criticism. He raised his eyebrows and broke into what Fontaine was saying. 'We usually hear about crimes before we get confessions.'

'I know that,' I said. 'It's more that I was wondering if Walter Dragonette heard about this crime before he confessed to it.'

'It was a good clean confession,' Fontaine said.

Fontaine was beginning to look irritated, and Hogan moved to mollify him. 'He knew where she was being held. That information was never released. There are eight hospitals in Millhaven. When we asked Dragonette the name of the hospital where he had killed April Ransom, he said Shady Mount.'

'Did he know her room number?'

'No,' Hogan said, and at the same time Fontaine said, 'Yes.'

'Paul means he knew the floor she was on,' Hogan said. 'He wouldn't know that unless he'd been here.'

'Then how did he know where to find her in the first place?' I asked. 'I don't suppose the switchboard gave out information about her.'

'We really haven't had the time to fully interrogate Mister Dragonette,' said Hogan.

The uniformed officers moving back and forth between April Ransom's room slowed down as they passed us.

'You could meet your friend Ransom down on Armory

216

Place,' Hogan said. 'He's waiting for Paul to begin Dragonette's interrogation. And Paul, I think you could usefully start matters down there.'

He turned back to me. 'You know where Armory Place is?'

I nodded.

'Follow Paul and park in the police lot. You and Mister Ransom could watch some of the interrogation.' He asked Fontaine, 'Is that okay with you?'

Fontaine nodded.

Downstairs, an elderly woman seated at a computer on one of the desks behind the counter looked up at us and twitched as if her chair had just given her an electric shock. April Ransom's murder had unsettled the entire hospital. Fontaine said he would wait for me at the entrance to the hospital parking lot.

'I know how to get to police headquarters,' I reminded him.

'Yeah, but if you try to get into the lot without me, somebody might mistake you for a reporter,' he said.

I trotted across the street and went up the block. Before I could put the key into the Pontiac's door, a heavyset man in Bermuda shorts and a blue button-down shirt came rushing out of the front door of the house with the flag and the yellow ribbon. 'Just hold it right there,' he shouted. 'I got something to say to you.'

I unlocked the door and waited for him to cross the lawn. He had a big belly and hairy legs, and his bulldog face was flushed pink. He came within ten feet of me and jabbed his finger at me. 'Do you see any signs saying HOSPITAL PARKING on this street? The parking places on this street are not for you people – you can park at the meters, or go around to the hospital lot. I am sick and tired of being abused.'

'Abused? You don't know what the word means.' I opened the car door.

217

'Wait up there.' He circled around the front of my car, still pointing at my chest. 'These – are – our – spaces. I paid a lot of money to live in this neighborhood, and people like you treat it like a public park. This morning, some guy was sitting on my lawn – on my lawn! He got out of his car and he sat down on my lawn, like he owned it, and then he went over to the hospital!'

'Your yellow ribbon made him feel at home,' I said, and got into the car.

'What the hell is that supposed to mean?'

'He thought it was a free country.' I started the car while he told me all about freedom. He was a patriot, and he had a lot of thoughts on the subject that people like me wouldn't understand.

10

Fontaine's blue sedan led me downtown through a city that seemed deserted.

The illusion of emptiness vanished as soon as we drove past the entrance to Armory Place. The newspaper articles had already brought perhaps a hundred people to the front of police headquarters. Signs bristled up over their heads. The crowd spilled down the wide steps of the huge gray building and flowed out onto the wide plaza between it and city hall. At the top of the steps, a man diminished by distance shouted into a bullhorn. Camera crews wound through his audience, recording it all for the evening news.

The blue sedan turned right at the end of the plaza, and a block later turned right again into an unmarked lane. A sign announced NO ACCESS   POLICE VEHICLES ONLY.

Red brick walls hemmed in the narrow lane. I followed

Fontaine's car into a wide rectangular parking lot crowded with police cars. Uniformed officers dwarfed by the high walls leaned against the cars, talking. The back of the police headquarters loomed on the opposite side of the lot. A few policemen turned their heads when the Pontiac came in. When I pulled into an empty space alongside Fontaine, two of them appeared at my door.

Fontaine got out of his car and said, 'Don't shoot him, he's with me.'

Without looking back, he took off toward a black metal door in the rear of the headquarters building. The two cops stepped aside, and I hurried after him.

Like an old grade school, the police building was a warren of dark corridors with scuffed wooden floors, rows of doors with pebbled glass windows, and clanging staircases. Fontaine charged ahead past a crowded bulletin board and the open door to a locker room. A half-naked man sitting on a bench called out, 'How's Mangelotti?'

'Dead,' Fontaine said.

He double-jumped up a staircase and banged open a door marked HOMICIDE. I followed him into a room where half a dozen men seated at desks froze at the sight of me. 'He's with me,' Fontaine said. 'Let's get down to business and interrogate that piece of batshit right now.' The men had already stopped paying attention to me. 'Let's give him the chance to explain himself.' Fontaine took off his suit jacket and put it over the back of a chair. Files and loose papers lay stacked on his desk. 'Let's wrap up every unsolved murder on our books and start all over again with a clean slate. And then everybody will go home happy.'

He rolled up his sleeves. The room smelled of sweat and stale cigarette smoke. It was a little bit hotter than the street. 'Now don't lose your head,' said a man at the back of the room.

'That's good,' Fontaine said.

'Say, Paul,' said a detective with a round, chubby face who looked up at him from the next desk, 'did it ever occur to you, and I'm sure it did, that your prisoner in there gave a whole new meaning to the expression, to give good head?'

'I'm grateful to you for that insight,' Fontaine said. 'When he starts to get hungry, I'll send one of you in to work things out with him.'

'Paul, is it my imagination, or is there a strange smell in here?' He sniffed the air.

'Ah, the smell,' Fontaine said. 'Do you know what our friend said when this odor was pointed out to him?'

'If you're not part of the solution, you're part of the problem?' said the other policeman.

'Not quite. He said, and I quote, *I've been meaning to do something about that*.'

Every man in the room cracked up. Fontaine regarded them stoically, as if he were resigned to their childishness. 'Gentlemen, gentlemen. I am using the suspect's exact words. He is a person of good intentions. The man fully intended to do something about the smell, which was as offensive to him as it was to his neighbors.' He raised his arms in mock appeal and slowly turned around in a complete circle.

A hidden connection that had struck me almost since I had walked into the detectives' office finally surfaced: these men reminded me of the body squad. The homicide detectives were as caustic and exclusionary as Scoot and Ratman and the others, and their humor was as corrosive. Because they handled death all day long, they had to make it funny.

'Are we set up for taping in Number One?' Fontaine asked.

'Are you kidding?' asked the detective with the chubby face. Short blond hair like feathers stuck flat to his head, and his peaceful blue eyes were set as far apart as an ox's. 'That baby is set to go.'

'Good,' Fontaine said.

'Can we, uh, watch this, if we want to?' asked the blond detective.

'I like to *watch*,' intoned a broad-shouldered detective with a heavy mustache that frothed over his upper lip. 'I want to *watch*.'

'You are free to join Mr Underhill and Mr Ransom in the booth,' Fontaine said, with as much dignity as possible.

'Show time,' said the detective across the room who had advised Fontaine not to lose his head. He was a slim man with skin the color of light coffee and an almost delicate, ironic face. Alone of all the men in the room, he still had on his suit jacket.

'My colleagues, the ghouls,' Fontaine said to me.

'These guys remind me of Vietnam.'

Something within Fontaine slowed down by an almost imperceptible degree. 'You were there? That's how you know Ransom?'

'I met him there,' I said. 'But I knew him from Millhaven.'

'You go to Brooks-Lowood, too?'

'Holy Sepulchre,' I said. 'I grew up on South Sixth Street.'

'Bastian there is from your part of town.'

Bastian was the corrupt cherub with feathery blond hair and wide-set blue eyes. 'I used to go to those athletes' suppers at your school,' he said. 'When I played football at St Ignatius. I remember your coach. A real character.'

'Christ wouldn't have dropped the ball,' I said, mystifying the other men.

'Jesus stands facing the goalposts,' Bastian said. He was looking upward, holding one hand on his heart and pointing toward an invisible horizon with the other.

'In his heart is a powerful will to win. He knows the odds are against him, but he also knows that at the end of the day, victory will be his.' I knew this even better than Bastian, having had to listen to it day after day for three years.

'Righteousness is a – is a what?' Bastian looked straight up at the fluorescent lights.

'Righteousness is a mighty – '

'*A mighty fire!*' Bastian yelled, sounding a lot more like Mr Schoonhaven than I did. He was still pointing at the distant goalposts with his hand clamped to his heart.

'That was it,' I said. 'It came with hamburgers and Hawaiian Punch.'

'Well, now that we're prepared,' Fontaine said. 'Bastian, get Dragonette out of the cell and put him in Number One. The rest of you who are coming, let's move, okay?'

At last I understood that he had not been trying to leave me behind when he came sprinting into the building. In spite of his exhaustion, he had been excited by the upcoming interrogation. His urgency was the expression of an intense desire to get into that room.

He moved toward the door, and the black detective and the big man with the energetic mustache stood up to follow. Bastian left the room through a side door and went down the long corridor I had briefly glimpsed.

The rest of us began moving down toward the front of the building. The hallway was slightly cooler than the squad room. 'First things first,' Fontaine said, and ducked into a room with an open door. Tube lighting fell on two formica-topped tables and a number of assorted chairs. Three men drinking coffee at one of the tables looked up at Fontaine. 'You were at the hospital?' one of them asked.

'Just got back.' Fontaine went up to one of two coffee

machines, took a thick paper cup off a stack, and poured hot black coffee into it.

'How's Mangelotti?'

'We could lose him.' He sipped from the coffee. I poured for myself.

On the side wall of the coffee room hung a big rectangle of white paper covered with names written in red or black marker. It was divided into three sections, corresponding to the three homicide shifts. Lieutenant Ross McCandless commanded the first shift. Michael Hogan and William Greider were his detective sergeants. From the list of names written in black and red marker beneath Hogan's, *April Ransom* jumped out at me. It was written in red marker.

The other two detectives helped themselves to coffee and introduced themselves. The black detective was named Wheeler, the big man Monroe. 'You know what bugs me about those people out in front?' Monroe asked me. 'If they had any sense, they'd be cheering because we got this guy behind bars.'

'You mean you want gratitude?' Fontaine drew another cup of coffee and led the three of us out of the lounge. Over his shoulder, he said, 'I'll tell you one good thing, anyhow. There's going to be a mile of black ink on the board in a couple of hours.'

On the other side of the lounge we entered the new part of the building. The floor was gray linoleum and the walls were pale blue with clear glass windows. The air conditioning worked, and the corridor felt almost cool. The three of us rounded a corner, and John Ransom looked up from a plastic chair pushed against one of the blue walls. He looked no more rested than Fontaine. John was wearing khaki pants and a white dress shirt, and he had obviously showered and shaved just before or after he had learned that his wife had been murdered. He looked like a half-empty sack. I wondered how long he had been sitting by himself.

'God, Tim, I'm glad you're here,' he said, jumping up. 'So you know? They told you?'

'Detective Fontaine told me what happened.' I did not want to tell him that I had seen April's body being taken from her room. 'John, I'm so sorry.'

Ransom held up his hands as if to capture something. 'It's unbelievable. She was getting better – this guy, this monster, found out she was getting better – '

Fontaine stepped before him. 'We're going to let you and your friend observe a portion of my interrogation. Do you still want to do it?'

Ransom nodded.

'Then let me show you where you'll be sitting. Want any coffee?'

Ransom shook his head, and Fontaine took us past the glass wall of a vast darkened room where a few people sat smoking as they waited to be questioned.

He nodded for Wheeler to open a blond wooden door. Six or seven feet down the corridor an identical door bore a dark blue plaque with the white numeral 1 at its center. Fontaine waved me in first, and I stepped into a dark chamber furnished with six chairs at a wooden table. In front of the table, a window looked into a larger, brighter room where a slim young man in a white T-shirt sat at a slight angle to a gray metal table. He was sliding a red aluminum ashtray back and forth across the table. His face was without any expression at all.

I sat down in the last chair, and Detective Monroe entered and took the chair beside me. John Ransom followed him. He made an involuntary grunt when he saw Walter Dragonette, and then he sat down beside the black detective. Monroe stepped inside and sat down on the other side of Ransom. Everything had been choreographed so that a couple of detectives would be able to restrain Ransom, if it turned out to be necessary.

Fontaine stepped inside. 'Dragonette can't see or hear you, but please don't make any loud noises or touch the glass. All right?'

'Yes,' Ransom said.

'I'll come back when the first part of the interrogation is over.'

He stepped outside, and Wheeler stood up and closed the door. Walter Dragonette looked like a man killing time in an airport. Every now and then he smiled at the *ting-ting-ting* of the flimsy ashtray as he tapped it against the table. A key turned in the door behind him, and he stopped toying with the ashtray to look over his shoulder.

A uniformed officer let in Paul Fontaine. He held a file clamped under his arm and a container of coffee in each hand.

'Hello, Walter,' Fontaine said.

'Hi! I remember you from this morning.' Walter sat up straight and folded his hands together on the table. He twisted to watch Fontaine go to the end of the table. 'Do we finally get to talk now?'

'That's right,' Fontaine said. 'I bought you some coffee.'

'Oh thanks, but I don't drink coffee.' Dragonette gave his torso a curious little shake.

'Whatever you say.' Fontaine removed the plastic top from one container and dropped it into a wastebasket. 'Sure you won't change your mind?'

'Caffeine's bad for you,' said Dragonette.

'Smoke?' Fontaine placed a nearly full packet of Marlboros on the table.

'No, but it's fine with me if you want to.'

Fontaine raised his eyebrows and tapped a cigarette from the pack.

'I just want to say one thing right at the start of this,' said Dragonette.

225

Fontaine lit the cigarette with a match and blew out smoke, extinguishing the match and quieting Dragonette with a wave of the hand. 'You will be able to say everything you want to, Walter, but first we have to take care of some details.'

'I'm sorry.'

'That's all right, Walter. Please give me your name, address, and date of birth.'

'My name is Walter Donald Dragonette, and my address is 3421 North Twentieth Street, where I have resided all of my life since being born on September 20, 1965.'

'And you have waived the presence of an attorney.'

'I'll get a lawyer later. I want to talk to you first.'

'The only other thing I have to say is that this conversation is being videotaped so that we can refer to it later.'

'Oh, that's a good idea.' Dragonette looked up at the ceiling, and then over his shoulder, and grinned and pointed at us. 'I get it! The camera's behind that mirror, isn't it?'

'No, it isn't,' Fontaine said.

'Is it on now? And are you sure it's working?'

'It's on now,' Fontaine said.

'So now we can start?'

'We're starting right now,' Fontaine said.

11

The following is a record of the conversation that followed.

WD: Okay. I have one thing I want to say right away, because it's important that you know about this. I was sexually abused when I was just a little boy, seven years old. The man who did it was a neighbor down the street, and his name was Mr Lancer. I don't know his first name. He moved away after that. But he used to invite me into his house, and then he'd, you know, he'd do things to me. I hated it. Anyhow, I've been thinking about things, about why I'm here and all, and I think that's the whole explanation for everything, right there, Mr Lancer.

PF: Did you ever tell anyone about Mr Lancer? Did you ever tell your mother?

WD: How could I? I hardly even know how to describe it to myself! And besides that, I didn't think my mother would believe me. Because she liked Mr Lancer. He helped keep up the tone of the neighborhood. Do you know what he was? He was a photographer, and he took baby pictures, and pictures of children. You bet he did. He took pictures of me without my clothes on.

PF: Is that all he did?

WD: Oh, no. Didn't I say he abused me? Well, that's what he did. Sexually. That's the really important part. He made me play with him. With his, you know, his thing. I had to put it in my mouth and everything, and he took pictures. I wonder if those pictures are in magazines. *He* had magazines with pictures of little boys.

PF: You took pictures, didn't you, Walter?

WD: Did you see them? The ones in the envelope?

PF: Yes.

WD: Well, now you know why I took them.

PF: Was that the only reason you took pictures?

WD: I don't know. I sort of had to do that. It's important to remember things, it's very important. And then there was one other reason.

PF: What was it?

WD: Well, I could use them to decide what I was going to eat. When I got home from work. That's why I sometimes called the pictures, the envelope of pictures,

227

the 'menu.' Because it was like a list of what I had. I was always going to get the pictures organized into a nice scrapbook, with the names and everything, but you got me before I got around to it. That's okay, though. I'm not mad or anything. It was really just having the pictures, really, not putting them in a book.

PF: And help you pick out what you were going to eat.

WD: It was the menu. Like those restaurants that have pictures of the food. And besides, you can wander down Memory Lane, and have those experiences again. But even after you sort of used up the picture, it's still a trophy – like an animal head you put on a wall. Because a long time ago, I figured out that that's what I was, a hunter. A predator. Believe me, I wouldn't have chosen it, there's a lot of work involved, and you have to have incredible secrecy, but it chose me and there it was. You can't go back, you know.

PF: Tell me about when you figured out that you were a predator. And I want to hear about how you got interested in the old Blue Rose murders.

WD: Oh. Well, the first thing was, I read this book called *The Divided Man*, and it was about this screwed-up cop who found out that he killed people and then he killed himself. The book was about Millhaven! I knew all the streets! That was really interesting to me, especially after my mother told me that the whole thing was real. So I learned from her that there used to be this man who killed people and wrote BLUE ROSE on the wall, or whatever, near the bodies. Only it wasn't the policeman.

PF: It wasn't?

WD: Couldn't be, never ever. No way. No. Way. That detective in the book, he wasn't a predator at all. I knew that – I just didn't know what you called it, yet. But whoever it really was, he was like my real dad. He was like me, but before me. He hunted them down, and he killed them. Back then, the only things I killed were

228

animals, just for practice, so I could see what it was like. Cats and dogs, a lot of dogs. You could use a knife, and it was pretty easy. The hard part was getting the skeletons clean. Nobody really knows how much work that is. You really have to *scrub*, and the smell can get pretty bad.

PF: You thought that the Blue Rose murderer was your father?

WD: No, I thought he was my *real* dad. No matter whether he was my actual father or not. My mother never told me much about my dad, so he could have been anybody. But after I read that book and found out how real it was, I knew I was like that man's real son, because I was like following in his footsteps.

PF: And so, a couple of weeks ago, you decided to copy what he had done?

WD: You noticed? I wasn't sure anyone would notice.

PF: Notice what?

WD: You know. You almost said it.

PF: You say it.

WD: The places – they were the same places. You knew that, didn't you?

PF: Those Blue Rose murders were a long time ago.

WD: There's no excuse for ignorance like that. You didn't notice because you never knew in the first place. I think that's really second-rate.

PF: I agree with you.

WD: Well, you should. It's shoddy.

PF: You went to a lot of trouble to recreate the Blue Rose murders, and nobody noticed. Noticed the details, I mean.

WD: People never notice anything. It's disgusting. They never even noticed that all those people were missing. Now I suppose nobody'll even notice that I got arrested, or all the things I did.

PF: You don't have to worry about that, Walter. You are becoming very well known. You're already notorious.

WD: Well, that's all wrong, too. There isn't anything special about me.

PF: Tell me about killing the man on Livermore Street.

WD: The man on Livermore Street? He was just a guy. I was waiting in that little alley or whatever you call it, in back of that hotel. A man came along. It was, let's see, about midnight. I asked him some question, who knows, like if he could help me carry something into the hotel through the back door. He stopped walking. I think I said I'd give him five bucks. Then he stepped toward me, and I stabbed him. I kept on stabbing him until he fell down. Then I wrote BLUE ROSE on the brick wall. I had this marker I brought along, and it worked fine.

PF: Can you describe the man? His age, his appearance, maybe his clothes?

WD: Real, real ordinary guy. I didn't even pay much attention to him. He might have been about thirty, but I'm not even too sure of that. It was dark.

PF: What about the woman?

WD: Oh, Mrs Ransom? That was different. Her, I knew.

PF: How did you know her?

WD: Well I didn't actually know her to speak to, or anything like that. But I knew who she was. My mother left some money when she died, about twenty thousand dollars, and I wanted to take care of it. So I used to go down to Barnett and Company to see Mr Richard Mueller, he invested the money for me? And I'd see him maybe once a month. For a while I did, anyhow, before things got kind of *hectic* around here. Mrs Ransom was in the office next to Mr Mueller's, and so I'd see her most times I went there. She was a really pretty woman. I liked her. And then her picture was in the paper that time she won the big award. So I decided to use her for the second Blue Rose person, the one in the St Alwyn, room 218. It had to be the right room.

PF: How did you get her to the hotel?

WD: I called her at the office and said that I had to tell her something about Mr Mueller. I made it sound like it was really bad. I insisted that she meet me at the hotel, and I said that I lived there. So I met her in the bar, and I said that I had to show her these papers that were in my room because I was afraid to take them anywhere. I knew room 218 was empty because I looked at it just before dinner, when I snuck in the back door. The locks are no good in the St Alwyn, and there are never any people in the halls. She said she'd come up to the see the papers, and when we got into the room I stabbed her.

PF: Is that all you did?

WD: No. I hit her, too. That was even in the newspapers.

PF: How many times did you stab Mrs Ransom?

WD: Maybe seven, eight times. About that many times.

PF: And where did you stab her?

WD: In the stomach and chest area. I don't really remember this.

PF: You didn't take pictures.

WD: I only took pictures at home.

PF: Did you get to the room by going through the lobby?

WD: We walked straight through the lobby and went up in the elevator.

PF: The clerk on duty claims he never saw Mrs Ransom that night.

WD: He didn't. We didn't see him, either. It's the St Alwyn, not the Pforzheimer. Those guys don't stay behind the desk.

PF: How did you leave?

WD: I walked down the stairs and went out the back door. I don't think anybody saw me.

PF: You thought you had killed her.

WD: Killing her was the whole idea.

PF: Tell me about what you did this morning.

WD: All of it?

PF: Let's leave out Alfonzo Dakins for now, and just concentrate on Mrs Ransom.

WD: Okay. Let me think about it for a second. All right. This morning, I was worried. I knew Mrs Ransom was getting better, and –

PF: How did you know that?

WD: First, I found out what hospital she was at by calling Shady Mount and saying I was Mrs Ransom's husband, and could they put me through to her room? See, I was going to keep calling hospitals until I got to the right one. I just started with Shady Mount because that's the one I knew best. On account of my mom. She worked there, did you know that?

PF: Yes.

WD: Good. So I called up and asked if they could put me through, and the switchboard lady said no, Mrs Ransom didn't have a phone, and if I was her husband I'd know that. Well, that was really dumb. If you wanted everybody to guess where she was right away, you put her in the right place. *Everybody* like Mrs Ransom goes to Shady Mount. My mom told me that when I was just a little boy, and it's still true. So I'm sorry to criticize you and everything, but you didn't even try to hide her. That's really sloppy, if you want my opinion.

PF: So you knew she was at Shady Mount, but how did you find out about her condition? And how did you learn her room number?

WD: Oh, those things were real easy. You know how I said that my mom used to work at Shady Mount? Well, sometimes, of course, she used to take me there with her, and I knew a lot of the people who worked in the office. They were my mom's friends – Cleota Williams, Margie Meister, Budge Dewdrop, Mary Graebel. They were a whole crowd. Went out for coffee and everything. When my mom died, I used to think that maybe I should kill

232

Budge or Mary so that she'd have company. Because dead people are just like you and me, they still want things. They look at us all the time, and they miss being alive. We have taste and color and smells and feelings, and they don't have any of those things. They stare at us, they don't miss *anything*. They really see what's going on, and we hardly ever really see that. We're too busy thinking about things and getting everything wrong, so we miss ninety percent of what's happening.

PF: I still don't know how you found out that –

WD: Oh, my goodness, of course you don't. Please forgive me! I'm really sorry. I was talking about my mom's friends, wasn't I? Really, my mouth should have a zipper on it, sometimes. Anyhow. Anyhow, as I was saying, Cleota died and Margie Meister retired and went to Florida, but Budge Dewdrop and Mary Graebel still work in the office at Shady Mount. Now Budge decided for some reason that I was a horrible person about the time my mother died, and she won't even talk to me anymore. So I think I *should* have killed her. After all, I saved her life! And she just turns her back on me!

PF: But your mother's other friend, Mary Graebel –

WD: She still remembers that I used to come in there when I was a little boy and everything, and of course I used to stop by the Shady Mount office every now and then and just chew the fat. So the whole thing was just as easy as pie. I stopped in on my lunch hour yesterday, and Mary and I had a nice long gabfest. And she told me all about their celebrity patient, and how she had a police guard and a private nurse, and how she was suddenly getting better up there on the third floor, and everything. And I could see fat old Budge Dewdrop fuming and fretting away all by herself over by the file cabinets, but Budge is too scared of me, I think, to do anything really *overt*. So she just gave us these *looks*, you know, these big *looks*. And I found out what I had to do.

233

PF: And this Mary Graebel told you that the private duty nurse took breaks every hour?

WD: No, I got lucky there. She was leaving the room just when I turned into the hallway. So I got in there fast. And I did it. Then I got out, fast.

PF: Tell me about the officer in the room.

WD: Well, I had to kill him, too, of course.

PF: Did you?

WD: What do you mean? Do you mean, did I really have to kill him or did I really kill him?

PF: I'm not really sure I follow that.

WD: I'm just – forget it. Maybe I don't remember the officer who was in the room very well. It's a little blurry. Everything had to happen very fast, and I was nervous. But I *know* I heard you tell someone that the officer from the hospital was dead. You were walking past the cells, and I overheard what you said. You said, 'He's dead.'

PF: I was exaggerating.

WD: Okay, so I was exaggerating too. When I said that I killed him.

PF: How did you *try* to kill the officer?

WD: I don't remember. It isn't clear. My mind was all excited.

PF: What happened to the hammer? You didn't have it when you came back to your house.

WD: I threw it away. I threw it into the river on my way back from the hospital.

PF: You threw it into the Millhaven River?

WD: From that bridge, the bridge right next to the Green Woman. You know, where they found that dead woman. The prostitute.

PF: What dead woman are we talking about now, Walter? Is this someone else you killed?

WD: God. You people don't remember *anything*. Of course she wasn't someone I killed, I'm talking about something that happened a long time ago. The woman

234

was the mother of William Damrosch, the cop. He was down there, too – he was a baby, and they found him on the riverbank, almost dead. Don't you ever *read*? This is all in *The Divided Man.*

PF: I'm not sure I know why you want to bring this up.

WD: Because it's what I was thinking about! When I was driving across the bridge. I saw the Green Woman Taproom, and I remembered what happened on the riverbank, the woman, the prostitute, and her poor little baby, who grew up to be William Damrosch. He was called Esterhaz in the book. I was driving across the bridge. I thought about the woman and the baby – I *always* think about them, when I drive over the river there, alongside the Green Woman Taproom. Because all that is connected into the Blue Rose murders. And they never caught that man, did they? He just got clean away. Unless you're dumb enough to think it was Damrosch, which I guess you are.

PF: Actually, I'm a lot more interested in you.

WD: Well, anyhow, I tossed the hammer right through the car window into the river. And then I drove right on home and met you. And I decided that it was time to tell the truth about everything. Time for everything to come out into the open.

PF: Well, we're grateful for your cooperation, Walter. I want to ask you about one detail before we break. You say that your mother's friend, her name was, let's see, her name was Budge Dewdrop, stopped talking to you after your mother's death. Do you have any idea why she did that?

WD: No.

PF: None? No idea at all?

WD: I told you! I don't have any idea.

PF: How did your mother die, Walter?

WD: She just died. In her sleep. It was very peaceful, the way she would have wanted it.

PF: Your mother would have been very unhappy if she

had discovered some of your activities, wouldn't she, Walter?

WD: Well, I suppose you could say that. She never liked it about the animals.

PF: Did she ever tell her friends about the animals?

WD: Oh, no. Well, maybe Budge.

PF: And she never knew that you had killed people, did she?

WD: No. Of course she didn't.

PF: Was she ever curious about anything that made you uneasy? Did she ever suspect anything?

WD: I don't want to talk about this.

PF: What do you think she said to her friend Budge?

WD: She never told me, but she must have said something.

PF: Because Budge acted like she was afraid of you.

WD: She should have been afraid of me.

PF: Walter, did your mother ever find one of your trophies?

WD: I said, I don't want to talk about this.

PF: But you said it was time for everything to come out into the open. Tell me what happened.

WD: What?

PF: You told me about the mother who was dead on the riverbank. Now tell me about your mother.

WD: (Inaudible.)

PF: I know this is hard to do, but I also know that you want to do it. You want me to know everything, even this. Walter, what did your mother find?

WD: It was a kind of diary. I used to hide it in a jacket in my closet – in the inside pocket. She wasn't snooping or anything, she just wanted to take the jacket to the cleaners. And she found the notebook. I had some things in there, and she asked me about them.

PF: What kind of things?

WD: Like initials. And some words like *tattoo* or *scar*.

Stuff like *red hair*. One of them said *bloody towel*. She must have talked to Budge Dewdrop about it. She shouldn't have!

PF: Did she ask you about the diary?

WD: Sure, of course. But I never thought she believed me.

PF: So she was suspicious before that.

WD: I don't know. I just don't know.

PF: Tell me how your mother died, Walter.

WD: It doesn't really matter anymore, does it? With all these other people, I mean.

PF: It matters to you, and it matters to me. Tell me about it, Walter.

WD: Well, this is what happened. It was the day after she found my diary. When she came home from work, she acted a little funny. I knew right away what it meant. She'd been talking to somebody, and she was guilty about that. I don't even know what she said, really, but I knew it had to do with the diary. I made dinner, like I always did, and she went to bed early instead of staying up and watching television with me. I was very distressed, but I don't think I showed it. I stayed up late, though I hardly understood what was going on in the movie, and I had two glasses of Harvey's Bristol Cream, which is something I *never* did. Finally the movie was over, even though I couldn't remember what happened in it. I only watched it for Ida Lupino, really – I always liked Ida Lupino. I washed my glass and turned off the light and went upstairs. I was just going to look in my mother's room before I went to bed. So I opened the door and went inside her room. And it was so dark in there I had to go up next to the bed to see her. I went right up next to her. And I said to myself, if she wakes up, I'll just say good night and go to bed. And I stood there next to her for a long time. I thought about everything. I even thought about Mr Lancer. If I hadn't had those two glasses of

Harvey's Bristol Cream, I don't think any of this would have happened.

PF: Go on, Walter. Do you have a handkerchief?

WD: Of course I have a handkerchief. I have a dozen handkerchiefs. It's okay, I mean, I'm okay. Anyhow, I was standing next to my, ah, my mother. She was really asleep. I didn't intend to do anything at all. And it didn't feel like I *was* doing anything. It was like nothing at all was happening. I leaned over and pulled the extra pillow over her face. And she didn't wake up, see? She didn't move at all. So nothing at all was happening. And then I just pushed down on the pillow. And I closed my eyes and I held the pillow down. And after a while I took it off and went to bed. In my own bedroom. The next morning, I made us both breakfast, but she wouldn't come when I said it was ready, so I went to her room and found her in her bed, and I knew right away that she was dead. Well, there it was. I called the police right from the bedroom. And then I went into the kitchen and threw away the food and waited until they came.

PF: And when the police came, what did you tell them about your mother's death?

WD: I told them she died in her sleep. And that was true.

PF: But not the whole truth, was it, Walter?

WD: No. But I hardly knew what the whole truth *was*.

PF: I can see that. Walter, we're going to take a break now, and I'm going to give you a couple of minutes to be by yourself. Will you be all right?

WD: Just let me be by myself for a while, okay?

12

Fontaine pushed back his chair and stood up. He nodded twice and turned away from Dragonette.

'Were you satisfied with that, Mr Ransom?' Wheeler asked. 'Is there any doubt in your mind as to the identity of your wife's murderer?'

'How could there be?' John asked.

Paul Fontaine saved me from speaking by opening the door and stepping inside the booth. 'I think that's all you'll have to watch, Mr Ransom. Go home and get some rest. If anything else turns up, we'll be in touch with you.'

'At least,' Wheeler said, 'you know why he killed your wife.'

'He killed her because he liked her,' Ransom said. 'She had the office next door to his broker's.' He sounded dumbfounded, almost stunned.

'That was good work, Paul,' Wheeler said, standing up.

We all stood up. Fontaine stepped out of the booth, and the rest of us followed him out into the light of the corridor.

'You did a number on him,' Monroe said.

Fontaine gave him a sad smile. 'I figure we'll have our charges ready by the end of the day. We have to get this one wrapped up with something more than our usual blinding speed, or the brass is going to have us cleaning toilets. I hate to admit this, but my getting Walter to admit that he killed his mother isn't going to mean anything to the lieutenant.'

'Well, McCandless didn't actually have a mother,' Monroe said. 'He came into the world via the Big Bang Theory.'

Fontaine stepped backward and regarded Wheeler and Monroe with mock horror. 'You two must have a couple of unsolved murders left to mull over.'

'There are no more unsolved murders in Millhaven,' said Monroe. 'Haven't you heard?'

He grinned at Ransom and me and turned away to walk back through the corridors to the Homicide office. Wheeler went with him.

'Seems you have another fan in Mr Dragonette,' Fontaine said to me.

'It's too bad he couldn't tell us who the original Blue Rose was, while he was telling us who he wasn't.'

Out of the interrogation room, Fontaine's skin appeared to be some shade halfway between yellow and green, like an old piece of lettuce.

'Did the new cases ever cause you to look up the records for the old ones?' I asked him.

'Blue Rose was way before my time.'

'Do you think I could look at those records?' He was staring at me, and I said, 'I'm still very curious about the Blue Rose case.'

'You do research for books *after* you write them?'

John Ransom turned ponderously toward me. 'What's the point?'

'Yes, what is the point, Mr Underhill?'

'It's a personal matter,' I said.

Fontaine blinked, twice, very slowly. 'Those records are a hot item. Well, since Mike Hogan is such an admirer of yours, we might be able to permit that breach of our normally fortresslike confidentiality. Of course, we have to *find* those records first. I'll let you know. Thank you for giving us your time, Mr Ransom. I'll be calling you as things progress.'

Ransom waved at him and began to move away toward the old part of the building.

Something else occurred to me, and I asked Fontaine

another question. 'Did you ever find out the name of the man was who was following John? The gray-haired man driving the Lexus?'

Fontaine pursed his lips. The lines around his eyes and mouth deepened, and the soft, saggy parts of his face seemed to get even more mournful. 'I forgot all about that,' he said. 'Do you think there's any point in – ?'

He smiled and shrugged, and it seemed to me that part of the meaning of all this courtesy was that, in some fashion or another, he had just lied to me. A second later, it seemed impossible that Fontaine would deceive me about such a trivial matter. I watched him walking back toward the interrogation room, hunched over in his shapeless suit. What he had done in the interrogation room had made me free again, but I did not feel free.

Fontaine looked sideways at a tall policeman who came out into the corridor holding a typed form and grabbed his elbow before he could get away. I remembered seeing the younger man at the hospital that morning.

'Sonny, will you see that these two gentlemen find their way downstairs to the parking lot? I'd do it myself, but I have to get back to an interrogation.'

'Yes, sir,' Sonny said. 'There must be a couple hundred people on the steps. How do they get those signs made so fast?'

'They don't have jobs.'

Sonny laughed and advanced toward us like Paul Bunyan moving in on a pine forest.

As we clanged down the metal stairs in the old part of the building, Sonny told John that he was sorry about his wife's death. 'The whole department's sorry,' he said. 'It was sort of like something you couldn't believe, when we first heard it in the car this morning. I was with Detective Fontaine, bringing that guy into the station.'

I asked, 'You were all in the car together when the report came in about Mrs Ransom?'

241

He turned around on the stairs and looked up at me. 'That's what I just said.'

'You were driving, and you could hear the report.'

'Clear as a bell.'

'What did it say?'

'For God's sake, Tim,' said John Ransom.

'I just want to know what the report said.'

'Well, the woman who called it in was pretty excited.' Sonny began moving more slowly down the stairs, gripping the handrail and looking back over his shoulder. 'She said that Mrs Ransom had been beaten to death in her room, excuse me, sir.'

'And did she say something about Officer Mangelotti?'

'Yeah, she said he was injured. She was new, and she must have been excited – she forgot to use the codes.'

'What the hell is this about, Tim? I don't want to know about this,' Ransom said. 'What difference does it make?'

'None, probably,' I said.

'Dragonette spilled the beans right away,' Sonny said. 'He told Fontaine, he says, If you guys had worked faster, you could have saved her, too. Fontaine says, Are you confessing to the murder of April Ransom, and he says, Of course. I killed her, didn't I?'

He got to the bottom of the stairs and strode down the corridor that had reminded me of an old grade school when I had pursued Paul Fontaine into the building. Now all of it felt tainted by what I had heard upstairs. The announcements and papers on the bulletin board looked like brutal jokes. GUNS FOR SALE GOOD | CHEAP. NEED A DIVORCE LAWYER WITH 20 YEARS POLICE EXPERIENCE? KARATE FOR COPS. Someone had already put up a yellow sheet with these words printed in block capitals at its top: PEOPLE WALTER DRAGONETTE SHOULD HAVE ASKED HOME. The name of Millhaven's mayor, Merlin Waterford, was first on the list.

'Here you go.' Sonny held the door to the parking lot

open with an outstretched arm and backed away so that he did not completely fill the frame. John Ransom squeezed past him grimacing, and I ducked through the space between the big cop and the frame. Sonny smiled down at me.

'Take it easy, now,' he said, and let the door close behind us.

All the cops standing around in the parking lot stared at us as we walked toward Ransom's car. The sides of the buildings around us, red brick and gray stone, leaned inward, and the watching policemen looked like caged animals. Everything was grimy with age and suppressed violence.

Ransom collapsed into the passenger seat. A few cops with cement faces started moving toward our car. I got in and started the engine. Before I could put it in gear, one of the cops appeared beside me and leaned in the open window. His face was very close to mine. Whiskey blotches burned on his fleshy cheeks, and his eyes were pale and dead. *Damrosch*, I thought. Two others stood in back of the car.

'You had business here?' he said.

'We were with Paul Fontaine,' I said.

'Were you.' It was not a question.

'This is John Ransom. The husband of April Ransom.'

The terrible face recoiled. 'Get out, get going.' He stood up and stepped back and waved me away. The cops behind the car melted away.

I drove through the jolting, pitted passage between the high municipal buildings and turned back out onto the street. Somewhere in the distance people were chanting. John Ransom sighed. I looked at him, and he leaned forward to switch on the radio. A bland radio voice said, '. . . accounts still coming in, and some of these are conflicting, but there seems to be little doubt that Walter Dragonette was responsible for a least twenty-five deaths.

243

Cannibalism and torture have been widely rumored. A spontaneous demonstration is now in progress in front of police head – '

Ransom punched a button, and trumpet music filled the car – Clifford Brown playing 'Joy Spring.' I looked at Ransom in surprise, and he said, 'The Arkham College radio station programs four hours of jazz every day.' He slumped back into his seat. He had just wanted to stop hearing about Walter Dragonette.

I turned the corner and drove past the entrance to Armory Place. Clifford Brown, dead for more than thirty years, uttered a phrase that obliterated death and time with a confident, offhand eloquence. The music nearly lifted me out of the depression Walter Dragonette had evoked. I remembered hearing the same phrase all those years ago in Camp Crandall.

Ransom turned his head to look at the big crowd filling half of Armory Place. Three times as many people as had been there earlier covered the steps of police head-quarters and the plaza. Signs punched up and down. One of them read VASS MUST GO. An amplified voice bawled that it was sick of living in fear.

I asked John Ransom who Vass was.

'Police chief,' he mumbled.

'Mind if we take a little detour?' I asked.

Ransom shook his head.

I left the yelling crowd behind me and continued on to Horatio Street, on the far side of the *Ledger* building and the Center for the Performing Arts. Horatio Street led us through a district given over to two-story brick ware-houses, gas stations, liquor stores, and two brave little art galleries that seemed to be trying to turn the area into another Soho.

Clifford Brown played on, and the sunlight dazzled off the glass windows and the tops of cars. Ransom sat back

244

in his seat without speaking, his right hand curled over his mouth, his eyes open but unseeing. At the entrance to the bridge, a sign announced that vehicles weighing over one ton were barred. I rolled across the rumbling old bridge and stopped on its far side. John Ransom looked as if he were sleeping with his eyes open. I got out and looked down at the river and its banks. Between high straight concrete walls, the black river moved sluggishly toward Lake Michigan. It was about fifteen or twenty feet deep and so dark that it would have been bottomless. Muddy banks littered with tires and rotting wooden crates extended from the concrete walls to the water.

Sixty years ago, this had been an Irish neighborhood, filled with the rowdy, violent men who had built roads and installed trolley tracks; for a brief time, the tenements had housed the men who worked in the warehouses across the river; for an even briefer time, students from Arkham and the local university campus had taken them over for their cheap rents. The crime they attracted had driven all the students away, and now these blocks were inhabited by people who threw their garbage and old furniture out onto the streets. The Green Woman Taproom had been affected by the same blight.

The tavern was a small two-story building with a slanting roof built on a concrete slab that jutted out over the river's east bank. Asymmetrical additions had been built onto its back end. Before the construction of Armory Place, the bar had been a hangout for civil servants and off-duty cops. During summers, hopeful versions of Irish food had been served at round white tables overlooking the river – 'Mrs O'Reilly's lamb shanks' and 'Paddy Murphy's Irish Stew.' Now the tables were gone, and spray-painted graffiti drooled across the empty concrete. SKUZ SUX. ROMI 22. KILL MEE DEATH. A Pforzheimer beer sign hung crookedly in a window zigzagged with strips of tape. On a bitter winter night, people had laughed and drunk in there while twenty feet away, someone murdered a woman holding an infant.

'Wasn't it a crazy story?' said a voice at my shoulder. Startled, I jumped and looked around to see John Ransom standing just behind me. The car gaped open at the side of the road. The two of us were alone in the sunny desolation. Ransom looked ghostly, insubstantial, his face bleached by the light and his pale clothing. For a second I thought he meant that William Damrosch's story was crazy, and I nodded.

'That lunatic,' he said, looking at the garbage strewn along the baked riverbank. 'He saw my wife in *his broker's office*.' He moved forward and stared down at the river. The black water was moving so slowly it seemed to be still. A shine coated it like a skin of ice.

I looked at Ransom. Some faint color had come back to his face, but he still looked on the verge of disappearing. 'To tell you the truth, I'm still bothered that he heard about April's murder before he confessed. And he didn't know that Mangelotti had been hit on the head with something instead of being stabbed.'

'He forgot. Besides, Fontaine didn't seem to mind.'

'That bothers me, too,' I said. 'Fontaine and Hogan want to get a lot of black marker on that board in the lounge.'

Ransom's face went white again. He moved back toward the car and sat down on the passenger seat. His hands were shaking. His whole face worked as he tried to swallow. He glanced up at me sidelong, as if he were checking to see if I were really taking all of this in. 'Could we get back to my house, please?'

He said nothing at all during the rest of the drive to Ely Place.

Inside, John pushed the playback button on his answering machine. Out of the harsh, dissolving sunlight, he looked more substantial, less on the verge of disappearance.

He straightened up when the tape had finished rewinding, and his eyes swam up to meet mine. The true lines of his face – the leaner, more masculine face I had seen years ago – rose through the cushion of flesh that had disguised them.

'One of those messages is from me,' I said. 'I called you here before going over to the hospital.'

He nodded.

I went through the arch into the living room and sat down on the couch facing the Vuillard painting. The first caller, I remembered, had left a message yesterday – Ransom had not been able to check his machine since we had left the house together yesterday afternoon. A tinny but clearly audible voice said, 'John? Mister Ransom? Are you home?' I leaned over the table and picked up one of the Vietnam books and opened it at random. 'I guess not,' the voice said. 'Ah, this is Byron Dorian, and I apologize for calling, but I really want to find out how, April, how Mrs Ransom is doing. Shady Mount won't even confirm that she's there. I know how hard this must be for you, but could you call me when you get back? It's important to me. Or I'll call you. I just want to hear something – not knowing is so hard. Okay. Bye.'

Another voice. 'Hello John, this is Dick Mueller. Everybody down at Barnett is wondering about April and hoping that there's been some improvement. We all sympathize completely with what you're going through,

John.' Ransom let go of an enormous sigh. 'Please give me a ring here at the office or at home to let me know the state of play. My home number is 474-0653. Hope to hear from you soon. Bye now.'

I bet the Meat Man's broker had gone through a queasy morning, once he sat down to his scrambled eggs with his copy of the *Ledger*.

The next call was mine from the St Alwyn, and I tried to block out that thicker, deeper, wheezier imitation of my real voice by focusing on the paintings in front of me.

Then a voice much deeper and wheezier than mine, erupted through the little speakers. 'John? John? What's going on? I'm supposed to be going on a *trip*. I don't understand – I don't understand where my daughter is. Can't you tell me something? Call me back or get over here soon, will you. Where the hell is *April*?' Loud breathing blasted through the tape hiss as the caller seemed to wait for an answer. 'Goddamn it anyhow,' he said, and breathed for another ten seconds. The caller banged the receiver on the body of the telephone a few times before he succeeded in hanging up.

'Oh, God,' Ransom said. 'Just what I need. April's father. I told you about him – Alan Brookner? Can you believe this? He's supposed to be teaching his course on Eastern Religions next year, as well as the course on the Concept of the Sacred that we do together.' He put his hands on top of his head, as if he were trying to keep it from exploding upward like a gusher, and wandered back through the arch.

I put the book back on the coffee table.

Still holding down the top of his head, Ransom released an enormous sigh. 'I guess I'd better call him back. We might have to go over there.'

I said that was okay with me.

'In fact, maybe I'll let you call back these other people,

too, after we're done with Alan.'

'Anything, fine,' I said.

'I'd better get back to Alan,' John said. He lowered his hands and returned to the telephone.

He dialed and then fidgeted impatiently during a long series of rings. Finally he said, 'Okay,' to me and turned to face the wall, tilting his head back. 'Alan, this is John. I just got your call . . . Yes, I can hear that . . . No, April isn't here, Alan, she had to go away. Look, do you want me to come over? . . . Sure, no problem, I'll be right there. Calm down, Alan, I'll be coming up the walk in a minute or two.'

He hung up and came back into the living room, looking so harassed that I wanted to order him to have a drink and go to bed. He had not even had breakfast, and now it was nearly two o'clock. 'I'm sorry about this, but let's get it over with,' he said.

'Aren't you going to drive?' I asked him when he went past the Pontiac and continued walking east on Ely Place.

'Alan only lives two blocks away, and even though we got lucky just now, you can never get a parking place around here. People are ready to kill each other for parking places.' He glanced back at me, and I sped up and joined him so that we were striding along together.

'A guy across from the hospital came out and yelled at me this morning for parking in front of his house,' I said. 'I guess I'm lucky he didn't shoot.'

Ransom grunted and jerked his thumb rightward as we got near the next corner. The collar of his white shirt was dark with moisture, and the front of his shirt stuck to his chest in amoeba-shaped damp patches.

'He was especially indignant because someone sat down on his lawn and then got up and headed for the hospital.'

Ransom gave me a startled look, like a deer spotting a

hunter in the forest. 'Well.' He looked forward again and plunged along. 'I'm sorry to put you through all this aggravation.'

'I thought Alan Brookner was a hero of yours.'

'He's been having a certain amount of trouble.'

'He doesn't even know that April was injured?'

He nodded and stuffed his hands in his pockets. 'I'd appreciate it if you'd sort of go along with me on this one. I can't tell him that April is dead.'

'Isn't he going to read it in the newspapers?'

'Not likely,' John said. 'This is it.'

The first house on the east side of the block was a substantial three-story red brick Georgian building with a fanlight over the door and symmetrical windows in decorative embrasures. Tall oak trees grew on the lawn, and the grass was wild and long, overgrown with knee-high weeds. 'I keep forgetting to have something done about the grass,' John said, sounding as if he wanted to asphalt the lawn. Rolls of yellowing newspaper in rubber bands peeked out of the weeds, some of them so weathered they looked like the artificial logs in gas fireplaces.

'It won't be too clean in there,' he told me. 'We hired a maid for him last year, but she quit just before April went into the hospital, and I haven't been . . .' He shrugged.

'Doesn't he ever go outside?' I asked.

Ransom shook his head and pounded on the door again, then flattened his hands over his face. 'He's having one of his *days*. I should have known.' He brought a heavy bunch of keys out of his pocket and searched through them before finding the one he inserted into the lock. He opened the door. 'Alan? Alan, I'm here, and I brought a friend.'

He stepped inside and motioned for me to follow him.

I waded through the unopened envelopes that littered the blue elephant-foot Persian rug in the entry. Untidy heaps of books and magazines covered all but a narrow footpath going up the bottom steps of a curving staircase. John stooped to pick up a handful of letters and carried them into the next room. 'Alan?' He shook his head in frustration and tossed the letters onto a brown leather chesterfield.

Large oil paintings of families arranged before English country houses hung on the long wall opposite me. Rows of books filled the other three walls, and unjacketed books lay over the larger rose-colored Indian carpet that rolled across the room. Splayed books, torn pages of typing paper, and plates of congealed fried eggs, curling slices of bread, and charred hot dogs covered the broad mantel and a wide leather-topped table in front of the chesterfield. All the lights burned. Something in the room made my eyes sting as if I'd been swimming in an overchlorinated pool.

'What a mess,' John said. 'Everything would be fine if the maid hadn't quit – look, he's been ripping up a manuscript.'

Big fluffy balls of gray dust fluttered away from his shoes. He pushed open a window set into the bookshelves on the side of the room.

I caught a faint but definite smell of excrement.

A big wheezy old man's baritone boomed out, 'John? Is that you, John?'

Ransom turned wearily to me and raised his voice. 'I'm downstairs!'

'Downstairs?' The old man sounded like he had a built-in megaphone. 'Did I call you?'

Ransom's face sagged. 'Yes. You called me.'

'You bring April with you? We're supposed to go on a *trip*.'

Footsteps came down the staircase.

'I don't know if I'm ready for this,' Ransom said.

'Who are you talking to? Grant? Is Grant Hoffman here?'

The footsteps reached the bottom of the stairs. John said, 'No, it's a friend of mine, not Grant Hoffman.'

An old man with streaming white hair and long, skinny arms and legs padded into the room wearing only a pair of underpants stained with successive layers of yellow. His knees and elbows looked too large for the rest of him, as big as boles on trees. White hair foamed from his skinny chest, and loose, gossamer hairs drifted around his neck and the underside of his chin. If he had not been hunched over, he would have been my height. A ripe, sour odor came in with him. His eyes were simian and very bright.

'Where's Grant?' he bellowed. 'I heard you talking to him.' The incandescent eyes focused on me, and his face closed like a clamshell. 'Who's this? Did he come for April?'

'No, Alan, this is my friend, Tim Underhill. April is out of town.'

'That's ridiculous.' The angry chimpanzee face swung back to scowl at Ransom. 'April would tell me if she went out of town. Did *you* tell me that she went out of town?'

'Several times.'

The old man walked up to us on his knotted stork's legs. His hair floated around his head. 'Well, I don't remember everything, I suppose. Friend of John's, are ye? You know my daughter?'

The odor increased as he got closer, and the stinging in my eyes got worse.

'I don't, no,' I said.

'Too bad. She'd knock your bobby sox off. You want a drink? A drink's what you need, if you're gonna tangle with April.'

'He doesn't drink,' John said. 'And you shouldn't have any more.'

'Come on in the kitchen with me, everything you need's in there.'

252

'Alan, I have to get you upstairs,' John said. 'You need to get cleaned up.'

'I had a shower this morning.' He jerked his head toward a door on the right-hand side of the room, grinning at me to let me know that we could cut loose in the kitchen if we got rid of this turkey. Then his face closed up again, and he gave John an unfriendly look. 'You can come in the kitchen too, if you tell me where April is. If you know. Which I doubt.'

He crunched my elbow in his bony claw and pulled at my arm.

'Okay, let's see what the kitchen is like,' John said.

'I don't drink to excess,' said Alan Brookner. 'I drink exactly the amount I want to drink. That's different. Drunks drink to excess.'

He tugged me across the room. Brown streaks and spatters had dried onto his legs.

'Ever meet my daughter?'

'No.'

'She's a pistol. Man like you would appreciate her.' He banged his forearm against the door in the wall of books, and it flew open as if on springs.

We were moving down a hallway lined with framed diplomas and awards and certificates. Among the awards were a few family photographs, and I saw a younger, robust Alan Brookner with his tweedy arm around a beaming blond girl only a few inches shorter than himself. They looked like they owned the world – confidence surrounded them like a shield.

Brookner went past the photograph without looking at it, as he must have done a dozen times every day. His smell was much more intense in the hallway. White fur like packed spiderwebs covered his bony shoulders. 'Get a good woman and pray she'll outlive you. That's the ticket.'

He thrust his way through another door and pulled me

into a cluttered junk pile of a kitchen before the door swung shut. The smell of rotting food helped mask Brookner's stench. The door swung back by itself and struck John Ransom, who said, 'Damn!'

'You ever think about damnation, John? Fascinating concept, full of ambiguity. In heaven we lose our characters in the perpetual glorification of God, but in hell we continue to be ourselves. What's more, we think we deserve damnation, and Christianity tells us our first ancestors cursed us with it, Augustine said that even Nature was damned, and – ' He dropped my arm and spun around. 'Now where the hell is that bottle? Those bottles, I should say.'

Empty Dewar's bottles stood against the splashboard of the sink counter, and a paper bag full of empty bottles stood beside the back door. Pizza delivery boxes lay strewn over the counters and tipped into the sink, where familiar brown insects roamed over and through them, scuttling across the crusty plates and upended glasses.

'Ask and ye shall receive,' Brookner said, fetching an unopened bottle of Scotch from a case beneath the sink. He slammed it down on the counter, and the roaches in the sink slipped inside the nearest pizza boxes. He broke the seal and twisted the cap off. 'Glasses up there,' he said to me, nodding at a cupboard near my head.

I opened the cupboard. Five highball glasses stood widely scattered on a shelf that could have held thirty. I brought down three and set them in front of Brookner. He looked a little like a disreputable Indian holy man.

'Oh, well, today I could use a drink,' Ransom said. 'Let's have one, and then we'll get you taken care of.'

'Tell me where April is.' Brookner gripped the bottle and glared at him out of his monkey face.

'April is out of town,' John said.

'Investment poo-bahs don't go dillydallying when their cutomers need them. Is she at home? Is she sick?'

254

'She's in San Francisco,' John said. He reached and took the bottle from his father-in-law the way a cop would take a handgun from a confused teenager.

'And what in Tophet is my daughter doing in San Francisco?'

Ransom poured half an inch of whiskey into a glass and gave it to the old man. 'Barnett is going to merge with another investment house, and there's been talk about April getting a promotion and running a separate office out there.'

'What's the other investment house?' Brookner drank all of the whiskey in two gulps. He held out his glass without looking at it. Liquid shone on his jutting lower lip.

'Bear, Stearns,' John said. He poured a good slug of whiskey into his own glass and slowly took a mouthful.

'She won't go. My daughter won't leave me.' He was still holding out his glass, and John poured another inch of whiskey into it. 'We were – we were supposed to go somewhere together.' He gestured at me with the bottle.

I shook my head.

'Go on, he wants one too, can't you see?'

Ransom twisted sideways, poured whiskey into the third glass, and handed it to me.

'Here's looking at you, kid,' Brookner said, and raised his glass to his mouth. He drank half of his whiskey and checked to see if I was still interested in having a good time.

I raised my glass and swallowed a tiny bit of the Scotch. It tasted hot, like something living. I moved away from the old man and set my glass on a long pine table. Then I noticed what else was on the table. 'Ta-ra-ra-boom-dee-ay,' Brookner boomed out in his disconcertingly healthy voice. 'All the whores are in luck today.' He sucked at his drink.

Next to my glass was a revolver and a stack of twenty-dollar bills that must have added up to at least four or five hundred dollars. Beside that was a stack of tens, just as high. A taller pile of fives stood beside that, and about a hundred singles lay in a heap like a pile of leaves at the end of the table. I made some sort of noise, and the old man turned around and saw what I was looking at.

'My bank,' he said. 'Worked it out myself. So I can pay the delivery boys. This way they can't cheat ya, get it? Make change lickety-split. The gun there is my security system. I grab it and watch them count it out.'

'Delivery boys?' John asked.

'From the pizza place, the one with the radio vans. And the liquor store. Generally I asks 'em if they'd like a little blast. Mostly they just take the money and run.'

'I bet they do,' John said.

'Uh-oh, my stomach feels bad.' The old man palped his stringy belly with his right hand. 'All of a sudden.' He groaned.

'Get upstairs,' John said. 'You don't want to have an accident in here. I'll come with you. You're going to have a shower.'

'I already had – '

'Then you'll have another one.' Ransom turned him around and pushed him through the swinging door.

Brookner bellowed about his stomach as they went up a second staircase at the back of the house. The loud voice went from room to room. I poured whiskey over the roaches, and they scampered back into the pizza boxes. When I got tired of watching them, I sat down next to the piles of money and waited. After a little while, I began stacking the pizza boxes and flattening them out so that I could squeeze them into the garbage can. Then I squirted soap over the heap of dishes in the sink and turned on the hot water.

14

About forty minutes later Ransom came back into the kitchen and stopped short when he saw what I was doing. His wide, pale face clouded over, but after a moment of hesitation, he pulled a white dish towel from a drawer and began wiping dishes. 'Thanks, Tim,' he said. 'The place was a mess, wasn't it? What did you do with all the *stuff* that was lying around?'

'I found a couple of garbage bags,' I said. 'There weren't all that many dishes, so I decided to take care of them while you hosed the old man down. Did he get sick?'

'He just complained a lot. I pushed him into the shower and made sure he used soap. He goes into these funny states, he doesn't remember how to do the simplest things. Other times, like when he was down here, he seems almost in control – not really rational, of course, but kind of on top of things.'

I wondered what the other times were like if I had seen Alan Brookner when he was on top of things.

We finished washing and drying the dishes.

'Where is he now?'

'Back in bed. As soon as he was dry, he passed out. Which is exactly what I want to do. Would you mind us getting out of here?'

I pulled the plug in the sink and wiped my hands on the wet towel. 'Did you ever figure out what that trip was that he kept talking about?'

He opened the kitchen door and fiddled with the knob so that the door would lock behind us when he closed it. 'Trip? April used to take him to the zoo, the museum, places like that. Alan isn't really up for any excursion, as you probably noticed.'

'And this was one of his good days?'

We went outside by the kitchen door and walked around the side of the house. The overgrown grass baked in the sunlight. One of the big oak trees had been split by lightning, and an entire side had turned black and leafless. Everything, house, lawn, and trees, needed care.

'Well, everything he said was coherent, as far as I remember. He would have been better if he hadn't been drinking for a couple of days.'

We came out of the tall grass onto the sidewalk and began walking back to Ely Place. Prickly little brown balls clung to my trousers like Velcro. I pulled fresh moist air into my lungs.

'He's supposed to teach next year?'

'He made it through last year with only a couple of funny episodes.'

I asked how old he was.

'Seventy-six.'

'Why hasn't he retired?'

John laughed – an unhappy bark. 'He's Alan Brookner. He can stay on as long as he wants. But if he goes, the whole department goes with him.'

'Why is that?'

'I'm the rest of the department.'

'Are you looking for a new job?'

'Anything could happen. Alan might snap out of it.'

We walked along in silence for a time.

'I suppose I ought to get him a new cleaning woman,' he said finally.

'I think you ought to start checking out nursing homes,' I told him.

'On my salary?'

'Doesn't he have money of his own?'

'Oh yes,' he said. 'I suppose there's some of that.'

258

15

When we got back to his house, Ransom asked me if I wanted something from the kitchen.

We went through a dining room dominated by a baronial table and into a modern kitchen with a refrigerator the size of a double bed and deep counters lined with two food processors, a pasta machine, a blender, and a bread maker. Ransom opened a cabinet and brought down two glasses from a crowded shelf. He shoved them one after the other into the ice-making contraption on the front of the refrigerator and filled them with silvery crescents of ice. 'Some kind of water? Soft drink?'

'Anything,' I said.

He swung open the refrigerator, took out a bottle of water with a picture of an iceberg on the label, broke the seal, and filled my glass. He handed me the glass, returned the bottle, and pulled bags of sliced meat and wrapped cheeses and a loaf of bread from the shelves. Mayonnaise, mustard in a stone crock, margarine, a head of romaine lettuce. He lined all of this up on the butcher block counter between us, and then set two plates and knives and forks beside them. Then he closed the refrigerator and opened the freezer door on shelves of frozen cuts of meat, a stack of frozen dinners, a big frozen pizza wedged in like a truck tire, and two shelves filled with bottles of vodka resting on their sides – Absolut Peppar and Citron; Finlandia; Japanese vodka; Polish vodka; Stolichnaya Cristal; pale green vodkas and pale brown vodkas and vodkas with things floating inside the bottles, long strands of grass, cherries, chunks of lemon, grapes. I leaned forward to get a better look.

He yanked out the Cristal, unscrewed the cap, and poured his glass half full. 'Really ought to chill the glass,' he mumbled, 'but it's not every day that your wife dies, and then you have to shove a seventy-six-year-old man into the shower and make sure he cleans off the shit smeared all over his legs.' He gulped down vodka and made a face. 'I practically had to climb in with him.' Another gulp, another grimace, another gulp. 'I did have to dry him off. That white hair all over his body – ugh. Sandpaper.'

'Maybe you should hire that nurse, Eliza Morgan, to spend at least the daytime with him.'

'You don't think my father-in-law seemed capable of caring for himself? I wonder what might have given you that impression.' John dropped more ice crescents into his glass and poured in another three inches of icy vodka. 'Anyhow, here's the sandwich stuff. Dig in.'

I began piling roast beef and swiss cheese on bread. 'Have you thought about how you'll tell him the truth about April?'

'The truth about April?' He set down his glass and almost smiled at me. 'No. I have not thought about that yet. Come to think of it, I'll have to tell a lot of people about what happened.' His eyes narrowed, and he drank again. 'Or maybe I won't. They'll read all about it in the paper.' Ransom set his glass back on the counter and rather absentmindedly began making a sandwich, laying a slice of roast beef on a piece of bread, then adding two slices of salami and a slice of ham. He peeled a strip from a slice of cheese and shoved it into his mouth. He stuck a spoon into the crock of mustard and stirred it aimlessly.

I put lettuce and mayonnaise on my own sandwich and watched him stir the mustard.

'What about funeral arrangements, a service, things like that?'

260

'Oh, yes,' he said. 'The hospital set up an undertaker.'

'Do you own gravesites, anything like that?'

'Who thinks about stuff like that, when your wife is thirty-five?' He drank again. 'I guess I'll have her cremated. That's probably what she would have wanted.'

'Would you like me to stay on here a few more days? I wouldn't mind if you wouldn't feel that I was intruding or becoming a burden.'

'Please do. I'm going to need someone to talk to. All this hasn't really hit me yet.'

'I'd be glad to,' I said. For a little while I watched him push the spoon around inside the grainy mustard. Finally he lifted it out and splatted mustard on his strange sandwich. He closed it up with a piece of bread.

'Was there any truth in what you told her father about her company's merger with the other brokerage house?' I asked him. 'It sounded so specific.'

'Made-up stories ought to be specific.' He picked the sandwich up and looked at it as if someone else had handed it to him.

'You made it all up?' It occurred to me that he must have invented the story shortly after April had been taken to the hospital.

'Well, I think something was, as they say, in the wind. Something was wafted here and there and everywhere, like dandelion seeds.' He put his sandwich down on the plate and lifted his glass and drank. 'You know the worst thing about people who do what April did, people in that kind of work? I don't mean April, of course, because she wasn't like that, but the rest of them? They were all absolutely full of hot air. They gab in their morning meetings, then they gab on the phone, then they gab to the institutional customers during lunch, then they gab some more on the phone – that's it, that's the job. It's all *talking*. They love *rumors*, God, do they love rumors. And the second-worst thing about these people is that they all believe every word every one of them says! So unless you are absolutely up-to-the-minute on all of this stupid, worthless gossip and innuendo they trade back and forth all day long, unless you already know what everybody is whispering into those telephones they're on day and night, you're out, boy, you are about to get *flushed*. People say that academics are unworldly, you know, people, especially these bullshit artists who do the kind of thing April did, they scorn us because we're not supposed to be in the real world? Well, at least we have real *subjects*, there's some intellectual and ethical content to our lives, it isn't just this big gassy bubble of spreading half-truths and peddling rumors and making *money*.'

He was breathing hard, and his face was a high, mottled pink. He drained the rest of his drink and immediately made another. I knew about Cristal. In just under ten minutes, John had disposed of about fifteen dollars' worth of vodka.

'So Barnett and Company wasn't really going to open a San Francisco office?'

'Actually, I have no real idea.'

I had another thought. 'Did she want to keep this house because it was so near her father's place?'

'That was one reason.' John leaned on the counter and lowered his head. He looked as if he wanted to lie down on the counter. 'Also, April didn't want to be stuck out in Riverwood with dodos like Dick Mueller and half the other guys in her office. She wanted to be closer to art galleries, restaurants, the, I don't know, the cultural life. You can see that, all you have to do is look at our house. We weren't like those dopes in the office.'

'Sounds like she would have enjoyed San Francisco,' I said.

'We'll never know, will we?' He gave me a gloomy look and bit into his sandwich. He looked down at it as he chewed, and his forehead wrinkled. He swallowed. 'What the hell is in this thing, anyhow?' He ate a little bit more. 'Anyhow, she would never have left Alan, you're right.' He took another bite. After he swallowed, he tilted his plate over the garbage can and slid most of the sandwich into it. 'I'm going to take this drink and go up to bed. That's about all I can face right now.' He took another long swallow and topped up his glass. 'Look, Tim, please do stay here for a little while. You'd be helping me.'

'Good,' I said. 'There is something I'd sort of like to look into, if I could stay around a couple of days.'

'What, some kind of research?'

'Something like that,' I said.

He tried to smile. 'God, I'm really shot. Maybe you could call Dick Mueller? He'd still be in the office, unless he's out at lunch somewhere. I hate to ask you to do this, but the people who knew April ought to be told what happened before they read it in the papers.'

'What about the other man who called? The one who didn't know whether to call you John or Mr Ransom?'

'Byron? Forget it. He can hear it on the news.'

He twirled his free hand in a good-bye and wavered out of the kitchen. I listened to him thudding up the stairs. His bedroom door opened and closed. When I had finished eating, I put my plate into the dishwasher and stowed all the lunch things back in the refrigerator.

In the quiet house, I could hear the cooled air hissing out of the vents. Now that I had agreed to keep John Ransom company, I was not at all certain about what I wanted to do in Millhaven. I went into the living room and sat down on the couch.

For the moment I had absolutely nothing to do. I looked at my watch and saw with more than surprise, almost with disbelief, that since I had staggered off the airplane and found an unrecognizable John Ransom waiting for me at the gate, exactly twenty-four hours had passed.

PART FIVE

Alan Brookner

1

A trio of reporters from the *Ledger* arrived about three in the afternoon. I told them that John was sleeping, identified myself as a family friend, and was told in return that they'd be happy to wait until John woke up. An hour later, the doorbell rang again when a Chicago deputation appeared. We had more or less the same exchange. At five, the doorbell rang once again while I was talking on the telephone in the entry. Gripping colorful bags of fried grease, notebooks, pens, and cassette recorders, the same five people stood on and around the steps. I refused to wake John up and eventually had to shake the telephone I was holding in the face of the most obstinate reporter, Geoffrey Bough of the *Ledger*. 'Well, can you help us out?' he asked.

Despite his name, which suggests a bulky middle-aged frame, a tweed jacket, and a tattersall vest, this Bough was a skinny person in his twenties with sagging jeans and a wrinkled chambray shirt. Forlorn black hair drooped over his thick eyeglasses as he looked down to switch on his tape recorder. 'Could you give us any information about how Mr Ransom is reacting to the news of his wife's death? Does he have any knowledge of how Dragonette first met his wife?' I shut the door in his face and went back to Dick Mueller, April Ransom's co-worker at Barnett and Company, who said, 'My God, what was that?' He spoke with an almost comically perfect Millhaven accent.

'Reporters.'

'They already know that, ah, that, ah, that . . .'

'They know,' I said. 'And it's not going to take them long to find out that you were Dragonette's broker, so you'd better start preparing.'

'Preparing?'

'Well, they're going to be very interested in you.'

'*Interested* in me?'

'They'll want to talk to everybody who ever had anything to do with Dragonette.' Mueller groaned. 'So you might want to figure out ways to keep them out of your office, and you might not want to enter or leave by the front door for a week or so.'

'Yeah, okay, thanks,' he said. He hesitated. 'You say you're an old friend of John's?'

I repeated information I had given him before Geoffrey Bough and the others had interrupted us. Through the narrow windows on either side of the front door I saw another car pull up and double-park in front of the house. Two men, one carrying a cassette recorder and the other a camera, slouched out and began walking toward the door, grinning at Bough and his two colleagues.

'How is John holding up?' asked Mueller.

'He had a couple of drinks and went to bed. He's going to have a lot to do over the next couple of days, so I think I'll stick around to help him out.'

Someone metronomically pounded his fist against the door four times.

'Is that John?' Mueller asked. He sounded worried, even alarmed.

'Just a gentleman of the press.'

Mueller gasped, imagining a gang bawling his name while pounding at the brokerage doors.

'I'll call you in the next few days.'

'When my secretary asks what you're calling about, tell her it's the bridge project. I'll have to start screening my

268

calls, and that'll remind me of who you are.'

'The bridge project?' More bawling and banging came through the door.

'I'll explain later.'

I hung up, opened the door, and began yelling. By the time I finished explaining that John was asleep in bed, my picture had been taken a number of times. I closed the door without quite slamming it. Through a slit of window I watched them retreat down to the lawn, munch on their goodies, and light up cigarettes while they worked out what to do. The photographers took a few desultory pictures of the house.

A quick check from the bottom of the stairs disclosed no movement upstairs, so John had managed either to sleep through the clamor or to ignore it. I picked up *The Nag Hammadi Library*, switched on the television, and sat on the couch. I turned to 'The Treatise on the Resurrection,' a letter to a student named Rheginos, and read only a few words before I realized that, like most of Millhaven, the local television had capitulated to Walter Dragonette.

I had been hoping that a combination of gnostic hugger-mugger and whatever was on the afternoon talk shows would keep me diverted until John surfaced again, but instead of Phil Donahue or Oprah Winfrey there appeared on the screen a news anchorman I remembered from the early sixties. He seemed almost eerily preserved, with the same combed-back blond hair, the same heavy brown eyeglasses, and the same stolid presence and accentless voice. With the air of unswerveable common sense I remembered, he was repeating, probably for the twentieth or thirtieth time, that regular programming had been suspended so that the All-Action News Team could 'maintain continuous reportage of this tragic story.' Even though I had seen this man read the evening news for years, I could not remember his name – Jimbo Somehow or Jumbo Somebody. He adjusted his glasses. The All-Action News Team would stay with events as they broke in the Walter Dragonette case until evening programming began at seven, giving us advice and commentary by experts in the fields of criminology and psychology, counseling us on how to discuss these events with our children, and trying in every way to serve a grieving community through good reportage by caring reporters. On a panel behind his face a mob of people occupying the middle of North Twentieth Street watched orange-clad technicians from the Fire Department's Hazardous Materials Task Force carry weighty drums out of the little white house.

Rheginos's teacher, the author of 'The Treatise on the Resurrection,' said 'do not think the resurrection is an illusion. It is the truth! Indeed, it is more fitting to say that the world is an illusion, rather than the resurrection.'

The news anchor slipped from view as the screen filled with a live shot of the multitude spilling across Armory Place. These people were angry. They wanted their innocence back. Jimbo explained: 'Already calls have been heard for the firing of the chief of police, Arden Vass, the dismissal of Roman Novotny, the police commissioner, and the fourth ward's aldermen, Hector Rilk and George Vandenmeter, and the impeachment of the mayor, Merlin Waterford.'

I could read the lettering on some of the signs punching up and down in rhythm to the crowd's chants: WHERE WERE YOU, MERLIN? and DISMEMBER HECTOR AND GEORGE. At the top of the long flight of marble steps leading to the front of police headquarters, a gray-haired black man in a dark double-breasted suit orated into a bull-horn. '. . . reclaim for ourselves and our children the safety of these neighborhoods . . . in the face of official neglect . . . in the face of official ignorance . . .' Seedy ghosts with cassette recorders, ghosts with dandruff on the shoulders of hideous purple shirts, with cameras and notebooks, with thick glasses sliding down their noses, prowled through the crowd.

A younger blond male head, as square as Jimbo's but attached to a sweating neck and a torso wrapped in a tan safari jacket, buried the speaker's words under the announcement that the Reverend Clement Moore, a longtime community spokesman and civil rights activist, had called for a full-scale investigation of the Millhaven Police Department and was demanding reparations for the families of Walter Dragonette's victims. Reverend Moore had announced that his 'protest prayer meetings' would continue until the resignations of Chief Vass, Commissioner Novotny, and Mayor Waterford. In a matter of days, the Reverend Moore expected that the protest prayer meetings would be joined by his fellow reverend, Al Sharpton, of New York City.

Back to you in the studio, Jimbo.

Jimbo tilted his massive blond head forward and intoned: 'And now for our daily commentary from Joe Ruddler. What do you make of all this, Joe?'

I perked up as another gigantic and familiar face crowded the screen. Joe Ruddler, another longtime member of the All-Action News Team, had been instantly celebrated for his absolute self-certainty and his passionate advocacy of the local teams. His face, always verging toward bright red and now a sizzling purple, had swollen to twice its earlier size. Ruddler had evidently been promoted to political commentary.

'What do I make of all this? I'll tell you what I make of this! I think it's a disgrace! What happened to the Millhaven where a guy could go out for a beer an' a bratwurst without stumbling over a severed head? And as for outside agitators – '

I used the remote to mute this tirade when the telephone rang.

As before, I picked it up to keep the ringing from

waking John Ransom, and as before, it was necessary to establish my identity as an old friend from out of town before the caller would reveal his own identity. But this time, I thought I knew the caller's name as soon as a hesitant voice asked, 'Mr Ransom? Could I speak to Mr Ransom?' A name I had heard on the answering machine came immediately into my mind.

I said that John was sleeping and explained why a stranger was answering his telephone.

'Oh, okay,' the caller said. 'You're staying with them for a while? You're a friend of the Ransoms?'

I explained that, too.

Long pause. 'Well, could you answer a question for me? You know what's happening with Mrs Ransom and everything, and I don't want to keep disturbing Mr Ransom. He never – I don't know if – . . .'

I waited for him to begin again.

'I wonder if you could just sort of fill me in, and everything.'

'Is your name Byron Dorian?'

He gasped. 'You've heard about me?'

'I recognize your style,' I said. 'You left a message on John's machine this morning.'

'Oh! Hah!' He gave a weak chuckle, as if he had caught me trying to amuse him. 'So, what's happening with April, with Mrs Ransom? I'd really like to hear that she's getting better.'

'Would you mind telling me your connection to the Ransoms?'

'My connection?'

'Do you work at Barnett?'

There came another uneasy laugh. 'Why, is something wrong?'

'Since I'm acting for the family,' I said, 'I just want to know who I'm talking to.'

'Well, sure. I'm a painter, and Mrs Ransom came to

my studio when she found out what sort of work I was doing, and she liked what she saw, so she commissioned me to do two paintings for their bedroom.'

'The nudes,' I said.

'You've seen them? Mrs Ransom liked them a lot, and that was really flattering to me, you've probably seen the rest of their collection, all that great work, you know, it was like having a patron, well, a patron who was a friend . . .'

His voice trailed off. Through one of the glass panels beside the front door I watched the reporters tossing crumpled candy bar wrappers toward the hedge. Five or six elderly people had taken up places on the steps and sidewalk across the street and settled in to enjoy the show.

'Well,' I said, 'I'm afraid I have bad news for you.'

'Oh, no,' said Dorian.

'Mrs Ransom died this morning.'

'Oh, no. Did she ever recover consciousness?'

'No, she didn't. Byron, Mrs Ransom did not die of her injuries. Walter Dragonette managed to find out that she was in Shady Mount and that her condition was improving, and he got past the guard this morning and killed her.'

'*On the day he got arrested?*'

I agreed that it seemed almost unbelievable.

'Well, what – what kind of *world* is this? What is going *on*? Did he *know* anything about her?'

'He barely knew her,' I said.

'Because she was, this was the most amazing woman, I mean there was so much *to* her, she was incredibly kind and generous and sympathetic – ' For a time I listened to him breathing hard. 'I'll let you go back to what you were doing. I just never thought – '

'No, of course not,' I said.

'It's too much.'

The reporters were gathering for another siege at the door, but I could not hang up on Byron Dorian while his grief pummeled him, and I peered out the slit of window while listening to his stifled moans and gasps.

When his voice was under control again, he said, 'You must think I'm really strange, carrying on like this, but you never knew April Ransom.'

'Why don't you tell me about her sometime?' I asked. 'I'd like to come to your studio and just have a talk.'

'That would probably help me, too,' he said, and gave me his phone number and an address on Varney Street, in the sad part of town, once a Ukrainian settlement, that surrounded the stadium.

I checked on the reporters, who had settled down to enjoy their third or fourth meal of the day under the appreciative eyes of a growing number of neighbors. Every now and then, some resident of Ely Place tottered through the litter to speak to Geoffrey Bough and his colleagues. I watched a bent old woman with a laden silver tray make her way down the steps of the house across the street, mount Ransom's lawn, and present the various lounging men with cups of coffee.

From my post by the door I saw Jimbo too retrace his steps, reminding his viewers of the extent and nature of Walter Dragonette's crimes, the public outcry, Mayor Waterford's assurances that all would continue to be done to ensure the safety of the citizens. At some point I did not quite mark as I kept watch on Bough and the others, April Ransom's murder passed into the public domain – so John too missed the appearance on the television screen of the *Ledger* photograph, minus himself, of his wife cradling a gigantic trophy. I know approximately when this happened, four o'clock, because at that time the gathering across the street suddenly doubled in size.

All afternoon, I alternated between watching television,

poking through the gnostic gospels, and peering out at the crowd and the waiting reporters. The faces of Walter Dragonette's victims paraded across the screen, from cowboy-suited little Wesley Drum on a rocking horse to huge leering Alfonzo Dakins gripping a beer glass. Twenty-two victims had been identified, sixteen of them black males. Hindsight gave their photographs a uniformly doomed quality. The unknown man found in Dead Man's Tunnel was represented by a question mark. April Ransom's *Ledger* photograph had been cropped down to her brilliant face. For the few seconds in which she filled the screen, I found that I was looking at the same person whose picture I had seen earlier, but that my ideas about her had begun to change: John's wife seemed smart and vibrant, not hard and acquisitive, and so beautiful that her murder was another degree more heartless than the others. Something had happened since the first time I had seen the photograph: I had become, like John, Dick Mueller, and Byron Dorian, one of her survivors.

A little while later, John came charging down the stairs. Wrinkles crisscrossed his shirt and trousers, and a long indentation from a sheet or pillowcase lay across his left cheek like a scar. He was not wearing shoes, and his hair was rumpled.

'What happened?' I asked.

'Some asshole threw stones at my window,' he said, and moved toward the door.

'Hold on,' I said. 'Did you look out the window before you came down? Do you know what's going on out there?'

'I don't care what's going on,' he said.

'Look,' I said, and pointed at the television. If he had bothered to look at the screen, he would have seen the façade of his own house from the perspective of his front lawn, where a good-looking young reporter with the strikingly literary name of Isobel Archer was doing a stand-up on the career of the Meat Man's most successful victim.

He shoved the door open.

Then for a second he froze, surprised by the camera, the reporters, and the crowd. It must have been like waking up to a bright light shining in his eyes. A low noise of surprise and pleasure came from the people assembled on the sidewalk and porches across the street. Ms Archer smiled and thrust a microphone into his face. 'Mr Ransom, what was your immediate reaction to the news that Walter Dragonette had made a second, successful attempt on your wife's life?'

'What?'

Geoffrey Bough and the others circled in, snapping pictures and holding their tape recorders in the air.

'Do you feel that Mrs Ransom was given adequate protection by the Millhaven Police Department?'

He turned around and looked at me in exasperation.

'What are your thoughts about Walter Dragonette?' Geoffrey Bough shouted. 'What can you tell us about the man?'

'I'd like you people to pack up and – '

'Would you call him sane?'

Other reporters, including Ms Archer, shouted other questions.

'Who's the man behind you?' Bough yelled.

'What's it to you?' John yelled back, pushed over the edge at last. 'You people throw rocks at my window, you ask these moronic questions – '

I moved alongside him, and cameras made popping gunfire noises. 'I'm a family friend,' I said. 'Mr Ransom has been through a great deal.' I could dimly hear my own voice coming through the television set behind me in the living room. 'All we can say now is that the case against Walter Dragonette, at least in regard to Mrs

Ransom, seems weaker than it should be.'

A confused tangle of shouted questions came from all the reporters, and Isobel Archer jammed her microphone under my nose and leaned forward so that her cool blue eyes and tawny hair were so close as to be disorienting. It was as if she were leaning forward for a kiss, but if I had kissed anything, it would have been the nubby head of the microphone. Her question was hard-edged and direct. 'So it's your position that Walter Dragonette did not murder Mrs Ransom?'

'No, I don't think he did,' I said. 'And I think the police will reject that portion of his confession, in time.'

'Do you share that view, Mr Ransom?'

The microphone expertly zipped in front of John's mouth. Ms Archer leaned forward and widened her eyes, coaxing words out of him.

'Get the hell out of here, right now,' John said. 'Take your cameras and your tape recorders and your sound equipment and get off my lawn. I have nothing more to say.'

Isabel Archer said, 'Thank you,' and then paused to smile at me. And that would have been that, except that something in the moment moved John a crucial step farther over the edge into outrage. The red wrinkle blazed on his cheek, and he started down the steps and went after the nearest male journalists, who happened to be Geoffrey Bough and his photographer. Isobel signaled to her own assistant, already swinging the camera toward John as he stiff-armed Bough exactly as he had stiff-armed me on the football field in the autumn of 1960.

The skinny reporter windmilled backward and went down with a howl of surprise. In the moment of shock that followed, John swung at Bough's photographer, who backed away while firing off a sequence of motor-driven pictures that appeared at the top of the next day's second section. John whirled away from him and rushed at the photographer from Chicago, who had prowled up beside him. John grasped the man's camera with one hand, his neck with the other, and bowled him over, snapping the camera's strap. John wound up like a pitcher and fired the camera toward the street. It struck a car and bounced off onto the concrete. Then he whirled on the man holding the Minicam.

Geoffrey Bough scrambled to his feet, and John turned away from the Minicam operator, who showed signs of a willingness to fight, and pushed Bough back down on the ground.

Reestablished in the middle of Ely Place, Isobel Archer held the microphone up to her American Sweetheart face and said something to the cameras that caused an outbreak of mirth among the assembled neighbors. John dropped his hands and stepped away from the scrambling, sputtering reporter. Bough jumped to his feet and followed the other reporters and camera people to the street. He brushed off his dirty jeans and inspected a grass stain on his right knee, missing the comparable stain on his right elbow. 'We'll be back tomorrow,' he said.

John raised his fists and began to charge. I grabbed his arm and pulled him back toward the steps – if he had not cooperated with me, I could not have held him. In the second or so that he resisted me, I knew that these days, for all his flab, John Ransom was considerably stronger than I was. We got up the steps and I opened the door. Ransom stormed inside and whirled around to face me.

'What the hell was that shit you were coming up with out there?'

'I don't think Dragonette killed your wife,' I said. 'I don't think he killed the man behind the St Alwyn, either.'

'Are you *crazy*?' Ransom stared at me as if I had just betrayed him. 'How can you say that? Everybody knows he killed April. We even heard him *say* he killed April.'

278

'I was thinking about everything while you were upstairs, and I realized that Dragonette didn't know enough about these murders to have done them. He doesn't even know what happened.'

He glared at me for a moment and then turned away in frustration and sat down on the couch and took in what the local TV stations were doing. Isobel Archer gloated beautifully into the camera and said, 'And so a startling new development in the Dragonette story, as a friend of the Ransom family casts doubt on the police case here.' She raised a notebook to just within camera range. 'We will have tape on this as soon as possible, but my notes show that the words were: "I don't think he did it. I think the police will reject that portion of his confession, in time."' She lowered the notebook, and an audible *pop!* whisked her into darkness and silence.

Ransom slammed the remote onto the table. 'Don't you get it? They're going to start blaming me.'

'John,' I said, 'why would Dragonette interrupt his busy little schedule of murder and dismemberment at home to reenact the Blue Rose murders? Don't they sound like two completely different types of crime? Two different kinds of mind at work?'

He looked sourly at me. 'That's why you went out there and threw raw meat to those animals?'

'Not exactly.' I went to the couch and sat down beside him. Ransom looked at me suspiciously and moved a few inches away. He began rearranging the Vietnam books into neater, lower stacks. 'I want to know the truth,' I said.

He grunted. 'What actual reasons do you have for thinking that Dragonette isn't guilty? The guy seems perfect to me.'

'Tell me why.'

'Okay.' Ransom, who had been slouching back against the couch, sat up straight. 'One. He confessed. Two. He's

279

crazy enough to have done it. Three. He knew April from his visits to the office. Four. He always liked the Blue Rose murders, just like you. Five. Could there really be two people in Millhaven who are crazy enough to do it? Six. Paul Fontaine and Michael Hogan, who happen to be very good cops and who have put away lots of killers, think the guy is guilty. Fontaine might be a little weird sometimes, but Hogan is something else – he's one smart, powerful guy. I mean, he reminds me of the best guys I knew in the service. There's no bullshit about Hogan, none.'

I nodded. Like me, John had been impressed by Michael Hogan.

'And last, what is it, seven? Seven. He could find out all about April and her condition from his mother's old pal Betty Grable at the hospital.'

'I think it was Mary Graebel, different spelling,' I said. 'And you're right, he did find out April was at Shady Mount. When I came down in the elevator with Fontaine this morning, an old lady working behind the counter almost passed out when she saw us. I bet that was Mary Graebel.'

'She knew she helped kill April,' John said. 'The cow couldn't keep her mouth shut.'

'She thought she helped her old friend's son kill April. That's different.'

'What makes you so sure he didn't?'

'Dragonette claimed that he couldn't remember anything he had done to that cop in April's room, Mangelotti. He overheard Fontaine joking that Mangelotti was dead – so he claimed that he had murdered him. Then Fontaine said he was exaggerating, so Dragonette said he was exaggerating, too!'

'He's playing mind games,' John said.

'He didn't know what happened to Mangelotti. Also, he had no idea that April had been killed until he heard

280

it over the police radio. That was the point that always bothered me.'

'Why would he confess if he didn't do it? That still doesn't make sense.'

'Maybe you didn't notice, but Walter Dragonette is not the most sensible man in the world.'

Ransom leaned forward and stared down at the floor for a time, considering what I had been saying. 'So there's another guy out there.'

I saw a mental picture of those drawings where the eye wanders over the leaves of an oak tree until the dagger leaps out of concealment, and the brickwork on the side of a house reveals a running man, a trumpet, an open door.

'You and your brainstorms.' He shook his head, now almost smiling. 'I'm going to have to live with the repercussions of shoving that reporter around.'

'What do you think they'll be?'

He shifted one of the stacks of novels sideways half an inch, back a quarter-inch. 'I suppose my neighbors are more convinced than ever that I killed my wife.'

'Did you, John?' I asked him. 'This is just between you and me.'

'You're asking me if I killed April?'

His face heated as before, but without the violence I had seen in him just before he had gone after Geoffrey Bough. He stared at me, trying to look intimidating. 'Is this something Tom Pasmore asked you to say?'

I shook my head.

'The answer is no. If you ask me that once more, I'll throw you out of this house. Are you satisfied?'

'I had to ask,' I said.

2

For the next two days, John Ransom and I watched the city fall apart on local television. When we were inside his house, we ignored the knot of reporters, varying from a steady core of three to a rumbling mob of fifteen, occupying his front lawn. We also ignored their efforts to lure us outside. They rang the bell at regular intervals, pressed their faces against the windows, yelled his name or mine with doglike repetitiveness . . . Every hour or so, either John or I would get up from the day's fifth, sixth, or fifteenth contemplation of the names and faces of the victims to check the enemy through the narrow window slits on either side of the door. It felt like a medieval siege, plus telephones.

We ate lunch in front of the set; we ate dinner in front of the set.

Someone banged imperiously on the front door. Someone else fingered open the mail slot and yelled, 'Timothy Underhill! Who killed April Ransom?'

'Who killed Laura Palmer?' muttered Ransom, mostly to himself.

This was on the day, Saturday, that Arkham's dean of humanities had left a message on the answering machine that Arkham's trustees, board of visitors, and alumni society had registered separate complaints about the televised language and behavior of the religion department's Professor Ransom. Would Professor Ransom please offer some assurance that all legal matters would be concluded by the beginning of the fall term? And it followed our struggles back and forth through the mob on our way to Trott Brothers Funeral Parlor.

So he wasn't doing too badly, considering everything. The worst aspect of our experience at Trott Brothers had been the manner of Joyce 'Just call me Joyce' Trott Brophy, the daughter and only child of the single remaining Mr Trott. Just Call Me Joyce made the reporters seem genteel. Obese and hugely pregnant, professionally oblivious to grief, she had long ago decided that the best way to meet the stricken people life brought her way was with the resolute self-involvement she would have called 'common sense.'

'We're doing a beautiful job on your little lady, Mr Ransom, you're going to say she looks as beautiful as she did on her wedding day. This here coffin is the one I'm recommending to you for display purposes during the service, we can talk about the urn later, we got some real beauties, but look here at this satin, plump and firm and shiny as you can get it – be the perfect frame around a pretty picture, if you don't mind my saying so. You wouldn't believe the pains I get carrying this baby back and forth around this showroom, boy, if Walter Dragonette showed up here he'd get two for the price of one, that'd give my daddy the job of his life, wouldn't it, by golly, that's gas this time. You ever get those real bad gas pains? I better sit down here while you and your friend talk things over, just don't pay any attention to me, Lord, I heard everything anyhow, people hardly know what they're saying when they come in here.'

We had at least two hours of Just Call Me Joyce, which demonstrated once again that when endured long enough, even the really horrible can become boring. In that time John rented the 'display' coffin, ordered the funeral announcements and the obituary notice, booked time at the crematorium, bought an urn and a slot in a mausoleum, secured the 'Chapel of Rest' and the services of a nondenominational minister for the memorial service, hired a car for the procession to the mausoleum, ordered flowers, commissioned makeup and a hairdo for the departed, bought an organist and an organ and ninety minutes' worth of recorded classical music, and wrote a check for something like ten thousand dollars. 'Well, I sure do like a man who knows what he wants,' said Just Call Me Joyce. 'Some of these folks, they come in here and dicker like they thought they could take it with them when they go. Let me tell you, I been there, and they can't.'

'You've been there?' I asked.

'Everything that happens to you after you're dead, I been there for it,' she said. 'And anything you want to know about, I can tell you about it.'

'I guess we can go home now,' Ransom said.

Early in the evening, Ransom was seated in the darkening room, staring at its one bright spot, the screen, which once again gave a view of the chanting crowd at Armory Place. I thought about Just Call Me Joyce and her baby. Someday the child would take over the funeral home. I saw this child as a man in his mid-forties, grinning broadly and pressing the flesh, slamming widowers on the back, breaking the ice with an anecdote about trout fishing, Lordy that was the biggest ole fish anybody ever pulled out of that river, oof, there goes my sciatica again, just give me a minute here, folks.

A door in my mind clicked open and let in a flood of light, and without saying anything to Ransom, I went back upstairs to my room and filled about fifteen sheets of the legal pad I had remembered at the last minute to slip into my carry-on bag. All by itself, my book had taken another stride forward.

3

What had opened the door into the imaginative space was the collision of Walter Dragonette with the certainty that Just Call Me Joyce's child would be just like his mother. When I had arrived at Shady Mount that morning, I'd had an idea which April Ransom's death had erased – but everything since then had secretly increased the little room of my idea, so that by the time it came back to me through imagination's door, it had grown into an entire wing, with its own hallways, staircases, and windows.

I saw that I could use some of Walter Dragonette's life while writing about Charlie Carpenter's childhood. Charlie had killed other people before he met Lily Sheehan: a small boy, a young mother, and two or three other people in the towns where he had lived before he had come back home. Millhaven would be Charlie's hometown, but it would have another name in the book. Charlie's deeds were like Walter Dragonette's, but the circumstances of his childhood were mine, heightened to a terrible pitch. There would be a figure like Dragonette's Mr Lancer. My entire being felt a jolt as I saw the huge head of Heinz Stenmitz lower itself toward mine – pale blue eyes and the odor of bloody meat.

During Charlie's early childhood, his father had killed several people for no better motive than revenge, and the five-year-old Charlie had taken his father's secret into himself. If I described everything through Charlie's eyes, I could begin to work out what could make someone turn out like Walter Dragonette. The *Ledger* had tried to do that, clumsily, by questioning sociologists, priests, and policemen; and it was what I had been doing when I put the photograph of Ted Bundy's mother up on my refrigerator.

For the second time that day, my book bloomed into life within me.

I saw five-year-old Charlie Carpenter in my old bedroom on South Sixth Street, looking at the pattern of dark blue roses climbing the paler blue wallpaper in a swirl of misery and despair as his father beat up his mother. Charlie was trying to *go into* the wallpaper, to escape into the safe, lifeless perfection of the folded petals and the tangle of stalks.

I saw the child walking along Livermore Avenue to the Beldame Oriental, where in a back row the Minotaur waited to yank him bodily into a movie about treachery and arousal. Reality flattened out under the Minotaur's instruction – the real feelings aroused by the things he did would tear you into bloody rags, so you forgot it all. You cut up the memory, you buried it in a million different holes. The Minotaur was happy with you, he held you close and his hands crushed against you and the world died.

Because columns of numbers were completely emotionless, Charlie was a bookkeeper. He would live in hotel rooms because they were impersonal. He would have recurring dreams and regular habits. He would never sleep with a woman unless he had already killed her, very carefully and thoroughly, in his head. Once every couple of months, he would have quick, impersonal sex with men, and maybe once a year, when he had allowed himself to drink too much, he would annoy some man he picked up in a gay bar by babbling hysterical baby talk while rubbing the stranger's erection over his face.

Charlie had been in the service in Vietnam.

He would kill Lily Sheehan as soon as he got into her lake house. That was why he stole the boat and let it drift into the reeds, and why he showed up at Lily's house so early in the morning.

I had to go back through the first third of the novel and insert the changes necessary to imply the background that I had just invented for Charlie. What the reader saw of him – his bloodless affection for his boring job, his avoidance of intimacy – would have sinister implications. The reader would sense that Lily Sheehan was putting herself in danger when she began her attempts to lure Charlie into the plot that had reminded me of Kent Smith and Gloria Grahame. You, dear heart, dear Reader, you without whom no book exists at all, who had begun reading what appeared to be a novel about an innocent lured into a trap would gradually sense that the woman who was trying to manipulate the innocent was going to get a nasty surprise.

The first third of the book would end with Lily Sheehan's murder. The second third of the book would be the account of Charlie's childhood – and it came to me that the child-Charlie would have a different name, so that at first you, dear Reader, would wonder why you were suddenly following the life of a pathetic child who had no connection to the events of the book's first two hundred pages! This confusion would end when the child, aged eighteen, enlisted in the army under the name Charles Carpenter. Charlie's capture would take up the final third.

The title of this novel would be *The Kingdom of Heaven*, and its epigraph would be the verses from the Thomas gospel I had read in Central Park.

The inner music of *The Kingdom of Heaven* would be the search for the Minotaur. Charlie would have returned to Millhaven (whatever it was called in the book) because, though he had only the most partial glimpse of this, he wanted to find the man who had abused him in the Beldame Oriental. Memories of the Minotaur would

haunt his life and the last third of the book, and once –
without quite knowing why – he would visit the shell of
the theater and have an experience similar to mine of
yesterday morning.

The Minotaur would be like a fearsome God hidden at
the bottom of a deep cave, his traces and effects scattered
everywhere through the visible world.

Then I had a final insight before going back downstairs.
The movie five-year-old Charlie Carpenter was watching
when a smiling monster slid into the seat next to his was
From Dangerous Depths. It did not matter that I had
never seen it – though I *could* see it, if I stayed in
Millhaven long enough – because all I needed was the
title.

Now I needed a reason for a child so young to be sent
to the movies on several days in succession, and that too
arrived as soon as I became aware of its necessity. Young
Charlie's mother lay dying in the Carpenter house. Again
the necessary image surged forward out of the immediate
past. I saw April Ransom's pale, bruised, unconscious
body stretched out on white sheets. A fresh understanding
arrived with the image, and I knew that Charlie's father
had beaten his wife into unconsciousness and was letting
her die. For a week or more, the little boy who grew up
to be Charlie Carpenter had lived with his dying mother
and the father who killed her, and during those terrible
days he had met the Minotaur and been devoured.

I put down my pen. Now I had a book, *The Kingdom of
Heaven*. I wanted to wrap it around me like a blanket. I
wanted to vanish into the story as little Charlie (not yet
named Charlie) yearned to melt into the blue roses
twining up the paler blue background of my bedroom
wallpaper – to become the twist of an elm leaf on
Livermore Avenue, the cigarette rasp of a warm voice in
the darkness, the gleam of silver light momentarily seen

on a smooth dark male head, the dusty shaft of paler light speeding toward the screen in a nearly empty theater.

4

With two exceptions, the weekend went by in the same fashion as the preceding days. At Ransom's suggestion, I brought my manuscript and new notes downstairs to the dining room table, where I happily chopped paragraphs and pages from what I had written, and using a succession of gliding Blackwing pencils sharpened to perfect points in a clever little electric mill, wrote the new pages about Charlie's childhood on a yellow legal pad.

Ransom did not mind sharing the legal pad, the electric sharpener, and the Blackwings, but the idea that I might want to spend a couple of hours working every day alternately irritated and depressed him. This problem appeared almost as soon as he had helped me establish myself on the dining room table.

He looked suspiciously at the pad, the electric sharpener, my pile of notes, the stack of pages. 'You had another brainstorm, I suppose?'

'Something like that.'

'I suppose that's good news, for you.'

He returned to the living room so abruptly that I followed him. He dropped onto the couch and stared at the television.

'John, what's the matter?'

He would not look at me. It occurred to me that he had probably acted like this with April, too. After a considerable silence, he said, 'If all you're going to do is work, you might as well be back in New York.'

Some people assume that all writing is done in between

drinks, or immediately after long walks through the Yorkshire dales. John Ransom had just put himself in this category.

'John,' I said, 'I know that this is a terrible time for you, but I don't understand why you're acting this way.'

'What way?'

'Forget it,' I said. 'Just try to keep in mind that I am not rejecting you personally.'

'Believe me,' he said, 'I'm used to being around selfish people.'

John didn't speak to me for the rest of the day. He made dinner for himself, opened a bottle of Chateau Petrus, and ate the dinner and drank the bottle while watching television. When the Walter Dragonette show ceased for the day, he surfed through the news programs; when they were over, he switched to CNN until 'Nightline' came on. The only interruption came immediately after he finished his meal, when he carried his wineglass to the telephone, called Arizona, and told his parents that April had been murdered. I was back in the dining room by that time, eating a sandwich and revising my manuscript, and was sure that Ransom knew that I could overhear him tell his parents that an old acquaintance from the service, the writer Tim Underhill, had come 'all the way from New York to help me deal with things. You know, handling phone calls, dealing with the press, helping me with the funeral arrangements.' He ended the conversation by making arrangements for picking them up from the airport. After 'Nightline,' Ransom switched off the set and went upstairs.

The next morning I went out for a quick walk before the reporters arrived. When I came back, Ransom rushed out of the kitchen and asked if I'd like a cup of coffee. Some eggs, maybe? He thought we ought to have breakfast before we went to his father-in-law's house to break the news.

Did he want me to come along while he told Alan? Sure he did, of course he did – unless I'd rather stay here and work. Honestly, that would be okay, too.

Either I wasn't selfish anymore, or he had forgiven me. The sulky, silent Ransom was gone.

'We can leave by the back door and squeeze through a gap in the hedges. The reporters'll never know we left the house.'

'Is there something I don't know about?' I asked.

'I called the dean at home last night,' he said. 'He finally understood that I couldn't promise to have everything settled by September. He said he'd try to calm down the trustees and the board of visitors. He thinks he can get some sort of vote of confidence in my favor.'

'So your job is safe, at least.'

'I guess,' he said.

The second exceptional event of the weekend took place before our visit with Alan Brookner. John came back into the kitchen while I was eating breakfast to report that Alan seemed to be having another one of his 'good' days and was expecting us within the next half hour. 'He's mixing Bloody Marys, so at least he's in a good mood.'

'Bloody Marys?'

'He made them for April and me every Sunday – we almost always went to his place for brunch.'

'Did you tell him why you wanted to see him?'

'I want him relaxed enough to understand things.'

The bell buzzed, and fists struck the door. A dimly audible voice asked that John open up, please. The hound pack was not usually so polite.

'Let's get out of here,' John said. 'Check the front to make sure they're not sneaking around the house.'

The phone started ringing as soon as I passed under the arch. A fist banged twice on the door, and a voice called,

'Police, Mr Ransom, please open up, we want to talk to you.'

The men at the door peered in through separate windows, and I found myself looking directly into the face of Detective Wheeler. The smirking, mustached head of Detective Monroe appeared at the window on the other side of the door. Monroe said, 'Open up, Underhill.'

Paul Fontaine's voice spoke through the answering machine. 'Mr Ransom, I am told that you are ignoring the presence of the detectives at your door. Don't be bad boys, now, and let the nice policemen come inside. After all, the policeman is your – '

I opened the door, beckoned in Monroe and Wheeler, and snatched up the phone. 'This is Tim Underhill,' I said into the receiver. 'We thought your men were reporters. I just let them in.'

'The policeman is your *friend*. Be good boys and talk to them, will you?' He hung up before I could reply.

John came steaming out from the hall into the living room, already pointing at our three dark shapes in the foyer. 'I want those people out of here *right now*, you hear me?' He charged forward and then abruptly stopped moving. 'Oh. Sorry.'

'That's fine, Mr Ransom,' said Wheeler. Both detectives went about half of the distance across the living room. When John did not come forward to meet them, they gave each other a quick look and stopped moving. Monroe put his hands in his pockets and gave the paintings a long inspection.

John said, 'You sat in the booth with us.'

'I'm Detective Wheeler, and this is Detective Monroe.' Monroe's mouth twitched into an icy smile.

'I guess I know why you're here,' John said.

'The lieutenant was a little surprised by your remarks the other day,' said Wheeler.

'I didn't say anything,' John said. 'It was him. If you

want to be specific about it.' He crossed his arms in front of his chest, propping them on the mound of his belly.

'Could we all maybe sit down, please?' asked Wheeler.

'Yeah, sure,' said John, and uncrossed his arms and made a beeline for the nearest chair.

Monroe and Wheeler sat on the couch, and I took the other chair.

'I have to see April's father,' John said. 'He still doesn't know what happened.'

Wheeler asked, 'Would you like to call him, Mr Ransom, tell him you'll be delayed?'

'It doesn't matter,' John said,

Wheeler nodded, 'Well, that's up to you, Mr Ransom.' He flipped open a notebook.

John squirmed like a schoolboy in need of the bathroom. Wheeler and Monroe both looked at me, and Monroe gave me his frozen smile again and took over.

'I thought you were satisfied with Dragonette's confession.'

Ransom exhaled loudly and slumped back against the couch.

'For the most part, I was, at least then.'

'So was I,' John put in.

'Did you have questions about Dragonette's truthfulness during the interrogation?'

'I did,' I said, 'but even before that I had some doubts.'

Monroe glared at me, and Wheeler said, 'Suppose you tell us about these doubts.'

'My doubts in general?'

He nodded. Monroe rocked back in his chair, jerked his jacket down, and gave me a glare like a blow.

I told them what I had said to John two days earlier, that Dragonette's accounts of the attacks on the unidentified man and Officer Mangelotti had seemed improvised and unreal to me. 'But more than that, I think his whole confession was contaminated. He only started talking

293

about John's wife after he heard a dispatcher say that she had just been killed.'

Monroe said, 'Suppose you tell us where this fairy tale about Dragonette and the dispatcher comes from.'

'I'd like to know the point of this visit,' I said.

For a moment the two detectives said nothing. Finally Monroe smiled at me again. 'Mr Underhill, do you have any basis for this claim? You weren't in the car with Walter Dragonette.'

John gave me a questioning look. He remembered, all right.

'One of the officers in the car with Dragonette told me what happened,' I said.

'That's incredible,' said Monroe.

'Could you tell me who was in the car with Walter Dragonette when that call from the dispatcher came in?' asked Wheeler.

'Paul Fontaine and a uniformed officer named Sonny sat in the front seat. Dragonette was handcuffed in the back. Sonny heard the dispatcher say that Mrs Ransom had been murdered in the hospital. Dragonette heard it, too. And then he said, "If you guys had worked faster, you could have saved her, you know." And Detective Fontaine asked if he were confessing to the murder of April Ransom, and Dragonette said that he was. At that point, he would have confessed to anything.'

Monroe leaned forward. 'What are you trying to accomplish?'

'I want to see the right man get arrested,' I said.

He sighed. 'How did you ever meet Sonny Berenger?'

'I met him at the hospital, and again after the interrogation.'

'I don't suppose anybody else heard these statements.'

'One other person heard them.' I did not look at John. I waited. The two detectives stared at me. We all sat in silence for what seemed a long time.

'I heard it, too,' John finally said.

'There we go,' said Wheeler.

'There we go,' said Monroe. He stood up. 'Mr Ransom, we'd like to ask you to come down to Armory Place to go over what happened on the morning of your wife's death.'

'Everybody knows where I was on Thursday morning.' He looked confused and alarmed.

'We'd like to go over that in greater detail,' Monroe said. 'This is normal routine, Mr Ransom. You'll be back here in an hour or two.'

'Do I need a lawyer?'

'You can have a lawyer present, if you insist.'

'Fontaine changed his mind,' I said. 'He went over the tape, and he didn't like that flimsy confession.'

The two detectives did not bother to answer me. Monroe said, 'We'd appreciate your cooperation, Mr Ransom.'

Ransom turned to me. 'Do you think I should call a lawyer?'

'I would,' I said.

'I don't have anything to worry about.' He turned from me to Wheeler and Monroe. 'Let's get it over with.'

The three of them stood up, and, a moment later, so did I.

'Oh, my God,' John said. 'We were supposed to see Alan.'

The two cops looked back and forth between us.

'Will you go over there?' John asked. 'Explain everything, and tell him I'll see him as soon as I can.'

'What do you mean, explain everything?'

'About April,' he said.

Monroe smiled slowly.

'Don't you think you ought to do that yourself?'

'I would if I could,' John said. 'Tell him I'll talk to him as soon as I can. It'll be better this way.'

'I doubt that,' I said.

He sighed. 'Then call him up and tell him that I had to go in for questioning, but that I'll come over as soon as I can this afternoon.'

I nodded, and the detectives went outside with John. Geoffrey Bough and his photographer trotted forward, expectant as puppies. The camera began firing with the clanking, heavy noise of a round being chambered. When Monroe and Wheeler assisted Ransom into their car, not neglecting to palm the top of his head and shoehorn him into the backseat, Bough looked back at the house and bawled my name. He started running toward me, and I closed and locked the door.

The bell rang, rang, rang. I said, 'Go away.'

'Is Ransom under arrest?'

When I said nothing, Geoffrey flattened his face against the slit of window beside the door.

Alan Brookner answered after his telephone had rung for two or three minutes. 'Who is this?'

I told him my name. 'We had some drinks in the kitchen.'

'I have you now! Good man! You coming here today?'

'Well, I was going to, but something came up, and John won't be able to make it for a while.'

'What does that mean?' He coughed loudly, alarmingly, making ripping sounds deep in his chest. 'What about the Bloody Marys?' More terrible coughing followed. 'Hang the Bloody Marys, where's John?'

'The police wanted to talk to him some more.'

'You tell me what happened to my daughter, young man. I've been fooled with long enough.'

A fist began thumping against the door. Geoffrey Bough was still gaping at the slit window.

'I'll be over as soon as I can,' I said.

'The front door ain't locked.' He hung up.

I went back through the arch. The telephone began to shrill. The doorbell gonged.

I passed through the kitchen and stepped out onto Ransom's brown lawn. The hedges met a row of arbor vitae like Christmas trees. Above them protruded the peaks and gables of a neighboring roof. A muted babble came from the front of the house. I crossed the lawn and pushed myself into the gap between the hedge and the last arbor vitae. The light disappeared, and the lively, pungent odors of leaves and sap surrounded me in a comfortable pocket of darkness. Then the tree yielded, and I came out into an empty, sun-drenched backyard.

I almost laughed out loud. I could just walk away from it, and I did.

5

This sense of escape vanished as soon as I walked up the stone flags that bisected Alan Brookner's overgrown lawn.

I turned the knob and stepped inside. A taint of rotting garbage hung in the air like perfume, along with some other, harsher odor.

'Alan,' I called out. 'It's Tim Underhill.'

I moved forward over a thick layer of mail and passed into the sitting room or library, or whatever it was. The letters John had tossed onto the chesterfield still lay there, only barely visible in the darkness. The lights were off, and the heavy curtains had been drawn. The smell of garbage grew stronger, along with the other stink.

'Alan?'

I groped for a light switch and felt only bare smooth wall, here and there very slightly gummy. Something small and black rocketed across the floor and dodged behind a curtain. A few more plates of half-eaten food lay on the floor.

'Alan!'

A low growl emerged from the walls. I wondered if Alan Brookner were dying somewhere in the house – if he'd had a stroke. The enormously selfish thought occurred to me that I might not have to tell him that his daughter was dead. I went back out into the corridor.

Dusty papers lay heaped on the dining room table. It looked like my own worktable back at John's house. A chair stood at the table before the abandoned work.

'Alan?'

The growl came from farther down the hallway.

In the kitchen, the smell of shit was as loud as an explosion. A few pizza boxes had been stacked up on the kitchen counter. The drawn shades admitted a hovering, faint illumination that seemed to have no single source. The tops of glasses and the edges of plates protruded over the lip of the sink. In front of the stove lay a tangled blanket of bath towels and thinner kitchen towels. A messy, indistinct mound about a foot high and covered with a mat of delirious flies lay on top of the towels.

I groaned and held my right hand to my forehead. I wanted to get out of the house. The stench made me feel sick and dizzy. Then I heard the growl again and saw that another being, a being not of my own species, was watching me.

Beneath the kitchen table crouched a hunched black shape. From it poured a concentrated sense of rage and pain. Two white eyes moved in the midst of the blackness. I was standing in front of the Minotaur. The stench of its droppings swarmed out at me.

'You're in trouble,' the Minotaur rumbled. 'I'm an old man, but I'm nobody's pushover.'

'I know that,' I said.

'Lies drive me crazy. *Crazy.*' He shifted beneath the

298

table, and the cloth fell away from his head. A white scurf of his whiskers shone out from beneath the table. The furious eyes floated out toward me. 'You are going to tell me the truth. Now.'

'Yes,' I said.

'My daughter is dead, isn't she?'

'Yes.'

A jolt like an electric shock straightened his back and pushed out his chin. 'An auto accident? Something like that?'

'She was murdered,' I said.

He tilted his head back, and the covering slipped to his shoulders. A grimace spread his features across his face. He looked as if he had been stabbed in the side. In the same terrible whisper, he asked, 'How long ago? Who did it?'

'Alan, wouldn't you like to come out from under that table?'

He gave me another look of concentrated rage. I knelt down. The buzzing of the flies suddenly seemed very loud.

'Tell me how my daughter was murdered.'

'About a week ago, a maid found her stabbed and beaten in a room at the St Alwyn Hotel.'

Alan let out a terrible groan.

'Nobody knows who did that to her. April was taken to Shady Mount, where she remained in a coma until this Wednesday. She began to show signs of improvement. On Thursday morning, someone came into her room and killed her.'

'She never came out of the coma?'

'No.'

He opened his Minotaur eyes again. 'Has anyone been arrested?'

'There was a false confession. Come out from under the table, Alan.'

Tears glittered in the white scurf on his cheeks. Fiercely, he shook his head. 'Did John think I was too feeble to hear the truth? Well, I'm not too damn feeble right now, sonny.'

'I can see that,' I said. 'Why are you sitting under the kitchen table, Alan?'

'I got confused. I got a little lost.' He glared at me again. 'John was supposed to come over. I was finally going to get the truth out of that damned son-in-law of mine.' He shook his head, and I got the Minotaur eyes again. 'So where is he?'

Even in this terrible condition, Alan Brookner had a powerful dignity I had only glimpsed earlier. His grief had momentarily shocked him out of his dementia. I felt achingly sorry for the old man.

'Two detectives showed up when we were about to leave. They asked John to come down to the station for questioning,' I said.

'They didn't arrest him.'

'No.'

He pulled the cloth up around his shoulders again and held it tight at his neck with one hand. It looked like a tablecloth. I moved a little closer. My eyes stung as if I had squirted soap into them.

'I knew she was dead.' He slumped down into himself, and for a moment had the ancient monkey look I had seen on my first visit. He started shaking his head.

I thought he was about to disappear back into his tablecloth. 'Would you like to come out from under the table, Alan?'

'Would you like to stop patronizing me?' His eyes burned out at me, but they were no longer the Minotaur's eyes. 'Okay. Yes. I want to come out from under the table.' He scooted forward and caught his feet in the fabric. Struggling to free his hands, he tightened the section of cloth across his chest. Panic flared in his eyes.

300

I moved nearer and reached beneath the table. Brookner battled the cloth. 'Damn business,' he said. 'Thought I'd be safe – got scared.'

I found an edge of the material and yanked at it. Brookner shifted a shoulder, and his right arm flopped out of the cloth. He was holding his revolver. 'Got it now,' he said. 'You bet. Piece of cake.' He wriggled his other shoulder out of confinement, and the cloth dropped to his waist. I took the gun away from him and put it on the table. He and I both pulled the length of fabric away from his legs, and Alan got one knee under him, then the other, and crawled forward until he was out from under the table. The tablecloth came with him. Finally, he accepted my hand and levered himself up on one knee until he could get one foot, covered with a powder-blue tube sock, beneath him. Then I pulled him upright, and he got his other foot, in a black tube sock, on the cloth. 'There we go,' he said. 'Right as rain.' He tottered forward and let me take his elbow. We shuffled across the kitchen toward a chair. 'Old joints stiffened up,' he said. He began gingerly extending his arms and gently raising his legs. Glittering tears still hung in his whiskers.

'I'll take care of that mess on the floor,' I said.

'Do what you like.' The wave of pain and rage came from him once more. 'Is there a funeral? There damn well better be, because I'm going to it.' His face stiffened with anger and the desire to suppress his tears. The Minotaur eyes flared again. 'Come on, tell me.'

'There's a funeral tomorrow. One o'clock at Trott Brothers. She'll be cremated.'

The fierce grimace flattened his features across his face again. He hid his face behind his knotted hands and leaned forward with his elbows on his knees and wept noisily. His shirt was gray with dust and black around the rim of the collar. A sour, unwashed smell came up from him, barely distinguishable in the reek of feces.

He finally stopped crying and wiped his nose on his sleeve. 'I knew it,' he said, looking up at me. The lids of his eyes were pink and inflamed.

'Yes.'

'That's why I wound up here.' He wiped most of the tears out of his silken white whiskers. A shadow of pain and confusion nearly as terrible as his grief passed over his face.

'April was going to take me – there was this place – ' The sudden anger melted into grief again, and his upper body shook with the effort of trying to look ferocious while he wanted to cry.

'She was going to take you somewhere?'

He waved his big hands in the air, dismissing the whole topic.

'What's the reason for this?' I indicated the buzzing mound on the towels.

'Improvised head. The one down here got blocked up or something, damn thing's useless, and I can't always get upstairs. So I laid down a bunch of towels.'

'Do you have a shovel somewhere around the place?'

'Garage, I guess,' he said.

I found a flat-bottomed coal shovel in a corner of a garage tucked away under the oak trees. On the concrete slab lay a collection of old stains surrounded by an ancient lawnmower, a long-tined leaf rake, a couple of broken lamps, and a pile of cardboard boxes. Framed pictures leaned back to front against the far wall. I bent down for the shovel. A long stripe of fluid still fresh enough to shine lay on top of the old stains. I touched it with a forefinger: slick, not quite dry. I sniffed my finger and smelled what might have been brake fluid.

When I came back into the kitchen, Alan was leaning against the wall, holding a black garbage bag. He straightened up and brandished the bag. 'I know this looks bad, but the toilet wouldn't work.'

302

'I'll take a look at it after we get this mess out of the house.'

He held the bag open, and I began to shovel. Then I tied up the bag and put it inside another bag before dropping it into the garbage can. While I mopped the floor, Alan told me twice, in exactly the same words, that he had awakened one morning during his freshman year at Harvard to discover that his roommate had died in the next bed. No more than a five-second pause separated the two accounts.

'Interesting story,' I said, afraid that he was going to tell me the whole thing a third time.

'Have you ever seen death close up?'

'Yes,' I said.

'How'd you come to do that?'

'My first job in Vietnam was graves registration. We had to check dead soldiers for ID.'

'And what was the effect of that on you?'

'It's hard to describe,' I said.

'John, now,' Alan said. 'Didn't something strange happen to him over there?'

'All I really know is that he was trapped underground with a lot of corpses. The army reported him killed in action.'

'What did that do to him?'

I mopped the last bit of the floor, poured the dirty water into the sink, filled it with hot soapy water, and began washing the dishes. 'When I saw him afterward, the last time I saw him in Vietnam, he said these things to me: *Everything on earth is made of fire, and the name of that fire is Time. As long as you know you are standing in the fire, everything is permitted. A seed of death is at the center of every moment.*'

'Not bad,' Alan said.

I put the last dish into the rack. 'Let's see if I can fix your toilet.'

I opened doors until I found a plunger in the broom closet.

In a lucid moment, Alan had blotted up the overspill from the toilet and done his best to clean the floor. Crushed paper towels filled the wastebasket. I stuck the plunger into the water and pumped. A wad of pulp that had once been typing paper bubbled out of the pipe. I trapped the paper in the plunger and decanted it in the wastebasket. 'Just keep this thing in here, Alan, and remember to use it if the same thing happens.'

'Okay, okay.' He brightened up a little. 'Hey, I made a batch of Bloody Marys. How about we have some?'

'One,' I said. 'For you, not me.'

Back in the kitchen, Alan took a big pitcher out of the refrigerator. He got some into a glass without spilling. Then he collapsed into a chair and drank, holding the glass with both hands. 'Will you bring me to the funeral?'

'Of course.'

'I have trouble getting around outside,' Alan said, glowering at me. He meant that he never left the house.

'What happens to you?'

'I lived here forty years, and all of a sudden I can't remember where anything *is*.' He glared at me again and took another big slug of his drink. 'Last time I went outside, I actually got lost. Couldn't even remember why I went out in the first place. When I looked around, I couldn't even figure out where I lived.' His face clouded over with anger and self-doubt. 'Couldn't find my *house*. I walked around for *hours*. Finally my head cleared or something, and I realized I was just on the wrong side of the street.' He picked up the glass with trembling hands and set it back down on the table. 'Hear things, too. People creeping around outside.'

I remembered what I had seen in the garage. 'Does anyone ever use your garage? Do you let somebody park there?'

'I've heard 'em sneaking around. They think they can fool me, but I know they're out there.'

'When did you hear them?'

'That's not a question I can answer.' This time he managed to get the glass to his mouth. 'But if it happens again, I'm gonna get my gun and blow 'em full of holes.' He took two big gulps, banged the glass down on the table, and licked his lips. 'Ta-ra-ra-boom-dee-ay,' he said. 'All the whores are in luck today.' A wet sound that was supposed to be a laugh came out of his mouth. He scrabbled a hand over the lower part of his face and uttered soft hiccuping wails. This injury to his dignity outraged him, and his crying turned into long shuddering choked-back sobs.

I stood up and put my arms around him. He fought me for a second, then sagged against me and cried evenly and steadily. When he wound down, both of us were wet.

'Alan, I'm not insulting you if I say that you need a little help.'

'I do need a little help,' he said.

'Let's get you washed up. And we have to get you a cleaning woman. And I don't think you ought to keep all your money on the kitchen table like that.'

He sat up straight and looked at me as sternly as he could.

'We'll figure out a place you'll be able to remember,' I said.

We moved toward the stairs. Alan obediently led me to his bathroom and sat on the toilet to pull off his socks and sweatpants while I ran a bath.

After he had succeeded in undoing his last shirt button, he tried to pull the shirt over his head, like a five-year-old. He got snared inside the shirt, and I pulled it over his head and yanked the sleeves off backward.

Brookner stood up. His arms and legs were stringy, and the silvery web of hair clinging to his body concentrated

305

into a tangled mat around his dangling penis. He stepped unself-consciously over the rim of the tub and lowered himself into the water. 'Feels good.' He sank into the tub and rested his head against the porcelain.

He began lathering himself. A cloud of soap turned the water opaque. He fixed me with his eyes again. 'Isn't there some wonderful private detective, something like that, right here in town? Man who solves cases right in his own house?'

I said there was.

'I have a lot of money salted away. Let's hire him.'

'John and I talked to him yesterday.'

'Good.' He lowered his head under the surface of the water and came up dripping and drying his eyes. 'Shampoo.' I found the bottle and passed it to him. He began lathering his head. 'Do you believe in absolute good and evil?'

'No,' I said.

'Me neither. Know what I believe in? Seeing and not seeing. Understanding and ignorance. Imagination and absence of imagination.' The cap of shampoo looked like a bulging wig. 'There. I've just compressed at least sixty years of reflection. Did it make any sense?'

I said it did.

'Guess again. There's a lot more to it.'

Even in his ruined state, Alan Brookner was like Eliza Morgan, a person who could remind you of the magnificence of the human race. He dunked his head under the water and came up sputtering. 'Need five seconds of shower.' He leaned forward to open the drain. 'Let me get myself up.' He levered himself upright, pulled the shower curtain across the tub, and turned on the water. After testing the temperature, he diverted the water to the shower and gasped when it exploded down on him. After a few seconds, he turned it off and yanked the shower curtain open. He was pink and white and steaming. 'Towel.' He pointed at the rack. 'I have a plan.'

'So do I,' I said, handing him the towel.

'You go first.'

'You said you have some money?'

He nodded.

'In a checking account?'

'Some of it.'

'Let me call a cleaning service. I'll do some of the initial work so they won't run away screaming as soon as they step into the house, but you have to get this place cleaned up, Alan.'

'Fine, sure,' he said, winding the towel around himself.

'And if you can afford it, someone ought to come in for a couple of hours a day to cook and take care of things for you.'

'I'll think about that,' he said. 'I want you to go downstairs and call Dahlgren Florist on Berlin Avenue and order two wreaths.' He spelled Dahlgren for me. 'I don't care if they cost a hundred bucks apiece. Have one delivered to Trott Brothers, and the other one here.'

'And I'll try the cleaning services.'

He tossed the towel toward the rack and walked on stiff legs out of the bathroom, for the moment completely in command of himself. He got into the hall and turned around slowly. I thought he couldn't remember the way to his own bedroom. 'By the way,' he said. 'While you're at it, call a lawn service, too.'

I went downstairs and left messages for the cleaning and lawn services to call me at John's house and then got another garbage bag and picked up most of the debris on the living room floor. I phoned the florist on Berlin Avenue and placed Alan's orders for two wreaths, and then called the private duty nursing registry and asked if Eliza Morgan was free to begin work on Monday morning. I dumped the dirty dishes in the kitchen sink, swearing to myself that this was the last time I was going to do Alan Brookner's housekeeping.

When I went back upstairs, he was sitting on his bed, trying to wrestle his way into a white dress shirt. His hair swirled around his head.

Like a child, he held out his arms, and I straightened the sleeves and pulled the two halves of the front together. I started buttoning it up. 'Get the charcoal gray suit out of the closet,' he said.

I got his legs into the trousers and took black silk socks out of a drawer. Alan slammed his feet into a pair of old black wingtips and tied them neatly and quickly, arguing for the endurance of certain kinds of mechanical memory in the otherwise memory-impaired.

'Have you ever seen a ghost? A spirit? Whatever you call it?'

'Well,' I said, and smiled. This is not a subject on which I ever speak.

'When we were small boys, my little brother and I were raised by my grandparents. They were wonderful people, but my grandmother died in bed when I was ten. On the day of her funeral, the house was full of my grandparents' friends, and my aunts and uncles had all come – they had to decide what to do with us. I felt absolutely lost. I wandered upstairs. My grandparents' bedroom door was open, and in the mirror on the back of the door, I could see my grandmother lying in her bed. She was looking at me, and she was smiling.'

'Were you scared?'

'Nope. I knew she was telling me that she still loved me and that I would have a good home. And later, we moved in with an aunt and an uncle. But I never believed in orthodox Christianity after that. I knew there wasn't any literal heaven or hell. Sometimes, the boundary between the living and the dead is permeable. And that's how I embarked upon my wonderful career.'

He had reminded me of something Walter Dragonette had said to Paul Fontaine.

'Ever since then, I've tried to *notice* things. To pay *attention*. So I hate losing my memory. I cannot bear it. And I cherish times like this, when I seem to be pretty much like my old self.'

He looked down at himself: white shirt, trousers, socks, shoes. He grunted and zipped his fly. Then he levered himself up out of the chair. 'Have to do something about these whiskers. Come back to the bathroom with me, will you?'

'What are you doing, Alan?' I stood up to follow him.

'Getting ready for my daughter's funeral.'

'Her funeral isn't until tomorrow.'

'Tomorrow, as Scarlett said, is another day.' He led me into the bathroom and picked up an electric razor from the top shelf of a marble stand. 'Will you do me a favor?'

I laughed out loud. 'After all we've been through together?'

He switched on the razor and popped up the little sideburn attachment. 'Mow down all that stuff under my chin and on my neck. In fact, run the thing over everything that looks too long to be shaved normally, and then I'll do the rest myself.'

He thrust out his chin, and I scythed away long silver wisps that drifted down like angel hair. Some of them adhered to his shirt and trousers. I made a pass over each cheek, and more silver fluff sparkled away from his face. When I was done, I stepped back.

Alan faced the mirror. 'Signs of improvement,' he said. He scrubbed the electric razor over his face. 'Passable. Very passable. Though I could use a haircut.' He found a comb on the marble stand and tugged it through the fluffy white cloud on his head. The cloud parted on the left side and fell in neat loose waves to the collar of his shirt. He nodded at himself and turned around for my inspection. 'Well?'

He looked like a mixture of Herbert von Karajan and Leonard Bernstein. 'You'll do,' I said.

He nodded. 'Necktie.'

We marched back into the bedroom. Alan wrenched open the closet door and inspected his ties. 'Would this make me look like a chauffeur?' He pulled out a black silk tie and held it up for inspection.

I shook my head.

Alan turned up his collar, wrapped the tie around his neck, and knotted it as easily as he had tied his shoes. Then he buttoned his collar and pushed the knot into place. He took the suit jacket from its hanger and held it out. 'Sometimes I have trouble with sleeves,' he said.

I held up the jacket, and he slid his arms into the sleeves. I settled the jacket on his shoulders.

'There.' He brushed some white fluff from his trousers. 'Did you call the florist?'

I nodded. 'Why did you want two wreaths?'

'You'll see.' From a bedside table he picked up a bunch of keys, a comb, and a fat black fountain pen and distributed these objects into various pockets. 'Do you suppose I'd be able to walk around outside without getting lost?'

'I'm sure of it.'

'Maybe I'll experiment after John turns up. He's basically a good fellow, you know. If I'd got stuck at Arkham the way he did, I'd be unhappy, too.'

'You were at Arkham your whole life,' I said.

'But I wasn't stuck.' I followed him out of the bedroom. 'John got to be known as my man – we collaborated on a few papers, but he never really did anything on his own. Good teacher, but I'm not sure Arkham will keep him on after I go. Don't mention this to him, by the way. I've been trying to figure out a way to bring up the subject without alarming him.'

We started down the stairs. Halfway down, he turned around to stare up at me. 'I'm going to be all right for my daughter's funeral. I'm going to be all present and accounted for.' He reached up and tapped my breastbone. 'I know something about you.'

I nearly flinched.

'Something happened to you when I was telling you about my grandmother. You thought of something – you *saw* something. It didn't surprise you that I saw my grandmother because' – here he began tapping his forefinger against my chest – 'because – you – have – seen – someone – too.'

He nodded at me and moved back down a step. 'I never thought there was any point in missing things. You know what I used to tell my students? I used to say there is another world, and it's *this* world.'

We went downstairs and waited for John, who failed to appear. Eventually, I persuaded Alan to salt away the money on the kitchen table in various pockets of his suit. I left him sitting in his living room, went back to the kitchen, and put the revolver in my pocket. Then I left the house.

Back at Ely Place, I put the revolver on the coffee table and then went upstairs to my manuscript. John had left a Post-It note in the kitchen saying that he had been too tired to go to Alan's house and had gone straight to bed. Everything was okay, he said.

PART SIX

Ralph and Marjorie Ransom

1

Just after one o'clock, I parked John's Pontiac in front of the Georgian house on Victoria Terrace. A man on a lawn mower the size of a tractor was expertly swinging his machine around the oak trees on the side of the house. A teenage boy walked a trimmer down the edge of the driveway. Tall black bags stood on the shorn lawn like stooks. John was shaking his head, frowning into the sunlight and literally champing his jaws.

'It'll go faster if you get him,' he said. 'I'll stay here with my parents.'

Ralph and Marjorie Ransom began firing objections from the backseat. In their manner was the taut, automatic politeness present since John and I had met them at the airport that morning.

John had driven to the airport, but after we had collected his parents, tanned and clad in matching black-and-silver running suits, he asked if I would mind driving back. His father had protested. John ought to drive, it was his car, wasn't it?

– I'd like Tim to do it, Dad, John said.

At this point his mother had stepped in perkily to say that John was tired, he wanted to talk, and wasn't it *nice* that his friend from New York was willing to drive? His mother was short and hourglass-shaped, big in the bust and hips, and her sunglasses hid the top half of her face. Her silver hair exactly matched her husband's.

– John should drive, that's all, said his father. Trimmer

315

than I had expected, Ralph Ransom looked like a retired naval officer deeply involved with golf. His white handsome smile went well with his tan. – Where I come from, a guy drives his own car. Hell, we'll be able to talk just fine, get in there and be our pilot.

John frowned and handed me the keys. – I'm not really supposed to drive for a while. They suspended my license. He looked at me in a way that combined anger and apology.

Ralph stared at his son. – Suspended, huh? What happened?

– Does it matter? asked Marjorie. Let's get in the car.

– Drinking and driving?

– I went through a kind of a bad period, yeah, John said. It's okay, really. I can walk everywhere I have to go. By the time it gets cold, I'll have my license back.

– Lucky you didn't kill someone, his father said, and his mother said *Ralph!*

In the morning, John and I had moved my things up to his office, so that his parents could have the guest room. John armored himself in a nice-looking double-breasted gray suit, I pulled out of my hanging bag a black Yohji Yamamoto suit I had bought once in a daring mood, found a gray silk shirt I hadn't remembered packing, and we were both ready to pick up his parents at the airport.

We had taken the Ransoms' bags up to the guest room and left them alone to change. I followed John back down to the kitchen, where he set out the sandwich things again. – Well, I said, now I know why you walk everywhere.

– Twice this spring, I flunked the breathalyzer. It's bullshit, but I have to put up with it. Like a lot of things. You know?

He seemed frazzled, worn so thin his underlying rage burned out at me through his eyes. He realized that I could see it and stuffed it back down inside himself like a burning coal. When his parents came down, they picked at the sandwich fillings and talked about the weather.

In Tucson, the temperature was 110. But it was dry heat. And you had air conditioning wherever you went. Golfing – just get on the course around eight in the morning. John, tell you the truth, you're getting way too heavy, ought to buy a good set of clubs and get out there on the golf course.

– I'll think about it, John said. But you never know. A tub of lard like me, get him out on the golf course in hundred-degree weather, he's liable to drop dead of a coronary right on the spot.

– Hold on, hold on, I didn't mean –

– John, you know your father was only –

– I'm sorry, I've been on –

All three Ransoms stopped talking as abruptly as they had begun. Marjorie turned toward the kitchen windows. Ralph gave me a pained, mystified look and opened the freezer section of the refrigerator. He pulled out a pink, unlabeled bottle and showed it to his son.

John glanced at the bottle. – Hyacinth vodka. Smuggled in from the Black Sea.

His father took a glass from a cupboard and poured out about an inch of the pink vodka. He sipped, nodded, and drank the rest.

– Three hundred bucks a bottle, John said.

Ralph Ransom capped the bottle and slid it back into place in the freezer. – Yeah. Well. What time does the train leave?

– It's leaving, John said, and began walking out of the kitchen. His parents looked at each other and then followed him through the living room.

John checked the street through the slender window.

– They're baa-ack.

His parents followed him outside, and Geoffrey Bough,

Isobel Archer, and their cameramen darted in on both sides. Marjorie uttered a high-pitched squeal. Ralph put his arm around his wife and moved her toward the car. He slid into the backseat beside her.

John tossed me the car keys. I gunned the engine and sped away.

Ralph asked where *they* had come from, and John said, They never leave. They bang on the door and toss garbage on the lawn.

– You're under a lot of pressure. Ralph leaned forward to pat his son's shoulder.

John stiffened but did not speak. His father patted him again. In the rearview mirror, I saw Geoffrey Bough's dissolute-looking blue vehicle and Isobel's gaudy van swinging out into the street behind us.

They hung back when I pulled up in front of Alan's. John locked his arms around his chest and worked his jaws as he chewed on his fiery coal.

I got out and left them to it. The man on the tractor-sized lawn mower waved at me, and I waved back. This was the Midwest.

Alan Brookner opened the door and gestured for me to come in. When I closed the door behind me, I heard a vacuum cleaner buzzing and humming on the second floor, another in what sounded like the dining room. 'The cleaners are here already?'

'Times are tough,' he said. 'How do I look?'

I told him he looked wonderful. The black silk tie was perfectly knotted. His trousers were pressed, and the white shirt looked fresh. I smelled a trace of aftershave.

'I wanted to make sure.' He stepped back and turned around. The back hem of the suit jacket looked a little crumpled, but I wasn't going to tell him that. He finished turning around and looked at me seriously, even severely. 'Okay?'

'You got the jacket on by yourself this time.'

'I never took it off,' he said. 'Wasn't taking any chances.'

I had a vision of him leaning back against a wall with his knees locked. 'How did you sleep?'

'Very, very carefully.' Alan tugged at the jacket of his suit, then buttoned it. We left the house.

'Who are the old geezers with John?'

'His parents. Ralph and Marjorie. They just came in from Arizona.'

'Ready when you are, C.B.,' he said. (I did not understand this allusion, if that's what it was, at the time, and I still don't.)

John was standing up beside the car, looking at Alan with undisguised astonishment and relief.

'Alan, you look great,' he said.

'I thought I'd make an effort,' Alan said. 'Are you going to get in back with your parents, or would you prefer to keep the front seat?'

John looked uneasily back at Geoffrey's blue disaster and Isobel's declamatory van and slid in next to his father. Alan and I got in at the same time.

'I want to say how much I appreciate your coming all the way from . . .' He hesitated and then concluded triumphantly, 'Alaska.'

There was a brief silence.

'We're so sorry about your daughter,' Marjorie said. 'We loved her, too, very much.'

'April was lovable,' said Alan.

'It's a crime, all this business about Walter Dragonette,' Ralph said. 'You wonder how such things could go on.'

'You wonder how a person like that can *exist*,' Marjorie said.

John chewed his lip and hugged his chest and looked back at the reporters, who hung one car behind us all the way downtown to the Trott Brothers' building.

Marjorie asked, 'Will you be back at the college with

319

John next year, or are you thinking about retiring?'

'I'll be back by popular demand.'

'You don't have a mandatory retirement age in your business?' This was Ralph.

'In my case, they made an exception.'

'Do yourself a favor,' Ralph said. 'Walk out and don't look back. I retired ten years ago, and I'm having the time of my life.'

'I think I've already had that.'

'You have some kind of nest egg, right? I mean, with April and everything.'

'It's embarrassing.' Alan turned around on his seat. 'Did you use April's services, yourself?'

'I had my own guy.' Ralph paused. 'What do you mean, "embarrassing"? She was too successful?' He looked at me again in the mirror, trying to work something out. I knew what.

'She was too successful,' Alan said.

'My friend, you wound up with a couple hundred thousand dollars, right? Live right, watch your spending, find some good high-yield bonds, you're set.'

'Eight hundred,' Alan said.

'Pardon?'

'She started out with a pittance and wound up with eight hundred thousand. It's embarrassing.'

I checked Ralph in the rearview mirror. His eyes had gone out of focus. I could hear Marjorie breathing in and out.

Finally, Ralph asked, 'What are you going to do with it?'

'I think I'll leave it to the public library.'

I turned the corner into Hillfield Avenue, and the gray Victorian shape of the Trott Brothers' Funeral Home came into view. Its slate turrets, gothic ginger-bread, peaked dormers, and huge front porch made it look like a house from a Charles Addams cartoon.

I pulled up at the foot of the stone steps that led up to the Trott Brothers' lawn.

'What's on the agenda here, John?' his father asked.

'We have some time alone with April.' He got out of the car. 'After that there's the public reception, or visitation, or whatever they call it.'

His father struggled along the seat, trying to get to the door. 'Hold on, hold on, I can't hear you.' Marjorie pushed herself sideways after her husband.

Alan Brookner sighed, popped open his door, and quietly got out.

John repeated what he had just said. 'Then there's a service of some kind. When it's over, we go out to the crematorium.'

'Keeping it simple, hey?' his father asked.

John was already moving toward the steps. 'Oh.' He turned around, one foot on the first step. 'I should warn you in advance, I guess. The first part is open coffin. The director here seemed to think that was what we should do.'

I heard Alan breathe in sharply.

'I don't like open coffins,' Ralph said. 'What are you supposed to do, go up and talk to the person?'

'I wish I *could* talk to the person,' Alan said. For a moment he seemed absolutely forlorn. 'Some other cultures, of course, take for granted that you can communicate with the dead.'

'Really?' asked Ralph. 'Like India, do you mean?'

'Let's go up.' John began mounting the steps.

'In Indian religions the situation is a little more complicated,' Alan said. He and Ralph went around the front of the car and began going up behind John. Bits of their conversation drifted back.

Marjorie gave me an uneasy glance. I aroused certain

misgivings within Marjorie. Maybe it was the ornamental zippers on my Japanese suit. 'Here we go,' I said, and held out my elbow.

Marjorie closed a hand like a parrot's claw on my elbow.

2

Joyce Brophy held open the giant front door. She was wearing a dark blue dress that looked like a cocktail party maternity outfit, and her hair had been glued into place. 'Gosh, we were wondering what was taking you two so long!' She flashed a weirdly exultant smile and motioned us through the door with little whisk-broom gestures.

John was talking to, or being talked at by, a small, bent-over man in his seventies whose gray face was stamped with deep, exhausted-looking lines and wrinkles. I moved toward Alan.

'No, now, no, mister, you have to meet my father,' Joyce said. 'Let's get the formalities over with before we enter the viewing room, you know, everything in its own time and all that kinda good stuff.'

The stooping man in the loose gray suit grinned at me ferociously and extended his hand. When I took it, he squeezed hard, and I squeezed back. 'Yessir,' he said. 'Quite a day for us all.'

'Dad,' said Joyce Brophy, 'you met Professor Ransom and Professor Brookner, and this is Professor Ransom's friend, ah – '

'Tim Underhill,' John said.

'Professor Underhill,' Joyce said. 'And this here is Mrs Ransom, Professor Ransom's mother. My dad, William Trott.'

'Just call me Bill.' The little man extended his already carnivorous smile and grasped Marjorie's right hand in his left, so that he could squeeze hands with both of us at once. 'Thought it was a good obituary, didn't you? We worked hard on that one, and it was all worth it.'

None of us had seen the morning paper.

'Oh, yes,' Marjorie said.

'Just want to express our sorrow. From this point on the thing is just to relax and enjoy it, and remember, we're always here to help you.' He let go of our hands.

Marjorie rubbed her palms together.

Just Call Me Bill gave a smile intended to be sympathetic and backed away. 'My little girl will be taking you into the Chapel of Rest. We'll lead your guests in at the time of the memorial service.'

By this time he had moved six paces backward, and on his last word he abruptly turned around and took off with surprising speed down a long dark hallway.

Just Call Me Joyce watched him fondly for a couple of seconds. 'He's gonna turn on the first part of the musical program, that's your background for your private meditations and that. We got the chairs all set up, and when your guests and all show up, we'd like you to move to the left-hand side of the front row, that's for immediate family.' She blinked at me. 'And close friends.'

She pressed her right hand against the mound of her belly and with her left gestured toward the hallway. John moved beside her, and together they stepped into the hallway. Organ music oozed from distant speakers. Alan drifted into the hallway like a sleepwalker. Ralph stepped in beside him. 'So you keep on getting born over and over? What's the payoff?'

I could not hear Alan's mumbled response, but the question pulled him back into the moment, and he raised his head and began moving more decisively.

323

'I didn't know you were one of John's professor friends,' Marjorie said.

'It was a fairly recent promotion,' I said.

'Ralph and I are so proud of you.' She patted my arm as we followed the others into a ballroom filled with soft light and the rumble of almost stationary organ music. Rows of folding chairs stood on either side of a central aisle leading to a podium banked with wreaths and flowers in vases. On a raised platform behind the podium, a deeply polished bronze coffin lay on a long table draped in black fabric. The top quarter of the coffin had been folded back like the lid of a piano to reveal plump, tufted white upholstering. April Ransom's profile, at an angle given her head by a firm white satin pillow, pointed beyond the open lid to the pocked acoustic tile of the ceiling.

'Your brochures are right here.' Just Call Me Joyce waved at a highly polished rectangular mahogany table set against the wall. Neat stacks of a folded yellow page stood beside a pitcher of water and a stack of plastic cups. At the end of the table was a coffee dispenser.

Everybody in the room but Alan Brookner took their eyes from April Ransom's profile and looked at the yellow leaflets.

'Yay Though I Walk is a real good choice, we always think.'

Alan was staring at his daughter's corpse from a spot about five feet inside the door.

Joyce said, 'She looks just beautiful, even from way back here you can see that.'

She began pulling Alan along with her. After an awkward moment, he fell into step.

John followed after them, his parents close behind. Joyce Brophy brought Alan up to the top of the coffin. John moved beside him. His parents and I took positions further down the side.

Up close, April's coffin seemed as large as a rowboat. She was visible to the waist, where her hands lay folded. Joyce Brophy leaned over and smoothed out a wrinkle in the white jacket. When she straightened up, Alan bent over the coffin and kissed his daughter's forehead.

'I'll be down the hall in the office in case you folks need anything.' Joyce took a backward step and turned around and ploughed down the aisle. She was wearing large, dirty running shoes.

Just Call Me Joyce had applied too much lipstick of too bright a shade to April's mouth, and along her cheekbones ran an artificial line of pink. The vibrant cap of blond hair had been arranged to conceal something that had been done at the autopsy. Death had subtracted the lines around April's eyes and mouth. She looked like an empty house.

'Doesn't she look beautiful, John?' asked Marjorie.

'Uh huh,' John said.

Alan touched April's powdered cheek. 'My poor baby,' he said.

'It's just so damn . . . awful,' Ralph said.

Alan moved away toward the first row of seats.

The Ransoms left the coffin and took the two seats on the left-hand aisle of the first row. Ralph crossed his arms over his chest in a gesture his son had learned from him.

John took a chair one space away from his mother and two spaces from me. Alan was sitting on the other side of the aisle, examining a yellow leaflet.

We listened for a time to the motionless organ music.

I remembered the descriptions of my sister's funeral. April's mourners had filled half of Holy Sepulchre. According to my mother, she had looked 'peaceful' and 'beautiful.' My vibrant sister, sometimes vibrantly unhappy, that furious blond blur, that slammer of doors, that demon of boredom, so emptied out that she had become peaceful? In that case, she had left everything to me, passed everything into my hands.

I wanted to tear the past apart, to dismember it on a bloody table.

I stood up and walked to the back of the room. I took the leaflet from my jacket pocket and read the words on the front of the cover.

Yea, though I walk through the Valley of the Shadow of Death,

I shall fear no evil.

I sat down in the last row of chairs.

Ralph Ransom whispered to his wife, stood up, patted his son's shoulder, and began wandering down the far left side of the chapel. When he got close enough to be heard if he spoke softly, he said, 'Hey,' as if he just noticed that I had moved to the last row. He jerked his thumb toward the back of the room. 'You suppose they got some coffee in that thing?'

That was not the question he wanted to ask.

We went to the table. The coffee was almost completely without taste. For a few seconds the two of us stood at the back of the room, watching the other three look at or not look at April Ransom in her enormous bronze boat.

'I hear you knew my boy in Vietnam.'

'I met him there a couple of times.'

Now he could ask me.

He looked at me over the top of his cup, swallowed, and grimaced at the heat of the coffee. 'You wouldn't happen to be from Millhaven yourself, would you, Professor Underhill?'

'Please,' I said, 'just call me Tim.'

I smiled at him, and he smiled back.

'Are you a Millhaven boy, Tim?'

'I grew up about a block from the St Alwyn.'

'You're Al Underhill's boy,' he said. 'By God, I *knew* you reminded me of somebody, and when we were in the car I finally got it – Al Underhill. You take after him.'

'I guess I do, a little bit.'

He looked at me as though measuring the distance between my father and myself and shook his head. 'Al Underhill. I haven't thought about him in forty years. I guess you know he used to work for me, back in the days when I owned the St Alwyn.'

'After John told me that you used to own the hotel, I did.'

'We hated like hell to let him go, you know. *I* knew he had a family. *I* knew what he was going through. If he could have stayed off the sauce, everything would have worked out all right.'

'He couldn't help himself,' I said. Ralph Ransom was being kind – he was not going to mention the thefts that had led to my father's firing. Probably he would not have stolen so much if he had managed to stay sober.

'Your sister, wasn't it? That started him off, I mean.'

I nodded.

'Terrible thing. I can remember it just like it was yesterday.'

'Me, too,' I said.

After a moment, he asked, 'How is Al these days?'

I told him that my father had died four years ago.

'That's a shame. I liked Al – if it hadn't been for what happened to your sister, he would have been fine.'

'Everything would have been different, anyhow.' I fought the annoyance I could feel building in me – when my father was in trouble, this man had fired him. I did not want his worthless reassurances.

'Was that kind of a bond between you and John, that your father worked for me?'

My annoyance with this silver-topped country club Narcissus escalated toward anger. 'We had other kinds of bonds.'

'Oh, I can see that. Sure.'

I expected that Ralph would go back to his seat, but he

still had something on his mind. Once I heard what it was, my anger shrank to a pinpoint.

'Those were funny days. Terrible days. You're probably too young to remember, but around then, there was a cop here in town who killed four or five people and wrote these words, BLUE ROSE, near the bodies. One of the victims even lived in my hotel. Shook us all up, I can tell you. Almost ruined our business, too. This lunatic, this Dragonette, I guess he was just imitating the other guy.'

I put down my cup. 'You know, Ralph, I'm very interested in what happened back then.'

'Well, it was like this thing now. The whole town went bananas.'

'Could we go out in the hallway for a second?'

'Sure, if you want to.' He raised his eyebrows quizzically – this was not in his handbook of behavior – and almost tiptoed out.

3

I closed the door behind me. Two or three yards away, Ralph Ransom leaned against the red-flocked wallpaper, his hands back in his pockets. He still had the quizzical expression on his face. He could not figure out my motives, and that made him uneasy. The unease translated into reflexive aggression. He pushed his shoulders off the wall and faced me.

'I thought it would be better to talk about this out here,' I said. 'A few years ago, I did some research that indicated that Detective Damrosch had nothing to do with the murders.'

'Research?' His shoulders went down as he relaxed.

'Oh, I get it. You're a history guy, a whaddayacallit. A historian.'

'I write books,' I said, trying to salvage as much of the truth as possible.

'The old publish or perish thing.'

I smiled – in my case, this was not just a slogan.

'I don't know if *I* can tell you anything.'

'Was there anybody you suspected, someone you thought might have been the killer?'

He shrugged. 'I always thought it was a guest, some guy who came and went. That's what we had, mostly, salesmen who showed up for a couple of days, checked out, and then came back again for a few more days.'

'Was that because of the prostitute?'

'Well, yeah. A couple girls used to sneak up to the rooms. You try, but you can't keep them out. That Fancy, she was one of them. I figured someone caught her stealing from him, or, you know, just got in a fight with her out in back there. And then I thought he might have known that the piano player saw it happen – his room looked right out onto the back of the hotel.'

'Musicians stayed at the St Alwyn, too?'

'Oh yeah, we used to get some jazz musicians. See, we weren't too far from downtown, our rates were good, and we had all-night room service. The musicians were good guests. To tell you the truth, I think they liked the St Alwyn because of Glenroy Breakstone.'

'He lived in the hotel?'

'Oh, sure. Glenroy was there when I bought it, and he was still there when I sold it. He's probably still there! He was one of the few who didn't move out, once all the trouble started. The reason that piano player lived in the hotel, Glenroy recommended him personally. Never any trouble with Glenroy.'

'Who used to cause trouble?'

'Well, sometimes guys, you know, might have a bad day and bust up the furniture at night – anything can happen in a hotel, believe me. The ones who went crazy, they got barred. The day manager took care of that. The man kept things shipshape, as much as he could. A haughty bastard, but he didn't stand for any nonsense. Religious fellow, I think. Dependable.'

'Do you remember his name?'

He laughed out loud. 'You bet I do. Bob Bandolier. You wouldn't want to go around a golf course with that guy, but he was one hell of a manager.'

'Maybe I could talk to him.'

'Maybe. Bob stayed on when I sold the place – guy was practically married to the St Alwyn. And I'll tell you someone else – Glenroy Breakstone. Nothing passed *him* by, you can bet on that. He pretty much knew everybody that worked at the hotel.'

'Were he and Bob Bandolier friends?'

'Bob Bandolier didn't have friends,' Ralph said, and laughed again. 'And Bob would never get tight with, you know, a black guy.'

'Would he talk to me?'

'You never know.' He checked his watch and looked at the door to the chapel. 'Hey, if you find something out, would you tell me? I'd be interested.'

We went back into the enormous room. John looked up at us from beside the table.

Ralph said, 'Who's supposed to fill all these chairs?'

John morosely examined the empty chairs. 'People from Barnett and clients, I suppose. And the reporters will show up.' He scowled down at a plastic cup. 'They're hovering out there like blowflies.'

There was a moment of silence. Separately, Marjorie Ransom and Alan Brookner came down the center aisle. Marjorie said a few words to Alan. He nodded uncertainly, as if he had not really heard her.

330

I poured coffee for them. For a moment we all word-lessly regarded the coffin.

'Nice flowers,' Ralph said.

'I just said that,' said Marjorie. 'Didn't I, Alan?'

'Yes, yes,' Alan said. 'Oh John, I haven't asked you about what happened at police headquarters. How long were you interrogated?'

John closed his eyes. Marjorie whirled toward Alan, sloshing coffee over her right hand. She transferred the cup and waved her hand in the air, trying to dry it. Ralph gave her a handkerchief, but he was looking from John to Alan and back to John.

'You were interrogated?'

'No, Dad. I wasn't interrogated.'

'Well, why would the police want to talk to you? They already got the guy.'

'It looks as though Dragonette gave a false confession.'

'What?' Marjorie said. 'Everybody knows he did it.'

'It doesn't work out right. He didn't have enough time to go to the hospital for the change of shift, go to the hardware store and buy what he needed, then get back home when he did. The clerk who sold him the hacksaw said they had a long conversation. Dragonette couldn't have made it to the east side and back. He just wanted to take the credit.'

'Well, that man must be crazy,' Marjorie said.

For the first time that day, Alan smiled.

'Johnny, I still don't get why the police wanted to question you,' said his father.

'You know how police are. They want to go over and over the same ground. They want me to remember everybody I saw on my way into the hospital, everybody I saw on the way out, anything that might help them.'

'They're not trying to – '

'Of course not. I left the hospital and walked straight home. Tim heard me come in around five past eight.'

John looked at me. 'They'll probably want you to verify that.'

I said I was glad I could help.

'Are they coming to the funeral?' Ralph asked.

'Oh, yeah,' John said. 'Our ever-vigilant police force will be in attendance.'

'You didn't say a word about any of this. We wouldn't have known anything about it, if Alan hadn't spoken up.'

'The important thing is that April is gone,' John said. 'That's what we should be thinking about.'

'Not who killed her?' Alan boomed, turning each word into a cannonball.

'Alan, stop *yelling* at me,' John said.

'The man who did this to my daughter is *garbage*!' Through some natural extra capacity, Alan's ordinary speaking voice was twice as loud as a normal person's, and when he opened it up, it sounded like a race car on a long straight road. Even now, when he was nearly rattling the windows, he was not really trying to shout. '*He does not deserve to live!*'

Blushing, John walked away.

Just Call Me Joyce peeked in. 'Is anything wrong? My goodness, there's enough noise in here to wake the know you what.'

Alan cleared his throat. 'Guess I make a lot of noise when I get excited.'

'The others will be here in about fifteen minutes.' Joyce gave us a thoroughly insincere smile and backed out. Her father must have been hovering in the hallway. Clearly audible through the door, Joyce said, 'Didn't these people ever hear of Valium?'

Even Alan grinned, minutely.

He twisted around to look for John, who was winding back toward us, hands in his pockets like his father, his eyes on the pale carpet. 'John, is Grant Hoffman coming?'

I remembered Alan asking about Hoffman when he

was dressed in filthy shorts and roaches scrambled through the pizza boxes in his sink.

'I have no idea,' John said.

'One of our best PhD candidates,' Alan said to Marjorie. 'He started off with me, but we moved him over to John two years ago. He dropped out of sight – which is odd, because Grant is an excellent student.'

'He was okay,' John said.

'Grant usually saw me after his conferences with John, but last time, he never showed up.'

'Never showed up for our conference on the sixth, either,' John said. 'I wasted an hour, not to mention all the time I spent going to and fro on the bus.'

'He came to your house?' I asked Alan.

'Absolutely,' Alan said. 'About once a week. Sometimes, he gave me a hand with cleaning up the kitchen, and we'd gab about the progress of his thesis, all kinds of stuff.'

'So call the guy up,' Ralph said to his son.

'I've been a little busy,' John said. 'Anyhow, Hoffman didn't have a telephone. He lived in a single room downtown somewhere, and you had to call him through his landlady. Not that I ever called him.' He looked at me. 'Hoffman used to teach high school in a little town downstate. He saved up some money, and he came here to do graduate work with Alan. He was at least thirty.'

'Do graduate students disappear like that?'

'Now and then they slink away.'

'People like Grant Hoffman don't slink away,' Alan said.

'I don't want to waste my time worrying about *Grant Hoffman*. There must be people who would notice if he got hit by a bus, or if he decided to change his name and move to Las Vegas.'

The door opened. Just Call Me Joyce led a number of men in conservative gray and blue suits into the chapel.

333

After a moment a few women, also dressed in dark suits but younger than the men, became visible in their midst. These new arrivals moved toward John, who took them to his parents.

I sat down in a chair on the aisle. Ralph and one of the older brokers, a man whose hair was only a slightly darker gray than his own, sidled off to the side of the big room and began talking in low voices.

The door clicked open again. I turned around on my seat and saw Paul Fontaine and Michael Hogan entering the room. Fontaine was carrying a beat-up brown satchel slightly too large to be called a briefcase. He and Hogan went to different sides of the room. That powerful and unaffected natural authority that distinguished Michael Hogan radiated out from him like an aura and caused most of the people in the room, especially the women, to glance at him. I suppose great actors also have this capacity, to automatically draw attention toward themselves. And Hogan had the blessing of looking something like an actor without at all looking theatrical – his kind of utterly male handsomeness, cast in the very lines of reliability, steadiness, honesty, and a tough intelligence, was of the sort that other men found reassuring, not threatening. As I watched Hogan moving to the far side of the room under the approving glances of April's mourners, glances he seemed not to notice, it occurred to me that he actually was the kind of person that an older generation of leading men had impersonated on the screen, and I was grateful that he was in charge of April's case.

Less conspicuous, Fontaine poured coffee for himself and sat behind me. He dropped the satchel between his legs.

'The places I run into you,' he said.

I did not point out that I could say the same.

'And the things I hear you say.' He sighed. 'If there's

one thing the ordinary policeman hates, it's a mouthy civilian.'

'Was I wrong?'

'Don't push your luck.' He leaned forward toward me. The bags under his eyes were a little less purple. 'What's your best guess as to the time your friend Ransom got home from the hospital on Wednesday morning?'

'You want to check his alibi?'

'I might as well.' He smiled. 'Hogan and I are representing the department at this municipal extravaganza.'

Cops and cop humor.

He noticed my reaction to his joke, and said, 'Oh, come on. Don't you know what's going to happen here?'

'If you want to ask me questions, you can take me downtown.'

'Now, now. You know that favor you asked me to do?'

'The lost license number?'

'The other favor.' He slid the scuffed leather satchel forward and snapped it open to show me a thick wad of typed and handwritten pages.

'The Blue Rose file?'

He nodded, smiling like a big-nosed cat.

I reached for the satchel, and he slid it back between his legs. 'You were going to tell me what time your friend got home on Wednesday morning.'

'Eight o'clock,' I said. 'It takes about twenty minutes to walk back from the hospital. I thought you said this was going to be hard to find.'

'The whole thing was sitting on top of a file in the basement of the records office. Someone else was curious, and didn't bother putting it back.'

'Don't you want to read it first?'

'I copied the whole damn thing,' he said. 'Get it back to me as soon as you can.'

'Why are you doing this for me?'

He smiled at me in his old way, without seeming to

move his face. 'You wrote that stupid book, which my sergeant adores. And I shall have no other sergeants before him. And maybe there's something to this ridiculous idea after all.'

'You think it's ridiculous to think that the new Blue Rose murders are connected to the old ones?'

'Of course it's ridiculous.' He leaned forward over the satchel. 'By the way, will you please stop trying to be helpful in front of the cameras? As far as the public is concerned, Mrs Ransom was one of Walter's victims. The man on Livermore Avenue, too.'

'He's still unidentified?'

'That's right,' Fontaine said. 'Why?'

'Have you ever heard of a missing student of John's named Grant Hoffman?'

'No. How long has he been missing?'

'A couple of weeks, I think. He didn't turn up for an appointment with John.'

'And you think he could be our victim?'

I shrugged.

'When was the appointment he missed, do you know?'

'On the sixth, I think.'

'That's the day after the body was found.' Fontaine glanced over at Michael Hogan, who was talking with John's parents. Her face toward the detective, Marjorie was drinking in whatever he was saying. She looked like a girl at a dance.

'Do you happen to know how old this student was?'

'Around thirty,' I said, wrenching my attention away from the effect Michael Hogan was making on John's mother. 'He was a graduate student.'

'After the funeral, maybe we'll – ' He stopped talking and stood up. He patted my shoulder. 'Get the file back to me in a day or two.'

He passed down the row of empty chairs and went up to Michael Hogan. The two detectives parted from the

Ransoms and walked a few feet away. Hogan looked quickly, assessingly at me for a long second in which I felt the full weight of his remarkable concentration, then at John. I still felt the impact of his attention. Rapt, Marjorie Ransom continued to stare at the older detective until Ralph tugged her gently back toward the gray-haired broker, and even then she turned her head to catch sight of him over her shoulder. I knew how she felt.

Someone standing beside me said, 'Excuse me, are you Tim Underhill?'

I looked up at a stocky man of about thirty-five wearing thick black glasses and a lightweight navy blue suit. He had an expectant expression on his broad, bland face.

I nodded.

'I'm Dick Mueller – from Barnett? We talked on the phone? I wanted to tell you that I'm grateful for your advice – you sure called it. As soon as the press found out about me and, ah, you know, they went crazy. But because you warned me what was going to happen, I could work out how to get in and out of the office.'

He sat down in front of me, smiling with the pleasure of the story he was about to tell me. The door clicked open again, and I turned my head to see Tom Pasmore slipping into the chapel behind a young man in jeans and a black jacket. The young man was nearly as pale as Tom, but his thick dark hair and thick black eyebrows made his large eyes blaze. He focused on the coffin as soon as he got into the big room. Tom gave me a little wave and drifted up the side of the room.

'You know what I go through to get to work?' Mueller asked.

I wanted to get rid of Dick Mueller so that I could talk to Tom Pasmore.

'I asked Ross Barnett if he wanted me to – '

I broke into the account of How I Get to My Office. 'Was Mr Barnett going to send April Ransom out to San

337

Francisco to open another office, some kind of joint venture with another brokerage house?'

He blinked at me. His eyes were huge behind the big square lenses. 'Did somebody tell you that?'

'Not exactly,' I said. 'It was more of a rumor.'

'Well, there was some talk a while ago about moving into San Francisco.' He looked worried now.

'That wasn't what you meant about the "bridge deal"?'

'Bridge deal?' Then, in a higher tone of voice: 'Bridge deal?'

'You told me to tell your secretary –'

He grinned. 'Oh, you mean the bridge project. Yeah. To remind me of who you were. And you thought I meant the Golden Gate Bridge?'

'Because of April Ransom.'

'Oh, yeah, no, it wasn't anything like that. I was talking about the Horatio Street bridge. In town here. April was nuts about local history.'

'She was writing something about the bridge?'

He shook his head. 'All I know is, she called it the bridge project. But listen, Ross' – he looked sideways and tilted his head toward the prosperous-looking gray-haired man who had been talking with Ralph Ransom – 'worked out this great little plan.'

Mueller told me an elaborate story about entering through a hat shop on Palmer Street, going down into the basement, and taking service stairs up to the fourth floor, where he could let himself into the Barnett copy room.

'Clever,' I said. I had to say something. Mueller was the sort of person who had to impose what delighted him on anyone who would listen. I tried to picture his encounters with Walter Dragonette, Mueller babbling away about bond issues and Walter sitting across the desk in a daze, wondering how that big schoolteacher head would look on a shelf in his refrigerator.

'You must miss April Ransom,' I said.

He settled back down again. 'Oh, sure. She was very important to the office. Sort of a star.'

'What was she like, personally? How would you describe her?'

He pursed his lips and glanced at his boss. 'April worked harder than anyone on earth. She was smart, she had an amazing memory, and she put in a lot of hours. Tremendous energy.'

'Did people like her?'

He shrugged. 'Ross, he certainly liked her.'

'You sound like you're not saying something.'

'Well, I don't know.' Mueller looked at his boss again. 'This is the kind of a person who's always going ninety miles an hour. If you didn't travel at her speed, too bad for you.'

'Did you ever hear that she was thinking of leaving the business to have a baby?'

'Would *Patton* quit? Would *Mike Ditka* quit? To have *babies*?' Mueller clamped a fat hand over his mouth and looked around to see if anyone had noticed his giggle. He wore a pinky ring with a tiny diamond chip and a big college ring with raised letters. Puffy circles of raised fat surrounded both rings.

'You could call her aggressive,' he said. 'It's not a criticism. We're supposed to be aggressive.' He tried to look aggressive as all get-out for a second and succeeded in looking a little bit sneaky.

People had been coming into the room in twos and threes while we talked, filling about three-fourths of the seats. I recognized some of John's neighbors from the local news. When Mueller stood up, I left my seat and carried the heavy satchel to the back of the room, where Tom Pasmore was drinking a cup of coffee.

'I didn't think you'd come,' I said.

'I don't usually have the chance to get a look at my murderers,' he said.

339

'You think April's murderer is here?' I looked around at the roomful of brokers and teachers. Dick Mueller had sidled up to Ross Barnett, who was angrily shaking his head, probably denying that he'd ever had any intention of moving April anywhere at all. Because you never know what you'll be able to use, I stepped sideways and took out my notebook to write down a phrase about a broker so feeble that he used his college ring to get business from other people who had gone to the same college. A combination of letters and numbers was already written on the last page, and it took me a moment to remember what they represented. Tom Pasmore was smiling at me. I put the notebook back in my pocket.

'I'd say there's an excellent chance.' He looked down at the case between my legs. 'The Blue Rose files wouldn't be in that thing, would they?'

'How did you work that out?'

He bent down and picked up the case to show me the dim, worn gold of the initials stamped just below the clasp: WD.

Fontaine had given me William Damrosch's own satchel – he had probably used it as a suitcase when he went on trips, and as a briefcase in town.

'Would you mind bringing this over to my place tonight, so I can make copies?'

'You have a copy machine?' Like Lamont von Heilitz, Tom often gave the impression of resisting technological progress.

'I even have computers.'

I thought he was being playful: I wasn't even sure that he used an electric typewriter.

'They're upstairs. These days, most of my information comes through the modem.' The surprise on my face made him smile. He held up his right hand. 'Honest. I'm a hacker. I'm tapped in all over the place.'

340

'Can you find out someone's name through their license plate number?'

He nodded. 'Sometimes.' He gave me a speculative look. 'Not in every state.'

'I'm thinking of an Illinois plate.'

'Easy.'

I began to tell him about the license number on the piece of paper I thought I had given to Paul Fontaine. At the front of the room, the young man who had come into the room behind Tom turned away from April Ransom's coffin and made a wide circle around John, who turned his back on him, either by chance or intentionally. The music became much louder. Mr Trott appeared through a white door I had not noticed earlier and closed the coffin. At the same time, everybody in the room turned around as the big doors at the back of the chapel admitted two men in their early sixties. One of them, a man about as broad as an ox cart, wore a row of medals on the chest of his police uniform, like a Russian general. The other man had a black armband on the sleeve of his dark gray suit. His hair, as silvery as Ralph Ransom's, was thicker, almost shaggy. I assumed that he must have been the minister.

Isobel Archer and her crew pushed themselves into the room, followed by a dozen other reporters. Isobel waved her staff to a point six feet from Tom Pasmore and me, and the other reporters lined up along the sides of the room, already scribbling in notebooks and talking into their tape recorders. The big silver-haired man marched up to Ross Barnett and whispered something.

'Who's that?' I asked Tom.

'You don't know Merlin Waterford? Our mayor?'

The uniformed man who had come in with him pumped John's hand and pulled him toward the first row. Bright lights flashed on and washed color from the room. The music ended. The pale young man in the black jacket bumped against a row of knees as he fought his way toward a seat. Isobel Archer held up a microphone to her face and began speaking into the camera and the floodlights. John leaned forward and covered his face with his hands.

'Ladies and gentlemen, fellow mourners for April Ransom.' The mayor had moved behind the podium. The white light made his hair gleam. His teeth shone. His skin was the color of a Caribbean beach. 'Some few weeks ago, I had the pleasure of attending the dinner at which a brilliant young woman received the financial community's Association Award. I witnessed the respect she had earned from her peers and shared her well-earned pride in that wonderful honor. April Ransom's profound grasp of business essentials, her integrity, her humanity, and her deep commitment to the greater good of our community inspired us all that night. She stood before us, her friends and colleagues, as a shining example of everything I have tried to encourage and represent during the three terms in which I have been privileged to serve as the mayor of this fine city.'

If you cared for that sort of thing, the mayor was a great speaker. He would pledge, in fact he would go so far as to promise, that the memory of April Ransom's character and achievements would never leave him as he worked night and day to bring good government to every citizen of Millhaven. He would dedicate whatever time was left to him to –

This went on for about fifteen minutes, after which the chief of police, Arden Vass, stumped up to the microphone, frowned, and pulled three sheets of folded paper from an inside jacket pocket. The papers crackled as he flattened them onto the podium with his fist. He was not actually frowning, I saw. That was just his normal expression. He tugged a pair of steel-rimmed glasses from a pocket below the rows of medals and rammed them onto his face.

'I can't pontificate like my friend, the mayor,' he said. His hoarse, bludgeoning voice slammed each of his short sentences to the ground before picking up the next. We had a great police department. Each man – and woman – in that department was a trained professional. That was why our crime rate was one of the lowest in the nation. Our officers had recently apprehended one of the worst criminals in history. That man was currently safe in custody, awaiting a full statement of charges and eventual trial. The woman whose life we were celebrating today would understand the importance of cooperation between the community and the brave men who risked their lives to protect it. That was the Millhaven represented by April Ransom. I have nothing more to say. Thank you.

Vass pushed himself away from the podium and lumbered toward the first row of seats. For a second everybody sat frozen with uncertainty, staring at the empty podium and the bleached flowers. Then the lights snapped off.

4

April's colleagues were moving in a compact group toward the parking lot. The pale young man in the black jacket had disappeared. Below the crest of the front lawn, Isobel and her crew were pulling away from the curb, and the Boughmobile was already moving toward the stop sign at the end of the street. John's neighbors stood near a long line of cars parked across the street, wistfully watching Isobel and the officials drive away.

Stony with rage, John Ransom stood with his parents

at the top of the steps. Fontaine and Hogan stood a few yards from Tom Pasmore and me, taking everything in, like cops. I was sure I could detect in Hogan's face an extra, ironic layer of impassivity, suggesting that he had thought his superiors' speeches ridiculously self-serving. He spoke a few words without seeming to move his lips, like a schoolboy uttering a scathing remark about his teacher, and then I knew I was right. Hogan noticed me looking at him, and amusement and recognition briefly flared in his eyes. He knew what I had seen, and he knew that I agreed with him. Fontaine left him and moved briskly across the dry lawn toward the Ransoms.

'Are you going with us to the crematorium?' I asked Tom.

He shook his head. In the sunlight, his face had that only partially smoothed-out parchment look again, and I wondered if he had ever been to bed. 'What is that detective asking John?' he asked me.

'He probably wants him to see if he can identify the victim from Livermore Avenue.'

I could almost see his mind working. 'Tell me more.'

I told Tom about Grant Hoffman, and a little color came into his face.

'Will you go along?'

'I think Alan Brookner might come, too.' I looked around, realizing that I had not yet seen Alan.

'Come over any time you can get away. I want to hear what happens at the morgue.'

The front door opened and closed behind us. Leaning on Joyce Brophy's arm, Alan Brookner moved slowly into the sunlight. Joyce signaled to me. 'Professor Underhill, maybe you'll see Professor Brookner down to the car, so we can start our procession. There's deadlines here too, just like everywhere else, and we're scheduled in at two-thirty. Maybe you can get Professor Ransom and his folks all set?'

Alan hooked an arm through mine. I asked him how he was doing.

'I'm still on my feet, sonny boy.'

We moved toward the Ransoms.

Paul Fontaine came up to us and said, 'Four-thirty?'

'Sure,' I said. 'You want Alan there, too?'

'If he can make it.'

'I can make anything you can set up,' Alan said, not looking at the detective. 'This at the morgue?'

'Yes. It's a block from Armory Place, on –'

'I can find the morgue,' Alan said.

The hearse swung around the corner and parked in front of the Pontiac. Two cars filled with people from Ely Place completed the procession.

'I thought the mayor gave a wonderful tribute,' Marjorie said.

'Impressive man,' Ralph said.

We got to the bottom of the stairs, and Alan wrenched his arm out of mine. 'Thirty-five years ago, Merlin was one of my students.' Marjorie gave him a grateful smile. 'The man was a dolt.'

'Oh!' Marjorie squeaked. Ralph grimly opened the back door, and his wife scooted along the seat.

John and I went up to the front of the car. 'They turned my wife's funeral into a sound bite,' he snarled. 'As far as I'm concerned, fifty percent of their goddamned bill is paid for in publicity.' I let myself into the silent car and followed the hearse to the crematorium.

5

'Why do you have to go to the morgue? I don't see the point.'

'I don't either, Dad.'

'The whole idea is ridiculous,' said Marjorie.

'The cops at the service must have overheard something,' John said.

'Overheard *what*?'

'About that missing student.'

'They didn't overhear it,' I said. 'I mentioned the student to Paul Fontaine.'

After a second of silence, John said, 'Well, that's okay.'

'But what was the *point*?' Ralph asked.

'There's an unidentified man in the morgue. It might have something to do with April's case.'

Marjorie and Ralph sat in shocked silence.

'The missing student might be the person in the morgue.'

'Oh, God,' Ralph said.

'Of course he isn't,' Marjorie said. 'The boy just dropped out, that's all.'

'Grant wouldn't do that,' Alan said.

'I might as well go to the morgue, if that's what the cops want,' John said.

'I'll do it myself,' Alan said. 'John doesn't have to go.'

'Fontaine wants me there. You don't have to come along, Alan.'

'Yes, I do,' Alan said.

There was no more conversation until I pulled up in front of John's house. The Ransoms got out of the backseat. When Alan remained in the passenger seat,

346

John bent to his window. 'Aren't you coming in, Alan?'

'Tim will take me home.'

John pushed himself off the car. His mother was zigzagging over the lawn, picking up garbage.

6

Alan pulled himself across the sidewalk on heavy legs. Shorn grass gleamed up from the lawn. We went into the house, and for a moment he turned and looked at me with clouded, uncertain eyes. My heart sank. He had forgotten whatever he had planned to do next. He hid his confusion by turning away again and moving through the entry into his hallway.

He paused just inside the living room. The curtains had been pulled aside. The wood gleamed, and the air smelled of furniture polish. Neat stacks of mail, mostly catalogues and junk mail, sat on the coffee table.

'That's right,' Alan said. He sat down on the couch, and leaned against the brown leather. 'Cleaning service.' He looked around at the sparkling room. 'I guess nobody is coming back here.' He cleared his throat. 'I thought people always came to the house after a funeral.'

He had forgotten that his daughter lived in another house.

I sat down in an overstuffed chair.

Alan crossed his arms over his chest and gazed at his windows. For a moment, I saw some fugitive emotion flare in his eyes. Then he closed them and fell asleep. His chest rose and fell, and his breathing became regular. After a minute or two, he opened his eyes again. 'Tim, yes,' he said. 'Good.'

'Do you still feel like going to the morgue?'

He looked confused for only a moment. 'You bet I do. I knew the boy better than John.' He smiled. 'I gave him some of my old clothes – a few suits got too big for me. The boy had saved up enough to be able to pay tuition and rent, but he didn't have much left over.'

Heavy footsteps came down the stairs. Whoever was in the house turned into the hall. Alan blinked at me, and I stood up and went to the entrance of the room. A heavy woman in black trousers and a University of Illinois T-shirt was coming toward me, pulling a vacuum cleaner behind her.

'I have to say that this was the biggest job I ever had in my whole entire life. The other girl, she had to go home to her family, so I finished up alone.' She looked at me as if I shared some responsibility for the condition of the house. 'That's six hours.'

'You did a very good job.'

'You're telling me.' She dropped the vacuum cleaner hose and leaned heavily against the molding to look at Alan. 'You're not a very neat man, Mr Brookner.'

'Things got out of hand.'

'You're going to have to do better than this if you want me to come back.'

'Things are already better,' I said. 'A private duty nurse will be coming every day, as soon as we can arrange it.'

She tilted her head and looked at me speculatively for a moment. 'I need a hundred and twenty dollars.'

Alan reached into a pocket of his suit and pulled out a flat handful of twenty-dollar bills. He counted out six and stood up to give them to the cleaning woman.

'You're a real humdinger, Mr Brookner.' She slid the twenties into a pocket. 'Thursdays are best from now on.'

'That's fine,' said Alan.

The cleaning woman left the room and picked up the hose of the vacuum cleaner. Then she dragged the vacuum back to the entrance. 'Did you want me

348

to do anything with that floral tribute thing?'

Alan looked at her blankly.

'Like, do you water it, or anything?'

Alan opened his mouth. 'Where is it?'

'I moved it into the kitchen.'

'Wreaths don't need watering.'

'Fine with me.' The vacuum cleaner bumped down the hall. A door opened and closed. A few minutes later, the woman returned and I walked her to the door. She kept darting little glances at me. When I opened the door, she said, 'He must be like Dr Jeckel and Mr Heckel, or something.'

Alan was carrying a circular wreath of white carnations and yellow roses into the hallway. 'You know Flory Park, don't you?'

'I grew up in another part of town,' I said.

'Then I'll tell you how to get there.' He carried the wreath to the front door. 'I suppose you can find the lake. It is due east.'

We went outside. 'East is to our right,' Alan said.

'Yes, sir,' I said.

He marched down the walkway and veered across the sidewalk to the Pontiac. He got into the passenger seat and hugged the big wreath against his chest.

On Alan's instructions, I turned north on Eastern Shore Drive. I asked if he wanted the little community beach down below the bluffs south of us.

'That's Bunch Park. April didn't use it much. Too many people.'

He clutched the wreath as we drove north on Eastern Shore Drive. After ten or twelve miles we crossed into Riverwood.

Eastern Shore Road shrank to a two-lane road, and it divided into two branches, one veering west, the other continuing north into a pine forest sprinkled with vast contemporary houses. Alan ordered me to go straight. At the next intersection, we turned right. The car moved forward through deep shadows.

Indented orange lettering on a brown wooden sign said FLORY PARK. The long drive curved into a circular parking lot where a few Jeeps and Range Rovers stood against a bank of trees. Alan said, 'One of the most beautiful parks in the county, and nobody knows it exists.'

He struggled out of the car. 'This way.' On the other side of the lot, he stepped over the low concrete barrier and walked across the grass to a narrow trail. 'I was here once before. April was in grade school.'

I asked him if he'd let me carry the wreath.

'No.'

The trail led into a stand of mixed pine and birch trees. I moved along in front of Alan, bending occasional branches out of his way. He was breathing easily and moving at a good walker's pace. We came out into a large clearing that led to a little rise. Over the top of the rise I could see the tops of other trees, and over them, the long flat blue line of the lake. It was very hot in the clearing. Sweat soaked through my shirt. I wiped my forehead. 'Alan,' I said, 'I might not be able to go any farther.'

'Why not?'

'I have a lot of trouble in places like this.'

He frowned at me, trying to figure out what I meant. I took a tentative step forward, and instantly pressure mines blew apart the ground in front of us and hurled men into the air. Blood spouted from the places where their legs had been.

'What kind of trouble?'

'Open spaces make me nervous.'

'Why don't you close your eyes?'

I closed my eyes. Little figures in black clothes flitted through the trees. Others crawled up to the edge of the clearing.

'Can I do anything to help you?'

'I don't think so.'

'Then I suppose you'll have to do it yourself.'

Two teenage boys in baggy bathing suits came out of the trees and passed us. They glanced over their shoulders as they went across the clearing and up the rise.

'You need me to do this?'

'Yes.'

'Here goes.' I took another step forward. The little men in black moved toward the treeline. My entire body ran with sweat.

'I'm going to walk in front of you,' Alan said. 'Watch my feet, and *step only where I step*. Okay?'

I nodded. My mouth was stuffed with cotton and sand. Alan moved in front of me. 'Don't look at anything but my feet.'

He stepped forward, leaving the clear imprint of his shoe in the dusty trail. I set my right foot directly on top of it. He took another step. I moved along behind him. My back prickled. The path began to rise beneath my feet. Alan's small, steady footprints carried me forward. He finally stopped moving.

'Can you look up now?' he asked.

We were standing at the top of the hill. In front of us, an almost invisible path went down a long forested slope. The main branch continued down to an iron staircase descending to a bright strip of sand and the still blue water. Far out on the lake, sailboats moved in lazy, erratic loops. 'Let's finish this,' I said, and went down the other side of the rise toward the safety of the trees.

As soon as I moved onto the main branch of the path, Alan called out, 'Where are you going?'

I pointed toward the iron stairs and the beach.

'This way,' he said, indicating the lesser branch.

I set off after him. He said, 'Could you carry this for a while?'

I held out my arms. The wreath was heavier than I had

expected. The stems of the roses dug into my arms.

'When she was a child, April would pack a book and something to eat and spend hours in a little grove down at the end of this path. It was her favorite place.'

The path disappeared as it met wide shelves of rock between the dense trees. Spangled light fell on the mottled stone. Birches and maples crowded up through the shale. Alan finally halted in front of a jagged pile of boulders. 'I can't get up this thing by myself.'

Without the wreath, it would have been easy; the wreath made it no more than difficult. The problem was carrying the wreath and pulling Alan Brookner along with my free hand. Alone and unhindered, I could have done it in about five minutes. Less. Three minutes. Alan and I made it in about twenty. When it was over, I had sweated through my jacket, and a torn zipper dangled away from the fabric.

I knelt down on a flat slab, took the wreath off my shoulder and looked at Alan grimly reaching up at me. I wrapped a hand around his wrist and pulled him toward me until he could grab the collar of my jacket. He held on like a monkey while I put my arms around his waist and lifted him bodily up onto the slab.

'See why I needed you?' He was breathing hard.

I wiped my forehead and inspected the wreath. A few wires and some stray roses protruded, and a dark green fern hung down like a cat's tail. I pushed the roses back into the wreath and wound the stray wires around them. Then I got to my feet and held out a hand to Alan.

We walked over the irregular surface formed by the juncture of hundreds of large boulders. He asked me for the wreath again.

'How far are we going?' I asked.

Alan waved toward the far side of the shelf of rock. A screen of red maples four or five trees thick stood before the long blue expanse of the lake.

On the other side of the maples, the hill dropped off gently for another thirty feet. A shallow groove of a path cut straight down through the trees and rocks to a glen. A flat granite projection lay in a grove of maples like the palm of a hand. Below the ridge of granite, sunlight sparkled on the lake. Alan asked me for the wreath again.

'That's the place.' He set off stiffly down the brown path.

After another half-dozen steps, he spoke again. 'April came here to be alone.' Another few steps. 'This was dear to her.'

He drew in a shuddering breath. 'I can *see* her here.'

He said no more until we stood on the flat shelf of granite that hung out over the lake. I walked up to the edge of the rock. Off to my right, the two boys who had passed us at the beginning of the clearing were bobbing up and down in a deep pool formed by a curve of the shoreline about twenty feet below the jutting surface of the rock. It was a natural diving board.

I stepped back from the edge.

'This is April's funeral,' Alan said. 'Her real funeral.'

I felt like a trespasser.

'I have to say good-bye to her.'

The enormity of his act struck me, and I stepped back toward the shade of the maples.

Alan walked slowly to the center of the shelf of rock. The little white-haired man seemed majestic to me. He had planned this moment almost from the time he had learned of his daughter's death.

'My dear baby,' he said. His voice shook. He clutched the wreath close to his chest. 'April, I will always be your father, and you will always be my daughter. I will carry you in my heart until the day of my death. I promise you that the person who did this to you will not go free. I don't have much strength left, but it will be enough for both of us. I love you, my child.'

353

He stepped forward to the lip of the rock and looked down. In the softest voice I had ever heard from him, he said, 'Your father wishes you peace.'

Alan took a step backward and dangled the wreath in his right hand. Then he moved his right foot backward, cocked his arm back, swung his arm forward, and hurled the wreath into the bright air like a discus. It sailed ten or twelve feet out and plummeted toward the water, turning over and over in the air.

The boys pointed and shouted when they saw the wreath falling toward the lake pool. They started swimming toward the spot where it would fall, but stopped when they saw Alan and me standing on the rock shelf. The ring of flowers smacked onto the water. Luminous ripples radiated out from it. The wreath bobbed in the water like a raft, then began drifting down the shoreline. The two boys paddled back toward the little beach at the bottom of the stairs.

'I'm still her father,' Alan said.

7

When we pulled up in front of John's house, only the shining gap between Alan's eyelids and his lower lids indicated that he was still awake.

'I'll wait,' he said.

John opened the door and pulled me inside. 'Where were you? Do you know what time it is?'

His parents were standing up in the living room, looking at us anxiously.

'Is Alan all right?' Marjorie asked.

'He's a little tired,' I said.

'Look, I have to run,' John said. 'We should be back in

half an hour. This can't take any longer than that.'

Ralph Ransom started to say something, but John glared at me and virtually pushed me outside. He banged the door shut and started down the path, buttoning his jacket as he went.

'My God, the old guy's asleep,' he said. 'First you make us late, and then you drag him out of bed, when he hardly even knows who he is.'

'He knows who he is,' I said.

We got into the car, and John tapped Alan's shoulder as I pulled away. 'Alan? Are you okay?'

'Are you?' Alan asked.

John jerked back his hand.

I decided to take the Horatio Street bridge, and then remembered something Dick Mueller had said to me.

'John,' I said, 'you didn't tell me that April was interested in local history.'

'She did a little research here and there. Nothing special.'

'Wasn't she especially interested in the Horatio Street bridge?'

'I don't know anything about it.'

The glittering strips at the bottom of Alan's eyelids were closed. He was breathing deeply and steadily.

'What took you so long?'

'Alan wanted to go to Flory Park.'

'What did he want to do in Flory Park?'

'April used to go there.'

'What are you trying to tell me?' His voice was flat with anger.

'There's a flat rock that overlooks a lake pool, and when April was in high school, she used to sun herself there and dive into the pool.'

He relaxed. 'Oh. That could be.'

'Alan wanted to see it once more.'

'What did he do? Moon around and think about April?'

'Something like that.'

He grunted in a way that combined irritation and dismissal.

'John,' I said, 'even after we listened to Walter Drago-nette talk about the Horatio Street bridge, even after we went there, you didn't think that April's interest in the bridge was worth bringing up?'

'I didn't know much about it,' he said.

'What?' Alan muttered. 'What was that about April?' He rubbed his eyes and sat up straight, peering out to see where we were going.

John groaned and turned away from us.

'We were talking about some research April was doing,' I said.

'Ah.'

'Did she ever talk to you about it?'

'April talked to me about everything.' He waited a moment. 'I don't remember the matter very well. It was about some bridge.'

'Actually, it was that bridge right ahead of us,' John said. We were on Horatio Street. A block before us stood the embankment of the Millhaven River and the low walls of the bridge.

'Wasn't there something about a *crime*?'

'It was a crime, all right,' John said.

I looked at the Green Woman Taproom as we went past and, in the second before the bridge walls cut it from view, saw a blue car drawn up onto the cement slab beside the tavern. Two cardboard boxes stood next to the car, and the trunk was open. Then we were rattling across the bridge. The instant after that, I thought that the car had looked like the Lexus that followed John Ransom to Shady Mount. I leaned forward and tried to see it in the rearview mirror, but the walls of the bridge blocked my view.

356

'You're hung up on that place. Like Walter Dragonette.'

'Like April,' I said.

'April had too much going on in her life to spend much time on local history.' He sounded bitter about it.

Long before we got close to Armory Place, voices came blasting out of the plaza. *'Waterford must go! Vass must go! Waterford must go! Vass must go!'*

'Guess the plea for unity didn't work,' John said.

'You turn right up here to get to the morgue,' Alan said.

8

A ramp led up to the entrance of the Millhaven County Morgue. When I pulled up in front of the ramp, Paul Fontaine got out of an unmarked sedan and waved me into a slot marked FOR OFFICIAL VEHICLES ONLY. He stood slouching with his hands in the pockets of his baggy gray suit. We were ten minutes late.

'I'm sorry, it's my fault,' I said.

'I'd rather be here than Armory Place,' Fontaine said. He took in Alan's weariness. 'Professor Brookner, you could sit it out in the waiting room.'

'No, I don't think I could,' Alan said.

'Then let's get it over with.' At the top of the ramp, Fontaine let us into an entry with two plastic chairs on either side of a tall ashtray crowded with butts. Beyond the next door, a blond young man with taped glasses sat drumming a pencil on a battered desk. Wide acne scars sandblasted the flesh under his chin.

'We're all here now, Teddy,' Fontaine said. 'I'll take them back.'

'Do the thang,' Teddy said.

Fontaine gestured toward the interior of the building. Two rows of dusty fluorescent tubes hung from the ceiling. The walls were painted the flat dark green of military vehicles. 'I'd better prepare you for what you're going to see. There isn't much left of his face.' He stopped in front of the fourth door on the right side of the corridor and looked at Alan. 'You might find this disturbing.'

'Don't worry about me,' Alan said.

Fontaine opened the door into a small room without furniture or windows. Banks of fluorescent lights hung from the ceiling. In the center of the room a body covered with a clean white sheet lay on a wheeled table.

Fontaine went to the far side of the body. 'This is the man we found behind the St Alwyn Hotel.' He folded back the sheet to the top of the man's chest.

Alan drew in a sharp breath. Most of the face had been sliced into strips of flesh that looked like uncooked bacon. The teeth were disturbingly healthy and intact beneath the shreds of skin. A cheekbone made a white stripe beneath an empty eye socket. The lower lip dropped over the chin. Long wounds separated the flesh of the neck; wider wounds on the chest continued beneath the sheet.

Fontaine let us adjust to the spectacle on the table. 'Does anything about this man look familiar? I know it's not easy.'

John said, 'Nobody could identify him – there isn't anything left.'

'Professor Brookner?'

'It could be Grant.' Alan took his eyes from the table and looked at John. 'Grant's hair was that light brown color.'

'Alan, this doesn't even look like hair.'

'Are you prepared to identify this man, Professor Brookner?'

358

Alan looked back down at the body and shook his head. 'I can't be positive.'

Fontaine waited to see if Alan had anything more to say. 'Would it help you to see his clothes?'

'I'd like to see the clothing, yes.'

Fontaine folded the sheet back up over the body and walked past us toward the door to the corridor.

Then we stood in another tiny windowless room, in the same configuration as before, Fontaine on the far side of a wheeled table, the three of us in front of it. Rumpled, bloodstained clothes lay scattered across the table.

'What we have here is what the deceased was wearing on the night of his death. A seersucker jacket with a label from Hatchett and Hatch, a green polo shirt from Banana Republic, khaki pants from the Gap, Fruit of the Loom briefs, brown cotton socks, cordovan shoes.' Fontaine pointed at each item in turn.

Alan raised his eagle's face. 'Seersucker jacket? Hatchett and Hatch? That was mine. It's Grant.' His face was colorless. 'And he told me that he was going to treat himself to some new clothes with the money I gave him.'

'You gave money to Grant Hoffman?' John asked. 'Besides the clothes?'

'Are you sure this was your jacket?' Fontaine lifted the shredded, rusty-looking jacket by its shoulders.

'I'm sure, yes,' Alan said. He stepped back from the table. 'I gave it to him last August – we were sorting out some clothes. He tried it on, and it fit him.' He pressed a hand to his mouth and stared at the ruined jacket.

'You're positive.' Fontaine laid the jacket down on the table.

Alan nodded.

'In that case, sir, would you please look at the deceased once more?'

'He already looked at the body,' John said in a voice too loud for the small room. 'I don't see any point in

359

subjecting my father-in-law to this torture all over again.'

'Sir,' Fontaine said, speaking only to Alan, 'you are certain that this was the jacket you gave to Mr Hoffman?'

'I wish I weren't,' Alan said.

John exploded. 'This man just lost his daughter! How can you think of subjecting him to – '

'Enough, John,' Alan said. He looked ten years older than when he had hurled the wreath into the lake.

'You two gentlemen can wait in the hall,' Fontaine said. He came around the table and put his hand high on Alan's back, just below the nape of his neck. This gentleness, his whole tone when dealing with Alan, surprised me. 'You can wait for us in the hall.'

A technician in a white T-shirt and white pants came through the adjoining door and crossed to the table. Without looking at us, he began folding the bloody clothes and placing them in transparent evidence bags. John rolled his eyes, and we went into the hall.

'What a setup,' John said. He was spinning around and around in the hallway. I leaned my back against a wall. Low voices came from inside the other room.

At the sound of footsteps, John stopped spinning. Paul Fontaine stayed inside the room while Alan marched out.

'I'll be in touch soon,' Fontaine said.

Alan walked down the hallway without speaking or looking back.

'Alan?' John called.

He kept on walking.

'It was someone else, right?'

Alan walked past Teddy and opened the door to the entry. 'Tim, will you drop me off?'

'Of course,' I said.

Alan moved through the door and let it close behind him. 'What the hell,' John said. By the time we got into the entry, the outside door had already closed behind

360

Alan. When we got outside, he was on his way down the ramp.

We caught up with him on the ramp. John put his arm through Alan's, and Alan shook him off.

'I'm sorry you had to see that,' John said.

'I want to go home.'

'Sure,' John said. When we got to the car, he opened the door for the old man, closed it behind him, and got into the backseat. I started the engine. 'At least that's over,' John said.

'Is it?' Alan asked.

I backed out of the space and turned toward Armory Place. John leaned forward and patted Alan's shoulder.

'You've been great all day long,' John said. 'Is there anything I can do for you now?'

'You could stop talking,' Alan said.

'It was Grant Hoffman, wasn't it?' I asked.

'Oh, God,' John said.

'Of course it was,' Alan said.

9

I slowed down as we drove past the Green Woman Taproom, but the blue car was gone.

'Why would anybody kill Grant Hoffman?' John asked.

No one responded. We drove back to his house in a silence deepened rather than broken by the sounds of the other cars and the slight breeze that blew in through the open windows. At Ely Place John told me to come back when I could and got out of the car. Then he paused for a second and put his face up to the passenger window and looked past Alan at me. A hard, transparent film covered his eyes like a shield. 'Do you think I should tell my parents about Grant?'

Alan did not move.

'I'll follow your lead,' I said.

He said he would leave the door unlocked for me and turned away.

When I followed Alan inside his house, he went upstairs and sat on his bed and held out his arms like a child so that I could remove his jacket. 'Shoes,' he said, and I untied his shoes and slipped them off while he fumbled with his necktie. He tried unbuttoning his shirt, but his fingers couldn't manage it, and I undid the buttons for him.

He cleared his throat with an explosive sound, and his huge, commanding voice filled the room. 'Was April as bad as Grant? I have to know.'

It took me a moment to understand what he meant. 'Not at all. You saw her at the funeral parlor.'

He sighed. 'Ah. Yes.'

I slid the shirt down his arms and laid it on his bed.

'Poor Grant.'

I didn't say anything. Alan undid his belt and stood up to push his trousers down over his hips. He sat again on the bed, and I pulled the trousers off his legs.

Dazed and unfocused, he watched me pull a handkerchief, keys, and bills from his trouser pockets and put them on his bedside table.

'Alan, do you know why April was interested in the Horatio Street bridge?'

'It had something to do with the Vuillard in their living room. You've seen it?'

I said that I had.

'She said one of the figures in the painting reminded her of a man she had heard about. A policeman – some policeman who killed himself in the fifties. She couldn't look at the painting without thinking about him. She did

362

some research on it – April was a great researcher, you know.' He wrenched the pillow beneath his head. 'I need to get some sleep, Tim.'

I went to the bedroom door and said that I'd call him later that evening, if he liked.

'Come here tomorrow.'

I think he was asleep before I got down the stairs.

10

Ralph and Marjorie Ransom, back in their black-and-silver running suits, sat side by side on one of the couches.

'I agree with John,' Ralph said. 'Thin stripes and puckered cotton, that's a seersucker jacket. That's the *point*. All seersucker jackets look alike. Hatchett and Hatch probably unloaded ten thousand of the things.'

By this time I was coming into the living room, and Marjorie Ransom leaned forward to look past her husband. 'You saw that poor boy too, didn't you, Tim? Did he look like John's student to you?'

Ralph broke in before I could respond. 'At this stage of the game, Alan Brookner couldn't tell Frank Sinatra from Gabby Hayes.'

'Well, I don't know,' I said.

'Mom,' John said loudly, carrying a fresh drink in from the kitchen, 'Tim has no idea what Grant Hoffman looked like.'

'Right,' I said. 'I'm a stranger here myself.'

'Get yourself a drink, son,' Ralph said. 'It's the Attitude Adjustment Hour.'

'That's what they call it at our center,' Marjorie said. 'Attitude Adjustment Hour. Isn't that cute?'

'I'll get myself something in the kitchen,' I said, and

went around the back of the couch and looked at the Vuillard over the tops of the Ransoms' heads.

Only one figure on the canvas, a child, looked forward and out of the painting, as if returning the viewer's gaze. Everyone else, the women and the servants and the other children, was caught in the shimmer of light and the circumstances of their gathering. The child who faced forward sat by himself on the lush grass, a few inches from a brilliant smear of golden light. He was perhaps an inch from the actual center of the painting itself, where the shape of a woman turning toward a tea service intersected one of the boughs of the juniper tree. As soon as I had seen him, he became the actual center of the painting, a sober, dark-haired boy of seven or eight looking unhappily but intently out of both the scene and the frame – right at me, it seemed. He knew he was in a painting, the meaning of which he contained within himself.

'Tim only came here to admire my art,' John said.

'Oh, it's just lovely,' Marjorie said. 'That big red one?'

I went into the kitchen and poured a glass of club soda. When I returned, Ralph and Marjorie were talking about something the day had brought back to them, a period that must have been the unhappiest of their lives.

'I'll never forget it,' Marjorie said. 'I thought I was going to faint.'

'That guy at the door,' Ralph said. 'God, I knew what it was as soon as the car pulled up in front of the house. He got out and stood there, making sure the address was right. Then the other one, the sergeant, got out, and handed him the flag. I didn't know whether to cry or punch him in the mouth.'

'And then we got that telegram, and there it was in black and white. Special Forces Captain John Ransom, killed in action at Lang Vei.'

'Nobody knew where I was, and another guy was identified as me.'

'Is that what happened?' I asked.

'What a foul-up,' said Ralph. 'If you made a mistake like that in business, you'd be out on your ear.'

'It's surprising more mistakes like that weren't made,' I said.

'In my opinion, John should have got at least a Silver Star, if not the Medal of Honor,' Ralph said. 'My kid was a hero over there.'

'I survived,' John said.

'Ralph broke down and cried like a baby when we found out,' Marjorie said.

Ralph ignored this. 'I mean it, kid. To me, you're a hero, and I'm damn proud of you.' He set down his empty glass, stood up, and went to his son. John obediently stood up and let himself be embraced. Neither of them looked as though he had done much embracing.

When his father let him go, John said, 'Why don't we all go out for dinner? It's about time.'

'This one's on me,' Ralph said, reminding me of his son. 'You better get me while you can, I'm not going to be around forever.'

When we got back from Jimmy's, I told John that I wanted to take a walk. Ralph and Marjorie headed in for a nightcap before going to bed, and I let myself out, took Damrosch's case from the trunk, and walked on the quiet streets beneath the beautiful starry night to Tom Pasmore's house.

PART SEVEN

Tom Pasmore

1

Familiar jazz music came from Tom's speakers, a breathy, authoritative tenor saxophone playing the melody of 'Star Dust.'

'You're playing "Blue Rose,"' I said. 'Glenroy Breakstone. I never heard it sound so good.'

'It came out on CD a couple of months ago.' He was wearing a gray glen plaid suit and a black vest, and I was sure that he had gone back to bed after the service. We emerged from the fabulous litter into the clearing of the sofa and the coffee table. Next to the usual array of bottles, glasses, and ice bucket lay the disc's jewel box. I picked it up and looked at the photograph reproduced from the original album – Glenroy Breakstone's broad face bent to the mouthpiece of his horn. When I was sixteen, I had thought of him as an old man, but the photograph showed a man no older than forty. Of course the record had been made long before I became aware of it, and if Breakstone were still alive, he had to be over seventy.

'I think I'm trying to get inspired,' Tom said. He bent over the table and poured an inch of malt whiskey into a thick low glass. 'Want anything? There's coffee in the kitchen.'

I said that I'd be grateful for the coffee, and he went back into his kitchen and returned a moment later with a steaming ceramic mug.

'Tell me about the morgue.' He sat down in his chair

and gestured me toward the couch in front of the coffee table.

'They had the man's clothes laid out, and Alan recognized the jacket as one he'd given to this student, Grant Hoffman.'

'And you think that's who it was?'

I nodded. 'I think it was Hoffman.'

Tom sipped the whiskey. 'One. The original Blue Rose murderer is torturing John Ransom. Probably he intends to kill him, too, eventually. Two. Someone else is imitating the original Blue Rose killer, and he too is trying to destroy John. Three. Another party is using the Blue Rose murders to cover up his real motives.' He took another little sip. 'There are other possibilities, but I want to stick with these, at least for now. In all three cases, some very determined character is still happily convinced the police think that Walter Dragonette committed his crimes.'

Tommy Flanagan began spinning out an ethereal solo on 'Star Dust.'

I told Tom about April Ransom's interest in the Horatio Street bridge and William Damrosch.

'Did she write up any of her findings?'

'I don't know. Maybe I could look around her office and find her notes. I'm not even sure John really knew anything about it.'

'Don't let him know you're interested in the notes,' he said. 'Let's just do things quietly, for a while.'

'You're thinking about it, aren't you? You already have ideas about it.'

'I want to find out who killed her. I also want to find out who killed this Grant Hoffman. And I want your help.'

'You and John.'

'You'll be helping John, too, but I'd rather you didn't tell him about our discussions until I say it's okay.'

I agreed to this.

'I said that I want to find out,' Tom said. 'That's what I meant. I want to know how and why April Ransom and that graduate student were killed. If we can help the police at that point, fine. If not, that's fine, too. I'm not in the justice business.'

'You don't care if April's murderer is arrested?'

'I can't predict what will happen. We might learn his identity without being able to do anything about it. That would be acceptable to me.'

'But if we find out who he is, we should be able to give our information to the police.'

'Sometimes it works out that way.' He leaned back in his chair, watching to see how I was taking this.

'What if I can't agree to this? I just go back to John's and forget about this conversation?'

'You go back to John's and do whatever you like.'

'I'd never know what happened. I'd never know what you did or what you found out.'

'Probably not.'

I couldn't stand the thought of walking away without knowing what he would do – I had to know what the two of us could discover.

'If you think I'm going to walk out now, you're crazy,' I said.

'Ah, good,' he said, smiling. He had never doubted that I would accept his terms. 'Let's go upstairs. I'll show you my toys.'

2

At the far left of the big downstairs room, past the cabinets for the sound system and the shelves packed with compact discs, a wide staircase led up to the second floor. Tom went up the stairs one step ahead of me now, already talking. 'I want us to begin at the beginning,' he said. 'If nothing else comes out of this, I want to understand the first Blue Rose murders. For a long time, Lamont thought it was solved, I guess – as you did, Tim. But I think it always bothered him.' At the top of the stairs, he turned around to look at me. 'Two days before his death, he told me the whole history of the Blue Rose murders. We were on the plane back from Eagle Lake, and we were going to stay at the St Alwyn.' He laughed out loud. 'A couple of nuns in the seats in front of us almost broke their necks, they were listening in so hard. Lamont said that you could call Damrosch's suicide a sort of wrongful arrest – by then he knew that my grandfather had killed Damrosch. Lamont was doing two things at once. He was preparing me to face the truth about my grandfather.'

He stepped back to let me reach the top of the stairs.

'And the second thing Lamont was doing – '

'Was to get me interested in the Blue Rose murders. I think the two of us would have worked on that one next. And do you know what that means? If he hadn't been killed, Lamont and I might have saved April Ransom's life.'

His face twitched. 'That's something I'd like to be clear about.'

'Me, too,' I said. I had my own reason for wanting to learn the identity of the original Blue Rose murderer.

'Okay,' he said. Now Tom did not look languid, bored, amused, indifferent, or detached. He didn't look lost or unhappy. I had seen all of these things in him many times, but I had never seen him in the grip of a controlled excitement. He had never let me see this steely side of him. It looked like the center of his being.

'Let's get to work.' Tom turned around and went down the hallway to what had been the door of Lamont van Heilitz's bedroom and went in.

The old bedroom was dark when I followed him in. My first impression was of a fire-sale chaos like the room downstairs. I saw the dim shapes of desks and cabinets and what looked like the glassy rectangles of several television sets. Books on dark shelves covered most of the walls. A thick dark curtain covered the window. In the depths of the room, Tom switched on a halogen lamp just as I finally grasped that the televisions were computer monitors.

He went methodically around the room, switching on lamps, as I took in that his office served two purposes: the mansion's old master bedroom was a much neater version of the room downstairs. It was where Tom both lived and worked. Against one wall of books, three office workstations held computers; a fourth, larger computer stood on the long wooden desk that faced the curtained window. File cabinets topped with microdiscs in plastic boxes stood beside each workstation and flanked his desk. Next to one of the workstations was a professional copy machine. Sound equipment crowded two tall shelves on the bookcase at the wall to my left. A long red leather chesterfield like Alan Brookner's, a plaid blanket folded over one of its arms, stood before the wall of books. A matching armchair sat at right angles to the chesterfield. Within reach of both was a glass table heaped with books and magazines, with a rank of bottles and ice bucket like the table downstairs. On the glossy white mantel of the room's fireplace, yellow orchids leaned and yawned out of tall crystal vases. Sprays of yellow freesias burst up out of a thick blue vase on a low, black piece of equipment that must have been a subwoofer.

The lamps cast mellow pools of light that burnished the rug lapping against the bookshelves. The orchids opened their lush mouths and leaned forward.

I wondered how many people had been invited into this room. I would have bet that only Sarah Spence had been here before me.

'My father told me something I never forgot, when we were flying back from Eagle Lake. *Occasionally, you have to go back to the beginning and see everything in a new way.*'

Tom set his glass down on his desk and picked up a book bound in gray fabric boards. He turned it over in his hands, and then turned it over again, as if looking for the title. 'And then he said, *Occasionally, there are powerful reasons why you can't or don't want to do that.*' He looked for the invisible writing again. Even the spine of the book was blank. 'That's what we're going to do to the Blue Rose case. We're going to go back to the beginning, the beginnings of a couple of things, and try to see everything in a new way.'

I felt a flicker, no more than that, of an absolute uneasiness.

Tom Pasmore placed the peculiar book back down on the desk and came toward me with his hands out, and I picked up the battered old satchel and gave it to him.

The moment of uneasiness had felt almost like guilt.

Tom switched on the copy machine. It began to hum. Deep in its interior, an incandescently bright light flashed once.

Tom took a wad of yellowing paper six or seven inches thick out of the satchel. The top page had long tears at top and bottom that looked like they had been made by someone trying to check the pages beneath without removing a rubber band, but there was no rubber band. Part of my mind visualized a couple of stringy, broken forty-year-old rubber bands lying limp in a leather crease at the bottom of the satchel.

He put the documents on the copy machine. 'Better err on the side of caution.' He lifted off the top sheet and repaired the rips with tape. Then he squared up the stack of pages and inserted the whole thing face down in a tray. He twisted a dial. 'I'll make a copy for each of us.' He punched a button and stepped back. The incandescent light flashed again, and two clean sheets fed out into trays on the side of the machine. 'Good baby,' Tom said to it, and turned to me with a wry smile and said, 'Don't put your business on the street, as a wise man once said to me.'

3

Clean white sheets pumped out of the copier. 'Do you know Paul Fontaine or Michael Hogan?' I asked.

'I know a little bit about them.'

'What do you know? I'm interested.'

Keeping an eye on the machine, Tom backed away and reached for his glass. He perched on the edge of the chesterfield, still watching the pages jump out of the machine. 'Fontaine is a great street detective. The man has an amazing conviction record. I'm not even counting the ones who confessed. Fontaine is supposed to be a genius in the interrogation room. And Hogan's probably the most respected cop in Millhaven – he did great work as a homicide detective, and he was promoted to sergeant two years ago. From what I've seen, even the people who

375

might be expected to be jealous are very loyal to him. He's an impressive guy. They're both impressive guys, but Fontaine clowns around to hide it.'

'Are there a lot of murders in Millhaven?'

'More than you'd think. It probably averages out to about one a day. In the early fifties, there might have been two homicides a week – so the Blue Rose murders caused a real sensation.' Tom stood up to inspect the progress of the old records through his machine. 'Anyhow, you know what most murders are like. Either they're drug-related, or they're domestic. A guy comes home drunk, gets into a fight with his wife, and beats her to death. A wife gets fed up with her husband's cheating and shoots him with his own gun.'

Tom checked the machine again. Satisfied, he sat back down on the edge of the couch. 'Still, every now and then, there's something that just *smells* different from the usual thing. A teacher from Milwaukee in town to see her cousins disappeared on her way to a mall and wound up naked in a field, with her hands and legs tied together. There was an internist murdered in a men's room stall at the stadium at the start of a ball game. Paul Fontaine solved those cases – he talked to everybody under the sun, tracked down every lead, and got convictions.'

'Who were the murderers?' I asked, seeing Walter Dragonette in my mind.

'Losers,' Tom said. 'Dodos. They had no connection to their victims – they just saw someone they decided they wanted to kill, and they killed them. That's why I say Fontaine is a brilliant street detective. He nosed around until he put all the pieces together, made his arrest, and made it stick. I couldn't have solved those cases. I need a kind of paper trail. A lowlife who stabs a doctor in a toilet, washes the blood off his hands, buys a hot dog and goes back to his seat – that's a guy who's safe from me.'

He looked at me a little ruefully. 'My kind of investigation sometimes seems obsolete.'

Tom took the original stack of papers from the copier and put them back into the satchel. One of the copies he put on his desk, and the other he gave to me.

'Let's leaf through these quickly tonight, just to see if anything will set off some sparks.'

I was still thinking about Paul Fontaine. 'Is Fontaine from Millhaven?'

'I don't really know where he's from,' Tom said. 'I think he came here about ten–fifteen years ago. It used to be that policemen always worked in their hometowns, but now they move around, looking for promotions and better pay. Half of our detectives are from out of town.'

Tom left the couch and went to the first workstation and turned on the computer by pressing a switch on the surge protector beneath it with his foot. Then he moved to the second and third workstations and did the same at each and finally sat down at his desk and bent over to turn on the surge protector there. 'Let's see what we can come up with for that license number of yours.'

I took my notebook out of my pocket and went over to the desk to see what he was going to do.

Tom's fingers moved over the keys, and a series of screens flashed across the monitor. The last one was just a series of codes in a single line. Tom put a plastic disc into the B drive – this much I could follow from my own experience – and punched in numbers on the telephone attached to his modem. The screen went blank for a moment and then flashed a fresh c prompt.

After the prompt, Tom typed in a code and pushed ENTER. The screen went blank again, and LC? appeared on the screen. 'What was that number?'

I showed him the paper, and he typed in the plate number under the prompt and pushed ENTER again. The number stayed on the screen. He pushed a button marked RECEIVE.

'You're in the Motor Vehicle Department records now?'

'Actually, I got to Motor Vehicles through the computer at Armory Place. It runs on a twenty-four-hour day.'

'You got directly into the police department central computer?'

'I'm a hacker.'

'Why couldn't you just get the Blue Rose file from the computer?'

'The computerized records only go back eight or nine years. Ah, here we go. It takes the system a little while to work through the file.'

Tom's computer flashed READY RECEIVE, and then displayed: ELVEE HOLDINGS, CORP   503 S 4TH ST   MILLHAVEN IL.

'Well, that's who owns your Lexus. Let's see if we can get a little farther.' Tom pushed ENTER again, rattled through a sequence of commands I couldn't follow, and typed in another code. 'Now we'll use the police computer to access Springfield, and see what this company looks like.'

He bounced past a blur of options and menus, going through different levels of state records, until he came to a list of corporations that filled the screen. All began with the letter A. The names and addresses of the officers followed the corporate names. He scrolled rapidly down the screen, reducing the names and numbers to a blur, until he got to E. EAGAN CORP   EAGAN MANAGEMENT CORP EAGLE CORP   EBAN CORP. When we got to ELVA CORP, he bumped down name by name and finally reached ELVEE HOLDINGS CORP.

Beneath the name was the same address on South Fourth Street in Millhaven, the information that the

378

company had been incorporated on 23 July 1973, and beneath that were the names of the officers.

ANDREW BELINSKI	503 S 4TH ST	MILHAVEN, P
LEON CASEMENT	503 S 4TH ST	MILLHAVEN, VP
WILLIAM WRITZMANN	503 S 4TH ST	MILLHAVEN, T

'Mysteriouser and mysteriouser,' Tom said. 'Who is the fugitive LV? I thought one of these guys would be named Leonard Vollman, or something like that. And does it seem likely that the officers of this corporation would all live together in a little tiny house? Let's take this one step further.'

He wrote down the names and the address on a pad and then exited back through the same steps he had used to access the state records. Then he switched from the modem to a program called NETWORK. He punched more buttons and pointed at the computer at the first workstation, which began to hum. 'I can use all my machines through this one. To keep from having to use a million different floppies, I have different kinds of information stored on the hard discs of these other computers. Over there, along with a lot of other stuff, I have reverse directories for a hundred major cities. Now let's punch up Millhaven in the reverse directory.'

'God bless macros.' He punched in a few random-looking letters, typed in the South Fourth Street address, and in a couple of seconds the machine displayed: EX-PRESSPOST MAIL & FAX, along with a telephone number.

'Damn.'

'Expresspost Mail?' I said. 'What's that?'

'Probably an office where you rent numbered boxes – like private post office boxes. Considering the address, I think it's a storefront with rows of these boxes and a counter with a fax machine.'

'It is legal to give a place like that as your address?'

'Sure, but we're not done yet. Let's see if these characters ever popped up in the ordinary Millhaven telephone directory over, let's say, the past fifteen years.'

He returned to the NETWORK slogan, punched in the same terminal code and more internal directory files. He keyed in the number 91, and a long list of names beginning with A followed with addresses and telephone numbers floated up on the monitors of both the first workstation and his desk computer.

'Go over to that station and make sure I don't miss one of these names.'

I sat down before the subsidiary computer and watched the screen jump to the B listings. 'We want Andrew Belinski,' Tom said, and rolled down the Bs until he came to BELI. Then he dropped line by line through BELIARD to BELITAS, then through to BELLIN, BELLINA, BELLINELLI, BELLING, BELLISSIMO, BELMAN.

'Did I miss it, or isn't it there?'

'There's no Belinski or Bellinski,' I said.

'Let's try Casement.'

He scrolled rapidly to the Cs and flipped down a row of names to CASE. CASEMENT followed. CASEMENT, ARTHUR; CASEMENT, HUGH; CASEMENT, ROGER. There was no LEON.

'Well, I think I know what we're going to find, but let's just try the last one.'

He jumped immediately to W, and rolled electronically through the pages. One WRITZMANN was listed in the 1991 Millhaven directory, OSCAR, of 5460 Fond du Lac Drive.

'What do you know? Either they don't exist, or they don't have telephones. Which seems more likely to you?'

'Maybe they have unlisted numbers,' I said.

'To me, no numbers are unlisted.' He smiled at me, proud of his toys. 'Maybe they're hiding – you can get a phone under another name, which makes it impossible to find you this way. But five years ago, maybe they didn't know they wouldn't want anybody to be able to find them in 1991. Let's try the listings for 1986.'

Another series of backward steps, another keystroke, and all the listed and unlisted telephone numbers in Millhaven for 1986 came up on both screens.

There were no BELINSKIS, the same three CASEMENTS, and OSCAR, but not WILLIAM, WRITZMANN.

'Let's zip back to 1981, and see if we can find them there.'

The 1981 directory contained no BELINSKI, CASEMENT, ARTHUR and ROGER but not HUGH, and WRITZMANN, OSCAR, at 5460 Fond du Lac Drive.

'I think I get the picture, but just for the hell of it, let's take a look at 1976.'

No BELINSKI. CASEMENT, ARTHUR, without the company of ROGER. WRITZMANN, OSCAR, already at 5460 Fond du Lac Drive.

'We struck out,' I said.

'Hardly,' Tom said. 'We've made great strides. We have discovered the very interesting fact that the car you saw following John is the property of a company incorporated in the State of Illinois under a convenience address and three phony names. I wonder if Belinski, Casement, and Writzmann are phony people, too.'

I asked him what he meant by 'phony people.'

'In order to incorporate, you need a president, a vice president, and a treasurer. Now *somebody* filed the papers for the Elvee Holding Corporation, or there wouldn't *be* an Elvee Holding Corporation. If I had to guess right now, I'd say that the person who filed for incorporation back in 1979 was good old LV. Anyhow, filing only takes one man. The filer can make up the names of his fellow officers.'

'So one of these three people actually has to exist.'

'That's right, but he may exist under some other name altogether. Now think, Tim. During the past few days,

381

has John ever mentioned anyone whose name began with the letter V?'

'I don't think so,' I said. 'He hasn't really talked about himself very much.'

'I don't suppose you ever heard Alan Brookner mention anybody with the initials LV.'

'No, I haven't.' This was a disturbing question. 'You don't think these murders could have anything to do with Alan, do you?'

'They have everything to do with him. Who are the victims? His daughter. His best graduate student. But I don't think Alan is in danger, if that's what you mean.'

I felt myself relaxing.

'You're fond of him, aren't you?'

'I think he has enough problems already,' I said.

Tom leaned forward, propped his elbows on his knees, and said, 'Oh?'

'I think he might have Alzheimer's disease. He managed to get himself together for the funeral, but I'm afraid that he's going to fall apart again.'

'Did he teach last year?'

'I guess so, but I don't see how he can do it again this year. The problem is that if he quits, the entire Religion Department at Arkham goes with him, and John loses his job. Even *Alan* is worried about that – he struggled through last year partly for John's sake.' I threw up my hands. 'I wish I could do something to help. I did make arrangements for a private duty nurse to come to Alan's place every day, but that's about it.'

'Can he afford that?' Tom was looking thoughtful, and I suddenly knew what he was considering. I wondered how many people he helped, quietly and anonymously.

'Alan's pretty well set up,' I said quickly. 'April saw to that.'

'Well, then, John should hardly have to worry, either.'

'John has complicated feelings about April's money.

I think it's a question of pride.'

'That's interesting,' Tom said.

He straightened up and looked at his monitor, still displaying Oscar Writzmann's name and address. 'Let's run these names through Births and Deaths. It's probably a wild goose chase, but what the hell?'

He began clicking at keys, and the screen before me went momentarily blank. Rows of codes marched across the dark gray background. John typed out Belinski, Andrew, Casement, Leon, and Writzmann, William, and the names appeared on my screen. More codes that must have been instructions to the modem replaced them. The screen went blank, and SEARCHING rose up out of the background and began pulsing on the screen.

'Now we just wait around?'

'Well, I'd like to take a look through the file,' Tom said. 'But before we do that, let's talk a little bit about the idea of *place*.' He swallowed a little more whiskey, stood up, and walked over to his couch and sat down. I took the chair beside the chesterfield. His eyes almost snapped with excitement, and I wondered how I could ever have thought they looked washed out. 'If William Damrosch didn't unite the Blue Rose victims, what did?'

During the brief moment in which Tom Pasmore and I waited for the other to speak, I would have sworn that we were thinking the same thing.

Finally I broke the silence. 'The St Alwyn Hotel.'

'Yes,' Tom said softly.

4

'When Lamont and I got off the plane from Eagle Lake, we went to the St Alwyn. We stayed there the last night of his life. The St Alwyn was where the murders happened – in it, behind it, across the street.'

'What about Heinz Stenmitz? His shop was five or six blocks from the St Alwyn. And there wasn't any connection between Stenmitz and the hotel.'

'Maybe there was a connection we don't know yet,' Tom said. 'And think about this, too. How much time elapsed between the murder of Arlette Monaghan and James Treadwell? Five days. How much time between Treadwell and Monty Leland? Five days. How much time between Monty Leland and Heinz Stenmitz? Almost two weeks. More than twice the time that separated the first three murders. Do you make anything of that?'

'He tried to stop, but couldn't. In the end, he couldn't restrain himself – he had to go out and kill someone again.' I looked at Tom glinting at me and tried to imagine what he was thinking. 'Or maybe someone else killed Stenmitz – maybe it was like Laing, a copycat murder, for entirely different motives.'

He smiled at me almost proudly, and despite myself, I felt gratified that I had guessed what he was thinking.

'I guess that's possible,' Tom said, and I knew that I had not followed his thinking after all. My pride curdled. 'But I think my grandfather was Blue Rose's only imitator.'

'So what are you saying?'

'I think you were half right. It was the same man, but with a different motive.'

384

I confessed that I was lost.

Tom leaned forward, eyes still snapping with excitement. 'Here we have a vindictive, ruthless man who does everything according to plan. What's his motive for the first three murders? A grudge against the St Alwyn?'

I nodded.

'Once every five days for fifteen days, he kills someone in the immediate vicinity of the St Alwyn, once actually *inside* the St Alwyn. Then he stops. By this time, how many people do you suppose are staying in the St Alwyn? It must be like a ghost town.'

'Sure, but . . .' I shut up and let him say what he had to.

'And then he kills Stenmitz. And who was Heinz Stenmitz? Pigtown's friendly neighborhood sex criminal. The other three victims could have been anybody – they were pawns. But when somebody goes out of his way to kill a molester of little boys, an active chickenhawk, I think that *is not a random murder*.'

He leaned back, finished. His eyes were still blazing.

'So what you need,' I said, 'is a vindictive, ruthless man who had a grudge against the St Alwyn – and – '

'And – '

'And a son.'

'And a son,' Tom said. 'You've got it. The kind of man we're talking about couldn't stand anybody violating his own child. If he found out about it, he'd have to kill the man who did it. The reason nobody ever thought of this before is that it looked as though that was exactly the reason that Stenmitz had been killed.' He laughed. 'Of course it was the reason he was killed! It just wasn't Damrosch who killed him!'

We looked at each other for a moment, and then I laughed, too.

'I think we know a lot about Blue Rose,' Tom said, still smiling at his own vehemence. 'He didn't stop because my grandfather had just guaranteed his immunity from arrest by killing William Damrosch. We've been assuming that all along, but, now that I have Blue Rose in a kind of focus, I think he stopped because he was finished – he was finished even before he murdered Heinz Stenmitz. He accomplished what he set out to do – he paid back the St Alwyn for whatever it did to him. If he thought the St Alwyn had still owed him something, he would have gone on leaving a fresh corpse draped around the place every five days until he was satisfied.'

'So what set him off all over again two weeks ago?'

'Maybe he started brooding about his old grudge and decided to make life miserable for the son of his old employer.'

'And maybe he won't stop until he kills John.'

'John is certainly the center of these new murders,' Tom said. 'Which puts you pretty close to that center, if you haven't noticed.'

'You mean Blue Rose might decide to make me his next victim?'

'Hasn't it occurred to you that you might be in some danger?'

It sounds stupid, but it had not occurred to me, and Tom must have seen the doubt and consternation I felt.

'Tim, if you want to go back to your life, there's no reason not to. Forget everything we talked about earlier. You can tell John that you have to meet a deadline, fly home to New York, and go back to your real work.'

'Somehow,' I said, trying to express what I had never put into words until this moment, 'my work seems related to everything we've been talking about. Every now and then I get the feeling that some answer, some *key*, is all around me, and that all I have to do is open my eyes.' Tom was looking at me very intently, not betraying anything. 'Besides, I want to learn Blue Rose's name. I'm not going to run out now. I don't want to go back to New

York and get a phone call from you a week from now telling me John was found knifed to death outside the Idle Hour.'

'As long as you remember that this isn't a book.'

'It isn't *Little Women*, anyhow,' I said.

'Okay.' He looked across the room at the monitor on his desk, where SEARCHING still pulsed on and off. 'Tell me about Ralph Ransom.'

5

After I described my conversation with John's father at the funeral, Tom said, 'I didn't know your father used to work at the St Alwyn.'

'Eight years,' I said. 'He ran the elevator. He was fired not too long after the murders ended. His drinking got worse after my sister was killed. About a year later, he straightened himself out and got a job on the assembly line at the Glax Corporation.'

'Your sister?' Tom said. 'You had a sister who was killed? I didn't know about that.' He looked at me hard, and I saw consciousness come into his face. 'You mean that she was murdered.'

I nodded, too moved by the speed and accuracy of his intelligence to speak.

'Did this happen near your house?' He meant: did it happen near the hotel?

I told him where April was murdered.

'When?'

I though he already knew, but I told him the date and then said that I had been running across the street to help her when I was hit by the car. Tom knew all about that, but he had known nothing else.

'Tim,' he said, and blinked. I wondered what was going through his mind. Something had amazed him. He began again. 'That was five days before Arlette Monaghan's murder.' He sat there looking at me with his mouth open.

I felt as if my mouth, too, was hanging open. I had always been secretly convinced that Blue Rose was my sister's murderer, but until this moment I had never thought about the sequence of the dates.

'That's why you're in Millhaven,' he said. Then he stared blindly at the table and said it to himself: 'That's why he's in Millhaven.' He turned almost wonderingly to me again. 'You didn't come back here for John's sake, you wanted to find out who killed your sister.'

'I came back to do both,' I said.

'And you *saw* him,' Tom said. 'By God, you actually *saw* Blue Rose.'

'For about a second. I never saw his face – just a shape.'

'You devil. You dog. You – you're a deep one.' He was shaking his head. 'I'm going to have to keep my eye on you. You've been sitting on this information since you were seven years old, and you don't come up with it until now.' He put a hand on top of his head, as if it might otherwise fly off. 'All this time, there was another Blue Rose murder that no one knew about. He didn't get to write his slogan, because you came along and got run over. So he waited five days and did it all over again.' He was looking at me with undiminished wonder. 'And afterward no one would ever connect your sister with Blue Rose because she didn't tie in with Damrosch in any way. You didn't even put it in your book.'

He took his hand off the top of his head and examined me. 'What else have you got locked up there inside yourself?'

'I think that's it,' I said.

'What was your sister's name?'

'April,' I said.

He was staring at me again. 'No wonder you had to come. No wonder you won't leave.'

'I'll leave when I learn who he was.'

'It must be like – like all the rest of your childhood was haunted by some kind of monster. For you, there was a real bogeyman.'

'The Minotaur,' I said.

'Yes.' Tom's eyes were glowing with intelligence, sympathy, and some other quantity, something like appreciation. Then the computer made a clicking sound, and both of us looked at the screen. Lines of information were appearing on the gray background. We stood up and went to the desk.

BELINSKI, ANDREW THEODORE   146 TURNER ST   VALLEY HILL   BIRTH: 6/1/1940   DEATH: 6/8/1940.

CONCLUSION BELINSKI SEARCH.

CASEMENT, LEON   CONCLUSION CASEMENT SEARCH.

'We must have been talking when the Belinski information came through. This Andrew Belinski was never an officer of Elvee Holdings, though – he was a week old when he died, which is the only reason his death date got into the computer. When they're that close, they usually punch them in. And there's nothing on the computer for Leon Casement. We should be getting Writzmann through in about ten minutes.'

We turned away from the machine. I went back to the chair and poured Poland water from a bottle on the coffee table into a glass and added ice from the bucket. Tom was walking backward and forward in front of the table with his hands in his pockets, sneaking little looks at me now and then.

Finally he stopped pacing. 'Your father probably knew him.'

That was right, I realized – my father had probably known the Minotaur.

'Ralph Ransom couldn't think of anyone else he fired

389

around that time? I think we ought to start with that angle, until we come up with something else. He or one of his managers fired this guy – the Minotaur. And in revenge, the Minotaur set out to ruin the hotel. If you start asking about that, and there was some other motive, it will probably come up.'

'You're asking people to remember a long way back.'

'I know.' He went to the second workstation and sat on the chair in front of the computer. 'What was that day manager's name again?'

'Bandolier,' I said. 'Bob Bandolier.'

'Let's see if he's still in the book.' Tom called up the directory on the other machine and scrolled down the list of names beginning with B. 'No Bandolier. Maybe he's in a nursing home, or maybe he moved out of town. Just for the fun of it, let's look for good old Glenroy.'

The blur of names rolled endlessly up the screen for a minute. 'This takes too long. I'll access it directly.' He made the screen go blank except for the directory code and punched in BREAKSTONE, GLENROY and ENTER.

The machine ticked, and the name, address, and telephone number appeared on the screen. BREAKSTONE, GLENROY   670 LIVERMORE AVE   542-5500.

He winked at me. 'Actually, I knew he was still living at the St Alwyn. I just wanted to show off. Didn't John's father say that Breakstone knew everybody at the hotel? Maybe you can get him to talk to you.' He wrote down the saxophone player's telephone number on a piece of paper, and I walked over to get it from him.

'Hold on, let's find out where this wonderful manager was living when the murders were committed.'

I stood behind him while he ordered up the Millhaven directory for 1950 and then jumped to the B listings. He found the address in five seconds.

BANDOLIER, ROBERT   17 S SEVENTH ST   LIVERMORE 2–4581.

'Old Bob had a short commute, didn't he? He lived about a block away from the hotel.'

'He lived right behind us,' I said.

'Maybe we can work out how long he was there.' Tom called up the directory for 1960. BANDOLIER, ROBERT was still living on South Seventh Street. 'Good stable guy.' He called up the 1970 directory and found him still there, same address but with a new telephone number. In 1971, still there, but with yet another new telephone number. 'Something funny happened here,' Tom said. 'Why do you change your phone number? Crank calls? Avoiding someone?'

By 1975, he was out of the book. Tom worked backward through 1974, and 1973, and found him again in 1972. 'So he moved out of town or into a nursing home or, if our luck just left us, died sometime in 1972.' He wrote the address down on the same slip of paper and handed it to me. 'Maybe you could go to the house and talk to whoever lives there now. It might be worth asking some of his old neighbors, too. Somebody'll know what happened to him.'

He stood up and took a look at the other computers, which were still SEARCHING. Then he went to the table and picked up his drink. 'Here's to research.' I raised my glass of water.

The computer clicked, and information began appearing on the two monitors.

'Well, what do you know?' Tom went back to his desk. 'Births and Deaths is talking to us.' He leaned forward and began writing something on his pad.

I got up and looked over his shoulder.

WRITZMANN, WILLIAM LEON   346 N 34TH STREET MILL-HAVEN   BIRTH: 4/16/48.

'We just found a real person,' Tom said. 'If this is the mystery man following John in the Elvee company car, I'd be surprised if he doesn't turn up again.'

'He already has,' I said, and told him what I had seen

391

when I had driven John Ransom and Alan Brookner to the morgue that afternoon.

'And you didn't tell me until now?' Tom looked indignant. 'You saw him at the Green Woman, doing something really *fishy*, and then you keep it to yourself? You just flunked Famous Detective School.'

He immediately sat down at the computer and began moving through another series of complicated commands. The modem clucked to itself. It looked to me as though he was calling up the city's registry of deeds.

'Well, for one thing I wasn't sure it was him,' I said. 'And I forgot about it once you started breaking into every office in the state.'

'The Green Woman closed down a long time ago,' Tom said, still punching in codes.

I asked him what he was doing.

'I want to see who owns that bar. Suppose it's – '

The screen went blank for a half-second, and RECEIVE flashed on and off. Tom whooped and clapped his hands.

THE GREEN WOMAN TAPROOM   21b HORATIO STREET
PURCHASED 01/07/1980   ELVEE HOLDINGS CORP
PURCHASE PRICE $5,000
PURCHASED 05/21/1935   THOMAS MULRONEY
PURCHASE PRICE $3,200

Tom combed his fingers through his hair so that it looked like a haystack. 'Who are these people, and what are they doing?' He wrenched himself away from the screen and grinned at me. 'I don't have the faintest idea where we're going, but we're certainly getting somewhere. And you certainly saw our friend in the blue Lexus, you sure did, and I take back every bad thing I ever said about you.' He returned to the screen and disarranged his hair a little more. 'Elvee bought the Green Woman Taproom, and looked how little they paid for it. Maybe, do you think, we could even say *he*, meaning

William Writzmann? Writzmann laid out a paltry five thousand. It was nothing but a leaky shell. What good is it? What could he use it for?'

'It looked like he was moving things into it,' I said. 'There were cardboard boxes next to the car.'

'Or taking something out,' Tom said. 'The place was a shed. The only thing it's good for is storage. Our boy Writzmann bought a five-thousand-dollar shed. Why?'

All this time, Tom was looking back and forth from the screen to me, torturing his hair. 'There's only one reason to buy the place. *It's the Green Woman Taproom*. Writzmann is interested in the Green Woman.'

'Maybe he was Mulroney's nephew, and he was helping out the starving widow.'

'Or maybe he was very, very interested in the Blue Rose case. Maybe our mysterious friend Writzmann has some connection to Blue Rose himself. He can't be Blue Rose himself, he's too young, but he could be – '

Tom was looking at me, a wild speculative delight shining out from his entire face.

'His son?' I asked. 'You think Writzmann is the son of Blue Rose? On the evidence that he bought a rundown bar and stored boxes in it?'

'It's a possibility, isn't it?'

'Writzmann was two years old at the time of the murders. That's pretty young, even for Heinz Stenmitz.'

'I'm not so sure about that. You don't like thinking about someone molesting a two-year-old child, but it happens. All you need is a Heinz Stenmitz.'

'Do you think this Writzmann murdered April because he found out about her research? Maybe he even saw her looking around the bridge and the taproom.'

'Maybe,' Tom said. 'But why would he murder Grant Hoffman?' He frowned and ran his hand through his soft blond hair, and it fell back into place. 'We have to find out what April was actually doing. We need her notes, or

her drafts, or whatever she managed to get done. But
before that – '

He left the desk, picked up one of the neat white stacks
of copied pages and handed it to me. 'We have to start
reading.'

6

So for another hour I sat in the comfortable leather chair,
leafing through the police files on the Blue Rose case,
deciphering the handwriting of half a dozen policemen
and two detectives, Fulton Bishop and William Damrosch. Bishop, who was destined for a long, almost
sublimely corrupt career in the Millhaven police department, had been taken off the case after two week: his
patrons had been protecting him from what they saw as a
kind of tar baby. I wished that they had let him investigate
for another couple of weeks. His small, tight handwriting
was as easy to read as print. His typed reports looked like
a good secretary's. Damrosch scribbled even when he was
relatively sober and scrawled when he was not. Anything
he wrote after about two in the afternoon was a hodge-
podge in which whole words disappeared into wormy
knots. He typed the way an angry child plays piano. After
ten minutes, my head hurt; after twenty, my eyes ached.

By the time I had gone through all the statements and
reports, all I had come up with was a sense that very few
people had liked Robert Bandolier. The only new thing I
learned was that the killings had not been savage mutila-
tions, like the murder of Grant Hoffman and Walter
Dragonette's performances: Blue Rose's victims had been
stabbed once, neatly, in the heart, and then their throats

had been cut. It was as passionless as ritual slaughter.

'Well, nothing jumped out at me, either,' Tom said. 'There are a few minor points, but they can wait.' He looked at me almost cautiously. 'I suppose you're about ready to go?'

'Well, your coffee is going to keep me awake for a while,' I said. 'I could stay a little longer.'

Tom's obvious gratitude at my willingness to stay made him seem like a child left alone in a splendid house.

'How about a little music?' he said, already getting up.

'Sure.'

He pulled a boxed set from the rows of CDs, removed one, and inserted the disc in the player. Mitsuko Uchida began playing the Mozart piano sonata in F. Tom leaned back into his leather couch, and for a time neither of us spoke.

Despite my exhaustion, I wanted to stay another half hour, and not merely to give him company. I thought it was a privilege. I couldn't banish Tom's sorrows any more than he could banish mine, but I admired him as much as anyone I've ever known.

'I wish we had discovered some disgruntled desk clerk named Lenny Valentine,' he said.

'Do you really think there's some connection between Elvee Holdings and the Blue Rose murders?'

'I don't know.'

'What do you think is going to happen?'

'I think a dead body is going to turn up in front of the Idle Hour.' He reached for his drink and took another sip. 'Let's talk about something else.'

I forgot I was tired, and when I looked at my watch I found that it was past two.

After we had gone over what I was going to do the next day, Tom went to his desk and picked up the book with the plain gray binding. 'Do you think you'll have time to look through this over the next few days?'

'What is it?' I should have known that the book wasn't on his desk by accident.

'The memoirs of an old soldier, published by a vanity press. I've been doing a lot of reading about Vietnam, and there are some questions about what John actually did during his last few months in the service.'

'He was at Lang Vei,' I said. 'There aren't any questions about that.'

'I think he was ordered to say he was there.'

'He wasn't at Lang Vei?'

Tom did not answer me. 'Do you know anything about a strange character named Franklin Bachelor? A Green Beret major?'

'I met him once,' I said, remembering the scene in Billy's. 'He was one of John's heroes.'

'Read this and see if you can get John to talk about what happened to him, but – '

'I know. Don't tell him you gave me the book. Do you think he's going to lie to me?'

'I'd just like to find out what actually *happened*.'

Tom handed me the book. 'It's probably a waste of time, but indulge me.'

I turned the book over in my hands and opened it to the title page. *WHERE WE WENT WRONG, or The Memoirs of a Plain Soldier*, by Col. Beaufort Runnel (Ret.). I turned pages until I got to the first sentence.

I have always loathed and detested deceit, prevarication, and dishonesty in all their many forms.

'I'm surprised he ever made it to colonel,' I said, and then a coincidence I trusted was meaningless occurred to me. 'Lang Vei starts with the initials LV,' I blurted.

'Maybe you didn't flunk out of Famous Detective School after all.' He grinned at me. 'But I still hope we come across Lenny Valentine one of these days.'

He took me downstairs and let me out into the warm

night. What looked like millions of stars hung in the enormous reaches of the sky. As soon as I got to the sidewalk, I realized that for something like four hours, Tom had nursed a single glass of malt whiskey.

7

The lights were turned off in all the big houses along Eastern Shore Road. Two blocks down from An Die Blumen, the taillights of a single car headed toward Riverwood. I turned the corner into An Die Blumen with a mind full of William Writzmann and an empty shell called the Green Woman Taproom.

The long empty street stretched out in front of me, lined with the vague shapes of houses that seemed to melt together in the night. Street lamps at wide intervals cast fuzzy circles of light on the cracked cement. Everything before me seemed deceptively peaceful, not so much at rest as in concealment. The scale of the black sky littered with stars made me feel tiny. I shoved my hands into my pockets and began to walk faster.

I had gone half a block down An Die Blumen before I fully realized what was happening to me – not a sudden descent of panic, but a gradual approach of fear that felt different from the way the past usually invaded me. No men in black flitted unseen across the landscape, no groans leaked out of the earth. I could not tell myself that this was just another bad one and sit down on someone else's grass until it went away. It wasn't just another bad one. It was something new.

I hurried along with my hands in my pockets, uncon-sciously huddled into myself. I stepped down off a curb and walked across an empty street, and the dread that had come over me slowly focused itself into the conviction that someone or something was watching me. Somewhere in the blanket of shadows on the other side of An Die Blumen, a creature that seemed barely human followed me with its eyes.

Then, with an absolute certainty, I knew: this was not just panic, but real.

I moved down the next block, feeling the eyes claiming me from their hiding place. The touch of those eyes made me feel appallingly dirty, soiled in some way I could not bear to define – the being that looked through those eyes knew that it could destroy me *secretly*, could give me *a secret wound* visible to no one but itself and me.

I moved, and it moved with me, sliding through the darkness across the street. At times it lagged behind, leaning against an invisible stone porch and smiling at my back. Then it melted through the shadows and passed among the trees and effortlessly moved ahead of me, and I felt its gaze linger on my face.

I walked down three more blocks. My palms and my forehead were wet. It was concealed in the darkness in front of a building like a tall blank tomb, breathing through nostrils the size of my fists, taking in enormous gulps of air and releasing fumes.

I can't stand this, I thought, and without knowing I was going to do it, I walked across the street and went up the edge of the sidewalk in front of the frame house. My knees shook. A tall shadow moved sideways in the dark and then froze before a screen of black that might have been a hedge of rhododendrons and became invisible again. My heart thudded, and I nearly collapsed. 'Who are you?' I said. The front of the house was a featureless slab. I took a step forward onto the lawn.

A dog snarled, and I jumped. A section of the darkness before me moved swiftly toward the side of the house.

My terror flashed into anger, and I charged up onto the lawn.

A light blazed behind one of the second-floor windows. A black silhouette loomed against the glass. The man at the window cupped his hands over his eyes. Light, pattering footsteps disappeared down the side of the house. The man in the window yelled at me.

I turned and ran back across the street. The dog pushed itself toward a psychotic breakdown. I ran as hard as I could down to the next corner, turned, and pounded up the street.

When I got to John's house, I waited outside the front door for my breathing to level out. I was covered in sweat, and my chest was heaving. I leaned panting against the door. I didn't think the man in the Lexus could have moved that quietly or quickly, so who could it have been?

An image moved into the front of my mind, so powerfully that I knew it had been hidden there all along. I saw a naked creature with thick legs and huge hands, ropes of muscle bulking in his arms and shoulders. A mat of dark hair covered his wide chest. On the massive neck sat the enormous horned head of a bull.

8

When I got into John's office, I turned on some lights, made up my bed, and got Colonel Runnel's book out of the satchel. Then I slid the satchel under the couch. After I undressed I switched off all the lights except the reading lamp beside the couch, lay down, and opened the book. Colonel Runnel stood in front of me, yelling about something he loathed and despised. He was wearing a starchy dress uniform, and rows of medals marched across his chest. After about an hour I woke up again and switched off the lamp. A car went past on Ely Place. Finally I went back to sleep.

9

Around ten-thirty Tuesday morning I rang Alan Brookner's bell. I'd been up for an hour, during which I had called the nursing registry to ensure that they had spoken to Eliza Morgan and that she had agreed to work with Alan, made a quick inspection of April Ransom's tidy office, and read a few chapters of *Where We Went Wrong*. As a stylist, Colonel Runnel was very fond of dangling participles and sentences divided. Into thunderous fragments. All three Ransoms had been eating breakfast in the kitchen when I came down, John and Marjorie in their running suits, John in blue jeans and a green polo shirt, as if the presence of his parents had changed him back into a teenager. I got John alone for a second and explained about the nursing registry. He seemed grateful that I had taken care of matters without bothering him with the details and agreed to let me borrow his car. I told him that I'd be back in the middle of the afternoon.

'You must have found some little diversion,' John said. 'What time did you get home last night, two o'clock? That was some walk.' He allowed himself the suggestion of a smirk.

When I told him about the man who had been following me, John looked alarmed and then immediately tried to hide it. 'You probably surprised some peeping Tom,' he said.

The usual reporters were slurping coffee on the front lawn. Only Geoffrey Bough intercepted me on the way to the car. I had no comments, and Geoffrey slouched away.

Eliza Morgan opened Alan's door, looking relieved to see me. 'Alan's been asking for you. He won't let me help him get his clothes on – he won't even let me get near his closet.'

'His suit pockets are full of money,' I said. I explained about the money. The house still smelled like wax and furniture polish. I could hear Alan bellowing, 'Who the hell was that? Is that Tim? Why the hell won't anybody talk to me?'

I opened his bedroom door and saw him sitting straight up in bed bare-chested, glaring at me. His white hair stuck up in fuzzy clumps. Silvery whiskers shone on his cheeks. 'All right, you finally got here, but who is this woman? A white dress doesn't automatically mean she's a nurse, you know!'

Alan gradually settled down as I explained. 'She helped my daughter?'

Eliza looked stricken, and I hurried to say that she had done everything she could for April.

'Humpf. I guess she'll do. What about us? You got a plan?'

I told him that I had to check out some things by myself.

'Like hell.' Alan threw back his sheet and blanket and swung himself out of bed. He was still wearing his boxer shorts. As soon as he stood up, his face went gray, and he sat down heavily on the bed. 'Something's wrong with me,' he said and held his thin arms out before him to inspect them. 'I can't stand up. I'm *sore*.'

'No wonder,' I said. 'We did a little mountain climbing yesterday.'

'I don't remember that.'

401

I reminded him that we had gone to Flory Park.

'My daughter used to go to Flory Park.' He sounded lost and alone.

'Alan, if you'd like to get dressed and spend some time with John and his parents, I'd be happy to drive you there.'

He started to push himself off the bed again, but his knees wobbled, and he sank back down again, grimacing.

'I'll run a hot bath,' Eliza Morgan said. 'You'll feel better when you're shaved and dressed.'

'That's the ticket,' Alan said. 'Hot water. Get the soreness out.'

Eliza left the room, and Alan gave me a piercing look. He held up his forefinger, signaling for silence. Down the hall, water rushed into the tub. He nodded. Now it was safe to speak. 'I remembered this man in town, just the ticket – brilliant man. Lamont von Heilitz. Von Heilitz could solve this thing lickety-split.'

Alan was somewhere back in the forties or fifties. 'I talked to him last night,' I said. 'Don't tell anybody, but he's helping us.'

He grinned at me. 'Mum's the word.'

Eliza returned and led him away to the bathroom, and I went downstairs and let myself out of the house.

10

I crossed the street and rang the bell of the house that faced Alan's. Within seconds, a young woman in a navy blue linen suit and a strand of pearls opened the door. She was holding a briefcase in one hand. 'I don't know who you are, and I'm already late,' she said. Then she gave me a quick inspection. 'Well, you don't look like a

Jehovah's Witness. Back up, I'm coming out. We can talk on the way to the car.'

I stepped down, and she came out and locked her door. Then she looked at her watch. 'If you start talking about the Kingdom of God, I'm going to stamp on your foot.'

'I'm a friend of Alan Brookner's,' I said. 'I want to ask you about something a little bit strange that happened over there.'

'At the professor's house?' She looked at me quizzically. 'Everything that happens over there is strange. But if you're the person who got him to cut his lawn, the whole neighborhood is lining up to kiss your feet.'

'Well, I called the gardener for him,' I said.

Instead of kissing my feet, she strode briskly down the flagged pathway to the street, where a shiny red Honda Civic sat at the curb.

'Better start talking,' she said. 'You're almost out of time.'

'I wondered if you happened to see someone putting a car into the professor's garage, one night within the past week or so. He thought he heard noises in his garage, and he doesn't drive anymore himself.'

'About two weeks ago? Sure, I saw it – I was coming home late from a big client dinner. Someone was putting a car in his garage, and the light was on. I noticed because it was past one, and there are never any lights on in there after nine o'clock.'

I followed her around the front of the car. She unlocked the driver's door.

'Did you see the car or the person who was driving it? Was it a black Mercedes sports car?'

'All I saw was the garage door coming down. I thought that the younger guy who visits him was putting his car away, and I was surprised, because I never saw him drive.' She opened the door and gave me another second and a half.

'What night was that, do you remember?'

She rolled her eyes up and jittered on one high heel. 'Okay, okay. It was on the tenth of June. Monday night, two weeks ago. Okay?'

'Thanks,' I said. She was already inside the car, turning the key. I stepped away, and the Civic shot down the street like a rocket.

Monday, the tenth of June, was the night April Ransom had been beaten into a coma and knifed in room 218 of the St Alwyn Hotel.

I got into the Pontiac and drove down to Pigtown.

11

South Seventh Street began at Livermore Avenue and extended some twenty blocks west, a steady, unbroken succession of modest two-story frame houses with flat or peaked porches. Some of the façades had been covered with brickface, and in a few of the tiny front yards stood garish plaster animals – Bambi deer and big-eyed collies. One house in twenty had a shrine to Mary, the Virgin protected from snow and rain by a curling scallop of cement. On a hot Tuesday morning in June, a few old men and women sat outside on their porches, keeping an eye on things.

Number 17 was on the first block off Livermore, in the same position as our house, the fifth building up from the corner on the west side of the street. The dark green paint left long scabs where it had peeled off, and a network of cracks split the remaining paint. All the shades had been drawn. I left the car unlocked and went up the steps while the old couple sitting outside on the neighboring porch watched me over their newspapers.

I pushed the bell. Rusting mesh hung in the frame of the screen door. No sound came from inside the house. I tried the bell again and then knocked on the screen door. Then I opened the screen door and hit my fist against the wooden door. Nothing. 'Hello, is anybody home?' I hit the door a few more times.

'Nobody's at home in there,' a voice called.

The old man on the neighboring porch had folded his newspaper across his lap, and both he and his wife were eyeing me expressionlessly. 'Do you know when they'll be back?'

'You got the wrong house,' he said. His wife nodded.

'This is the right address,' I said. 'Do you know the people who live here?'

'Well, if you say it's the right house, keep on pounding.'

I walked to the end of the porch. The old man and his wife were no more than fifteen feet away from me. He was wearing a faded old plaid shirt buttoned up tight against the cords in his neck. 'What are you saying, no one lives here?'

'You could say that.' His wife nodded again.

'Is it empty?'

'Nope. Don't think it's empty.'

'Nobody's home, mister,' his wife said. 'Nobody's ever home.'

I looked from husband to wife and back again. It was a riddle: the house wasn't empty, but nobody was ever home. 'Could I come over and talk to you?'

He looked at his wife. 'Depends on who you are and what you want to talk about.'

I told them my name and saw a trace of recognition in the man's face. 'I grew up right around the corner, on South Sixth. Al Underhill was my father.'

'You're Al Underhill's boy?' He checked with his wife. 'Come on up here.'

When I got up onto their porch, the old man stood and

held out his hand. 'Frank Belknap. This is the wife, Hannah. I knew your father a little bit. I was at Glax thirty-one years, welding. Sorry we can't give you a chair.'

I said that was fine and leaned against the railing.

'How about a glass of lemonade? We got August in the middle of June, now that the politicians poisoned the weather.'

I thanked him, and Hannah got up and moved heavily through the door.

'If your father's still alive and kicking, tell him to drop in sometime, chew the fat. I was never one of the old Idle Hour gang, but I'd like to see Al again.' Frank Belknap had worked thirty-one years in the purposeful, noisy roughhouse of the factory, and now he spent all day on the porch with his wife.

I told him that my father had died a few years ago. He looked resigned.

'Most of that bunch died,' he said. 'What brings you to the place next door?'

'I'm looking for a man that used to live there.'

Hannah came back through the door, carrying a green plastic tray with three tall glasses filled with ice and lemonade. I had the feeling that she had been waiting to hear what I was after. I took a glass and sipped. The lemonade was cold and sweet.

'Dumkys lived there,' she said, and held the tray out to her husband.

'Them, all their kids, and a couple of brothers.'

'Dumkys rented.' Hannah took her seat again. 'You like the lemonade?'

'It's very good.'

'Make up a fresh jug every morning, stays cold all day long.'

'It was one of the Dumkys you wanted?'

'I was looking for the man that used to own the house, Bob Bandolier. Do you remember him?'

406

Frank cocked his head and regarded me. He took a slow sip of the lemonade and held it in his mouth before swallowing. He was not going to say anything until I told him more.

'Bandolier was the manager at the St Alwyn for a long time.'

'That right?'

I wasn't telling him anything he didn't know.

'My father worked there, too, for a while.'

He turned his head to look at his wife. 'Al Underhill worked at the hotel for a while. Knew Mr Bandolier.'

'Well, well. Guess he would have.'

'That would have been before Al came to the plant,' Frank said to me.

'Yes. Do you know where I could find Bandolier?'

'Couldn't tell you,' Frank said. 'Mr Bandolier wasn't much for conversation.'

'Dumkys rented *furnished*,' Hannah said.

'So Mr Bandolier moved out and left his furniture behind?'

'That's what the man did,' said Frank. 'Happened when Hannah and me were up at our cottage. Long time ago. Nineteen seventy-two, Hannah?'

Hannah nodded.

'We came back from vacation, there were the Dumkys, every one of them. Dumkys weren't very neighborly, but they were a lot more neighborly than Mr Bandolier. Mr Bandolier didn't encourage conversation. That man would look right through you.'

'Mr Bandolier dressed like a proper gentleman, though. A suit and tie, whenever you saw him. When he did work in his garden, the man put on an apron. Kept his sorrows inside himself, and you can't fault him for that.'

'Mr Bandolier was a widower,' Frank said. 'We heard that from old George Milton, the man I bought this house from. Had a wife who died two–three years before we

407

moved in. I suppose she used to keep things quiet for him.'

'The man liked quiet. He'd be firm, but not rude.'

'And his upstairs tenants, the Sunchanas, were nice folks, foreigners, but nice. We didn't really know them either, of course, no more than to say hello to. Sunchanas stuck to themselves.'

'Talked a little bit funny,' Frank said. 'Foreign. She was one pretty woman, though.'

'Would they know how I could get in touch with Mr Bandolier?'

The Belknaps smiled at each other. 'Sunchanas didn't get on with Mr Bandolier,' Hannah said. 'There was bad blood there. The day they moved out, they were packing boxes into a trailer. I came out to say good-bye. Theresa said she hoped she'd never have to see Mr Bandolier again in all her life. She said they had a tiny little nest egg saved up, and they put a downpayment on a house way on the west side. When *Dumkys* left, one of the girls told me a young man in a military uniform came around and told them they'd have to pack up and leave. I told her the army didn't act like that in the United States of America, but she wasn't a real intelligent child.'

'She didn't know who the soldier was?'

'He just turned up and made them skedaddle.'

'There's no sense to it, except that Mr Bandolier could do things that way,' Frank said. 'What I thought was, Mr Bandolier wanted to live there by himself, and he got some fellow to come along and scare off his tenants. So I reckoned we'd be seeing Mr Bandolier back here. Instead, the place stayed empty ever since. Mr Bandolier still owns it, I believe – never saw a FOR SALE sign on the place.'

I thought about it for a moment while I finished my lemonade. 'So the house has been empty all this time? Who cuts the grass?'

'We all do, taking turns.'

'You've never seen that soldier the Sunchanas told you about?'

'No,' Frank said.

'Well,' Hannah said.

'Oh, that old foolishness.'

'You *have* seen him?'

'Hannah didn't see anything.'

'It might not have been a *soldier*,' Hannah said. 'But it isn't just foolishness, either.'

I asked her what she had seen, and Frank made a disgusted noise.

Hannah pointed at him. 'He doesn't believe me because he never saw him. He goes to sleep at nine every night, doesn't he? But it doesn't matter if he believes me, because I know. I get up in the middle of the night, and I saw him.'

'You saw someone going into the house?'

'*In* the house, mister.'

'Hannah's ghost,' Frank said.

'I'm the one who saw him, and he wasn't a ghost. He was just a man.' She turned away from Frank, toward me. 'Every two or three nights, I get up because I can't sleep. I come downstairs and read.'

'Tell him what you read,' Frank said.

'Well, it's true, I like those scary books.' Hannah smiled to herself, and Frank grinned at me. 'I got a whole collection of them, and I get new ones at the supermarket. I always got one going, like now I'm reading *Red Dragon*, you know that one? I like those real gooshy ones.'

Frank covered his mouth and cackled.

'But that doesn't mean I made it all up. I saw that man walking around in the living room next door.'

'Just walking around in the dark,' Frank said. 'Yep.'

'Sometimes he has a little flashlight, but most times, he

409

just goes in there and walks around for a while and sits down. And – '

'Go on,' Frank said. 'Say the rest.'

'And he cries.' Hannah looked at me defiantly. 'I use this little tiny light to read by, and from where I'm sitting in my chair, I can see him through the window on the side of the house – there's only a net curtain on that window over there. He's there maybe one night every two weeks. He walks around the living room. Sometimes he disappears into some other room, and I think he's gone. But then I look up later, and he's sitting down, talking to himself or crying.'

'He never noticed your light?'

'Those red dragons probably don't see real good,' Frank said.

'It's little,' she said. 'Like a pinpoint.'

'You never saw him go into the house?'

'I think he goes around the far side and comes in the back,' she said.

'Probably he comes down the chimney.'

'Did you ever call the police?'

'No.' For the first time, she seemed embarrassed.

'*Tears from Beyond the Grave*,' Frank said, 'by I. B. Looney.'

'Welders are all that way,' Hannah said. 'I don't know why, but they all think they're comedians.'

'Why didn't you call the police?'

'I think it's one of those poor little Dumkys, all grown up now, come back to a place where he used to be happy.'

'Hillbillies don't act like that,' Frank said. 'And hillbillies is what they were. Even the little ones got so drunk they passed out on the lawn.' He grinned at his wife again. 'She liked them because they called her ma'am.'

She gave him a disapproving look. 'There's a big difference between being ignorant and being bad.'

410

'Did you ever ask other people on the street if they saw him, too?'

She shook her head. 'There's nobody in this neighborhood is up at night except me.'

'Mr Bandolier lived alone?'

'He did everything alone,' Frank said. 'He was a whole separate country.'

'Maybe it's him,' I said.

'You'd need a microscope to find any tears in Mr Bandolier,' Frank said, and for once his wife seemed to agree with him.

Before I left, I asked Hannah Belknap to call me the next time she saw the man in the house next door. Frank pointed out the houses of the two other couples who had been on the block since the Belknaps had moved in, but he didn't think they'd be able to help me find Robert Bandolier.

One of these couples lived up at the end of the block and had only the vaguest memories of their former neighbor. They thought he was, in their words, 'a stuck-up snob with his nose in the air,' and they had no interest in talking about him. They still resented his renting to the Dumkys. The other couple, the Millhausers, lived two houses up from Livermore, on the other side of the street. Mr Millhauser came outside the screen door to talk to me, and his wife shouted from a wheelchair stationed far back in a gloomy hallway. They shared the universal dislike of Bob Bandolier. It was a shame that house just sat empty year after year, but they too had no wish to see more of the Dumkys. Mrs Millhauser bawled that she thought the Sunchanas had moved to, what was that place called, Elm Hill? Elm Hill was a suburb on Millhaven's far west side. Mr Millhauser wanted to get back inside, and I thanked him for talking to me. His wife shouted, 'That Bandolier, he was handsome as Clark Gable, but

411

no good! Beat his wife black and blue!' Millhauser gave me a pained look and told her to mind her own business. 'And you might as well mind yours, mister,' he said to me. He went back inside his house and slammed the door.

12

I left the car on South Seventh and walked toward the St Alwyn through the steaming day. Everything I had heard in the past two days went spinning through my head. The farther I got from South Seventh Street, the less I believed that Hannah Belknap had seen anyone at all. I decided to give myself the pleasure of meeting Glenroy Breakstone even though it would probably turn out to be another blind alley, and after that I would try to find the Sunchanas.

My stomach growled, and I realized that I hadn't eaten anything since dinner with the Ransoms at Jimmy's, last night. Glenroy Breakstone could wait until after lunch – he was probably still in bed, anyhow. I got a *Ledger* from a coin-operated dispenser on the corner of Livermore and Widow Street and carried it through the street entrance of Sinbad's Cavern.

The restaurant had relaxed since the morning of Walter Dragonette's arrest. Most of the booths were filled with neighborhood people and hotel residents eating lunch, and the young woman behind the bar was pulling draft beers for workmen covered in plaster dust. The waitress I had spoken to that morning came out of the kitchen in her blue cocktail dress and high heels. There was a lively buzz of conversation. The waitress waved me toward a table in a rear corner of the room. At a table directly across the room, four men ranging in age from over fifty

412

to about twenty sat around a table, drinking coffee and paying no attention to one another. They were very much like the different men who had been at the same table on the day of April Ransom's murder. One of them wore a summer suit, another a hooded sweatshirt and dirty trousers. The youngest man at the table was wearing baggy jeans, a mesh undershirt, and a heavy gold chain around his neck. They ignored me, and I opened my paper.

Millhaven was still tearing itself apart. Half of the front page dealt with the protest meetings at Armory Place. The Reverend Al Sharpton had appeared as promised and declared himself ready to storm City Hall by himself if the policemen who had failed to respond to calls from Walter Dragonette's neighbors were not put on suspension or dismissed. Pictures of the chief and Merlin Waterford orating at April Ransom's funeral, complete with full texts of both remarks, filled the top of the next page. All three editorials blasted Waterford and the performance of the police department.

While I read all of this and ate a club sandwich, I gradually began to notice what the men across the room were doing. At intervals, they stood up and disappeared through an unmarked door in the wall behind their table. When one came out, another went in. I caught glimpses of a gray hallway lined with empty metal kegs. Sometimes the man coming back out left the restaurant, sometimes he went back to the table and waited. The men smoked and drank coffee. Whenever one of the original men left, another came in from outside and took his place. They rarely spoke. They did not look arrogant enough to be mobsters or furtive enough to be drug dealers making pickups.

When I left, only the man with the gold chain was left of the original four, and he had already been once in and out of the back room. None of them looked at me when I paid up and left through the arched door into the St Alwyn's lobby.

I forgot about them and went up to the desk clerk to ask if Glenroy Breakstone was in his room.

'Yeah, Glenroy's up there,' he said and pointed to a row of house phones. One old man in a gray suit with fat lapels sat on the long couch in the lobby, smoking a cigar and mumbling to himself. The clerk told me to dial 925.

A thick, raspy voice said, 'You have reached Glenroy Breakstone's residence. He *is* home. If you have a message, now's the time.'

'Mr Breakstone?'

'Didn't I say that? Now it's your turn.'

I told him my name and said that I was downstairs in the lobby. I could hear the sound of Nat 'King' Cole singing 'Blame It on My Youth' in the background. 'I was hoping that I could come up to see you.'

'You some kind of musician, Tim Underhill?'

'Just a fan,' I said. 'I've loved your playing for years, and I'd be honored to meet you, but what I wanted to talk about with you was the man who used to be the day manager here in the fifties and sixties.'

'You want to talk about Bad Bob Bandolier?' I had surprised him, and he laughed. 'Man, nobody wants to talk about Bad Bob anymore. That subject is talked *out*.'

'It has to do with the Blue Rose murders,' I said.

There was a long pause. 'Are you some kind of reporter?'

'I could probably tell you some things you don't know about those murders. You might be interested, if only for James Treadwell's sake.'

Another pause while he considered this. I was afraid that I had gone too far, but he said, 'You claim you're a jazz fan?'

I said that I was.

'Tell me who played the tenor solo on Lionel

414

Hampton's "Flyin' Home," who played tenor for the Billy Eckstine band with Charlie Parker, and the name of the man who wrote "Lush Life."'

'Illinois Jacquet, I think both Gene Ammons and Dexter Gordon, and Billy Strayhorn.'

'I should have asked you some *hard* questions. What was Ben Webster's birthday?'

'I don't know.'

'I don't know, either,' he said. 'Pick up a pack of Luckies at the desk before you come up.'

Before I had taken three steps back toward the desk, the clerk was already holding out a pack of Lucky Strikes. He waved away the bills I offered him. 'Glenroy's got an account, but I almost never charge him for cigarettes. What the hell, he's Glenroy Breakstone.'

'Don't I know it,' I said.

13

On the St Alwyn's top floor, the dull black door of 925 stood at the end of the long corridor to the right of the elevators. Patterned yellow paper covered the walls. I knocked on the door, and a wiry man of about five-eight with tight, close-cropped white hair and bright, curious eyes opened it and stood before me. He was wearing a black sweatshirt that said LAREN JAZZFEST across its front and loose black trousers. His face was thinner and his cheekbones sharper than when he had recorded *Blue Rose*. He held out his hand for the cigarettes and smiled with strong white teeth. I could hear Nat Cole singing behind him.

'Get in here, now,' he said. 'You got me more interested than an old man ought to be.' He tossed the pack onto a table and shooed me into the room.

Sun streaming in the big windows at the front of the room fell on a long, colorful Navaho rug, a telescope on a black metal mount, an octagonal table stacked with sheet music, compact discs, and paperback books. Just out of the sunlight, a group of chairs faced a fifteen-foot-long hotel dresser unit flanked with speakers. Two large, framed posters hung on the exposed wall, one for the Grande Parade du Jazz in Nice, the other for a concert at the Concertgebouw in Amsterdam. Glenroy Breakstone's name figured prominently on both. Framed photographs were propped against his shelves of records – a younger Breakstone in a dressing room with Duke Ellington, with Benny Carter and Ben Webster, playing side by side on a stage with Phil Woods and Scott Hamilton.

Two tenor saxophone cases sat on the floor like suitcases, and a baritone saxophone and a clarinet capped with mouthpieces stood upright on a stand beside them. The room smelled faintly of cigarette smoke only partially masked by incense.

I turned around to find Glenroy Breakstone smiling at me and knew that he had seen my surprise. 'I didn't know you played clarinet and baritone,' I said.

'I don't play them anywhere but in this room,' he said. 'About 1970, I bought a soprano in Paris, but I got so frustrated with the thing I gave it away. Now I'm thinking of getting another one, so I can get frustrated all over again.'

'I love *Blue Rose*,' I said. 'I was just listening to it last night.'

'Yeah, people go for those ballad albums.' He looked at me a second, half-amused. 'People like you, you ought to go out and get new records instead of playing the old ones over and over. I made one with Tommy Flanagan in Italy last year. We used Tommy's trio – I like that one.' He moved toward the bedroom door. 'You want fruit juice or something? I got a lot of good juice in here, mango, papaya, passion fruit, all kinds of stuff.'

I said I'd have whatever he was having, and he went into the bedroom. I began inspecting the posters and photographs.

He came back carrying two tall glasses and handed me one. He gestured with his own glass toward what I had been looking at. 'See, this is how it goes. Everything's overseas. In a week, I go to France for the festivals. When I'm there I'm gonna make a record with Warren Vaché, that's all set up, then I spend the rest of the summer in England and Scotland. If I'm lucky, I get on a cruise and do a couple of the jazz parties. It sounds like a lot, but it ain't. I spend a lot of time in this place, practicing my horns and listening to the people I like. Tell you the truth.' He smiled again. 'I almost always listen to old records, too. You like that juice?' He was waiting for me to tell him what it was.

I sipped it. I had no idea what it was. 'Is it mango?'

He gave me a disgusted look. 'You don't know much about fruit juice, I guess. What you have there is papaya. See how sweet that is? That's a natural sweetness.'

'How long have you been living at the St Alwyn?'

He nodded. 'Long time. First year I moved in here, in '45, I had a room on the third floor. *Little* tiny room. I was with Basie in those years, hardly ever got home. When I quit to form my own group, they moved me up to the fifth floor, way at the back, because I wanted to be able to have rehearsals in my room. In '61, Ralph Ransom said I could have one of the big rooms on the seventh floor, same rent, after the guy who lived there died. Ralph was being good to me, because right around then the music business went to hell, and sometimes I couldn't make the rent. After Ralph sold out, I made a deal with the new people and moved up here and made the place safe.'

417

I asked him what he meant.

'I got the only rooms in the place with new locks.'

I remembered someone telling me that the locks in the St Alwyn were no good. 'So someone could keep his key when he checked out, come back a year later and get back into the same room?'

'All I know is, I lost my Balanced Action tenor and a new clarinet, and that ain't gonna happen *any*more. The way things are now, you have one of those locks, you can come home, find a body parked in your bed. And if you're a cop in Millhaven, maybe you're even dumb enough to think a boy called Walter Dragonette put her there.' He stepped away from the wall and gestured toward the chairs. 'I been doing a lot of talking, but I think it's your turn now, Mr Underhill.'

We sat down on two sides of a low square table with an ashtray, a lighter, a pack of Luckies, and a flat black object that looked like a mirror folded into a case. A picture of Krazy Kat was stamped onto the case. Beside it was a flat wooden box with decorative inserts. Breakstone set his glass beside the box and lit a cigarette. 'You think you can tell me something new about the Blue Rose murders? I'd be interested in hearing what that would be.' He looked at me without a trace of humor. 'For James Treadwell's sake.'

I told him about Glendenning Upshaw and Buzz Laing and how I thought William Damrosch had died. Breakstone got more excited as I went along.

'I know damn well everybody was tellin' themselves a lie about Bill Damrosch,' he said. 'For one thing, Bill used to come to see us now and then, when we were playing in that club on Second Street, the Black and Tan Review Bar. He used to get out there, you know, he'd have blackouts, but I never saw any of that. He just liked our music.'

418

He drew in smoke, exhaled, and looked at me grimly. 'So old Upshaw killed Bill. But who killed James? James grew up around the corner from my folks, and when I heard how he could play, I put him in my band. That was forty years ago. Hardly as much as a week goes by without my thinking about James.'

'Murder injures the survivors,' I said.

He looked up at me, startled, and then nodded. 'Yeah. It does that. I was no good for about two months afterward – couldn't touch my horn.' He went inward for a moment, and the Nat Cole record stopped playing. Breakstone seemed not to hear it. 'Why do you say that the man who killed him probably knew him to look at?'

'I think he worked in the hotel,' I said, and went over some of what Tom Pasmore and I had talked about.

He tilted his head and looked at me almost slyly. 'You know Tom? You sit around with Tom at his nice crib up there on the lake and talk with the man?'

I nodded, remembering Tom's wink when he looked up Breakstone's address.

'Why didn't you say so? Once every blue moon, Tom and I spend a night hanging out and listening to music. He likes hearing those old Louis Armstrong records I got.' He pronounced the final *s* in Louis. He thought for a second, and then grinned at me, astonished by what had just occurred to him. 'Tom's finally going to start thinking about that Blue Rose business. He must have been waiting for you to come along and help him.'

'No, it's because of the new murders – the woman left in James's old room, and the other one, downstairs in the alley.'

'I knew he'd see that,' Breakstone said. 'I knew it. The police don't see it, but Tom Pasmore does. And you do.'

'And April Ransom's husband. He's the one who called me first.'

419

Glenroy Breakstone asked about that, and I told him about John and *The Divided Man* and wound up telling him about my sister, too.

'So that little girl was your sister? Then your father was that elevator man, Al.' He looked at me wonderingly.

'Yes, he was,' I said.

'Al was a nice guy.' He wanted to change the subject, and looked toward the bright windows. 'I always thought your sister was part of what happened afterward. But when Bill wound up dead, they didn't care if it was *right*, as long as it was *neat.*'

'Damrosch thought so, too?'

'Told me that right downstairs in the bar.' He finished off his juice. 'You want me to think about who got fired way back then? First of all, Ralph Ransom never fired anybody directly. Bob Bandolier and the night manager, Dicky Lambert, did that.'

So maybe it had been Blue Rose who had forced Bandolier to change his telephone number a couple of times.

'Okay. I remember a bellhop name of Tiny Ruggles, he got fired. Tiny sometimes used to go into empty rooms, help himself to towels and shit. Bad Bob caught him at it and fired him. And there was a guy named Lopez, Nando we used to call him, who worked in the kitchen. Nando was crazy about Cuban music, and he had a couple Machito records he used to play for me sometimes. Bob Bandolier got rid of him, said he ate too much. And he had a friend called Eggs – Eggs Benson, but we called him Eggs Benedict. Bob axed him too, and him and Nando went to Florida together, I think. That happened a month or two before James and the others got killed.'

'So they didn't kill anybody.'

'Just a lot of bottles.' He frowned at his empty glass. 'Drinking and stealing, that's what most of 'em got fired for.' He looked embarrassed for a moment, then tried to soften it. 'Truth is, everybody who works in a hotel helps themselves to stuff now and then.'

'Can you think of anyone else who would have had a grudge against Ralph Ransom?'

Glenroy shook his head. 'Ralph was okay. The man never had enemies or anything like that. Dicky and Bob Bandolier, they might have made some enemies, because of letting people go and playing a few angles here and there. I think Dicky had a deal going with the laundry, stuff like that.'

'What happened to him?'

'Dropped dead right at the bar downstairs twenty years ago. A stroke.'

'What about Bandolier?'

Glenroy smiled. 'Well, that's the one who should have had the stroke. Dicky was easygoing, but old Bob never relaxed a day in his life. Most uptight guy I ever knew. Heart attack and Vine! Bad Bob, that's right. He had the wrong job – they should of put Bad Bob in charge of the *toilets*, man, he would of made them sparkle and shine like Christmas lights. He never should of been in charge of *people*, 'cause people are never gonna be as neat as Bob Bandolier wanted them to be.' He shook his head and lit a fresh cigarette. 'Bob kept his cool in front of the guests, but he sure raised hell with the staff. The man acted like a little god. He never really *saw* you, the man never really *saw* other people, he just saw if you were going to mess him up or not. And once he got going on religion – '

'Ralph told me he was religious.'

'Well, there's different ways of being religious, you know. Church I went to when I was a little boy was about being happy. Everybody sang all the time, sang that gospel music. Bob, Bob thought religion was about

421

punishment. The world was nothing but wickedness, according to Bob. He came up with some crazy shit, once he got going.'

He laughed, genuinely amused by some memory. 'One time, Bad Bob thought everybody on days ought to get together for a prayer meeting at the start of the shift. They had to get together in the kitchen five minutes before work started. I guess most showed up, too, but Bob Bandolier started off telling how God was always watching, and if you didn't do your job right, God was gonna make you spend eternity having your fingernails pulled out. He got so wound up, the shift started ten minutes late, and Ralph told him there wouldn't be any more prayer meetings.'

'Is he still alive?'

'Far as I know, the man was too nasty to die. He finally retired in nineteen seventy-one or 'two, sometime around there. 'Seventy-one, I think. Probably went somewhere he could make a whole new lot of people feel miserable.'

Bandolier had retired a year before he had vanished and left his house to the Dumkys. 'Do you have any idea where I could find him?'

'Travel around until you find a place where you hear the sound of everybody grinding their teeth at once, that's all I can say.' He laughed again. 'Let's put on some more music. Anything you'd like to hear?'

I asked if he would play his new CD with Tommy Flanagan.

'I can take it if you can.' He jumped up and pulled a disc from the shelf, put it in the player, and punched a couple of buttons. That broad, glowing sound floated out of the speakers, playing a Charlie Parker song called 'Bluebird.' Glenroy Breakstone was playing with all of his old passionate invention, and he could still turn long, flowing phrases over in midair.

I asked him why he had always lived in Millhaven,

instead of moving to New York.

'I can travel anywhere from here. I park my car at O'Hare and get to New York in less than two hours, if I have something to do there. But Millhaven's a lot cheaper than New York. And by now I know most of what's going on, you see? I know what to stay away from – like Bob Bandolier. Just from my window I see about half the action in Millhaven.'

That reminded me of what I had seen in the restaurant downstairs, and I asked him about it.

'Those guys at the back table? That's what I was talking about, the stuff you want to stay away from.'

'Are they criminals?'

He narrowed his eyes and smiled at me. 'Let's say, those are guys who know things. They talk to Billy Ritz. He might help them or not, but they all know one thing. Billy Ritz can make sure their lives'll take a turn for the worse, if they hold out on him.'

'He's a gangster? Mafia?'

He grinned and shook his head. 'Nothing like that. He's in the middle. He's a *contact*. I'm not saying he doesn't do something dirty from time to time, but mainly he makes certain kinds of deals. And if you don't talk to Billy Ritz, so he can talk to the people *he* talks to, you could wind up taking a lot of weight.'

'What happens if you don't play the game?'

'I guess you could find out you were playing the game all along, only you didn't know it.'

'Who does Billy Ritz talk to?'

'You don't want to know that, if you live in Millhaven.'

'Is Millhaven that corrupt?'

He shook his head. 'Someone in the middle, he helps out both sides. See, everybody needs someone like Billy.' He looked at me, trying to see if I was as naive as I sounded. Then he checked his watch. 'Tell you what, there's a chance you can get a look at him, you're so curious. Around this time, Billy generally walks across Widow Street and does a little business in the Home Plate Lounge.'

He stood up, and I followed him to the window. We both looked down nine stories to the pavement. The shadow of the St Alwyn darkened Widow Street and fell in a harsh diagonal across the brick buildings on the other side. A dwarf man in a tiny baseball cap walked into the grocery store down the block, and a dwarf woman pushed a stroller the size of a pea toward Livermore Avenue.

'A man like Billy has to be regular,' Glenroy said. 'You have to be able to find him.'

A police car came up from the bottom of Widow Street and parked in front of the old redbrick apartment building on the other side of the pawnshop. One of the uniforms in the car got out and walked up the block to the grocery store. It was Sonny Berenger, the cop who looked like a moving blue tree. The door of the Home Plate swung open, and a barrel of a man in a white shirt and gray trousers stepped outside and leaned against the front of the bar. Sonny walked past without looking at him.

'Is that him?'

'No, that's a guy named Frankie Waldo. He's in the wholesale meat business. Idaho Meat. Except for a couple of years, Idaho used to supply all the meat used in this hotel, back when we had room service. But Billy's late, see, and Frankie wants to talk to him. He's wondering where he is.'

Frankie Waldo stared at the entrance of the St Alwyn until Sonny came back out of the grocery store with two containers of coffee. Before Sonny reached him, Waldo went back into the bar. Sonny returned to his car. A van and a pickup truck went by and turned onto Livermore. The patrol car left the curb and rolled up the street.

'Here he comes,' Glenroy said. 'Now look out for Frankie.'

I saw the top and brim of a dark gray hat tilted back on the head of a man who was crossing the sidewalk in front of the hotel's entrance. Frankie Waldo popped out of the bar again and held the door open. Billy Ritz stepped down off the curb and began moving across Widow Street. He was wearing a loose wide-shouldered gray suit, and he walked without hurrying, almost indolently.

Ritz went up to Waldo and said something that made the other man seem almost to melt with relief. Waldo clapped Ritz on the back, and Ritz marched through the open door like a crown prince. Waldo was after him before the door swung shut.

'See, Billy spread some goodwill.' Glenroy moved back from the window. 'Anyhow, this is about as close as you want to get to Billy Ritz.'

'Maybe he told him the St Alwyn is going to start delivering room service again.'

'I wish they would.' We moved away from the window, and Glenroy Breakstone gave me a look that said I had already taken up enough of his time.

I began to go toward the door, and a stray thought came to me. 'I guess it was the Idaho Meat Company that sold meat to the hotel at the time of the Blue Rose murders?'

He smiled. 'Well, it was supposed to be. But you know who really did it.'

I asked him what he meant.

'Remember I said the managers worked a few angles? Lambert got a cut on the laundry work, and Bad Bob worked out a deal on the meat. Ralph Ransom never found out about it. Bob got phony bills printed up, and they were all marked paid by the time they crossed Ralph's desk.'

'How did you find out about it?'

'Nando told me, one night when he was loaded. Him and Eggs used to unload the truck every morning, right at

425

the start of their shift. But you knew that already, right?'

'How could I?'

'Didn't you say that the St Alwyn connected all the Blue Rose victims?'

Then I saw what he was talking about. 'The local butcher who took over the meat contract was Heinz Stenmitz?'

'Sure it was. How else could he be connected to the hotel?'

'Nobody ever said anything about it to the police.'

'No reason to.'

I thanked Glenroy and took a step toward his door, but he did not move. 'You never asked me what I thought about the way James died. That's the reason I let you come up here in the first place.'

'I thought you let me come up because I knew who wrote "Lush Life."''

'Everybody ought to know who wrote "Lush Life,"' he said. 'Are you interested, or not? I can't tell you who was fired right around then, and I can't tell you where to find Bob Bandolier, but I can tell you what I know about James. If you have the time.'

'Please,' I said. 'I should have asked.'

He took a step toward me. 'Damn right. Listen to me. James was killed in his room, right? In his bed, right? Do you know what he was wearing?'

I shook my head, cursing myself for not having read the police reports more carefully.

'Nothing at all. You know what that means?' He did not give me time to answer. 'It means he got up out of bed to open his door. He knew whoever was out there. James might have been young, but he wasn't a fool about anything but one thing. Pussy. James did want to fuck just about anything good-looking that came his way. There used to be some pretty maids in this hotel, and James got tight with one of them, a girl named Georgia

McKee, during the time we were playing at the Black and Tan.'

'When was that?'

'September 1950. Two months before he got killed. He dropped her, just like he dropped every other girl he used to run with. He started seeing a girl who worked at the club. Georgia used to come around and make trouble, until they barred her from the club. She wanted James *back*.' He was making sure that I understood what he was saying. 'I always thought that Georgia McKee went into James's room and killed him and made it look like the same person who did that whore did him, too. He *opened the door*. Or she let herself in with her key. Either way. James wouldn't make any fuss, if he thought she was coming back to go to bed with him.'

'You never told the police?'

'I told Bill Damrosch, but by that time, Georgia McKee was out of here.'

'What happened to her?'

'Right after James got killed, she quit the hotel and moved to Tennessee. I guess she had people there. Tell you the truth, I hope she got knifed in a bar.'

After that, the two of us stood facing each other for a couple of seconds.

'James should have had more life,' Glenroy finally said. 'He had something to offer.'

14

It was still too early to call Tom Pasmore, so I asked the desk clerk if he had a Millhaven directory. He went into his office and came back with a fat book. 'How's Glenroy doing today?'

'Fine,' I said. 'Isn't he always?'

'No, but he's always Glenroy,' the clerk said.

I nodded, and leafed through the book to the S's. David Sunchana was listed at an address on North Bayberry Lane, which sounded like it belonged in Elm Hill. I wrote down the number on the paper Tom had given me, and then, on an afterthought, looked up Oscar Writzmann on Fond du Lac Drive. Maybe he would be able to tell me something about the mysterious William Writzmann.

From the pay phone in the St Alwyn's lobby, I dialed the Sunchanas' number and let it ring a long time before I hung up. They must have been the only people in Elm Hill who didn't have an answering machine.

I went outside and began walking back toward Bob Bandolier's old house. He must have known something, I thought – maybe he had seen Georgia McKee coming out of James Treadwell's room and blackmailed her instead of turning her over to the police.

I turned into South Seventh, looking down, and walked past the Millhauser place before I saw Frank Belknap waving at me from his front lawn. He motioned for me to stay where I was and began walking quickly down the block. When he got closer, he looked back at his front porch and then motioned me backward, toward Livermore. 'Told Hannah I was going out for a walk,' he said. 'Went up and down the street four times, waiting for you to come back.'

He jerked his head toward the avenue, and we walked far enough so he could be sure his wife wouldn't see him talking to me.

'What is it?' I asked.

He was still fighting with himself. 'I met that soldier, the one who threw the Dumkys out of the house next door. He came back the day after to check on the place. Hannah was out shopping. I went out to talk to the fella when I saw him leaving, and he was worse than rude,

428

mister. Tell you the truth, he scared me. He wasn't big, but he looked dangerous – that fella would have killed me in a minute, and I knew it.'

'What happened? Did he threaten you?'

'Well, he did.' Belknap frowned at me. 'I think that fella had just got back from Vietnam, and I don't think there was anything he wouldn't have done. I respect our soldiers, I want you to know, and I think what we did to those boys was a damn shame. But this fella, he was something special.'

'What did he say to you?'

'He said I had to forget I ever saw him. If I ever let on anything about him or his doings, he'd burn my house down. And he meant it. He looked like he'd burned down a few houses in his time, like you saw them on the news, with their Zippos.' Frank moved closer to me, and I could smell his stale breath. 'See, he said there'd never be any trouble as long as I acted like he didn't exist.'

'Oh,' I said. 'I see.'

'You get the picture?'

'He's the man Hannah sees at night,' I said.

He nodded wildly, as if his head were on a ball bearing. 'I keep telling her she's making it all up. Maybe it's *not* him – that was all the way back in '73, when he warned me off. But I tell you one thing, if it is him, I don't know what he's doing in there, but he sure as hell isn't crying.'

'Thanks for telling me,' I said.

He looked at me doubtfully, wondering if he had made a mistake. 'I was thinking you might know who he is.'

'He was in uniform when you met him?'

'Sure. I kind of had the feeling he didn't have civilian clothes yet.'

'What kind of uniform was it?'

'He had on a jacket with brass buttons, but all the stuff, the insignia was torn off.'

That was no help. 'And then there was no sign of him

until Hannah saw him in the house at night.'

'I was hoping he died. Maybe it's someone else she sees in there?'

I said that I didn't know, and he walked slowly back to his house. He looked back at me a couple of times, still wondering if he'd done the right thing.

15

I got into the white Pontiac and drove back onto Livermore and through the shadow of the valley.

I left the freeway at the Elm Hill turnoff and drove randomly through a succession of quiet streets, looking for Bayberry Lane. In Elm Hill, they liked two-story imitation colonials and raised ranch houses with elaborate swing sets in the long backyards and ornate metal nameplates on posts next to the driveway – THE HARRISONS. THE BERNHARDTS. THE REYNOLDS. Almost all of the mailboxes were half the size of garbage cans and decorated with painted ducks in flight, red barns by millponds, or leaping salmon.

At the center of Elm Hill, I drove into the parking lot of a semicircle of gray colonial shops. You could tie your car to a hitching rail, if you had a rope. Across the street was the hill where the elms had grown. Now it had a historical marker and two intersecting paths with granite benches. I bought a map at the Booky, Booky Bookshoppe and took it across the street to one of the benches. Bayberry Lane began just behind the shopping center at Town Hall, curved around a pond and wandered for about half a mile until it intersected Plum Barrow Way, which banged straight north back to the freeway.

The first half-dozen houses closest to squat Town Hall,

modest, rundown wooden boxes with added porches, were the oldest buildings I had seen in Elm Hill, dating from the twenties and thirties. Once Bayberry Lane got past the pond, I was back among the white and gray colonials. I kept checking the addresses as the numbers went up. Finally I came to a long straight line of oak trees that had once marked the boundary of a farm.

On the other side of the oak border stood a two-story, slightly ramshackle farmhouse with a screen porch, utterly out of character with the rest of the neighborhood. Two gray propane tanks clung to the side of the house, and a rutted driveway went straight from the road to a leaning clapboard garage with a hinged door. The fading number on the plain mailbox matched the number on my piece of paper. The Sunchanas had bought the original farmhouse on this land and then watched an optimistic re-creation of Riverwood grow up around them. I drove up the ruts until I was in front of the garage, turned off the engine, and got out of the car.

I walked along the screen porch and tried the door, which opened. I stepped onto the long narrow porch. Sunbleached wicker chairs stood beneath a window in the middle of the porch. I knocked on the front door. There was no answer. I knew there wouldn't be. After all, I was just getting away from the Ransoms. I turned around and saw a man staring at me from beside the straight row of oaks across the street.

The mesh of the screen door turned him into a standing arrangement of black dots. I felt an instant of absolute threat, and without thinking about it at all, moved sideways and crouched next to one of the wicker chairs. The man had not moved, but he was gone.

I stood up, slowly. My nerves shrieked. The man had vanished into the column of oaks. I went back out the screen door and walked toward Bayberry Lane, looking for movement in the row of great trees. It could have

431

been a neighbor, I thought, wondering what I was doing on the Sunchanas' porch.

But I knew it wasn't any neighbor.

There was no movement in the row of oak trees. I walked across the street on a diagonal, so that I could see between the trees. About six feet of grass separated them. There wasn't another human being in sight. The row of oaks ended at the street behind Bayberry, which must have been the property line of the old farm. Out of sight in the tangled lanes of eastern Elm Hill, a car started up and accelerated away. I turned toward the noise, but all I saw were swing sets and the backs of houses. My heart was still pounding.

I went back across the street and waited in the Pontiac for half an hour, but the Sunchanas did not come home. Finally, I wrote my name and John's phone number at the bottom of a note saying that I wanted to talk with them about Bob Bandolier, tore the page from my notebook, and went back up onto the screened porch. I turned the knob of their front door, and the door opened. A residue of the sense of danger I had just experienced went through me, as if the empty house held a threat. 'Hello, anybody home?' I called out, leaning into the room, but I didn't expect an answer. I put the note on the polished floor-boards in front of the brown oval rug on the living room floor, closed the door, and went back to the car.

16

Two exits east of the stadium, I took Teutonia Avenue and slanted north, deep into Millhaven's wide residential midsection. I wasn't quite sure of the location of Fond du Lac Drive, but I thought it intersected Teutonia, and I drove along a strip of little shops and fast-food restaurants, watching the street signs. When I came to the traffic light at Fond du Lac Drive, I made a quick guess and turned right.

Fond du Lac Drive was a wide six-lane street that began at the lake before crossing central Millhaven on a diagonal axis. This far west, no trees stood along the white sidewalks, and the sun baked the rows of 1930s apartment buildings and single-family houses that stood on both sides of the street. As I had been doing since leaving Elm Hill, I looked in my rearview mirror every couple of seconds.

One of three identical poured concrete houses, 5460 had black shutters and a flat roof. All three had been painted the same pale yellow. The owners of the houses on either side of it had tried to soften the stark exteriors by planting borders of flowers along their walks and around their houses, but Oscar Writzmann's house looked like a jail with shutters.

Before I knocked on the door, I checked up and down the empty block.

'Who's there?' said a voice on the other side of the door.

I gave my name.

The door opened part of the way. Through the screen I saw a tall, heavyset bald man in his seventies taking a good look at me. Whatever he saw didn't threaten him, because he pulled the door open the rest of the way and came up to the screen. He had a big chest and a thick neck, like an old athlete, and was wearing khaki shorts and a tired blue sweatshirt. 'You looking for me?'

'If you're Oscar Writzmann, I am,' I said.

He opened the screen door and stepped forward far enough to fill the frame. His shoulder held the door open. He looked down at me, curious about what I was up to. 'Here I am. What do you want?'

'Mr Writzmann, I was hoping that you could help me

locate one of the officers of a corporation based in Millhaven.'

He rotated his chin sideways, looking skeptical and amused at once. 'You sure you want *Oscar* Writzmann? *This* Oscar Writzmann?'

'Have you ever heard of a company called Elvee Holdings?'

He thought for a second. 'Nope.'

'Have you ever heard of an Andrew Belinski or a Leon Casement?'

Writzmann shook his head.

'The other officer was named Writzmann, and since you're the only Writzmann listed in the book, you're sort of my last shot.'

'What is this all about?' He leaned forward, not yet hostile but no longer friendly. 'Who are you, anyhow?'

I told him my name again. 'I'm trying to help an old friend of mine, and we want to acquire more information about his company, Elvee Holdings.'

He was scowling at me.

'It looks like the only genuine officer of Elvee Holdings is a man named William Writzmann. We can't go to the offices, because – '

He came out through the open door, stepped down, and jabbed me hard in the chest. 'Does Oscar sound like William to you?'

'I thought you might be his father,' I said.

'I don't care what you thought.' He poked me in the chest again and stepped forward, crowding me backward. 'I don't need tricky bastards like you coming around bothering me, and I want you to get off my property before I knock your block off.'

He meant it. He was getting angrier by the second.

'I was just hoping you could help me find William Writzmann. That's all.' I held my hands up to show I didn't want to fight him.

434

His face hardened, and he stepped toward me. I jumped back, and an enormous fist filled my vision, and the air in front of my face moved. Then he stood a yard from me, his fists ready and his face burning with rage.

'I'm going,' I said. 'I didn't mean to disturb you.'

He dropped his hands.

He stayed on the lawn until I got into the car. Then he turned himself around and trudged back toward his house.

I went back to Ely Place and my real work.

PART EIGHT

Colonel Beaufort Runnel

1

I let myself into the house and called out a greeting. The answering silence suggested that the Ransoms were all napping. For a moment I felt like Goldilocks.

In the kitchen I found the yellow flap of a Post-It note on the central counter beside a bottle of Worcestershire sauce and three glasses smeary with red fluid. *Tim – Where are you? We're going to a movie, be back around 7 or 8. Monroe and Wheeler dropped in, see evidence upstairs. John.*

I dropped the note into the garbage and went upstairs. Marjorie had arranged little pots and bottles of cosmetics on the guest room table. A copy of the AARP magazine lay splayed open on the unmade bed.

Nothing had been disturbed in John's bedroom, except by John. He had stashed his three-hundred-dollar vodka on the bedside table, no doubt to keep Ralph from sampling it. Shirts and boxer shorts lay in balls and tangles on the floor. Byron Dorian's two big paintings, powerful reminders of April's death, had been taken down and turned to the wall.

On the third floor, Damrosch's satchel still lay underneath the couch.

I crossed the hall into April's office. A pile of corporate reports had been squared away, and old faxes lay stacked on the shelves. I finally noticed that most of the white shelves were bare.

Monroe and Wheeler had packed up most of April's

files and papers and taken them away. By nightfall, an Armory Place accountant would be examining her records, looking for a motive for her murder. Monroe and Wheeler had probably emptied her office at Barnett that morning. I pulled open a desk drawer and found two loose paper clips, a tube of Nivea skin cream, and a rubber band. I was a couple of hours too late to discover what April had learned about William Damrosch.

I went back to John's office and picked up Colonel Runnel's book. Then I stretched out on the couch to read until the Ransoms came back from the movies.

2

Happily unaware of the disadvantages of being a terrible writer with nothing to say, Beaufort Runnel had marshaled thirty years of boneheaded convictions, pointless anecdotes, and heartfelt prejudices into four hundred pages. The colonel had ordered himself to his typewriter and carved each sentence out of miserable, unyielding granite, and it must have been infuriating for him when no commercial publisher would accept his masterpiece.

I wondered how Tom Pasmore had managed to find this gem.

Colonel Runnel had spent his life in supply depots, and his most immediate problems had been with thievery and inaccurate invoices. His long, sometimes unhappy experiences in Germany, Oklahoma, Wisconsin, California, Korea, the Philippines, and Vietnam had inexorably led him to certain profound convictions.

3

The finest fighting force on the globe is beyond doubt the Army of the United States of America. This is cold fact. Valorous, ready to dig in and fix bayonets at any moment, prepared to fight until the last man, this is the Army as we know and love it. Working on many bases around the world over a long and not undistinguished (though unsung) career, the Army has placed me in many 'hot' spots, and to these challenges this humble Colonel of the Quartermaster Corps, with his best efforts, has responded. I have seen our fighting forces worldwide, at ease and under pressure, and never have they deserved less than my best and most devoted efforts.

What makes our Army the foremost in the world? Several factors, each of them important, come into play when we ask this question.

Discipline, which is forged in training.

Loyalty, our American birthright.

Strength, physical and of numbers.

Here I skipped a handful of pages.

I will recount some experiences in setting up a well-stocked, orderly depot in places around the world by way of explanation. I promise the reader that the amusing 'touches' are in no way the inventions or embellishments of the author. This is the way it happened, from the twin perspectives of long experience and the front porch of my modest but comfortable retirement home in a racially unified section of Prince George's County, Maryland.

4

Groaning, I turned to Runnel at Cam Ranh Bay, Runnel in Saigon, Runnel in the field. Then a familiar place-name caught in my eye like a fishhook. Runnel had been at Camp White Star, my first stop in Vietnam. I saw another name I knew and started reading in earnest.

5

It was during my overburdened weeks at Camp White Star that one of the single most unpleasant events of my career took place. Unpleasant and revealing it was, for it told me in no uncertain terms that the old army I loved had fallen prey to unhealthy ideas and influences. Noxious trends were loose in its bloodstream.

Here I began skimming again, and turned a couple of pages.

I had, of course, heard of the Green Berets created by the Catholic demagogue put into office by the corrupt expenditure of his father's ill-gained millions, as who had not? This was trumpeted throughout the land, and many otherwise bright and patriotic young fellows tumbled into the trap. But I had never come into contact with the breed until a certain Captain, later, incredibly, Major, Franklin Bachelor entered my depot at Camp White Star. It was an education.

He strode in, in no discernible uniform but clearly an officer with an officer's bearing. One gave leeway to the men in the field. I should explain the normal procedure, at least as I ran my operations. It can be stated in one simple maxim. Nothing in without paperwork, nothing out without paperwork. That is the basis. Of course, every Quartermaster has known what it is to 'improvise,' and I, when called upon to do so, acquitted myself splendidly, as in the case of the six oxen of Cho Kin Reservoir. The reader will remember the episode. I rest my case.

In the normal instance, papers are presented at the desk, the goods requested are assembled and then loaded into the waiting vehicle or vehicles, and copies of the forms are sent to the relevant authority. It goes without saying that Captain Bachelor observed none of the usual amenities.

IIe ignored me and began ordering his minions to take articles of clothing from the shelves. These were, emphatically, not soldiers of the United States Army. Aboriginal in stature, ugly in face and form, some even smeared gaudily with dye. Such were the 'Yards,' the tribesmen with whom many Green Berets were forced to consort. My command to return the stolen goods to the shelves was completely ignored. I struck my counter and asked, in what I hoped was an ironic tone, if I might see the officer's requisition forms. The man and his goons continued to ignore me. Whirling, bestial little creatures daubed in mud and crested with feathers had taken over my depot.

I emerged from behind the counter, sidearm conspicuously in hand. This, I said, was not acceptable, and would cease forthwith. I approached the officer and as I did so heard from behind me the sound of an M-16 being readied to fire. The officer advised me to remain calm. Slowly, very slowly indeed, I turned to face one of the most astounding spectacles with which the Asian conflict had thus far provided me. A woman of considerable beauty, dressed in conventional fatigues, held the weapon pointed at my head. She too was a 'Yard,' but more highly evolved than her scampering compatriots. I knew two things almost at once: this beauty would shoot me where I stood, with the well-known Asian indifference to life. Secondly, she was the mate of the Green Beret officer. I use no more elevated word. They were mates, as creatures of the barnyard are mates. This indicated to me that the officer was insane. I relinquished all resistance to the pair and their tribe. My staff had scattered, and I stood mute.

I proceeded on the instant to the office of the commanding officer, a gentleman who shall remain nameless. He and I had had our disagreements over the course of my reorganization of various matters. Despite our differences, I expected full and immediate cooperation. Restoration of the stolen goods. Full reports and documentation. Disciplinary action appropriate to the deed. To my amazement, the CO at White Star refused to lift a finger.

I had merely been visited by Captain Franklin Bachelor, I was told. Captain Bachelor stopped in once every two years or so to outfit his soldiers. The Captain never bothered with paperwork, the Quartermaster assessed what had been taken and filled out the forms himself. Or he wrote it off to pilferage. My problem was that I tried to *stop* him – you couldn't stop Captain Bachelor. I enquired why one could not, and received the stupefying reply that the Captain was a legend.

It was this asinine CO who told me that Franklin Bachelor was known as 'The Last Irregular.' Irregular, indeed, I allowed *sotto voce*.

As the reader will understand, I thenceforth took a great interest in the developing career of young Captain Franklin Bachelor.

I declared myself a convert to such as Bachelor, a partisan of the 'Irregulars.' I probed for tales, and heard such stories as those with which the Moor did seduce Desdemona.

The picture that emerged from the tales about Bachelor became disturbing. If so for me, how much more so for Those Who Must Not Be Named, who had encouraged him? Incalculably, yes. It was because of this disturbance, registered in the highest places in the land, that the hapless Jack (I believe) Ransom, a Captain of Special Forces, first became enmeshed in the insane Bachelor's treacherous web, resulting in the final conspiracy – the ultimate conspiracy – of silence. From which silence, leaks an undying shame. I intend to expose it in these pages.

6

The task of a man like Bachelor was to exploit the existing hostility between ordinary Vietnamese and local tribesmen by organizing individal tribal villages into virtual commando units, strike forces capable of the same stealth as our guerila enemy. Another goal was to win support for our government by actively assisting the life of the villager. To build dams, to dig wells, to develop healthier crops. It was imperative that these men speak the language of their tribesmen, live as they did, eat the food they ate. The goal was the training of guerila soldiers to be used in guerila warfare.

Bachelor soon showed his true colors by turning his villagers into a traveling wolf pack. After several months, the pack established permanent camp deep in a valley of the Vietnamese highlands.

It was at this time that Bachelor's reputation was at its peak. The ordinary soldier idealized Bachelor's achievements. His superiors valued him because he consistently provided intelligence on the movements of the enemy. The rogue elephant kept in communication with the pack.

Here we come to the heart of the matter.

It is my belief that Bachelor had begun to dip into that most dangerous of waters, the role of intermediary – you could say, double agent.

Operating first from his secret base in the highlands and then an even more heavily defended redoubt further north, Major Bachelor became a trafficker in information, a source for intelligence about troop movements and military strategy that could be gained in no other way.

Even I, deep in my duties, heard of instances in which our forces went out to surprise a battalion of North Vietnamese, reported (by Whom?) to be making its way south by devious routes, only to encounter no more than a few paltry squads. Were we victorious? Absolutely. On the scale to which we had been led, by our intelligence, to expect? The response is negative. It must have been some such reasoning that caused They Who Must Not Be Named to dispatch a young Special Forces Captain, Jack Ransom, into the highlands to contact Major Bachelor and return him to the leafy vales of suburban Virginia for interrogation and debriefing.

7

My feet hurt, and my back never gives me a moment's peace. Writing is as I have found an activity draining, depleting, and infinitely interruptable. No sooner does a good sentence billow up to the mind's forefront, than some wretch appears at the door of my modest but comfortable retirement cottage in a sensible sector of Prince George's County. He is delivering an unwanted package, he is begging for food, he is looking for some phantom person represented by an illegible name scribbled on a dirty scrap of paper. I return to my desk, attempting to recapture the lost words, and the telephone goes off like an exploding shell. When I answer the demonic thing, a heavily accented voice inquires if I really do wish the delivery of twenty-four mushroom and anchovy pizzas.

And! At all hours a juvenile from the neighboring house, a once presentable house now gone sadly to seed, is likely to be throwing a tennis ball against the wall before my desk, retrieving the ball, hurling it again at my wall, so that a steady drumming of THUMP THUMP THUMP intercedes between me and my thoughts. The child's parents own no sense of decorum, duty, discipline, or neighborly feeling. On the one occasion I visited their pestiferous hovel, they greeted my complaints with jeers. It is, I am certain, from these pathetic folk that the pizza orders, etc, etc, originate. I hereby inscribe their name so that it may reverberate with shame: Dumky. Is that what we fought for, that a whey-faced, slat-sided, smudge-eyed spawn of the Dumkys is free to hurl a tennis ball at my modest dwelling? When a man is trying to *write* in here, a

man already working against backache and sore feet,
sweating over his words to make them memorable?

There it goes, the tennis ball. THUMP THUMP
THUMP.

8

The reader will forgive the above outburst. It is this
damnable subject that raises my ire and my blood pressure,
not my squalid neighbors.

I heard from many of my confidants that Ransom and
another officer were sent into the highlands to locate
Bachelor and bring him, as they say, 'in from the cold.'
They Who Must Not Be Named wished to question the
man, but doomed their own venture by permitting word of
Ransom's mission to reach Bachelor before the Captain
did himself. This can happen in a thousand ways – a
whisper in the wrong ear, an overseen cable, an ill-advised
conversation in the officers' club. The results were foresee-
able but tragic nonetheless.

After a difficult and dangerous journey, Ransom succeeded in locating the degenerate officer's secret encampment. I have heard differing versions of what he came
upon, some of which I reject on grounds of sheer implaus-
ibility. I believe that Ransom and his fellow officer entered
the camp and came upon a scene of mass carnage. Bodies
of men and women littered the camp – their prey had fled.

What followed was another strange increment in the
legend of Franklin Bachelor. Captain Ransom entered a
roofless shed and discovered a Caucasian American male
in the remains of a military uniform cradling the stripped
and cleaned skull of an Asian female. This man, half-
crazed with exhaustion and grief, declared that he was
Franklin Bachelor. The skull was his wife's. He and his
subordinate, he said, a Captain Bennington, had been
away from the encampment when it had been overrun by
the Vietcong who had been searching for him for years –
the enemy had slaughtered more than half of his people,

447

burned down the camp, and then *boiled the bodies, eaten the flesh, and reduced Bachelor's people to skeletons.* Bennington had pursued the cadre and been killed.

When Captain Ransom delivered his man to The Shadows, it was discovered that he was in reality the Captain Bennington supposed murdered by the VC. What had happened was that Franklin Bachelor had actually persuaded his subordinate to submit to interrogation and possible arrest in his place, while Bachelor himself fled into the jungle with the remnant of his wolf pack. Bennington was found to be hopelessly insane, and was confined to a military hospital, where I am sure he repines to this day for his lost commander.

The official story stops here. Yet an awkward question must be asked. How likely is it that there would be a VC assault on Bachelor's camp only a short time before the arrival of Captain Ransom? And that Bachelor would behave, in this case, as reported?

Here is what transpired. Bachelor knew that Captain Ransom was on his way to take him back to the United States for questioning. At that point he murdered his own followers. In cold blood, he dispatched those who could not keep up on a high-speed escape through rough terrain. Women. Children. The old and the weak, all were executed or mortally wounded, along with any able-bodied men who opposed Bachelor's scheme. Then Bachelor and his remaining men boiled the flesh off some of the bodies and made a last meal of their dead. I believe it is even possible that Bachelor's people *voluntarily accepted death, cooperated in their own destruction.* He held them under his sway. They believed he possessed magical powers. If Bachelor ate their flesh, *they would live in him.*

9

Bachelor retained his core group of tribesmen, and I have no doubt that not a few of the spinning, whirling savages daubed in mud and covered with feathers who looted my orderly shelves at Camp White Star were among them. Those fellows, barbaric to the core, would be hard to kill and impossible to discourage. To this core group of fanatical savages he had added stray VC and other lawless bandits. They had armed and outfitted themselves so stealthily, and with such deadly force, that the Army that supported it never suspected its existence. What they had been looking for was another secret encampment, far enough north in the rugged, fog-shrouded terrain of I Corps to be safe from accidental discovery by conventional American troops and to be strategically well-positioned for intelligence purposes. Bachelor was now about to begin playing his most dangerous game.

His legend increased when he began again transmitting infallibly accurate reports of North Vietnamese troop movements from his newfound redoubt. To all intents and purposes, 'the Last Irregular' had indeed returned from the dead. His reports concerned the North Vietnamese divisions moving toward Khe Sanh and vicinity.

The following is a mere outline of the story of Khe Sanh for those unfamiliar with this unhappy episode. Special Forces set up a camp around a French Fort at Khe Sanh in 1964 – CIDG, some say at its best. When its airfield became crucially important in 1965, the marines were sent in to Khe Sanh, and for a time shared it with Special Forces and their ragtag battalion of tribesmen. The marines gradually squeezed out the Green Berets, who were unused to dealing with the efficiency, discipline, and superior organization of the Gyrenes. The 'Bru' and their masters relocated in Lang Vei, where they built another camp, despite the existence a mere twenty kilometers away in Lang Vo of *another* CIDG camp of 'Bru,' this under the command of Captain Jack Ransom.

Had Ransom succeeded in bringing Bachelor back to mainland America eight months before, he would have been rewarded with a promotion and a more significant post. Having failed, the Shadow Masters had relegated Ransom to a secondary post in I Corps, where his role would have been to ensure that his 'Bru' were instructed in matters of personal hygiene and rudimentary agriculture.

Now enter Franklin Bachelor.

Some time after the Green Berets and their savages had fortified Lang Vei, the camp was bombed and strafed by a

US aircraft. The camp was destroyed, and many women and children killed. The explanation given was that the aircraft had become lost in the foggy mountains. This tale is patently false, though believed to this day. The true story is much worse than this invention of a confused pilot. This time, Bachelor had made a crucial error. The rogue major had long harbored an insane hatred for the Captain who had forced him to leave his own best camp, and provided false information that would lead to the destruction of the Special Forces camp. But the *wrong* false camp was selected – Bachelor had sent deadly destruction down upon Lang Vei, not Lang Vo, twenty kilometers distant. Ransom still lived, and when he discovered his error, Bachelor's wrath led him into deeper treachery.

By 1968, both Khe Sanh and the lesser-known Lang Vei were under perpetual siege. Then came the assault the world knows well – the North Vietnamese descended on tiny Lang Vei with tanks, troops, and mortars.

What is not known, because this information has been suppressed, is that Lang Vo, an otherwise insignificant Montagnard village under command of a single Green Beret, was likewise attacked, by North Vietnamese tanks and troops, at the same time. Why did this occur? There can be but one answer. Franklin Bachelor had duped his North Vietnamese contacts into believing that Lang Vo would be the next thorn in their side, after the destruction of Khe Sanh. And he sold out his country for one purpose only: the killing of Jack Ransom.

Lang Vo was flattened, and Ransom and most of the hapless 'Bru' were trapped in an underground command post. There they were discovered, machine-gunned, and their bodies sealed up.

10

In 1982, five years after my retirement here to an idyllic backwater such as had always been my fondest dream, a much-traveled letter was delivered to my door. I might have committed the ghastly error of pitching it immediately into the trash, had I not noticed the strange assortment of stamps arrayed across its back. By following the travels of this heroic missive, as revealed by the stamps of successive postmasters, I learned that it had passed through army bases in Oregon, Texas, New Jersey, and Illinois before traveling finally to the house of my sister Elizabeth Belle in Baltimore, my first residence upon leaving the security of the United States Army, and where I lived until I relocated to PG County, as we residents know it. It had reached each destination just after my departure from it – a hurried, unhappy, unfortunate departure, in the final case.

My correspondent, a Fletcher Namon of Ridenhour, Florida, had heard many a time during his three hitches in the service of both the elusive Franklin Bachelor and that odd duck, Colonel Runnel of the Quartermaster Corps, who had tirelessly sought out stories of the former. Being so intensely interested in the adventures and lore of 'the Last Irregular,' he wanted me to be apprised of a story that had come his way. Mr Namon could vouch for the integrity of the man who told it to him, a top-notch Ridenhour bartender who was like himself a combat veteran, but could not speak for the man who had told it to Namon's own informant.

The man had claimed to be a visitor at Lang Vo on the day before its invasion by the North Vietnamese: a certain Francis Pinkel on the staff of the much-loved Senatorial hawk, Clay Burrman, conducting his yearly tour of his favorite projects in Vietnam. These being so many, he had dispatched Pinkel, his aide, alone, to a CIDG camp assumed to be in no great danger. Pinkel arrived, quickly saw that nothing in Lang Vo would interest the Senator, and penned the usual pack of lies lauding the work of the Special Forces. Pinkel had come to praise Caesar, not to bury him. The helicopter returned to bring Pinkel back to his boss at Camp Crandall, and lifted off before sundown.

Once they were up in the air, Pinkel saw – imagined he saw, as he was later advised – something he did not understand. Beneath the helicopter, less than a kilometer from Lang Vo, *was another tribe of 'Yards' under the command of a Caucasian male*. What were they doing there? Who were they? There was no second officer detailed to Lang Vo, and the tribesmen in the little encampment could not have been so numerous. The tribe and their leader scattered across the ridge where the helicopter had come upon them, fleeing for cover.

Pinkel made an addendum to his puff of a report.

The next day the North Vietnamese struck. Pinkel mentioned his odd sighting, and was ignored. The Senator mentioned it, to loud protestations of ignorance and impossibility.

Fletcher Namon of Ridenhour, FL, wondered if the white man seen by Francis Pinkel – seen lurking on the outskirts of the camp under the command of Captain Ransom – was none other than Franklin Bachelor. Francis Pinkel and Senator Clay Burrman had suggested this possibility, once returned to Washington. They were suggesting that Bachelor had come down from his mountain redoubt to assist a fellow Green Beret in time of trouble. But how could Bachelor have known what the rest of the command did not? Or if he knew, why not issue a warning, as he had done at other times?

The upshot, Pinkel had told the bartender, was that the Shadow Masters had come to unwelcome conclusions and expunged the disaster at Lang Vo from military records. Everybody who had been there was dead, their survivors informed that they had died as a result of enemy action at Lang Vei. Pinkel and Burrman were put under order of silence, in the name of national security.

The letter ended with the wish that I would find this information interesting. It may have been no more than 'a tale told over a bar,' but if the man Pinkel saw was not Bachelor – who was he?

I did find this 'interesting,' mild word, interesting indeed. It is the final bit of evidence that locks all else into place. To conceal the treachery of one of its favorite sons, the army instituted a massive cover-up which has been in place to this day.

I replied to my correspondent in Ridenhour, but soon my grateful screed returned to me stamped with the information that no town of that name exists in the state of Florida. And I have since observed that 'Namon' is *No man* spelled backwards. This in no way shakes my belief in the veracity of the much-traveled letter. Mister 'Namon' is a man who takes sensible precautions, and I salute him for it!

452

11

Franklin Bachelor disappeared once again, it was said into North Vietnam. This rumor was false.

In 1971 a marine patrol near the DMZ came upon an old camp, long since destroyed, littered with the remains of dead tribesmen. Amongst these bodies lay the severely decomposed corpse of a white male of indeterminate age. Franklin Bachelor had met, too late it is true, his proper fate. His entrails had been picked apart by birds, and wild foxes had torn his flesh. After a fruitless search for his relatives, Bachelor was buried by the army in an unmarked grave – sprung from nowhere, he was returned to the selfsame place.

For all the oddities we have observed in the case of Major Franklin Bachelor, this is perhaps the oddest of all, that the man *never existed at all*. It was one of those cases where a lad enlists in the service under a false name, hiding his origins or his identity, and so enters from the dream world, the shadow world, the night world. Though he was responsible for untold tragedy, this figment was tolerated, nay embraced by the army's great sheltering arms, and encouraged toward an unwise independence that led to a dishonorable death. Call me foolish, hidebound, what you will, but in this progression from the dark dream world to success, thence to corruption and a return to nothingness and the dark, I see an epitome. Franklin Bachelor – 'Franklin Bachelor,' a true unknown soldier, he is the ghost that haunts us when our principles are laid aside.

Here I closed the book to resume my own work.

PART NINE

In the Realm of the Gods

1

The three Ransoms came in through the front door on a
wave of talk a few minutes after eleven. They had seen a
double feature of *Double Indemnity* and *Kiss Me Deadly*
and then stopped in for a drink at Jimmy's. It was the first
time I had seen them relaxed and comfortable with each
other. 'So you finally came home,' John said. 'What have
you been doing all day, shopping?'

'You spent the day shopping, big guy?' Ralph fell into
the couch beside me, and Marjorie sat beside him.

'I talked to a few people,' I said, looking at John to let
him know that I wanted him to stay up after his parents
left for bed.

'Just let the cops handle everything, that's what they're
paid for,' Ralph said. 'You should have come to the show
with us.'

'Honestly, I don't know why we stayed for the whole
thing,' Marjorie said. She leaned forward to give me the
full effect of her eyes. 'Gloomy? Oh, Lord.'

'Hey!' Ralph said. 'Weren't you going to see if old
Glenroy is still at the hotel?'

'Were you?' John said.

'I had a long talk with him, that's right.'

'How is old Glenroy?'

'Busy – he's getting ready to go to France.'

'What for?' He really could not figure it out.

'He's playing in a jazz festival and making a record.'

'The poor bastard.' He shook his head, evidently at the

notion of an ancient wreck like Glenroy Breakstone trying to play jazz in front of a crowd of French people. Then his eyes lighted up, and he pointed his index finger at me. 'Did Glenroy tell you about the time he introduced me to Louis Armstrong? Satchmo? What a thrill. Just a little guy, did you know that? No bigger than Glenroy.'

I shook my head, and he dropped his hand, disappointed.

'Ralph,' Marjorie said. 'It's late, and we're traveling tomorrow.'

'You're leaving?'

'Yeah,' John said.

'We figure we've done everything we could, here,' Ralph said. 'There isn't much point in sticking around.'

So that was why they had been able to relax.

Marjorie said, '*Ralph*,' and tugged at his arm. Both of them got up. 'Okay, guys,' Ralph said. Then he looked at me again. 'It's probably a waste of time, anyhow, you know. I don't think I ever fired more than one person, myself, and that didn't last long. Bob Bandolier pretty much took care of that kind of thing.'

'Who was the person you did fire?'

He smiled. 'I remembered it when we were sitting in the movie – it seems kind of funny now, to think of it.'

'Who was it?' I asked.

'I bet you could tell me. There were only two people in the hotel that I *would* fire, me personally, I mean.'

I blinked at him, and then understood. 'Bob Bandolier and Dicky Lambert. Because they were directly subordinate to you.'

'Why is this important?' Marjorie asked.

'John's friend is *interested*, that's why it's important,' Ralph said. 'It's research, you heard him.'

Marjorie waved a dismissive hand, turned, and walked away from us. 'I give up. Come up soon, Ralph, and I mean it.'

He watched her walk away and then turned back to me. 'It just came to me, watching *Double Indemnity*. I remembered how Bob Bandolier started shaving hours off his time, coming in late, leaving early, making all kinds of excuses. Finally the guy came out and said his wife was sick and he had to take care of her. Sure surprised *me*. I didn't even think he was married. That was some thought, Bob Bandolier with a wife, I tell you.'

'He came in late because his wife was sick?'

'He damn near missed a couple of days. I told Bob he couldn't do that, and he gave me a lot of guff about how he was a better manager in two hours than anybody else would be in eight, or some crap like that, and finally I fired him. Had no choice.' He held his hands out, palms up. 'He wasn't doing the job. The guy was a fixture, but he put me over a barrel. So I gave him the axe.' The hands went into his pockets and his shoulders went up, in that gesture common to father and son. 'Anyhow, I hired him back in a couple of weeks. When Bob was gone, things didn't *go* right. The meat orders went completely haywire, for one thing.'

'What happened to his wife?' John asked.

'She died – during that time before he came back. Dicky Lambert told me, he got it out of him somehow. Bob wouldn't have ever said anything about it to me.'

'When was this?' I asked.

Ralph shook his head, amused by my persistence. 'Hey, I can't remember everything. In the early fifties sometime.'

'When James Treadwell was found dead in his room, did Bandolier handle the details?'

Ralph opened his mouth and blinked at me. 'Well. I guess not. I remember wishing that he *could* handle the details, because I moved Dicky to days, and he was no good at all.'

'So you fired Bob Bandolier around the time of the murders.'

'Well, yeah, but . . .' He gave me a sharp, disbelieving look, and then started shaking his head. 'No, no, that's way off base. We're talking about *Bob Bandolier* – this upright character who organized prayer meetings.'

I remembered something Tom Pasmore had said to me. 'Did he have any children? A son, maybe?'

'God, I hope not.' Ralph smiled at the notion of Bob Bandolier raising a child. 'See you guys in the morning.' He gave us an awkward half-wave and started up the stairs.

John said good night to his father and then turned to me. He looked tense and irritated. 'Okay, what have you been doing all day?'

2

'Mostly, I was looking for traces of Bob Bandolier,' I said.

John uttered a disgusted sound and waved me toward his couch. Without bothering to look at me, he went into his kitchen and returned with a lowball glass filled to the brim with ice and vodka. He came to the chair and sipped, glowering at me all the while. 'And what were you up to last night?'

'What's the matter with you, John? I don't deserve this.'

'And I don't deserve *this*.' He sipped again, unwilling to sit down until he had come out with whatever it was that troubled him. 'You told my mother you were a college professor! What are you these days, some kind of imposter?'

'Oh, John, Joyce Brophy called me Professor Underhill, that's all.'

He glared at me, but finally sat down. 'I had to tell my parents all about your illustrious academic career. I didn't want them to know you're a liar, did I? So you're a full professor at Columbia, and you've published four books. My parents are proud that I know a guy like you.'

'You didn't have to lay it on so thick.'

John waved this away. 'You know what she said to me? My mother?'

I shook my head.

'She said that some day I'd meet a wonderful young woman, and that she was still hoping to be a grandmother some day. I'm supposed to remember that I'm still a healthy young man with a wonderful house and a wonderful job.'

'Well, they're leaving tomorrow, anyway. You're not sorry they came, are you?'

'Hey, I got to hear my father talk about Indian theology with Alan Brookner.' He raised his eyebrows and laughed. Then he groaned, and flattened his hands against his temples, as if trying to press his thoughts into order. 'You know what it is? I don't have time to catch up with myself. Is Alan okay, by the way? You got him a nurse?'

'Eliza Morgan,' I said.

'Swell. We all know what a fine job – ' He flapped a hand in the air. 'No, I take it back, I take it back. I'm grateful. I really am, Tim.'

'I don't really expect you to act as if the worst thing that ever happened to you was a parking ticket,' I said.

'The problem is, I'm angry. I hardly even *know* it most of the time. I only figure it out when I look back and realize that all day I went around slamming doors.'

'Who are you angry with?'

He shook his head and drank again. 'I guess actually,

the person I'm angry with is April. How can I be angry with April?'

'She wasn't supposed to die.'

'Yeah, you went to shrink school at the same time you were becoming this English professor at Columbia.' He leaned back and gazed at his ceiling. 'Which is not to say that I don't think you're right. I just don't want to accept it. Anyhow, I'm grateful that you can overlook my acting like an asshole.' He slouched further down in the chair and cocked his feet on the coffee table. '*Now* will you tell me what happened to you today?'

I took him through my day: Alan, the Belknaps, Glenroy Breakstone, the trip to Elm Hill, the irate old man on Fond du Lac Drive.

'I must have missed something. What made you go to this man's house in the first place?'

Without mentioning Tom Pasmore, I told him about Elvee Holdings and William Writzmann. 'The only Writzmann in the book was Oscar, on Fond du Lac. So I stopped in to see him, and as soon as I said that I was looking for William Writzmann, he called me a tricky bastard and tried to clobber me.'

'He tried to hit you?'

'I think he was sick of people coming around his place to talk about William Writzmann.'

'Isn't William in the phone book?'

'He's listed at Expresspost, on South Fourth. And so are the other two directors of Elvee.'

'Who may or may not be real.'

'Exactly,' I said. 'But there was another reason I wanted to find William Writzmann.'

John Ransom sat slouched into his chair, his feet up on the table, drink cradled in his lap. He watched me, waiting, still not sure how interesting this was going to be.

I told him about seeing the blue Lexus beside the Green

462

Woman. Before I finished, he lifted his feet off the table and pushed himself upright.

'The same car?'

'It was out of sight before I could be certain. But while I was looking up Elvee Holdings, I thought I might as well find out who owned the Green Woman.'

'Don't tell me it's this Writzmann character,' he said.

'Elvee Holdings bought the bar in 1980.'

'So it is Writzmann!' He put his glass down on the table, looked at me, back at the glass, and picked it up and bounced it on his palm, as if weighing it. 'Do you think April was killed because of the damn *history project*?'

'Didn't she talk to you about it?'

He shook his head. 'Actually, she was so busy, we didn't have that much time to talk to each other. It wasn't a problem or anything.' He looked up at me. 'Well, to tell you the truth, maybe it was a problem.'

'Alan knew that it had something to do with a crime.'

'Did he?' John visibly tried to remember the conversation we'd had in the car. 'Yeah, she probably talked more to him about it.'

'More to him than to you?'

'Well, I wasn't too crazy about these projects of April's.' He hesitated, wondering how much he should say. He stood up and began yanking his shirt down into the waistband of his trousers. After that he adjusted his belt. These fussy maneuvers did not conceal his uneasiness. John bent down and grabbed the glass from the table. 'Those projects got on my nerves. I didn't see why she'd take time away from our marriage to do these screwy little things she'd never even get paid for.'

'Do you know how she first got interested in the Blue Rose business?'

He frowned into the empty glass. 'Nope.'

'Or what she managed to get done?'

'No idea. I suppose Monroe and Wheeler took away the file, or whatever, this morning, along with everything else.' He dropped his hands and sighed. 'Hold on. I'm going to have another drink.'

After John had taken a couple of steps toward the kitchen, he stopped moving and twisted around to say something else. 'It's not like we were having trouble or anything – I just wanted her to spend more time at home. We didn't fight.' He turned the rest of his body and faced me directly. 'We did argue, though. Anyhow, I didn't want to talk about this in front of the cops. Or my parents. They don't have to know that we were anything but happy together.'

'I understand,' I said.

John took a step forward, gesturing with his glass. 'Do you know what it takes to put together an art collection like this? When April had a lull in business, she'd just hop on a plane to Paris and spend a couple of days hunting down a painting she wanted. It was the whole way she was raised – there were no limits for little April Brookner, no sir, April Brookner could do anything that came into her head.'

'And you're angry with her because she left you,' I said.

'You don't get it.' He whirled around and went into the kitchen. I heard rattles and splashes, the big freezer door locking on its seal. John came back and stopped at the same point on the rug, holding his glass out toward me, his elbow bent. Clear liquid slid down the sides. 'April could be hard to live with. Something in her was off-balance.'

John saw the dark spots on the carpet, wiped the bottom of the glass with his hand, and drank to lower the level. 'I was the best thing that ever happened to April, and somewhere inside that head of his, Alan knows it.

Once she married me, he relaxed – I did him a real favor. He knew I could keep her from going off the deep end.'

'She was a gifted woman,' I said. 'What did you want her to do, spend all day baking cookies?'

He sipped from the drink again and went back to his chair. 'What was this gift of hers? April was good at making money. Is that such a wonderful goal?'

'I thought she didn't care much about the money. Wasn't she the only postmodern capitalist?'

'Don't fool yourself,' he said. 'She got caught up in it.' He held the glass before his face in the tips of his fingers and stared at it. A deep vertical line between his eyebrows slashed up into his forehead.

John let out a huge sigh and leaned forward to rest the cold glass against his forehead.

'I'm sure she was grateful for the stability you gave her,' I said. 'Think of how long you were married.'

His mouth tightened, and he clamped his eyes shut and leaned over, still holding the glass to his forehead. 'I'm a basketcase.' He laughed, but without any cheer. 'How did I ever make it through Vietnam? I must have been a lot tougher then. Actually, I wasn't tougher, I was just a lot crazier.'

'So was everybody else.'

'Yeah, but I was on a separate track. After I graduated from wanting to put an end to communism, I wanted something I hardly understood.' He smiled, wryly.

'What was that?'

'I guess I wanted to see through the world,' he said.

3

He exhaled with what seemed his whole being, making a sound like one of Glenroy Breakstone's breathy final notes. 'I didn't want any veils between me and whatever reality was. I thought you could sort of burst out into the open.' He let out that long, regretful sound again. 'You understand me? I thought you could *cross the border*.'

'Did you ever think you got close?'

He jumped up from the chair and turned off the lamp nearest him. 'Sometimes I thought I did, yeah.' He picked up his glass and turned off the lamp on the far side of the couch. 'It's too bright in here, do you mind?'

'No.'

John walked around the table and switched off the lamp at my end of the couch. Now the one light left burning was in a tall brass standard lamp near the entrance to the foyer, and the flared, bell-like shape of the lamp threw its illumination into a yellow circle on the ceiling. Dim silver light floated in from the windows across the room.

'There was this time I was doing hard traveling, going away incountry. I was with another man, Jed Champion, superb soldier. We'd been traveling on foot, mostly at night. We had a jeep, but it was way back there, *way* off the trail, covered up so it'd still be there when we got back.'

He was moving to a complicated pattern that sent him from the window to the mantel to his chair, then past the wall of paintings to the open floor near the brass lamp, and finally returning to the window, carving the shape of an arrow into the darkness with his body.

'After two or three days, we stopped talking entirely. We knew what we were doing, and we didn't have to talk about it. If we had a decision to make, we just acted together. It was like ESP – I knew *exactly* what was going on in his mind, and he knew what was going on in mine.

'We were working through relatively empty country, but there had been some VC activity here and there. We weren't supposed to make any contact. If we saw them we were supposed to just let them go their sweet way. On our sixth night, I realized that I was seeing better than I had the night before – in fact, all of my senses were amazingly acute. I heard *everything*.

'I could practically feel the roots of the trees growing underground. A VC patrol came within thirty feet of us, and we sat on our packs and watched them go by – we'd heard them coming for about half an hour, and you remember how quiet they could be? But I could smell their sweat, I could smell the oil on their rifles. And they couldn't even *see* us.

'The next night, I could have caught birds with my bare hands. I was beginning to hear something new, and at first I thought it was some noise made by my own body – it was that intimate. Then, right before dawn, I realized that I was hearing the voices of the trees, the rocks, the ground.

'The night after that, my body did things completely by itself. I was just up there behind my eyes, floating. I couldn't have put a foot wrong if I tried.'

Ransom stopped talking and turned around. He had come back to the window, and when he faced into the room, a sheet of darkness lay over his features and the entire front of his body. The cold silver light lay across the top of his head and the tops of his shoulders. 'Do you know what I'm talking about? Does this make any sense to you?'

'Yes,' I said.

'Good. Maybe the next part won't sound totally crazy to you.'

For an uncomfortably long time, he stared at me without saying anything. At last he turned away and went toward the fireplace. Cold light from the window touched his back. 'Maybe I wouldn't even want to be that alive anymore. You're right up next to death when you're that alive.'

He reached the fireplace, and in the darkness of that part of the room, I saw him raise an arm and caress the edge of the marble. 'No, I'm not saying it right. Being alive like that *includes* death.'

He turned from the mantel and walked back into the silver wash of light. He looked as dispassionate as a bank examiner. 'Not long before this, I lost a lot of people. Tribesmen. We had two "A" teams in our encampment, one under an officer named Bullock. Bullock and his team went out one night, and none of them ever came back. We waited an extra twelve hours, and then I took my team out to look for them.'

He had stepped into the darkness between the windows. 'It took three days to find them. They were in the woods not far from a little ville, about a hundred feet off the trail, in only moderately thick growth. Bullock and his five men were tied to trees. They'd been cut open – slashed across the gut and left to bleed to death. One more thing.'

He moved past the far window without turning to look at me, and the light turned his shirt and skin to silver again. 'Their tongues had been cut out.' John began moving toward the brass lamp, and now did turn, half in and half out of the soft yellow light. 'After we cut down the bodies and made litters to carry them back, I wrapped their tongues in a cloth and took them with me. I dried

468

them out and treated them, and wore them everywhere after that.'

'Who killed Bullock and his team?' I asked.

I saw the flicker of a smile in the darkness. 'VC cut out tongues, sometimes, to humiliate your corpse. So did the Yards, sometimes – to keep you silent in the other world.'

Ransom walked around the lamp and began heading back to the windows and the wall of paintings.

'So it's about the eighth night out. And then something says *Ransom*.

'I thought it must have been my partner, but I tuned to his frequency, you know, I focused on him and he wasn't making any more sound than a beetle. He sure as hell wasn't talking.

'Then I hear it again. *Ransom*.

'I came around the side of a tree about twenty feet wide, and standing off a little way under a big elephant fern like a roof, standing up and looking right at me, is Bullock. Right next to him is his number one guy, his team leader. Their clothes are covered with blood. They just stand there, waiting. They know I can see them, and they're not surprised. Neither am I.'

Ransom had made it past the windows again, and now he was stationed before the fireplace, in the darkest part of the room. I could barely make out his big figure moving back and forth in front of the fireplace.

'I was in the place where death and life flow into each other. Those little tongues felt like leaves on my skin. They let me pass through them. They knew what I was doing, they knew where I was going.'

I waited for more of the story, but he faced the fireplace in silence. 'You're talking about going to bring Bachelor back.'

I could hear him smiling. 'That's right. He knew I was coming, and he got out way ahead of me.' He was softly

469

beating a hand on the fireplace, like a mockery of self-punishment. 'That way I was? He was like that all the time. He lived in the realm of the gods.'

I was still waiting for the end of the story.

'Have you ever experienced anything like that? Are you qualified to judge it?'

'Something like that,' I said. 'But I don't know if I'm qualified to judge it.'

John pushed himself off the fireplace like a man doing a standing push-up. He switched on the lamp on the end table, and the room expanded into life and color. 'I felt extraordinary – like a king. Like a god.'

He turned around and gazed at me.

'What's the end of the story?' I asked.

'That is the end.'

'What happened when you got there?'

He was frowning at me, and when he spoke, it was to change the subject. 'I think I'd like to take a look inside the Green Woman Taproom tomorrow. Want to come with me?'

'You want to break in?'

'Hey, my old man owned a hotel,' John said. 'I have a lot of skeleton keys.'

4

The next morning I learned that while John Ransom and I had talked about seeing death moving through life, Mr and Mrs David Sunchana of North Bayberry Lane, Elm Hill, had nearly died in a fire caused by a gas explosion. I remembered the propane tanks and wondered what had caused the explosion. The thought that I might have caused it sickened me. Maybe the person who had followed me to Elm Hill had wanted to keep Bob Bandolier's old tenants from talking to me so badly that he had tried to kill them.

5

Ralph and Marjorie had gone back upstairs after their breakfast to pack for the return to Arizona, and John had gone out. Ralph had left the *Ledger* folded open to the sports pages, which crowed about the 9 to 4 victory of the Millhaven team over the Milwaukee Brewers. I flipped the paper back to the front page and read the latest dispatches from Armory Place. Local civic and religious leaders had formed the 'Committee for a Just Millhaven' and demanded a room at City Hall and secretarial help.

The Reverend Clement Moore was leading a protest march down Illinois Avenue at three o'clock in the afternoon. The mayor had issued a permit for the march and assigned all off-duty policemen to handle security and crowd control. Illinois Avenue would be closed to traffic from one-thirty until five o'clock.

A two-paragraph story on the fifth page reported that the previously unknown man murdered on Livermore Avenue had been positively identified as Grant Hoffman, 31, a graduate student in religion at Arkham College.

I turned the page and saw a small photograph of what looked like a farmhouse that had been half-destroyed by fire. The left side of the house had sunk into a wasteland of ashes and cinders from which protruded a freestanding porcelain sink surrounded by snapped-off metal pipes. The fire had blackened the remaining façade and left standing the uprights of what must have been a sort of porch. Beside the house stood a windowless little garage or shed.

I did not even recognize it until I saw the name Sunchana in the caption beneath the photograph. My breath stopped in my throat, and I read the article.

An Elm Hill patrolman named Jerome Hodges had been driving down North Bayberry Lane at the time of the explosion and had immediately radioed for a fire truck from the joint Elm Hill-Clark Township station. Patrolman Hodges had broken into the house through a bedroom window and led Mr Sunchana back out through the window while carrying Mrs Sunchana in his arms. The fire truck had arrived in time to save some of the house and furniture and the Sunchanas had been released from Western Hills hospital after examination had proven them unharmed. The explosion was not suspected to have been of suspicious origin.

I carried the newspaper to the counter, looked up the number of the Millhaven police headquarters in the directory, and asked to speak to Detective Fontaine. The police operator said she would put me through to his desk.

I shouldn't have been surprised when he answered, but I was.

After I identified myself, he asked, 'You get anything out of Damrosch's old records?'

'No, not much. I'll get them back to you.' Then something occurred to me. 'Didn't you tell me that someone else had been looking through the Blue Rose file?'

'Well, the little case, whatever, was sitting on top of the files down in the basement.'

'Did you remove anything from the file?'

'The nude pictures of Kim Basinger will cost you extra.'

'It's just that it was obvious that the records had been

472

held together by rubber bands – they were ripped that way – but the rubber bands were gone. So I wondered if whoever looked at the file before me went through it, trying to find something.'

'A forty-year-old rubber band was no longer in evidence. Do you have any other gripping information?'

I told him about going out to Elm Hill to talk to the Sunchanas, and that I had seen someone following me.

'This is the couple who had the fire?'

'Yes, the Sunchanas. When I was on the porch, I turned around and saw someone watching me from a row of trees across the street. He disappeared as soon as I saw him. That doesn't sound like much, but someone has been following me.' I described what had happened the other night.

'You didn't report this incident?'

'He got away so quickly. And John said he might have been just a peeping Tom.'

Fontaine asked me why I had wanted to talk to the Sunchanas in the first place.

'They used to rent the top floor of a duplex owned by a man named Bob Bandolier. I wanted to talk to them about Bandolier.'

'I suppose you had a reason for that?'

'Bandolier was a manager at the St Alwyn in 1950, and he might remember something helpful.'

'Well, as far as I know, there wasn't anything suspicious about the explosion out there.' He waited a second. 'Mr Underhill, do you often imagine yourself at the center of a threatening plot?'

'Don't you?' I asked.

Overhead, the Ransoms squabbled as Ralph pulled a wheeled suitcase down the hall.

'Anything else?'

I felt an unreasonable reluctance to share William Writzmann's name with him. 'I guess not.'

'Propane tanks aren't the safest things in the world,' he said. 'Leave the Sunchanas alone from now on, and I'll get back to you if I find out anything you ought to know.'

In a bright pink running suit, Ralph came down with the other, smaller suitcase, and carried it to the door, where he set it beside the wheeled case. He came back toward the kitchen and stood in the door. 'Are you talking to John?'

'Is John back?' Marjorie said. She came down in pink Reeboks and a running suit that matched her husband's. Maybe that was what the Ransoms had been arguing about. They looked like a pair of Easter Bunnies.

'No,' Ralph said. 'No, no, no.'

'As you could probably guess, things are a little crazy down here,' Fontaine was saying. 'Enjoy our beautiful city. Join a protest march.' He hung up.

Marjorie pushed past Ralph and stood scowling at me through her sunglasses. She put her hands on her pink, flaring hips. 'That's not John, is it?' she asked in a loud voice. 'If it is, you might remind him that we have to get to the airport.'

'I told you,' Ralph said. 'He's not talking to John.'

'You told me John wasn't back,' Marjorie said. Her voice was even louder. 'That's what you *told* me.' She zoomed out of the kitchen so quickly she nearly left a vapor trail.

Ralph went to the sink for a glass of water, raised the glass, and looked at me with a mixture of bravado and uncertainty. 'She's a little on edge. Getting to the airport, getting on the plane, you know.'

'It wasn't *me*,' Marjorie called from the living room. 'If my son isn't back here in ten minutes, we're going to the airport in a cab.'

'I'll drive you,' I said. Both of them began refusing before I had finished making the offer.

Ralph glanced toward the living room and then sat at

the other end of the kitchen table from me.

'It's about this driving business – John isn't the kind of person who ought to have his license suspended. I asked him what kind of troubles he had that made him get picked up three times for drunken driving. It does you good to talk about these things, get them out in the open.'

'He's home,' Marjorie announced in a thunderous stage whisper. Ralph and I heard the sound of the front door opening.

'I hope he can put it all behind him,' Ralph said.

John's voice, full of loud false cheer, called out, 'Is everybody okay? Everything all set?'

Ralph wiped his hand across his mouth and shouted back, 'Have a nice walk?'

'Hot out there,' John said. He walked into the kitchen, and Marjorie came trailing behind him, smiling and showing all her teeth. John was wearing loose, faded jeans and a dark green linen sports coat buttoned over his belly. His face shone with perspiration. He glanced at me, twisting his mouth to demonstrate his exasperation, and said, 'Those two the only bags?'

'That and your mother's carryon,' Ralph said. 'We're all set, think we ought to get moving?'

'Plenty of time,' John said. 'If we leave in twenty minutes, you'll still have about an hour before they call your flight.'

He sat down between Ralph and myself at the table. Marjorie stood behind him and put her hands on his shoulders. 'It's good for you to walk so much,' she said. 'But, honey, you could sure use a little loosening up. Your shoulders are so tight!' She stood behind him and kneaded his shoulders. 'Why don't you take off that jacket? You're all *wet*!' John grunted and twitched her off.

6

At the airport, Ralph insisted that we not walk them to the gate. 'Too much trouble to park – we'll say good-bye here.' Marjorie tilted her head for a kiss beside the suitcases. 'Just take it easy until your teaching starts again,' she said.

Ralph hugged his stiff, resisting son, and said, 'You're quite a guy.' We watched them go through the automatic doors in their Easter Bunny suits. When the glass doors closed, John got in the passenger seat and cranked down the window. 'I want to break something,' he said. 'Preferably something nice and big.' Ralph and Marjorie were moving uncertainly toward the lines of people at the airline desks. Ralph groped in a zippered pocket of the running suit, brought out their tickets, and stooped over to pull his suitcase toward the end of the line. 'I guess they'll get there,' John said. He leaned back against the seat.

I pulled away from the curb and circled around the terminals back to the access road.

'I have to tell you what happened last night,' I said. 'The people I went out to see in Elm Hill were nearly killed in a fire.'

'Oh, Jesus.' John turned to look behind us. 'I saw you checking the mirror on the way out here. Did anyone follow us out here?'

'I don't think so.'

He was almost kneeling on the seat, scanning the cars behind us. 'I don't see any blue Lexus, but probably he's got more than one car, don't you think?'

'I don't even know who *he* is,' I said.

'William Writzmann. Wasn't that the name you said last night?'

'Yes, but who is he?'

He waved the question away. 'Tell me about the fire.'

I described what I had read in the newspaper and told him about my conversation with Fontaine.

'I'm fed up with these cops.' John hoisted himself around, pulled his left leg up onto the seat, and twitched down the hem of the green jacket. 'After it turned out that Walter Dragonette's confession was false, all they think of is hauling me down to the station. Whose negligence got her killed in the first place?'

He twitched his jacket down over his belly again and put his left arm up on the back of the seat. He kept an eye on the traffic behind us. 'I'm not letting Fontaine stand in my way.' He turned his head to give me a hard look. 'Still willing to stay and help me?'

'I want to find Bob Bandolier.'

'William Writzmann is the one I went to find,' John said.

'We're going to have to be careful,' I said, meaning no more than that we would have to keep out of Fontaine's way.

'You want to see careful?' John tapped my shoulder. 'Look.' I turned my head, and he unbuttoned the linen jacket and held it out from his side. The curved handle of a handgun stuck up out of the waistband of his trousers. 'After you took it away from Alan, I put it in my safety deposit box. This morning, I went down to the bank and got it out.'

'This is a bad idea,' I said. 'In fact, it's a really terrible idea.'

'I know how to handle a firearm, for God's sake. So do you, so stop looking so disapproving.'

My effort to stop looking as disapproving as I felt was at least good enough to make him stop smirking at me.

'What were you going to do next?' he asked me.

'If I can find the Sunchanas, I'd like to talk to them. Maybe I could learn something if I knocked on a few more doors on South Seventh Street.'

'There's no reason to go back to Pigtown,' John said.

'Do you remember my telling you about the old couple I talked to, the ones who lived next to the Bandolier house? The woman, Hannah Belknap, told me that late at night she sometimes sees a man sitting alone in the living room.' I then went through Frank Belknap's response to his wife's story and his private words to me on the sidewalk.

'It's Writzmann,' John said. 'He burns down houses.'

'Hold on. This soldier threatened Belknap twenty years ago. Fontaine says propane tanks aren't the safest things in the world.'

'Do you really believe that?'

'No,' I confessed. 'I think somebody followed me to the Sunchanas and decided to stop them from talking to me. That means we're not supposed to learn something about Bob Bandolier.'

'I'd like to pay a call on Oscar Writzmann before we do anything else. Maybe I can get something out of him. Will you let me try?'

'Not if you're going to pull that gun on him.'

'I'm going to ask him if he has a son named William.'

7

Against my better judgment, I left the north-south expressway at the point in downtown Millhaven where it connects with the east-west expressway. Once again I

478

turned west. From the loop of the interchange, the tall square shapes of the Pforzheimer and the Hepton hotels stood like ancient monuments among the scoops and angles, the peaks and slabs of the new buildings east of the Millhaven River.

John watched the skyline as we curved down the ramp into the sparse traffic moving west.

'Every cop in town is going to be watching the marchers this afternoon. I think we could take the Green Woman to pieces and put it back together again without anybody noticing.'

At Teutonia, I began the long diagonal north through the strip of Piggly Wiggly supermarkets, bowling alleys, and fast-food franchises. 'Do you know if Alan lets anyone use his garage?'

'He might have let Grant use it for storage.' John looked at me as if I were playing some game he did not understand yet. 'Why?'

'The woman who lives across the street saw someone in his garage on the night April was attacked.'

Unconsciously, he touched the butt of the gun through his jacket. His face looked blander than ever, but a nerve under his right eye started jumping. 'What did she see, exactly?'

'Only the door going down. She thought it might have been Grant, because she'd seen him around. But Grant was already dead.'

'Well, actually, that was me,' John said. 'I didn't know anybody saw me, or I would have mentioned it before this.'

I pulled up at the light and switched on the turn indicator. 'You went there the night April disappeared?'

'I thought she might have been over at Alan's – we had a little argument. Anyhow, when I got there, all the lights were off, and I didn't want to make a scene. If April wanted to spend the night there, what the hell?'

The light changed, and I turned toward Oscar Writzmann's cheerless little house.

'We have some old stuff in his garage. I thought I might bring some old photographs, blowups of April, back home with me, so I went in and took a look around, but they were too big to carry, and the whole idea seemed crazy, once I actually saw them.' The nerve under his eye was still jittering, and he placed two fingers over it, as if to push it back into place.

'I thought it might have had something to do with her Mercedes,' I said.

'That car is probably in Mexico by now.'

Out of habit, I checked the rearview mirror. Writzmann's car was nowhere behind us on our three lanes of the drive. Nor was it among the few cars trolling through the dazzle of sunlight ahead of us. I pulled over to the curb in front of the yellow concrete jail.

John put his hand on the door handle.

'I think this is a mistake,' I said. 'All you're going to do is rile this guy. He isn't going to say anything you want to hear.'

John tried to give me his all-knowing look again, but the nerve was still pumping under his eye. 'I hate to say this, but you don't know everything.' He leaned toward me. His eyes pinned mine. 'Give me some rope, Tim.'

I said, 'Is this about Franklin Bachelor?'

He froze with his hand against the lump in the jacket. His eyes looked like stones. He slowly moved his hand from the gun handle to the door.

'Last night, you didn't tell me the end of that story.'

John opened his mouth, and his eyes moved wildly. He looked like an animal in a trap. 'You can't talk about this.'

'It doesn't matter if it really happened or not,' I said. 'It was Vietnam. I just want to know the end. Did

Bachelor kill his own people?'

John's eyes stopped moving.

'And you knew it,' I said. 'You knew he was already gone. You knew Bennington was the man you were bringing back with you. I'm surprised you didn't shoot him on the way to Camp Crandall, and then say that he got violent and tried to escape.' Then I understood why he had brought Bennington back. 'Oh. Jed Champion didn't understand things the way you did. He thought Bennington was Franklin Bachelor.'

'I got there two days before Jed,' John said in the same small voice. He cleared his throat. 'I was moving that much faster, at the end. I could smell the bodies for hours before I got to the camp. The bodies and a . . . a smell of cooking. Corpses were lying all over the camp. There were little fires everywhere. Bennington was just sitting on the ground. He had been burning the dead, or trying to.'

'Was he eating them?'

John stared at me for a time. 'Not the people he was burning.'

'What about Bachelor's wife?' I said. 'Her skull was in the back of your jeep.'

'He slit her throat and he gutted her. Her hair was hanging from a pole. He dressed and cleaned her, like a deer.'

'Bachelor did,' I said.

'He sacrificed her. Bennington was still boiling the meat off her bones when I got there.'

'And you ate some of her flesh,' I said.

He did not answer.

'You knew it was what Bachelor would do.'

'He already had.'

'You were in the realm of the gods,' I said.

He looked at me through his flat eyes, not speaking. He didn't have to speak.

'Do you know what happened to Bachelor?'

'Some Marines found his body up near the DMZ.' Now the pebbles in his eyes shone with defiance.

'Somebody found your body, too,' I said. 'I'm just asking.'

'Who have you been talking to?'

'Ever hear of a colonel named Beaufort Runnel?'

He blinked again, and the defiance left his eyes. 'That pompous twerp from the supply depot at Crandall?' He looked at me with something like amazement. 'How did you happen to meet *Runnel*?'

'It was a long time ago,' I said. 'A veterans' meeting, or something like that.'

'Veterans' groups are for bullshit artists.' Ransom opened his door. When I got out of the car, he was reaching up under the hips of the buttoned jacket to yank at the waist of the jeans. He did a little wiggle to get everything, presumably including Alan's pistol, into place. Then he pulled the jacket firmly down. He was in control again. 'Let me handle this,' he said.

8

Ransom plunged across Oscar Writzmann's brittle yellow lawn as if in flight from what he had said to me.

At the doorstep, I came up beside him, and he glared at me until I stepped back. He hitched his shoulders and rang the bell. I felt a premonition of disaster. We were doing the wrong thing, and terrible events would unfold from it.

'Go easy,' I said, and his back twitched again.

From my post one step beneath John, I saw only the top of the front door moving toward John's head.

'You wanted to see me?' Writzmann asked. He sounded a little weary.

'You're Oscar Writzmann?'

The old man did not answer. He shifted sideways and pushed the door fully open, so that John had to move back a step. Writzmann's face was still hidden from me. He was wearing a dark blue sweat suit with a zippered jacket, like the Ransoms' running suits but limp from a thousand trips through the washing machine. His bare feet were heavy, square, and rampant with exploding blue veins.

'We'd like to come in,' John said.

Writzmann looked over John's shoulder and saw me. He lowered his cannonball head like a bull.

'What are you, this guy's keeper?' he said. 'I have nothing to say to you.'

John gripped the door and held it open. 'You want to cooperate with us, Mr Writzmann. It'll go easier for you.'

Writzmann surprised me by backing away from the door. John stepped inside, and I followed him into the living room of the yellow house. Writzmann moved around a rectangular wooden table and stood beside a reclining chair. There was a cuckoo clock on the wall, but no pictures. A worn green love seat stood in front of the hatch to the kitchen. On the other side of the love seat stood a rocking chair with a seal set into the headpiece above the curved spindles.

'Nobody's here but me,' Writzmann said. 'You don't have to mess the place up, looking.'

'All we want is information,' John said.

'That's why you're carrying a gun. You want information.' His fear had left him, and what I saw was the same distaste, nearly contempt, that he had shown before. John had given him a look at the handle of the revolver. He sat down in the recliner, looking hard at us both.

I looked at the seal on the rocker. Around the number

25 the words *Sawmill Paper Company* were described in an ornate circle full of flourishes and ornamentation.

'Tell me about Elvee, Oscar,' John said. He was about four feet from the old man.

'Good luck.'

'Who runs it? What do they do?'

'No idea.'

'Tell me about William Writzmann. Tell me about the Green Woman Taproom.'

I saw something flicker in the old man's eyes. 'There is no William Writzmann,' he said. He leaned forward and put his hands together. His shoulders bunched. The heavy blue feet slid back under his knees.

John took a step backward, reached into his jacket, and yanked out the pistol. He didn't look much like a gunfighter. He pointed it at the old man's chest. Writzmann exhaled and bit down, pouching out his upper lip.

'That's interesting,' John said. 'Explain that to me.'

'What's to explain? If there ever was a person by that name, he's dead.' Writzmann looked straight at the barrel of the pistol. He slid his feet forward slowly and carefully, until only the thick blue-spattered heels touched the floor and the stubby, crooked toes pointed up.

'He's dead,' John said.

Writzmann took his eyes from the gun and looked at John's face. He did not seem angry or frightened anymore. 'People like you should stay down there on Livermore, where you belong.'

John lowered the gun. 'What about the Green Woman Taproom?'

'Used to be a pretty seedy place, I guess.' Writzmann pulled back his feet and shoved himself upright. 'But I don't want to talk about it very much.' John raised the gun waist-high and pointed it at his gut. 'I don't want to talk about anything with you two.' Writzmann stepped forward, and John moved back. I stood up from the rocking chair. 'You're not going to shoot me, you sorry piece of shit.'

He took another step forward. John jerked up the gun, and a flash of yellow burst from the barrel. A wave of sound and pressure clapped my eardrums tight. Clean white smoke hung between John and Oscar Writzmann. I expected Writzmann to fall down, but he just stood still, looking at the gun. Then he slowly swiveled around to look behind him. There was a hole the size of a golf ball in the wall above the recliner.

'Stay where you are,' John said. He had straightened his right arm and was gripping the wrist with his left hand. The ringing in my ears made his voice sound small and tinny. 'Don't tell anybody that we came here.' John backed up, holding the pistol on Writzmann's head. 'You hear me? You never saw us.'

Writzmann put his hands in the air.

John backed toward the door, and I went outside beforc him. Heat fell on me like an anvil. I heard John say, 'Tell the man in the blue Lexus he's finished.' He was improvising. I felt like grabbing him by the belt and throwing him into the street. So far, nobody had come outside to investigate the noise. Two cars rolled down the broad drive. My whole head was ringing.

John walked backward through the door, still holding his arms in the shooter's position. As soon as he was outside, he lowered his arms, turned toward the sidewalk, and began to run. Wc rushed across the sidewalk and John opened the back door and jumped in. Swearing, I dug the keys out of my pocket and started the Pontiac. Writzmann appeared in the frame when I pulled away from the curb. John was yelling, 'Floor it, floor it!'

I smashed my foot on the accelerator, and we moved sluggishly down the street.

'Floor it!'

'I am flooring it,' I yelled, and the car, though still

moving with dreamlike slowness, picked up some speed. Writzmann began walking gingerly across his dry lawn. The Pontiac swayed like a boat, then finally began to charge. When I turned right at the next corner, the car heeled over and the tires squealed.

'Whoo!' Ransom shouted. He leaned over the back of the front seat, still holding the pistol. 'Did you *see* that? Did that stop the bastard cold, or what?' He started laughing. 'He came toward me – I just lifted this sucker – and WHAM! Just like that!'

'I could murder you,' I said.

'Don't be mad, it was too good,' John gasped. 'Did you see that *fire*? Did you see that *smoke*?'

'Did you mean to fire?' I took a couple more rights and lefts, waiting to hear the sirens.

'Sure. Sure I did. That old thug was going to take it away from me. I had to stop him, didn't I? How else could I show him I meant business?'

'I ought to brain you with that thing,' I said.

'You know what that guy was? He used to take guys apart with his bare hands.' He sounded hurt.

'He worked in a paper mill for twenty-five years,' I said. 'When he retired, they gave him a rocking chair.'

I could hear John turning the revolver in his hands, admiring it.

I took another turn and saw Teutonia two blocks ahead of me. 'Why do you suppose he told us to go back to Livermore Avenue, where we belonged?'

'No offense, but it's not the classiest part of town.'

I did not say another word until I turned into Ely Place, and then what made me speak was not forgiveness but shock. A police car was pulled up in front of John's house.

'He got your license number,' I said.

'Shit,' John said. He bent over, and I heard him sliding the pistol under the passenger seat. 'Keep going.'

It was too late to keep going. The driver's door of the

police car swung open, and a long blue leg appeared. A giant blue trunk appeared, and then a second giant leg emerged from the car. It was like watching a circus trick – the enormous man could not have fit into the little car, but here he came anyhow. Sonny Berenger straightened up and waited for us to park in front of him.

'Deny everything,' John said. 'It's our only chance.'

I got nervously out of the car. I did not think denial would do much good against Sonny. He towered over his patrol car, watching us coldly.

'Hello, Sonny,' I said, and his face hardened. I remembered that Sonny had good reason to dislike me.

He looked from me to John and back. 'Where is it?' he asked.

John couldn't help taking a quick look back at the Pontiac.

'You have it in the car?'

'There's a reason for everything,' John said. 'Don't fly off the handle until you hear our side of the story.'

'Get it for me, please. Sergeant Hogan wants it back today.'

John started walking back to the Pontiac, and as Sonny's last sentence sank in, his steps became slower. I thought he nearly staggered. 'Oh, did I say it was in the *car*?' He stopped and turned around.

'What does Sergeant Hogan want you to give him?' I asked.

Sonny looked from me to John and back to me. He stood up even straighter. His chest looked about two axe handles wide. 'An old case file. Will you get it for me, sir, wherever it happens to be?'

'Ah,' John said. 'Yes. You saw it last, didn't you, Tim?'

Sonny focused on me.

'Wait right here,' I said, and started up the path with John right behind me. I waited by the door while John fumbled for his key. Sonny crossed his arms and managed

487

to lean against the patrol car without folding it in half.

As soon as we got inside, John let out a whoop of laughter. He was happier than I had seen him during all the rest of my stay in Millhaven.

'After that speech about denying everything, you were all set to hand him the gun.'

'Trust me,' he said. 'I would have figured something out.' We started up the stairs. 'Too bad Hogan didn't wait another couple of hours before sending Baby Huey over. I wanted to look at the file.'

'You still can,' I said. 'I made a copy.'

John followed me up to the third floor and stood in the door of his study while I reached under the couch and pulled out the satchel. I wiped off some of the dust with my hands and opened the satchel to take out the thick bundle of the copy. I handed this to John.

He winked at me. 'While I start reading this, why don't you stop off and see how Alan is doing?'

Sonny was still leaning against the car with his arms crossed when I closed the door. His immovability power-fully communicated the message that I was worth no extra effort. When I held the satchel out toward him, he uncoiled and took it from me in one motion.

'Thank Paul Fontaine for me, will you?'

Sonny's reply consisted of getting into the patrol car and placing the satchel on the seat beside him. He pushed the key into the ignition.

'In the long run,' I said, 'you did everybody a favor by talking to me that day.'

He regarded me from what seemed a distance of several miles. He didn't even bother getting me into focus.

'I owe you one,' I said. 'I'll pay you back when I can.'

The expression in his eyes changed for something like a nano-second. Then he turned the key and whipped the patrol car around into a U-turn and sped away toward Berlin Avenue.

9

Talking softly, Eliza Morgan led me to the living room. 'I
just got him settled down with lunch in front of the TV.
Channel Four is having a discussion with the press, and
then they're showing live coverage of the march down
Illinois Avenue.'

'So that's where all the reporters went,' I said.

'Would you like some lunch? Mushroom soup and
chicken salad sandwich? Oh, there he goes.'

Alan's voice came booming down the hall. 'What the
dickens is going on?'

'I'm starved,' I told Eliza. 'Lunch sounds wonderful.'

I followed her as far as the living room. Alan was
seated on the chesterfield, threatening to upset the
wooden tray on his lap as he twisted to look at me. A
small color television on a wheeled stand stood in the
middle of the room. 'Ah, Tim,' Alan said. 'Good. You
don't want to miss this.'

I sat down, taking care not to upset his tray. Beside the
bowl of soup and a small plate containing the crusts of
what had been a sandwich stood a bud vase with a pink,
folded rose. A linen napkin was flattened across Alan's
snowy white shirt and dark red tie. He leaned toward me.
'Did you see that woman? That's Eliza. You can't have
her. She's mine.'

'I'm glad you like her.'

'Splendid woman.'

I nodded. Alan leaned back and started on his soup.

Geoffrey Bough, Isobel Archer, Joe Ruddler, and three
reporters I did not recognize sat at a round table under
Jimbo's kindly, now slightly uncertain gaze.

' – extraordinary number of brutal murders in a community of this size,' Isobel purred, 'and I wonder at the sight of Arden Vass parading himself in front of television cameras during the funerals of persons whose murders may as yet be unsolved, despite – '

'*Despite what, get your foot out of your mouth,*' Joe Ruddler yelled, his red face exploding up from his collar without the usual buffer provided by the neck.

' – despite the ridiculous readiness of certain of my colleagues to believe everything they're told,' Isobel smoothly finished.

Eliza Morgan handed me a tray identical to Alan's, but without a rose. A delicious odor of fresh mushrooms drifted up from the soup. 'There's more, if you'd like.' She crossed in front of me to sit in a chair near Alan.

Jimbo was trying to wrestle back control of the panel. Joe Ruddler was bellowing, '*If you don't like it here, Miss Archer, try it in Russia, see how far you get!*'

'I guess it's interesting to imagine, Isobel,' said Geoffrey Bough, but got no further.

'*Oh, we'd all imagine that, if we could!*' yelled Ruddler.

'Miss Archer,' Jimbo desperately interposed, 'in the light of the widespread civic disturbance in our city these days, can you think it is responsible to bring further criticism against – '

'*Exactly!*' Ruddler bellowed.

'Is it responsible not to?' Isobel asked.

'*I'd shoot myself right now if I thought it would protect one good cop!*'

'What an interesting concept,' Isobel said, with great sweetness. 'More to the point, and for the moment setting aside the two recent Blue Rose murders, let's consider the murder of Frank Waldo, a local businessman with an interesting reputation – '

'I'm afraid you're getting off the subject, Isobel.'

'*We'll get 'em and put 'em away! We always do!*'

'We always put somebody away.' Isobel turned, grinning Geoffrey Bough into a smoking ruin with a glance.

'Who?' I asked. 'What was that?'

'Are you done, Alan?' Eliza asked. She stood up to remove his tray.

'Who did she say was killed?' I asked.

'A man named Waldo,' Eliza said, returning to the room. 'I read about it in the *Ledger*, one of the back pages.'

'Was he found dead on Livermore Avenue? Outside a bar called the Idle Hour?'

'I think they found him at the airport,' she said. 'Would you like to see the paper?'

I had read only as far as the article about the fire in Elm Hill. I said that I would, yes, and Eliza left the room again to bring me the folded second section.

The mutilated body of Francis (Frankie) Waldo, owner and president of the Idaho Wholesale Meat Co., had been found in the trunk of a Ford Galaxy located in the long-term parking garage at Millhaven airport at approximately three o'clock in the morning. An airport employee had noticed blood dripping from the trunk. According to police sources, Mr Waldo was nearing criminal indictment.

I wondered what Billy Ritz had done to make Waldo look so happy and what had gone wrong with their arrangement.

'Oh, Tim, I suppose you'd be interested in that thing April was writing? The bridge project?'

Alan was looking at me hopefully. 'You know, the history piece about the old Blue Rose murders?'

'It's here?' I asked.

Alan nodded. 'April used to work on it in my dining room, off and on. I guess John hardly let her work on it at home, but she could always tell him she was coming over here to spend time with the old man.'

I remembered the dust-covered papers on Alan's dining room table.

'I plain forgot about the whole thing,' he said. 'That cleaning woman, she must have thought they were my papers, and she just picked 'em up, dusted underneath, and put 'em back. Eliza asked me about them yesterday.'

'I'll get them for you, if you like,' Eliza said. 'Have you had enough to eat?'

'Yes, it was wonderful,' I said, and lifted the tray and hitched forward.

In seconds, Eliza returned with a manila folder in her hands.

10

The manuscript was not the chronological account of the Blue Rose murders I had assumed it would be, given my stereotypical preconceptions concerning the sorts of books likely to be written by stockbrokers. April Ransom's manuscript was an unclassifiable mix of genres. *The Bridge Project* was the book's actual title, not merely a convenient reference. It was clear that April intended this title to mean that the book itself was a bridge of sorts – between historical research and journalism, between event and setting, between herself and the boy in the painting called *The Juniper Tree*, between the reader and William Damrosch. She had taken an epigraph from Hart Crane.

> Through the bound cable strands, the arching path
> Upward, veering with light, the flight of strings, –
> ....
> As though a god were issue of the strings . . .

April had begun by examining the history of the Horatio Street bridge. In 1875, one citizen had complained in the columns of the *Ledger* that a bridge connecting Horatio Street to the west side of the Millhaven River would carry the infections of crime and disease into healthy sections of the city. One civic leader referred to the bridge as 'That Ill-Starred Monstrosity which has supplanted an honest Ferryman.' Immediately upon completion, the bridge had been the site of a hideous crime, the abduction of an infant from a carriage by a wild, ragged figure on horseback. The man boarded the carriage, snatched the child from its nurse, and then remounted his horse, which had kept pace. The kidnapper had spun his mount around and galloped off into the warren of slums and tenements on the east side of the river. Two days later, an extensive police search discovered the corpse on a crude altar in the Green Woman's basement. The abductor was never identified.

April had uncovered the old local story of the ancient man with battered white wings discovered in a packing case on the riverbank by a band of children who had stoned him to death, mocking the creature's terrible, foreign cries as the stones struck him. I too had run across the story, but April had located old newspaper accounts of the legend and related the angel figure to the epidemic of influenza which had killed nearly a third of the Irish population that lived near the bridge. Nonetheless, she reported, an individual known only as M. Angel had been listed in police documents from 1911 as a death from stoning and had subsequently been buried in the city's old potter's field (now vanished beneath a section of the east-west freeway).

The Green Woman Taproom, originally the ferryman's shanty, made frequent appearances in the police documents of the late nineteenth and early twentieth centuries. Apart from being the scene of the occasional brawls, stabbings, and shootings not uncommon in rough taverns of the period, the Green Woman had distinguished itself as the informal headquarters of the Illuminated Ones, the most vicious gang in the city's history. The leaders of the Illuminated Ones, said to be the same men who as children had killed the mysterious M. Angel, organized robberies and murders throughout Millhaven and were said to have controlled criminal activity in both Milwaukee and Chicago. In 1914, the taproom burned down in a suspicious fire, killing three of the five leaders of the Illuminated Ones. The remaining two appeared to divert themselves into legal activity, bought vast houses on Eastern Shore Drive, and became active in Millhaven politics.

It was from the steps of the rebuilt Green Woman Taproom that a discharged city clerk shot and wounded Theodore Roosevelt; and the psychotic city employee who shot at, but failed to hit, Dwight D. Eisenhower, stepped out from the shadows of the Green Woman when he raised his pistol.

The god who had issued from these strings, April Ransom implied, spoke most clearly through the life and death of William Damrosch, originally named Carlos Rosario. As an infant, he had been carried to the foot of the Horatio Street bridge by his mother, who had been summoned there by her murderer.

For weeks after the discovery of the living baby and the dead woman on the frozen riverbank beneath the Green Woman, wrote April, the old legend of the winged man resurfaced, changed now to account for the death of Carmen Rosario: this time the angel was robust and healthy instead of weakened by age, his golden hair flowed in the dark February wind, and he killed instead of being killed.

How did April know that the old legend had returned?

On the second Sunday following the discovery of the infant, two churches in Millhaven, Matthias Avenue Methodist and Mt Horeb Presbyterian, had advertised sermons entitled, respectively, 'The Angel of Death, A Scourge to the Sinful' and 'The Return of Uriel.' An editorial in the *Ledger* advised residents of Millhaven to remember that crimes of violence have human, not supernatural, origins.

Three weeks after the murder of his mother, the child was released into the first of the series of orphanages and foster homes that would lead him in five years to Heinz Stenmitz, a newly married young butcher who had recently opened a shop beside his house on Muffin Street in the section of Millhaven long known as Pigtown.

At this stage of his life, April wrote, Stenmitz was a striking figure who, with his long blond hair and handsome blond beard, bore a great resemblance to the conventional Christian portrait of Jesus; moreover, he conducted informal church services in his shop on Sundays. Long after, at his trial for child abuse, it was introduced as evidence of the preacher-butcher's good character that he had often sought his parishioners at the train and bus stations and had given special attention to those frightened and confused immigrants from Central and South American countries who were handicapped by an ignorance of English as well as poverty.

11

April Ransom was quietly making the case that Heinz Stenmitz had murdered William Damrosch's mother. She believed that, on a dark cold night in February, gullible and intoxicated witnesses had seen the butcher's flowing hair and remembered the old stories of the persecuted angel.

I looked up to see that Alan had returned from his nap. His hands were clasped at his waist, his chin was up, and his eyes were bright and curious. 'Do you think it's good?'

'It's extraordinary,' I said. 'I wish she had been able to finish it. I don't know how she ever managed to get even this much together.'

'Efficiency. And she was my daughter, after all. She knew how to do research.'

'I'd like to be able to read the whole thing,' I said.

'Keep it as long as you like,' Alan said. 'For some reason, I can't seem to make much headway on it.'

For a moment I was unable to keep from registering the shock of the understanding Alan had just given me. He could not read his daughter's manuscript, which meant that he could no longer read at all. I turned to the television to hide my dismay. The screen showed a long view of Illinois Avenue. People stood three and four deep along the sidewalks, yelling along with someone chanting through a bullhorn.

'Oh, my God,' I said, and looked at my watch. 'I have to meet John.' I stood up.

'I knew it'd be good,' Alan said.

PART TEN

William Writzmann

1

In shirtsleeves, Ransom motioned me inside and went into the living room to turn off the television, which showed the same roped-off stretch of Illinois Avenue I had just seen on Alan's set. The books had been pushed to the side of the coffee table, and loose pages of the Blue Rose file lay over the rest of its surface. The green linen jacket was draped over the back of the couch. Just before John reached the television, a slightly breathless Isobel Archer appeared on its screen, holding a microphone and saying, 'The stage is set for an event unlike any which has occurred in this city since the early days of the civil rights movement, and which is sure to inspire controversy. As the tensions in Millhaven grow more and more intense, religious and civic leaders demand – '

John bent over to turn the set off. 'I thought you'd be back before this.' He noticed the thick folder in my hand. 'What's that, the other part of the file?'

I placed the folder beside the telephone. 'April's manuscript has been at Alan's house all this time.'

He lifted the green jacket off the couch and slipped it on. 'You must have taken a look at it, then.'

'Of course I did,' I said, opening the upside-down file to its last pages. I had looked through only something like the first quarter of *The Bridge Project*, and I wondered what April had written last. A letterhead was darkly visible through the paper on the top of the pile, and, curious, I lifted up the sheet and turned it over. It was a sheet of April's personal stationery, and the letterhead was her name and address. The letter had been dated some three months ago and was addressed to the chief of police, Arden Vass.

John came toward me from the living room, adjusting the linen jacket.

The letter explained that April Ransom had become interested in writing a paper that would touch upon the Blue Rose murders of forty years before and hoped that Chief Vass would give her permission to consult the original police files for the case.

I turned over the next letter, dated two weeks later, expressing the same desire in somewhat stronger terms.

Beneath this was a letter addressed to Sergeant Michael Hogan and dated five days after the second letter to Arden Vass. April wondered if the sergeant might assist her in her research – the chief had not responded to her requests, and if Sergeant Hogan had any interest in this fascinating corner of Millhaven history, Ms Ransom would be most grateful. Sincerely yours.

Another letter to Michael Hogan followed, regretting what might seem the writer's bad manners, but hoping to make amends for them by her willingness to spend her own time trying to locate a forty-year-old file in whatever storage facility it was kept.

'Hogan knew she was interested in the old Blue Rose case,' I said. John was reading the letter over my shoulder. He nodded. 'He plays it pretty close to the vest, doesn't he?'

John stepped beside me and turned over the next sheet, also a letter. This was to Paul Fontaine.

Dear Detective Fontaine: I turn to you in something like desperation, after failing to receive replies from Chief Vass and Sergeant Michael Hogan. I am an amateur historian whose latest project concerns the history and origins of the Horatio Street bridge, the Green Woman Taproom, and

500

among other topics, the connections of these sites to the Blue Rose murders that took place in Millhaven in 1950. I would very much like to see the original police file for the Blue Rose case, and have already expressed my absolute willingness to search for this file myself, wherever it may be stored.

Detective Fontaine, I am writing to you because of your splendid reputation as an investigator. Can you see that I too am talking about an investigation, one back into a fascinating time? I trust that you will at least give me the courtesy of a reply.

Yours in hope,
April Ransom

'She was jiving him,' John said. 'Yours in hope? April would never say anything like that.'

'Do you think she might ever have taken a look at the Green Woman?'

He straightened up and looked at me. 'I'm beginning to wonder if I was ever qualified to answer questions like that.' He threw up his arms. 'I didn't even really know what she was working on!'

'She didn't either, exactly,' I said. 'It was only partly a historical paper.'

'She couldn't be satisfied!' John said, stepping toward me. 'That's it. She wasn't satisfied with being a star at Barnett, she wasn't satisfied with doing the same kind of articles anybody else would write, she wasn't . . .' He clamped his mouth shut and looked moodily at the manuscript file. 'Well, let's get downtown before the damn march is all over.' He threw open the door and stormed outside.

As soon as he was in the car, he bent over, placed a hand on my thigh and his head on my knee, and reached under my seat. 'Oh, no,' I said.

'Oh, *yes*.' John straightened up, holding the revolver. 'I hate to say it, but we might need this.'

'Then count me out.'

501

'Okay, I'll go alone.' He leaned back, held in his stomach, and slid the gun into his trousers. Then he looked back at me. '*I* don't think we'll need a gun, Tim. But if we meet someone, I want to have something to fall back on. Don't you want to take a look at the place?'

I nodded.

'This is just backup.'

I started the car, but did not take my eyes off him. 'Like at Writzmann's?'

'I made a mistake.' He grinned, and I turned the car off. He held up his hands, palms out. 'No, I mean it, I shouldn't have done that, and I'm sorry. Come on, Tim.'

I started the car again. 'Just don't do that again. Ever.'

He was shaking his head and hitching the jacket around the curved tusk of the handle. 'But suppose some guy walks in when we're there. Wouldn't you feel easier if you knew we had a little firepower?'

'If it were in my hands, maybe,' I said.

Wordlessly, John opened his jacket, pulled the gun out of his trousers, and handed it to me. I put it on the seat beside me and felt it press uncomfortably into my thigh. When I came to a red light, I picked it up and pushed the barrel into the left side of my belt. The light turned green, and I jerked the car forward.

'Why would Alan buy a gun?'

John smiled at me. 'April got it for him. She knew he kept a lot of cash in the house, in spite of her efforts to get the money into the bank. I guess she figured that if someone broke in, all Alan had to do was wave that cannon around, and the burglar would get out as soon as he could.'

'If he was just supposed to wave it around, she shouldn't have bought him any bullets.'

'She didn't,' John said. 'She just told him to point the gun at anyone who broke in. One day last year when she was out of town, Alan called, all pissed off that April didn't trust him enough to give him bullets, he could handle a gun better than I could – '

'Is that true?' Alan Brookner did not seem like a man who would have spent a great deal of time firing guns.

'Got me. Anyhow, he chewed me out until I gave up and took him to a shop down on Central Divide. He bought two boxes of hollow points. I don't know if he ever told April, but I sure didn't.'

As I drove down Horatio Street, distant crowd noises came to us from the direction of Illinois Avenue and the other side of the river. Voices shouting slogans into bullhorns rose above mingled cheers and boos.

I looked south toward Illinois at the next cross street. A thick pack of people, some of them waving signs, blocked the avenue. As gaudy and remote as a knight in armor, a mounted policeman in a riot helmet trotted past them. As soon as I got across the street, the march vanished again into distant noise.

The tenements along this section of Horatio Street looked deserted. A few men sat drinking beer and playing cards in parked cars.

'You looked through the file?' I asked.

'Funny, isn't it?'

'Well, they never did ask about who had been fired recently.'

'You didn't notice? Come on.' He sat up on the car seat and stared at me to see if I was just pretending to be unobservant. 'Who is the one guy they should have talked to? Who knew more about the St Alwyn than anyone else?'

'Your father.'

'They *talked* to my father.'

I remembered that and tried another name. 'Glenroy Breakstone, but I read his statements, too.'

'You're not thinking.'

'Then tell me.'

He sat there twisted sideways, looking at me with an infuriating little smile on his lips. 'There are no statements from the famous Bob Bandolier. Isn't that a little bit strange?'

2

'You must be mistaken,' I said.

He snorted.

'I'm sure I read about Bob Bandolier in those statements.'

'Other people mention him from time to time. But he wasn't working in the hotel when the murders took place. So for Damrosch – probably Bandolier never crossed his mind at all.'

With the bridge directly before us, I turned left onto Water Street. Forty feet away, the Green Woman Taproom sat on its concrete slab across from the tenements. Pigeons waddled and strutted over the slashes of graffiti.

Ten feet beyond the front of the bar, a fifteen-foot section of the concrete sloped down smoothly to meet the roadbed. Pigeons ambled and flapped away from my tires. I drove slowly up past the left side of the bar. The second, raised section of the tavern ended in a flat frame wall with an inset door.

I swung around the back of the building and swerved in behind it. Tarpaper covered the back of the building. Above the back door, two windows were punched into the high blank façade. Ransom and I softly closed our doors. Now nearly at the Illinois Avenue bridge, cut from view by the curve of the river and the prisonlike walls of an abandoned factory, the army advanced. An outsize, brawling voice bellowed, '*Justice for all people! Justice for all people!*'

Pigeons moved jerkily across SKUZ SUKS and KILL MEE DEATH.

A blaze of whiteness caught my eye, and I turned toward it – the harsh sunlight poured down like a beam onto a dove standing absolutely still on the concrete.

I looked at Ransom's white, shadowless face across the top of the car. 'Maybe someone took those pages out of the file.'

'Why?'

'So April wouldn't see them. So we wouldn't see them. So nobody would ever see them.'

'Suppose we try to get inside this place before the march breaks up?' Ransom said.

3

John pulled open the screen door and fought with the knob. Then he banged his shoulder against the door.

I pulled out the revolver and came up beside him. He was fighting the knob again. I got closer and saw that he was pulling on a steel padlock. I pushed him aside and pointed the gun barrel at the lock.

'Cool it, Wyatt.' John pushed down the barrel with a forefinger. He went back to the car and opened the trunk. After an excruciating period that must have been shorter than it seemed, he pushed down the lid and came toward me carrying a jack handle. I stepped aside, and John slid the rod into the shackle of the padlock. Then he twisted the rod until the lock froze it and pulled down heavily on the top end of the rod. His face compressed, and his shoulders bulged in the linen jacket. His face turned dull red. I pulled up on the bottom of the rod. Something between us suddenly went soft and malleable, like putty, and the shackle broke.

John staggered forward, and I almost fell on my backside. He dropped the rod, yanked the broken lock away from the clip and set it on the concrete beside the jack handle. 'What are you waiting for?' he said.

I pushed the door aside and walked into the Green Woman Taproom.

4

We stood in a nearly empty room about ten feet square. On the far wall, a staircase with a handrail led up to the room above. A brown plastic davenport with a slashed seat cover stood against the far wall, and a desk faced out from the wall to my left. A tattered green carpet covered the floor. Another door faced us from the far wall. John closed the door, and most of the light in the old office disappeared.

'Was this where you saw Writzmann taking stuff out of his car?' John asked me.

'His car was pulled up alongside the place, and the front door was open.'

Something rustled overhead, and both of us looked up at the pockmarked ceiling tiles.

'You want to look in front, and I'll check up there?'

I nodded, and Ransom moved toward the stairs. Then he stopped and turned around. I knew what was on his mind. I tugged the Colt out of my waistband and passed it to him, handle first.

He carried the pistol toward the staircase. When he set

his foot on the first tread, he waved me into the next rooms, and I went across the empty office and opened the door to the intermediate section of the building.

A long wooden counter took up the middle of the room. Battered tin sinks and a ridged metal counter took up the far wall. Once, cabinets had been attached to thick wooden posts on the rough plaster walls. Broken pipes jutting up from the floor had fed gas to the ovens. A beam of buttery light pooled on the far wall. Upstairs, Ransom opened a creaking door.

An open hatch led into the barroom. Thick wads of dust separated around my feet.

I stood in the hatch and looked around at the old barroom. The tinted window across the room darkened the day to an overcast afternoon in November. Directly before me was the curved end of the long bar, with a wide opening below a hinge so the bartender could swing up a section of the wood. Tall, ornate taps ending in the heads of animals and birds stood along the bar.

Empty booths incongruously like seventeenth-century pews lined the wall to my right. A thick mat of dust covered the floor. As distinct as tracks in snow, a double set of footprints led up to and away from a three-foot-square section of the floor near the booths. I stepped through the hatch. When I looked down, I saw tiny, long-toed prints in the dust.

The sense came to me of having faced precisely this emptiness at some earlier stage of my life. I took another step forward, and the feeling intensified, as if time were breaking apart around me. Some dim music, music I had once known well but could no longer place, sounded faintly in my head.

A chill passed through my entire body.

Then I saw that someone else was in the empty room, and I went stiff with terror. A child stood before me on the dusty floor, looking at me with a terrible, speaking urgency. Water rushed beneath Livermore Avenue's doomed elms and coursed over dying men screaming in the midst of dead men dismembered in a stinking green wilderness. I had seen him once before, long ago.

And then it seemed to me that another boy, another child, stood behind him, and that if this child should reach out for me, I myself would instantly be one of the dismembered dead.

The Paradise Garden, the Kingdom of Heaven.

I took another step forward, and the child was gone.

Another step took me closer to the window. Two square outlines had been stamped into the cushion of felt near the window. Brown pellets like raisins lay strewn over the streaky floor.

Heavy footsteps came through the old kitchen. Ransom said, 'Something chewed a hole the size of Nebraska in the wall up there. Find the boxes?'

'They're gone,' I said. I felt light-headed.

'Shit.' He came up beside me. 'Well, that's where they were, all right.' He sighed. 'The rats went to work on those boxes – maybe that's why Writzmann moved them.'

'Maybe – ' I didn't finish the sentence, and it sounded as if I were agreeing with him. I didn't want to say that the boxes might have been moved because of his wife.

'What's over here?' John followed the double trail of footprints to the place where they reversed themselves. The pistol dangled from his hand. He bent down and grunted at whatever he saw.

I came up behind him. At the end of a section of boards, a brass ring fit snugly into a disc.

'Trap door. Maybe there's something in the basement.' He bent down and tugged at the ring. The entire three-foot section of floor folded up on a concealed hinge, revealing the top of a wooden ladder that descended straight down into darkness. I smelled blood, shook my head, and smelled only must and earth.

I had already lived through this moment, too. Nothing on earth could get me to go into that basement.

'Okay, it doesn't seem likely,' John said, 'but isn't it worth a look?'

'Nothing's down there but . . .' I could not have said what might be down there.

My tone of voice caught his attention, and he looked at me more closely. 'Are you all right?'

I said I was fine. He pointed the revolver down into the darkness underneath the tavern. 'You have a lighter, or matches, or anything?'

I shook my head.

He clicked off the safety on the revolver, bent over and put a foot on the second rung. With one hand flat on the floor, he got his other foot on the first rung, and then almost toppled into the basement. He let go of the pistol and used both hands to steady himself as he took another couple of steps down the ladder. When his shoulders were more or less at the level of the opening, he snatched up the pistol, glared at me, and went the rest of the way down the ladder. I heard him swear as he bumped against something at the bottom.

The ripe odor of blood swarmed out at me again. I asked him if he saw anything.

'To hell with you,' he said.

I looked at his thinning hair swept backward over pink, vulnerable-looking scalp. Below that his right hand ineffectually held out the pistol at the level of his spreading belly. Beside one of his feet was a bar stool with a green plastic seat. He had stepped on it when he came down off the ladder. 'Way over at the side are a couple of windows. There's an old coal chute and a bunch of other shit. Hold on.' He moved away from the opening.

I bent over, put my hand on the floor, and sat down and swung my legs into the abyss.

John's voice reached me from a hundred miles away.

'They kept the boxes down here for a while, anyway. I can see some kind of crap . . .' He kicked something that made a hollow, gonging sound, like a barrel. Then: 'Tim.'

I did not want to put my feet on the rungs of the ladder. My feet put themselves on the ladder. I swung the rest of myself around and let them lead me down.

'Get the hell down here.'

As soon as my head passed beneath the level of the floor, I smelled blood again.

My foot came down on the same bar stool over which Ransom had almost fallen, and I kicked it aside before I stepped down onto the packed earth. John was standing with his back to me about thirty feet away in the darkest part of the basement. The dusty oblong of a window at the side let in a beam of light that fell onto the old coal chute. Beside it, a big wooden keg lay beached on its side. A few feet away was a mess of shredded cardboard and crumpled papers. Half of the distance between myself and John, a druidical ring of bricks marked the site where the tavern's furnace had stood. The smell of blood was much stronger.

John looked over his shoulder to make sure I had come down the ladder.

I came toward him, and he stepped aside.

An old armchair drenched in black paint stood like a battered throne on the packed earth. Black paint darkened the ground in front of it. I held my breath. The paint glistened in the feeble light. I came up beside John, and he pointed the Colt's barrel at three lengths of thick, bloodstained rope. Each had been cut in half.

'Somebody got shot here,' Ransom said. The whites of his eyes flared at me.

'Nobody got shot,' I said. The eerie rationality of my voice surprised me. 'Whoever he was, he was probably killed with the same knife they used to cut the ropes.' This came to me, word by word, as I was saying it.

510

He swallowed. 'April was stabbed with a knife. Grant Hoffman was killed with a knife.'

And so were Arlette Monaghan and James Treadwell and Monty Leland and Heinz Stenmitz.

'I don't think we'd better tell the police about this, do you? We'd have to explain why we broke in.'

'We can wait until the body turns up,' I said.

'It already did. The guy in the car at the airport.'

'A guard found him because blood was dripping out of the trunk,' I said. 'Whoever killed him put him in the trunk alive.'

'So this is someone else?'

I nodded.

'What the hell is going on around here?'

'I'm not sure I want to know anymore,' I said, and turned my back on the bloody throne.

'Christ, they might come back,' John said. 'Why are we standing around like chumps?' He moved toward the ladder, shooting wild glances at me over his shoulder. 'What are you doing?'

I was walking toward the rubble of cardboard and crumpled paper near the side of the basement.

'Are you crazy? They might come *back*.'

'You have a gun, don't you?' Again, the words that came out of my mouth seemed to have no connection to what I was actually feeling.

Ransom stared at me incredulously and then went the rest of the way to the ladder and began going up. He gained the top of the ladder about the time I reached the mess of chewed paper. John sat down on the edge of the opening and raised his legs. I heard him scramble to his feet. His footsteps thudded toward the kitchen.

The impressions of two boxes, partially obscured by bits of ragged cardboard, were stamped like footprints into the basement floor. The rats searching for food or insulation had left largely untouched whatever had been

511

inside the boxes, but a few scraps of paper lay among the bits of tattered cardboard.

I squatted to poke through the mess. Here and there a fragment of handwriting, no more than two or three letters, was visible on some of the scraps. I flattened out one of these. Part of what looked like the letter *a* was connected to an unmistakable letter *r*. *ar*. Harp? Scarf? Arabesque? I tried another. *vu*. Ovum? Ovulate? A slightly larger fragment lay a few feet away, and I stretched to read it. John thudded toward the rear of the building. The quality of his impatience, a sweaty anxious anger, permeated the sound of his footsteps.

I flattened out the section of paper. Compared to the other scraps, it was as good as a book. I stood up and tried to make out the writing as I went toward the ladder.

At the top of the paper, in capitals, was *Alle* (gap) *to* (gap) *n*. I had the feeling, like the sense of the uncanny, that it meant something to me. After another missing section appeared the numerals *5,77*. Beneath this legend has been written: *5–10, 120. 26. Jane Wright. Near tears, brave smile in par* (gap) *tight jeans, cowboy boots, black tank top. Appealing white trash trying val* (gap) *to move up. No kids, husband* (here the paper ended).

I folded the paper in half and slid it into my shirt pocket. Afraid that John might really have driven away, I went straight up the ladder without touching its sides and jumped off the final rung onto the floor.

Outside, he was walking around in circles on the cement, banging the car keys against his leg and gripping the Colt with his free hand. He tossed me the keys, too forcefully. 'Do you know how close you came?' he said, and picked up the broken lock and the jack handle. He meant: how close to being left behind. A few blocks east of us, the crowd bellowed and chanted. John clipped the lock's shackle through the metal loop.

In spite of his panic, I felt no urgency at all. Everything

that was going to happen would happen. It already had. Things would turn out, all right, but whether or not they turned out well had nothing to do with John and me.

When I got into the car, John was drumming on the dashboard in frustration. I pulled around the corner of the tavern. John tried to look two or three directions at once, as if a dozen men carrying guns were sneaking up on us. 'Will you get us out of here?'

'Do you want me to drop you at home?' I asked.

'What the hell are you talking about?'

'I want to go to Elm Hill to find the Sunchanas.'

He groaned, extravagantly. 'What's the point?'

I said he knew what the point was.

'No, I don't,' he said. 'That old stuff is a waste of time.'

'I'll drop you at Ely Place.'

He collapsed back into the seat. I made the light onto Horatio Street and turned onto the bridge. John was shaking his head, but he said, 'Okay, fine. Waste my gas.'

I stopped at a gas station and filled the tank before I got back on the east-west expressway.

5

Plum Barrow Lane intersected Bayberry at a corner where a tall gray colonial that looked more like a law office than a house lorded it over the little saltbox across the street. What we had seen inside the tavern made Elm Hill ugly and threatening.

The houses with their nameplates, huge mailboxes, and neat lawns faced the narrow streets bluntly, like the tenements along Horatio Street. They might have been as empty as the tenements. The garage doors had been sealed tight to the asphalt driveways by remote control.

Ours was the only car in sight. Ransom and I could have been the only people in Elm Hill.

'Do you really know where you're going?'

This, the first sentence Ransom had spoken since inviting me to waste his gasoline, was a grudging snarl directed to the side window. His entire upper body was twisted to rest his head on his right shoulder.

'This is their street,' I said.

'Everything looks alike.' He had transferred his anger to our surroundings. Of course, he was correct: all the streets in Elm Hill did look very much alike.

'I hate these brain-dead toytowns.' A second later: 'They put their names on those signs so they can come home to the right house at night.' After another pause: 'You know what I object to about all this? It's so tacky.'

'I'll drive you home and come back by myself,' I said, and he shut up.

From the end of the block, the house looked almost undamaged. A woman in jeans and a gray sweatshirt was shoving a cardboard box into the rear of an old blue Volvo station wagon drawn up onto the rutted tracks to the garage. A tall, curved lamp ending in a round white bubble stood on the grass behind her. Her short white hair gleamed in the sun.

I pulled the Pontiac onto the tracks and parked behind the Volvo. John pushed the Colt under his seat. The woman moved away from the station wagon and glanced at the house before coming toward us. When I got out of the car, she gave me a shy, almost rueful smile. She thought we were from the fire department or the insurance company, and she gestured at her house. 'Well, there it is.' A light, vaguely European accent tugged at her voice. 'It wouldn't have been so bad, except the explosion buckled the floor all the way into the bedroom.'

The prettiness her old neighbors had mentioned was still visible in her round face, clean of makeup, beneath the thick cap of white hair. A streak of black ash smudged her chin. She wiped her hands on her jeans and stepped forward to take my hand in a light, firm handshake. 'The whole thing was pretty scary, but we're doing all right.'

A thin man with an angular face and a corona of graying hair came off the porch with a heap of folded clothes in his arms. He said he'd be right with us and went to the back of the Volvo and pushed the pile of clothes in next to the box.

John came up beside me, and Mrs Sunchana turned with us to look at what had happened to her house. The explosion had knocked in the side of the kitchen, and the roof had collapsed into the fire. Roof tiles curled like leaves, and wooden spars jutted up through the mess. Charred furniture stood against the far wall of the black-ened living room. A glittering chaos of shattered glass and china covered the tilted floor of the living room. The heavy, deathlike stench of burned fabric and wet ash came breathing out of the ruin.

'I hope we can save the sections of the house left standing,' said Mr Sunchana. He spoke with the same light, lilting accent as his wife, but not as idiomatically. 'What is your opinion?'

'I'd better explain myself,' I said, and told them my name. 'I left a note yesterday, saying that I wanted to talk to you about your old landlord on South Seventh Street, Bob Bandolier. I realize that this is a terrible time for you, but I'd appreciate any time you can give me.'

Mr Sunchana was shaking his head and walking away before I was halfway through this little speech, but his wife stayed with me to the end. 'How do you know that we used to live in that house?'

'I talked to Frank and Hannah Belknap.'

'Theresa,' said her husband. He was standing in front of the ruined porch and the fire-blackened front door. He gestured at the rubble.

'I found your note when we came home, but it was after ten, and I thought it might be too late to call.'

'I'd appreciate any help you can give me,' I said. 'I realize it's an imposition.'

John was leaning against the hood of the Pontiac, staring at the destruction.

'We have so much to do,' said her husband. 'This is not important, talking about that person.'

'Yesterday, someone followed me out here from Millhaven,' I told her. 'I just caught a glimpse of him. When I read about your house in the paper this morning, I wondered if the explosion was really accidental.'

'What do you mean?' Mr Sunchana came bristling back toward his wife and me. His hair looked like a wire brush, and red veins threaded the whites of his eyes. 'Because you came here, someone did this terrible thing to us? It's ridiculous. Who would do that?'

His wife did not speak for a moment. Then she turned to her husband. 'You said you wanted to take a break.'

'Sir,' David said, 'we haven't seen or spoken to Mr Bandolier in decades.' He pushed his fingers through his hair, making it stand up even more stiffly.

His wife focused on me again. 'Why are you so interested in him?'

'Do you remember the Blue Rose murders?' I asked. The irises snapped in her black eyes. 'I was looking for information that had to do with those killings, and his name came up in connection with the St Alwyn Hotel.'

'You are – what? A policeman? A private detective?'

'I'm a writer,' I said. 'But this is a matter of personal interest to me. And to my friend too.' I introduced John, and he moved forward to nod hello to the Sunchanas. They barely looked at him.

'Why is it personally interesting to you?'

I couldn't tell what was going on. Theresa and David Sunchana were both standing in front of me now,

David with a sort of weary nervousness that suggested an unhappy foreknowledge of everything I was going to say to him. His wife looked like a bird dog on point.

Maybe David Sunchana knew what I was going to say, but I didn't. 'A long time ago, I wrote a novel about the Blue Rose murders,' I said. David looked away toward the house, and Theresa frowned. 'I followed what I thought were the basic facts of the case, so I made the detective the murderer. I don't know if I ever really believed that, though. Then Mr Ransom called me about a week ago, after his wife was nearly murdered by someone who wrote Blue Rose near her body.'

'Ah,' Theresa said. 'I am sorry, Mr Ransom. I saw it in the papers. But didn't the Dragonette boy kill her?' She glanced at her husband, and his face tightened.

I explained about Walter Dragonette.

'We can't help you,' David said. Frowning, Theresa turned to him and then back to me again. I still didn't know what was going on, but I knew that I had to say more.

'I had a private reason for trying to find out about the old Blue Rose murderer,' I said. 'I think he was the person who killed my sister. She was murdered five days before the first acknowledged victim, and in the same place.'

John opened his mouth, then closed it, fast.

'There was a little girl,' Theresa said. 'Remember, David?'

He nodded.

'April Underhill,' I said. 'She was nine years old. I want to know who killed her.'

'David, the little girl was his sister.'

He muttered something that sounded like German played backward.

'Is there somewhere in Elm Hill where I could get you a cup of coffee?'

517

'There's a coffee shop in the town center,' she said. 'David?'

He glanced at his watch, then dropped his hand and carefully, almost fearfully, inspected my face. 'We must be back in an hour to meet the men from the company,' he said. His wife touched his hand, and he gave her an almost infinitesimal nod.

'I will put my car in the garage,' David said. 'Theresa, will you please bring in the good lamp?'

I moved toward the lamp behind the Volvo, but he said, 'Theresa will do it.' He got into the car. Theresa smiled at me and went to pick up the lamp. He drove the station wagon into the wooden shell of the garage with excruciating slowness. She followed him in, set the lamp down in a corner, and went up beside the car. They whispered to one another before he got out of the car. As they came toward me, Theresa's eyes never left my face.

John opened the back door of the Pontiac for them. Before they got in, David took a white handkerchief from his pocket and wiped the smudge from his wife's chin.

6

As if by arrangement, the Sunchanas did not mention either their former landlord or the Blue Rose murders while we were in the car. Theresa described how the policeman had miraculously walked into the smoke to carry them out through the bedroom window. 'That man saved our lives, really he did, so David and I can't be too tragic about the house. Can we, David?'

She was their public voice, and he assented. 'Of course we cannot be tragic.'

'Then we'll live in a trailer while we build a new one.

We'll put it on the front lawn, like gypsies.'

'They'll love that, in Elm Hill,' John said.

'Are you staying in a hotel?' I asked.

'We're with my sister. She and her husband moved to Elm Hill years before us – that's why we came here. When we bought our house, it was the only one on the street. There were fields all around us.'

Other questions drew out the information that they had moved to Millhaven from Yugoslavia, where in the first days of their marriage they had rented out rooms in their house to tourists while David had gone to university. They had moved to America just before the war. David had trained as an accountant and eventually got a job with the Glax Corporation.

'The Glax Corporation?' I remembered Theresa's saying 'the Dragonette boy.' On our left, sunlight turned half the pond's surface to a still, rich gold. Mallards floated in pairs on the gilded water. 'You must have known Walter Dragonette.'

'He came to my department a year before I retired,' David said. I didn't want to ask the question anyone with even a tenuous connection to a famous or infamous person hears over and over. Neither did John. There was silence in the car for a few seconds.

Theresa broke it. 'David was shaken when the news came out.'

'Were you fond of him?' I asked.

'I used to think I was fond of Walter, once.' He coughed. 'He had the manner of a courteous young man. But after three or four months, I began to think that Walter was nonexistent. His body was there, he was polite, he got his work done even though he sometimes came in late, but he was not *present*.'

We drove past the low, red town hall. Visible around a bend in the road, the bare hill that gave the suburb its name raised itself into the sunlight. Mica glittered and dazzled in the gray paths that crossed its deep green.

'Don't you think they suffer, people like that?' asked Theresa.

Her question startled me with its echo of some barely conscious thought of my own. As soon as she spoke, I knew I agreed with her – I believed in the principle behind her words.

'No,' her husband said flatly. 'He was not *alive*. If you're not alive, you do not feel anything.'

I moved my head to see Theresa in the rearview mirror. She had turned toward her husband, and her surprisingly sharp, clear profile stood out like a profile on a coin. She moved her eyes to meet mine in the mirror. I felt a shock of empathy.

'What do you think, Mr Underhill?'

I wrenched my eyes away to check for traffic before turning into the parking lot of the little shopping center. 'We saw part of his interrogation,' I said. 'He said that he had been sexually abused by a neighbor when he was a small boy. So yes, I do think he suffered once.'

'That is not an excuse,' David said.

'No,' Theresa sighed. 'It is not an excuse.'

I pulled into a space, and David said something to her in the language they had spoken in their garage. Whatever he said ended with the word *Tresich*. I am spelling it the only way I can, phonetically. She had anglicized her name for the sake of people like me and the Belknaps.

We got out of the car.

John said, 'If that communication was too private to disclose, please tell me, but I can't help but be curious about what you just said.'

'It was – ' David stopped, and raised his hands in a gesture of helplessness.

'My husband mentioned to me how awful it is, that we have known two murderers.' That same forceful compassion came out of her again, straight at me. 'When we lived upstairs from Mr Bandolier, he killed his wife.'

7

'We didn't know what to do,' Theresa said. Cups of coffee steamed on the pale wood of the window table between us. She and I sat beside the window onto the parking lot, David and John opposite each other. Two children rolled down the long green hill across the street, spinning through the grass with flying arms and legs. 'We were so frightened of that man. David is right. He was like a Nazi, a Nazi of the private life. And we were so new in America that we thought he could put us in jail if we went to the police. We lived in his house, we didn't know what rights he had over us.'

'Violent,' David said. 'Always shouting, always yelling.'

'Now we would know what to do,' she said. 'In those days, we didn't think anyone would believe us.'

'You have no doubt that he killed his wife?'

David shook his head emphatically, and Theresa said, 'I wish we did.' She picked up her coffee and sipped it. 'His wife was named Anna. She was a beautiful woman, blond, always very quiet and shy. He didn't want her talking to anyone. He didn't want people to know that he beat her.' Her eyes met mine again. 'Especially on weekend nights, when he was drunk.'

'Drunker,' said David. 'On the weekends, he drank more, even more than usual. Then began the yelling, yelling, yelling. And it got louder and louder, until the screaming began.'

'I would see Anna outside in back when we hung up

521

our wash, and she had so many bruises. Sometimes it hurt her to raise her arms.'

'He beat her to death?' I asked.

She nodded. 'One night, I think in October, we heard the shouts, the curses. She was crying so pitifully. He started smashing furniture. They were in their bedroom, just below ours. That big loud voice, cursing at her. It went on and on, and then it just stopped. There was silence.' She glanced at her husband, who nodded. 'Their fights usually ended with Anna crying, and Mr Bandolier, Bob, calming down and . . . *crooning* at her. This time the noise just stopped.' She was looking down at the table. 'I felt sick to my stomach.'

'But you didn't go downstairs?' John asked.

'No,' David said. 'Bob would not permit that.'

'What did he do, call an ambulance?' I asked.

Theresa shook her head vigorously. 'I think Anna was in a coma. The next morning, he must have put her in bed and cleaned up the room.'

This description was so close to what had happened to April Ransom that I looked to see how John was taking it. He was leaning forward with his chin propped on his head, listening calmly.

'We never saw Anna anymore. He began doing all the washing. Eventually, he washed her sheets every night, because we could see them on the line in the mornings. And a smell began to come from their apartment. That smell got worse and worse, and finally I stopped him one day and asked about Anna. He said she was ill, but he was taking care of her.'

David stirred. 'Theresa told me he was home all day, and I was worried because of the thought of my wife in the same house with that, that mad creature.'

'But I was fine, he never bothered *me*.'

'Bandolier stayed home all day?' I asked.

'I think he must have been fired.'

'He was,' I said. 'Later, his boss took him back because he was good at his job.'

'I can imagine,' Theresa said. 'He probably made the trains run on time.' She shook her head and sipped her coffee again. 'One day, David and I couldn't take anymore, thinking about what was going on downstairs. David knocked on their door, and when it opened, we could see straight through into their bedroom – and then we really knew.'

'Yes,' David said.

'Her face was covered in blood. There was a smell of – of rot. That's what it was. He didn't know enough to turn her in bed, and she had bedsores. Her sheets were filthy. It was obvious that she was dying. He came out bellowing and ordered us upstairs.'

'And a little while after that, we saw a doctor come to their door,' said David. 'A terrible doctor. I knew she was dead.'

'I thought he must have finally understood that she was dying and decided to get real medical help. But David was right. A little while after the doctor left, two men came and took her out. She was covered in a sheet. There was never an obituary, there was no funeral, nothing.'

Theresa put her chin in her hand, like John, and turned her head to look out of the big bright window. She sighed, distancing herself from what she was remembering, and leaned back and pushed her hair off her forehead with one hand. 'We didn't know what could happen next. It was a terrible time. Mr Bandolier had some kind of job, because he went out of the house dressed in his suits. We thought the police would come for him. Even a doctor as terrible as that man who came to his apartment must have known how Mrs Bandolier had died. But nothing happened, and nothing happened. And then something did happen, Mr Underhill. But it was nothing like what we expected.'

She looked straight into my eyes again. 'Your sister was killed outside the St Alwyn Hotel.'

Though she had been leading me toward this connection all the way through her story, I still could not be certain that I understood her. I had become interested in Bob Bandolier, but chiefly as a source for other information and only secondarily as himself, and therefore my next question sounded doubtful. 'You mean, you thought that he was the person who murdered my sister?'

'Not at first,' she said. 'We did not think that at all. But then about a week later, maybe less – ' She looked at her husband, and he shrugged.

'Five days,' I said. My voice did not seem to be working properly. They both looked at me, and I cleared my throat. 'Five days later.'

'Five days later, after midnight, the sound of the front door of the building opening and closing woke us both up. Maybe half an hour later, the same sound woke us up again. And when we read the papers the next day – when we read about that woman who was killed in the same place as the little girl, your sister, we wondered.'

'You wondered,' I said. 'And five nights later?'

'We heard the same thing – the front door opening and closing. After David went to work, I went out to buy a newspaper. And there it was. Another person, a musician, had been killed right in the hotel. I ran home and locked myself in our apartment and called David at work.'

'Yes,' David said. 'And what I said to Theresa was, you cannot arrest a man for murder because he leaves his house at night.' He seemed more depressed by what he had said forty years ago than by what had happened to his house within the past twenty-four hours.

'And five days later?'

'It was the same,' David said. 'Exactly the same. *Another* person is killed.'

524

'And you still didn't go to the police?'

'We might have, even though we were so frightened,' Theresa said. 'But the next time someone was attacked, Mr Bandolier was home.'

'And what about the time after that?'

'We heard him go out, exactly as before,' said David. 'Theresa said to me, what if another person tried to kill the young doctor? I said, what if the same person tried to kill the doctor, Theresa? But on the weekends, we began looking for another place to live. Neither of us could sleep in that house anymore.'

'Someone else tried to kill Dr Laing,' I said. My feelings were trying to catch up with my mind. I thought that there must be hundreds of questions I should ask these two people. 'What did you think after the detective was found dead?'

'What did I think? I did not think. I felt relief,' David said.

'Yes, tremendous relief. Because all at once, everyone knew that he was the one. But later – '

She glanced at her husband, who nodded unhappily.

'You had doubts?'

'Yes,' she said. 'I still thought that some other person might have tried to kill the doctor. And the only person that poor policeman really had any reason to hate so much was that terrible man, the butcher on Muffin Street. And what we thought, what David and I thought – '

'Yes?' I said.

'Was that Mr Bandolier had murdered people because the hotel had fired him. He could have done a thing like that, he was capable of that. *People* didn't mean anything to him. And then, of course, there were the roses.'

'What roses?' John and I said this more or less in unison.

She looked at me in surprise. 'Didn't you say you went to the house?'

I nodded.

'Didn't you see the roses at the front of the house?'

'No.' I felt my heart begin to pound.

'Mr Bandolier loved roses. Whenever he had time, he was out in front, caring for his roses. You would have thought they were his children.'

8

Time should have stopped. The sky should have turned black. There should have been a bolt of lightning and crashes of thunder. None of these things happened. I did not pass out, I didn't leap to my feet, I didn't knock the table over. The information I had been searching for, consciously or unconsciously, all of my life had just been given to me by a white-haired woman in a sweatshirt and blue jeans who had known it for forty years, and the only thing that happened was that she and I both picked up our cups and drank more steaming coffee.

I knew the name of the man who had taken my sister's life – he was the horrible human being named Bob Bandolier, Bad Bob, a Nazi of the private life – I might never be able to prove that Bob Bandolier had killed my sister or that he had been the man who called himself Blue Rose, but being able to prove it was weightless beside the satisfaction of knowing his name. I knew his name. I felt like a struck gong.

I looked out of the window. The children who had been rolling down the hill were scampering up over the dense green, holding their arms out toward their parents. Theresa Sunchana reached out to rest her cool hand on my hand.

'I guess the neighbors pulled out the roses after he left,'

I said. 'The house has been empty for years.' This statement seemed absurdly empty and anticlimactic, but so would anything else I could have said. The children rushed into the arms of their parents and then spun away, ready for another long giddy flip-flop down Elm Hill. Theresa's hand squeezed mine and drew away.

If he was still alive, I had to find him. I had to see him put in jail, or my sister's hungry spirit would never be free, or I free of it.

'Should we go to the police now?' David asked.

'We must,' said Theresa. 'If he's still alive, it isn't too late.'

I turned away from the window, able to look at Theresa Sunchana now without disintegrating. 'Thank you,' I said.

She slid her hand across the table again. I put mine on top of it, and she neatly revolved her hand to give me another squeeze before she took her hand back. 'He was such a completely terrible human being. He even sent away that adorable little boy. He *banished* him.'

'The boy was better off,' David said.

'What little boy was that?' I thought they must have been talking about some boy from the neighborhood, some Pigtown boy like me.

'Fee,' she said. 'Don't you know about Fee?'

I blinked at her.

'Mr Bandolier banished him, he cast out his own son,' she said.

'His son?' I asked, stupidly.

'Fielding,' said David. 'We called him Fee – a sweet child.'

'I loved that little boy,' Theresa told me. 'I felt so *sorry* for him. I wish David and I could have taken him.'

Theresa looked down into her cup when the inevitable objection came from David. When he had finished listing the reasons why adopting the child had been an impossibility, she raised her head again. 'Sometimes I would see him sitting on the step in front of the house. He looked so cold and abandoned. His father made him go to the movies alone – a five-year-old boy! Sending him to the movies by himself!'

All I wanted to do was to get out of the coffee shop. A number of distressing symptoms had decided to attack simultaneously. I felt hot and slightly dizzy. My breath was caught in my throat.

I looked across the table, but instead of the reassuring figure of Theresa Sunchana, saw the boy from the Green Woman Taproom, the imagined boy who was fighting to come into this world. Behind every figure stood another, insisting on being *seen*.

9

Allerton, I remembered. Or Allingham, on the side of a stalled truck. Where I dip my buckets, where I fill my pen. David Sunchana's polite, unswervably gentle voice brought me back to the table. 'The insurance men. And we have so many things to take from the house.'

'Oh, we have a thousand things to do. We'll do them.' She was still sitting across from me, and the sun still fell on the scene across the street, where a boy carried a big kite shaped like a dragon uphill.

Theresa Sunchana had not taken her eyes from me. 'I'm glad you found us,' she said. 'You needed to know.'

I looked around for the waitress, and John said, 'I already paid.' He looked a little smug about it.

We stood up from the table and, with the awkwardness and hesitancies of a party of four, moved toward the door.

When I pulled back out of the lot, I found Theresa's

eyes in the rearview mirror again. 'You said Bandolier sent Fee away. Do you know where he sent him?'

'Yes,' she said. 'I asked him. He said that Fee went to live with Anna's sister Judy in some little town in Iowa, or somewhere like that.'

'Can you remember the name of the town?'

'Is that of any importance, at this point?' David asked.

We drove around the pretty little pond. A boy barely old enough to walk clapped his hands at a foot-high sailboat. We followed the meandering curves of Bayberry Lane. 'I don't think it was Iowa,' she said. 'Give me a minute, I'll remember it.'

'This woman remembers everything,' said David. 'She is a phenomenon of memory.'

From this end of Bayberry Lane, their house looked like a photograph from London after the blitz. A long length of glinting rubble led into a room without an exterior wall. Both of the Sunchanas fell silent as soon as it came into view, and they did not speak until I pulled up behind the station wagon. David opened the door on his side, and Theresa leaned forward and patted my shoulder. 'I knew I'd remember. It was Ohio – Azure, Ohio. And the name of Anna's sister was Judy Leatherwood.'

'Theresa, you amaze me.'

'Who could forget a name like Leatherwood?' She got out of the car and waved at us as David put his fingers in his wiry hair and walked toward what was left of his house.

10

'Bob Bandolier?' John said. 'That asshole, Bob Bandolier?'

'Exactly,' I said. 'That asshole, Bob Bandolier.'

'I met him a couple of times when I was a little boy. The guy was completely phony. You know how when you're a kid you can sometimes see things really clearly? I was in my father's office, and a guy with a waxy little mustache and slicked-down hair comes in. Meet the most important man in this hotel, my father says to me. *I just do my job, young man*, he says to me – and I can see that he does think he's the most important man in the hotel. He thinks my father's a fool.'

'All killers can't be as congenial as Walter Dragonette.'

'*That* guy,' John said again. 'Anyhow, you were brilliant, coming up with that sister.'

'I was telling them the truth. He murdered my sister first.'

'And you never told me?'

'John, it just never – '

He muttered something and moved away from me to lean against the door, indications that he was about to descend into the same wrathful silence of the journey out to the suburbs.

'Why should you be upset?' I asked. 'I came here from New York to help you with a problem – '

'No. You came here to help yourself. You can't concentrate on the problems of another person for longer than five seconds, unless you have some personal interest in the matter. What you're doing has nothing to do with me. It's all about that book you're writing.'

I waited until my impatience with him died down. 'I suppose I should have told you about my sister when you first called. I wasn't hiding it from you, John. Even I couldn't really be sure that the man who had killed her had done the other murders.'

'And now you know.'

'Now I know,' I said, and felt a return of that enormous relief, the satisfaction of being able to put down a weight I had carried for four decades.

'So you're done, and you might as well go back home.' He flicked his eyes in my direction before looking expressionlessly out the car window again.

'I want to know who killed your wife. And I think it might be safer if I stay with you for a while.'

He shrugged. 'What are you going to do, be my bodyguard? I don't think anybody is going to try to take me to the Green Woman and tie me up in a chair. I can protect myself from Bandolier. I know what he looks like, remember?'

'I'd like to see what else I can turn up,' I said.

'I guess you're pretty much free to do whatever you want.'

'Then I'd like to use your car this evening.'

'For what? A date with that gray-haired crumpet?'

'I ought to talk to Glenroy Breakstone again.'

'You sure don't mind wasting your time,' he said, and that was how we left it for the rest of the drive back to Ely Place. John pulled the Colt out from under the seat and took it into the house with him.

11

I made a right turn at the next corner, went past Alan's house, and saw him walking up the path to his front door beside Eliza Morgan. It was getting a little cooler by now, and she must have taken him for a walk around the block. He was waving one arm in big circles, describing something, and I could hear the boom of his voice without being able to distinguish the words. They never noticed the Pontiac going down the street behind them. I turned right again at the next corner and went back to Berlin Avenue to go back downtown to the east-west expressway.

Before I saw Glenroy I wanted to fulfill an obligation I had remembered in the midst of the quarrel with John.

At the time I had spoken to Byron Dorian, my motive for suggesting a meeting had been no more than my sense that he needed to talk; now I actively wanted to talk to him. The scale of what April Ransom had been trying to do in *The Bridge Project* had given me a jolt. She was discovering her subject, watching it unfold, as she rode out farther and farther on her instincts. She was really *writing*, and that the conditions of her life meant that she had to do this virtually in secret, like a Millhaven Emily Dickinson, made the effort all the more moving. I wanted to honor that effort – to honor the woman sitting at the table with her papers and her fountain pen.

Alan Brookner had been so frustrated by his inability to read April's manuscript that he had tried to flush thirty or forty pages down the toilet, but what was left was enough to justify a trip to Varney Street.

12

I had been relying on my memory to get me there, but once I turned off the expressway, I realized that I had only a general idea of its location, which was past Pine Knoll Cemetery, south of the stadium. I drove past the empty stadium and then the cemetery gates, checking the names on the street signs. One Saturday a year or two after my sister's death, my father had taken me out to Varney Street to buy a metal detector he had seen advertised in the *Ledger* – he was between jobs, still drinking heavily, and he thought that if he swept a metal detector over the east side beaches, he could find a fortune. Rich people didn't bother picking up the quarters and half dollars that dropped out of their pockets. It was all lying there to be picked up by a clever entrepreneur like Al Underhill. He had steered his car to Varney Street unhesitatingly – we had gone past Pine Knoll, made a turn, perhaps another. I remembered a block of shops with signs in a foreign language and overweight woman dressed in black.

Varney Street itself I remembered as one of the few Millhaven neighborhoods a step down from Pigtown, a stretch of shabby houses with flat wooden fronts and narrow attached garages. My father had left me in the car, entered one of the houses, and come out twenty minutes later, gloating over the worthless machine.

I turned a corner at random, drove three blocks while checking the street signs, and found myself in the same neighborhood of little shops I had first seen with my father. Now all the signs were in English. Spools of thread in pyramids and scissors suspended on lengths of string filled the dusty window of a shop called Lulu's Notions. The only people in sight were on a bench in the laundromat beside it. I pulled into an empty place behind a pickup truck, put a quarter in the meter, and went into the laundromat. A young woman in cutoff shorts and a Banana Republic T-shirt went up to the plate-glass window and pointed through houses at the next street down.

I went to the back of the laundromat, took the paper on which I had written Dorian's phone number and address from my wallet, and dialed the number.

'You're who?' he asked.

I told him my name again. 'We spoke on the phone once when you called the Ransom house. I'm the person who told you that she had died.'

'Oh. I remember talking to you.'

'You said I might come to your place to talk about April Ransom.'

'I don't know . . . I'm working, well, I'm sort of trying to work . . .'

'I'm just around the corner, at the laundromat.'

'Well, I guess you could come over. It's the third house from the corner, the one with the red door.'

The dark-haired, pale young man I had seen at April's funeral cracked open the vermillion door in the little brown house and leaned out, gave me a quick, nervous glance, and then looked up and down the block. He was dressed in a black T-shirt and faded black jeans. He pulled himself back inside. 'You're a friend of John Ransom's, aren't you? I saw you with him at the funeral.'

'I saw you there, too.'

He licked his lips. He had fine blue eyes and a handsome mouth. 'Look, you didn't come here to make trouble or anything, did you? I'm not sure I understand what you're doing.'

'I want to talk about April Ransom,' I said. 'I'm a

writer, and I've been reading her manuscript, "The Bridge Project." It was going to be a wonderful book.'

'I guess you might as well come in.' He backed away.

What had been the front room was a studio with drop cloths on the floor, tubes of paint and a lot of brushes in cans strewn over a paint-spattered table, and a low daybed. At its head, large, unframed canvases were stacked back to front against the wall, showing the big staples that fastened the fabric to the stretchers; others hung in an uneven row along the opposite wall. An opening on the far side of the room led into a dark kitchen. Tan drop cloths covered the two windows at the front of the house, and a smaller cloth that looked like a towel had been nailed up over the kitchen window. A bare light bulb burned on a cord in the middle of the room. Directly beneath it, a long canvas stood on an easel.

'Where did you find her manuscript? Did John have it?'

'It was at her father's house. She used to work on it there.'

Dorian moved to the table and began wiping a brush with a limp cloth. 'That makes sense. You want some coffee?'

'That would be nice.'

He went into the kitchen to pour water into an old-fashioned metal percolator, and I walked around the room, looking at his paintings.

Nothing like the nudes in the Ransoms' bedroom, they resembled a collaboration between Francis Bacon and panels from a modernist graphic novel. In all of the paintings, dark forms and figures, sometimes slashed with white or brilliant red, moved forward out of a darker background. Then a detail jumped out at me from the paintings, and I grunted with surprise. A small, pale blue rose appeared in each of the paintings: in the buttonhole of the suit worn by a screaming man, floating in the air above a bloody corpse and a kneeling man, on the cover of a notebook lying on a desk beside a slumped body, in the mirror of a crowded bar where a man in a raincoat turned a distorted face toward the viewer. The paintings seemed like responses to April's manuscript, or visual parallels to it.

'Sugar?' Dorian called from the kitchen. 'Milk?'

I realized that I had not eaten all day, and asked for both.

He came out of the kitchen and gave me a cup filled to the top with sweet white coffee. He turned to look at the paintings with me and raised his cup to his lips. When he lowered the cup, he said, 'I've spent so much time with this work, I hardly know what it looks like anymore. What do you think?'

'They're very good,' I said. 'When did you change your style?'

'In art school, this was at Yale, I was interested in abstraction, even though no one else was, and I started getting into that flat, outlined, Japanese-y Nabi kind of work right around the time I graduated. To me, it was a natural outgrowth of what I was doing, but everybody *hated* it.' He smiled at me. 'I knew I wouldn't have a chance in New York, so I came back here to Millhaven, where you can live a lot cheaper.'

'John said that a gallery owner gave your name to April.'

He looked away abruptly, as if this was an embarrassing subject. 'Yeah, Carol Judd, she has a little gallery downtown. Carol knew my work because I took my slides in when I first got back. Carol always liked me, and we used to talk about my having a show there sometime.' He smiled again, but not at me, and the smile faded back into his usual earnestness when I asked another question.

'So that was how you first met April Ransom?'

He nodded, and his eyes drifted over the row of

paintings. 'Uh huh. She understood what I was after.' He paused for a second. 'There was a kind of appreciation between us right from the start. We talked about what she wanted, and she decided that instead of buying any of the work I'd already done, she would commission two big paintings. So that's how I got to know her.'

He took his eyes off the paintings, set his cup on the table covered with paints and brushes, and swung around a sway-backed chair in front of the easel so that it faced the bed. Two tapestry cushions were wedged into the tilted back support. When I sat down, the cushions met my back in all the right places.

Dorian sat on the camp bed. Looking at his paintings had comforted him, and he seemed more relaxed.

'You must have spent a lot of time talking with her,' I said.

'It was wonderful. Sometimes, if John was out of town or teaching late, she'd invite me to her house so I could just sit in front of all those paintings she had.'

'Didn't she want you to meet John?'

He pursed his lips and narrowed his eyes, as if he were working out a problem. 'Well, I did meet John, of course. I went there for dinner twice, and the first time was all right, John was polite and the conversation was fine, but the second time I went, he barely spoke to me. It seemed like their paintings were just possessions for him – like sports cars, or something.'

I had the nasty feeling that, for John, having Byron Dorian around the house would have been something like an insult. He was young and almost absurdly good-looking while appearing to be entirely without vanity – John would have accepted him more easily if his looks had been undermined by obvious self-regard.

Then something else occurred to me, something I should have understood as soon as I saw the paintings on the walls.

'You're the one who got April interested in the Blue Rose case,' I said. 'You were the person who first told her about William Damrosch.'

He actually blushed.

'That's what all these paintings are about – Damrosch.'

His eyes flew to the paintings again. This time, they could not comfort him. He looked too anguished to speak.

'The boy in the Vuillard painting reminded you of Damrosch, and you told her about him,' I said. 'That doesn't make you responsible for her death.'

This sentence, intended to be helpful, had the opposite effect.

Like a girl, Dorian pushed his knees together, propped his elbow on them, and twisted sideways with his chin in his hand. An almost visible cloud of pain surrounded him.

'I'm fascinated by Damrosch, too,' I said. 'It's hard not to be. When I was in Vietnam, I wrote two novels in my head, and the second, *The Divided Man*, was all about Damrosch.'

Dorian shot me a blue-eyed glance without altering his posture. 'I must have looked at that boy in the Vuillard three or four times before I really *saw* him – it's so subtle. At first, you just take him for granted, and then the way he's looking out at you takes over the whole painting.'

He paused to struggle with his feelings. 'That's how we started talking about Bill Damrosch and everything. She was excited about the idea of the bridge, that he was found under a *bridge*. That sort of ignited her.'

I asked him how he had first become interested in Damrosch's story.

'Oh, I heard about him from my father. Lots and lots of times. They were partners for a long time. My dad didn't get on very well with his first wife, so he spent a lot of time with Bill Damrosch. I guess you could say he loved him – he used to say he tried everything he could think of to stop Bill from drinking, but he couldn't, so he started drinking with him.' He gave me a frank look. 'My father was an alcoholic, but after Bill died, he straightened himself out. In the sixties, when he was getting close to retirement age, he met my mother in a grocery store. Even she says she picked him up. She was twenty-five years younger, but they got married, and a year later I happened along, not exactly according to plan, I gather.'

It made sense, if Dorian took after his father – as long as he didn't get fat, women would be trying to pick him up for the next three decades.

'Your father must have been disturbed about the outcome of the Blue Rose case.'

He gave me a fierce look. 'What outcome? You mean the junk in the papers? That drove him crazy. He almost quit the force, but he loved the work too much.' He had calmed down, and now I was getting the frank, level look again. This time there was a touch of censure in it. 'He hated your book, by the way. He said you got everything wrong.'

'I guess I did.'

'What you did was irresponsible. My father knew that Bill Damrosch never killed anybody. He was set up.'

'I know that now,' I said.

Dorian hooked one foot around his other ankle and started looking stricken again. 'I should never have mentioned Damrosch to her. That's how everything started.'

'The only people who knew what she was doing with her spare time were one or two brokers at Barnett and the police.'

'I told her she should write to the police department.'

'It should have worked.' I told him what Paul Fontaine had done for me.

Outrage and scorn darkened his face. 'Then they're as fucked up as my father said they were. That doesn't make any sense. They *should* have let her see those records.' He glared at the paint-spattered floor for a couple of seconds. 'My dad told me he didn't like what happened to the force after he retired – all the new people, like Fontaine. He didn't like the way they worked. He didn't trust their methods. Except for Mike Hogan. My dad thought Mike Hogan was a real cop, and he had a lot of respect for him.' Dorian looked suspiciously back up at me.

'So your father was still alive when Fontaine and Hogan joined the force.' He was describing any veteran's natural resentment of a brilliant new arrival.

'He's still alive, period. My father is eighty-five, and he's as strong as an ox.'

'If it's any consolation, Paul Fontaine told me that he liked my book because it was so ridiculous.'

'I'll tell him that.' He flashed me a nice white smile. 'No, on second thought, maybe I won't.'

'Do you think I could talk to your father?'

'I guess.' Dorian rubbed his face and looked at me grudgingly for a moment before reaching down behind the end of the day bed to pick up a spiral notebook with a ballpoint pen clipped into its metal rings. He flipped out the page and walked across the floor to hand it to me.

He had printed the name George Dubbin above an address and telephone number.

'George Dubbin?'

'That's his name.' Dorian sat down on the bed again. 'My name used to be Bryan Dubbin. I thought I could never be a famous painter with a name like that. Francesco Clemente and Bryan Dubbin? As soon as I graduated from UI-Millhaven, I changed it to something that sounded better to me. You don't have to tell me that I was being silly. But it could have been worse – the other name I was considering was Beaumont Darcy. I guess my head was in a pretty decadent place back then.'

We both smiled.

'You actually had your name changed officially? You

went to city hall, or wherever?'

'It's easy to change your name. You just fill out a form. I did the whole thing through the mail.'

'Your father must have been a little . . .'

'He was, a lot. Big time upset. I see his point. I even agree with him. But he knows I wouldn't do it all over again, and that helps. He says, Well, kid, at least you kept your goddamn initials.' This was delivered in a forceful raspy growl that communicated both affection and exasperation and summoned up George Dubbin with eerie clarity.

'That was good,' I said. 'I bet he sounds just like that.'

'I was always a good mimic.' He smiled at me again. 'At school, I used to drive the teachers crazy.'

The revelation about his name had dissipated the tension between us.

'Talk to me about April Ransom,' I said.

13

Instead of answering, Byron reached for his cup, stood up, and walked to the table, where he began lining up the bottles filled with brushes. He got them all into a nice straight row at the far end of the table. In order to be able to see him, I stood up, too, but all I could see was his back.

'It's hard to know what to say.' Next he started lining up the tubes of paint. He looked over his shoulder and seemed surprised to see me up on my feet, looking at him. 'I don't think I could just sum her up in a couple of sentences.' He turned all the way around and leaned back against the table. The way he did it made the table seem as if it had been built specifically for this purpose, to be leaned against in precisely that easy, nonchalant way.

'Try. See what comes out.'

He looked up, elongating his pale neck. 'Well, at first I thought she was a sort of ideal patron. She was married, she lived in a good house, she had a lot of money, but she wasn't even a little bit snobbish – when she came here, the first time I met her, she acted like ordinary people. She didn't mind that I lived in a dump, by her standards. After she was here about an hour, I realized that we were getting along really well. It was like we turned into friends right away.'

'She was perceptive,' I said.

'Yeah, but it was more than that. There was a lot going on inside her. She was like a huge hotel, this place with a thousand different rooms.'

'She must have been fascinating,' I said.

He walked to the covered windows and brushed the drop cloths with the side of his hand. Once again, I could not see his face. 'Hotel.'

'Excuse me?'

'I said hotel. I said she was like a hotel. That's kind of funny, isn't it?'

'Have you ever been to the St Alwyn?'

He turned around, slowly. His shoulders were tight, and his hands were slightly raised. 'What's that supposed to mean? Are you asking if I took her there and beat her up and knifed her?'

'To tell you the truth, that thought never occurred to me.'

Dorian relaxed.

'In fact, I don't think she was assaulted in the hotel.'

He frowned at me.

'I think she was originally injured in her Mercedes. Whoever assaulted her probably left a lot of blood in the car.'

'So what happened to it?'

'The police haven't found it yet.'

Dorian wandered back to the day bed. He sat down and drank some of his coffee.

'Do you think her marriage was happy?'

His head jerked up. 'Do you think her husband did it?'

'I'm just asking if you thought she had a happy marriage.'

Dorian did not speak for a long time. He swallowed more coffee. He crossed and uncrossed his legs. He grazed his eye along the row of paintings. He put his chin in his hand. 'I guess her marriage was okay. She never complained about it.'

'You thought about it for a long time.'

He blinked at me. 'Well, I had the feeling that if April weren't so busy, she would have been lonely.' He cleared his throat. 'Because her husband didn't really share her interests, did he? She couldn't talk to him about a lot of stuff.'

'Things she could talk about with you.'

'Well, sure. But I couldn't talk with her about her business – whenever she started up about puts and calls and all that, the only words I ever understood were Michael and Milken. And her job was tremendously important to her.'

'Did she ever say anything to you about moving to San Francisco?'

He cocked his head, moving his jaw as if he were chewing on a sunflower seed. 'Did you hear something about that?' His eyes had become cautious. 'It was more like a remote possibility than anything else. She probably just mentioned it once, when we were out walking, or something.' He cleared his throat again. 'You heard something about that, too?'

'Her father mentioned it to me, but he wasn't too clear about it, either.'

His face cleared. 'Yeah, that makes sense. If April had

543

ever moved anywhere, she would have brought him along. Not to live with her, I mean, but to make sure she could still take care of him. I guess he's getting kind of out of it.'

'You said you went for walks?'

'Sure, sometimes we'd just go walk around.'

'Did you go out for drinks, or anything like that?'

He pondered that. 'When we were still talking about the paintings, we went out for lunch a couple of times. Sometimes we went for drives.'

'Where would you go?'

He threw up his hands and looked rapidly from side to side. I asked if he minded my asking these questions.

'No, it's just hard to answer. It's not like we went for drives every day or anything. Once we went to the bridge, and April told me about what used to go on at that bar on Water Street, right next to the bridge.'

'Did you ever try to go in there?'

He shook his head. 'It's closed up, you can't go in.'

'Did she ever mention someone named William Writzmann?'

He shook his head again. 'Who's he?'

'It probably isn't important.'

Dorian smiled at me. 'I'll tell you a place we used to go. I never even knew it existed until she showed it to me. Do you know Flory Park, way out on Eastern Shore Drive? There's a rock shelf surrounded by trees that hangs out over the lake. She loved it.'

'Alan took me there,' I said, seeing the two of them going down the trail to the little glen above the lake.

'Well, then, you know.'

'Yes,' I said. 'I know. It's very private.'

'It was private,' he said. He stared at me for a moment, chewing on the nonexistent seed, and jumped up again. He carried the cup into the kitchen. I heard him rinse the

544

cup and open and close the refrigerator. He came out carrying a bottle of Poland Water. 'You want some of this?'

'I still have some coffee left, thanks.'

Dorian went to his table and poured bottled water into his cup. Then he moved one of the tubes of paint a fraction of an inch. 'I ought to get back to work soon.' He closed both hands around the cup. 'Unless you want to buy a painting, I don't think I can spare much more time.'

'I do want to buy one of your paintings,' I said. 'I like your work a lot.'

'Are you trying to bribe me, or something like that?'

'I'm trying to buy one of your paintings,' I said. 'I've been thinking about doing that since I first saw them.'

'Really?' He managed to smile at me again. 'Which one do you want?' His hands were all right now, and he moved toward the paintings on the wall.

'The men in the bar.'

He nodded. 'Yeah, I like that one, too.' He turned doubtfully to me. 'You really want to buy it?'

I nodded. 'If you can pack it for shipping.'

'I can do that, sure.'

'How much do you want?'

'God. I never thought about that yet.' He grinned. 'Nobody but April ever even saw them before this. A thousand?'

'That's fine,' I said. 'I have your address, and I'll send you a check from John's house. Have UPS ship it to this address.' I took one of my cards from my wallet and gave it to Dorian.

'This is really nice of you.'

I told him I was happy to have the painting, and we went toward the door. 'When you looked up and down the street before you let me in, did you think that John might be out there?'

He stopped moving, his hand already on the doorknob. Then he opened the door and let in a blaze of sudden light.

'Anything you did is okay with me, Byron,' I said. He looked as if he wanted to flee back into the artificial light. 'You were tremendously helpful to her.'

Dorian shuddered, as if a winter wind were streaming through the open door. 'I'm not going to say any more to you. I don't know what you want.'

'All I want from you is that painting,' I said, and held out my hand. He hesitated a second before taking it.

14

After all that, I did not want to just drive back to Ely Place. I had to let everything sort itself out in my mind before I went back to John's house. The satisfaction of knowing that Bob Bandolier was the Blue Rose murderer had left me. Before anything like it could return, I had to know who had killed April Ransom. I sat behind the wheel of the Pontiac until I noticed that Dorian was peeking out at me through a dimple in one of the drop cloths.

I drove away without any idea of where I would go. I would be like April Ransom, I thought, like April Ransom at the wheel of her Mercedes, Byron Dorian in the other seat. I'd just drive, and see where I wound up.

15

I had gone no more than five blocks when it occurred to me that I had, in effect, done no more than to swap one ghost for another. Where I had seen April Underhill's disgruntled spirit, now I would find myself seeing April Ransom's.

A series of images marched across my inner eye. I saw Walter Dragonette sitting across the battered table from Paul Fontaine, crying *victim, victim, victim*; then saw Scoot, my old partner in the body squad at Camp White Star, bending to dismember the corpse of Captain Havens. I saw the human jigsaw puzzles sealed up in the body bags; the boy in the hut at Bong To; April Ransom and Anna Bandolier lying unconscious on their beds, separated by space and time. A meaning which seemed nearly close enough to touch connected these images. The figure with an outstretched hand stepping out of death or the imaginative space offers the pearl. On the open palm is written a word no one can read, a word that cannot be spoken.

16

I had returned on automatic pilot to my old neighborhood and was turning from South Sixth Street onto Muffin Street. It was one of those sleepy pockets of commerce that had long ago inserted itself into a residential area, like the row of shops near Byron Dorian's studio but even less successful, and two little shops with soaped windows flanked a store where bins of bargain shoes soaked up sunlight on the pavement.

On the other side of the shoe store was the site of Heinz Stenmitz's two-story frame house. A wide X of boards blocked the entrance to the porch, and vertical pallets of nailed boards covered the windows. On the other side of the house, the site of the butcher shop with its triangular sign, was an empty lot filled with skimpy yellow ragweed and bright sprays of Queen Anne's lace. The weeds led down into a roughly rectangular hollow in the middle of the lot. Red bricks and gray concrete blocks lay among the weeds around the perimeter of the hollow. That vacancy seemed right to me. No one had debased the site with an apartment building or a video shop. Like his house, it had been left to rot away.

At the end of the block, I turned onto South Seventh Street. Next to Bob Bandolier's empty house, the Belknaps were drinking Hannah's lemonade and talking to one another on their porch. Hannah was smiling at one of Frank's jokes, and neither of them noticed me driving past. I stopped at Livermore Avenue, turned right on Window Street, parked in an empty spot a block away from the St Alwyn, and walked past Sinbad's Cavern to the hotel.

The same old man I had seen before sat smoking a cigar in the lobby; the same feeble bulb burned behind its green shade beside the same worn couch; but the lobby seemed bleaker and sadder.

Under the lazy scrutiny of the desk clerk, I walked toward the pay phone and dialed the number on the slip of paper in my wallet. I spoke for a short time to a gruff, familiar voice. George Dubbin, Byron's father, told me that Damrosch had questioned Bob Bandolier – 'Sure he did. Bill was a good cop.' Then he said, 'I wish my kid would go out with women his own age.' When the conversation was over, I went across the lobby to the house phone and punched Glenroy Breakstone's room number.

'You again. Tom's friend.'

'That's right. I'm down in the lobby. Can I come up for a short talk?'

He sighed. 'Tell me the name of the great tenor player in Cab Calloway's band.'

'Ike Quebec,' I said.

'You know what to get before you come up.' He put the phone down.

I went up to the clerk, who had recognized me and was already bending under the desk. He came up with two packs of Luckies and rapped them down on the counter. 'Surprised he let you come up. Bad day for old Glenroy, *bad* day.'

'I'll watch my back.'

'Better watch your head, because that's what he's gonna mess with.' He raised his right hand and shot me with his index finger.

When I knocked on Breakstone's door, loud jazz muffled his voice. 'What'd you do, fly? Give me a minute.'

Under the music, I heard the sound of wood clicking against wood.

Glenroy opened the door and scowled at me with red-rimmed eyes. He was wearing a thin black sweatshirt that said SANTA FE JAZZ PARTY. 'You got 'em?' He held out his hand.

I put the cigarettes in his hand, and he wheeled away from me, jamming one pack into each of his pockets, as if he thought I might try to steal them. He took two steps and stopped, pointing an imperious finger into the air. The music surrounded us, as did a faint trace of marijuana. 'You know who that is?'

It was a tenor saxophone player leading a small group, and at first I thought he was playing an old record of his own, one I didn't know. The tune was 'I Found a New Baby.' Then the saxophone started to solo.

'Same answer as before. Ike Quebec. On Blue Note, with Buck Clayton and Keg Johnson, in 1945.'

'I should of thought of a harder question.' He lowered his hand and proceeded across the bright rug to the same low table where we had been sitting before. Beside the Krazy Kat mirror and the wooden box sat a round white ashtray crowded with mashed butts, a nearly full pack of Luckies and a black lighter, a bottle of Johnny Walker Black, and a highball glass containing an inch of whiskey. Breakstone dropped into a chair and looked at me sourly. I took the other chair without being invited.

'You messed me up,' he said. 'Ever since you were here, I been thinking about James. I gotta start getting my shit together to go to France, and I can't do anything but remember that boy. He never had his chance. We ought to be sitting up here together right now, talking about what tunes we'll play and the assholes we'll have to play 'em with, but we can't, and that's not *right*.'

'It still affects you so much, after forty years?'

'You don't understand.' He picked up his glass and swallowed half of the whiskey. 'What he was starting, nobody could finish but him.'

I thought of April Ransom and her manuscript.

He was glaring at me with his red eyes. 'All of that music he would have made, nobody else can make it. I should have been standing right next to him, listening to the things he would have done. That boy was like my son, you understand? I play with lots of piano players, and some of them are great, but no piano player except James ever grew up right under my wing, you know?' He finished the whiskey in his glass and thumped the glass down on the table. His eyes moved to the wooden box, then back to me. 'James played so pretty – but you never heard him, you don't know.'

550

'I wish I had,' I said.

'James was like Hank Jones or Tommy, and nobody heard him except me.'

'He was like you, you mean.'

The red eyes gave me a deep, deep look. Then he nodded. 'I wish I could go to Nice with him. I wish I could see through his eyes again.'

He poured another inch of whiskey into his glass, and I looked around the room. Subtle signs of disorder were everywhere – the telescope tilted wildly upward, records and compact discs were spread on the floor in front of the shelves, record sleeves covered the octagonal table. Gray smears of ash dirtied the wrinkled Navaho rugs.

The record came to an end, and he glanced up at the turntable. 'If you want to hear something, put it on. I'll be right back.'

Glenroy slid the box toward him, and I said, 'You can do what you like. It's your place.'

He shrugged and swung back the top of the box. Two two-gram bottles, one about half full and the other empty, lay in a rounded groove along one side. A short white straw lay beside them. In the middle of the box was a baggie filled with marijuana buds resting on a layer of loose, crumbled shreds. He had lots of different kinds of rolling paper. Glenroy flipped back the lid of the mirror, took out a vial, unscrewed the top, and used the spoon to dump two fat white piles of powder on the mirror. He pushed them into rough lines with the long spoon attached to the screw top. Then he worked an end of the straw into one of his nostrils and sucked up one of the lines. He did the same thing with the other nostril.

'You get high?'

'Not anymore,' I said.

He screwed the cap back on the bottle and put it into the groove in the box. 'I been trying to get in touch with Billy, but I can't find him in any of his places. I want to

551

get some for the plane over, you know.'

Glenroy wiped his finger over the white smears on the glass, rubbed his gums, and closed the box and the mirror. He gave me the first halfway friendly look of the night and looked at the box again. 'Billy better show up before tomorrow, man.' He leaned back in his chair, wiping his finger under his nose.

'Does Tom do coke?' I asked.

He grinned derisively at me. 'Tom won't hardly do anything at all anymore. That cat hardly even *drinks*. He acts like he juices all day and all night, but you watch him. He takes one tiny little sip, and that's it. That's *that*. He's funny, man. He looks like he's half asleep, you know what he's doing? The man is working.'

'I noticed that the other night,' I said. 'He nursed one drink all night long.'

'He's a *sneaky* mother.' Breakstone stood up and went to the turntable. He removed the Ike Quebec record, grabbed its plastic inner sleeve from a shelf, and slid it into the sleeve. 'Duke, I want some Duke.' He moved along the shelves, running his hand over the tops of the albums, and pulled out an Ellington record. With the same rough delicacy, he set the record on the turntable. Then he turned down the volume knob on the amplifier. 'I don't suppose you came over here just to listen to my records.'

'No, I didn't,' I said. 'I came here to tell you how James Treadwell was killed.'

'You found that bitch!' His whole face brightened. He took his chair again, picked the burning cigarette out of the ashtray, and squinted at me through the smoke as he inhaled. 'Tell me about it.'

'If Bob Bandolier came to James's room late at night, would James have let him in?'

Nodding, he said, 'Sure.'

'And if Bandolier wanted to get in without knocking, he could just have let himself in.'

His eyes widened. 'What are you trying to tell me?'

'Glenroy, Bandolier murdered James Treadwell. And the woman, and Monty Leland, and Stenmitz. His wife was dying because he beat her into a coma, and he got angry because Ransom fired him when he had to take extra time to care for her. He killed all of them to ruin the hotel's business.'

'You're saying Bob killed all these people, and then afterward, he just came back here like nothing happened?'

'Exactly.' I told him what I had learned from Theresa Sunchana, and I watched him take it all in.

When I was done, he said, 'Roses?'

'Roses.'

'I don't know if I can believe this.' Breakstone shook his head slowly, smiling. 'I saw Bob Bandolier every day, almost every day, when I was here at home. He was a miserable bastard, but outside of that, he was normal, if you know what I mean.'

'Did you know he had a wife and a son?'

'First I ever heard of it.'

For a time we said nothing. Glenroy stared at me, shaking his head now and then. Once or twice he opened his mouth and closed it without saying anything. 'Bob Bandolier,' he said, but not to me. Finally, he said, 'This lady heard him going out every night someone was killed?'

'Every night.'

'You know, he could have done it. I know he didn't give a damn about anybody but himself.' He frowned at me for a little time.

Glenroy was changing an idea he had held firmly for forty years. 'He was the kind of man who'd beat a woman, that's right.' He gave me a sharp look. 'I tell you, what I

553

think, Bob would sort of like his woman helpless. She wouldn't walk around, messing things up. That kind of guy, he could *go* for that.'

He was silent for another couple of seconds, and then he stood up, walked away a couple of steps, turned around and sat back down again. 'There isn't any way to prove all this, is there?'

'No, I don't think it can be proved. But he was Blue Rose.'

'Goddamn.' He smiled at me. 'I'm starting to believe it. James probably didn't even know Bob was fired. I didn't know for maybe a week, when I asked one of the maids where he was. You know, they didn't even uncover his meat scam – he was back in time to switch back to Idaho.'

'Speaking of the meat business,' I said, and asked him if he'd heard about Frankie Waldo.

'We better not talk about that. I guess Frankie got too far out of line.'

'It sounds like a mob killing.'

'Yeah, maybe it's supposed to look that way.' He hesitated, then decided not to say any more.

'You mean it had something to do with Billy Ritz?'

'Frankie just got out of line, that's all. That day we saw him, he was one worried man.'

'And Billy reassured him that everything was going to be okay.'

'Looked that way, didn't it? But we weren't supposed to see that. If you don't get in Billy's way, everything's cool. Someday, they'll nail somebody for Waldo's murder.'

'Paul Fontaine has a great arrest record.'

'He sure does. Maybe pretty soon he'll get whoever killed your friend's wife.' There was an odd smile on his face.

'I have an idea about that,' I said.

554

Glenroy refused to say any more. He was casting glances at his box again, and I left a few minutes later.

17

The clerk asked me if Glenroy was feeling any better, and when I said that I thought he was, he said, 'Will he let the maids in there tomorrow?'

'I doubt it,' I said, and went back to the pay phone. I could hear him sighing to himself while I dialed.

Twenty minutes later, I pulled up in front of Tom Pasmore's house on Eastern Shore Drive. Tom had still been in bed when he answered, but he said he'd be up by the time I got there.

On the telephone, I'd asked Tom if he would like to know the name of the Blue Rose murderer.

'That's worth a good breakfast,' he told me.

My stomach growled just as Tom opened the door, and he said, 'If you can't control yourself better than that, get in the kitchen.' He looked resplendent in a white silk robe that came down to a pair of black slippers. Under the robe, he was wearing a pink shirt and a crimson necktie. His eyes were clear and lively.

The smell of food hit me as soon as I reached the table, and saliva filled my mouth. I walked into the kitchen. In separate pans on two gas rings on the range, diced ham, bits of tomatoes, and a lot of whitish cheese lay across irregular circles of egg. Two plates had been set out on the counter, and four brown pieces of toast jutted up out of a toaster. I smelled coffee.

Tom rushed in behind me and immediately picked up a spatula and experimentally slid it under each of the omelettes. 'You butter the toast, if you want some, and

I'll take care of these. They'll be ready in a minute.'

I took out the hot slices of toast, put two on each plate, and smeared butter over them. I heard one of the omelettes slapping into its pan and looked sideways to see him fold over the edges of the second one and toss it neatly into the air and field it with the pan. 'When you live alone, you learn to amuse yourself,' he said, and slid them onto the plates.

I had finished a quarter of my omelette and an entire piece of toast before I could speak. 'This is wonderful,' I said. 'Do you always flip them like that?'

'No. I'm a show-off.'

'You're in a good mood.'

'You're going to give me the name, aren't you? And I have something to give you.'

'Something besides this omelette?'

'That's right.'

Tom took the plates into the kitchen and brought out a glass cylinder of strong filtered coffee and two cups. I leaned back into the sturdy, comfortable chair. Tom's coffee was another sort of substance from Byron Dorian's, stronger, smoother, and less bitter.

'Tell me everything. This is a great moment.'

I started with the man who had followed me back to John's from his house and finished with Glenroy Breakstone's final remark. I talked steadily for nearly half an hour, and all Tom did was to smile occasionally. Every now and then he raised his eyebrows. Once or twice he closed his eyes, as if to see exactly what I was describing. He read the fragment from the taproom and handed it back without comment.

When I had finally finished, he said, 'Most of Glenroy's clothes come from festivals or jazz parties, have you noticed that?'

I nodded. *This* was what he had to say?

'Because he almost always wears black, those outfits

always look pretty good on him. But their real function is to declare his identity. Since the only people he sees at all regularly, at least while he's at home, are the desk clerk, his dealer, and me, the person to whom he's announcing that he is Glenroy Breakstone, the famous tenor player, is mostly Glenroy Breakstone.' He smiled at me. 'Your case is a little different.'

'My case?' I looked at the clothes I had on. They mainly announced that I didn't spend a lot of time thinking about what I wore.

'I'm not talking about your clothes. I mean, the child who appears to you from time to time – from what you call the imaginative space.'

'That's work.'

'Of course. But a lot of children are scattered through your whole story. It's as though you're fitting everything that happens to you into a novel. And the main element of this novel isn't Bob Bandolier or April Ransom, but this nameless boy.'

So far Tom had said nothing at all about Bob Bandolier, and all of this seemed like an unnecessary indirection. I had mentioned the boy, maybe vaingloriously, to give Tom some insight into the way I worked, and now I had begun feeling a bit impatient with him, as if he were ignoring some splendid gift I had laid before him.

'Do you know what movie was playing at your old neighborhood theater during the last two weeks of October in 1950?'

'I don't have any idea.'

'A film noir called *From Dangerous Depths*. I looked back at old issues of the paper. Isn't it interesting to think that everyone we're talking about might have seen that movie over those two weeks?'

'If they went to the movies, they all did,' I said.

He smiled at me again. 'Well, it's a minor point, but I'm intrigued that even when you're doing my job for me, going around and investigating, you're still doing yours – even when you're in the basement of the Green Woman.'

'Well, in a way they're the same job.'

'In a sense,' Tom said. 'We just look through different frames. Different windows.'

'Tom, are you trying to let me down gently? Don't you think Bob Bandolier was the Blue Rose killer?'

'I'm sure he was. I don't have doubt about that. This *is* a great moment. You know who killed your sister, and I know the real name of Blue Rose. Those people who knew him, the Sunchanas, are finally going to tell the police what they've been sitting on for forty years, and we'll see what happens. But your real mission is over.'

'You sound like John,' I said.

'Are you going to go back to New York now?'

'I'm not done yet.'

'You want to find Fee Bandolier, don't you?'

'I want to find Bob.' I thought about it. 'Well, I'd like to know about Fee, too.'

'What was the name of that town?'

I was sure he remembered it, but I told him anyhow. 'Azure, Ohio. The aunt was named Judy Leatherwood.'

'Do you suppose Mrs Leatherwood is still alive? It would be interesting to know if Fee went off to college, or if he, what, killed himself driving a stolen car while he was drunk. After all, when he was five years old, he all but saw his father beat his mother to death. And at some level, he would have known that his father went out and killed other people.' He interrogated me with a look. 'Do you agree?'

'Children always pick up on what's going on. They might not admit it, or acknowledge it, but they understand.'

'All of which amounts to substantial disturbance. And there's one other terrible thing that happened to him.'

I must have looked blank.

'The reason his father murdered Heinz Stenmitz,' Tom said. 'Didn't that woman you liked so much say that Bob sent him to the movies? Fee went along to see *From Dangerous Depths*, and who should the boy meet but his father's partner in a business arrangement?'

I had managed to forget this completely.

'Do you want to see what I found?' His eyes sparkled. 'I think it'll interest you.'

'You found where Writzmann lives?'

He shook his head.

'You found out something about Belinski or Casement?'

'Let me show you upstairs.'

Tom bounded up the stairs and led me into his office. He threw his robe on the couch, waved me to a chair, and went around the room, turning on the lights and the computers. Suspenders went up the front of the pink shirt like dark blue stripes. 'I'm going to hook into one of the data bases we used the last time.' He put himself in front of the desk computer and began punching in codes. 'There's a question we didn't ask, because we thought we already knew the answer.' He turned sideways on the chair and looked at me with a kind of playful expectancy. 'Do you know what it was?'

'I have no idea,' I admitted.

'Bob Bandolier owned a property at Seventeen South Seventh Street, right?'

'You know he did.'

'Well, the city has records of all leaseholders and property owners, and I thought I'd better make sure that address was still listed under his name. Just watch, and see what turned up.'

He had linked his computer to the mainframe at Armory Place and through it to the Registrar of Deeds. The modem burped. 'I just keyed in the address,' Tom said. 'This won't take long.'

I looked at the blank gray screen. Tom leaned forward with his hands on his knees, smiling to himself.

Then I knew. 'Oh, it can't be,' I said.

Tom put his finger to his lips. 'Shhh.'

'If I'm right . . .' I said.

'Wait.'

RECEIVE flashed in the upper left corner of the screen.

'Here we go,' Tom said, and leaned back.

A column of information sped down the screen.

17 SOUTH SEVENTH STREET

PURCHASED 04/12/1979   ELVEE HOLDINGS CORP   314 SOUTH FOURTH STREET   MILLHAVEN IL

PURCHASE PRICE $1,000

PURCHASED 05/01/1943   ROBERT BANDOLIER   14B SOUTH WINNETKA STREET   MILLHAVEN IL

PURCHASE PRICE $3,800

'Good old Elvee Holdings,' Tom said, virtually hugging himself in gleeful self-congratulation and smiling like a new father.

'My God,' I said. 'A real connection.'

'That's right. A real connection between the two Blue Rose cases. What if Bob Bandolier is the man who's been following you?'

'Why would he do that?'

'If he tried to kill the Sunchanas after seeing you in Elm Hill, he didn't want them to tell you something.'

I nodded.

'What is it?'

'They knew that he killed his wife. They told me about the roses.'

'The Belknaps could have told you about the roses. And a doctor signed Anna Bandolier's death certificate. She's been dead so long that no one could prove that she had been beaten. But the Sunchanas knew about the existence of Fielding Bandolier.'

'But anyone who asked the Sunchanas the right questions would find out what he had done.'

'And find out that he had a son. I think the person who followed you was Fee.'

I stopped breathing. Fee Bandolier had tried to kill the Sunchanas. Then I realized what a long leap Tom had made. 'Why do you even think that Fee came back to Millhaven? He's had forty years to get as far away as he can.'

Tom asked me if I remembered the price Elvee had paid for the house on South Seventh.

I looked at the screen of the monitor, but the letters and numbers were too small to read from across the room. 'I think it was something like ten thousand dollars.'

'Take a look.'

I walked up beside him and looked at the screen.

'A thousand?'

'You saw ten thousand because you expected to see something like that. Elvee bought the house for next to nothing. I think that means that Elvee Holdings is Fee Bandolier. And Fee protects himself here, too, by putting up a smoke screen of fake directors and a convenience address.'

'Why would Bob give him his house? He sent him away when he was five. As far as we know, he never saw him again.' Tom held up his hands. He didn't know. Then another of Tom's conclusions fell into place for me. 'You think Fee Bandolier was the man in uniform, the soldier who threatened Frank Belknap.'

'That's right. I think he came back to take possession of the house.'

'He's a scary guy.'

'I think Fee Bandolier is a very scary guy,' Tom said.

18

'I want to see if we can talk to Judy Leatherwood,' he said. 'Go down the hall to the bedroom and pick up the telephone next to the bed when I tell you. In the meantime, I'll try to get her number from Information.'

He pulled a telephone book out of a drawer and started looking for dialing codes in Ohio. I went into the hall, pushed open the door to a darkened room, and went inside and turned on the light. A telephone stood on an end table at the side of a double bed.

'Success,' Tom called out. 'Pick up now.'

I put the receiver to my ear and heard the musical *plunk, plunk, plunk* of the dialing. The Leatherwood telephone rang three times before a woman picked it up and said, 'Hello?' in a quavery voice.

'Am I speaking to Mrs Judith Leatherwood?' Tom asked.

'Well, yes, you are,' said the quavery voice. She was faintly alarmed by the official-sounding voice coming from Tom's mouth.

'Mrs Leatherwood, this is Henry Bell from the Mid-States Insurance Company. I'm in the Millhaven office, and I promise you I'm not trying to sell you insurance. We have a five-thousand-dollar death benefit to pay out, and I am trying to locate the beneficiary. Our field agents have discovered that this beneficiary was last known to be living with you and your husband.'

'Someone left money to my son?'

'The name of the recipient, at least as it's listed on the policy here in front of me, is Fielding Bandolier. Did you adopt Mr Bandolier?'

562

'Oh, no. We didn't adopt him. Fee was my sister's boy.'

'Could you tell me Fielding Bandolier's present location, ma'am?'

'Oh, I know what happened,' she said. 'It must be, Bob died. Bob Bandolier, Fee's dad. Is he the one who left that money to Fee?'

'Robert Bandolier was our policy holder, that's right, ma'am. He was the beneficiary's father?'

'Well, yes, he was. How did Bob die? Are you allowed to tell me that?'

'I'm afraid it was a heart attack. Were you close?'

She uttered a shocked little laugh. 'Oh my, no. We were never close to Bob Bandolier. We hardly ever saw him, after the wedding.'

'You said that Fielding Bandolier no longer resides at your address?'

'Oh, no,' she said. 'There's nobody here but senior citizens. Only about five or six of us have our own telephones. The rest of them wouldn't know what to *do* with a telephone.'

'I see. Do you have a current address for the beneficiary?'

'No, I don't.'

'How long did he reside with you, ma'am?'

'Less than a year. After I got pregnant with my Jimmy, Fee went to live with my brother Hank. Hank and his wife, my sister-in-law, Wilda? They had a real nice home in Tangent, that's about a hundred miles east of here. They were real nice people, and Fee lived with them until he graduated high school.'

'Could I trouble you for your brother's telephone number?'

'Hank and Wilda passed away two years ago.' She did not speak for about fifteen seconds. 'It was a terrible thing. I still don't like to think about it.'

'They did not die of natural causes?' I heard a suppressed excitement in his voice.

'They were on that Pan Am flight – 103, the one that blew up right in the air? Over Lockerbie, in Scotland? I guess they have a nice memorial over there, with my brother's name and Wilda's on a kind of a *plaque*? I'd go over there to see it, but I don't get around too good these days, with the walker and everything.' There was another long pause. 'It was a terrible, terrible thing.'

'I'm sorry for your loss.' What probably sounded like sympathy to her sounded like disappointment to me. 'You said that your nephew graduated from high school in Tangent?'

'Oh, yes. Hank always said Fee was a good student. Hank was the vice-principal of the high school, you know.'

'If your nephew went on to college, we might get his address from the alumni records.'

'That was a big disappointment to Hank. Fee went down and joined up in the army right after he graduated. He didn't even tell anyone until the day before he was supposed to be inducted.'

'What year would that have been?'

'Nineteen sixty-one. So we all thought he must have gone to Vietnam. But of course we couldn't know.'

'He didn't tell your brother where he was assigned to duty?'

'He didn't tell him *anything*. But that wasn't all! My brother wrote to him where he said he was going, for basic training? At Fort Sill? But his letters all came back. They said they didn't have any soldier named Fielding Bandolier. It was like running up against a stone wall.'

'Was your nephew a troubled boy, ma'am?'

'I don't like to say. Do you have to know about things like that?'

'There's a particular feature of Mr Bandolier's policy that might come into play. It allowed him to make smaller payments. What the provision states is that payment of the death benefit is no longer in effect should the beneficiary, I'm reading this right off the form here, be incarcerated in any penal institution, on parole, or in a mental institution of any kind at the time of the death of the policy holder. As I say, this provision seldom comes into force, as you can imagine, but we do have to have assurance on this point before we are allowed to issue payment.'

'Well, I wouldn't know anything about that.'

'Did your brother have any feeling for what sort of work our beneficiary was interested in taking up? It might help us locate him.'

'Hank told me once that Fee said he was interested in police work.' She paused. 'But after he disappeared like that, Hank sort of wondered if – you know, if he really knew Fee. He wondered if Fee was truthful with him.'

'During the year he lived with you, did you notice any signs of disturbance?'

'Mr Bell, is Fee in some sort of trouble? Is that why you're asking these questions?'

'I'm trying to give him five thousand dollars.' Tom gave her a good, hearty insurance man laugh, the laugh of a member of the Million Dollar Round Table. 'That may be trouble to some, I don't know.'

'Could I ask you a question, Mr Bell?'

'Of course.'

'If Fee is somewhere like you say, or if you flat can't find him, does that insurance money go to the family? Does that ever happen?'

'I'll have to tell you the simple truth. It happens all the time.'

'Because I'm the only family left, you see. Me and my son.'

'In that case, anything you can tell me could be even more useful. You said that Fee went to Tangent, Ohio, when you found you were pregnant?'

'With my Jimmy, that's right.'

'Was that because you did not feel that you could cope with two children?'

'Well, no.' Pause. 'That was why I asked about, you know. I could have brought up two children, but Fee was like a boy who – like a boy a normal person couldn't *understand*. He was such a little boy, but he was so *private*. He'd just sit staring into space for so long! And he'd wake you up screaming at night! But never talk about it! So closed-mouthed! But that's not the worst.'

'Go on,' Tom said.

'Well, if what you say is right, my Jimmy could use that money to help get a downpayment.'

'I understand.'

'It's not for me. But that money can come to the family if Fee is like you say. Incarcerated.'

'We'll be going over the policy to make that determination, ma'am.'

'Well, I know that Fee took a knife from my knife drawer once and went outside with it, and that same day, I mean that night, one of our neighbors found their old dog dead. That dog was *cut*. I found the knife under Fee's little bed, all covered with dirt. I didn't think he killed that dog, of course – he was just a little boy! I didn't even connect it with my knife. But a while later, a dog and a cat were killed about a block away from our house. I asked Fee right out if he was the one who did those things, and he said no. I was so relieved! But then he said, "There isn't any knife missing from the drawer, is there, Mama?" He called us Mama and Papa. And I just, I don't know, felt a chill. It was like he knew that I counted those knives.'

The quavery voice stopped talking. Tom said nothing.

'I just never felt right about Fee after that. Maybe I was wrong, but I couldn't stand the thought of bringing a

566

baby into the house if he was still living with us. So I called Hank and Wilda.'

'Did you tell them anything about your doubts?'

'I couldn't. I felt terrible, having all these bad thoughts about my sister's boy. What I said to Hank was, Fee wasn't screaming at night anymore, which was the truth, but I still thought he might upset the baby. And then I went and talked to Fee. He cried, but not for very long, and I told him he had to be a good boy in Tangent. He had to be a normal boy, or Hank would have to put him in the orphan home. It sounds just awful, but I wanted to help him.'

'He did well in Tangent, didn't he?'

'Just fine. He behaved himself. But when we drove over to Tangent, Thanksgiving and such, Fee never looked at me. Not once.'

'I see.'

'So I wondered,' she said.

'I understand,' Tom said.

'No, sir, I don't think you do. You said you're in Millhaven?'

'At the Millhaven office, yes.'

'That Walter Dragonette was on the front page right here in Azure. And when I first heard about him, I just started to shake. I couldn't eat a bite at dinner. Couldn't sleep at all that night – I had to go down to the lounge and watch the television. And there was his picture on the news, and he was so much younger, and I could go back up to my room.'

Tom did not say anything.

'I'd do the same thing I did back then,' she said. 'With a new baby in the house.'

'We'll be in touch, ma'am, if we cannot locate the beneficiary.'

She hung up without saying good-bye.

19

Tom had tilted himself back in his desk chair and was staring at the ceiling, his hands laced together behind his head, his legs straight out before him and crossed at the ankle. He looked like a bored market trader waiting for something to show up on his Quotron. I leaned forward and poured water from a crystal jug on the table into a clean glass. On second thought, he looked too pleased with himself to be bored.

'Extraordinary place names they have in Ohio,' he said. 'Azure. Tangent. Cincinnati. They're positively Nabokovian. Parma. Wonderful names.'

'Is there a point to this, or are you just enjoying yourself?'

He closed his eyes. 'Everything about this moment is extraordinary. *Fee Bandolier* is extraordinary. That woman, Judy Leatherwood, is extraordinary. She knew exactly what her nephew was. She didn't want to admit it, but she knew. Because he was her sister's child, she tried to protect him. She told him he had to act like a normal child. And the incredible child could do it.'

'Aren't you making a lot of assumptions?'

'Assumptions are what I have to work with. I might as well enjoy them. Do you know what is really extraordinary?'

'I have the feeling you're going to tell me.'

He smiled without opening his eyes. 'This city. Our mayor and chief of police get up on their feet at April Ransom's funeral and tell us that we are a haven of law and order, while against odds of about a million to one, we have among us two very dedicated, utterly ruthless serial killers, one of them of the disorganized type and only recently apprehended, and the other of the organized type and still at large.' He opened his eyes and brought his hands forward and clasped them in his lap. 'That really is extraordinary.'

'You think Fee killed April Ransom and Grant Hoffman.'

'I think he probably killed a lot of people.'

'You're going too fast,' I said. 'I don't see how you can pretend to know that.'

'Do you remember telling me why Walter Dragonette thought he had to kill his mother?'

'She found his notebook. He made lists of details like "red hair".'

'And this is pretty common with people like that, isn't it? They want to be able to remember what they've done.'

'That's right,' I said.

There was an anticipatory smile on his face. 'You wouldn't want anyone else to find your list, would you?'

'Of course not.'

'And if you kept detailed notes and descriptions, you'd have to put them in a safe place, wouldn't you?'

'As safe as possible.'

Still smiling, Tom waited for me to catch up with him.

'Someplace like the basement of the Green Woman, you mean?'

His smile widened. 'You saw the impressions of two boxes. Suppose he wrote narratives of every murder he committed. How many of these narratives would it take to fill two boxes? Fifty? A hundred?'

I took the folded paper from my shirt pocket. 'Can you get into the Allentown police records? We have to find out if this woman, Jane Wright, was murdered there. We even have an approximate date: May 'seventy-seven.'

'What I can do is scan the Allentown newspapers for her name.' He stood up and put his hands in the small of his back and stretched backward. This was probably Tom's morning exercise program. 'It'll take a couple of hours. Do you want to wait around to see what turns up?'

I looked at my watch and saw that it was nearly seven. 'John's probably going out of his mind again.' As soon as I said this, I gave an enormous yawn. 'Sorry,' I said. 'I guess I'm tired.'

Tom put a hand on my shoulder. 'Go back to John's and get some rest.'

20

Paul Fontaine stepped out of a dark blue sedan parked in front of the Ransom house as I walked down the block from the spot where I'd left the Pontiac. I stopped moving.

'Get over here, Underhill.' He looked almost incandescent with rage.

Fontaine unbuttoned the jacket of his baggy suit and stepped back from the sedan. I smiled at him, but he wasn't having any smiles today. As soon as I got within a couple of feet of him, he jumped behind me and jammed his hands into the small of my back. I fell toward his car and caught myself on my arms. 'Stay there,' he said. He patted my back, my chest, my waist, and ran his hands down my legs.

I told him I wasn't carrying a gun.

'Don't move, and don't talk unless I ask you a question.'

Across the street, a little white face appeared at a downstairs window. It was the elderly woman who had brought coffee to the reporters the day after April

Ransom was killed in Shady Mount. She was getting a good show.

'I've been sitting here for *half an hour*,' Fontaine said. 'Where the hell were you? Where's Ransom?'

'I was driving around,' I said. 'John must have gone out somewhere.'

'You've been doing a lot of driving around lately, haven't you?' He made a disgusted sound. 'You can stand up.'

I pushed myself off the car and faced him. His rage had quieted down, but he still looked furious. 'Didn't I talk to you this morning? Did you think I was trying to *amuse* you?'

'Of course not,' I said.

'Then what do you think you're doing?'

'All I did was talk to some people.'

His face turned an ugly red. 'We got a call from the Elm Hill police this afternoon. Damn you, instead of paying attention to me, you and your pal went out there and made everybody crazy. Listen to me – you have no role in what is going on in Millhaven. You get that? The last thing we need right now is bullshit about some – some – ' He was too angry to continue.

He jabbed his index finger at me. 'Get in the car.'

His eyes were blazing.

I moved to open the back door of the sedan, and he growled, 'Not there, dummy. Go around and get in the front.'

He opened his door and kept blazing at me as I walked around the front of the car and got in the front seat. He got behind the wheel, slammed his door, and wrenched the ignition key to the side. We streaked off down the street, and he tore through the stop sign on Berlin Avenue and turned left in a blare of horns.

'Are we going to Armory Place?'

He told me to shut up. The police radio crackled and spat, but he ignored it. Fontaine simmered in silence all the way downtown, and when he hit the on-ramp to the east-west expressway, he thumped the accelerator. We hurtled out into the westbound traffic. Fontaine careened through the other cars, ignoring the cacophony, and got us into the fast lane without actually hitting another car. I managed not to put my arms in front of my face.

He kept his foot down until we reached seventy-five. When a red Toyota refused to get out of his way, he flashed his lights and held down the horn until it swerved into the next lane, and then he roared past it.

I asked where we were going.

His glare was as solid as a blow. 'I'm taking you to Bob Bandolier. Do me a favor and keep your mouth shut until we get there.'

Fontaine blew the cars in front of us into smoke. When the stadium floated into view, he flicked the turn indicator and changed lanes at the same time. Brakes squealed behind us. Fontaine kept moving in an implacable diagonal line until he got across the expressway. He was still doing seventy when we squirted onto the off-ramp. Holding down the horn, he blasted through a red light. The tires whined and the car heeled over to the left as he dodged through the traffic and turned south. We roared past the stadium and slowed down only when we reached Pine Knoll.

Fontaine turned in through the gates and rolled up to the guardhouse. He cut off the engine. 'Okay, get out.'

'Where am I going to meet him, in the afterlife?' I asked, but he left the car and stood in the slanting sun until I got out and walked toward him, and then he began moving quickly up a gravel path toward the area where my parents and my sister were buried. By now, I was regretting my crack about the afterlife. The sprinklers were quiet, and the groundskeeper had gone home. We were the only people in the cemetery. Fontaine moved steadily and without looking back toward the stone wall at the far left.

He left the path about thirty feet before the row of graves I had visited earlier and led me up along a row of graves with small white headstones, some decorated with bright, wilting roses and lilies. He stopped at a bare white marker. I came up beside him and read what was carved into the stone. ROBERT C. BANDOLIER   21 SEPTEMBER 1919–22 MARCH 1972.

'You have anything to say?'

'A Virgo. That figures.'

I thought he was going to hit me. Fontaine unclenched his fists. His saggy face twitched. He didn't look anything like a comedian. He stared at the ground, then looked back up at me. 'Bob Bandolier has been dead for twenty years. He did not ignite the propane tanks at the house in Elm Hill.'

'No,' I said.

'Nobody is interested in this man.' Fontaine's voice was flat and emphatic. 'You can't prove he was the Blue Rose killer, and neither can anyone else. The case came to an end in 1950. That's *that*. Even if we wanted to open it up again, which would be absurd, the conclusion would be exactly the same. *And*. If you keep wandering around, stirring things up, I'll have you shipped back to New York on the next available flight. Or I'll arrest you myself and charge you with disturbing the peace. Is that clear?'

'Can I ask you a couple of questions?'

'Is that *clear*? Do you understand me?'

'Yes. Now can I ask you a few things?'

'If you have to.' Fontaine visibly settled himself and stared off toward the row of hemlocks, far in the distance.

'Did you hear the substance of what the Sunchanas had to say about Bob Bandolier?'

'Unfortunately.'

'Didn't you think there was some chance they might be right?'

He grimaced as if he had a headache. 'Next question.'

'How did you know how to find this grave?'

He turned his head and squinted at me. His chest rose and fell. 'That's a hell of a question. It's none of your business. Are you through?'

'Do the Elm Hill police think that the explosion at the Sunchana house was accidental?'

'That's none of your business, either.'

I couldn't ask him any of the questions I really wanted answered. What seemed a safer, more neutral question suddenly occurred to me, and, thoughtlessly, I asked it. 'Do you know if Bandolier's middle initial stood for Casement?' As soon as I said it, I realized that I had announced a knowledge of Elvee Holdings.

He stared up at the sky. It was just beginning to get dark, and heavy gray clouds were sailing toward us from over the hemlocks, their edges turned pink and gold by the declining sun. Fontaine sighed. 'Casement was Bandolier's middle name. It was on his death certificate. He died of a longstanding brain tumor. Is that it, or do you have some more meaningless questions?'

I shook my head, and he shoved his hands in his pockets and stamped back toward the car.

Might as well go for broke, I thought, and called out, 'Does the name Belinski mean anything to you? Andrew Belinski?'

He stopped walking to turn around and glower at me. 'As a matter of fact, not that it's any business of yours, that was what we called the head of the homicide unit when I came to Millhaven. He was one of the finest men I ever met. He took on most of the people I work with now.'

'That's what you called him?'

Fontaine kicked at the gravel, already sorry he had

574

answered the question. 'His name was Belin, but his mother was Polish, and people just called him Belinski. It started off as a joke, I guess, and it stuck. Are you coming with me, or do you want to walk back to the east side?'

I followed him toward the car, looking aimlessly at the headstones and thinking about what he had told me. Then a name jumped out at me from a chipped headstone, and I looked at it again to make sure I had seen it correctly. HEINZ FRIEDREICH STENMITZ, 1892–1950. That was all. The stone had not merely been chipped; chunks had been knocked off, and parts of the curved top were vaguely serrated, as if someone had attacked it with a hammer. I stared at the battered stone for a moment, feeling numb and tired, and then walked back to the car. Fontaine was revving the engine, sending belches of black smoke out of the exhaust pipe.

As soon as I got back into the car, I realized Fee Bandolier had to be a Millhaven policeman – he had appropriated a name only a cop would know.

21

By the time Fontaine rolled up the looping ramp to the expressway, the heavy clouds I had seen coming in from the west had blotted out the sky. The temperature had dropped at least twenty degrees. Fontaine got to the end of the ramp and moved slowly forward until a truck hummed past, then nudged the sedan into the space behind it. He checked his rearview mirror before changing into the second lane. I rolled up my window against the sudden cold and looked over at him. He was pretending I wasn't there. I leaned back against the seat, and we drove peacefully back toward the middle of the town.

A raindrop the size of an egg struck my side of the windshield; a few seconds later, another noisily landed in the center of the windshield. Fontaine sighed. The radio spooled out crackling nonsense. Two more fat raindrops plopped onto the windshield.

'Are you going to go back to New York soon, Underhill?'

The question surprised me. 'In a little while, probably.'

'We all make mistakes.'

After a little silence, Fontaine said, 'I don't know why you'd want to hang around here now.' The big raindrops were landing on the windshield at the rate of one per second, and we could hear them striking the roof of the car like hailstones.

'Have you ever had doubts about this police department?'

He looked at me sharply, suspiciously. 'What?'

The clouds opened up, and a cascade of water slammed against the windshield. Fontaine snapped on the wipers, and peered forward into the blur until they began to work. He pulled out the knob for the headlights, and the dashboard controls lit up.

'I probably didn't phrase that well,' I said.

'I have plenty of doubts about you, which is something you ought to know about.' He scowled into the streaming windshield until the blade swept it clean again. 'You don't understand cops very well.'

'I know you're a good detective,' I said. 'You have a great reputation.'

'Leave me out of this, whatever it is.'

'Have you ever heard of – '

'Stop,' he said. 'Just stop.'

About thirty seconds later, the intensity of the rain slackened off to a steady drumming against the windshield and the top of the car. It slanted down from the clouds in visible gray diagonals. Sprays of water flew away from the wheels of the cars around us. Fontaine loosened his hands on the wheel. We were going no more than thirty-five miles an hour. 'Okay,' he said. 'For the sake of my great reputation, tell me what you were going to ask me.'

'I wondered if you ever heard of the Elvee Holdings Corporation.'

For the first time, I saw genuine curiosity in his glance. 'You know, I'm wondering about something myself. Is everyone in New York like you, or are you some kind of special case?'

'We're full of meaningless little queries,' I said.

The police radio, which had been sputtering and hissing at intervals, uttered a long, incomprehensible message. Fontaine snatched up the receiver and said, 'I'm on the expressway at about Twentieth Street, be there in ten minutes.'

He replaced the receiver. 'I can't take you back to Ransom's. Something came up.' He checked the mirror, looked over his shoulder, and rocketed into the left lane.

Fontaine unrolled his window, letting in a spray of rain, pulled a red light from under his seat, and clapped it on the top of the car. He flicked a switch, and the siren began whooping. From then on, neither of us spoke. Fontaine had to concentrate on controlling the sedan as he muscled it around every car that dared to get in front of him. At the next exit, he swung off the expressway and went zooming up Fifteenth Street Avenue the same way he had terrorized the expressway on our way to Pine Knoll. At intersections, Fontaine twirled the car through the traffic that stopped to let him go by.

Fifteenth Street Avenue brought us into the valley, and factory walls rose up around us. Fontaine turned south on Geothals and rocketed along until we swerved onto Livermore. The streetlights were on in my old neighborhood. The pouring sky looked black.

A long way ahead of us, blinking red-and-blue lights

filled the inside lane on the other side of the street. Yellow sawhorses and yellow tape gleamed in the lights. Men in caps and blue rain capes moved through the confusion. As we got closer to the scene, I saw where we were going. I should have known. It had happened again, just as Tom had predicted.

Fontaine didn't even bother to look as we went past the Idle Hour. He went down the end of the block, his siren still whooping, made a tight turn onto the northbound lanes of Livermore, and pulled up behind an ambulance. He was out of the car before it stopped ticking. Curls of steam rose up off the sedan's hood.

I got out of the car, hunched myself against the rain, and followed him toward the Idle Hour.

Four or five uniformed officers were standing just inside the barricades, and two others sat smoking in the patrol car that blocked off the avenue's inside lane. The rain had kept away the usual crowd. Fontaine darted through a gap in the barricades and began questioning a policeman trying to stand in the shelter of the tavern's overhang. Unlike the others, he was not wearing a rain cape, and his uniform jacket was sodden. The policeman took a notebook from his pocket and bent over the pages to keep them dry as he read to Fontaine. Directly beside him at the level of his shoulders, a red marker spelling the words BLUE ROSE burned out from the dirty white planks. I stepped forward and leaned over one of the yellow barricades.

A sheet of loose black plastic lay over a body on the sidewalk. Rainwater puddled and splashed in the hollows in the plastic, and runnels of rainwater sluiced down from the body onto the wet pavement. From the bottom end of the black sheet protruded two stout legs in soaked dark trousers. Feet in basketweave loafers splayed out at ten to two. The cops standing behind the barricade paid no attention to me. Steady rain beat down on my head and shoulders, and my shirt glued itself to my skin.

Fontaine nodded to the rain-drenched young policeman who had found the body and pointed at the words on the side of the tavern. He said something I couldn't hear, and the young policeman said, 'Yes, sir.'

Fontaine crouched down beside the body and pulled back the plastic sheet. The man who had followed John Ransom down Berlin Avenue in a blue Lexus stared unseeing up at the overhang of the Idle Hour. Rain spattered down onto his chest and ran into the slashes in a ragged, blood-soaked shirt. Ridges of white skin surrounded long red wounds. The gray ponytail lay like a pointed brush at the side of his neck. I wiped rain off my face. Dark blood had stiffened on his open suit jacket.

Fontaine took a pair of white rubber gloves from his pocket, pulled them on, and leaned over the body to slide his hand under the bloody lapel. The fabric lifted away from the shirt. Fontaine drew out the slim black wallet I had seen before. He flipped it open. The little badge was still pinned to a flap on the right side. Fontaine lifted the flap. 'The deceased is a gentleman named William Writzmann. Some of us know him better under another name.' He stood up. 'Is Hogan here yet?' The young officer held out a plastic evidence bag, and Fontaine dropped the wallet into it.

One of the men near me said that Hogan was on his way.

Fontaine noticed me behind the barricade and came frowning toward me. 'Mr Underhill, it's time for you to leave us.'

'Is that Billy Ritz?' I asked. As much rain was falling on the detective as on me, but he still did not look really wet.

Fontaine blinked and turned away.

'He was the man who followed John. The one I told you about at the hospital.' The policemen standing near

579

me edged away and put their hands under their capes.

Fontaine turned around and gave me a gloomy look. 'Go home before you get pneumonia.' He went back to the body, but the young policeman was already pulling the plastic sheet over Writzmann's wet, empty face.

The two closest policemen looked at me with faces nearly as empty as Writzmann's. I nodded to them and walked along the barricades past the front of the tavern. Two blocks away, another dark blue sedan wearing a flashing red bubble like a party hat was moving down South Sixth Street toward the tavern. Rain streaked through the beams of its headlights. I went across Sixth and looked up at the side of the St Alwyn. A brass circle at the tip of a telescope angled toward the Idle Hour from the corner window of the top floor. I waited for a break in the line of cars moving north in the single open lane and jogged toward the St Alwyn's entrance.

22

The night clerk watched me leave a trail of damp footprints on the rug. My shoes squished, and water dripped down inside my collar.

'See all that excitement outside?' He was a dry old man with deep furrows around his mouth, and his black suit had fit him when he was forty or fifty pounds heavier. 'What they got there, a stiff?'

'He looked dead to me,' I said.

He hitched up his shoulder and twitched away, disappointed with my attitude.

When Glenroy Breakstone picked up, I said, 'This is Tim Underhill. I'm down in the lobby.'

'Come up, if that's what you're here for.' No jazz trivia this time.

Glenroy was playing Art Tatum's record with Ben Webster so softly it was just a cushion of sound. He took one look at me and went into his bathroom to get a towel. The only light burning was the lamp next to his records and sound equipment. The windows on Widow Street showed steady rain falling through the diffuse glow thrown up by the streetlights.

Glenroy came back with a worn white towel. 'Dry yourself off, and I'll find you a dry shirt.'

I unbuttoned the shirt and peeled it off my body. While I rubbed myself dry, Glenroy returned to hand me a black long-sleeved sweatshirt like the one he was wearing. His said TALINN JAZZFEST across the front; when I unfolded the one he gave me, it said BRADLEY'S above a logo of a toothy man strumming a long keyboard. 'I never even worked that place,' he said. 'A bartender there likes my music, so he mailed it to me. He thought I was about your size, I guess.'

The sweatshirt felt luxuriously soft and warm. 'You moved the telescope into your bedroom.'

'I went into the bedroom when I heard the sirens. After I got a look across the street, I fetched my telescope.'

'What did you see?'

'They were just pulling that blanket thing over the dead guy.'

'Did you see who it was?'

'I need a new dealer, if that's what you mean. You mind coming into the bedroom? I want to see what happens.'

I followed Glenroy into his neat, square bedroom. None of the lights had been turned on, and glass over the framed prints and posters reflected our silhouettes. I stood next to him and looked down across Livermore Avenue.

The big cops in rain capes still stood in front of the barricades. A long line of cars crawled by. The plastic sheet had been folded down to Billy Ritz's waist, and a stout, gray-haired man with a black bag squatted in front of the body, next to Paul Fontaine. Billy looked like a ripped mattress. The gray-haired man said something, and Fontaine pulled the sheet back up over the pale face. He stood up and gestured at the ambulance. Two attendants jumped out and rolled a gurney toward the body. The gray-haired man picked up his bag and held out his hand for a black rod that bloomed into an umbrella in front of him.

'What do you think happened to him?' I asked.

Glenroy shook his head. 'I know what they'll say, anyhow – they'll call it a drug murder.'

I looked at him doubtfully, and he gave a short, sharp nod. 'That's the story. They'll find some shit in his pockets, because Billy *always* had some shit in his pockets. And that'll take care of that. They won't have to deal with any of the other stuff Billy was into.'

'Did you see the words on the wall over there?'

'Yeah. So what?'

'Billy Ritz is the third Blue Rose victim. He was killed –' I stopped myself, because I suddenly realized where Billy Ritz had been killed. 'His body was found exactly where Monty Leland was killed in 1950.'

'Nobody cares about those Blue Rose murders,' Glenroy said. He stepped back and put his eye to the end of the telescope. 'Nobody is gonna care about Billy Ritz, either, any more than they cared about Monty Leland. Is that Hogan, that one over there now?'

I leaned toward the window and looked down. It was Michael Hogan, all right, rounding the corner in front of the tavern: the charge of his personality leapt across the great distance between us like an electrical spark.

Ignoring the rain, Hogan began threading through the

582

police outside the Idle Hour. As soon as they took in his presence, the other men parted for him as they would have for Arden Vass. Instantly in charge, he got to the body and asked one of the policemen to fold back the sheet. Ritz's face was a white blotch on the wet sidewalk. The ambulance attendants waited beside their gurney, hugging themselves against the chill. Hogan stared down at the body for a couple of seconds and commanded the sheet to be raised again with an abrupt, angry-looking gesture of his hand. Fontaine slumped forward to talk to him. The attendants lowered the gurney and began maneuvering the body onto it.

Glenroy left the telescope. 'Want a look?'

I adjusted the angle to my height and put my eye to the brass circle. It was like looking through a microscope. Startlingly near, Hogan and Fontaine were facing each other in the circle of my vision. I could almost read their lips. Fontaine looked depressed, and Hogan was virtually luminous with anger. With the rain glistening on his face, he looked more than ever like a romantic hero from forties movies, and I wondered what he made of the end of Billy Ritz. Hogan spun away to speak to the officer who had found the body. The other policemen edged away from him. I moved the telescope to Fontaine, who was watching the attendants wheel the gurney down the sidewalk.

'That writing is red,' Glenroy said. I was still looking at Fontaine, and as Glenroy spoke, the detective turned his head to look at the slogan on the wall. I couldn't see his face.

'Right,' I said.

'Wasn't it black, the other time? Behind the hotel?'

'I think so,' I said.

Fontaine might have been comparing the two slogans, too: he turned around and stared fixedly across the street, toward the passage where three people had been killed.

Rain streamed off the tip of his nose.

'It's funny, you mentioning Monty Leland,' Glenroy said.

I straightened up from the telescope, and Fontaine shrank to a damp little figure on the sidewalk, facing in a different direction from all of the other damp little figures. 'Why is it funny?'

'He was kind of in the same business as Billy. You know much about Monty Leland?'

'He was one of Bill Damrosch's informers.'

'That's right. He wasn't much else, but he was that.'

'Billy Ritz was an informer?'

'Like I told you – the man was in the middle. He was a contact.'

'Whose informer was he?'

'Better not to know.' Glenroy tilted up the telescope. 'Show's over.'

We went back into the living room. Glenroy switched on a lamp near his table and sat down. 'How did you wind up out there in the rain?'

'Paul Fontaine took me out to see Bob Bandolier's grave, and he got called here on the way back. He wasn't in a very good mood.'

'He was saying – okay, maybe he did it, but he's dead. Right? So leave it alone.'

'Right,' I said. 'I think I'm beginning to see why.'

Glenroy hitched himself up in the chair. 'Then you better watch who you talk to. On the real side.'

The record ended, and Glenroy jumped up and flipped it over. He put the needle down on the second side. 'Night and Day' breathed out into the room. Glenroy stood next to his shelves, looking down at the floor and listening to the music. 'Nobody like Ben. Nobody.'

I thought he was about to take the tension out of the air by telling me some anecdote about Ben Webster, but he clamped his arms around his chest and swayed in time to the music for a few seconds. 'Suppose some doctor got killed out at the stadium,' he said. 'I'm not saying this happened, I just supposing. Suppose he got killed *bad* – cut up in a toilet.'

He looked up at me, and I nodded.

'Suppose I'm a guy who likes to go to ball games now and then. Suppose I was there that day. Maybe I might happen to see a guy I know. He's got some kind of name like . . . Buster. Buster ain't worth much. When he ain't breaking into someone's house, he's generally drunk on his ass. Now suppose one time when I'm coming back from the food stand, I happen to see this no-good Buster all curled up under the steps to the next level in a puddle of Miller High Life. And if this ever happened, which it didn't, the only reason I knew this was a human being and not a blanket was that I knew it was Buster. Because the way this *didn't* happen was, he was jammed so far up under the steps you had to look for him to see him.'

I nodded.

'Then just suppose a detective gets word that Buster was out at the game that day, and Buster once did four years at Joliet for killing a guy in a bar, and when the detective goes to his room, he finds the doctor's wallet in a drawer. What do you *suppose* happens next?'

'I suppose Buster confesses and gets a life sentence.'

'Sounds about right to me,' Glenroy said. 'For a made-up story, that is.'

I asked Glenroy if he knew the number of a cab company. He took a business card from the top of the dresser and carried it to me. When I reached for the card, he held onto it for a second. 'You understand, I never said all that, and you never heard it.'

'I don't even think I was here,' I said, and he let go of the card.

A dispatcher said that a cab would pick me up in front of the hotel in five minutes. Glenroy tossed me my wet shirt and told me to keep the sweatshirt.

23

Laszlo Nagy, from my point of view a mass of dark curls erupting from the bottom of a brown tweed cap, began talking as soon as I got into his cab. Some guy got killed right there across the street, did I know that? Makes you think of that crazy guy Walter Dragonette, didn't it? What makes a guy do things like that, anyhow? You have to be God to know the answer to that one, right? Laszlo Nagy had arrived from Hungary eight years ago, and such terrible things never happened in Hungary. Other terrible things happened instead. Do I see this terrible rain? It will last six hours exactly. And what will come next? A fog will come next. The fog will be equally terrible as the rain, because no driver will be able to see what is in front of him. We will have fog two days. Many accidents will take place. And why? Because Americans do not drive well in the fog.

I grunted in all the appropriate places, thinking about what I knew and what it meant. William Writzmann was the son of Oscar Writzmann – now I understood Oscar's remark to John and me about going back to Pigtown, where we belonged. As Billy Ritz, Writzmann had carried on an interesting criminal career under the protection of a murderous Millhaven policeman until the day after John and I had come crashing in on his father. Writzmann had been the front man for Elvee Holdings; Elvee's two fictitious directors had been named after Fee Bandolier's father and an old head of homicide named Andy Belin.

Tom Pasmore had been right all along. And Fee Bandolier was a policeman in Millhaven.

I had no idea what to do next.

Laszlo drew up in front of John's house. When I paid him, he told me that American money should be different sizes and colors, like bills in England and France – and Hungary. He was still talking about the beauty of European money when I closed the door.

I ran up the walk and let myself into the dark house with the extra key. In the kitchen, I rubbed the rain off my face with a paper towel, and then I went upstairs to do some work until John came home.

PART ELEVEN

Jane Wright and Judy Rollin

1

After I had showered, dressed in clean, dry clothes, and worked for an hour or so, I sat on the bed and called Tom Pasmore. No woman named Jane Wright had been killed in Allentown, Pennsylvania, in May or any other month of 1977, but there were lots of other Allentowns in the United States, and he was gradually working through them. He told me he was going to look into Tangent's history as soon as he found the right Allentown. Tom had a lot to say about Fee Bandolier. He also had a few ideas of how to proceed, all of which sounded dangerous to me. When we finished, I felt hungry again and decided to go downstairs to see if there was anything in the refrigerator except vodka.

As I was going toward the stairs, I heard a car splashing to a stop at the front of the house and went to the window at the front of the hallway. A dark green cab stood near the curb. Sheets of water washed down the street, the rain bounced crazily off the roof of the cab. Through the streaming water I could read the words MONARCH CAB CO. and a local telephone number on the front door. John Ransom was leaning over the front seat, wrangling with the driver. I ran back to the guest room and dialed the number on the cab door.

'This is Miles Darrow, the accountant for Mr John Ransom. I understand that my client has used the services of your cab company within the past few hours. He has a problem saving his receipts, and I wonder if you could tell me where your driver picked him up, where he was going, and what the average fare would be to Ely Place on the east side from that location. No reason letting the IRS get it all.'

'Gee, you're a good accountant,' said the woman I was speaking to. 'I took the call from Mr Ransom myself. Pickup was at his house and destination was the Dusty Roads Sunoco Service Station on Claremont Road in Purdum, then to return back to Ely Place. The average fare, that's kind of hard to say, but it would have to be about sixty–seventy dollars, except more on a day like this. And waiting time would add some more, but I don't know about that.'

'Dusty Rhoades?' I asked.

She spelled the name for me. 'Not like the baseball player,' she said. 'It's more like a kind of a cute kind of a name.'

That was about right. Purdum was an affluent town about twenty miles up the shoreline. There was a well-known boarding school in Purdum; a famous polo player, if you knew about things like that, owned a stable and a riding school there. In Purdum, every traffic accident involved at least two Mercedes. I thanked her for her help, hung up, and listened to John moving through the living room. I went to the head of the stairs. The television began to babble. A heavy body hit the couch.

I started down the stairs, telling myself that John would have stowed Alan's gun somewhere in his room.

He didn't say anything until he had given me a long, disapproving look from the couch. Streaks of moisture still dampened his scalp, and widening dark spots covered the shoulders of the dark green linen jacket. On the television screen, a beautifully dressed, handsome black family sat around a dining room table in what looked like a million-dollar house. John took a big mouthful from a glass filled with clear liquid and a lot of ice cubes, still giving me the full weight of his disapproval. Maybe it was disappointment. Then he looked back at the black family. The soundtrack told us that they were hugely enjoyable. 'I didn't know you were home,' he said, stressing the pronoun.

'I had a busy day,' I said.

He shrugged, still watching the television.

I walked behind the couch and leaned against the mantel. The bronze plaque with April's name on it still lay on the pink-and-grey marble. 'I'll tell you what I did, if you tell me what you did.'

He gave me a look of pure annoyance and turned theatrically back to the set. 'Actually, I thought I'd get home long before you came back. I had a little errand to get out of the way, but it look longer than I thought.' Loud, sustained laughter came from the television. The father of the black family was strutting around the table in an exaggerated cakewalk. 'I had to go to my office at Arkham to go over the curriculum for next year. What took so long was that I had to hand in Alan's reading list, too.'

'I suppose you called a taxi service,' I said.

'Yeah, and I waited an extra twenty minutes for the driver to find the place. You shouldn't be able to drive a cab until you know the city. And the suburbs, too.'

The Monarch driver hadn't known how to find Claremont Road. Maybe he hadn't even known how to find Purdum.

'So what did you do?' he asked.

'I discovered some interesting information. Elvee Holdings has owned Bob Bandolier's house since 1979.'

'What?' John finally looked up at me. 'Elvee has a connection to Bandolier?'

'I was coming back here to tell you when Paul Fontaine

jumped out of an unmarked car, frisked me, and yelled at me because a cop in Elm Hill bugged him about Bandolier.'

John smiled when I said I had been frisked. 'Did you assume the position?'

'I didn't have much choice. When he was done yelling, he pushed me into his car and drove like a madman to the expressway, *down* the expressway, and finally got off at the stadium exit. He was taking me to Bob Bandolier.'

John stretched his arm along the top of the couch and leaned toward me.

'Bandolier is buried in Pine Knoll Cemetery. He's been dead since 1972. You know how much Elvee paid for his house? A thousand dollars. What must have happened was that he left the house to his son, who sold it to the company he set up as soon as he came home from Vietnam.'

'Writzmann,' John said. 'I get it. This is *great*.'

'Before we could get back to the east side, just about the time it started to rain, Fontaine answered a call and took me down to Sixth and Livermore. And there, lying in front of the Idle Hour beneath the slogan Blue Rose, was William Writzmann. Oscar Writzmann's son.'

For once, John looked stupefied. He even forgot about his drink.

'Also known as Billy Ritz. He was a small-time coke dealer down around the St Alwyn. He also had connections to some police officer in Millhaven. I think that policeman is Fee Bandolier, grown up. I think he murders people for pleasure and has been doing it for a long time.'

'And he can cover up these murders because he's a cop?'

'That's right.'

'So we have to find out who he is. We have to nail him.'

I began saying what I had to say. 'John, there's a way to look at things that makes everything I just told you

594

irrelevant. William Writzmann and Bob Bandolier and the Green Woman would have nothing to do with the way your wife died.'

'You just lost me.'

'The reason none of that would matter is that you killed April.'

He started to say something, but stopped himself. He shook his head and tried to smile. I had just announced that the earth was flat, and if you went too far in any one direction you fell off. 'You're kidding me, I hope. But I have to tell you, it isn't funny.'

'Just suppose these things are true. You knew Barnett offered her a big new job in San Francisco. Alan knew about it, too, even though he was too mixed up to really remember anything about it.'

'Well, exactly,' John said. 'This is still supposed to be a joke, right?'

'If April was offered that kind of job, would you want her to take it? I think you would have been happier if she'd quit her job altogether. April's success always made you uneasy – you wanted her to stay the way she was when you first met her. Probably she did say that she was going to quit after a couple of years.'

'I told you that. She wasn't like the rest of those people at Barnett – it was a big joke to April.'

'She wasn't like them because she was so much better than they were. In the meantime, let's admit that you saw your own job disappearing. Alan only got through last year because you were holding his hand.'

'That's not true,' John said. 'You saw him at the funeral.'

'What he did that day was an astonishing act of love for his daughter, and I'll never forget it. But he knows he can't teach again. In fact, he told me he was worried about letting you down.'

'There are other jobs,' John said. 'And what does this

make-believe have to do with April, anyhow?'

'You were Alan Brookner's right-hand man, but how much have you published? Can you get a professorship in another department?'

His body stiffened. 'If you think I'm going to listen to you trash my career, you're wrong.' He put his drink on the table and swiveled his entire body toward me.

'Listen to me for a minute. This is how the police will put things together. You resented and downplayed April's success, but you needed her. If someone like April can make eight hundred thousand dollars for her father, how much could she make for herself? A couple of million? Plenty of money to retire on.'

John made himself laugh. 'So I killed her for her money.'

'Here's the next step. The person I went to see downtown was Byron Dorian.'

John rocked back on the couch. Something was happening to his face that wasn't just a flush.

'Suppose April and Dorian saw each other a couple of times a week. They were interested in a lot of the same things. Suppose they had an affair. Maybe Dorian was thinking about going to California with her.' John's face darkened another shade, and he clamped his mouth shut. 'I'm pretty sure she was going to bring Alan along with her. I bet she had a couple of brochures squirreled away up in her office. That means the police have them now.'

John licked his lips. 'Did that pretentious little turd put you on this track? Did he say he slept with April?'

'He didn't have to. He's in love with her. They used to go to this secluded little spot in Flory Park. What do you suppose they did there?'

John opened his mouth and breathed in and out, so shocked he couldn't speak. Years ago, I thought, April had taken him there, too. John's face softened and lost all its definition. 'Are you almost done?'

'You couldn't stand it,' I said. 'You couldn't keep her, and you couldn't lose her, either. So you worked out a plan. You got her to take you somewhere in her car. You got her to park in a secluded place. As soon as she started talking, you beat her unconscious. Maybe you stabbed her after you beat her. Probably you thought you killed her. There must have been a lot of blood in the car. Then you drove to the St Alwyn and carried her in through the back door and up the service steps to room 218. They don't have room service, the maids don't work at night, and almost everybody who lives there is about seventy years old. There's no one in those halls after midnight. You still have master keys. You knew the room would be empty. You put her on the bed and stabbed her again, and then you wrote BLUE ROSE on the wall.'

He was watching me with assumed indifference – I was explaining that the earth was flat all over again.

'Then you took the car to Alan's house and stashed it in his garage. You knew he'd never see it – Alan never even left his house. You cleaned up all the obvious bloodstains. As far as you knew, you could keep it there forever, and no one would ever find it. But then you got me here, in order to muddy the water by making sure everybody thought about the old Blue Rose murders. I started spending time with Alan, so the garage wasn't safe anymore. You had to move the Mercedes. What you did was find a friendly garage out of town, put it in for a general service and a good cleaning, and just left it there for a week.'

'Are we still talking about a hypothesis?'

'You tell me, John. I'd like to know the truth.'

'I suppose I killed Grant Hoffman. I suppose I went to the hospital and killed April.'

'You wouldn't be able to let her come out of her coma, would you?'

'And Grant?' He was still trying to look calm, but red-

and-white blotches covered his face.

'You were setting up a pattern. You wanted me and the cops to think that Blue Rose was back to work. You picked a guy who would have remained unidentified forever if he hadn't been wearing your father-in-law's old sport jacket. Even when we saw the body, you still pretended he was a vagrant.'

John was rhythmically clenching and unclenching his jaws.

'It wouldn't be hard for me to think you just got me out here to use me.'

'You just turned into a liability – if you talk to anybody, you could convince them that all of this bullshit is real. Go upstairs and start packing, Tim. You're gone.'

He started to get up, and I said, 'What would happen if the police went to Purdum, John? Did you take her car to Purdum?'

'Damn you,' he said, and rushed at me.

He was on me before I could stop him. The odors of sweat and alcohol poured out of him. I punched him in the stomach, and he grunted and wrenched me away from the fireplace. His arms locked around my middle. It felt like he was trying to crush me to death. I hit the side of his head two or three times, and then I got my hands under his chin and tried to pry him off of me. We struggled back and forth, rocking between the fireplace and the couch. I shoved up on his meaty chin, and he released his arms and staggered back. I hit him once more in the belly. John clutched his stomach and stepped backward, glaring at me.

'You killed her,' I managed to say.

He lunged toward me, and I put my hands on his shoulders and tried to push him aside. John rode in under me, clamped his right arm around my waist, and pulled me into his shoulder. His head was a boulder in my side. I grabbed the brass plaque off the mantel and pounded it into his neck. Ransom pushed me backward with all of his weight. My feet vanished beneath me, and I landed on the marble apron of the fireplace so hard I saw actual stars. Ransom reached wildly up toward my head and got a hand on my face and pulled himself up onto my chest. Both hands closed around my neck. I bashed the plaque into the side of his head. Because of the way I was holding the award, I couldn't use the edge, only the flat surface. I hit him with the plaque again. A creaky squawk came from my throat, and I merely tapped the plaque against the side of his head. My muscles felt like water. I used the last of my strength to bash the metal plaque against his head again.

John's hands loosened on my throat. All the tension went out of his body. He was a huge slack weight pressing down on me. His chest heaved. Strangled, wheezing noises came from his mouth. After a couple of seconds, I realized that he wasn't dying right on top of me. He was weeping. I crawled out from under him and lay panting on the carpet. I unwrapped my fingers from the plaque. John curled up like a fetus and continued to cry, his arms tented over his head.

After a little while, I got upright and slid along the marble apron and leaned against the edge of the fireplace. We'd been fighting for no more than a minute or two. Someone had been slamming a baseball bat into my arms, my back, my legs, my chest, and my head. I still felt Ransom's hands around my neck.

John lowered his arms and lay curled up with his chest on the marble apron and his hips and legs on the carpet. An ugly wound bled down into his hair. He reached into his trouser pocket for a dark blue handkerchief and put it up against the cut. 'You're a real bastard.'

'Tell me what happened,' I said. 'Try to get in the truth this time.'

He looked at the handkerchief. 'I'm bleeding.' He

placed the handkerchief back over the wound.

'You can put a bandage on it later.'

'How did you know about Purdum?'

'I was sneaky,' I said. 'Where is her car now, John?'

He tried to push himself up and groaned. He lay back down again. 'It's out there in a storage garage. In Purdum. April and I could have retired there. It's a beautiful place.'

People like Dick Mueller moved to Riverwood. People like Ross Barnett retired to estates in Purdum.

John sat up, holding the handkerchief to the side of his head, and slid on his bottom until his back hit the other side of the fireplace. We sat there like andirons. He wiped his free hand down over his face and snorted back mucus. Then he looked at me, red-eyed. 'I'm sorry I went for you like that, but you pushed my buttons, and I snapped. Did I hurt you?'

'Was that what happened with April? You snapped?'

'Yeah.' He nodded very carefully, wincing. I got another darting look from the red eyes. 'I wasn't going to tell you about any of this, because it makes me look so bad. But I didn't invite you here to use you – you have to know that.'

'Then tell me what happened.'

He sighed. 'You got a lot of it right. Barnett spoke to April confidentially about going into business in San Francisco. I wasn't crazy about that. I wanted her to keep to the agreement we made – that she'd quit after she proved she could do a good job at Barnett. But then she had to prove she was the best broker and analyst in the whole damn Midwest. It got so I never saw her except on weekends, and not always then. But I didn't want her to go to California. She could open her own office here, if that was what she wanted. Everything would have been all right, if it hadn't been for that fourth-rate, womanizing twerp.' He glared at me. 'Dorian had an affair with Carol

Judd, the dealer who put him onto April, did you know that?'

'I guessed,' I said.

'The guy is slime. He goes after older women. I will never, never know what April saw in him. He was *cute*, I guess.'

'How did you find out about it?'

John inspected the handkerchief again. I couldn't see the wound, but the handkerchief was bright with blood. 'Could we move? I have to take care of this gash.'

I got up, all my joints aching, and held out a hand for him. John grabbed my hand and levered himself up. He steadied himself on the mantel for a moment and then began moving across the living room toward the stairs.

2

Leaning over to let the blood drip into the sink, John dipped a washcloth into the stream of cold water and dabbed at the inch-long abrasion on the side of his head, where his hair began to get thin. It didn't look so bad now that it was clean. He had placed a square white bandage on the edge of the sink. I was sitting on the tub, looking up at him and holding a wad of folded tissues.

'April told me she was working late at the office. Just to see if she was telling me the truth, I called her line every half hour for three hours. Every half hour, on the button. Maybe six times. She was never there. Around eleven-thirty, I went up to her office here and looked in the file where she kept her charge slips and credit card records. Okay.'

He held out his hand, and I passed him the tissues. He clamped them down on the gash to dry it and then tossed them into the wastebasket and snatched up the bandage square. He centered it over the wound, pushed wisps of hair out of the way, and flattened it down on his scalp. 'That'll do. I guess I won't need any stitches.' He turned his head to see the bandage from different angles. 'Now all I have is one hell of a headache.'

He opened his medicine chest, shook two aspirin tablets onto his palm, and swallowed them with a gulp of water from a surprisingly humble red plastic cup.

'You know what I found? Charges from Hatchett and Hatch. She bought *clothes* for that little turd.'

'How do you know they weren't yours?'

He sneered at me in the mirror. 'I haven't bought anything there in years. All my suits and jackets are made for me. I even get my shirts made to order at Paul Stuart, in New York. And I order my shoes from Wilkes Bashford in San Francisco.' He lifted a foot so that I could admire a dark brown pigskin cap-toe. 'About all I buy in Millhaven is socks and underwear.' He patted the bandage and stepped away from the sink. 'Could we go downstairs so I could get a drink? I'm going to need one.'

I followed him into the kitchen, and he gave me a chastened look as he opened the freezer. Now that his father was gone, the three-hundred-dollar bottle was back in the vodka library. 'I'm not going to run away or anything, Tim, you don't have to act like my shadow.'

'What did you do when she finally came home?'

He poured about three inches of hyacinth vodka into a glass. He tasted it before answering me. 'I should never put ice cubes in this stuff. It's too refined to dilute – such a delicate flavor. Would you like a sip?'

'A sip wouldn't help me. Did you confront her directly?'

He took another taste and nodded. 'I had the charge slips right in front of me – I was sitting out there in the living room, and she came in about a quarter past twelve.

God, I almost died.' He looked up at the ceiling and let out a nearly soundless sigh. 'She looked so beautiful. She didn't see me for a second. And as soon as she noticed me, she *changed*. All the life went out of her. She might have just seen her jailer. Right up until that moment, I was still thinking that there could be another explanation for everything. The clothes could have been for her father – he used to like that store. But the second I saw her mood change like that, I knew.'

'Did you lose your temper?'

He shook his head. 'I felt like someone had just shoved a knife in my back. "Who is it?" I said. "Your little pet, Byron?" She said she didn't know what I was talking about. So I told her I knew that she hadn't been at her office all night, and she gave me some kind of story about not answering the *phone*, about being in the *copy* room, in another *office* . . . so I said, April, what are these charge slips? and she kept giving me lies, and I kept saying Dorian, Dorian, Dorian, and finally she plunked herself down in a chair and said, okay, I've been seeing Byron. What's it to you? God, it was like she was *killing* me. Anyhow, she got less defensive as we went along, and she said she was sorry I had to find out like this, she didn't like being underhanded, and she was almost glad I'd found out, so we could talk about ending our marriage.'

'Did she mention the job in San Francisco?'

'No, she saved that for the car. I want to go into the other room, Tim. I'm a little bit dizzy, okay?'

In the living room, he noticed the bronze plaque on the floor and bent down to pick it up. He showed it to me. 'Is this what you were clobbering me with?' I said that it was, and he shook his head over the irony of it all. 'Damn thing even looks like a murder weapon,' he said, and put it back on the mantel.

'Whose idea was it to go for a ride?'

John looked slightly peevish for a second, but no more than that. 'I'm not used to being grilled. This is still a very touchy subject.'

He went to the couch. The cushions exhaled when he sat down. He drank and held the liquid in his mouth for a moment as he looked around the room. 'We didn't break anything. Isn't that amazing? The only reason I know I was in a fight is that I feel like shit.'

I sat down on the chair and waited.

'Okay. I got everything I thought about that weasel, Dorian, out of my system, and finally I started telling her what I should have said at the beginning – I said I loved her and I wanted to stay married. I said that we had to give ourselves another chance. I said she was the most important person in my life. Hell, I said she *was* my life.'

Tears spilled out of his eyes. 'And that was true. Maybe I wasn't much of a husband, but April was my whole life.' He got his handkerchief halfway to his face before noticing its condition. He checked his trousers for bloodstains and dropped the handkerchief in a clean ashtray. 'Tim, do you happen to have . . .?'

I fished mine out of my pocket and tossed it to him. It was two days old, but still clean, mostly. John pressed it to his eyes, wiped his cheeks, and threw it back to me.

'Anyhow, she said she couldn't sit still any longer, she had to go out for a drive or something. I even asked if I could come along. If you want to talk to me, you'd better, hadn't you? she said. So we drove around, I don't even remember where. We kept saying the same things over and over – she wouldn't *listen* to me. Finally, we ended up somewhere around Bismarck Boulevard, on the west side.'

John pushed out air between his lips. 'She pulled over on Forty-sixth, Forty-fifth, I don't remember. There was a bar down at the end of the block. The Turf Lounge, I think it was.' He looked at me, and his mouth twitched.

His glance shot away again, and he made a wild inventory of the things in the room. 'Tim, you remember how I kept looking for a car following us, after we dropped off my parents? I think someone was following April and me that night. I wasn't too straight, you know, I was really screwed up. But I still pick up on things, I haven't lost all the old radar. But sometimes I get that feeling, and no one's there, you know? Doesn't that happen to you?'

I nodded.

'Anyhow, there wasn't anybody else on the street. All the lights were out, except in the bar. I was begging for my life. I told her about this place I found in Purdum, good price, fifteen acres, a pond, a beautiful house. We could have had our own art gallery there. I got done telling her about it, and she said, Ross might want me to go to San Francisco. I'd head my own office, she said. Forget that stuffed shirt Ross, I said, what do you want? I've been thinking of taking it, she said. I said, Without discussing it with me first? And she said – I didn't see any point in bringing you into it. *Bringing me into it*. She was giving me broker talk! I couldn't help myself, Tim.' He sat forward and stared at me. His mouth worked while he figured out a way to say it. 'I couldn't help myself. Literally.' His face reddened. 'I just – smacked her. I reached up and belted her in the face. Twice.' His eyes got swimmy, bleary with tears. 'I, I felt so shocked – I felt so dirty. April was crying. I couldn't *take* it.'

His voice crumbled, and he closed his eyes and reached a big pink hand out toward me. For an odd second I thought he wanted me to grasp it. Then I realized what he wanted and passed him my handkerchief again. He held it over his eyes and bent forward and wept.

'Oh, God,' he said at last, sitting up. His voice was soft and cottony. 'April just sat there with tears all over her face.' His chest was jerking, and he mopped his eyes until he could speak again. 'She didn't *say* anything. I couldn't

605

sit in that car anymore. I got out and walked away. I'm pretty sure I heard a car starting up, but I wasn't paying attention to things like that. I didn't think I was going up to the bar, but when I got to the door, I went inside. I never even noticed if anyone else was in the place. I put down about four drinks, boom boom boom boom, one right after the other. I have no idea how long I was in there. Then this sumo wrestler type of guy was standing in front of me, telling me that they were closing and I had to pay up. I guess he was the bartender, but I couldn't even remember seeing him before. He said – get this – '

John's chest and belly started jerking up and down again. He was laughing and crying at the same time. 'He said, "Don't come back here again, pal, we don't need your business."' It took him a long time to get the sentence out. He passed my handkerchief over his face. His mouth flickered in and out of a crazy grin.

'I put a fifty-dollar bill on the bar and walked out. April was gone, of course – I hardly expected her to be waiting for me. It took about an hour to walk home. I was making all these speeches in my head. When I got here, her car was right out in front, and I thought, Oh God, at least she's home. I went upstairs, but she wasn't in the bedroom. I checked all over the house, calling her name. Finally I went back outside to see if she was still sitting in the car. When I opened the door, I almost fell over in a faint – there was blood all over both seats. A *lot* of blood. I went crazy. I ran up and down the block, thinking I must have hurt her a lot worse than I had imagined. I could see her getting out of the car and collapsing on someone's lawn. Jesus. I went all over the neighborhood, twice, out of my mind, and then I came back inside and called Shady Mount and said that I'd seen a dazed, bleeding woman walking down Berlin Avenue, and had anyone brought her to the Emergency Room? This very suspicious woman said she wasn't there. I didn't think I could call the cops – my story would have sounded so fishy! Down deep, Tim, down deep, I already knew she was dead. So I put a towel over the driver's seat and took the car to Alan's and put it in his garage. A couple of nights later, when I knew I'd really be in trouble if anyone found it, I went back there in the middle of the night and cleaned it up. That night, I went home and waited to hear something. Finally I just went to bed – well, actually, I slept on this couch here. I wasn't sober. But I don't suppose I have to tell you that. The day before you came, I took her car out to this place in Purdum.'

He noticed the handkerchief balled up in his hands and unfolded it and blew his nose in it. Then he dropped it in the ashtray on top of the bloody one.

'At the time, I thought, after Vietnam, this must be the worst night I'll ever have, all my life. Little did I know.'

'And the next day, the police called.'

'Just after noon.'

'When did you learn about the slogan, or the signature, or whatever it is?'

'At Shady Mount. Fontaine told me. He asked me if I had any idea what it meant.'

'You didn't tell him about April's project?'

He shook his head. He looked stunned and resentful. 'She wasn't sharing a lot with me by that time.' The resentfulness went up a notch. 'All I knew was that it was something that creep started her thinking about.'

'Dorian's father was one of Bill Damrosch's old partners.'

'Oh? I suppose that would be interesting, if you cared about that sort of thing.'

He grabbed his drink, swallowed, moaned, and fell back against the cushions. Neither of us spoke for a time.

'Tell me what you think happened after you went into the bar.'

John pressed the cold glass against one cheek, then

another. Then he rolled the glass back and forth across his forehead. His eyes were slits. 'First, I have to know that you believe me. You know I couldn't have killed April.'

This was the question I had been putting off. I answered the only way I could. 'I guess I do believe you, John.' As soon as I spoke, I realized that I had told him the truth – I guessed that I did believe him.

'I could have sweetened it up, Tim. I could have said that I just got out of the car and walked away as soon as she started crying. I didn't have to tell you I hit her. I didn't make myself sound any better than I was.'

'I know that,' I said.

'This is the truth. It's ugly, but it's the truth.'

'Do you think you were right about being followed?'

'Sure I was right,' he said. 'If I hadn't been so screwed up, I would have been paying more attention.' He shook his head and groaned again. 'Here's what happened. Someone parked about a block away from us and waited. They must have been surprised when I got out of the car – maybe they even thought I spotted them. That's why they started their car. They saw me go into the bar. When I didn't come right out with a pack of cigarettes or something, they went to the Mercedes and – and did what they did. So if I hadn't hit her – if I hadn't been so stupid I had to leave her alone – '

He clamped his eyes shut and pressed his lips together in a tight line. I waited for him to get back in control of himself.

'There had to be two of them, because – '

'Because one drove her car here before they took her to the St Alwyn.'

Sudden anger made me shout. 'Why didn't you tell me the truth when I first got here? All this subterfuge! Didn't you realize how it would look if the police found the car?'

Ransom stayed calm. 'Well, they didn't find it, did

they?' He drank again and swished the vodka around in his mouth. 'After you left town, I was going to drive it to Chicago and leave it on the street with the keys in it. A present for the hoodlums. Then it wouldn't matter if the police found it.'

He registered my impatience. 'Look, I know it was a dumb scheme. I was scared, and I panicked. But forget about me for a second. Writzmann had to be one of the men in the car. That's why he hung around the hospital. He was waiting to see if April was going to wake up.'

'All right, but that makes twice you lied to me,' I said.

'Tim, I didn't think I could ever tell anyone what really happened. I was wrong. I'm apologizing. Just *listen* to me. There was another guy in that car, the cop you were talking about. And he must be the one who killed Writzmann.'

'Yes,' I said. 'He met him in the Green Woman.' John nodded slowly, as if this was utterly new and fascinating.

'Go on,' he said.

'Writzmann probably asked for the meeting. His father called him up and said, Billy, I want you to keep your thugs away from me.'

'Didn't I tell you we'd get something moving?' John said. 'It worked like a charm.'

'Is this really the kind of thing you had in mind?'

'I don't mind the bad guys bumping each other off. That's fine by me. Go on.'

'Writzmann said that two people had come to his father's house asking about Elvee Holdings. That was all he had to say. The cop had to cut his connections to everything that would lead us to him. I don't know what he did. Probably he waited for Writzmann to turn his back and clubbed him with the butt of his gun. He dragged him to that chair, tied him up, and cut him to pieces. That's what he likes.'

'Then he left him there overnight,' John said. 'He knew

609

we were in for a hell of a storm, so yesterday morning he put him in the trunk of his car, waited until it started to really come down, and dumped him in front of the Idle Hour. Nobody'd be on the streets, and it was dark anyhow. It's beautiful. He's got his third Blue Rose victim, and nobody can tie him to Writzmann. He killed Grant Hoffman and my wife and his own stooge, and he's completely in the clear.'

'Except that we know he's a cop. And we know he's the son of Bob Bandolier.'

'How do we know the part about his being a cop?'

'The names given for the other two directors of Elvee Holdings were Leon Casement and Andrew Belinski. Casement was Bob Bandolier's middle name, and about ten years ago, the head of the homicide division in Millhaven was a guy named Andy Belin. Belin's mother was Polish, and the other detectives called him Belinski.' I tried to smile at him, but the smile didn't turn out right. 'I suppose that's station house humor.'

'Wow,' John said. He looked at me admiringly. 'You're good.'

'Fontaine told me,' I said. 'I'm not so sure I should have asked.'

'Goddamn,' John said. He sat up straight and leveled his entire arm at me. 'Fontaine took his father's statements out of the Blue Rose file before he gave them to you. He ordered you to stay away from the Sunchanas, and when that didn't work, he hauled you all the way out to his father's grave. See? he said. Bob Bandolier is dead and buried. Forget this crap and go home. Right?'

'Basically. But he couldn't have taken Writzmann's body to the Idle Hour. I was with him when it started to rain.'

'Think of how the man works,' John said. 'He had one stooge, right? Now he's got another one. He *paid* somebody to dump the body. It's perfect. You're his alibi.'

It wouldn't even have to be money, I thought. Information would be better than money.

'So what do we do?' John asked. 'We can hardly go to the police. They love Fontaine down there at Armory Place. He's Millhaven's favorite detective – he's Dick Tracy, for God's sake!'

'Maybe we can get him out in the open,' I said. 'Maybe we can even get him to put himself out in the open.'

'How do we do that?'

'I told you that Fee Bandolier has been slipping into his father's old house in the middle of the night about once every two weeks. The woman who lives next door catches glimpses of him. She promised to call me the next time she saw him.'

'To hell with that. Let's break into the place.'

I groaned. 'I'm too tired and sore to play cowboy.'

'Think about it. If it isn't Fontaine, it's some other guy at Armory Place. Maybe there are family pictures in the house. Maybe there's, I don't know, something, with his name on it. Why did he keep the house? He's keeping something in there.'

'Something was always in there,' I said. 'His childhood. I'm going to bed, John.' My muscles complained when I stood up.

He put his empty glass on the table and touched the bandage on the side of his head. Then he leaned back into the chair. For a second, we both listened to the rain beat against the windows.

I turned away to go toward the stairs. Gravity pulled at every cell in my body. All I wanted in the world was to get into bed.

'Tim,' he said.

I turned around slowly. He was getting up, and he fixed me with his eyes. 'You're a real friend.'

'I must be,' I said.

'We'll see this thing through together, won't we?'

'Sure,' I said.

He came toward me. 'From now on, I promise, there'll be nothing but the truth. I should have – '

'It's okay,' I said. 'Just don't try to kill me anymore.'

He moved up close and put his arms around me. His head pressed against mine. He hugged me tight into his padded chest – it was like being hugged by a mattress. 'I love you, man. Side by side, all right?'

'*De Opresso Libri*,' I said, and patted him on the back.

'There it is.' He slammed his fist into my shoulder and gripped me tighter. 'Tomorrow we start fresh.'

'Yeah,' I said, and went upstairs.

I undressed and got into bed with *The Nag Hammadi Library*. John Ransom was moving around in his bedroom, now and then bumping against the furniture. The hard, steady rain pounded the window and rattled against the side of the house. By the light of the bedside lamp, I opened the book to 'The Thunder, Perfect Mind,' and read:

> For what is inside of you is what is outside of you,
>   and the one who fashions you on the outside
>   is the one who shaped the inside of you.
> And what you see outside of you,
>   you see inside of you;
>   it is visible and is your garment.

Before long, the words swam together and became different words altogether, and I managed to close the book and turn off the light before I dropped into sleep.

3

At four o'clock, I came irretrievably awake from a dream
in which a hideous monster searched for me in a dark
basement, and lay in bed listening to my heart thud
against my chest. After a moment I realized that the rain
had stopped. Laszlo Nagy was a better meteorologist than
most weathermen.

For a while I followed the advice I always give myself
on sleepless nights, that rest is the next best thing, and
stayed in bed with my eyes closed. My heart slowed down,
and I breathed easily and regularly while my body
relaxed. An hour passed. Every time I turned the pillow
over, I caught the traces of some florid scent and finally
realized that it must have been whatever perfume or
cologne Marjorie Ransom put on before she went to bed.
I threw back the sheet and went to the window. Black,
oily-looking fog pressed against the glass. The street lamp
out on the sidewalk was only a dim, barely visible yellow
haze, like the sun in a Turner painting. I turned on the
overhead light, brushed my teeth and washed my face,
and went downstairs in my pajamas to work on my book.

For another hour and a half I inhabited the body of a
small boy whose bedroom walls were papered with climbing blue roses, a boy whose father said he struck him out
of a great, demanding love, and whose mother lay dying
in a stink of feces and decaying flesh. We're taking good
care of this woman here, his father said, our love is better
for her than any hospital. Beneath Charlie Carpenter's
skin, Fee Bandolier watched his mother drifting out into
blackness. I was in the air around him, Fee and not-Fee,
Charlie and not-Charlie, watching and recording. When

the sorrow became too great to continue, I put down the pencil and went back upstairs on trembling legs.

It was about six. I had this odd sense – that I was *lost*. John's house seemed no more or less real than the smaller house I had imagined around me. If I had still been drinking, I would have had two inches of John's hyacinth vodka and tried to get to sleep again. Instead, I checked the window – the fog had turned to a thick, impenetrable silver – took a quick shower, dressed in jeans and Glenroy's black sweatshirt, put my notebook in my pocket, and went back down to go outside.

4

The world was gone. Before me hung a weightless gauze of light grayish silver which parted as I passed through and into it, reforming itself at a constant distance of four or five feet before and behind me. I could see the steps going down to the walk, and the tall hedges on either side of the lawn tinged the silver dark green. The moist, chill air settled like mist against my face and hands. I moved toward the haze of the street lamp.

Out on the sidewalk, I could see the dim, progressively feebler and smaller points of light cast by the row of street lamps marching down Ely Place toward Berlin Avenue. If I counted them as I went along, as the child-me had counted the rows in the movie theater to be able to return to my seat, the lamps would be my landmarks. I wanted to get out of John's house for a little while; I wanted to replace Marjorie Ransom's tropical perfume with fresh air, to do what I did in New York, let the blank page fill itself with words while I moved thoughtlessly along.

I went three blocks and passed six lamps without seeing

a house, a car, or another person. I turned around and looked back, and all of Ely Place except the few feet of sidewalk beneath my feet was a shimmering silver void. Seeming a long way away, much more distant than I knew it was, a circular yellow haze burned feebly through the bright emptiness. I put my back to it again and tried to look across what had to be Berlin Avenue.

But it didn't *look* like Berlin Avenue – it looked exactly like the other three intersections I had come to, with a low rounded curb and a flat white roadbed partially and intermittently revealed through gaps in the stationary fog. The gleam of the next streetlight cut through the fog ahead of me. Ely Place ended at Berlin Avenue, and there should have been no streetlight ahead of me. Maybe, I thought, one stood directly opposite Ely Place, on the other side of the avenue. But in that case, shouldn't it have been farther away?

Of course I could not really tell the distance between me and the next lamp. The fog made that impossible, distancing objects where it was thickest, bringing them nearer where it was less dense. I almost certainly had to be standing on the corner of Ely Place and Berlin Avenue. Starting at John's house, I had walked three blocks west. Therefore, I had reached Berlin Avenue.

I'll walk across the avenue, I thought, and then go back to John's. Maybe I could even get some sleep before the day really began.

I stepped down onto the roadbed, looking both ways for the circular yellow shine of headlights. There was no noise at all, as if the fog had muffled everything around in cotton. I took six slow steps forward into a gently yielding silver blankness that sifted through me as I walked. Then my foot struck a curb I could only barely see. I stepped up onto the next section of sidewalk. Some unguessable distance ahead of me, the next street lamp burned a circle of dim yellow the size of a tennis ball through the silver.

Whatever I had crossed, it wasn't Berlin Avenue.

Three feet away, the green metal stalk of a street sign shone out of the fog. I went toward the sign and looked up. The green pole ascended straight up into thick cloud, like a skyscraper. I couldn't even see the signs, much less read the names stamped on them. I got right beside the pole and tilted back my head. Far up in a silver mass that seemed to shift sideways as I looked into it, a darker section of fog vaguely suggested a rectangle. Above that the shining silver fog appeared to coalesce and solidify, like a roof.

There must have been four blocks, not three, between John's house and Berlin Avenue. All I had to do was follow the lamps and keep counting. I began walking toward the glow of the lamp, and when I drew level with it, I said *five* to myself. As soon as I walked past the lamp, the world disappeared again into soft bright silvery emptiness. Berlin Avenue had to be directly ahead of me, and I moved along confidently until the dime-sized glow of yet another street lamp reached me through the fog from somewhere far ahead. Then I reached another intersection with a rounded curb down into a gray-white roadbed. Ely Place had stretched itself off into a dimensionless infinity.

But as long as I kept counting the street lamps, I was secure – the street lamps were my version of Ariadne's thread; they would lead me back to John's house. I stepped down into the narrow road and walked across.

Mystified, I walked another two blocks and passed three more lamps without hearing a car or seeing another human being. At the beginning of the next block, the ninth street lamp glowing just ahead of me, I realized what must have happened – I had turned the wrong way when I left John's house and was now far east of Berlin Avenue, nearing the Sevens and Eastern Shore Drive. The invisible houses around me had grown larger and grander, the lawns had become longer and more immaculate. In a few blocks, I would be across the street from the big bluffs falling away to the lakeshore.

Another block went by in a chilly silver emptiness, and then another. I had counted eleven lamps. If I had turned east instead of west on Ely Place, I was very nearly at Eastern Shore Road. Ahead of me lay another block and another dim circle of yellow light.

Two thoughts came to me virtually simultaneously: this street was never going to lead me either to Berlin Avenue or to Eastern Shore Road, and if John Ransom and I were going to break into Bob Bandolier's old house, this was the day to do it. I even thought there was an excellent reason for taking a look inside the Bandolier house. I'd dismissed John's statement that Fee was keeping something in the house by telling him yes, he kept his childhood there: now I thought that probably his adulthood – the records of his secret life – would be in the house, too. Where else could he have taken the boxes from the Green Woman? Elvee Holdings couldn't own property all over town. It was so obvious that I didn't see why I hadn't thought of it before.

Now all I had to do was to count off eleven street lamps and wait for John to get out of bed. I turned around and started moving back through the bright vacancy.

The sequence of lamps burned toward me, increasing in size from dull yellow pinpoints to glowing pumpkins and illuminating nothing but the reflective haze surrounding them. Once I heard a car moving down the street, so slowly that I could almost hear the tread of the tires flattening against the road. It crept up behind me and then finally inched past. The engine hissed. All I could see of the car were two ineffectual lines of light slanting abruptly toward the street, as if they were trying to read the concrete. It was like watching some huge invisible animal slide past me. Then the animal was gone. For a long moment I still heard it hissing, and then the sound was gone, too.

At the eleventh lamp I moved toward the edge of the sidewalk, trying to locate one of the hedges that marked the boundaries of John's lot. No tinge of dark green shone through the fog, and I held out my hands and groped back and forth without finding the hedge. I took another step toward the edge of the sidewalk and stumbled off the curb into the street. For a second I stood looking right and left, seeing nothing, half-stupefied with confusion. I could not be in the street – the car had gone past me *on the other side*. I took another step into the street, leaving the lamp behind me, and thrust my hands out in front of me, blindly reaching for anything I could actually touch.

I turned around and saw the reassuring yellow light reflecting itself off smoky particles that reflected onto other particles, then onto others, so that the lamp had become a smoky yellow ball of haze without edges or boundaries, continuing on beyond itself into the illusion of a reflection, like a fiction of itself.

I went back over the empty invisible street and came up onto the sidewalk again. When I got close enough to the pole so that it stood out shining and green against the silver, I brushed my fingers against it. The metal was cold and damp with tiny invisible droplets, solid as a house. I moved to the other side of the sidewalk, the side where the huge hissing animal had swept past me, and felt my way forward until I felt the sidewalk give way to short coarse grass.

I both understood and imagined that somehow I had walked all the way across the city to my old neighborhood, where snow fell in the middle of summer and angels blotted out half the sky. I came fearfully up the lawn, hoping to see John's sturdy, deceptive building come into being in front of me, but knowing that I was back in Pigtown and would see some other house altogether.

A dwelling with wide steps leading up to a porch gradually drifted toward me out of the silver mist. Beyond the porch, flaking boards dotted with sparkling silver drops led up to a broad black window. I stood a few feet from the edge of the porch, waiting. My heart went into overdrive. A small boy came forward out of the darkness behind the window and stopped moving as soon as he saw me looking in. *Don't fear me*, I thought, *I have a thing to tell you*, but the thing I wished to say instantly fractured into incoherence. The world is made of fire. You will grow up. Bunny is Good Bread. We can, we *can* come through. The boy blinked, and his eyes went out of focus. He would not hear me – he couldn't hear me. A huge white curl of fog swam out of the void like a giant paw, cutting me off from the boy, and when I stepped forward to see him again, the window was empty.

Don't be afraid, I wanted to say, but I was afraid, too.

I went blindly across the lawn, holding my hands out before me, and fifteen paces brushed me against a thick green hedge. I moved down the side of the tough, springy border until it fell away in a square corner at the edge of the sidewalk. Then I groped my way around it and went diagonally up across the next lawn until I saw familiar granite steps and a familiar door flanked by narrow windows.

Pigtown – either the real Pigtown or the one I carried within me – had melted away, and I was back on Ely Place.

5

Pink from the shower and dressed in gray slacks, a charcoal gray cotton turtleneck, and a dark blue silk jacket, John came downstairs a couple of hours later. A smaller, flesh-colored bandage was taped to his head. He smiled at me when he came into the living room, and said, 'What a day! We don't usually get fogs like this, in the middle of summer.' He clapped his hands together and regarded me for a moment, shaking his head as if I were a tremendous curiosity. 'You get up early to do some work?' Before I could answer, he asked, 'What's that mighty tome? I thought the gnostic gospels were my territory, not yours.'

I closed the book. 'How many blocks is it from here to Berlin Avenue?'

'Three,' he said. 'Can't you find the answer in the Gospel of Thomas? I like the verse where Jesus says, If you understand the world, you have found a corpse, but if you have found a corpse, you're superior to the world. That has the real gnostic *thing*, don't you think?'

'How many blocks is it to Eastern Shore Drive?'

He looked up and counted on his fingers. 'Seven, I think. I might have left one out. Why?'

'I went out this morning and got lost. I went about nine blocks in the fog, and then I realized that I wasn't even sure what direction I was going.'

'It must have been up,' he said. 'Or sideways. You can't go nine blocks in either of the usual directions. Look, I'm starved. Did you eat anything yet?'

I shook my head.

'Let's get something in the kitchen.'

He turned around, and I followed him into the kitchen. 'What do you want? I'm going to have some fried eggs.'

'Just toast,' I said.

'Suit yourself.' Ransom put bread into the toaster, greased a pan with margarine, and broke two eggs into the sizzling grease.

'Who lives in the house next door?' I asked him. 'The one to the right?'

'Them? Bruce and Jennifer Adams. They're in their late sixties. Bruce used to own a travel agency, I guess. The one time we went to their house, it was full of these folk art sculptures from Bali and Indonesia. The stuff looked like it would walk around the house at night after all the lights were out.'

'Have you ever seen any children over there?'

He laughed. 'I don't think they'd let a kid within twenty feet of the place.'

'What about the neighbors on the other side?'

'That's an old guy named Reynolds. April liked him enough to invite him over for dinner now and then. Used to teach French literature at the university. Reynolds is okay, I guess, but a little bit swishy.' He was working a spatula under one of the eggs and stopped moving before he swung his head to glance at me. 'I mean, you know what I mean. I don't have anything against the guy.'

'I understand,' I said. 'But I guess there wouldn't be any children in that house, either.'

Four slices of toast popped up in the toaster, and I put them on a plate and began spreading margarine on them.

'Tim,' John said.

I looked up at him. He slid the eggs onto a plate, met my eyes, looked away, and then met my eyes again. 'I'm really glad we had that conversation last night. And I'm grateful to you. I respect you, you know that.'

'How long do you think this fog is going to last?'

He looked at the window. 'Hard to say. Might even last

until the afternoon, it's so thick. Why? You want to do something?'

'I think we might see if we can get into that house,' I said.

'In this?' He was carrying his plate to the table, and he flapped a hand at the window. 'Let's give it another half hour or so, and see what happens.' He gave me a curious half-smile. 'What made you change your mind?'

I spread a spoonful of jam on top of my toast. 'I was thinking about what you said last night – that there had to be something in that house. Do you remember that little piece of paper I found in the Green Woman?'

He stopped shaking his head after I spoke a couple of sentences and began getting interested after I reminded him of Walter Dragonette's notebook.

'Okay,' he said. 'So *if* this guy kept detailed notes about every murder he committed, then we can really nail him. All we have to do is trace him back to the town where he was working.'

'Tom Pasmore would probably be able to help us with that.'

'I'm not putting any faith in that guy,' he said. 'This is our baby.'

'We'll think about that after we get the notes,' I said.

For the rest of the morning, we listened to weather reports on the radio and kept checking the windows. The fog was as thick at ten as it had been at eight, and the radio advised everybody to stay home. There had been half a dozen accidents on the freeways, as well as another five or six minor crashes at intersections. No planes had left Millhaven airport since before midnight, and all incoming flights were being diverted to Milwaukee or Chicago.

John kept jumping up from the couch to take a few steps outside the front door, coming back in to razz me about getting lost.

622

I was glad he was in a good mood. While he ran in and out, checking to see if we could see far enough to drive, I leafed through 'The Paraphrase of Shem' and 'The Second Treatise of Great Seth.'

'Why are you *bothering* with that drivel?' John asked.

'I'm hoping to find out,' I said. 'What do you have against it?'

'Gnosticism is a dead end. When people allude to it now, they make it mean anything they want it to mean by turning it into a system of analogies. And the whole point of gnosticism in the first place was that any kind of nonsense you could make up was true because you made it up.'

'I guess that's why I like it,' I said.

He shook his head in cheerful derision.

At twelve-thirty we ate lunch. The planes were still sitting on the runways and the announcers hadn't stopped telling people to stay home, but from the kitchen window, we could see nearly halfway to the hemlocks at the back of John's property. 'You won't lose your mind again if I bring that pistol, will you?' John asked me.

'Just don't shoot the old lady next door,' I said.

6

I turned on the fog lights and pulled out into the street. The stop sign at the end of the block swam up out of the fog in time for me to brake to a halt.

'You can do this, right?' John asked.

Experimentally, I flicked on the headlights, and both the stop sign and the street ahead disappeared into a shimmering gray fog pierced by two useless yellow tunnels. Ransom grunted, and I punched the lights to low beam. At least other people would be able to see us coming.

'Let's hire a leper to walk in front of us, ringing a bell,' Ransom said.

On a normal day, the drive to South Seventh Street took about twenty minutes; John and I got there in a little more than two and a half hours. We made it without accident, though we had two close calls and one miraculous intervention, when a boy on a bicycle suddenly loomed up directly in front of me, no more than two or three feet away. I veered around him and kept driving, my mouth dry and my bowels full of water.

We got out of the car a block away from the house. The fog obscured even the buildings across the sidewalk. 'It's this way,' I said, and led him across the street and down toward Bob Bandolier's old house.

7

I heard low voices. Hannah and Frank Belknap were sitting on their porch, looking out at nothing. From the sidewalk, I could just make out the porch of the Bandolier place. The Belknaps' voices came through the fog as clearly as voices on a radio that had been dialed low. They were talking about going to northern Wisconsin later in the summer, and Hannah was complaining about having to spend all day in a boat.

'You always catch more fish than I do, you know you do,' Frank said.

'That doesn't mean it's all I want to do,' said Hannah's disembodied voice.

John and I began walking slowly and softly across the

lawn, making as little noise as possible.

The side of the house cut off Frank's reply. John and I walked over wet brown grass, keeping close to the building. At the corner we turned into the backyard. At the far end, barely visible in the fog, a low wooden fence with a gate stood along a narrow alley. We came up to the back door, set on a concrete slab a little larger than a welcome mat.

John bent down to look at the lock, whispered, 'No problem,' and hauled the big ball of keys out of his pants pocket. He riffled through them, singled out one, and tried it in the lock. It went a little way in and stopped. He pulled it out, flicked through the keys again, and tried another one that looked identical to the first. That didn't work, either. He turned to me, shrugged and smiled, and singled out another. This one slid into the lock as if it had been made for it. The lock mechanism clicked, and the door opened. John made an after you, Alfonse gesture, and I slid inside behind his back while he turned to close the door behind us.

I knew where everything was. It was the kitchen of the house where I had grown up, a little dusty and battered, but entirely familiar. A rectangular table with a scarred top stood a few feet from the door. In the dim light, I could make out the names BETHY JANEY BILLY scratched into the wood, along with a lot of random squiggles. Ransom took a couple of steps forward on the cracked yellow linoleum. 'What are you waiting for?' he said.

'Decompression,' I said. A section of wallpaper with images of shepherds and shepherdesses holding crooks dropped away from the wall. Someone, probably Bethy, Janey, and Billy, had scribbled over the images, and ancient yellow grease spots spattered the wall behind the little electric stove. An enormous cock and balls, imperfectly covered with a palimpsest of scrawled lines, sprouted from one of the shepherds near the loose seam of wallpaper. The Dumkys had left plenty of signs of their brief residence.

John said, 'You should be used to a life of crime by now,' and walked through the kitchen into the hallway. 'What are there, three or four rooms?'

'Three, not counting the kitchen,' I said. I came into the dark little hallway and put my hand on a doorknob. 'The boy's bedroom would have been here,' I said, and opened the door.

The narrow rectangle of Fee's old bedroom matched mine exactly. There was a narrow bed with a dark green army surplus blanket and a single wooden chair. A small chest of drawers, stained so dark it was almost black, stood against the wall. At the far end, a narrow window exposed a moving layer of fog. I stepped inside, and my heart shrank. John knelt to look under the bed. 'Cooties.' A frieze of stick figures, round suns with rays, and cartoon houses all interconnected by a road map of scribbled lines, covered the walls to the level of my waist. The light blue paint above the graffiti had turned dingy and mottled.

'This Fee kid got away with a lot of crap,' John said.

'The tenants did this,' I said. I went to the bed and pulled down the blanket. There were no sheets, just an ancient buttoned mattress covered in dirty stripes. John gave me a curious look and began opening the drawers. 'Nothing,' he said. 'Where would he stash the boxes?'

I shook my head and escaped the bedroom.

The three windows at the front of the living room were identical to those in my old house, and the whole long rectangular room brought me back to childhood as surely as the bedroom. An air of leftover misery and rage seemed to intensify the musty air. I knew this room – I had *written* it.

I had placed two tables in front of the windows – the

place where our davenport had stood – and there they were, more ornate than I had imagined, but the same height, and of the same dark wood. A telephone sat on the table to the left, beside a worn overstuffed chair – Bob Bandolier's throne. The long couch I had described stood against the far wall, green, not yellow, but with the same curved arms I had described.

And yet, I thought, it was more unlike than like the room I had imagined. I had thought that Bob Bandolier would provide his family with devotional pictures, the Sermon on the Mount or the Feeding of the Multitude, but there were no reproductions or chromographs on the walls, only wallpaper. I had imagined a small shelf of books with the Bible and paperback Westerns and mysteries, but the only shelves in the living room were shallow, glass, and rimmed with black metal piping – once they had held china figurines. A high-backed brocade chair with rolled arms stood beside the telephone table, and another matching chair without arms faced into the room from beside the other, empty table. His and hers.

'It's like a – like a museum of 1945,' John said, turning to me with an incredulous smile.

'That's what it is,' I said.

I sat down on the chaise and looked sideways. Through a window in the unadorned wall, I could just about make out the side of the Belknap house. Through a matching window in her own living room, Hannah had seen the adult Fee sitting just where I was now. John was looking behind the chairs and beneath the couch. Fee came at night and used only a flashlight, so he had never noticed the grease spots on the brocade chairs or the rim of grime along the edges of the couch cushions.

John opened the door opposite that into the common entry. I stood up and followed him into the bedroom where Anna Bandolier had died of starvation and neglect.

A rusty black stain wavered down the middle of the

bare mattress on the double bed. John looked under the bed, and I opened Bob Bandolier's walnut clothing press. Two wire hangers hung from a metal rail, and a third lay deep in forty-year-old dust on the bottom of the press. 'The drawers,' John said, and we both opened one of the big drawers on either side of the little mirrored vanity table against the wall. Mine was empty. John pushed his drawer closed and looked at me with both impatience and exasperation.

'Okay,' he said. 'Where are they?'

'After Bob Bandolier got rid of the Sunchanas, there were no more upstairs tenants. So he might have put the boxes there.' Then I remembered something else. 'And there's a basement, where they used to do the washing.'

'I'll look upstairs.' He brushed the dust off his knees and gave me another tight-mouthed look. 'Let's get out of here as soon as we can. I don't trust this fog.'

I could almost *see* little Fee Bandolier standing on the side of the bed on a cold night in November of 1950, holding onto his dying mother's arm while his father lay unconscious on the floor, surrounded by empty beer bottles.

'All right?' John asked.

I nodded, and he left the bedroom. I turned my back on the boy and walked out through the mists and vapors that emanated from everything I thought about him and went back through the living room toward the kitchen.

As in my old house, the basement door was next to the stove. I went down the wooden steps in the dark, letting my eyes adjust.

A long wooden workbench stood across the gray concrete floor from the bottom of the stairs. Against the wall above the back of the bench hung a row of coffee cans and jam jars filled with nails and screws. Soon I made out the shapes of boxes beneath the bench, and I exhaled with mingled relief and triumph and went to the bench

628

and bent down and pulled the nearest box toward me.

It was about the size of a case of whiskey, and the top of the box had been folded, not taped, shut. I wrestled with the interlocking cardboard panels before all four of them sprang free at once, revealing a layer of dark fabric. Fee had wrapped his notes in cloth after seeing what the rats had done to them in the Green Woman. I grabbed a loose handful of cloth and pulled up. The cloth came out of the box without resistance. Sleeves flopped out of the bundle. It was a suit jacket. I dropped it on the floor and put my hands back into the box. This time I pulled out the trousers to the suit. Beneath the trousers, carelessly folded, were two more suits, one dark blue, the other dark gray. I stuffed the first suit back into the box, pushed it back under the workbench, and pulled another carton toward me. When I got the top open, I found a pile of white shirts with Arrow labels. They were grimy from the dust sifting down from the workbench and stiff with starch.

The next box held three more suits folded onto a layer of wrinkled boxer shorts and balled-up undershirts, the next a jumble of black shoes, and the final one at least a hundred wide, late-forties neckties tangled together like snakes. My knees creaked when I stood up.

Fee Bandolier had expelled the Dumkys, cleaned up what was important to him, and turned the lock on the door, sealing the past inside a bell jar.

A wide gray spiderweb hung between the wringer of the old washing machine and the slanting ledge of the small rectangular basement window in the wall behind it. I walked slowly down the length of the basement. A black bicycle the size of a Shetland pony leaned against the wall. I turned toward the bulky furnace in the center of the basement, seeing another row of boxes in the darkness. I moved forward, and the row of boxes mutated into the long rectangular dish of a coaster wagon. I pushed it with my foot, and it rolled backward on squeaking wheels, dragging its wooden handle with it. When it moved, I saw another box hidden between the coaster and the furnace.

'There,' I said, and bent down to get my hands on it. Wisps and tatters of old spiderwebs hung from the box. It had been moved recently. I braced my muscles and jerked the box off the ground. It was nearly weightless. Whatever it contained was not hundreds of handwritten pages. I carried the box around the furnace toward the foot of the stairs and heard John walking across the kitchen floor.

I set the box down and opened the four flaps on its top. There was another box inside it. 'Damn it,' I said, and jumped up to go to the front of the furnace.

'Find anything?' John was at the top of the stairs.

'I don't know,' I said. I pulled down the handle and swung open the door.

'There's nothing upstairs. Just bare rooms.' Every other stair groaned beneath his weight. 'What are you doing?'

'Checking the furnace,' I said. 'I just found two empty boxes.'

The interior of the furnace was about the size of a baby carriage. Fine white ash lay across the bottom of the furnace, and black soot coated the grate. John came up beside me.

'I think we lost them,' I said.

'Hold on,' John said. 'He didn't burn anything here. See that stuff?' He pointed at a nearly invisible area on the furnace wall, a section slightly lighter in color than the rest of the interior that I had taken for some kind of stain. John reached into the furnace and dragged it down with his fingers – the ancient spiderweb pulled toward him, then broke and collapsed into a single dirty gray rope.

The boxes lay where I had left them, the flaps of the outer box open on the smooth side of the one inside it. When I shook them, something rattled. 'Let's pull them apart,' I said.

John came foward and flattened his hands on the box. I thrust my fingers inside and tugged. The inner box slid smoothly out. The brown tape across its top flaps had been slit down the middle. I bent up the flaps. Another, smaller box was inside it. I pulled out the third box. About the size of a toaster, it too had been cut open before being inserted into the nest. When I shook it, a papery, slithery sound came from inside the box.

'Guess you found the easter egg,' John said.

I righted the box on the floor and opened it. A square white envelope lay in the bottom of the carton. I picked it up. The envelope was thicker and heavier than I expected. I carried it to the light at the head of the stairs. John watched me open the flap.

'Pictures,' he said.

The old square, white-bordered photographs looked tiny by contemporary standards. I took them out of the envelope and stared at the first one. Some Dumky child had scribbled over its surface. Beneath the crazy lines, the tunnel behind the St Alwyn was still visible. I moved the photograph to the bottom of the pile and looked at the next. At first, it looked like a copy of the photograph I had just seen. There were fewer scribbles on this one. Then I saw that the photographer had moved a few feet nearer the opening of the tunnel, and the fan of vertical bricks at the top of the arch showed more clearly through the overlay of scribbles.

The next one showed a neatly made bed beneath a framed painting invisible behind the mirrored explosion of the flash. Beside the bed, half of a door filled the frame. A little Dumky had scratched XXXXXXXXXXX across the door and the wall. He had run out of patience before he got to the bed, and the X's broke down into scrawls and loops.

'What's that?' John asked.

The next photograph was of the same bed and door

taken from an angle that included the corner of a dressing table. The details of the room lay buried under a lot more scribbled ink.

'A picture of room 218 at the St Alwyn,' I said, and looked up at Ransom's face. 'Bob Bandolier took pictures of the sites before he did the murders.'

I uncovered the next image, scarcely touched by the little Dumkys. Here, rendered in soft brown tones, was the Livermore Avenue side of the Idle Hour, where Monty Leland had been murdered. The photograph beneath had been taken from a spot nearer the corner of South Sixth and showed more of the tavern's side. A zigzag of ink ran across the wooden boards like a bolt of lightning.

'The guy was an obsessive's obsessive. It was planned out, like a campaign.'

I moved the photograph to the bottom of the pile and found myself looking at a photograph almost unreadable beneath inky loops and scratches. I lifted it nearer my face. It had to be a picture of Heinz Stenmitz's butcher shop, but something about the size or shape of the building buried beneath the ink bothered me.

The next was nearly as bad. The edge of the building that might equally have been the Taj Mahal, the White House, or the place where I lived on Grand Street dove beneath a hedge of scribbles.

'They worked that one over,' John said.

I peered down at the picture, trying to figure out what troubled me about it. I could only barely remember the front of Stenmitz's shop. One side of the sign that projected out in a big V above the window read HOME-MADE SAUSAGES; the other side, QUALITY MEATS. Something like that seemed visible underneath the scrawls, but the proportions of the building seemed wrong.

'It must be the butcher shop, right?'

'I guess,' I said.

'How come they're squirreled away in these boxes?'

'Fee must have found them in a drawer – wherever his father kept them. He put them down here to protect them – he must have thought that no one would ever find them.'

'What do we do with them?'

I already had an idea about that.

I sorted through the photographs and chose the clearest of each pair. John took the envelope, and I passed him the others. He slid them into the envelope and tucked in the flap. Then he turned over the envelope and held it up close to his face, as I had done with the last photograph. 'Well, well.'

'What?'

'Take a look.' He pointed to faint, spidery pencil marks on its top left-hand corner.

In faint, almost ladylike thin gray letters, the words BLUE ROSE appeared on the yellowing paper.

'Let's leave these here,' I said, and put the envelope in the smallest box, folded the top shut, and slid the box into the next, and then inserted this one into the largest box, folded its flaps shut, and pushed it back behind the furnace.

'Why?' John asked.

'Because we know they're here.' He frowned and pushed his eyebrows together, trying to figure it out. I said, 'Someday, we might want to show that Bob Bandolier was Blue Rose. So we leave the envelope here.'

'Okay, but where are the notes?'

I raised my shoulders. 'They have to be somewhere.'

'Great,' John walked to the end of the basement, as if trying to make the boxes of notes materialize out of the shadows and concrete blocks. After he passed out of sight behind the furnace, I heard him coming up on the far side of the basement. 'Maybe he hid them under the furnace grate.'

We went back around to the front of the furnace. John

633

opened the door and stuck his head inside. 'Ugh.' He reached inside and tried to pick up the grate. 'Stuck.' He withdrew his hand, which was streaked with gray and black on the back and completely blackened on the palm. The sleeve of the blue silk jacket had a vertical black stripe just below the elbow. John grimaced at the mess on his hand. 'Well, I don't think they're in here.'

'No,' I said. 'They're probably still in the boxes. He doesn't know that we know they exist.'

I took another, pointless look around the basement.

John said, 'What the hell, let's go home.'

We went upstairs and back out into the fog. John locked the door behind us.

I got lost somewhere north of the valley and nearly ran into a car backing out of a driveway. It took me nearly two hours to get back to Ely Place, and when we pulled up in front of his house, John said, 'Got any other great ideas?'

I didn't remind him that the idea had been his.

8

'What do we do now?' John asked. We were in the kitchen, eating a big salad I had made out of a tired head of lettuce, half of an onion, some old Monterey jack cheese, and cut-up slices of the remaining luncheon meat.

'We have to do some shopping,' I said.

'You know what I mean.'

I chewed for a little while, thinking. 'We have to work out a way to get him to take us to those notes. And I've been running a few lines of research. I want to continue with those.'

'What kind of research?'

'I'll tell you when I have some results.' I didn't want to tell him about Tom Pasmore.

'Does that mean that you want to use the car again?'

'A little later, if that's all right,' I said.

'Okay. I really do have to get down to the college to take care of my syllabus and a few other things. Maybe you could drive me there and pick me up later?'

'Are you going to set up Alan's courses, too?'

'I don't have any choice. April's estate is still locked up, until it gets out of probate.'

I didn't want to ask him about the size of April's estate.

'It'll be a couple of million,' he said. 'Two something, according to the lawyers. Plus about half a million from her life insurance. Taxes will eat up a lot of it.'

'There'll be a lot left over,' I said.

'Not enough.'

'Enough for what?'

'To be comfortable, I mean, really comfortable, for the rest of my life,' he said. 'Maybe I'll want to travel for a while. You know what?' He leaned back and looked at me frankly. 'I have gone through an amazing amount of shit in my life, and I don't want any more. I just want the money to be *there*.'

'While you travel,' I said.

'That's right. Maybe I'll write a book. You know what this is about, don't you? I've been locked up inside Millhaven and Arkham College for a long time, and I have to find a new direction.'

He looked at me, hard, and I nodded. This sounded almost like the old John Ransom, the one for whose sake I had come to Millhaven.

'After all, I've been Alan Brookner's constant companion for about ten years. I could bring his ideas to the popular audience. People are always ready for real

635

insights packaged in an accessible way. Think about Joseph Campbell. Think about Bill Moyers. I'm ready to move on to the next level.'

'So let's see if I get this right,' I said. 'First you're going to travel around the world, and then you're going to popularize Alan's ideas, and after that you're going to be on television.'

'Come off it, I'm serious,' he said. 'I want to take time off to rethink my own experience and see if I can write a book that would do some good. Then I could take it from there.'

'I like a man with a great dream,' I said.

'I think it *is* a great dream.' John looked at me for a couple of beats, trying to figure out if I was making fun of him and ready to feel injured.

'When you do the book, I could help you find the right agent.'

He nodded. 'Great, thanks, Tim. By the way.'

I looked attentively at him, wondering what was next.

'If the fog lets up by tomorrow, I'm going to take the car out of Purdum and drive it to Chicago. You know, like I said? Feel like coming along?'

He wanted me to drive him to Purdum – he probably wanted me to drive the Mercedes to Chicago, too. 'I have lots of things to do tomorrow,' I said, not knowing how true that statement was. 'We'll see what happens.'

John seemed inclined to stay downstairs with the television. Jimbo was telling us that police had reported half a dozen cases of vandalism and looting in stores along Messmer Avenue, the main shopping street in Millhaven's black ghetto. Merlin Waterford had refused to acknowledge the existence of the Committee for a Just Millhaven, claiming that 'the capture of one lunatic does not justify tinkering with our superb system of local government.'

I picked up *365 Days*, a book by a doctor named

636

Ronald Glasser who had treated servicemen wounded in Vietnam, and took it upstairs with me.

9

I laid the four photographs on the bed and stretched out beside them. In soft brown-gray tones, visible to various degrees beneath the ballpoint scribbles, the brick passage behind the St Alwyn, room 218, the flank of the Idle Hour, and what had to be Heinz Stenmitz's butcher shop looked back at me. A powerful sense of time passed – of *difference* – came from them. The arched passage and the exterior of the Idle Hour had not changed in forty years, but everything around them had been through wars, recessions, and the long disillusionment that followed the narcotic Reagan years.

I looked at the photograph of the hotel room where James Treadwell had died, set it aside and held the fourth photograph under the bedside lamp. It had to be the butcher shop, but something still troubled me – then I remembered the stench of blood and Mr Stenmitz bending his great blond beast-head toward me. I dropped the photo onto the bed and picked up *365 Days*.

Around three-thirty, John began hollering up the stairs that we'd better get going if we wanted to get to Arkham by four. I got into a jacket and put the four photographs in the pocket.

John was standing at the bottom of the stairs, holding a black briefcase. His other hand was balled into a pocket of the silk jacket. 'Where will you be going, anyhow?' he asked me.

'I'll probably hit the computers at the university library,' I said.

637

'Ah,' he said, as if now he had everything finally figured out.

'There might be some more information about Elvee.'

He leaned forward and peered at my eyes. 'Are you all right? Your eyes are red.'

'I ran out of Murine. If I get involved in something at the library, would you mind taking a cab home?'

'Try to wrap it up before seven,' he said, looking grumpy. 'After that, everything snaps shut like a trap. Budget cuts.'

Twenty minutes later, I dropped John off in front of Arkham's seedy quadrangle and watched him disappear into the heavy gray clouds. A few dim lights burned down from windows in the dark shapes of the college buildings. In the fog, Arkham looked like an insane asylum on the moors. Then I cruised slowly down the street. When a pay telephone swam up out of the murk, I double-parked the car and called Tom's number.

After his message ended, I said that I had to see him as soon as possible, he should call me as soon as he got up, I had to be back at John's –

The line clicked. 'Come on over,' Tom said.

'You're up already?'

'I'm *still* up,' he said.

10

'Do you know how many Allentowns there are in America?' Tom asked me. 'Twenty-one. Some of them aren't even in the standard atlases. I didn't bother with Allentown, Georgia, Allentown, Florida, Allentown, Utah, or Allentown, Delaware, because they all have populations under three thousand – it's an arbitrary cutoff, but not even Fee Bandolier could get away with committing a string of murders in a town that size.'

The start-up menus glowed from the monitors of his computers. Tom looked a little pale and his hair was rumpled, but the only other indication that he hadn't slept in twenty-four hours was that his necktie had been pulled below the undone top button of his shirt. He was wearing the same long silk robe he'd had on the other day.

'So I went through every one of the sixteen other Allentowns, looking for a Jane Wright who had been murdered in May 1977. Nothing. No Jane Wright. Most of these towns are so small that there were no murders at all in that month. All I could do then was go back to Allentown, Pennsylvania, and take another look.'

'And?'

'I found something good.'

'Are you going to tell me about it?'

'In time.' Tom smiled at me. 'You sounded like you had something pretty good yourself, on the phone.'

There was no point in trying to get him to say anything until he was ready. I took a sip of his coffee and said, 'April Ransom's car is in a garage in Purdum. John panicked when he found it in front of his house with blood all over the seats, and he took it to Alan's garage and cleaned it up and then stashed it out of town.'

'Did he, now?' Tom tilted his head back and regarded me through half-closed eyes. 'I thought he knew where that car was.' He was smiling again, that same slow, almost luxuriant smile I had seen on the day I had brought John Ransom to meet him. 'Somehow, I see that we do not think he is a guilty party here. Tell me the rest of it.'

'After I left your house the other day, Paul Fontaine pushed me into an unmarked car and drove me out to Pine Knoll.' I told him everything that had happened – Bob Bandolier's middle name and Andy Belin, Billy Ritz, my brawl and John's account of the night April was beaten. I described our visit to the house on South Seventh Street and brought the photographs out of my jacket pocket and put them on the table in front of us. Tom scarcely moved during my long recital – his eyes opened a bit when I got to Andy Belin, he nodded when I described calling the cab company, and he smiled again when I described the fight with John, but that was all.

Finally, he said, 'Hadn't it already occurred to you that Fee Bandolier was a Millhaven policeman?'

'No,' I said. 'Of course it hadn't.'

'But someone took Bob Bandolier's statements out of the Blue Rose file – only a policeman could do that, and only his son would want to.'

He took in my response to these remarks. 'Don't get angry with me. I didn't mention it because you wouldn't have believed me. Or was I wrong about that?'

'You weren't wrong.'

'Then let's think about what else we have here.' He closed his eyes and said nothing for at least an entire minute. Then he said, 'Preservation.' He smoothed out the front of the silk robe and nodded to himself.

'Maybe you could elaborate on that a little bit,' I said.

'Didn't John say Fee's house looked like a museum of the year 1945?'

I nodded.

'It's his power source – his battery. He keeps that house to step back into his childhood and taste it again. It's a kind of shrine. It's like that ghost village in Vietnam you told me about.'

Finally, he bent forward and looked at the photographs. 'So here we are,' he said. 'The sites of the original Blue Rose murders. With a slight overlay of static provided by the annoying tenants.'

He pulled the fourth photograph towards him. 'Hmmm.'

'It has to be Stenmitz's shop, doesn't it?'

640

Tom looked sharply up at me. 'Do you have some doubts about that?'

I said I wasn't sure.

'It's almost unreadable,' he said. 'Wouldn't it be interesting if it were a photograph of something else?'

'What about your computers? Do you have a way to lift off the ink and expose what's underneath?'

Tom thought about it for a couple of seconds, frowning down at the ruined photograph with his chin in his hand. 'The computer can extrapolate from the bits and pieces that are still visible – suggest a reconstruction. There's so much damage here it'll probably offer several versions of the original image.'

'How long would that take?'

'At least a couple of days. It'll have to go through a lot of variations, and some of them will be worthless. To tell you the truth, nearly all of them will be worthless.'

'Are you willing to do it?'

'Are you kidding?' He grinned at me. 'I'll start as soon as you leave. Something bothers you about this picture, doesn't it?'

'I can't put my finger on it,' I said.

'Maybe Bandolier originally intended to kill Stenmitz somewhere else,' Tom said, more to himself than to me. He was looking at an invisible point in space, like a cat.

Then he focused on me again. 'Why did Fee kill April Ransom?'

'To finish what his father started?'

'Did you read that book I gave you?'

We looked at each other for a moment. Finally I said, 'You think that Franklin Bachelor could be Fee Bandolier?'

'I'm sure of it,' Tom said. 'I bet that Fee called his father twice, in '70 and '71, and that's why Bob changed his phone number. When Bob died, Fee inherited the house and sold it to Elvee.'

'Can you get into the draft records from Tangent? We know Fee enlisted under another name right after he graduated from high school, in 1961.'

'None of that information was ever computerized. But if you'd be willing to make a little trip, there's a good chance we could find out.'

'You want me to go to Tangent?'

'I looked through almost every issue of the Tangent *Herald* published during the late sixties. I finally managed to find the name of the head of the local draft board, Edward Hubbel. Mr Hubbel retired from the hardware business about ten years ago, but he's still living in his own home, and he's quite a character.'

'Wouldn't he give you the information over the phone?'

'Mr Hubbel is a little cranky. Apparently, war protestors gave him a lot of trouble during the late sixties. Someone tried to blow up the draft office in 1969, and he's still mad. Even after I explained that I was writing a book about the careers of veterans from various areas, he refused to talk to me unless I saw him in person. But he said he kept his own records of every boy from Tangent who went into the army while he ran the board, and if someone will take the trouble to see him in person, he'll make the effort of checking his files.'

'So you do want me to go to Tangent,' I said.

'I booked a ticket on a flight for eleven o'clock tomorrow. If the fog lifts, you can be back for dinner.'

'What name did you use?'

'Yours,' he said. 'He won't talk to anyone but a veteran.'

'Okay. I'll go to Tangent. Now will you tell me what you found in the police records in Allentown, Pennsylvania?'

'Sure,' he said. 'Nothing.'

I stared at him. Tom was almost hugging himself in self-satisfaction.

'And that's the information you uncovered? Could you explain why that's so wonderful?'

'I didn't find anything in the police records because I don't have any access to them. You can't get there from here. I had to do it the hard way, through the newspapers.'

'So you looked in the newspaper and found Jane Wright.'

He shook his head, but he was still bubbling over with suppressed delight.

'I don't get it,' I said.

'I didn't find Jane Wright anywhere, remember? So I went back to the Allentown, Pennsylvania, records for anything that even looked close to the name and date on that piece of paper you found in the Green Woman.'

Tom grinned at me again and stood up to walk around the side of the chesterfield. He picked up a manila folder lying next to the computer keyboard on his desk and tucked it under his elbow.

'Our man wants to keep a narrative account of every murder he's done as a kind of written memory. At the same time, someone as intelligent as Fee might work out a way to defuse these records, to make them harmless if anyone else found them. If he turned his own records into a kind of code, he'd have it both ways.'

'A code? You mean, change the names or the dates?'

'Exactly. I ploughed through microfilm of the Allentown paper from the mid-seventies. And in the papers from May 1978, I came across a very likely little murder.'

'Same month, one year off.'

'The victim's name was Judy Rollin. Close enough to Jane Wright to suggest it, but so different that it amounts to a good disguise.' He took the folder from under his elbow, opened it up, and took out the sheet of paper on the bottom. Then he walked back to me and handed me the file. 'Take a look.'

I opened the file, which held copies of three pages of newsprint. Tom had circled one story on each page. The pages had been reduced in size, and the type was just large enough to be read without a magnifying glass. On the first page, the circled story was about the discovery by three teenage boys of the corpse of a young woman who had been knifed to death and then dumped behind an abandoned steel mill. The second story gave the dead woman's name as Judy Rollin, twenty-six, a divorced hairdresser employed at the Hi-Tone Hair Salon last seen at Cookie's, a club five miles from the old steel mill. Mrs Rollin had gone to the club with two friends who had gone home together, leaving her behind. The third article, headed DOOMED BY LIFE IN FAST LANE, was a salacious description of both Judy Rollin and Cookie's. The dead woman had indulged in drugs and alcohol, and the club was said to be 'a well-known place of assignation for drug dealers and their customers.'

The last article was ARRESTED GOOD-TIME GIRL MURDERER KILLS SELF IN CELL. A bartender at Cookie's named Raymond Bledsoe had hanged himself in his cell after confessing to Mrs Rollin's murder. An informant had provided police with information that Bledsoe regularly sold cocaine to the victim, and Mrs Rollin's handbag had been found in the trunk of his car. The detective in charge of the case said, 'Unfortunately, it isn't possible for us to provide full-time surveillance for everyone who expresses an unwillingness to spend the rest of their lives in prison.' The name of the detective was Paul Fontaine.

I handed the sheet of paper back to Tom, who slid it into his file.

'Paul Fontaine,' I said. I felt a strange sense of letdown, almost of disappointment.

'So it seems. I'm going to do some more checking, but . . .' Tom shrugged and spread out his hands.

'He was so confident that he'd never get caught that he

didn't bother changing his name when he came to Mill-haven.' Then I remembered the last time I'd seen Fontaine. 'My God, I asked him if he'd ever heard of Elvee Holdings.'

'He still doesn't know how close we are. Fontaine just wants you to get out of town. If we can get our friend in Tangent to identify him as Franklin Bachelor, we'll have a real weapon in our hands. And maybe you could fit in a visit to Judy Leatherwood, too.'

'I suppose you have a picture,' I said.

Tom nodded and went back to his desk to pick up a manila envelope. 'I clipped this out of the *Ledger*.'

I opened the envelope and took out the photograph of Paul Fontaine standing in front of Walter Dragonette's house in the midst of a lot of other officers. Then I looked back up at Tom and said that Judy Leatherwood wasn't going to believe that I was showing her the photograph to straighten out an insurance matter.

'That part's up to you,' Tom said. 'You have a well-developed imagination, don't you?'

The last thing he said to me before he closed the door was 'Be careful.' I didn't think he was talking about driving in the fog.

PART TWELVE

Edward Hubbel

1

The flight to Tangent, Ohio, took off at twelve fifty-five, nearly two hours late. For most of the morning, I thought the plane would never leave, and I kept calling the airport to see if the flight had been canceled. A young man at the ticket counter assured me that although some arriving aircraft had been rerouted, there were no problems with takeoffs. So while John took a cab to the suburbs to pick up his wife's car, I drove out to the airport at a rousing twenty-five miles an hour, passed a couple of fender-benders without having one, and left the Pontiac in the long-term parking garage.

Our flight boarded at a quarter to eleven, and at a quarter after, the captain announced that the tower was going to take advantage of a reduction in the fog to land aircraft that had been stacked up above us for several hours. He apologized for the delay, but said that it would not last much longer than thirty minutes.

After an hour, the stewardess passed out free drinks and extra packets of honey-roasted nuts. I spent the time reading the last two days' issues of the *Ledger*, which I'd brought along.

The death of William Writzmann, alias Billy Ritz, took up only three inches of type on page five of the second section of yesterday's paper. Five grams of cocaine, divided into a dozen smaller quantities and double-wrapped in plastic pill envelopes, had been found in his suit pockets. Detective Paul Fontaine, interviewed at the scene, speculated that Writzmann had been murdered during a drug transaction, although other possibilities were under investigation. When questioned about the words written above the body, Fontaine replied, 'At present, we think this was an attempt to mislead our investigation.'

The next day, two patrons of the Home Plate Lounge remembered seeing Billy Ritz with Frankie Waldo. Geoffrey Bough examined the life of Frankie Waldo and came to certain conclusions he was careful, over the course of three long columns, not to state. Over the past fifteen years, the Idaho Meat Company had lost ground to national distributors organized into vertical conglomerates; yet Waldo's salary had tripled by 1990. In the mid-eighties, he had purchased a twelve-room house on four acres in Riverwood; a year later, he divorced his wife, married a woman fifteen years younger than himself, and bought a duplex apartment in the Waterfront Towers.

The source of this affluence was his acquisition of Reed & Armor, a rival meat company that had gone into disarray after its president, Jacob Reed, disappeared in February of 1983 – Reed had gone out for lunch one day and never been seen again. Waldo immediately stepped in, bought the disintegrating company for a fraction of its real value, and merged the resources of the two firms. It was the operations of this new company that had roused the suspicions of various regulatory agencies, as well as the Internal Revenue Service.

Various persons who chose to remain anonymous reported having seen William Writzmann, known as Billy Ritz, in restaurants, bars, and nightclubs with Mr Waldo, beginning in late 1982. I would have bet a year's royalties that these persons were all Paul Fontaine, rewriting history to suggest that Billy Ritz had killed Jacob Reed so that Ritz and Waldo could launder drug money through a profitable meat company.

I thought that Waldo was just a guy who spent too much money on stupid things. Eventually, he made the error of turning to Billy Ritz to get himself out of the hole. After that, he was nothing more than a victim with a glitzy apartment and a lakefront view. Paul Fontaine had Ritz murder Waldo in a way that looked like a gang killing. When Billy's body turned up, it was just the bigger dealers taking out the little ones. I wondered if anyone but me would ever wonder why a big-time dealer like Billy Ritz was walking around with separate grams and half grams in his pockets.

And then I reminded myself that I still had no real evidence that Paul Fontaine was Fee Bandolier. That was part of the reason I was sitting on a stalled airplane, waiting to take off for Ohio. I didn't even want Fee to be Paul Fontaine – I liked Fontaine.

2

The plane took off into a clinging layer of fog that soon thickened into dark wool. Then we shot out of the soft, clinging darkness into radiant light. The plane made a wide circle in the sudden light, and I looked down at Millhaven through the little window. A dirty, wrinkled blanket lay over the city. After ten minutes, the blanket had begun to admit shafts of light. Five minutes later, the land lay clear and green beneath us.

The speakers overhead hissed and crackled. The pilot's unflappable voice cut through the static. 'You people might be interested in knowing that we departed Millhaven just before the tower decided to shut down operations until further notice. That inversion bowl that caused all the trouble is still stickin' around, so I congratulate you on not having chosen a later flight. Thank you for your patience.'

An hour later, we landed at a terminal that looked like a ranch house with a conning tower. I walked through a long waiting room with rows of plastic chairs to the pay telephones and dialed the number Tom Pasmore had given me. A deep voice jerky with anxiety answered after four or five rings.

'You're the writer fellow I was talking to? Suppose you tell me what outfit you were in.'

I told him.

'You bring your discharge papers?'

'No, sir,' I said. 'Was that part of the agreement?'

'How do I know you're not some peacenik?'

'I have a few genuine scars,' I said.

'What camp were you stationed at and who was the CO there?'

It was like talking to Glenroy Breakstone. 'Camp Crandall. The CO was Colonel Harrison Pflug.' After a second, I said, 'Known as the Tin Man.'

'Come out and let me get a look at you.' He gave me a complicated set of directions involving a shopping mall, a little red house, a big rock, a dirt road, and an electric fence.

At the rental counter, I signed up for every available kind of insurance and took the keys to a Chrysler Imperial. The young woman waved her hand toward the glass doors at what looked like a mile of parking lot. 'Row D, space 20. You can't miss it. It's red.'

I carried my briefcase out into the sun and walked across the lot until I came up to a cherry-red car about the size of a houseboat. It should have had a raccoon tail on the antenna and a pair of fuzzy dice in the front window. I opened the door and let the ordinary heat trickle into the oven of the interior. When I got in, the car smelled like a Big Mac box.

About forty minutes later, I finally backtracked to a boulder slightly smaller than the one I had chosen, found my way to a dirt road that vanished into an empty field, and bounced the Chrysler's tires along the ruts until the road split into two forks. One aimed toward a far-off farmhouse, and the other veered left into a grove of oak trees. I looked into the trees and saw flashes of yellow and the glint of metal. I turned left.

Huge yellow ribbons had been tied head-high around each of the trees, and on the high cross-hatched metal fence that ran through them a black-and-white sign said: DANGER ELECTRIFIED FENCE NO TRESPASSERS. I got out of the car and went up to the fence. Fifty feet away, the dirt road ended at a white garage. Beside it stood a square, three-story white house with a raised porch and fluted columns. I pushed a button in the squawk box next to the gate.

The same deep, anxious voice came through the box. 'You're a little late. Hold on, I'll let you in.'

The box buzzed, and I pushed open the gate. 'Close the gate behind you,' the voice ordered. I drove in, got out of the car, and pushed the gate shut behind me. An electronic lock slammed home a bolt the size of my fist. I got back in the car and drove up toward the garage.

Before I stopped the car, a bent old man in a white short-sleeved shirt and a polka-dot bow tie appeared on the porch. He hobbled along the porch, waving at me to stop. I cut the engine and waited. The old man glowered at me and got to the white steps that came down to the lawn. He used the handrail and made it down the steps. I opened the door and stood up.

'Okay,' he said. 'I checked you out. Colonel Pflug was the CO at Camp Crandall right up until seventy-two. But

I have to tell you, you have pretty flashy taste in vehicles.'

He wasn't kidding – Hubbel didn't look like a man who had ever wasted much time on humor. He got up to within a yard of me and squinted at the car. Distaste narrowed his black little eyes. He had a wide flabby face and a short hooked nose like an owl's beak. Liver spots covered his scalp.

'It's a rental,' I said, and held out my hand.

He turned his distaste to me. 'I want to see something in that hand.'

'Money?'

'ID.'

I showed him my driver's license. He bent so far over that his nose nearly touched the plastic covering. 'I thought you were in Millhaven. That's in Illinois.'

'I'm staying there for a while,' I said.

'Funny place to stay.' He straightened up as far as he could and glared at me. 'How'd you learn my name?'

I said that I had looked through copies of the Tangent newspaper from the sixties.

'Yeah, we were in the paper. Irresponsibility, plain and simple. Makes you wonder about the patriotism of those fellows, doesn't it?'

'They probably didn't know what they were doing,' I said.

He glared at me again. 'Don't kid yourself. Those commie dupes put a bomb right in our front door.'

'That must have been terrible for you,' I said.

He ignored my sympathy. 'You should have seen the hate mail I got – people used to scream at me on the street. Thought they were doing *good*.'

'People have different points of view,' I said.

He spat onto the ground. 'The pure, they are always with us.'

I smiled at him.

'Well, come on in. I got complete records, like I said

on the phone. It's all in good order, you don't have to worry about *that*.'

We moved slowly toward the house. Hubbel said that he had moved out of town and put up his security fence in 1960. 'They made me live in the middle of a field,' he said. 'I tell you one thing, nobody gets into *this* office unless they stood up for the red, white, and blue.'

He stumped up the stairs, getting both feet on one step before tackling the next. 'Used to be, I kept a rifle right by the front door there,' he said. 'Would have used it, too. In defense of my country.' We made it onto the porch and crawled toward the door. 'You say you got some scars over there.'

I nodded.

'How?'

'Shell fragments,' I said.

'Show me.'

I took off my jacket, unbuttoned my shirt, and pulled it down over my shoulders to show him my chest. Then I turned around so that he could see my back. He shuffled forward, and I felt his breath on my back. 'Pretty good,' he said. 'You still must have some of that stuff inside you.'

My anger disappeared when I turned around and saw that his eyes were wet. 'Every now and then, I set off metal detectors,' I said.

'You come on in, now.' Hubbel opened the door. 'Just tell me what I can do for you.'

3

The crowded front parlor of the old farmhouse was dominated by a long wooden desk with high-backed armchairs behind and before it. An American flag stood between the desk and the wall. A framed letter on White House stationery hung on the wall behind the desk. A couch, a shaky-looking rocker, and a coffee table filled most of the rest of the room. The rocker faced a television set placed on the bottom shelf of a unit filled with books and large journals that looked like the records of his hardware business.

'What's this book you want to write?' Hubbel got himself behind his desk and let out a little puff of exertion. 'You interested in some of the boys you served with?'

'Not exactly,' I said, and gave him some stuff about how representative soldiers had been affected by their wartime experience.

He gave me a suspicious look. 'This wouldn't be one of those damn pack of lies that show our veterans as a bunch of criminals, I s'pose.'

'Of course not.'

'Because they aren't. People go on and on gassing about Post-Traumatic Whatzit, but the whole damn thing was made up by a bunch of journalists. I can tell you about boys right here in Tangent who came back from the war just as clean-cut as they were when they got drafted.'

'I'm interested in a very special group of people,' I said, not adding that it was a group of one.

'Of course you are. Let me tell you about one boy, Mitch Carver, son of a fireman here, turned out to be a good little soldier in Airborne.' He went on to tell me the story, the point of which seemed to be that Mitch had come back from Vietnam, married a substitute school-teacher, become a fireman just like his dad, and had two fine sons.

After the children had been produced like a merit badge, I said, 'I understand that you also have records of the volunteers from your area.'

'Why shouldn't I? I made a point of meeting each and every one of our boys who enlisted. A fine, fine bunch. And I kept up with them, too – just like the boys I helped get into the service. I was proud of all of them. You want to see the names?'

He gestured toward the row of record books. 'See, I wrote down the name of every one of those boys. I call it my Roll Call of Honor. Fetch me a couple of those books, I'll show you.'

I stood up and went to the bookshelves. 'Could we look at the list from 1961?'

'You want to see something, get me the book for 1968 – that's a whole volume all by itself, there's a million good stories in that one.'

'I'm working on 1961,' I said.

His venomous face distorted itself into a smile. A hooked old finger jabbed the air in my direction. 'I bet that's the year you went in.'

I had been drafted in 1967. 'Got me,' I said.

'Just remember you can't pull anything over on me. 'Sixty–'sixty-one is the second book in line.'

I pulled the heavy book off the shelf and brought it to his desk. Hubbel opened the cover with a ceremonious flourish. ROLL CALL OF HONOR had been written in broad black strokes on the first page. He flipped through pages covered with names until he came to 1961 and began moving his finger down the line. The names were listed in the order in which they had been drafted and had been written very carefully in the same broad strokes of Hubbel's fountain pen.

'Benjamin Grady,' Hubbel said. 'There's one for your book. Big, handsome kid. Took him right after high school. I wrote to him two or three times, but the letters never got through. I wrote a lot of my boys.'

'You knew where he had been assigned?'

He peered up at me. 'Took a special interest. Grady came back in 'sixty-two, but he didn't stay long. Went to college in New Jersey and married some Jewish girl, his dad told me. See?' He moved his finger across the line, where he had written NJ.

The finger traveled down the column again. 'Here's a boy for you. Todd Lemon. Used to work at Bud's Service Station here in town, cutest little guy you ever saw in your life. Spunky. I can still remember him at the physical – when the doc asked him about drugs, he said, "My body is my temple, sir," and all the other fellows standing in line gave a big laugh of appreciation.'

'You went to the physicals?'

'That was how I met the boys who enlisted,' he said, as if that should have been obvious. 'Every day of the physicals, I turned over the business to my clerks and went down there. Can't tell you what a thrill it was, seeing all those wonderful boys lined up – God, I was proud of all of them.'

'Is there a separate list for the volunteers?'

My question made him indignant. 'What kind of record-keeper would I be if there weren't? That's a separate category, after all.'

I asked to see that list.

'Well, you're missing out on some fine, upstanding boys, but . . .' He turned over another page. Under the heading ENLISTED was a column of about twenty-five names. 'If you'd let me show you 1967 or 1968, you'd have a lot more to choose from.'

I scanned down the list, and my heart stopped about two-thirds of the way down, when I came to Franklin Bachelor. 'I think I've heard of one of these people,' I said.

'Bobby Arthur? You'd know him, of course. Great golfer – turned pro for a couple of years after the war.'

'I was thinking of this one.' I pointed at Bachelor's name.

He bent over to peer at the name, and then he brightened. 'That boy, oh, yes. Very, very special. He got into Special Forces, had a wonderful career. One of our heroes.' He nearly beamed at me. 'What a boy. There was some kind of story there, I always thought.'

He would have told me even if I hadn't asked.

'I didn't know him – I didn't know most of my boys, of course, but I never even heard of a family named Bachelor living in Tangent. By God, I believe I even checked the telephone book when I got to my place that evening, and damned if there were no Bachelors listed. I had a feeling this was one of those lads who signs up under another name. I didn't say anything, though – I let the boy go through. I knew what he was doing.'

'What was he doing?'

Hubbel lowered his voice. 'That boy was *escaping*.' He looked up at me and nodded. He looked more like an owl than ever.

'Escaping?' I wondered if Hubbel had managed to guess that Fee had been avoiding arrest. He wouldn't have even begun to imagine the sorts of crimes Fee had committed: all of his 'boys' had been as sinless as his own ideas of himself.

'That boy had been mistreated. I saw it right away – little round scars on his chest. Sort of thing that makes you sick inside. Idea that his own mother or father would do a thing like that to a handsome little lad.'

'They scarred him?' I asked.

He almost whispered. 'Burned him. With cigarettes. Until they left scars.' Hubbel shook his spotted head, staring down at the page. His hands were spread out over the names, as if to conceal them. Maybe he just liked touching them. 'Doc asked him about the scars, and the boy said he ran into bob wire. I knew – I could see. Bob wire doesn't leave scars like that. Small, like dimes. Shiny. I knew what happened to that boy.'

'You have a wonderful memory,' I said.

'I go over these journals pretty often, being here by myself.' His face hardened. 'Now I got so feeble, I can't get the books down so easy anymore, need a little help sometimes.'

He moved his hands and stared down at the pages. 'You probably want to copy down some of my boys' names.'

I let him read out half a dozen names from the enlisted men and the draftees while I copied them into my notebook. They were all still living in Tangent, he said, and I'd have no trouble finding them in the telephone book.

'Do you think you'd still be able to identify Franklin Bachelor from a photograph?' I asked.

'Maybe. You got one?'

I opened my briefcase and took out the manila envelope. Tom had cut off the caption. I put it on top of the list of names, and Hubbel bent over so that his nose was only an inch away from it. He moved his head back and forth over the picture as if he were smelling it. 'Policeman,' he said. 'He went into law enforcement?'

'Yes,' I said.

'I'm going to write that in my book.'

I watched the top of the spotted head drift back and forth over the photograph. Sparse gray hairs grew up out of his mottled scalp.

'Well, I believe you're right,' he said. 'It sure could be that boy I saw at the induction center.' He blinked up at me. 'Turned out fine, didn't he?'

'Which one is he?'

'You're not going to trick *me*,' he said, and planted the tip of his right index finger on top of Paul Fontaine's face. 'There he is, right there, that's the boy. Yep. Franklin Bachelor. Or whatever his real name was.'

I packed the photograph away in my briefcase and told him how helpful he had been.

'Would you do me a favor before you leave?'

'Of course,' I said.

'Fetch my journals for 1967 and 1968, will you? I'd like to remember some more of my boys.'

I pulled the books from the shelf and piled them on his desk. He spread his hands out on top of them. 'Tell you what, you honk the horn of that flashy car when you want me to open the gate. I'll push the button for you.'

When I let myself out onto the porch, he was pushing his beaky nose down a long column of names.

4

I still had two hours before the flight back to Millhaven, and Tangent was only two miles down the highway past the airport. I drove until I came to streets lined with handsome houses set far back on wide lawns. After a while, the quiet streets led into a part of town with four-story office buildings and old-fashioned department stores.

I parked on a square with a fountain and walked around the square until I found a diner. The waitress at the counter gave me a cup of coffee and the telephone book.

I took the book to the pay telephone near the kitchen and called Judy Leatherwood.

The same quavery voice I had heard at Tom's house said hello.

I couldn't remember the name of the insurance company Tom had invented. 'Mrs Leatherwood, do you remember getting a call from the Millhaven branch of our insurance company a few nights ago?'

'Oh, yes, I do,' she said. 'Mr Bell? I remember speaking to him. This is about my brother-in-law's insurance?'

'I'd like to come out to speak to you about the matter,' I said.

'Well, I don't know. Have you located my nephew?'

'He may have changed his name,' I said.

For about ten seconds, she said nothing. 'I just don't feel right about all this. I've been worried ever since I talked to Mr Bell.' Another long pause. 'Did you give me your name?'

'Mister Underhill,' I said.

'I think I shouldn't have said those things to Mr Bell. I don't really know what that boy did – I don't feel right about it. Not at all.'

'I understand that,' I said. 'It might help both of us if we could have a talk this afternoon.'

'My son said he never heard of any insurance company doing things that way.'

'We're a small family firm,' I said. 'Some of our provisions are unique to us.'

'What was the name of your company again, Mr Underhill?'

Then, blessedly, it came to me. 'Mid-States Insurance.'

'I just don't know.'

'It'll only take a minute or two – I have to get on a flight back to Millhaven.'

'You came all this way just to see me? I guess it would be okay.'

I said I'd be there soon, hung up, and showed her address to the waitress. The directions she gave took me back the way I had come.

When I drove up to the nursing home, I realized that I had mistaken it for a grade school when I had driven past it on the way into town. It was a long low building of cream-colored brick with big windows on either side of a curved entrance. I parked in front of a sign that read FAIRHOME CENTER FOR THE AGED and walked toward a concrete apron beneath a wide red marquee. An electronic door whooshed open and let out a wave of cool air.

A woman who looked like Betty Crocker smiled when I came up to a white waist-high counter and asked if she could help me. I said that I wanted to see Mrs Leatherwood.

'It'll be nice for Judy to have a visitor,' she said. 'Are you family?'

'No, I'm a friend,' I said. 'I was just speaking to her on the phone.'

'Judy is in the Blue Wing, down the hall and through the big doors. Room six, on your right. I can get an aide to show you the way.'

I said that I could find it by myself, and went down the hall and pushed open a bright blue door. Two uniformed nurses stood at a recessed station, and one of them came toward me. 'Are you looking for one of the residents?'

'Judy Leatherwood,' I said. She smiled, said, 'Oh, yes,' and took me past the nurses' station to an open door and a room with a hospital bed and a bulletin board crowded with pictures of a young couple and two blond little boys. An old woman in a print dress sat on a wooden chair in front of a desk below the bright window at the end of the room. The light behind her head darkened her face. An aluminum walker stood beside her legs. 'Judy, you have a visitor,' the nurse said.

Her white hair gleamed in the light from the window. 'Mister Underhill?'

'It's nice to meet you,' I said, and came toward her. She lifted her face, showing me the thick, milky glaze over both of her eyes.

'I don't like this business,' she said. 'I don't want to be rewarded for my nephew's misfortune. If the boy is in trouble, won't he need that money himself?'

'That may not be an issue,' I said. 'May I sit down for a minute?'

She kept her face pointed toward the door. Her hands twisted in her lap. 'I suppose.'

Before I sat down, she asked, 'Do you know where my nephew is? I'd like to know that.'

'I want to ask you a question,' I said.

She turned briefly to me and then back to the door. 'I don't know what I should say.'

'When your nephew lived with you, did you notice any scars on his body? Small, circular scars?'

Her hand flew to her mouth. 'Is this important?'

'It is,' I said. 'I understand that this must be difficult for you.'

She lowered her hand and shook her head. 'Fee had scars on his chest. He never said how he got them.'

'But you thought you knew.'

'Mister Underhill, if you're telling me the truth about any of this rigamarole, please tell me where he is.'

'Your nephew was a major in the Green Berets, and he was a hero,' I said. 'He was killed leading a team on a special mission into the DMZ in 1972.'

'Oh, heavens.' She said it twice more. Then she started to cry, softly, without moving in any way. I took a tissue from the box on her dresser and put it into her hands, and she dabbed her eyes.

'So there won't be any trouble about the money,' I said.

I make an extravagant amount of money from writing, not as much as Sidney Sheldon or Tom Clancy but a lot anyhow, a matter I talk about only with my agent and my accountant. I have no family, and there's no one to spend it on except myself. I did what I had decided to do on the airplane if I learned conclusively that Fee Bandolier had grown up to be Franklin Bachelor, took my checkbook out of my briefcase, and wrote her a check for five thousand dollars.

'I'll give you a personal check right now,' I said. 'It's a little irregular, but there's no need to make you wait for our accounting office to process the papers, and I can get reimbursement from Mr Bell.'

'Oh, this is wonderful,' she said. 'I never dreamed – you know, what makes me so happy is that Fee – '

'I'm happy for you.' I put the check in her hands. She clenched it into the tissue and dabbed her eyes again.

'Judy?' A man in a tight, shiny suit bustled into the room. 'I'm sorry I couldn't get here right away, but I was on the phone. Are you all right?'

Before she could answer, he whirled toward me. 'Bill Baxter. I run the business office here. Who are you, and what are you doing?'

I stood up and told him my name. 'If Mrs Leatherwood spoke to you about our earlier conversation – '

'You bet she did, and I want you out of here right now. We're going to my office, and I'm calling the police.'

'Mr Baxter, this man – '

'This man is a fraud,' Baxter said. He grabbed my arm.

'I came here to give Mrs Leatherwood a check,' I said. 'It represents the death benefit on a small insurance policy.'

'He gave me a check, he did,' Judy Leatherwood said. She extricated it from the tissue and flapped it at Baxter.

He snatched the check away from her, looked at me,

back at the check, and then at me again. 'This is a personal check.'

'I didn't see any reason to make Mrs Leatherwood wait two or three months for our office to issue the payment,' I said, and repeated my statement about reimbursement.

Baxter dropped his arms. I could almost see the question mark floating over his head. 'This doesn't make any sense. Your check is on a New York bank.'

'I'm a troubleshooter for my company. I was in Millhaven when Mrs Leatherwood's problem came up.'

'He told me about my nephew – Fee was a major in Vietnam.'

'Special Forces,' I said. 'He had quite a career.'

Baxter scowled at the check again. 'I think we'll use your phone to get in touch with Mr Underhill's company.'

'Why not call the bank to see if the check is covered?' I asked him. 'Isn't that the main point?'

'You're giving her this money yourself?'

'You could look at it like that,' I said.

Baxter stewed for a moment and then picked up the telephone and asked for directory assistance in New York. He put the call through the home's switchboard and asked to speak to the manager of my branch. He spoke for a long time without getting anywhere and finally said, 'I'm holding a five-thousand-dollar check this man made out to one of our residents. I want to be assured that he can cover it.'

There was a long pause. Baxter's face grew red.

'I knew I should have called Jimmy,' said Judy Leatherwood.

'All right,' Baxter said. 'Thank you. I'll personally deposit the check this afternoon.' He hung up and looked at me for a moment before handing the check back to her. The question mark still hung over his head. 'Judy, you just got five thousand dollars, but I'm not sure why. When you first talked to this insurance company, did someone tell you the amount you were supposed to get?'

'Five thousand,' she said, with an extra wobble in her voice.

'I'll walk Mr Underhill to the door.' He stepped out into the hall and waited for me to follow him.

I said good-bye to Judy Leatherwood and joined Baxter in the hallway. He set off at a quick march toward the big blue doors and the entrance, giving me sharp, inquisitive glances as we went. Betty Crocker waved good-bye to me. Once we got outside, Baxter stuffed his hands into the pockets of his shiny suit. 'Are you going to explain what you just did in there?'

'I gave her a check for five thousand dollars.'

'But you don't work for any insurance company.'

'It's a little more complicated than that.'

'Was her nephew really a Green Beret major?'

I nodded.

'Does this money come from him?'

'You might say that he owes a lot of people,' I said.

He thought it over. 'I think my responsibility ends at this point. I'm going to say good-bye to you, Mr Underhill.' He didn't offer to shake hands. I walked to my car, and he stood in the sun on the concrete apron until I drove past the entrance.

5

I turned in the keys to the Chrysler and paid for the gas I had used at the counter. There was still half an hour to fill before boarding, so I went to the telephones to call Glenroy Breakstone. 'Tangent?' he asked me. 'Tangent, Ohio? Man, that's a dead place. Back in the fifties, we played a place called the French Quarter there, and the owner used to pay us in one-dollar bills.' I asked if I could come up to see him after I got back to Millhaven. 'How soon?' he asked. I told him that I'd be there in about two hours. 'As long as you're here before eight,' he said. 'I got a little business to do around then.'

After that I tried Tom Pasmore's number, on the off-chance that he might be up, and when his machine answered, I began describing what I had learned from Edward Hubbel and Judy Leatherwood. He picked up before I was able to say more than a couple of sentences. 'This case is turning my day around,' he said. 'I went to bed about an hour after you left, and I got up about noon to play with my machines a little more. So you found out, did you?'

'I found out, all right,' I said, and told him about it in detail.

'Well, that's that,' he said, 'but I still feel like exploring matters for a while, just to see if anything interesting turns up.'

Then I told him about giving Judy Leatherwood a check.

'Oh, you didn't! No, no, no.' He was laughing. 'Look, I'll pay you back as soon as I see you.'

'Tom, I'm not criticizing you, but I couldn't leave her stranded.'

'What do you think I am? I sent her a check for five thousand yesterday.' He started laughing again. 'She's going to love Mid-States Insurance.'

'Oh, hell,' I said.

He offered once again to pay me back.

'One white lie shouldn't cost you ten thousand dollars,' I said.

'But it was *my* white lie.' He was still laughing.

We talked for a few more minutes. There was still a lot of fog in Millhaven, and a small-scale riot had begun on Messmer Avenue. No one had been injured, so far.

I asked the cheerful blond person at the airline desk if the flight would be delayed. He said there were no problems.

Twenty minutes after we left the ground, the pilot announced that atmospheric problems in Millhaven meant that our flight was being diverted to Milwaukee, where we could either wait until conditions improved or arrange for connecting flights.

At about a quarter to seven, we touched down at Mitchell Field in Milwaukee, where another cheerful blond person told us that if we remained in the departure lounge, we would be able to reboard and continue on to our original destination in no less than an hour. I had lost faith in cheerful blond persons and walked through the departure lounge, trudged along a series of corridors, took an escalator downstairs, and rented another car. This one was a gunmetal gray Ford Galaxy, and all it smelled of was new leather. They spray it into the cars, like air freshener.

6

South of Milwaukee, the city flattens out into miles of suburbs and then yields to the open farmland of the original Midwest. After I crossed the border into Illinois, the sunlight still fell on the broad green-and-yellow fields, and the billboards advertised high-yield fertilizer and super-effective crop spray. Herds of Holstein cows stood unmoving in vast pastures. Fifteen miles farther, the air darkened; and a little while after that, wisps and tendrils of fog floated between the cars ahead of me. Then the fields disappeared into misty gray. I turned on my fog lights when a Jeep Cherokee two hundred feet down the highway turned into a pair of tiny red eyes. After that, we crawled along at thirty miles an hour. The first Millhaven exit jumped up out of the emptiness barely in time for me to make the turn. After that, the ten-minute drive to the airport took half an hour, and it was seven-thirty before I found the rental parking spaces. I went into the terminal, turned over the keys, and walked back across the access road and down a long stretch of pavement to the long-term parking garage.

On the second floor, twenty or thirty cars stood parked at wide intervals on the gray cement. Overhead bulbs in metal cages shone down on cement pillars and bright yellow lines. The exit signs glowed red across empty space. I turned on the Pontiac's lights and rolled toward the curving wall before the ramp. Another pair of head-lights shot out into the gloom. When I stopped to pay the attendant, long yellow beams elongated on the ramp behind me. The attendant handed back my change with-out looking at me, and the gate floated up. I sped out of the garage and across the pedestrian walkway, swerved onto the circular access road, and got up to forty on the empty drive to the highway. I wanted to vanish into the fog.

I paused at the stop sign long enough to be sure that nothing was coming, cramped the wheel, hit the acceler-ator and the horn at the same time, and cut into the middle lane. A huge sign flashing FOG WARNING 25MPH burned toward me from the side of the road. As soon as I got up to fifty, the taillights of a station wagon jumped toward me, and I swerved into the fast lane before I rammed into the puzzled face of the Irish retriever staring at me through the wagon's rear window. I whisked past the wagon. I thought that if I drove Paul Fontaine-style for another mile or two, I could put to rest the fear that Billy Ritz's replacement was gaining on me, back in the fog. And then I thought that probably no one was following me, cars drove out of the long-term garage night and day, and I slowed to twenty-five miles an hour. Taillights appeared before me in the fast lane, and I moved as slowly as a rowboat back into the center lane. Then I began to imagine a thug creeping toward me out of the sludge in my rearview mirror, and I moved the accelerator down until I was nipping along at forty. It seemed dangerously slow. I swerved around a little powder-blue hatchback that appeared in front of me with vivid, dreamlike suddenness, and ploughed through the drifting lengths and thicknesses of batting, of wool, of white gauze and gray gauze, and whipped past another flashing red FOG WARNING sign. A pain I had not felt in a good five years declared itself in a circle about eight inches in diameter on the upper right side of my back.

I remembered this pain, a combination of burn and puncture, though it is neither. Generally speaking, it is the legacy of the metal fragments embedded in my back, and specifically, the result of some flesh-encrusted screw, some rusty bolt, working its way toward the air like a restless corpse. I felt it now exactly in the place where Edward Hubbel, who had never understood why he had been mesmerized by lines of seminaked boys, had breathed on me while he scrutinized my scars. Edward Hubbel's breath had seeped through my skin and awakened the sleeping bolt. Now it was moving around, crawling toward the surface like Lazarus, where first a sharp edge, then a blunt curl, would emerge. For a week, I'd print spotty bloodstains on my shirts and sheets.

I slowed down before I slammed into the back of a truck and puttered along behind it while I tried rubbing my back on the seat. The truck picked up a little speed. I could feel the exact dimension of the little hatchet buried at the bottom of my shoulder blade. Pressing it against the seat seemed to calm it. The painful circle on my back shrank by half an inch. I looked into the rearview mirror, saw nothing, and moved out to get around the truck.

A horn blared; brakes shrieked. I jammed the accelerator. The Pontiac wavered ahead, and the massive wheels of the truck filled my side window. The horn blasted again. The Pontiac made up its mind and shot forward. The rear end of another car jumped into the windshield, and I hauled the Pontiac into the fast lane with my heart skipping and my mind in the clear empty space of panic. I never even ticked it. When I saw red lights ahead of me, I slowed down and waited for my heart to get back to normal. The screw in my back declared itself again. A few other little knots and bumps began to throb. Hubbel had breathed them all into wakefulness. Headlights appeared in my rearview mirror, and I sped up by another five miles an hour. The headlights grew larger and sharper. I swung back into the middle lane.

The car behind me came up alongside me and stuck with me for a long time. I thought it must have been someone I had irritated or frightened during my Fontaine phase. The other car drifted toward my lane, and I swerved right far enough to put my tires on the yellow line. The other car swerved with me. It was dark blue, pocked with brown primer, with crumpled corrugations behind the headlight. I sped up; he sped up. I slowed down; he slowed down. Now he was only inches from the side of my car, and my heart began to trip again. I looked sideways at a curly dark head, heavy bare shoulders, and a flash of gold. The other driver was watching the front of the Pontiac. He moved his wheel, and his car whapped into mine just above the left front tire.

I slammed down the accelerator, and the Pontiac zoomed into the slow lane. There was a screech of metal as he dug a long strip down my side. The Pontiac jumped ahead. The other man raced up alongside to hit me again, and I zagged sideways. The rows of warning lights at the back of another semi zoomed toward me. When I saw its mudflaps, I swerved off the road and shuddered onto the gravel. I kept pace with the semi for half a mile, telling myself that the other driver would think I had driven off the road. The truck driver blasted his air horn. I was glad I didn't have to hear what he was saying. Sooner or later, I was going to run into an exit sign or a stalled car, so I edged forward until I could see past the front of the cab, gunned the Pontiac, and scrambled back onto the road. The truck driver gave another enraged blast of his air horn. *

The dark blue car swam up beside me again. This time he hit me hard enough to jolt my hands off the wheel. The semi's headlights filled my rearview mirror. The blue car veered away and then came back and ground against the side of the Pontiac. If he got me to slow down, or if he jarred me into an angle, the semi would flatten me. A calm little voice in the midst of my panic said that Fontaine had learned that I had tickets to Tangent and had someone watch the Pontiac until I came back. The same voice told me that a couple of witnesses would testify that I had been driving recklessly. The thug in the blue car would just disappear.

The semi's enormous radiator filled my rearview mirror. It looked carnivorous. The blue car swung into me again, and I fastened onto the wheel and slammed into him, just for the satisfaction. Sparks flew up between us. I could taste adrenaline. The big green rectangle of an exit sign took shape in the fog ahead of me. I took my foot off the accelerator, yanked the wheel to the right, and took off over the gravel. In seconds, I was shuddering over bumpy ground. The steel posts of the sign flew past the sides of the Pontiac, and the blue car sailed away into the fog only feet away from the cab of the semi. I went bumping through weeds. The bottom of the Pontiac scraped rock. Then a curb led down to the off ramp, and I thumped down onto the roadbed, drove without seeing or thinking for thirty seconds, pulled up at the stop sign, and started to shake.

7

I wiped my face with a handkerchief and got out to look at the damage. The man in the blue car would be swept along until the next exit, at least a mile away. He had put three long silver slashes down the side, buckled in the metal between the wheel and the door, and punched a lot of dents along the entire length of the car. I leaned against the car and breathed hard for a while, watching the ghostly traffic move along the highway in the fog. After a while I realized that I was on the off ramp to the south side of Millhaven, twenty minutes from Livermore Avenue. In all the excitement, I had reached the exit I wanted in the first place. I think I had forgotten that I had a destination.

I got back into the car and pointed it toward Pigtown. The uneasy thought came to me that the man in the blue car would already be traveling back toward me.

8

I didn't look at my watch until I saw the vague shapes of the St Alwyn towering over Livermore Avenue, and then I was surprised to see that it was ten to eight. Time seemed to have simultaneously speeded up and slowed down. The little hooks and ratchets in my back pulsed and burned, and I kept hearing air horns and seeing the blue car slamming toward me. As soon as I saw a parking spot, I moved up and reversed in. The right front tire rubbed against the dented shell, and the entire body of the Pontiac shuddered and moaned.

I paid the meter an hour's worth of quarters. Maybe Glenroy's appointment had been called off; maybe his visitor was delayed by the fog. I had a feeling I knew what kind of appointment it was, anyhow. Meetings like that don't take long. I locked the car, shivering a little in the fog.

The hotel was two blocks away. I hugged myself against the cold, walking through the thin layers of gauze. The street lamps cast feeble yellow orbs, like Japanese lanterns. All of the shops were closed, and there was no one else on the street. The St Alwyn receded as I walked toward it, as a mountain backs away when you approach it. Behind me, a distant, momentary crackle tugged at my subconscious, then died. I took another couple of steps and heard it again. This time I recognized the sound of gunfire. I turned around, and there came another rattling burst from off on the other side of the valley and a little way south. The sky held a faint orange tinge. If I'd been closer to Messmer Avenue, I would have heard fire gobbling up stores and houses.

The hot circle below my right shoulder blade began to sing more loudly, but that was a phantom, like the pain in a severed leg. It was just memory, brought back by the sound of small arms' fire. I crossed the next street in the fog, and then I couldn't take it anymore. Directly to my side, rising up two stories of solid darkened brick, was the old annex of the St Alwyn, now a Valu-Rite pharmacy. I went over to the wall, bent my knees, and pressed my back against the cold brick. After a couple of seconds, the heat and pressure began to shrink. Real relief from phantom pain, as good as a Percodan. If I could press my back against the cold wall for an hour, I thought, all the

675

bolts and fish hooks could go back to their rusty sleep.

I was standing half-crouched against the wall when a curly-haired young character in a black sleeveless T-shirt and baggy black pants came hurrying out of the arched little alleyway. He took a quick, automatic glance in my direction, turned away, then gave me a double take. He stopped moving with a kind of indolent, theatrical slowness. I pushed myself away from the wall. He was going to say something about the rattle of gunfire coming to us from the ghetto at that moment.

He grinned. That was disconcerting. He said, 'You stupid fuck,' even more disconcerting. Then he took a step near me, and I recognized him. Somewhere on the other end of the brick alley, tucked behind a dumpster or nestled in at the back of a liquor store, was a dark blue car with a lot of dents and scratches on its left side. He laughed at the recognition in my face. 'This is beautiful,' he said. 'I don't believe it, but it's beautiful.' He looked up and spread out his hands, as if thanking the god of lowlifes.

'You must be the new Billy Ritz,' I said. 'The old one had a little more style.'

'Nobody is gonna help you now, shithead. There's nowhere you can go.' He reached behind his back with his right hand, the muscles popping in his biceps and shoulders, and the hand came back filled with a solid black rod with shiny steel tips on both ends. A long blade popped out of the case. He was grinning again. He was going to have a good day, after all, and his boss was going to think he was a hot shot.

Ice formed in my stomach, in my lungs, along the inside of my chest. This was fear, a lot less of it than I had felt on the highway, and useful because of the anger that came along with it. I was safer here on the sidewalk than I had been tearing along on a fogbound highway. Nothing was going to come at me that I couldn't already see. I was

676

probably twenty-five years older than this creep and a lot less muscular, but at his age, I had spent an entire summer in a sweatbox in Georgia, dealing with lousy food and a lot of determined men coming at me with knives and bayonets.

He jabbed at me, just having fun. I didn't move. He jabbed again. I kept my feet planted. We both knew he was too far away to touch me. He wanted me to run, so that he could trot up behind me and clamp his left arm around my neck.

He prowled toward me, and I let my arms dangle, watching his hands and his feet. 'Jesus, you got nothing, you got no moves at all,' he said.

His right foot stabbed out, and his right arm came up toward me. I felt a blast of mingled adrenaline and rage and twisted to my left. I grabbed his wrist with my right hand and closed my left just above his elbow. In the half-second he could have done something to get his momentum back, he swiveled his head and looked into my eyes. I brought up my right knee and slammed my hands down as hard as I could. I even grunted, the way they recommended back in Georgia. His arm came apart in my hands – the two long bones snapped away from the elbow, and the big one, the radius, sliced through the skin of his inner arm like a razor. The knife clunked down onto the sidewalk. He made a small astonished sound, and I got both hands on his forearm and yanked it, using as much torque as I could. I was hoping it would come off, but it didn't. Maybe I was standing too close to him. He stumbled in front of me, and I saw his eyes bulge. He started screaming. I pushed him down, but he was already crumpled. He landed on his side with his knees drawn up. His chest was sprayed with blood, and blood pumped through the ragged hole in his arm.

I walked around him and picked up the knife. He was still screaming, and his eyes looked glazed. He thought he was going to die. He wasn't, but he'd never really use his right arm again. I walked up to him and kicked the place where his elbow used to be. He passed out.

I looked up and down the street. There wasn't a person in sight. I knelt down beside him and shoved my hand into the pocket of his pants. I found a set of keys and a number of slippery little things. I threw the keys into the storm drain and put my hand back into his pocket and came out with four double-wrapped little plastic envelopes filled with white powder. These I dropped into my jacket pocket. I rolled him over and picked the pocket on the other side. He had a fat little wallet with about a hundred dollars and a lot of names and addresses written on little pieces of paper. I lifted the flap and looked at his driver's license. His name was Nicholas Ventura, of McKinney Street, about five blocks west of Livermore. I dropped the wallet and walked away on legs made of air. At the end of the block I realized that I was still holding his knife. I threw it into the street. It bounced and clattered until it was a dark spot in the fog.

I had seen him before, waiting with three other men at a round table at the back of Sinbad's Cavern. He was part of the talent pool. I turned into Widow Street and got myself up the steps to the St Alwyn's entrance on my air-legs. I felt sick and weary, more sick than weary, but weary enough to lie down for a week. Instead of adrenaline, I could taste disgust.

The dried-out night clerk looked up at me and elaborately looked away. I went to the pay telephone and called 911. 'There's an injured man on the sidewalk alongside the St Alwyn Hotel,' I said. 'That's on Livermore Avenue, between South Sixth and South Seventh. He needs an ambulance.' The operator asked my name, and I hung up. Out of the sides of his eyes, the clerk watched me move toward the elevators. When I pushed the button, he said, 'You don't go up without you go through me.'

'I'll go through you, if that's what you really want,' I said. He moved like a ghost to the far end of the counter and began playing with a stack of papers.

9

I rapped twice on Glenroy's door. Nat Cole was singing about Frim-Fram sauce with shifafa on the side, and Glenroy called out, 'Okay, I'm coming.' I could barely hear him through the music. The door opened, and Glenroy's eager smile vanished as soon as he saw my face. He leaned out and looked around me to see if anyone else was in the corridor.

'Hey, man, I said for you to come before eight. Why don't you go downstairs, get a drink at the bar, and then call me from the lobby? It'll be okay, I just need some time, you know.'

'It's okay now,' I said. 'I have something for you.'

'I got some private business to do.'

I palmed two of the packets and showed them to him. 'Your man had an accident.'

He backed away from the door. I walked toward the table with the box and the mirror. Glenroy kept his eyes on me until I sat down. Then he closed the door. I could see caution, worry, and curiosity working in his eyes. 'I guess I should hear this story,' he said, and came toward the table like a cat padding into a strange room.

Glenroy took the chair across from me, put the palms of his hands on the table, and stared at me as if I were some neighborhood child who had suddenly displayed a tendency toward arson.

'Were you waiting for a grown-up delinquent named Nicholas Ventura?' I asked.

He closed his eyes and blew air through his nose.

'I want you to talk to me,' I said.

He opened his eyes as soon as I began to speak, and now he looked at me with an unhappy pity. 'I thought I told you about staying out of trouble. You looked like you understood me.'

'I had to take a trip today,' I said. 'Ventura was waiting for me. He tried to run me off the highway, and he nearly managed to do it.'

Glenroy let one hand drop to the table and pressed the other against his cheek. He wanted to close his eyes again – he'd have closed his ears, if he could.

'Then I came here,' I said. 'I parked a couple of blocks away. The accident was that he saw me when he was coming here to make his delivery. He brightened right up.'

'I got nothing to do with him, except for one thing,' he said. 'I can't explain him to you.'

'He pulled out a knife and tried to kill me. I took care of that. He isn't going to talk about it, Glenroy. He'll be too embarrassed. But I don't think he'll be around anymore.'

'You took his merchandise away from him?'

'I went through his pockets. That's how I learned his name.'

'I suppose it could be worse,' Glenroy said. 'As it is, I'm glad I'm getting on that plane to Nice the day after tomorrow.'

'You're not in any danger. I just want you to give me a name.'

'You're a fool.'

'I already know the name, Glenroy. I just want to make sure all the edges are nailed down. And then I want you to do something for me.'

He rolled his head sidways on his palm. 'If you want to

be my friend, give me that merchandise and leave me out of it.'

'I'm going to give it to you,' I said. 'After you tell me the name.'

'I'd rather stay alive,' he said. 'I can't tell you anything. I don't even know anything.' But he straightened up and pulled his chair closer to the table.

'Who was the detective that Billy Ritz worked for? Who helped him plant evidence, after he killed people?'

'Nobody knows that.' Glenroy shook his head. 'Some people might have worked out that that kind of business was goin' on, but those people made sure they stayed on the right side of Billy. That's all I can tell you.'

'You're lying,' I said. 'I'm going to flush that shit down the toilet – I need your help, Glenroy.'

He glowered at me for a moment, trying to work out how he could get what he wanted without endangering himself. 'Billy was *connected*,' he said. 'You know what I mean? He was all over the place.'

'What are you saying? That he was an informant for more than one detective?'

'That was the word.' He was deeply uncomfortable.

'You don't have to tell me any names. Just nod when I say the name of anyone who used Billy as a source.'

He chewed on it for a time and finally nodded.

'Bastian.'

He did not react.

'Monroe.'

He nodded.

'Fontaine.'

He nodded again.

'Wheeler.'

No response.

'Hogan.'

He nodded.

681

'Good God,' I said. 'What about Ross McCandless?'

Glenroy pursed his lips, and then nodded again.

'Any more?'

'Someone like Billy keeps his business to himself.'

'You didn't tell me a thing,' I said. This was far truer than I wished it to be. At least Glenroy had nodded when I said Paul Fontaine's name, but he had not given me the confirmation I wanted.

'What was that thing you wanted me to do?' he asked. 'Throw myself in front of a bus?'

'I want you to show me room 218,' I said.

'Shoo,' he said. 'Is that all? Show me what you got in your pocket.'

I took out the four packets and put them on the table in front of him. Glenroy picked up each in turn and hefted it for weight, smiling to himself. 'Guess I was his first stop of the night. This is a double eightball. Nick was gonna eyeball it down into packets, probably cut off a little for himself every time he did it.'

'Congratulations,' I said.

'Nick still out there?'

'I called 911. He's in a hospital by now. He'll have to stay there for a couple of days.'

'Maybe you and me will both stay alive for a while, after all.'

'To tell you the truth, Glenroy, it could have gone either way.'

'Now I *know* you're dangerous.' He pushed himself away from the table and stood up. 'You said you want to see James's old room?'

Before we left, he scooped up the plastic envelopes and put them in the wooden box.

10

Glenroy pushed the button marked 2 on the panel and leaned back on the wooden bar. 'What did you find out?'

'Bob Bandolier had a son,' I said. 'After Bob's wife died, he sent him away to live with relatives. I think he started killing people when he was a teenager. He enlisted under a phony name and went to Vietnam. He worked in a couple of police departments around the country and finally came back here.'

'Lot of detectives here were in Vietnam.' The elevator came to a stop, and the doors slid open. A corridor painted a dark, gloomy shade of green stretched out before us. 'But only one of them looks like he takes after Bad Bob.'

We stepped out, and Glenroy looked up at me speculatively, beginning to get worried again. 'You think this guy killed your friend's wife?'

I nodded. 'Which one?'

Glenroy motioned me down the hallway. He did not speak until we came around a corner and came up to the door of room 218. Yellow police tape was strung tautly across the frame, and a white notice on the door announced that entrance was a crime punishable by a fine and a jail term. 'All this trouble, and they never bothered to lock the door,' Glenroy said. 'Not that the locks would stop you, anyhow.'

I bent down to look at the keyhole in the doorknob. I didn't see any scratches.

Glenroy didn't even bother to look up and down the corridor. He just put his hand on the knob and opened the door. 'No sense in hanging around.' He bent under the tape and walked into the room.

I crouched down and followed him. Glenroy closed the door behind us.

'I was thinking of Monroe,' Glenroy said. 'He looks like Bob Bandolier. Monroe is a mean son of a bitch, too. He got a few people alone, you know, and they didn't look so good, time he got through with them.'

He was looking at the floor as he spoke. I couldn't take my eyes off the bed, and what he was telling me fought for space in my mind with the shock of what was before me. The bed reminded me of the chair in the basement of the Green Woman. Whoever had brought April Ransom into this room had not bothered to pull back the long blue quilt or uncover the pillows. A dark stain lay like a shadow across the bed, and runners and strings of the same dark noncolor dripped down the sides of the quilt. Brown splashes and spatters surrounded the words above the bed. BLUE ROSE had been written in the same spiky letters I had seen in the alleyway behind the hotel.

'A cop like that turns up, every now and then,' Glenroy said. He had wandered over to the window, which looked down into the passage behind the hotel.

'Goddamn, I hate being in this room.' Glenroy drifted off to the dresser unit that ran along the wall opposite the bed. Cigarette butts filled the ashtray on top of the dresser. 'Why did you want me to come here, anyhow?'

'I thought you might notice something,' I said.

'I notice I want to get out.' Glenroy finally glanced at the bed. 'Your buddy has a lot of those pens.'

I asked him what he meant.

'The words. They're blue. That makes three. Red, black, and blue.'

I looked at the wall again. Glenroy was right – the slogan was written in dark blue ink.

'If it's all the same to you, I'm going back upstairs.' Glenroy went to the door, cracked it open, and glanced back at me. His face was tight with impatience. I took in the slanting words for as long as I thought he could stand it, tingling with a recognition that would not come into focus.

I followed Glenroy back under the tape. 'You better not come back here for a while,' he said, and started toward the elevator.

I wandered down the hall until I came to a pair of wide metal doors. They led down to another pair of doors that must have opened into the lobby, and then continued down another few steps to the back entrance. I walked outside into the narrow alley behind the hotel, half-expecting a couple of policemen to come toward me with drawn guns. Cold fog moved up the alley from the brick passage, licking against the back of the pharmacy that had taken over the old annex. Up to my left, I could see the crumpled nose of Nick Ventura's car poking past the rear of the hotel.

I hurried through the passage. A few gunshots came from Messmer Avenue, a little more orange tinted the sky. A long smear of blood lay across the sidewalk. I walked around it and plodded through the fog until I got to the Pontiac. I kept seeing room 218 in my mind without understanding what had been wrong up there.

When I got close enough to the car to see it clearly, I groaned out loud. Some wayward child had happened along with a baseball bat and clubbed in the rear window. The Pontiac looked like it had been driven away from a junkyard. I didn't think John was going to react very gracefully to the sight of his car. I was surprised that I still cared.

PART THIRTEEN

Paul Fontaine

1

Back at John's, I took a couple of aspirins for the pain in my back and went upstairs. I didn't even bother with a book, I just stretched out on the guest bed and waited for unconsciousness. John must have been still on his way home from Chicago – I wasn't looking forward to his reaction to what had happened to his car. I had just decided to tell him about my meetings with Tom Pasmore when I witnessed my hand picking up the fourth, most disfigured photograph from the blood-soaked bed in the St Alwyn. I understood that if I shook the photograph while holding it upside down, the markings would fall away like hair cuttings. I upended and shook the little square. Dried-up ink fragments obediently dropped to the floor. I turned the photograph over and saw an image I knew – a photograph my mother had taken in front of the house on South Sixth Street. A three-year-old me stood on the sidewalk while my father, Al Underhill, crouched behind me, his hat slanted back on his head, his hand loose and proprietorial on my shoulder.

2

Some time later, an actual hand on my shoulder brought me back up into the real world. I opened my eyes to the gloating face of John Ransom, six or seven inches away from mine. He was almost demonic with glee. 'Come on,' he said, 'let's hear about it. You tell me your adventures, and I'll tell you mine.'

'Did you see your car?'

He pulled away from me, waving the trouble away with his thick hands.

'Don't worry about that, I understand. I almost had a real crack-up myself on the way to Chicago. You must have been sideswiped, right?'

'Someone ran me off the road,' I said.

He laughed and pulled the chair closer to the bed. 'Listen to this. It was perfect.'

John had made it from Purdum to Chicago in four hours, narrowly missing several incidents of the sort he'd assumed I'd had. The fog had vanished about thirty miles this side of Chicago, and he'd parked a block from the train station.

He had left the keys in the unlocked car and walked up the street. Two potential thieves had been chased away on the basis of being dressed too well. 'I mean, some yuppie, what's he going to do, actually *steal* it? Give me a break. I had to shut up some guy who started yelling for a cop, and he gave me a big lecture about leaving the keys in my car. Anyhow, this white kid finally comes up, gold chain around his neck, his pants halfway down his ass, no laces in his shoes, and when *this* jerk sees the keys he

690

starts ambling around the car, checking out the street to make sure nobody's watching him – I'm standing there, looking into a window, practically praying that he'll try the door.' And finally the boy had tried the open door, nearly fainted when it opened, and jumped in and driven away in the car of his dreams.

'The kid'll beat the shit out of it for a couple of weeks, total it, and I'll get the insurance. Perfect.' He all but covered his own face with kisses. Then he remembered that I had been in an accident and looked at me with a sort of humorous concern. 'So you got run off the road? What happened?'

I went into the bathroom, and he stood outside the door while I splashed water on my face and told him about coming back from Tangent.

I rubbed my face with a towel. John was standing in the doorway, chewing on the inside of his cheek.

'He pulled a knife on me, but I got lucky. I broke his arm.'

'Jesus,' John said.

'Then I went inside the hotel and took a look at the room where they found April.'

'What happened to the guy?'

'He's in the hospital now.'

I went toward the door, and John backed away and slapped me on the back as I came through. 'What was the point of going to the room?'

'To see if I'd notice anything.'

'It must be pretty bad,' John said.

'I have the feeling I missed something, but I can't work out what it was.'

'The cops have been over that room a million times. Ah, what am I saying? A cop is the one who did it.'

'I know who he is,' I said. 'Let's go downstairs, and I'll tell you the rest of my adventures.'

'You found out his name in Tangent? Somebody described him?'

'Better than that,' I said.

3

'John,' I said, 'I want to know where you were assigned after you brought the man you thought was Franklin Bachelor back to the States.'

We were sitting at the table, eating a dinner both of us had made up out of food we had come across in the refrigerator and the freezer. John wolfed down the meal as if he hadn't eaten in a week. He'd had two substantial glasses of the hyacinth vodka while we worked in the kitchen and opened another bottle of the Chateau Petrus from his cellar.

Since we had come downstairs, he had been debating out loud with himself whether he should really go back to Arkham next year. If you thought about it, he said, his book was really a higher duty than meeting his classes. Maybe he should admit that he had to move on to a new phase of his life. My question interrupted this self-absorbed flow, and he looked up from his plate and stopped chewing. He washed down the food in his mouth with wine.

'You know exactly where I was. Lang Vei.'

'Weren't you really somewhere else? A camp not far from Lang Vei?'

He frowned at me and sliced off another bit of veal. He took some more of the wine. 'Is this more wild stuff you got from that quartermaster colonel?'

'Tell me.'

He set down his knife and fork. 'Don't you think the

692

name of the cop is a lot more important? I've been really patient with you, Tim, I let you do your Julia Child number at the stove, but I don't feel like rooting around in ancient history.'

'Did someone tell you to say that you'd been at Lang Vei?'

He gave me the look you'd give a mule that had decided to stop moving. Then he sighed. 'Okay. After I finally made it to Khe Sanh, a colonel in Intelligence showed up and ordered me to tell people I'd been at Lang Vei. My orders were all rewritten, so as far as history goes, I *was* at Lang Vei.'

'Did you know why you were given those orders?'

'Sure. The army didn't want to admit how badly it fucked up.'

'Where were you, if you weren't at Lang Vei?'

'A little encampment called Lang Vo. We got wiped out right after Lang Vei was overrun. Me and a dozen Bru. The North Vietnamese took us apart.'

'After you came back from Langley, they sent you off to a postage stamp in the jungle.' So far, Colonel Runnel had been telling the truth. 'Why did they do that?'

'Why do they do anything? That's the kind of thing we did.'

'Did you think you were being punished for having brought back the wrong man?'

'It wasn't *punishment*.' He glared at me. 'I didn't lose any rank.'

Maybe he was right. But I thought that Runnel was right, too. John was beginning to flush, turning red from the neck up. 'Tell me what happened at Lang Vo.'

'It was a massacre.' He was looking straight into my eyes. 'First they shelled us, and then North Vietnamese regulars swarmed in, and then the tanks blasted the hell out of whatever was left standing.' His entire face had turned red. 'I felt like fucking Custer.'

'Custer didn't get out alive,' I said.

'I don't have to defend myself to you.' He jammed his fork into the home fries, brought one up to his mouth, and looked at it as if it had turned into a cockroach. He put the fork back down on his plate.

I said that I wanted to know what had happened.

'I made a mistake,' he said, and met my eyes again. 'You want to know what happened, that's what happened. I didn't think they'd send so much force after us. I didn't think it'd be a goddamn siege.'

I waited for him to explain how he had survived.

'Once things got hairy, I ordered everybody into this bunker, with firing slits raised above the ground. Two tunnels. It was a good system. It just didn't work against that many men. They pounded the shit out of us. They fired a grenade in through one of the slits, and that was pretty much that. I wound up flat on the ground with about a dozen guys lying on top of me. I couldn't see or hear. I could hardly breathe. All the blood almost drowned me. Finally, some guy got in through the tunnel and emptied a clip into us. Two, I think, but I wasn't really counting.'

'You couldn't see him.'

'I couldn't see anything,' he said. 'I thought I was dead. The way it turned out, I caught a round in my ass, and I had some grenade fragments in my legs. When I realized I was still alive, I crawled out. It took a long time.' He picked up his fork and stared at the fried bit of potato again before putting it back on his plate. 'A hell of a long time. The tunnels had collapsed.'

I asked him if he remembered Francis Pinkel.

John almost smiled. 'The little twerp who worked for Burrman? Sure. He came in the day before the shit hit the fan, gave us an hour of his precious time, and climbed back into the helicopter.'

According to Runnel's mysterious informant, Pinkel had visited Lang Vo on the day of the assault. It made more sense as John told it: the assault on John's camp would have taken at least a day to coordinate.

'Well,' I said, 'the twerp reported sighting an A Team under an American officer after he lifted off.'

'Really?' John raised his eyebrows.

'Do you remember Tom Pasmore asking if anyone might have a reason to want to injure you?'

'Pasmore? He's just living off his reputation.'

I said I didn't think that was true, and John snorted in contempt. 'What if I'd offered him a hundred thousand? Don't kid yourself.'

'But the point is, can you think of anyone with a grudge against you?'

'Sure,' he said. He was beginning to get irritated again. 'Last year I flunked a kid out of graduate school because he could hardly read. He has a grudge against me, but I don't think he'd murder anybody.' John looked at me as if I were being deliberately simpleminded. 'Am I wrong, or is there actually some point to this?'

'Did you ever think about the name of Fee Bandolier's corporation?'

'Elvee? No. I never thought about it. I'm getting a little tired of this, Tim.' He pushed his plate away and poured more wine into his glass.

'Lang Vei,' I said. 'Lang Vo.'

'This is *nuts*. I ask you a question, and you give me gobbledygook.'

'Fielding Bandolier enlisted in the army in 1961.'

'Great.'

'Under the name Franklin Bachelor,' I said. 'I guess he has a thing about initials.'

John had been raising his glass to his mouth. His arm stopped moving. His mouth opened a little wider, and his eyes turned cloudy. He took a big gulp of the wine and wiped his mouth with a napkin. 'Are you accusing me of something?'

'I'm accusing him, not you,' I said. 'Bachelor is resourceful enough to have made it back to the States under someone else's name. And he blamed you for his wife's death.'

Anger flared in John's eyes, and for a second I thought he might try to strangle me again. Then I saw a curtain of reflection pass across his face, and he began to look at me with a growing sense of understanding.

'Why would he wait all this time to get his revenge?'

'Because after he came into your bunker and emptied a couple of clips into the bodies, he thought you were dead.'

'So he wound up back here.' He said it flatly, as if this was to have been expected.

'He's been living in Millhaven since 1979, but he had no idea that you were back here, too.'

'How did he find out that I was alive?'

'He saw your picture in the paper. He killed Grant Hoffman two days later. Five days after that, he tried to kill your wife. His father murdered people at five-day intervals, and he was just following the pattern, even writing the same words.'

'To make the murders look like they were connected to the old Blue Rose case.'

'When April began writing to the department about the case, he went into the files and removed his father's statements. And moved his notes out of the Green Woman, in case anyone else got curious.'

'Franklin Bachelor,' John said. 'The Last Irregular.'

'Nobody knew what he really was,' I said. 'He had a lifetime of pretending to be someone else.'

'Tell me his name,' John said.

'Paul Fontaine,' I said.

John repeated the detective's name, slowly, his voice rising at the end. 'I can't believe it. Are you sure?'

'The man I saw in Ohio put his finger right on Fontaine's face,' I said.

The telephone went off like a bomb, and I jumped no more than a foot or two.

The answering machine cut in, and we heard Alan Brookner's conversational bellow, raised about 10 percent above its usual volume. 'Goddamn it, will you answer the phone? I'm sitting here all alone, the whole city's going crazy, and – '

John was already on his feet. Alan's voice clicked off as soon as John picked up the receiver, and from then on I could hear only half of the conversation. John was being placating, but to judge from the number of times he said, 'Alan, I can hear you' and 'No, I haven't been avoiding you,' placation did not occur. 'No, the police haven't been in touch,' he said, and moved the receiver a few inches from his ear. 'I will, I will,' he said. 'Of course you're worried. Everybody's worried.' He moved the receiver away from his ear again. Then: 'I know you don't care about what everybody else does, Alan, you never have.' He endured another long tirade, during which my guilt at not having visited Alan Brookner increased exponentially.

He put down the receiver and did a brief mime of exhausted patience, wobbling his knees and shaking his hands and his head. 'He assured me that he was going to call again. Is that startling news? No, it is not.'

'I guess we've been ignoring him,' I said.

'Alan Brookner has never been ignored for five whole minutes at a time.' John came back into the living room and collapsed into his chair. 'The problem is that Eliza goes home at five o'clock. All he has to do is eat the dinner she has warming in the oven, take off his clothes, and go to bed. But of course he doesn't do that. He has a couple of drinks and forgets about dinner. He watches the news, imagining it will be about himself and his daughter, there can't possibly be any other topic, the concept is ridiculous, and when he sees burning buildings and gunmen flitting through the fog he imagines that he is in danger' – John paused for a deep breath – 'because it cannot be possible that what's on the news is not directly related to him.'

'Isn't he just alarmed?'

'I've known him a lot longer than you have,' John said. 'He's going to keep on calling until I go over there.' He looked up at me with a speculative gleam. 'Unless you go. He adores *you*.'

'I don't mind visiting Alan,' I said.

'You must be some kind of frustrated nurse,' John grumbled. 'Anyhow, what do you say? If we're going to take a look inside Fontaine's house, this is the night.' He made a third attempt at eating the home fry on his fork, and this time got it into his mouth. Chewing, he challenged me with a look. I did not respond. He shook his head in disgust and polished off the last of the veal. Then he slugged down a mouthful of wine and kept his eyes on me, trying to provoke me into agreement.

'God, Tim, I hate to say this, but I seem to be the only guy around here who's willing to see a little action.'

I stared at him, and then I began to laugh.

'Okay, okay,' he said. 'I spoke out of turn. Let's see how bad it is before we make up our minds.'

4

We settled onto the couch in the living room, and John flicked on the television with the remote.

Looking more distressed than I had ever seen him, his hair slightly rumpled, his conservative tie out of plumb, Jimbo appeared on the screen, announcing for the hundredth time that the members of the Committee for a Just Millhaven had appeared at City Hall, led by the Reverend Clement Moore and accompanied by several hundred demonstrators, demanding a meeting with Merlin Waterford and a reconsideration of their demands. The mayor had sent out his deputy with the message that unscheduled appointments had never been and never would be permitted. The delegation had refused to leave the building. Arden Vass had sent in police to disperse the crowd, and after demands, counterdemands, and speeches, a teenage boy had been shot and killed by an officer who thought he had seen a pistol in the boy's hand. From a jail cell, the Reverend Clement Moore had issued the statement that 'Decades of racial injustice, racial insensitivity, and economic oppression had finally come home to roost, and the fires of rage will not be banked.'

A police car had been overturned and set on fire on North Sixteenth Street. Homemade incendiary bombs thrown into two white-owned businesses on Messmer Avenue had spread through the neighboring buildings, and fire fighters responding to the emergency had been fired upon from rooftops across the street.

Behind Jimbo's face, a camera showed figures running through the fog carrying television sets, piles of suits and dresses, armloads of groceries, mufflers, running shoes tied together by their laces. People trotted out of the fog, waved steaks and halogen lamps and cane-backed chairs at the camera, and disappeared again into the haze.

'Damage is presently estimated at the five-million-dollar level,' Jimbo said. 'For a report on some other disturbing aspects of the situation, here is Isobel Archer, live from Armory Place.'

Isobel appeared on the near side of a solid line of policemen separating her from a chaotic mob. She raised her voice to be heard over chants and howls. 'Reports of isolated fires and incidents of shooting have begun to come in from other sections of the city,' she said. A faint but distinct noise of breaking glass made her look over her shoulder. 'There have been several accounts of drivers being dragged from their cars on Central Divide and Illinois Avenue, and several downtown merchants have hired private security firms to protect their stores. I'm told that gangs of armed rioters are traveling in cars and shooting at other vehicles. Lone pedestrians have been attacked and beaten on Livermore Avenue and Fifteenth Street Avenue.' She winced at loud gunshots from somewhere on the far side of the line of police. 'At this point, I'm told that we are moving to the top of police head-quarters, where we may be able to show you something of the scale of the destruction.'

The anchor's stolid face appeared again on a split screen. 'On a personal note, Isobel, do you feel in danger yourself?'

'I believe that's why we're going to try to get to the roof,' she said.

Jimbo filled the entire screen again. 'While Isobel moves to a safer location, we advise all residents to draw their curtains, stay away from their windows, and refrain from leaving the house. Now. This just in. There are unconfirmed reports of arson and random gunfire in the fifteen hundred block of Western Boulevard, the twelve hundred block of Fifteenth Street Avenue, and sections of the near west side near the Galaxy Shopping Center. And now, Joe Ruddler with a commentary.'

Mouth already open, eyes flaring, cheeks blazing, Joe Ruddler's irate, balloonlike visage zoomed onto the screen. He looked as if he had just charged out of a cage. *'If any good comes out of this, it ought to be that those uninformed, soft-headed idiots who babble about gun control will finally come to their senses!'*

'This is the ideal time to take Fontaine's house apart,' John said. He went into the kitchen and came back with his glass and the rest of the wine. A little windblown and out of breath, Isobel Archer appeared on top of police headquarters to point at the places where we would be able to see fires, had we been able to see them.

'This place is going to look like San Francisco after the great quake,' John said.

'The fog won't last that long,' I said. 'It'll be gone by about midnight.'

'Oh, yeah,' John said. 'And Paul Fontaine will turn up at the front door, tell us he found Jesus too, and apologize for all the trouble he caused me.'

Alan Brookner called back around ten o'clock and held John on the phone for twenty minutes, ten of which John spent with the receiver a foot away from his head. When he hung up, he went straight into the kitchen and made a fresh drink.

A smiling young black face filled the screen as Jimbo announced that the teenager killed by a police bullet in City Hall was now identified as Lamar White, a seventeen-year-old honor student at John F. Kennedy High School. 'White seems to have been unarmed at the time of his shooting, and the incident will be under departmental investigation.'

The telephone rang again.

'John, John, John, John, John, John,' Alan said

through the answering machine. 'John, John, John, John, John, John.'

'You ever notice how they always turn into honor students as soon as they're dead?' John asked me.

'John, John, John, John, John . . .'

John got up and went to the telephone.

Jimbo said that Ted Koppel would be hosting a special edition of 'Nightline' from the Performing Arts Auditorium tomorrow night. A police spokesman announced that all roads and highways in and out of Millhaven were to be blocked by state troopers.

Clutching one hand to the side of his head, John wandered back into the living room. 'I have to go over there and get him,' he said. 'Do you think it's safe?'

'I don't think there's been any trouble up here,' I said.

'I'm not going out without that gun.' John looked at me as if he expected me to protest, and when I did not, he went upstairs and came back down buttoning the linen jacket over a lump at his waistband. I said I'd hold the fort. 'You think this is all a joke,' he said.

'I think it'd be better for Alan to spend the night here.'

John went to the door, opened it carefully, looked both ways, gave me a last mournful glance, and went outside.

I sat watching pictures of fire lapping up entire blocks while men and women trotted past the camera carrying what they had looted. Stocks must have been getting low – their arms were full of toilet paper and light bulbs and bottles of mineral water. When the phone rang again, I got up to answer it.

Alan was hiding in a closet. Alan was sitting in a pile of feces on his kitchen floor. Whatever the crisis was, John had given up.

I answered the telephone, and a voice I did not recognize asked to speak to Tim Underhill.

'Speaking,' I said.

The man on the other end of the line said he was Paul Fontaine.

5

When I didn't respond, he asked, 'Are you still there?'

I said I was still there.

'Are you alone?'

'For about five minutes,' I said.

'We have to talk about a certain matter. Informally.'

'What did you have in mind?'

'I have some information you might be interested in, and I think you have some I could use. I want you to meet me somewhere.'

'This is a funny time for a meeting.'

'Don't believe everything you hear on television. You'll be okay as long as you stay away from Messmer Avenue. Look, I'm at a pay phone near Central Divide, and I don't have much time. Meet me across Widow Street from the St Alwyn at two o'clock.'

'Why should I come?'

'I'll explain the rest there.' He hung up.

I put down the telephone and instantaneously found myself, as if by teleportation, seated again on the couch in front of the babbling television. Of course I had no intention of meeting Fontaine on a deserted street at two in the morning – he wanted to put me in a position where my death could be attributed to random violence.

John Ransom and I had to get out of Millhaven as soon as we could. If the fog lifted, we could get to the airport before Fontaine realized that I was not going to show up across from the St Alwyn. In Quantico, the FBI had experts who did nothing but think about people like Paul Fontaine. They could look into every homicide Fontaine had handled in Allentown and wherever else he had worked before returning to Millhaven. What I most needed was what I didn't have – the rest of the notes.

Where were Fontaine's narratives of his murders? Now it seemed to me that Ransom and I had merely rushed in and out of the house on South Seventh Street. We should have pried up floorboards and punched holes in the walls.

Once Fontaine realized that I was not going to show up to be murdered, he'd check every flight that left Millhaven during the night. Then he'd go to South Seventh Street and make a bonfire in the old furnace.

My thoughts had reached this unhappy point when the front door opened on a loud burst of talk, and John came in, literally leading Alan Brookner by the hand.

6

Alan wore the wrinkled top of a pair of pajamas under a gray suit jacket paired with tan trousers. John had apparently dressed his father-in-law in whatever he had pulled first out of his closet. Alan's hair drifted around his head, and his wild, unfocused eyes communicated both belligerence and confusion. He had reached a stage where he had to express himself as much through gesture as verbally, and he raised his hands to his head, carrying John's hand along. John released him.

Alan smacked his forehead with the hand John had just released. 'Don't you get it?' He boomed this question toward John's retreating back. 'It's the answer. I'm giving you the solution.'

John stopped moving. 'I don't want that answer. Sit

down, Alan. I'll get you a drink.'

Alan extended his arms and yelled, 'Of *course* you want it! It's exactly what you want.' He took in my presence and came through the foyer into the living room. 'Tim, talk sense to this guy, will you?'

'Come over here,' I said, and Alan moved toward the couch while keeping his eyes on John until he had passed through into the kitchen. Then he sat down beside me and ran both hands through his hair, settling most of it into place.

'He thinks he can solve everything by running away. You have to stay in place and face it.'

'Is that the answer you're trying to give him?' I asked. John had evidently told the old man of his plans to move abroad.

'No, no, no.' Alan shook his head, irritated by my inability to understand the matter all at once. 'I have an endowed chair, and all I have to do is make sure that John gets the chair, starting next term. I can *give* it to him.'

'Can you appoint your own successor?'

'Let me tell you something.' He gripped my thigh. 'For thirty-eight years, the administration has given me every single thing I ever asked for. I don't think they'll stop now.'

Alan addressed these last words to John, who had returned to set a dark brown drink in front of him.

'It's not that simple.' John took the chair at the end of the couch and turned to look at the television.

'Of course it is,' Alan insisted. 'I didn't want to admit what was happening to me. But I'm not going to pretend anymore.'

'I'm not going to carry on for you,' John said.

'Carry on for yourself,' Alan said. 'I'm giving you a way to keep yourself whole. What you want to do is run away. It's no good, kid.'

'I'm sorry you feel rejected,' John said. 'It isn't personal.'

'Of *course* it's personal,' Alan roared.

'I'm sorry I brought it up,' John said. 'Don't make me say any more, Alan.'

Alan overflowed with all he felt – he had been waving his arms while he spoke, splashing whiskey onto himself, the couch, and my legs. Now he gulped from the glass and groaned. I had to get John away from Alan and talk to him in private.

Alan came out of his sulk long enough to give me a way to do this.

'Talk to him, Tim. Make him see reason.'

I stood up. 'Let's go in the kitchen, John.'

'Not you, too.' He gave me a disbelieving glare.

I said John's name in a way that was like kicking him in the foot, and he looked sharply up at me. 'Oh,' he said. 'Okay.'

'Attaboy,' Alan said.

I set off for the kitchen. John trailed along behind me. I opened the door and stepped outside. What was left of the fog curled and hung above the grass. John came out and closed the door.

'Fontaine called,' I said. 'He wants to trade information. We're supposed to meet at two o'clock on Widow Street, across from the St Alwyn.'

'That's *great*,' John said. 'He still thinks we trust him.'

'I want to get out of town tonight,' I said. 'We can go to the FBI and tell them everything we know.'

'Listen, this is our chance. He'll hand himself to us on a plate.'

'You want me to meet him on a deserted street in the middle of the night?'

'We'll go down early. I'll hide in that little alley next to the pawnshop and hear everything he says. Together, we can handle him.'

'That's crazy,' I said, and then I understood what he really intended to do. 'You want to kill him.'

Alan shouted our names from within the kitchen, and John bit his lip and checked to see how persuasive he had been. 'Running away won't work,' he said, unconsciously echoing what Alan had just said.

The door swung open, and Alan stood framed in a spill of yellow light. 'You getting him to see reason?'

'Give us a little more time,' I said.

'The rioting seems to be pretty much over,' Alan said. 'Looks like four people got killed.' When we said nothing, he backed away from the door. 'Well, I won't get in your way.'

When Alan had retreated from the door, I said, 'You want to kill him. Everything else is just window dressing.'

'How bad is that, as a last resort? It's probably the only safe way to deal with the guy.' He waited for me to see the force of this. 'I mean, there's no doubt in your mind that he's Bachelor, is there?'

'No,' I said.

'He murdered my wife. And Grant Hoffman. He wants to murder you, and after that he wants to murder me. How concerned are you about the civil rights of a guy like that?'

'Two more!' Alan bawled through the window. 'Total of six dead! Ten million dollars in damage!'

'I won't con you,' John said. 'I think it's a lot more likely that Fontaine will wind up dead than on trial.'

'I do, too,' I said. 'You better make sure you know what you're doing.'

'It's my life too.' John held out his hand, and when I took it, I felt my uneasiness double on itself.

Hovering near the sink when we came back inside, Alan looked at our faces for clues to what had been decided. He had shucked the suit jacket, and parts of his pajama top had worked their way out of his trousers.

'You get things straightened out?'

'I'll think about it,' John said.

'Okay!' Alan boomed, taking this as surrender. 'That's all I wanted to hear, kiddo.' He beamed at John. 'This calls for a celebration, what d'ya say?'

'Help yourself, please.' John waved his hand at the evidence that Alan had already been helping himself. A scotch bottle and a glass with slivers of ice floating in dark brown liquid stood on the counter. Alan poured more whiskey into the glass and turned again to John. 'Come on, join me, otherwise it's not a celebration.'

John went into the living room, and I looked at my watch. It was about eleven-thirty. I hoped John was going to have sense enough to keep sober. Alan gripped me by the shoulder. 'God bless you, boy.' He pulled another glass from the shelf and splashed whiskey into it. 'It's not a celebration unless you join in.'

John was going to lead Alan on until I left town, and then he'd refuse the chair. That would be the end of it. I felt as though I'd just assented to a second murder. When John returned, he raised his eyebrows at the drink before me and then smiled. 'Something to calm the nerves.'

Alan clinked glasses with John, then with me. 'I feel better than I have all day.'

'Cheers,' John said, raising his glass and giving me an ironic glance. His jacket shifted far enough to catch on the handle of the revolver, and he quickly pulled it back into place.

I tasted the scotch. My whole body shuddered.

'Thirsty, eh?' Alan took a gulp and grinned at both of us. He seemed almost half-crazy with relief.

He and Alan left the kitchen, and I poured the drink out into the sink. When I came back into the living room, the two of them were back in their old places, staring at the television.

Alan's pajama top had come all the way out of his

708

trousers, and a bright, unhealthy flush covered his cheek-bones. He was saying, 'We should go into the ghetto, set up storefront classrooms, really work with these people. You start with a pilot program and then you expand it until you have a couple of real classes going.'

For another thirty minutes, we stared at the screen. The family of the boy who had been killed in City Hall announced through a lawyer that they were praying for peace. A pale blue map indicated burned-out neighbor-hoods with little red flames and areas where gunfire had taken place with little black pistols. John refilled Alan's glass. His hair and necktie back in place, Jimbo declared that the worst of the rioting seemed to be over and that police had restored order to all but the most troubled neighborhoods. Fire fighters trained hoses on a long row of blazing shop fronts.

At ten past twelve, when Alan's head had begun to loll forward on his chest, the telephone rang again. John jumped up and then waved me off the couch. 'Go on, get it, he's checking in,' he said.

Alan raised his head and blinked.

'You said I should call,' a woman whispered. 'Well, I'm calling.'

'You have the wrong number,' I said.

'Is this Al Underhill's boy? You said I should call. He's back. I just saw him go into the living room.'

I opened my mouth, but no words came out.

'Don't you remember?'

'Yes, Hannah, I remember,' I said.

'Maybe you don't want to do anything, it's such a terrible night – '

'Stay in the house and keep your lights off,' I said.

7

I came back into the living room and told Alan that I had to speak privately to John again. Before Alan had time to ask any questions, John was up on his feet and leading me into the kitchen. He went as far as the back door and then whirled to face me. 'What did he say? Does he want you to come now?'

'Hannah Belknap called to tell me that she saw someone in the house next door.'

'What is he doing there *now*?'

'He might be taking advantage of the chaos to move his notes again.'

'What are you talking about?'

'Maybe we didn't look hard enough,' I said. 'They have to be there – it's the safest place.'

John pursed his lips. 'He might have decided to destroy them.'

This possibility had occurred to me the second before John spoke it. Then I realized that Hannah had seen Fontaine in his old living room. 'He's upstairs now,' I said. 'If we get down there fast enough, we might be able to catch him with them.'

John opened his mouth, making up his mind. His eyes were large and clear and unreadable. 'Let's go,' he said. 'It's even better.'

I thought it was better, too, but for different reasons. If we could catch Fontaine with his records, we had a better chance of bringing him to justice than if we simply met him on an empty street. All we had to do was get down to South Seventh Street before Fontaine got away or burned the records of his secret life. My next thought was

710

that we actually had plenty of time – if Fontaine had returned to his old house on this night, it was probably to wait out the two hours before the meeting he had arranged.

Alan appeared in the kitchen door. 'What's going on? What was that phone call?'

'Alan, I'm sorry, but there's no time to explain,' John said. 'Tim and I have to go somewhere. We might have some good news for you.'

'Where are you going?'

'Sorry, but it's none of your business.' John pushed his way past the old man, who glanced at me and then took off after his son-in-law.

'I'll decide if it's my business or not,' Alan said, a little louder than before but still a long way from shouting.

They were standing in the middle of the living room, about two feet from each other. Alan jabbed his finger at John. 'Obviously, this mission of yours does concern me, if you say that you'll come back with good news. I'm coming along.'

John turned to me in total exasperation.

'There might be some danger,' I said.

'That settles it.' Alan grabbed his jacket from the couch and wrenched it on. 'I am *not* going to be left in the dark. That's that.'

'Alan – '

Alan walked to the front door and opened it.

Something happened to John's face – it was not just that he gave up on the spot, but all resistance left him. 'Fine,' he said. 'Come along. But you're going to sit in the backseat, and you're not going to do anything until we tell you to do it.'

Alan looked at him as if he'd just smelled something nasty, but he turned away and went outside without protest.

'This is nuts,' I said to John. '*You're* nuts.'

711

'I didn't notice you doing much to stop him,' John said. 'We'll make him stay in the car. Maybe a witness will come in handy.'

'A witness to what?'

The car door slammed.

Instead of responding, John went outside. I went after him and closed the door. Alan was already enthroned in the backseat, facing forward, ignoring us. John walked around to the passenger door. I looked up and saw that the night was perfectly clear. The row of street lamps marched down toward Berlin Avenue, and a scattering of stars lay across the black sky. I got into the car and started the engine.

'This has something to do with April's death,' Alan boomed from the backseat. It was a statement, not a question.

'Maybe,' John said.

'I can see right through you. You're made of glass.'

'Would you please shut up, maybe?'

'Fine,' Alan said. 'I'll do that.'

8

Gangs of boys standing outside the taverns and the factory walls stared at us when we drove through the valley. John put his hand on the butt of the revolver, but the boys stepped back deeper into the shadows and followed us with their eyes.

A police car turned out of a side street and stayed with us all the way down Goethals. I waited for the flashing lights and the siren. The car followed us onto Livermore. 'Lose him,' John said, and I made a careful right turn onto South Second and looked in the rearview mirror.

The police car kept moving in a straight line down Livermore.

On Muffin Street, I turned left and drove past the rows of quiet houses. Through most of the dark windows flickered the gray-green of the television screen. They were sitting in the dark in front of their sets, watching what was left of the excitement. Finally, I came to South Seventh and turned down toward Bob Bandolier's old house. Two blocks away, I cut off the headlights and drifted past the darkened houses until I reached the same place where John and I had parked in the fog. I pulled in next to the curb and looked at John.

'Okay.' He turned around to speak to Alan. 'We're going to go into a house in the next block. If you see a man come out through the front door, lean over the seat and tap the horn. Tap it, Alan, don't honk the thing, just give it enough of a touch to make a short, sharp sound.' He looked at me, still thinking, and then turned back to Alan. 'And if you see lights come on in the window, in any window, or if you hear shots, get out of the car and hustle up there as fast as you can and start banging on the front door. Make a hell of a lot of noise.'

'What *is* this about?' Alan asked.

'In a word, April,' John said. 'Do you remember what I told you to do?'

'April.'

'That's right.'

'I'm not going to sit in this car,' Alan said.

'For God's sake,' John said. 'We can't waste any more time arguing with you.'

'Good.' Alan decided the issue by opening his door and climbing out of the car.

I got out and went around the rear to stand in front of him. John softly closed the passenger door and moved a couple of feet away, deliberately distancing himself. Haggard and defiant, Alan tilted his chin up and tried to stare

713

me down. 'Alan,' I whispered, 'we need you to stand watch for us. We're meeting a policeman inside that house' – I pointed at it – 'and we want to get some boxes of papers from him.'

'Why – ' he began in his normal voice, and I put my finger in front of my mouth. He nodded and, in his version of a whisper, asked, 'Why didn't you ask me along in the first place, if you needed me to stand watch?'

'I'll explain when we're done,' I said.

'A policeman.'

I nodded.

He leaned forward, curling his fingers, and I bent down. He put his mouth next to my ear. 'Does John have my gun?'

I nodded again.

He stepped back, his face rigid. He wasn't giving anything away. John moved up the block, and I went toward him, looking back at Alan. He had the monkey-king look again, but at least he was standing still. John began walking across the street, and I moved along the side of the car and caught up with him before he reached the next curb. I looked back at Alan. He was walking past the front of the car, clearly intending to keep pace with us on the other side of the street. I waved him back toward the car. He didn't move. A single gunshot came from what I thought was the northwest. When I looked back at Alan, he was standing in the same place.

'Let the old fool do what he wants,' John said. 'He will, anyhow.'

We went toward the Bandolier house with Alan trailing along on the other side of the street. When we reached the boundary of the property, John and I walked up onto the lawn at the same instant. I looked back at Alan, who was dithering on the sidewalk across the street. He stepped forward and sat on the curb. From one of the houses on our side of the street, Jimbo's bland, slow-moving voice drifted through an open window.

I went up toward the side of the house, hearing John pull the fat wad of keys out of his pocket. I hoped he could remember which one had worked the last time. We began working our way down the peeling boards.

When we reached the corner of the house, I grasped John's shoulder and kept him from walking into the backyard.

'Wait,' I whispered, and he turned around to face me. 'We can't go in the back.'

'Sure we can,' he said.

'We wouldn't make it halfway across the kitchen before he knew we were in the house.'

'So what do you want to do?'

'I want to get on the porch,' I said. 'You stand against the building, where he can't see you when he opens the door.'

'And then what?'

'I knock on the door and ask if I can see him now. He has to open it. He doesn't have any choice. As soon as he opens the door, Alan'll stand up and shout, and then I'll go in low and you come in high.'

I jerked my head sideways, and we crept back along the side of the house.

Alan looked up at us as we crept back into view on the side of the porch. I put my finger to my lips, and he squinted at me and then nodded. I pointed up toward the porch and the door. He stood up from the curb. *Stay there*, I motioned. I mimed knocking and pretended to open a door. He nodded again. I poked my head forward, as if I were looking out, then put my hands on the sides of my mouth and waggled my head. He made a circle with his thumb and forefinger and stepped back off the sidewalk into the deeper darkness of the lawn behind it.

We came around the side of the porch and moved silently over the site of Bob Bandolier's old rose garden.

715

Alan came a little forward off the lawn. Someone in the old Bandolier living room stood up on a creaking board and began pacing. Fontaine was walking around in his childhood, charging himself up.

Everything fell apart before John and I reached the porch steps.

Alan bellowed, '*Stop! Stop!*'

'Goddamn,' John said, and took off across the lawn. Alan had misunderstood what he was supposed to do. I came up out of my own crouch and ran toward the steps before Fontaine could open the door.

But the front door was already open – that was what Alan had been yelling about. Paul Fontaine stepped outside, and a squad car, the same car we had seen patroling, turned into South Seventh from Livermore. Its light bar had not been turned on.

'Goddamn you, Underhill,' Fontaine said.

Alan blared, '*Is that him?*'

A light came on in the living room of the house behind him and in bedrooms of the houses on either side.

'*Is that the man?*'

Fontaine swore, either at me or at the world in general. He came running down the steps, and I tried to get away from him by cutting across the lawn toward John.

'Come back here, Underhill,' Fontaine said.

I stopped running, not because of his words, but because I thought I saw someone moving through the darkness between the houses behind John and Alan Brookner. Alan was staring wildly from Fontaine to me and back, and John was still trying to calm him down.

'I'm not letting you get away,' Fontaine said. The man between the houses across the street had vanished, if he had ever been there at all. The patrol car swung up to the curb about thirty feet away, and Sonny Berenger and another patrolman stepped out. As he uncurled, Sonny was looking straight at John and Alan – he had not even seen us yet.

'*Underhill*,' Fontaine said.

Then Alan ripped the big revolver out from under John's jacket and jumped down into the street. Instead of going after him, John flattened out on the sidewalk. Alan raised the gun. He fired, and then fired again in a chaos of flares and explosions that filled the street. I heard people yelling and saw Alan drop the gun a second before I realized that I was lying down. I tried to get up. Pain yanked me back down into the grass. I had been hit in the front, but the pain blared out from the hot circle in my back. It felt as if I'd been hit with a sledgehammer.

I turned my head to see Fontaine. The big wheel of the world spun around me. Part of the wheel was a black shoe at the end of what looked like a mile-long gray leg. When the world came right-side up again, I turned my head very slowly in the other direction. I saw the stitching around a buttonhole of a gray suit. The reek of smoke and ashes came from his clothes. On the other side of the buttonhole a white shirt printed with a huge red blossom jerkily rose and fell. Alan had managed to hit us both. I got the elbow of my good arm under me, hitched up my knees, and pushed myself toward him. Then I rolled up on my elbow and saw the other patrolman running toward us.

A few inches away from mine, Fontaine's face was dull with shock. His eyes focused on mine, and his mouth moved.

'Tell me,' I said. I don't know what I meant – tell me everything, tell me how Fee Bandolier turned into Franklin Bachelor.

He licked his lips. 'Shit,' he said. His chest jerked up again, and blood gouted out of him and drenched my arm. 'Bell.' Another gout of blood soaked my arm, and the policeman's upper body appeared above us. Two rough hands dragged me away from Fontaine. I said, 'Ouch,' using what felt like commendable restraint, and the cop said, 'Hang in there, just hang in there,' but not to me.

I stared up at the black, starry sky and said, 'Get Sonny.' I hoped I would not die. I was floating in blood.

Then Sonny bent over me. I could hear the other cop doing something to Fontaine and visualized him slapping a big pressure bandage over the wound in his chest. But that was not where we were, that was somewhere else. 'Are you going to make it?' Sonny asked, looking as if he hoped the answer were no.

'I owe you one, and here it is,' I said. 'Along with a lot of other people, Fontaine killed that graduate student and Ransom's wife. He was a Green Beret officer named Franklin Bachelor, and he grew up in this house as Fielding Bandolier. Check up on a company named Elvee Holdings, and you'll find out he was tied into Billy Ritz. Somewhere in this house, you'll find two boxes of notes Fontaine made on all his killings. And inside a couple of boxes in the basement, you'll find his father's photographs of the places where he killed the original Blue Rose victims.'

As I said all this, Sonny's face went from rigid anger to ordinary cop impassivity. I figured that was a long distance. 'I don't know where the notes are, but the pictures are behind the furnace.'

His eyes flicked toward the house. 'Fontaine owns it, through Elvee Holdings. Also the Green Woman Taproom. Look at the Green Woman's basement, you'll see where Billy Ritz died.'

He took it all in – his world was whirling over on itself as sickeningly as mine had just done, but Sonny was not going to fail me. I nearly fainted from sheer relief. 'The ambulance'll be here in a second,' he said. 'That old guy was April Ransom's father?'

I nodded. 'How is he?'

'He's talking about the kingdom of heaven,' Sonny said.

Oh yes, of course. The kingdom of heaven. Where a certain man had wished to kill a noble, tested his sword by striking it against the wall, and gone out and killed the noble. What else would he be talking about?

'How's Fontaine?'

'I think the crazy old bastard killed him,' he said, and then the huge space he had occupied above me was filled again with black, starry night. Sirens came screaming into the street.

PART FOURTEEN

Ross McCandless

1

During the journey in the ambulance, as endless as if we were going to some hospital on the moon, my body detached itself from my anxiety and settled into its new condition. I was awash in blood, bathed in it, blood covered my chest and my arms and hung like a sticky red syrup on my face, but most of it belonged to the dead or dying man on the next stretcher. I was going to live. One paramedic labored over Paul Fontaine's body while another cut off my shirt and looked at my wound. He held up two fingers in front of my face and asked how many I saw. 'Three,' I said. 'Just kidding.' He jabbed me with a needle. I heard Fontaine's body leap up off the stretcher as they tried to jump-start him, once, twice, three times. 'Holy moly,' said the paramedic whose face I had not seen, 'I think this guy is Paul Fontaine.' 'No shit,' said the other. His face loomed again above mine, friendly, reassuringly professional, and black. 'And you a cop, too? What's your name, partner?'

'Fee Bandolier,' I said, and startled him by laughing.

Whatever he had goosed into my veins put my pain to sleep and caused my anxiety to retreat another three or four feet toward the roof of the ambulance, where it hung like an oily cloud. We, the anxiety, the paramedics, the leaping corpse, and myself, whirled forward on our journey to the moon. 'This Fontaine, he's a DOA,' said the other paramedic, and from the oily cloud came the information that I had heard Fontaine's last words, but understood only one of them. He had struggled to speak – he had licked his lips and forced out a syllable he wanted me to hear. *Bell*. The bell tolls, ask not for whom. The tintinnabulation that so musically wells, what a tale their terror tells, how the danger sinks and swells. I wondered what was happening to Alan Brookner, I wondered if Sonny Berenger would be able to remember everything I'd told him. I had the feeling that a lot of policemen would be coming to see me, in my hospital on the moon. Then I floated away.

2

I woke up with the enormous drill-like head of an X-ray machine aimed at the right side of my chest, most of which was covered with a bloody pad. A technician armored in a diving helmet and a lead vest was ordering me to stand still. Instead of my clothes, I was wearing a flimsy blue hospital gown unbuttoned at the back and draped down off my right shoulder like a toga. Someone had cleaned all the blood off me, and I smelled like rubbing alcohol. It came as a surprise that I was standing up by myself. 'Could you *please* try to stand still?' asked the surly beast in the armor, and the drill clicked and whirred. 'Now turn around, and we'll do your back.' I found that I could turn around. Evidently I had been performing miracles like this for some time. 'We'll have to get that arm up,' said the beast, and came out from behind his machine to take my right arm by the elbow and firmly rip it away from my shoulder. He paid no attention to the noises I made. 'Hold it like that.' Click. Whir. 'You can go back to your room now.'

'Where am I?' I asked, and he laughed. 'I'm serious. What hospital is this?'

He walked out without speaking, and a nurse hurried forward out of nowhere with a long blue splint festooned with dangling white strips of Velcro and the information that I was in St Mary's Hospital. Here was another homecoming: it was in St Mary's that I had spent two months of my seventh year, and where a nurse named Hattie Bascombe had told me that the world was half night. A great dingy pile of brown brick occupying about a quarter-mile of Vestry Street, the hospital was a block away from my old high school. In real time, if there is such a thing, the whole endless journey in the ambulance could have taken no more than five minutes. The nurse clamped the sling onto my arm, tied up my gown, deposited me in a wheelchair, pushed me down a corridor, loaded me into an empty elevator, unloaded me, and then navigated me through a maze of hallways to a room with a high bed, both evidently mine. A lot of people wanted to talk to me, she said, I was a pretty popular guy. I said, 'I vant to be alone.' She was too young to know about Greta Garbo, but she left me alone anyhow.

A bemused-looking doctor with a long manila envelope in one hand came in about ten minutes later. 'Well, Mr Underhill,' he said, 'you present us with an unusual problem. The bullet that struck you traveled in a nice straight line past your lung and came to rest beneath your right shoulder blade. But according to these X rays, you're carrying so much metal around in your back that we can't distinguish the bullet from everything else. Under the circumstances, I think we'll just leave it there.'

Then he shifted on his feet and smiled down at me with the envelope of X rays dangling over his crotch in his joined hands. 'Would you mind settling a little dispute between me and the radiologist? What happened to you, some kind of industrial accident?'

He had clear blue eyes, a thick flop of blond hair on his forehead, and no lines at all, none, not even crow's feet. 'When I was a little boy,' I said, 'I swallowed a magnet.'

A tiny, almost invisible horizontal wrinkle, as fine as a single hair on a baby's head, appeared in the center of his forehead.

'Okay,' I said. 'It was more in the nature of foreign travel.' He didn't get it. 'If you're not going to operate, does that mean that I get to go home tomorrow?'

He said that they wanted to keep me under observation for a day or two. 'We want to keep you clear of infections, see that your wound begins to heal properly.' He paused. 'And a police lieutenant named McCandless seemed concerned that you stay in one place. I gather that you can expect a lot of visitors over the next few days.'

'I hope one of them brings me something to read.'

'I could pick up some magazines from the lounge, if you like, and bring them to you the next time I'm in this wing.'

I thanked him, and he smiled and said, 'If you tell me how foreign travel can put about a pound of metal fragments in your back.'

I asked how old the radiologist was.

That little baby-hair wrinkle turned up in his forehead again. 'About forty-six, forty-seven, something like that.'

'Ask him. He'll explain it to you.'

'Get some rest,' he said, and turned off the lights when he left.

As soon as he was gone, whatever they had given me while I was still only semiconscious began to wear off, and a wide track through my body burst into flame. I groped around for the bell to ring the nurse and finally found it hanging on a cord halfway down the side of the mattress. I pushed the button twice, waited a long time, and then pushed it again. A black nurse with stiff, bristling orange hair came in about twenty minutes later and said that I was due for a painkiller in about an hour. I didn't need it now, I just *thought* I needed it now. Out she went. The flames laughed and caroused. An hour later, she turned on the lights, wheeled in a tray with a row of needles lined up like dental tools, told me to roll over and jabbed me in the butt. 'See?' she said. 'You didn't really need it until now, did you?'

'Anticipation is half the fun,' I said. She turned off the light and went away. The darkness started to move over me in long, smooth waves.

When I woke up, the window at the end of the room shone with a delicate pink light. The happy flames were already racing around and organizing another shindig. A little stack of magazines stood on the bedside table. I picked them up to see what they were. The doctor had brought me copies of *Redbook*, *Modern Maturity*, *Modern Bride*, and *Longevity*. I guessed the hospital didn't subscribe to *Soldier of Fortune*. I opened *Redbook* and began reading the advice column. It was very interesting on the subject of menopause, but just when I was beginning to learn something new about progesterone, my first visitor of the day arrived. Two visitors, actually, but only one of them counted. The other was Sonny Berenger.

3

The man who followed Sonny through the door had a wide, deeply seamed brick-colored face and short reddish hair shot with gray that rolled back from his forehead in tight waves. His tweed jacket bracketed a chest about four feet across. Next to Sonny Berenger, he looked like a muscular dwarf who could bend iron bars and bite nails in half. The detective gave me a quick, unsettling glance and ordered Sonny to close the door.

He came up to the bed and said, 'My name is Ross McCandless, and I'm a lieutenant in Homicide. We have a lot to talk about, Mister Underhill.'

'That's nice,' I said.

Sonny came back from shutting the door and went to the foot of the bed. He looked about as animated as an Easter Island statue, but at least he didn't look hostile.

McCandless pulled up the chair and parked himself about two feet from my head. His light blue eyes, set close to his sharp little pickax of a nose, were utterly flat and dead, far past the boundary where they could have been called expressionless. They did not even have enough life in them to be lifeless. I was suddenly aware that the three of us were alone in the room and that whatever happened between us was going to shape reality. Sonny was going to contribute, or he would have been left out in the hall, I was going to contribute, but whatever reality we created together was mainly going to suit McCandless.

'How are you feeling? You doing all right?'

'No serious damage,' I said.

'Yeah. I talked to your doctor.' That took care of the social portion of our encounter. 'I understand you feel you have some interesting information about the late Detective Fontaine, and I want to know about that. All about it. I've been talking with your friend Ransom, but it seems that you're the key to what happened on South Seventh Street last night. Why don't you just explain that whole situation to me, as you see it.'

'Is Officer Berenger going to take a statement?'

'There's no need for that right now, Mr Underhill. We are going to proceed with a certain amount of care here. In due time, you will be asked to sign a statement all of us will be able to live with. I assume you already knew

728

that Detective Fontaine died of his wounds.'

He had already cut Fontaine loose – now he was trying to control the damage. He wanted me to give him a quick route out of the chaos. I nodded. 'Before I begin, could you tell me what happened to John and Alan Brookner?'

'When I left Armory Place, Mr Ransom was being questioned by Detective Monroe. Professor Brookner is being held under observation at County Hospital. Bastian is trying to get a statement from him, but I don't think he's having much luck. The professor isn't very coherent.'

'Has he been charged with anything?'

'You might say this conversation is part of that process. Last night, you made certain statements to Officer Berenger concerning Paul Fontaine and a company called Elvee Holdings. You also mentioned the names Fielding Bandolier and Franklin Bachelor. Why don't you start by telling me how you became aware of Elvee Holdings?'

'I had dinner with John on my first night in Millhaven,' I said. 'Just as we were finishing, he called the hospital and heard that his wife was showing signs of improvement, and he immediately left the restaurant to walk to Shady Mount.' I described how I had noticed that a car was following him, taken down the license number in my notebook, trailed after both of them to Shady Mount, spoken to the driver in the hospital lobby, and recognized him from my visit earlier that day. 'The driver turned out to be Billy Ritz.'

'And what did you do with the license number?'

'The next day I went to the hospital without knowing that April had been killed, saw Paul Fontaine along with a lot of policemen on her floor, and gave him the license number.'

McCandless looked briefly at Sonny. 'You gave it to Fontaine?'

'Actually, I read it to him out of my notebook. I

729

thought I had given him the sheet of paper, but at April's funeral, I opened my notebook and saw that I still had it. That afternoon, when John and Alan and I went to the morgue to identify Grant Hoffman's body, I saw the same car parked next to the Green Woman Taproom.' I told him about seeing Billy Ritz putting cardboard boxes in his trunk. McCandless was still waiting to see how all this led to Elvee Holdings. I repeated what I had told John about working with a computer at the university library. 'It turned out that a company named Elvee Holdings owned both the car and the Green Woman. I got the names and addresses of the corporate officers.' When I gave him the names, McCandless could not keep from registering surprise – he'd been busy with the consequences of the riot, and he was starting his own research with me.

'We're checking on Elvee right now, and I suppose we'll come up with the same information,' he said. 'Did you understand the significance of the name Andrew Belinski?'

'Not at the time.'

'And you say you got all this information by using a computer at the university library?'

'That's right,' I said.

He didn't believe me – he must have known that I wouldn't be able to get motor vehicle records through a university computer – but he wasn't going to press the point. 'Someday, you'll have to show me how you did that.'

'I guess I got lucky,' I said. 'Did John tell you that I have a long-standing interest in the old Blue Rose murders? That's why he called me.'

'Go on,' he said.

For something like ten minutes, I told him about meeting the Belknaps, hearing about Bob Bandolier, visiting the Sunchanas, and for the first time learning of the existence of Fielding Bandolier. The computer told

730

me that Elvee owned Bob Bandolier's old house. A vanity press book by a retired colonel gave me an idea about a soldier, supposedly killed in action, who had an old grudge against John Ransom. I talked about Judy Leatherwood and Edward Hubbel.

'You saw no need to come to the police with all this information.'

'I did go to the police,' I said. 'I went to Fontaine. He was the detective in charge of April's case. Once I mentioned the Sunchanas, Fontaine ordered me to stay away from the old Blue Rose murders, and then he suggested that I get out of town. When I didn't, he took me himself to Bob Bandolier's grave, in order to prove that Bandolier couldn't have had anything to do with the new deaths. He was the one who told me about Andy Belin's nickname, by the way, but he denied knowing anything about Elvee.'

McCandless nodded. 'Ransom said he called you to arrange a meeting near the St Alwyn.'

'He found out that I had gone to his old hometown in Ohio. When I came back, somebody tried to run me off the highway in the fog. Fontaine wanted me dead, but he didn't know what I had learned from Hubbel.'

McCandless hitched his chair an inch closer to the bed. 'Then this woman on South Seventh Street called you.' We were getting to the red meat now, and I had the feeling that something was going on that I did not quite understand. McCandless seemed to grow heavier and denser with concentration, as if he were now willing me to put things in a way that would match a prearranged pattern. The only pattern I could see grew out of what I had already told him, and I alluded again to the agreement Hannah Belknap had made with me.

He nodded. That was explanatory, but unimportant.

A cart rattled past the door, and someone down the hall began shouting.

'What did you have in mind when you decided to go to the Bandolier house?'

'I wanted to surprise Fontaine. John and I thought we could knock him out or overpower him and find the boxes of notes.' I looked down the bed at Sonny, but Sonny was still made of stone.

'What was the point of bringing that old man along with you?'

'Alan can be extremely insistent. He didn't give us much choice.'

'Apparently, a lot of people heard Professor Brookner threaten to kill the man who murdered his daughter. I guess he was insistent then, too.'

I remembered the funeral – John must have told them about Alan's outburst. 'I ordered him to stay in the car, but he wanted to be close to the action, and he followed us on the other side of the street.'

'You had already been inside the house.'

I nodded. 'Looking for his records – those boxes he moved out of the Green Woman. You found them, didn't you?'

'No,' McCandless said.

I felt my stomach sinking toward the mattress.

'How'd you happen to get in, that first time?'

'The back door wasn't locked,' I said.

'Really,' McCandless said. 'He left the place open. Like the Green Woman, right? You went up there, you found the lock broken.'

'Right,' I said. 'So I went in and had a look around.'

'That's probably a real common activity in New York, breaking and entering. Out here, we sort of frown on it.' The man down the hall started shouting again, but the dead eyes never left mine. 'Anyhow, let's say you and your buddy got in there. There's an interesting little present down in the basement, but no boxes full of good

732

stuff. On the other hand, you picked up something, didn't you? A piece of paper.'

I'd been carrying that paper around in my jacket pocket ever since Tom gave it back to me. I had forgotten all about it, and someone at the hospital had turned it over to the police.

'Tampering with evidence carries a little weight, too.'

John had told him all about getting into the house and the tavern, and they were keeping him at Armory Place until McCandless decided what to do with me. The decision had to do with the way I answered his questions – unless I helped him push reality into the shape he wanted, he'd be happy to mess up my life with as many criminal charges as he could think up.

'I might even be tempted to think that you and your pal brought along the old man because you knew he'd shoot Fontaine as soon as he had the chance.'

'We told him to stay in the car,' I said, wearily. 'We didn't want him anywhere near us. This is crazy. John didn't let him have the gun, he took it. We didn't even have a real plan.' The pain dialed itself up a couple of notches. It was a long time until my next injection. 'Look, if you saw the paper, you understood what it was, right? You saw that it was about a woman in Allentown. Fontaine worked in Allentown.'

'Yeah.' McCandless sighed. 'But we don't have anything that proves he killed anybody there. And this conversation isn't really about Paul Fontaine anymore. It's about you.'

He abruptly stood up and walked over to the window. He rubbed his face, looking out at the street. Sunlight blazed on the building across the street. McCandless tugged at his belt and turned slowly around. 'I have to think about this city. At this point, things could go a couple of different ways. There's going to be a lot of changes in the department. You got a guy in Ohio who says Fontaine was somebody else. What *I* got is a dead detective and the tail end of a riot. What I don't need is a lot of publicity about another serial killer in Millhaven, *especially* one on the force. Because then, what we get is even more trouble than we already have.' He sighed again. 'Am I making sense to you?'

'Too much,' I said.

'Everything in the world is politics.' He walked back to the chair, planted his hands on its back, and leaned forward. 'Let's talk about what happened when Fontaine got shot.'

He looked up as the door swung open. The blonde doctor I had met last night took two steps into the room, froze, and turned right around and walked out again.

'When we're done,' McCandless said, 'all this is settled for good. After this, there are going to be no surprises. On the night of the riot, you went down to that house with the intention of overpowering and capturing a man you had reason to believe had killed two people. You intended to turn him over to the police.'

'Exactly,' I said.

'Did you hear gunfire in the neighborhood?'

'Not then. No, I'm wrong. I heard shots from the area of the riot.'

'What happened when you got to the house?'

'John and I were going around to the back door, but I took him along the side of the house again to go up onto the porch. When John and I got near the porch steps, Alan saw the front door open and started yelling.'

'The patrol car was about a block away at that point.'

'That's right,' I said. 'Alan saw Fontaine and started screaming, "Is that him?" Fontaine said something like, "Damn you, Underhill, you're not going to get away." I don't think the men in the car had seen us yet.'

McCandless nodded.

'John ran up to Alan and tried to get him to calm down, but Alan yanked the gun away from him and started shooting. The next thing I knew, I was lying down in a pool of blood.'

'How many shots did you hear?'

'There must have been two,' I said.

He waited a significant beat. 'I asked, how many did you hear?'

I thought back. 'Well, I saw Alan fire twice,' I said. 'But I think I might have heard more than two shots.'

'Brookner fired twice,' McCandless said. 'Officer Berenger fired a warning shot into the air. The couple who live across the street from where you were say they heard at least five shots, and so does the woman next door. Her husband slept through the whole thing, so he didn't hear anything. Berenger's partner thinks he heard five shots, fired very close together.'

'It's like the grassy knoll,' I said.

'You were facing Ransom and Brookner. What did you see? There had been some trouble in that area during the rioting.'

I remembered what I had seen. 'I had an impression that there was a person between the houses behind Alan and Ransom.'

'Good for you, Mr Underhill. Did you see this person?'

'I thought I saw movement. It was dark. Then everything went crazy.'

'Have you ever heard of someone named Nicholas Ventura?'

A second too late, I said, 'No.'

'No, I don't suppose so,' McCandless said. He must have known that I was lying. 'Ventura was an up-and-coming young sleazeball who ran into some trouble on Livermore Avenue during the rioting. Somebody took a knife away from him and almost broke off his arm.' McCandless almost smiled at me and then came around

735

the chair and sat down, facing me. 'Some party called 911 from the St Alwyn Hotel almost immediately afterward, but I don't imagine that it was the same party that kicked the shit out of Ventura, do you?'

'No,' I said.

'In fact, what happened to Ventura was riot-related, wouldn't you say?'

I nodded.

'Probably you heard about the death of a man named Frankie Waldo.'

'I heard something about it,' I said. 'If you want to know what I think – '

'So far, you don't think anything about it,' McCandless said. 'Unofficially, I can tell you that Waldo was tied into Billy Ritz's drug business. And Ritz was killed in retribution for his murder.'

'Do you think you can really do this?' I asked.

'I didn't hear you.'

'Ritz was payback for Waldo.'

'Like I told you, everything is politics.' He stood up. 'By the way, Officer Berenger found some old photographs in the basement of that house. I think some good might come out of this, despite what you idiots tried to do.'

'You're not too unhappy that Fontaine is dead, are you?'

McCandless moved away from the chair. Sonny stepped back and looked down toward his feet. He was deaf and blind. 'You know what makes me happy?' McCandless asked me. 'I can protect him one hell of a lot better the way things are.'

'You didn't have much trouble believing that he was really Franklin Bachelor. All you have is what I told you about Edward Hubbel. I don't get it.'

McCandless gave me a long, utterly unreadable look. Then he glanced down the bed at Sonny, who snapped his head up like a soldier on parade. 'Tell him.'

'Detective Monroe made a search of Detective Fontaine's apartment this morning.' Sonny directed his words to the bright window. 'He located Major Bachelor's discharge papers in his desk.'

If I hadn't known how much it would hurt, I would have laughed out loud. 'I wonder if he also came across some boxes of notes.'

'There never were any boxes of notes,' McCandless said.

'Not now, I bet,' I said. 'Congratulations.'

McCandless let it roll right off him. Maybe they hadn't destroyed the notes, after all. Maybe Fontaine had flushed them down the toilet, page by page, before we had shown up at his old house.

'You'll be protected from journalists as long as you are here,' McCandless said. He sounded like he was reading me my Miranda rights. 'The hospital will screen all your calls, and I'm stationing an officer at the door to secure your privacy. In about an hour, Officer Berenger will bring you your statement, based on your responses to my questions. Is that correct, Sonny?'

'Yes, sir,' Sonny said.

'And you might think about booking your ticket home for the day of your release. You'll be taken to the airport in a patrol car, so after you arrange the ticket, give the officer your flight information.'

'All in the interest of my security,' I said.

'Take care of yourself,' McCandless said. 'You look lousy, if you want to know the truth.'

'Glad to help you out,' I said. They were already moving toward the door.

I opened the magazine and tried to revive my interest in menopause. Some of the symptoms had an ironic familiarity – heavy bleeding, increased pain, depression. The columnist had nothing to say about sudden flare-ups of anger against authority figures who looked like retired circus performers. I understood some of what McCandless had been after, but his insistence on there having been more than three gunshots puzzled me. Whatever I had said had satisfied him, but I couldn't figure out why. Then I started worrying about Alan. I reached across my chest to get the telephone and call County Hospital, but the operator almost apologetically told me that I was restricted by police order to incoming calls. I picked up *Modern Bride* and discovered that today's young woman got married in pretty much the same kind of thing as yesterday's. I was just getting into *Longevity* and 'Exercises for the Recently Bereaved' when a short, pudgy young policeman stuck his head in the door and said, 'I'll be right out here, okay.' We recognized each other at the same moment. It was Officer Mangelotti, minus the white head bandage he'd been wearing when I last saw him. 'Nobody said I had to talk to you, though,' he said, and gave me what he thought was a truly evil scowl. His folding chair squeaked when he sat down.

4

Geoffrey Bough conned his way past the receptionist and turned up outside my door about an hour after Ross McCandless left. I was playing with the cold oatmeal the kitchen had sent up, coaxing it into a mound and then mushing it flat. The first indication I had of the reporter's arrival was the sound of Mangelotti saying, 'No. No way. Get out of here.' I thought he was ordering John Ransom away from my room, and I shoved away the oatmeal and called out, 'Come on, Mangelotti, let him in.'

738

'No way,' Mangelotti said.

'You heard him,' said a voice I knew. Bough squeezed his skinny chest past Mangelotti and leaned into the room. 'Hi, Tim,' he said, as if we were old friends. Maybe we were, by now – I realized that I was glad to see him.

'Hello, Geoffrey,' I said.

'Tell this officer to give me five minutes, will you?'

Mangelotti planted his hand on Bough's chest and pushed him part of the way into the hall. Geoffrey gesticulated at me over the cop's head, but Mangelotti gave him another push, and the reporter disappeared.

I heard him protesting all the way down the hallway to the elevator. Mangelotti was so angry with me that he closed the door when he came back.

The next time the door opened, I was beginning to wish that I had eaten the oatmeal. Sonny Berenger came in with a single sheet of paper on a clipboard. 'Your statement's ready,' he said, and handed it to me. He pulled a ballpoint out of his pocket. 'Sign it anywhere on the bottom.'

Most of the sentences in the statement began with 'I' and contained fewer than six words. There was at least one typing mistake in every sentence, and the grammar was casual. It was a bare-bones account of what had happened outside Bob Bandolier's old house. The last two sentences were: 'Professor Brookner fired two shots, striking me. I heard the shooting to continue.' McCandless had probably made him rewrite it three times, taking new details out each time.

'I have to make some changes in this before I sign it,' I said.

'What do you mean, changes?' Berenger asked.

I began writing in 'with one of them' after 'striking me,' and Berenger leaned over the clipboard to see what I was doing. He wanted to grab the pen out of my hand, but he relaxed when he saw what I was doing. I crossed out the 'to' in the last sentence, and then wrote my name under the statement.

He took back the clipboard and the pen, puzzled but relieved.

'Just editing,' I said. 'I can't help myself.'

'The lieutenant's a big believer in editing.'

'I got that part.'

Sonny stepped back from the bed and glanced toward the door to make sure it was closed. 'Thanks for not saying that you told me about the photographs.'

'Will Monroe let John go home after you get back with that statement?'

'Probably. Ransom's just sitting at his desk, trading Vietnam stories.' He still did not want to go, towering near the bed with his clipboard like Officer Friendly in a high school auditorium.

For the first time, he looked openly at the pad of gauze taped to my shoulder. I saw him decide not to say anything about it, and then he took a step backward toward the door. 'Should I tell Ransom you'd like to see him?'

'I'd like to see anybody except Mangelotti,' I said.

After Sonny left, a black-haired, energetic young doctor bounced in to tape fresh gauze over the bloody hole. 'You're going to have to run around your backhand for a month or so, but otherwise, you'll be fine.' He pressed the last of the tape into place and straightened up. Curiosity was fairly boiling out of him. 'The police seem to feel you'll be safer in here.'

'I think it's the other way around,' I said.

After that, I read *Modern Maturity*. Cover to cover, every word of it, including the advertisements. I had to change my running shoes and do something about my IRA account. For lunch, I had a piece of chicken so pale that it nearly disappeared into the plate. I ate every scrap, even the gristly little bits that clung to the bones.

When John turned up several hours later, Mangelotti refused to let him in until he got permission from the department. Permission took a long time to get, and while they were at the desk, I got out of bed and hauled my glucose pole across the room to the sink and looked at myself in the mirror. I had a little more color than the chicken, and I needed a shave. As revenge for the magazines, I peed into the sink. By the time Mangelotti learned he would not be suspended for letting John into my room, I had hobbled back to bed, feeling as though I had just climbed one of the minor Alps.

John came in carrying a beat-up white canvas bag, closed the door, and leaned back against it, shaking his head from side to side in frustration. 'Can you believe that guy is still on the force? What's he doing here anyhow?'

'Defending me from the press.' John snickered and pushed himself off the door. I looked greedily at the canvas bag. ARKHAM COLLEGE was printed on its side in big red letters.

'Funny thing, you look like a guy who just got shot. I stopped off at the house and picked up some books. Nobody was willing to tell me how long you'd be in here, so I got a lot of them.' He set the bag next to me and began piling books on the table. *The Nag Hammadi Library*, Sue Grafton, Ross Macdonald, Donald Westlake, John Irving, A. S. Byatt, Martin Amis. 'Some of these belonged to April. And I thought you'd be interested in seeing this.' He took a thick, green-jacketed book out of the bag and held it up so that I could see the cover. *The Concept of the Sacred*, Alan Brookner. 'Probably his best book.'

I took it from him. As battered as an old suitcase, smudged, soft with use, it looked as if it had been read a hundred times. 'I'm really grateful,' I said.

'Keep it.' He reared back in the chair and shook out his arms. 'What a night.'

I asked what happened to him after I'd been taken away.

'They jammed Alan and me into a police car and hauled us off to Armory Place. Then they locked us up in a little room and asked the same questions over and over.' After a couple of hours, they had driven him home and let him get some sleep, and then picked him up again and started the questioning all over again. Eventually, McCandless had taken a statement and then let him go. He had not been charged with anything.

He took hold of my wrist. 'You didn't say anything about the car, did you? Or about that other stuff?' He meant Byron Dorian.

'No. I stuck to Elvee and Franklin Bachelor and the Blue Rose business.'

'Ah.' He leaned back in the chair and looked up, giving thanks. 'I didn't know what shape you were in. Good. I had a few worried moments there.'

'What about Alan? I heard he was at County Hospital.'

John groaned. 'Alan fell apart. For a long time, he kept quoting one of those damned gnostic verses. Then he started on baby talk. I don't know what he did when they interrogated him, but Monroe finally told me that he was under sedation at County. I guess they have to charge him with reckless use of a weapon, or reckless endangerment, or something like that, but Monroe told me that he would probably never have to go to trial or anything. I mean, he won't end up in *jail*. But God, you should see him.'

'You visited him?'

'I feel like he's taken over my life. I went to County and there's Alan, lying in a bed and saying things like "I live in a little white house. Is my daddy home yet? My brother made pee-pee off the bridge." Literally. He's about four years old. To tell you the truth, I don't think he's ever going to be anything else.'

'Oh, my God,' I said.

'So then his lawyer gets ahold of me and tells me that since he appointed April the trustee of his estate a couple of years ago, now I'm his trustee by default, unless I elect to turn the job over to him. Fat chance. He's about eighty years old, a lawyer straight out of Dickens. So I have to deal with the bank, I have to sign a million papers, I have to see his case through the court, I have to sell his house.'

'Sell his house?'

'He can't live there anymore, he's *gone*. I have to find a home that'll take him, which is a good trick, given his condition.'

I pictured Alan babbling about a little white house and felt a wave of pity and sorrow that nearly made me dizzy. 'What's happening out in the world? Is it on the news?'

'Are we on the news, do you mean? I put on the radio when I got home, and all I heard about us was that Detective Paul Fontaine had been killed in an incident that took place in the Livermore Avenue area. I'll tell you one thing – Armory Place is keeping a very tight lid on things.'

'I guessed,' I said.

'Tim, I have to get moving. All this business about Alan – you know.' He stood up and looked benignly down. 'I'm glad you're on the mend. Man, I couldn't tell *what* happened to you last night.'

'Alan hit me in the shoulder.' Of course, John knew that, but I felt that it deserved a little more attention.

'You nearly flipped over. I'm not kidding. Your feet flew straight out in front of you. *Wham*, you're down.'

My hand moved automatically to the gauze pad. 'You know what's funny about all this? Nobody seems to doubt that Fontaine killed April and Grant Hoffman. They don't have the notes, or they claim they don't, and they

743

don't have any evidence. All they have is what we gave them, and they knew him for better than ten years. His own department, people who thought he was God yesterday morning, did a 360-degree turn twelve hours later.'

'Of course they did.' John smiled and shook his head, looking at me as if I'd flunked an easy test. 'McCandless and Hogan found out that they never really knew the guy at all. They might not be showing it to us, but they're feeling betrayed and angry. Just when they have to convince this entire city that their cops are hot shit after all, their best detective turns out to be very, very dirty.'

John came forward, buttoning his suit, his eyes alight with a private understanding. 'And Monroe searched his apartment, right? He found the discharge papers, but who knows what else he found? Just the fact they're not telling us that they came up with knives or bloodstains on his shoes means that they did.'

When he saw I took the point that they would have been much tougher on us if they had not, he glanced toward the door and then lowered his voice. 'What I think is, I bet Monroe found those notes we were looking for, took them straight to McCandless, and after McCandless read them, he put them through a shredder. Case closed.'

'So they'll never officially clear April's murder?'

'McCandless told me he'd get me for breaking and entering if he ever heard that I was talking to the press.' He shrugged. 'Why is that fat little shit sitting outside your door? He's useless at saving lives, but he's good enough to keep Geoffrey Bough out of your room.'

'You can live with that?' I asked, but the answer had been present since he had walked into the room.

'I know who murdered my wife, and the son of a bitch is dead. Can I live with that? You bet I can.' John looked at his watch. 'Hey, I'm already late for a meeting at the bank. You're okay? Need anything else?'

744

I asked him to arrange airline tickets for the day after tomorrow and to give the flight information to McCandless.

5

Alan Brookner's book made two or three hours zoom by in happy concentration, even though I probably understood about one-fourth of what I was reading. The book was as dense and elegant as an Elliot Carter string quartet, and about as easy to grasp on first exposure. After a bright-faced little nurse rolled in the magic tray and injected me, the book began speaking with perfect clarity, but that may have been illusory.

I heard the door close and looked up to see Michael Hogan coming toward me. His long face seemed about as expressive as Ross McCandless's rusty iron mask, but as he got closer I saw that the effect was due to exhaustion not disdain. 'I thought I'd check up on you before I went home,' he said. 'Mind if I sit down?'

'No, please do,' I said, and he slipped into the chair sideways, almost languidly. A stench of smoke and gunpowder floated toward me from his wrinkled pinstripe suit. I looked at Hogan's weary, distinguished face, still distinguished in spite of the marks of deep exhaustion, and realized that the odor was nothing more than the same smell of ashes that I had caught at the Sunchanas' burned-out house. Along with Fontaine, Hogan had spent a lot of the night near burning buildings, and he had not been home since then.

'You look better than I do,' he said. 'How are things going? In much pain?'

'Ask me again in about an hour and a half.'

He managed to smile through the tangle of emotions visible in his weary face.

'I guess the riot is over,' I said, but he sent the riot into oblivion with a wave of his hand and an impatient, bitter glance that touched me like an electric shock.

Hogan sighed and slumped into the chair. 'What you and Ransom were trying to do was incredibly stupid, you know.'

'We didn't know who to trust. We didn't think anybody would believe us unless we caught him in his old house and made him talk.'

'How did you think you were going to get him to talk?'

He was avoiding the use of the name – the process John had predicted was already beginning.

'Once we had him tied up' – this was the image I'd had of the conclusion of our attack on Fontaine – 'I was going to tell him that I knew who he really was. I could prove it. There wouldn't be any way out for him – he'd have to know he was trapped.'

'The proof would be this man Hubbel?'

'That's right. Hubbel identified him immediately.'

'Imagine that,' Hogan said, meaning that it was still almost too much to imagine. 'Well, we'll be sending someone out there tomorrow, but don't expect to be reading much about Franklin Bachelor in the *New York Times*. Or the *Ledger*, for that matter.' The look in his eyes got even smokier. 'When we got in touch with the army, they stonewalled for most of the day, and finally some character in the CIA passed down the word that Major Bachelor's file is not only closed, it can't be opened for fifty years. Officially, the man is dead. And anything printed about him that isn't already a matter of public record must be approved first by the CIA. So there you are.'

'There we all are,' I said. 'But thanks for telling me.'

746

'Oh, I'm not done yet. I understand you met Ross McCandless.'

I nodded. 'I understand what he wants.'

'He doesn't tend to leave much doubt about that. But probably he didn't tell you a couple of things you ought to know.'

I waited, fearing that he was going to say something about Tom Pasmore.

'The old man's gun is at ballistics. They move slow, over there. The report won't come back for about a week. But the bullet that killed our detective couldn't have come from the same gun as the one that hit you.'

'You're going too far,' I said. 'I was there. I saw Alan fire, twice. What's the point of this, anyhow?' And then I saw the point – if Alan had not killed Fontaine, then our whole story disappeared into a fiction about the riot.

'It's the truth. You saw Brookner fire twice because his first shot went wild. The second one hit you – if the first one had hit you, you'd never have seen him fire the second one.'

'So the first one hit Fontaine.'

'Do you know what happened to him? His whole chest blew apart. If you'd been hit by the same kind of round, you wouldn't have anything left on your right side below the collarbone. You wouldn't even be alive.'

'So who shot him?' As soon as I had spoken, I knew.

'You told McCandless that you saw a man between the houses across the street.'

Well, I had – I thought I had, anyhow. Even if I hadn't, McCandless would have suggested that I probably had. I'd conveniently given him exactly what he wanted.

'We still have a police department in this town,' Hogan said. 'We'll get him, sooner or later.'

I saw a loose end and seized it. 'McCandless mentioned someone named Ventura, I think. Nicholas Ventura.'

'That's the other thing I wanted you to know. Ventura

was operated on, put into a cast, and given a bed at County. Not long after the riot started, he disappeared. Nobody's seen him since. Somehow, I don't think anybody ever will.'

'How could he disappear?' I asked.

'County's a disorganized place. Maybe he walked out.'

'That's not what you think.'

'I don't think Ventura could have stood up by himself, much less walked away from the hospital.' The flat rage in his eyes seemed connected to the stink of ashes that floated out from his clothing, as if his body produced the smell. 'Anyhow, that's what I had to say. I'll leave you alone now.'

He pushed himself to his feet and looked grimly down at me. 'It's been real.'

'A little too real,' I said, and he nodded and walked out of the room. The stench of his rage and frustration stayed behind, like a layer of ashes on my skin, the sheets, the book I had forgotten I was holding.

6

'I warned you that something like this might happen,' Tom Pasmore said to me the next morning, after I had described my conversation with Hogan. 'But I didn't think it would be so complete.' That ashy layer of frustration still covered me so absolutely that I came close to being grateful for the distraction of the steady thudding into which my pain had retreated. Tom's uncharacteristically discreet charcoal suit seemed like another form of it, unrelieved by any of the flashes of color, the pink tie or yellow vest or blooming red pocket cloth, with which he would normally have brightened his general aspect. Tom's general aspect seemed as wan as mine.

Both of us held copies of the morning's *Ledger*, which was dominated by photographs of burned-out buildings and articles about volunteers engaged in the monumental cleanup necessary before rebuilding could begin. At the top of the third page, ordered like the pictures of Walter Dragonette's victims, lay a row of photographs of the eight people killed during the rioting. They were all male, and seven were African-Americans. The white man was Detective Paul Fontaine. Beneath the square of his photograph, a short paragraph referred to his many commendations, the many successes in solving difficult homicide cases that had given him the nickname 'Fantastic,' and his personal affability and humor. His death, like most of the others, had been due to random gunfire.

On the second page of the next section, a column-length article headed FORTY-YEAR-OLD CASE SOLVED reported that recent investigations led by Lieutenant Ross McCandless had brought to light the identity of the Blue Rose killer, who had murdered four people in Millhaven in October of 1950, as Robert C. Bandolier, at the time the day manager of the St Alwyn Hotel. 'It is a great satisfaction to exonerate Detective William Damrosch, who has had an undeserved stain on his reputation for all this time,' said McCandless. 'Evidence located in Mr Bandolier's old residence definitely ties him to the four killings. Forty years later, we can finally say that justice has been done for William Damrosch, who was a fine and dedicated officer, in the tradition of Millhaven's Homicide Division.'

And that was it. Nothing about Fielding Bandolier or Franklin Bachelor, nothing about Grant Hoffman or April Ransom. 'It's complete, all right,' I said.

Tom dropped his copy of the newspaper to the floor, raised one foot to prop his ankle on a knee, and leaned forward with his elbow on the other knee. Chin in hand, his eyes bright with inward curiosity, he suggested an almost comic awareness of his own depression. 'The thing is, if I knew what was coming, why do I feel so bad about it?'

'They're just protecting themselves,' I said.

He knew that – it didn't interest him. 'I think you feel left out,' I said.

'This certainly isn't what I had in mind,' he said. 'I don't blame you in any way, but I sort of pictured that it would be you and me instead of you and John. And Alan should have been nowhere in sight.'

'Naturally,' I said. 'But if you hadn't been insistent on keeping yourself out – '

'I wouldn't have been *kept* out, I know.' He jiggled his foot. 'John put me off. He tried to buy one of my paintings, and then he tried to buy me.'

I agreed that John could be off-putting. 'But if you ever spent half an hour with his parents, you'd know why. And underneath it all, he's a pretty good guy. He just wasn't quite what I expected, but people change.'

'I don't,' Tom said, sounding disconsolate about it. 'I guess that's part of my problem. I've always got two or three things on the fire, but this was the most exciting one in years. We really did something tremendous, and now it's all over.'

'Almost,' I said. 'Don't you still have the two or three other things to take up the slack?'

'Sure, but they're not like this one. In your terms, they're just short stories. This was a whole novel. And now, nobody will ever read it but you and me and John.'

'Don't forget Ross McCandless,' I said.

'Ross McCandless always reminded me of the head of the secret police in a totalitarian state.' Realizing that he could pass on a fresh bit of gossip, he brightened. 'Have you heard that Vass is probably on the way out?'

I shook my head. 'Because of Fontaine?'

'Fontaine's probably the real reason, but the mayor will imply that he's resigning because of the combination of Walter Dragonette, the riot, and the boy who was shot in City Hall.'

'Is this public yet?'

'No, but a lot of people – the kind of people who really know, I mean – have been talking about it as though it's a foregone conclusion.'

I wondered whom he meant, and then remembered that Sarah Spence spent her life among the kind of people who really know.

'How about Merlin?'

'Merlin's a gassy liquid – he takes the shape of whatever container he puts himself into. I think we'll be seeing a lot of the elder statesman act for a while. What he'll probably do is find a good black chief in some other part of the country, sing lullabies to him until he loses his mind, and then announce the appointment of a new chief. Right up until that moment, he'll be behind Vass a thousand percent.'

'Everything is politics,' I said.

'Especially everything that shouldn't be.' He gloomily regarded the stack of books on my table without seeming to take in the individual titles. 'I should have protected you better.'

'Protected me?'

He looked away. 'Oh, by the way, I brought some of those computer reconstructions of the last photograph, if there's any point in looking at them anymore.' He reached into his jacket pocket, brought out three folded sheets of paper, and then met my eyes with a flash of embarrassment at what he saw there.

'That was you – you followed me back to John's that night.'

'Do you want to look at these, or not?'

I took the papers without releasing him. 'It was you.'

The red dots appeared in his cheeks. 'I couldn't just let you walk nine blocks in the middle of the night, could I? After everything I'd just said to you?'

'And was that you I saw out in Elm Hill?'

'No. That was Fontaine. Or Billy Ritz. Which proves that I should have stuck to you like a burr.' He smiled, at last. 'You weren't supposed to see me.'

'It was more like I felt you,' I said, troubled by the evil I had sensed dogging me that night, and the memory of the Minotaur's knowledge of a hidden shame. From where had I dredged that up, if not out of myself? Cloudy with doubt, I flattened the pages and looked at each of the computer images in turn.

They were of buildings that had never existed, buildings with recessed ground floors beneath soaring blank upper reaches like pyramids, oblongs, ocean liners. Empty sidewalks devoid of cracks led up to boxy windows and glassed-in guardhouses. They looked like an eccentric billionaire's vision of a modern art museum. I spread the papers out between us. 'This is it?' I asked.

'The other ones were even worse. You know what they say – garbage in, garbage out. There just wasn't enough information for it to work with. But I guess we know what it really is, anyhow, don't we?'

'Stenmitz's shop had a kind of triangular sign over the window. That must be what suggested all this – ' I pointed at the rearing structures of the upper floors.

'I guess.' Tom swept the pages together in a gesture of disappointment and disgust. 'It would have been nice if . . .'

'If I recognized some other building?'

'I don't want it to be over yet,' Tom said. 'But boy, is it over. You want to keep these? Bring a souvenir home with you?'

I didn't say that I already had a souvenir – I wanted to

752

keep the computer's hallucinations. I'd fasten them to the refrigerator, beneath the picture of Ted Bundy's mother.

7

Tom came back the next day with the news that Arden Vass had offered to resign as soon as a suitable replacement could be found. He had expected the mayor to refuse his offer, but Merlin Waterford had immediately announced that he was accepting the resignation of his old friend, albeit with the greatest sorrow, and the Committee for a Just Millhaven would be given a voice in the selection of the new chief. The officer who had killed the teenage boy was under suspension, pending a hearing. Tom stayed for an hour, and when he left, we promised to stay in touch.

John Ransom came in half an hour before the end of visiting hours and told me that he had decided what he wanted to do – buy a farmhouse in the Dordogne where he could work on his book and rent an apartment in Paris for weekends and vacations in the city. 'I need a city,' he said. 'I want a lot of quiet for my work, but I'm no country mouse. Once I'm set up, I want you to come over, spend some time with me. Will you do that?'

'Sure,' I said. 'It'd be nice. This visit turned out to be a little hectic.'

'Hectic? It was a nightmare. I was out of my mind most of the time.' John had stayed on his feet during his visit, and he jammed his hands in his pockets and executed a hesitant half-turn, clocking toward the sunny window and then back to me again. 'I'll see you tomorrow when you come around to get your things. Ah, I just have to say how much I appreciate everything you did here, Tim. You were great. You were fantastic. I'll never forget it.'

'It was quite a ride,' I said.

'I want to give you a present. I've been giving this a lot of thought, and while nothing could really repay you for everything you did, I want to give you that painting you liked so much. The Vuillard. Please take it. I want you to have it.'

I looked up at him, too stunned to speak.

'I can't look at the thing anymore, anyhow. There's too much of April in it. And I don't want to sell it. So do me a favor and take it, will you?'

'If you really want to give it to me,' I said.

'It's yours. I'll take care of the paperwork and have some good art handlers pack it up and ship it to you. Thanks.' He fidgeted for a while, having run out of things to say, and then he was gone.

8

Four hours before my flight was scheduled to take off, John called to say that he was in a meeting with his lawyers and couldn't get out. Would I mind letting myself in with the extra key and then pushing it through the mail slot after I locked up again? He'd get the painting off to me as soon as he had the time and be in touch soon to let me know how his plans were developing. 'And good luck with the book,' he said. 'I know how important it is to you.'

Five minutes later, Tom Pasmore called. 'I tried to wangle a ride out to the airport with you, but Hogan turned me down. I'll call you in a day or two to see how you're doing.'

'Tom,' I said, suddenly filled with an idea, 'why don't you move to New York? You'd love it, you'd make hundreds of interesting friends, and there'd never be any shortage of problems to work on.'

'What?' he said in a voice filled with mock outrage. 'And abandon my roots?'

Officer Mangelotti stood beside me like a guard dog as I signed myself out of the hospital, drove me to Ely Place, and trudged around the house while I struggled with the problem of one-armed packing. The curved blue splint covering my right arm from fingers to shoulder made it impossible for me to carry downstairs both the hanging bag and the carryon, and Mangelotti stood glumly in the living room and watched me go back up and down the stairs. When I came down the second time, he said, 'These are real paintings, like oil paintings, right?'

'Right,' I said.

'I wouldn't put this crap in a doghouse.' He watched me pick up both bags with my left hand and then followed me out through the door, waited while I locked up, and let me put the bags in the trunk by myself. 'You don't move too fast,' he said.

I looked at my watch as he turned onto Berlin Avenue – it was still an hour and a half before my flight. 'I want to make a stop before we get to the airport,' I said. 'It won't take long.'

'The sergeant didn't say anything about a stop.'

'You don't have to tell him about it.'

'You sure get royal treatment,' he said. 'Where's this stop you want me to make?'

'County Hospital.'

'At least it's on the way to the lousy airport,' Mangelotti said.

9

A nurse in a permanent state of rage took me at quick-march tempo down a corridor lined with ancient men and women in wheelchairs. Some of them were mumbling to themselves and plucking at their thin cotton robes. They were the lively ones. The air smelled of urine and disinfectant, and a gleaming skin of water had seeped halfway out into the corridor, occasionally swelling into puddles that reached the opposite wall. The nurse flew over the puddles without explaining, apologizing, or looking down. They had been there a long time.

Unasked, Mangelotti had refused to leave the car and told me that I had fifteen minutes, tops. It had taken about seven minutes to get someone to tell me where Alan was being kept and another five of jogging along behind the nurse through miles of corridors to get this far. She rounded another corner, squeezed past a gurney on which an unconscious old woman lay covered to the neck by a stained white sheet, and came to a halt by the entrance to a dim open ward that looked like a homeless shelter for the aged. Rows of beds no more than three feet apart stood in ranks along each wall. Dirty windows at the far end admitted a tired substance more like fog than light.

In a robot voice, the nurse said, 'Bed twenty-three.' She dismissed me with her eyes and about-faced to disappear back around the corner.

The old men in the beds were as identical as clones, so institutionalized as to be without any individuality – white hair on white pillows, wrinkled, sagging faces, dull eyes and open mouths. Then the details of an arched, beaky

756

nose, a crusty bald head, a protruding tongue, began to emerge. The mumbles of the few old men not asleep or permanently stupefied sounded like mistakes. I saw the numeral 16 on the bed in front of me and moved down the row to 23.

Flyaway white hair surrounded a shrunken face and a working mouth. I would have walked right past him if I hadn't looked first at the number. Alan's thrusting eyebrows had flourished at the expense of the rest of his body. I supposed he had always possessed those branchy, tangled eyebrows, but everything else about him had kept me from noticing them. Even his extraordinary voice had shrunk, and whatever he was saying vanished into a barely audible whisper. 'Alan,' I said, 'this is Tim. Can you hear me?'

His mouth went slack, and for a second I saw something like awareness in his eyes. Then his lips began moving again. I bent down to hear what he was saying.

'. . . standing on the corner and my brother had a toothpick in his mouth because he thought it made him look tough. All it did was make him look like a fool, and I told him so. I said, you know why those fools hang around in front of Armistead's with toothpicks in their mouths? So people will think they just ate a big dinner there. I guess everybody can recognize a fool except one of its own kind. And my aunt came out and said, You're making your brother cry, when are you ever going to learn to control that mouth of yours?'

I straightened up and rested my left hand on his shoulder. 'Alan, talk to me. It's Tim Underhill. I want to say good-bye to you.'

He turned his head very slightly in my direction. 'Do you remember me?' I asked.

Recognition flared in his eyes. 'You old son of a gun. Aren't you dead? I shot the hell out of you.'

I knelt beside him, the sheer weight of my relief pushing

757

me close to tears. 'Alan, you only hit me in the shoulder.'

'*He's* dead.' Alan's voice recovered a tiny portion of its original strength. Absolute triumph widened his eyes. 'I *got* him.'

'You can't stay in this dump,' I said. 'We have to get you out of here.'

'Listen, kiddo.' A smile stretched the loose mouth, and the shrunken face and enormous eyebrows summoned me nearer. 'All I have to do is get out of this bed. There's a place I once showed my brother, over by the river. If I can watch my big motormouth, uh, . . .' He blinked. Fluid wobbled in the red wells of his eyelids. 'Curse of my life. Talk first, think later.' Alan closed his eyes and sank into the pillow.

I said, 'Alan?' Tears leaked from his closed eyelids and slipped into the gauze of his whiskers. After a second, I realized that he had fallen asleep.

When I let myself back into the car, Mangelotti glowered at me. 'I guess you don't have a watch.'

I said, 'If you bitch one more time, I'll ram your teeth down your throat with this cast.'

PART FIFTEEN

Lenny Valentine

1

When I got back to New York, I did my best to settle
back into my abnormal normal life, but settling was
exactly what I couldn't do. Everything had been taken
away while I was gone and replaced with other objects
that only appeared to resemble them – the chairs and
couches, my bed and writing table, even the rugs and
bookshelves, were half an inch narrower or shorter, the
wrong width or height, and subtly shifted in a way that
turned my loft into a jigsaw puzzle solved by forcing
pieces into places where other pieces belonged. Part of
this sense of dislocation was the result of having to type
with only the index finger of my left hand, which refused
to work in the old way without the assistance of its
partner, but all the rest of it, most of it, was simply me. I
had returned from Millhaven so disarranged that I no
longer fit my accustomed place in the puzzle.

Wonderfully, my friends distracted me from this sense
of disarrangement by fussing over my injury and demanding to hear the story of how I had managed to get myself
shot in the shoulder by a distinguished professor of
religion. The story was a long story, and it took a long
time to tell. They wouldn t settle for summations, they
wanted details and vivid recreation. Maggie Lah was
particularly interested in what had happened on the
morning I got lost in the fog and told me that it was
simple, really. 'You walked into your book. You saw your
character, and he was yourself. That's why you told the

man in the ambulance that your name was Fee Bandolier. Because what else is the point of this book you're writing?'

'You're too smart,' I said, flinching a little at her perception.

'You better write this book, get it out of your system,' she answered, and that was perceptive, too.

When Vinh brought plates of delicious Vietnamese food up from Saigon's kitchen – an internal takeout – Maggie insisted that he go back downstairs for soup. 'This is a person who requires a great deal of soup,' she said, and Vinh must have agreed, because he went right back down and came back with enough soup to feed us all for a week, most of it parceled out into containers that he put into my refrigerator.

Michael Poole wanted to know about the Franklin Bachelor period of Fee Bandolier's life and if I thought I understood what had happened when John Ransom reached Bachelor's encampment. 'Didn't he say that he got there two days before the other man? What did he do there, for two whole days?'

'Eat soup,' Maggie said.

These friends clustered around me like a family, which is what they are, at various times and for various periods, separately and together, for two or three days, and then, because they knew I needed it, began giving me more time by myself.

Using one finger, turned at an unfamiliar angle to the keyboard, I started typing what I had written in John's house into the computer. What would normally have taken me about a week dragged out to two weeks. The hooks and ratchets in my back heated up and rolled over, and every half hour or so I had to stand up and back into the wall to press them back into place. My doctor gave me a lot of pills that contained some codeine, but after I discovered that the codeine slowed me down even further and gave me a headache, I stopped using them. I typed on for another couple of days, trying to ignore both the pain in my back and the sensation of a larger disorder.

Byron Dorian's painting arrived via UPS, and five days later April's Vuillard turned up, wrapped in foot-thick bubble wrap within a wooden case. The man who delivered it even hung it for me – all part of the service. I put the paintings on the long blank wall that faced my desk, so that I could look up and see them while I worked.

Tom Pasmore called, saying that he was still 'fooling around,' whatever that meant. John Ransom called with the news that he had found a place for Alan in Golden Manor, a nursing home with lake views from most of the rooms. 'The place looks like a luxury hotel and costs a fortune, but Alan can certainly afford it,' John said. 'I hope I can afford it, or something like it, when I'm his age.'

'How is he doing?' I asked.

'Oh, physically, he's improved a lot. He's up and around, he doesn't look so *small* anymore, and he's eating well. I meant that in both senses. The food at the place is better than it is in most restaurants around here.'

'And mentally?'

'Mentally, he goes in and out. Sometimes, it's like talking to the old Alan, and other times, he just disconnects and talks to himself. To tell you the truth, though, I think that's happening less and less.' Without transition, he asked if I had received the painting. I said I had and thanked him for it.

'You know it cost about a thousand bucks to get it packed and shipped by those guys?'

Around eight o'clock one night, three in the morning for him, Glenroy Breakstone called me from France and announced that he wanted to talk about Ike Quebec. He talked about Ike Quebec for forty minutes. Whatever Glenroy was using these days, they had a lot of it in

France. When he had finished, he said, 'You're on my list now, Tim. You'll be hearing from me.'

'I hope I will,' I said, telling him nothing but the truth.

The next morning, I finished typing out everything I had written in Millhaven. To celebrate, I went straight to bed and slept for an hour – I'd hardly been able to sleep at night ever since I'd returned. I went downstairs and ate lunch at Saigon. After I got back up to my loft, I started writing new scenes, new dialogue again. And that's when my troubles really began.

2

Sleeplessness must have been part of the trouble. In the same way that the fingers of my left hand had mysteriously lost the ability to type, my body had lost its capacity to sleep. During my first nights back in New York, I came awake about four in the morning and spent the rest of the night lying in bed with my eyes closed, waiting until long past dawn for the gradual mental slippage, the loosening of rationality, which signals the beginning of unconsciousness. To make up for the lost sleep, I took hour-long naps after lunch. Then I began waking at three in the morning, with the same results. I tried reading and wound up reading until morning. By the end of the first week, I was going to bed at eleven and waking up at two in the morning. After another four or five nights, I never went to sleep at all. I took off my clothes and brushed my teeth, got into bed, and instantly felt as though I'd just gulped down a double espresso.

I couldn't blame the cast or the pains in my back and shoulder. These were uncomfortable, awkward, and irritating, but they were not the problem. My body had forgotten how to sleep at night. I went back to my doctor, who gave me sleeping pills. For two nights, I took the pills before going to bed, with the alarming result that I'd come out of a lengthy daze at six in the morning, standing by the window or sitting on the couch, with no memory of what had happened since I had stretched out on my bed. Instead of sleep, I'd had amnesia. I threw the pills away, took two-hour naps in the middle of the day, and waited it out. By the time I began writing fresh material, I had stopped going to bed – I took a shower around midnight, changed clothes, and alternately worked, read, and walked around my loft. Sometimes I turned off the lights and wrote in the dark. I took a lot of aspirin and vitamin C. Sometimes I wandered into the kitchen and gazed at the surreal buildings that Tom's computer had invented. Then I went back to my desk and lost myself in my made-up world.

Despite my fatigue, my work went leaping ahead of me like some animal, tiger or gazelle, that I was trying to capture. I was scarcely conscious of writing – the experience was more like *being written*. I saw everything, smelled everything, touched everything. During those hours, I ceased to exist. Like a medium, I just wrote it down. By the time I began to awaken to my various aches, it was seven or eight in the morning. I tottered to my bed, lay down, and rested while my mind kept pursuing the leaping tiger. After fifteen minutes of exhausted nonsleep, I got up and went back to the machine.

Sometimes I noticed that I had spent an entire night writing *Fee Bandolier* instead of *Charlie Carpenter*.

All of this should have been joyous, and most of the time it was. But even when I was most absorbed in my work, during those periods when I had no personal existence, some dormant part of me flailed about in an emotional extremity. After I stopped typing, my fingers trembled – even the fingers trapped in the cast were quivering. I had entered the childhood of Fielding Bandolier, and dread and terror were his familiars. But not all of the trouble came from what I was writing.

During my two-hour naps, I dreamed of being back on the body squad and plunging my hands into dead and dismembered bodies. I encountered the skinny young VC on Striker Tiger and froze, blank and mindless, while he raised his ancient rifle and sent a bullet into my brain. I stepped on a mine and turned into red mist, like Bobby Swett. I walked across a clearing so crowded with dead men that I had to step over their bodies, looked down to see purple-and-silver entrails spilling out of my gut, and fell down in acknowledgment of my own death. Paul Fontaine sat up on his gurney with his gun in his hand and said, *Bell*, and blew my chest apart with a bullet.

For twenty years, the afternoons had been the hours when I did the bulk of my work. After I forgot how to sleep at night, after I began walking into hell every time I took a nap, those hours turned to stone. What I wrote came out forced and spiritless. I couldn't sleep, and I couldn't write. So I tucked my notebook into my pocket and went out on long walks.

I trudged through Soho. I passed unseeing through Washington Square. I hovered distracted in the Three Lives bookstore and came back to myself in Books & Co., miles away. Now and then, some grudging little incident found its way into the notebook, but most of the time I was in Millhaven. People I had never seen before turned into John Ransom and Tom Pasmore. The lightless eyes and rusty face of Ross McCandless slanted toward me from the window of a passing bus. Block after block, I walked along Livermore Avenue, finally saw the sign outside the White Horse Tavern, and realized that I was on Hudson Street.

Around seven o'clock on what turned out to be the last

of these miserable journeys, I walked past a liquor store, stopped moving, and went back and bought a bottle of vodka. If what I needed was unconsciousness, I knew how to get it. I carried the bottle home in the white plastic carrier bag, set it on the kitchen shelf and stared at it. Sweating, I paced around the loft for a long time. Then I went back into the kitchen, twisted the cap off the bottle, and poured the vodka into the sink.

As soon as the last of it disappeared into the drain, I went downstairs for dinner and told everybody I was feeling much better today, thank you, just a little trouble sleeping. I forced myself to eat at least half of the food on my plate, and drank three bottles of mineral water. Maggie Lah came out of the kitchen, took a long look at me, and sat down across the table. 'You're in trouble,' she said. 'What's going on?'

I said I wasn't too sure.

'Sometimes I hear you walking around in the middle of the night. You can't sleep?'

'That's about it.'

'You could try going to one of those veterans' meetings. They might help you.'

'Veterans of Millhaven don't have meetings,' I said, and told her not to worry about me.

She said something about therapy, stood up, kissed the top of my head, and left me alone again.

When I got back into my loft, I double-checked my locks, something I'd been doing four and five times a night since my return, took a shower, put on clean clothes, and went to my desk and turned on the computer. When I saw that my hands were still shaking, Maggie's words came back to me. They sounded no more acceptable now than they had the first time. Years before, I'd gone twice to a veterans' group, but the people there had been in another war altogether. As for therapy, I'd rather go directly to the padded rooms and the electroshock table.

I tried to get back into the world of my work and found that I could not even remember the last words I'd written. I called up the chapter, pushed HOME HOME and the button with the arrow that pointed down, which instantly delivered me to the point where I had stopped work that morning. Then the nightly miracle took place once again, and I fell down into the throat of my novel.

3

Something astounding, no other word will do, happened to me the next day. Its cause was an ordinary moment, banal in every outward way; but what it called up was another moment, not at all ordinary, from the archaic story ringed with warnings about looking back I had imagined concealed behind Orpheus and Lot's wife, and this glimpse did turn me into something like a pillar of salt, at least for a while.

My own cries had jerked me up out of the usual daymares, napmares mingling Vietnam and Millhaven. My shirt was stuck to my skin, and the cushion I used as a pillow was slick with sweat. I ripped off the shirt and groaned my way into the bathroom to splash cold water over my face. In a fresh shirt, I went up to my desk, sat down before the computer and searched for that capacity for surrender which gave me access to my book. I hated the whole idea of going outside again. As it had on every other afternoon for the past two weeks, the door into the book refused to open. I gave up, left the machine, and paced around my loft in a state suspended between life and death. My loft seemed like a cage built for some other prisoner altogether. It came to me that my strange afternoon treks around Manhattan might be an essential part of the night's work – that they might be what allowed my imagination to fill itself up again. It also came to me that this was magical thinking. But worthless as it was, it was the best idea I had, and I let myself out of the cage and went out onto Grand Street.

Warm summer light shone on the windows of art galleries and clothing stores, and women from New Jersey and Connecticut strolled like travelers from a more affluent planet among the locals. Today, most of the locals seemed to be young men in pressed jeans and rugby shirts. They were Wall Street trainees, embryo versions of Dick Mueller, who had taken over artists' lofts when the rents in Soho had pushed the artists into Hoboken and Brooklyn. I tried to picture Dick Mueller hovering over the arugala at Dean & DeLuca, but failed. Neither could I see Dick bragging to his friends about the Cindy Sherman photograph he had picked up for a good price at Metro Gallery. My mood began to improve.

I stopped in front of my local video shop, thinking about renting *Babette's Feast* for the twentieth time. I could catch up on all the Pedro Almodovar films I hadn't seen, or have a private Joan Crawford retrospective, beginning with *Strait-Jacket*. Along with all the usual Mel Gibson and Tom Cruise posters in the window was one for a line of film noir released on video for the first time. Now we're talking, I thought, and moved up to inspect the poster. Alongside a reproduction of the box for *Pickup on South Street* was that for *From Dangerous Depths*, the movie that Tom said had been playing in our neighborhood at the time of the Blue Rose murders. I peered at the picture on the box, looking for details. *From Dangerous Depths* starred Robert Ryan and Ida Lupino and had been directed by Robert Siodmak. I told myself that I would rent it someday and moved on.

At the Spring Street Bookstore, I bought John Ashbery's *Flow Chart* and took a quick, unforeseen spin into desperation while I signed the credit slip. I saw myself pouring the vodka into the drain the previous night. I wanted it back, I wanted a big cold glass of liquid narcotic in my hand. As soon as I got out of the bookstore, I went into a cafe and took a table at the opposite end of the room from the bar to order whatever kind of mineral water they had. The waiter brought me an eight-ounce bottle of Pellegrino, and I made myself drink it slowly while I opened the Ashbery book and read the first few pages. The desperation began to recede. I finished the water and devoured another hundred lines of *Flow Chart*. Then I left some bills on the table and walked back out into the sunlight.

What happened next might have been the culmination of all these events. It might have been the result of getting only two hours of sleep every day or of the wretched dreams that jumped out at me during those hours. But I don't think it was any of those things. I think it happened because it had been waiting to happen.

A long gray Mercedes pulled into a parking space across the street, and a huge bearded blond man got out and locked his door. He looked like Thor dressed in artist uniform, black shirt and black trousers. His hair fell in one long wave to just above his collar, and his beard foamed and bristled. Although I'd never met him, I recognized him as a painter named Allen Stone who had become famous in the period between Andy Warhol and Julian Schnabel. He'd just had a retrospective, negatively reviewed almost everywhere, at the Whitney. Allen Stone turned away from his car and glanced at me with cold, pale blue eyes.

I *saw*. That was all that happened, but it was enough. I saw.

On a mental screen that obliterated the street before me, Heinz Stenmitz's great blond head loomed over me. He was grinning like a wolf, pressing one hand against the back of my neck as I knelt in semidarkness, crowded between his vast legs, my arm across his lap, my fingers held tight around the great veiny red thing straining up at me out of his trousers. This, the center and foreground of the scene, pulsed in my hand. 'Put it in your mouth, Timmy,' he said, almost pleading, and urged my head toward the other head, my mouth toward the other little mouth.

I shuddered, recoiled, and the vision blew apart. Allen Stone had turned away from whatever he saw in my face and was moving past the front of his car toward a set of double black doors set into an ornate building at the level of the sidewalk.

Heat blazed in my face. My scalp tried to peel itself away from my skull. My stomach flipped inside-out, and I stepped forward and deposited a pink mixture of Italian water and partially digested Vietnamese food into the gutter. Too shocked to be embarrassed, I stood looking down at the mess. When my insides contracted again, I drooled out another heap of the pink lava. I wobbled back on the sidewalk and saw two of the well-dressed suburban women, their faces stiff with disgust, standing stock-still about six feet away from me. They jerked their eyes away and hurried across the street.

I wiped my mouth and moved toward the corner, separating myself from the spatter in the gutter. My legs seemed disconnected and much too long. *Fee Bandolier*, I said to myself.

When I got back to Grand Street, I fell into a chair and began to cry, as if I had needed the safety of my own surroundings to experience the enormity of whatever I felt – shock and grief. Anger, too. A glance on the street had just unlocked a moment, a series of moments, I had stuffed into a chest forty years ago. I had wrapped chain after chain around the chest. Then I had dropped the chest down into a psychic well. It had been bubbling and simmering ever since. Among all the feelings that rushed up from within was astonishment – this had happened to me, to *me*, and I had deliberately, destructively forgotten all about it.

Memory after memory came flooding back. Partial, fragmentary, patchy as clouds, they brought my own life back to me – they were the missing sections of the puzzle that allowed everything else to find its proper place. I had met Stenmitz in the theater. Slowly, patiently, saying certain things and not saying others, playing on my fear and his adult authority, he had forced me to do what he wanted. I did not know how many days I had met him to kneel down before him and take him in my mouth, but it had gone on for a time that the child-me had experienced as a wretched eternity – four times? Five times? Each occasion had been a separate death.

Around ten, I reeled out to a restaurant where I wouldn't see anyone I knew, reeled through some kind of dinner, then reeled back to my loft. I realized that I had done exactly what I wished: instead of therapy, I had gone straight to electric shocks. At midnight, I took the usual second shower – not, this time, to get ready for work, but to make myself feel clean. About an hour later, I went to bed and almost immediately dropped into the first good eight-hour sleep in two weeks. When I came awake the next morning, I understood what Paul Fontaine had been trying to tell me on Bob Bandolier's front lawn.

4

I spent most of the next day at my desk, feeling as though I were shifting a pile of gravel with a pair of tweezers – real sentences, not instruction-manual sentences, came out, but no more of them than filled two pages. Around four, I turned off the machine and walked away, figuring that it would take me at least a few weeks to adjust to what I had just learned about myself. Too restless to read a book or sit through a movie, I met the old urge to get on my feet and walk somewhere, but two weeks of wandering in an aimless daze were enough. I needed somewhere to go.

Eventually I picked up the telephone book and started looking for veterans' organizations. My sixth call turned up information about a veterans' group that met at six o'clock every night in the basement of a church in the East Thirties – Murray Hill. They took drop-ins. Without being what I wanted, it was what I was looking for, a long walk to an actual destination. I left Grand Street at five-fifteen and turned up at the low, fenced-in brick church ten minutes early. A sign with inset white letters told me to use the vestry door.

5

When I came down into the basement, two skinny guys with thinning hair and untrimmed beards and dressed in parts of different uniforms were arranging a dozen folding chairs in a circle. An overweight, heavily mustached priest in a cassock striped with cigarette ash stood in front of a battered table drinking coffee from a paper cup. All three of them glanced at my splint. An old upright piano stood in one corner, and Bible illustrations hung on the cinder block walls alongside colored maps of the Holy Land. Irregular brown stains discolored the concrete floor. I felt as though I had walked back into the basement of Holy Sepulchre.

The two skinny vets nodded at me and continued setting up the chairs. The priest came up and grabbed my hand. 'Welcome. I'm Father Joe Morgan, but everybody usually calls me Father Joe. It's your first time here, isn't it? Your name is?'

I told him my name.

'And you were in Nam, of course, like Fred and Harry over there – like me, too. Before I went to the seminary, that was. Ran a riverboat in the Delta.' I agreed that I had been in Nam, and he poured me a coffee from the metal urn. 'That's how we started out, of course, guys like us getting together to see if we could help each other out. These days, you never know who could turn up – we get fellows who were in Grenada, Panama, boys from Desert Storm.'

Fred or Harry sent me a sharp, dismissive look, but it didn't refer to me.

'Anyhow, make yourself at home. This is all about sharing, about support and understanding, so if you feel like letting it all hang out, feel free. No holds barred. Right, Harry?'

'Not many,' Harry said.

By six, another seven men had come down into the basement, three of them wearing old uniform parts like Harry and Fred, the others in suits or sport jackets. Most of them seemed to know each other. We all seemed to be about the same age. As soon as we took our chairs, five or six men lit cigarettes, including the priest.

'Tonight we have two new faces,' he said, exhaling an enormous cloud of gray smoke, 'and I'd like us to go around the circle, giving our names and units. After that, anybody who has something to say, jump right in.'

Bob, Frank, Lester, Harry, Tim, Jack, Grover, PeeWee, Juan, Buddy, Bo. A crazy quilt of battalions and divisions. The jumpy little man called Buddy said, 'Well, like some of you guys know from when I was here a couple of weeks ago, I was a truck driver in Cam Ranh Bay.'

I immediately tuned out. This was what I remembered from the veterans' meeting I'd attended four or five years before, a description of a war I never saw, a war that hardly sounded like war. Buddy had been fired from his messenger job, and his girlfriend had told him that if he started acting crazy again, she'd leave him.

'So what do you do when you act crazy?' someone asked. 'What does that mean, crazy?'

'It gets like I can't talk. I just lay up in bed and watch TV all day long, but I don't really see it, you know? I'm like blind and deaf. I'm like in a hole in the ground.'

'When I get crazy, I run,' said Lester. 'I just take off, man, no idea what I'm doin', I get so scared I can't stop, like there's something back there comin' after me.'

Jack, a man in a dark blue suit, said, 'When I get scared, I take my rifle and go up on the roof. It's not loaded, but I aim it at people. I think about what it would be like if I started shooting.'

We all looked at Jack, and he shrugged. 'It helps.'

Father Joe talked to Jack for a while, and I tuned out again. I wondered how soon I could leave. Juan told a long story about a friend who had shot himself in the chest after coming back from a long patrol. Father Joe talked for a long time, and Buddy started to twitch. He wanted us to tell him what to do about his girlfriend.

'Tim, you haven't said anything yet.' I looked up to see Father Joe looking at me with glistening eyes. Whatever he had said to Juan had moved him. 'Is there anything you'd like to share with the group?'

I was going to shake my head and pass, but a scene rose up before me, and I said, 'When I first got to Nam, I was on this graves registration squad at Camp White Star. One of the men I worked with was called Scoot.' I described Scoot kneeling beside Captain Havens's body bag, saying *He nearly got in and out before I could pay my respects*, and told them what he had done to the body.

For a moment no one spoke, and then Bo, one of the men in clothing assembled from old uniforms, said, 'There's this thing, this place I can't stop thinking about. I didn't even see what the hell happened there, but it got stuck in my head.'

'Let it out,' said the priest.

'We were in Darlac Province, way out in the boonies, way north.' Bo leaned forward and put his elbows on his knees. 'This is gonna sound a little funny.' Before Father Joe could tell him to let it out again, he tilted his head and glanced sideways in the circle at me. 'But what, Tim? what Tim said reminded me. I mean, I never saw any American do that kind of junk, and I hate it when people talk like that's all we ever did. You want to make *me* crazy, all you gotta do is tell me about so-called atrocities we did over there, right? Because personally, I never saw one. Not one. What I did see, what I saw plenty of times, was Americans doing some good for the people over there. I'm talking about food and medicine, plus helping kids.'

Every man in the circle uttered some form of assent – we had all seen that, too.

'Anyhow, this one time, it was like we walked into this ghost town. The truth is, we got lost, we had this lieutenant fresh out of training, and he just got lost, plain and simple. He had us moving around in a big circle, which he was the only one who didn't understand what we were doing. The rest of us, we said, fuck it, he thinks he's a leader, let him lead. We get back to base, let *him* explain. So we're out there three–four days, and the lieutenant is just beginning to get the picture. And then we start smelling this fire.

'Like an old fire, you know? Not like a forest fire, like a burning building. Whenever the wind comes in from the north, we smell ashes and dead meat. And pretty soon, the smell is so strong we know we're almost on top of it, whatever it is. Now the lieutenant has a mission, he can maybe save his ass if he brings back something good – hell, it doesn't even have to be good, it just has to be something he can bring back, like he was looking for it all along. So we hump along through the jungle for about another half hour, and the stench gets worse and worse. It smells like a burned-down slaughterhouse. And besides that, there's no *noise* around us, no birds, no monkeys, none of that screeching we heard every other single day. The jungle is deserted, man, that fucker's *empty*, except for us.

'So in about half an hour we come up to this place, and we all freeze – it isn't a hamlet, it isn't a ville, it's out in the jungle, right? But it looks like some kind of town or something, except most of it's burned down, and the rest of it is still burning. You could tell from the charred stakes that there used to be a big stockade fence around it – some of it's still sticking up. But we can see this goddamn *grid*, with little tiny lots and everything, where these people had their huts all lined up on these narrow streets. All this was straw, I guess, and it's gone – there's nothing left but holes in the ground, and some flooring here and there. And the bodies.

'Lots of bodies, lots and lots of bodies. Someone pulled a lot of them into a big pile and tried to burn them, but all that happened was they split open. These were all women and children, and a couple of men. Yards – the first Yards I ever saw, and they're all dead. It looked like that Jonestown, that Jim Jones thing, except these bodies had bullet holes. The stink was incredible, it made your eyes water. It looked like someone had all these people stand in a big ring and then just blasted them to pieces. We didn't say a word. You can't talk about what you don't understand.

'At the far end of this place, there's part of a mud wall and a lot of blood on the ground. I saw a busted-up M-16 lying next to a big iron cookpot hung up over a burned-out fire. Somebody had did a job on that M-16. They busted the stock right off, and the barrel was all bent out of true. I looked into the cookpot and wished I hadn't even thought of it. Through the froth on top, I could see bones floating down in this kind of jelly, this soupy jelly. Long bones, like leg bones. And a rib cage.

'And then I saw what I really didn't want to see. Next to the pot was a baby. Cut in half – just sliced in half, right across the belly. There was maybe a foot of ground between the top half and the bottom half, where his guts were. It was a boy. Maybe a year old. And he wasn't any ordinary Yard baby, because he had blue eyes. And his nose was different – straight, like ours.'

Bo knotted his hands together and stared at them. 'It was like we were killing our own, you know? Like we were killing our own. I couldn't take it anymore. I said to myself, This is too weird, all I'm doing from now on is concentrating on getting out of this place. I said, I'm through with seeing things. This right here is it. I said, From now on, all I'm doing is following orders – man, I'm already done.'

Father Joe waited a second, nodding like a sage. 'Do you feel better about this incident, now that you've told the group about it?'

'I don't know.' Bo retreated into himself. 'Maybe.'

Jack hesitantly raised his hand a couple of inches off his lap. 'I don't want to keep going up on my roof. Could we talk about that some more?'

'You never heard of willpower?' Lester asked.

The meeting broke up a little while later, and Bo disappeared almost instantly. I helped Harry and Frank stack the chairs while Father Joe told me how much I'd gotten out of the meeting. 'These feelings are hard to let go of. Lots of times I've seen men experience things they couldn't even grasp until a couple of days went by.' He put a hand on my shoulder. 'You might not believe this, Tim, but something happened to you while Bo was sharing with us. He reached you. Come back soon, will you, and let the others help you get through it?'

I said I'd think about it.

6

When I opened the door to my loft, the red light on the answering machine flashed like a beacon in the darkness, but I ignored it and went into the kitchen, turning on lights along the way. I couldn't even imagine *wanting* to talk to anyone. I wondered if I would ever know the truth about anything at all, if the actual shape of my life, of other lives too, would ever remain constant. What had really happened in Bachelor's encampment? What had John met there and what had he done? I made myself a cup of herbal tea, carried it back into the main part of the loft, and sat down in front of the paintings that had been shipped from Millhaven. I had looked at them during the long nights of work, been pleased and delighted by them, but until this moment I had never really *seen* them – seen them together.

The Vuillard was a much greater painting than Byron Dorian's, but by whose standards? John Ransom's? April's? By mine, at least at this moment, they had so much in common that they spoke in the same voice. For all their differences, each seemed crammed with possibility, with utterance, like Glenroy Breakstone's saxophone or like the human throat – overflowing with expression. It occurred to me that for me, both paintings concerned the same man. The isolated boy who stared out of Vuillard's deceptively comfortable world would grow into the man turned toward Byron Dorian's despairing little bar. Bill Damrosch in childhood, Bill Damrosch near the end of his life – the painted figures seemed to have leapt onto the wall from the pages of my manuscript, as if where Fee Bandolier went, Damrosch trailed after. Heinz Stenmitz meant that I was part of that procession, too.

The red light blinked at my elbow, and I finished the tea, set down the cup, and pushed the playback button.

'It's Tom,' said his voice. 'Are you home? Are you going to answer? Well, why aren't you home? I wanted to talk to you about something kind of interesting that turned up yesterday. Maybe I'm crazy. But do you remember talking about Lenny Valentine? Turns out he's not fictional, he's real after all. Do we care? Does it matter? Call me back. If you don't, I'll try you again. This is a threat.'

I rewound the tape, looking across the room at the paintings, trying to remember where I had heard or read the name Lenny Valentine – it had the oddly unreal 'period' atmosphere of an old paperback with a tawdry cover. Then I remembered that Tom had used Lenny Valentine as one of the possible sources for the name Elvee Holdings. How could this hypothetical character be 'real after all'? I didn't think I wanted to know, but I picked up the receiver and dialed.

7

I waited through his message, and said, 'Hi, it's Tim. What are you trying to say? There is no Lenny – '

Tom picked up and started talking. 'Oh, good. You got my message. You can deal with it or not, that's up to you, but I think this time I'm going to have to do *something*, for once in my life.'

'Slow down,' I said, slightly alarmed and even more puzzled than before. Tom's words had flown past so quickly that I could now barely retain them. 'We have to decide about *what*?'

'Let me tell you what I've been doing lately,' Tom said. For a week or so, he had busied himself with the two or three other cases he had mentioned to me in the hospital, but without shedding the depression I had seen there. 'I was just going through the motions. Two of them turned out all right, but I can't take much credit for that. Anyhow, I decided to take another look through all those Allentowns, and any other town with a name that seemed possible, to see if I could find anything I missed the first time.'

'And you found Lenny Valentine?'

'Well, first I found Jane Wright,' he said. 'Remember Jane? Twenty-six, divorced, murdered in May 1977?'

'Oh, no,' I said.

'Exactly. Jane Wright lived in Allerton, Ohio, a town of about fifteen thousand people on the Ohio River. Nice little place, I'm sure. From 1973 to 1979, they had a few random murders – well, twelve actually, two a year, bodies in fields, that kind of thing – and about half of them went unsolved, but I gather from the local paper that most people assumed that the killer, if there was one single killer, was some kind of businessman whose work took him through town every now and then. And then they stopped.'

'Jane Wright,' I said. 'In Allerton, Ohio. I don't get it.'

'Try this. The name of the homicide detective in charge of the case was Leonard Valentine.'

'It can't be,' I said. 'This is impossible. We had this all worked out. Paul Fontaine was in Allentown, Pennsylvania, in May of 'seventy-seven.'

'Precisely. He was in Pennsylvania.'

'That old man I talked to, Hubbel, pointed right at Fontaine's picture.'

'Maybe his eyesight isn't too good.'

'His eyesight is terrible,' I said, remembering him pushing his beak into the photograph.

Tom said nothing for a moment, and I groaned. 'You know what this means? Paul Fontaine is the only detective in Millhaven, as far as we know, who could *not* have killed Jane Wright. So what was he doing at that house?'

'I suppose he was beginning a private little investigation of his own,' Tom said. 'Could it be a coincidence that a woman named Jane Wright is killed in a town with the right sort of name in the right month of the right year? And that the detective in charge of the case has the initials LV, as in Elvee? Is there any way you can see that as coincidental?'

'No,' I said.

'Me, neither,' Tom said. 'But I don't understand this LV business anymore. Would someone call himself Lenny Valentine because it starts with the same letters as Lang Vo? That just doesn't sound right.'

'Tom,' I said, remembering the idea I'd had that morning, 'could you check on the ownership of a certain building for me?'

'Right now, you mean?'

I said yes, right now.

'Sure, I guess,' he said. 'What building is it?'

I told him, and without asking any questions, he switched on his computer and worked his way into the civic records. 'Okay,' he said. 'Coming up.' Then it must have come up, because I could hear him grunt with astonishment. 'You know this already, right? You know who owns that building.'

'Elvee Holdings,' I said. 'But it was just a guess until I heard you grunt.'

'Now tell me what it means.'

'I guess it means I have to come back,' I said, and fell silent with the weight of all *that* meant. 'I'll get the noon flight tomorrow. I'll call you as soon as I get there.'

'As soon as you get here, you'll see me at the gate. And you have your pick of the Florida Suite, the Dude Ranch, or the Henry the Eighth Chamber.'

'The what?'

'Those are the names of the guest rooms. Lamont's parents were a little bit eccentric. Anyhow, I'll air them out, and you can choose between them.'

'Fontaine wasn't Fee,' I said, finally stating what both of us knew. 'He wasn't Franklin Bachelor.'

'I'm partial to the Henry the Eighth Chamber myself,' Tom said. 'I'd suggest you stay away from the Dude Ranch, though. Splinters.'

'So who is he?'

'Lenny Valentine. I just wish I knew *why*.'

'And how do we find out who Lenny Valentine is?' Then an idea came to me. 'I bet we can use that building.'

'Ah,' Tom said. 'Suddenly, I'm not depressed anymore. Suddenly, the sun came up.'

PART SIXTEEN

From Dangerous Depths

1

And so, again because of an unsolved murder, I flew back to Millhaven, carried the same two bags out again into the bright, science-fictional spaces of its airport, and again met the embrace of an old friend with my own. A twinge, no more, blossomed and faded in my shoulder. I had removed the blue cast shortly after putting down the telephone the night before. Tom snatched my hanging bag and stepped back to grin at me. He looked revived, younger, and more vital than when he had visited me in the hospital. Everything about him seemed fresh, and the freshness was more than an aura of soap, shampoo, and clear blue eyes: it was the result of an awakened excitement, a readiness to join the fray.

Tom asked about my shoulder and said, 'This might be crazy – it's so little evidence, to bring you all the way back here.'

We were walking through the long gray tube, lined with windows on the runway side, that led from the gate into the center of the terminal.

'I don't care how little it is.' I felt the truth of it as soon as I had spoken – the size of the evidence didn't matter when the evidence was right. If we could apply pressure in the right place, a dead woman in a small town in Ohio would let us pry open the door to the past. Tom and I had worked out a way to do that on the telephone last night. 'I liked Paul Fontaine, and even though I had what looked like proof, I never – '

787

'I could never quite believe it, either,' Tom said. 'It all fit together so neatly, but it still felt wrong.'

'But this old queen in Tangent, Hubbel, pointed right at him. He couldn't see very well, but he wasn't blind.'

'So he made a mistake,' Tom said. 'Or we're making one. We'll find out, soon enough.'

The glass doors opened before us, and we walked outside. Across the curving access road, hard bright sunlight fell onto the miles of pale concrete of the short-term parking lot. I stepped down off the curb, and Tom said, 'No, I parked up this way.'

He gestured toward the far end of the passenger loading zone, where a shiny blue Jaguar Vanden Plas sat in the shade of the terminal just below a NO PARKING sign. 'I didn't know you had a car,' I said.

'It mainly lives in my garage.' He opened the trunk and put my bags inside, then lowered the lid again. The trunk made a sound like the closing of a bank vault. 'Something came over me, I guess. I saw it in a showroom window, and I had to have it. That was ten years ago. Guess how many miles it has on it.'

'Fifty thousand,' I said, thinking I was being conservative. In ten years, you could put fifty thousand miles on your car just by driving once a week to the grocery store.

'Eight,' he said. 'I don't get out much.'

The interior of the car looked like the cockpit of a private jet. When Tom turned the key, the car made the noise of an enormous, extremely self-satisfied cat being stroked in a pool of sunlight. 'Lots of times, when I can't stand being in the house anymore, when I'm stuck or when there's something I know I'm not seeing, I go out into the garage and take the car apart. I don't just clean the spark plugs, I clean the *engine*.' We rolled down the access road and slipped without pausing into the light traffic on the expressway. 'I guess it isn't transport, it's a hobby, like fly fishing.' He smiled at the picture he had just evoked, Tom Pasmore in one of his dandy's suits sitting on the floor of his garage in the middle of the night, polishing up the exhaust manifold. Probably his garage floor sparkled; I thought the entire garage probably resembled an operating theater.

He brought me out of this reverie with a question. 'If we're not wasting our time and Fontaine was innocent, who else could it be? Who is Fee Bandolier?'

This was what I had been considering during the flight. 'He has to be one of the men who used Billy Ritz as an informant. According to Glenroy, that means he's either Hogan, Monroe, or McCandless.'

'Do you have a favorite?'

I shook my head. 'I think we can rule out McCandless on grounds of age.'

Tom asked me how old I thought McCandless was, and I said about fifty-seven or fifty-eight, maybe sixty.

'Guess again. He's no older than fifty. He just looks that way.'

'Good Lord,' I said, realizing that the intimidating figure who had questioned me in the hospital was about my own age. He instantly became my favorite candidate.

'How about you?' I asked. 'Who do you think he could be?'

'Well, I managed to get into the city's personnel files, and I went through most of the police department, looking for their hiring dates.'

'And?'

'And Ross McCandless, Joseph Monroe, and Michael Hogan were all hired from other police departments within a few months of each other in 1979. So was Paul Fontaine. Andy Belin hired all four of them.'

'I don't suppose one of them came from Allerton?'

'None of them came from anywhere in Ohio –

McCandless claims to be from Massachusetts, Monroe says he's from California, and Hogan's file says he's from Delaware.'

'Well, at least we each have the same list,' I said.

'Now all we have to do is figure out what to do with it,' Tom said, and for the rest of the drive to Eastern Shore Road we talked about that – what to do with the people on our list.

2

His garage looked a lot more like the service bays in the gas stations on Houston Street than an operating room. I think it might have been even messier than the service bays. For some reason, I found this reassuring. We got the bags out of the Jaguar's trunk, walked through the piles of rags and boxes of tools, and after Tom swung down the door of the old garage, went into the house through the kitchen door. I felt a surge of pleasure – it was good to be in Tom Pasmore's house again.

He led me upstairs and past his office to a narrow, nearly vertical staircase which had once led up to the servants' rooms on the third floor. An only slightly worn gray-and-blue carpet with a floral pattern covered the stairs and extended into the third-floor hallway. Over each of the three doors hung an elaborately hand-painted sign announcing the name of the room. Dude Ranch Bunkhouse, Henry VIII Chamber, Florida Suite.

'I bet you thought I was kidding,' Tom said. 'Lamont's parents really were a little strange, I think. Now Dude Ranch has saddles and Wanted posters and bleached skulls, Henry has a suit of armor and an enclosed bed that's probably too small for you, and Florida has violent wallpaper, rattan chairs, and a stuffed alligator. But it's big.'

'I'll take it,' I said. 'Delius once wrote something called "Florida Suite."'

He opened the door to a set of rooms with dormer windows and white wallpaper printed with the flat patterns of enormous fronds – it reminded me of Saigon's dining room. Yellow cushions brightened the rattan furniture, and the eight-foot alligator grinned toward a closet, as if waiting for dinner to walk out.

'Funny you should remember that,' Tom said. 'There's a picture of Delius in the bedroom. Do you need help hanging up your things? No? Then I'll meet you in my office, one floor down, whenever you're ready.'

I took my bags into the bedroom and heard him walk out of the suite. Over a glass-topped bamboo table with conch shells hung a photograph of Delius that made him look like the physics master in a prewar English public school. Frederick Delius and an alligator, that seemed about right. I washed my hands and face, wincing a little when I moved my right arm the wrong way, dried myself off, and went downstairs to give Tom the last part of the plan we had been working out in the car.

3

'Dick Mueller was the first person to mention April's project to you, wasn't he? So he hints that he came across something in the manuscript.'

'Something worth a lot of money.'

'And then he arranges our meeting. And our boy gets rattled.'

'We hope,' I said. We were seated on the chesterfield

in Tom's office, with the three surreal computer dreams spread out on the table before us. Now that we knew the identity of the building in the defaced photograph, the computer's lunatic suggestions made a kind of sense – the pyramids and ocean liners were exaggerations of the marquee, and the glass guardhouses had grown out of the ticket booth. Bob Bandolier had intended to murder Heinz Stenmitz in the most fitting place possible, in front of the Beldame Oriental. The presence of either other people or Stenmitz himself had caused a change in Bandolier's plans, but the old theater had retained its importance to his son.

'It has to be where he's keeping his notes,' I went on. 'It's the last place left.'

Tom nodded. 'Do you think you can really convince him that you're Dick Mueller? Can you do that voice?'

'Not yet, but I'm going to take lessons,' I said. 'Do you have a phone book in this room?'

Tom got up and pulled the directory off a shelf beside his desk. 'Lessons in how to speak Millhaven?' He handed me the book.

'Just wait,' I said, and looked up Byron Dorian's number.

4

Dorian sounded unsurprised to hear from me: what did surprise him, mildly, was that I was back in Millhaven. He told me that he was working on getting a show in a Chicago gallery and that he had done another Blue Rose painting. He asked me how my writing was going. I spoke a couple of meaningless sentences about how the writing was going, and then I did succeed in surprising him.

792

'You want to learn how to talk with a Millhaven accent?'

'I'll have to explain later, but it's important that the poeple I talk to think I'm who I say I am.'

'This is wild,' Dorian said. 'You're even from here.'

'But I don't have the accent anymore. I know you can do it. I heard you do your father's voice. That's the accent I want.'

'Oh, boy. I guess I can try. What do you want to say?'

'How about "The police will be very interested"?'

'The p'leece 'll be very innarestud,' he said immediately.

'"This could be important for your career."'

'This cud be importint f'yore c'reer. What's this about, anyhow?'

'"Hello."'

'H'lo. Does this have anything to do with April?'

'No, it doesn't. "I don't want to go off on a tangent."'

'Are you saying that really, or do you want me to say it in Millhaven?'

'Say it in Millhaven.'

'I doan wanna go off onna tangunt. The whole thing is to put your voice up into your head and keep things flat. When you want emphasis, you just sort of stretch the word out. You know how you say Millhaven?'

'Muhhaven,' I said.

'Close. It's really M'avun. Just listen to the guys on the news sometime – they all say M'avun. It's almost *maven*, but not quite.'

'M'avun,' I said. 'H'lo. This cud be importint f'yore c'reer.'

'That was good. Anything else?'

I tried to think what else I would need. '"Movie theater. Beldame Oriental. This manuscript has some interesting information."'

'Movee thee*a*dur. Beldayme Orientul. This manyewscrip has got sum innaresteen infermashun. Oh, and if you want to say a time, you know? Like five o'clock? You just say five clock, unless it's twelve – you always say twelve o'clock, I don't know why.'

'I wanna meet yoo at five clock to talk about sum innaresteen infermashun.'

'Tock, not talk – tock about. And ta, not to. Ta tock. Otherwise, you're sounding pretty good.'

'Tock,' I said.

'Now you're tockin',' he said. 'Good luck, whatever this is.'

I hung up and looked over at Tom. 'Do you realize,' he asked, 'that you're probably trying to learn to talk in exactly the same way you did when you were a little boy?'

'I'm tryna lurn ta tock like Dick Mueller,' I said.

5

While Tom paced around the room, I called each of them in turn – McCandless, Monroe and Hogan – saying that I was Dick Mueller, a good friend and colleague of April Ransom's. I put my voice up into my head and kept it flat as Kansas. H'lo. I jus happena to cum across this innaresteen manyewscrip April musta hid beheyn the books in my office, because that's where I founnit. Iss fulla innaresteen infurmashun, ya know? Very innaresteen infurmashun, speshally if yur a p'leeceman in M'aven. In fact, this cud be importint f'yore c'reer.

McCandless said, 'If what you found is so important, Mr Mueller, why don't you bring it in?'

Hogan said, 'The April Ransom case is over. Thanks for calling, but you might as well just throw the manuscript away.'

Monroe said, 'What is this, some kind of threat? What kind of information are you talking about?'

I doan wanna go off onna tangent, but I think iss importunt for you ta tock ta me.

McCandless: 'If you want to talk about something, come down here to Armory Place.'

Hogan: 'I have the impression that we *are* talking. Why don't you just say what you have to say?'

Monroe: 'Maybe you could be a little more specific, Mr Mueller.'

I wanna meet you inside the ol movie thee*a*dur, the Beldame Orientul, five clock tomorrow morneen.

McCandless: 'I don't think we have any more to say to each other, Mr Mueller. Good-bye.'

Hogan: 'If you want to see me, Mr Mueller, you can come to Armory Place. Good-bye.'

Monroe: 'Sure. I love it. Give my best wishes to your doctor, will you?' He hung up without bothering to say good-bye.

I put down the receiver, and Tom stopped pacing.

6

'How much time do you think we have?' I asked.

'At least until dark.'

'How are we going to get in?'

'Who do you think inherited the Lamont von Heilitz collection of picklocks and master keys? Give me enough time, and I can get in anywhere. But it won't take five minutes to get into the Beldame Oriental.'

'How can you be so sure?'

Tom let his mouth drop open, raised his shoulders,

spread his hands, and gazed goggle-eyed around the room.

'Oh. You went down and looked at it.'

He came back to the couch and sat beside me. 'The entry doors on Livermore Avenue open with a simple key that works a deadbolt. The same key opens the doors on the far side of the ticket booth.' He pulled an ordinary brass Medeco key from his jacket pocket and set it on the table. 'There's an exit to the alley behind the theater – double doors with a push-bar that opens them from the inside. On the outside, a chain with a padlock runs between the two bracket handles. So that's easy, too.' From the same pocket, he removed a Yale key of the same size and color and placed it beside the first. 'We could also go in through the basement windows on the alley, but I imagine you've had enough B&E to last you a while.'

'So do you want to go in through the front or the back?'

'The alley. No one will see us,' Tom said. 'But it has one drawback. Once we're inside, we can't replace the chain. On the other hand, one of us could go in, and the other one could reattach the chain and wait.'

'In front?'

'No. On the other side of the alley there's a wooden fence that juts out from the back of a restaurant. They line up the garbage cans inside the fence. The top half of the fence is louvered – there are spaces between the slats.'

'You want us to wait out there until we see someone let himself into the theater?'

'No, I want you inside, and me behind the fence. When I see someone go in, I come around to the front. Those old movie theaters have two entrances to the basement, one in front, near the manager's office, and the other in back, close to the doors. In the center of the basement there's a big brick pillar, and behind that is the boiler. On the far side are old dressing rooms from the days when they used to have live shows between the movies. If I come down in front, he'll hear me, but he won't know you are already there. I could drive him right back to the pillar, where you'd be hiding, and you could surprise him.'

'Have you already been inside the theater?'

'No,' he said. 'I saw the plans. They're on file at City Hall, and this morning I went down there to check them out.'

'What am I supposed to do when I "surprise" him?'

'That's up to you, I guess,' Tom said. 'All you have to do is hold him still long enough for me to get to you.'

'You know what I think you really want to do? I think you want to stick a gun in his back while he's unlocking the chain, march him downstairs, and make him take us to the notes.'

'And then what do I want to do?'

'Kill him. You have a gun, don't you?'

He nodded. 'Yes, I have a gun. Two, in fact.'

'I'm not carrying a gun,' I said.

'Why not?'

'I don't want to kill anyone again, ever.'

'You could carry it without using it.'

'Okay,' I said. 'I'll carry the other gun if you come inside the theater with me. But I'm not going to use it unless I absolutely have to, and I'm only going to wound him.'

'Fine,' he said, though he looked unhappy. 'I'll go in with you. But are you absolutely clear about your reasons? It's almost as if you want to protect him. Do you have any doubts?'

'If one of those three turns up at the theater tonight, how could I?'

'That's just what I was wondering,' Tom said. 'Whoever

turns up is going to be Fielding Bandolier-Franklin Bachelor. Alias Lenny Valentine. Alias whatever his name is now.'

I said that I knew that.

He went to his desk and opened the top drawer. The computer hid his hands, but I heard two heavy metal objects thunk against the wood. 'You get a Smith & Wesson .38, okay? A Police Special.'

'Fine,' I said. 'What do you have, a machine gun?'

'A Glock,' he said. 'Nine millimeter. Never been fired.' He came around the desk with the guns in his hands. The smaller one was cupped in a clip-on brown holster like a wallet. The .38 looked almost friendly, next to the Glock.

'Someone I once helped out thought I might need them sometime.'

They had never been sold. They were unregistered – they had come out of the air. 'I thought you helped innocent people,' I said.

'Oh, he was innocent – he just had a lot of colorful friends.' Tom pushed himself up. 'I'm going to make the coffee and put it in a thermos. There's food in the fridge, when you get hungry. We'll leave here about eight-thirty, so you have about three hours to kill. Do you want to take a nap? You might be grateful for it, later.'

'What are you going to do?'

'I'll be around. There are a few projects I'm working on.'

'You have somebody watching the theater, don't you? That's why we're not already on the way there.'

He smiled. 'Well, I do have two boys posted down there. They'll call me if they see anything – I don't think our man will show up until after midnight, but there's no sense in being stupid.'

I carried the revolver upstairs and lay down on the bed with my head propped against the pillows. Three floors below, the garage door squeaked up on its metal track.

After a couple of minutes, I heard a steady tapping of metal against metal float up from inside the garage. I aimed the revolver at the dormer window, the alligator, the tip of Delius's pointed nose. Fee Bandolier aroused so much sorrow and horror in me, such a mixture of sorrow and horror, that shooting him would be like killing a mythical creature. I lowered my arm and fell asleep with my fingers around the grip.

7

By eight-fifteen we were back in the Jaguar, heading south toward Livermore Avenue. My stomach was full, my mind was clear, and because Tom's .38 hung on its clip from my belt, I felt like I was pretending to be a cop. A fat red thermos full of coffee stood between us. Tom seemed to have nothing on his mind but driving his pampered car. He was wearing black slacks and a black T-shirt under a black linen sports jacket, and he looked like Allen Stone without the beard and the paranoia. In more or less the same clothes, black jeans, one of Tom's black T-shirts, and a black zippered jacket, I looked like a middle-aged burglar. About twenty minutes later, we were moving past the St Alwyn, and five blocks farther south, the Jaguar slowly cruised past the front of what once had been the Beldame Oriental. On the far side of the street, a black teenager in a Raiders sweatshirt and a backward baseball cap squatted on his haunches and leaned against the yellow brick wall of a supermarket. When Tom glanced at him through the Jaguar's open window, the teenager shook his head sharply and bounced to his feet. He flipped a wave toward the Jaguar and started walking north on Livermore, rolling from side to side and tilting his head back as if listening to some private music.

'Well, no one's gone in through the front yet, anyhow,' Tom said.

'Who's that?' I indicated the swaggering boy.

'That's Clayton. When we get to the alley, you'll see Wiggins. He's very reliable, too.'

'How did you happen to meet them?'

'They came to visit me one day after seeing a story in the *Ledger*. I think they were about fourteen, and I believe they took the bus.' Tom smiled to himself and turned off to the right. Directly ahead of us on the left was a white building with a sign that read MONARCH PARKING. 'They wanted to know if the story in the paper was true, and if it was, they wanted to work for me.' Tom turned into the garage and drove up to the STOP HERE sign. 'So I tried them out on a few little things, and they always did exactly what I asked. If I said, stand on the corner of Illinois Avenue and Third Street and tell me how many times a certain white car goes past you, they'd stand there all day, counting white cars.'

We got out of the Jaguar, and a uniformed attendant trotted toward us on the curved drive sloping down to the lower floor. He saw the Jaguar and his face went smooth with lust. 'Could be any time between two and six in the morning,' Tom said. The attendant said that was fine, he'd be there all night, and took the keys, barely able to look away from the car. He went into his booth and returned with a ticket.

Tom and I walked out of the garage into the beginning of twilight. Grains of darkness bloomed in the midst of the fading light. Tom turned away from Livermore, crossed the street, and led me into the alley at the end of the block. Ten feet wide, the alley was already half in night. A tall boy leaning against a dumpster up at the far end straightened up when we moved in out of the light.

'Wiggins?' Tom asked. 'Nope,' said Wiggins, his voice soft but carrying, 'but check that chain.' He gave Tom a mock salute and sauntered off.

Tom moved ahead of me as the boy slipped out of the alley by the other end. Thirty feet along, opposite a high brown half-louvered fence, stood the long flat windowless back of the Beldame Oriental. Whorls of spray paint covered the gray cement blocks and surrounded the two wide black doors. I came up beside Tom. The thick length of chain that should have joined the two doors hung from the left bracket, and the padlock dangled from the right. Tom frowned at me, thinking.

'Is he in there?' I whispered.

'I think I should have sent Clayton and Wiggins down here right after you did your Dick Mueller act. I thought he'd wait until the end of his shift.'

'To do what?'

'Move the papers, of course.' At what must have been my expression of absolute dismay, he said, 'It's just a guess. He'll come back, anyhow.'

He pulled at the right bracket, and both doors moved forward a quarter of an inch and then clanked to a stop. 'Ah, there's another lock,' Tom said. 'I forgot that one.' Until Tom spoke, I had not seen the round, slightly indented shape of the lock beneath the bracket.

From the inside of his jacket he pulled a long dark length of fabric, held it by one end, and let its own weight unroll it. Keys of different sizes and long, variously shaped metal rods fit into slots and pockets all along the heavy, ribbed fabric. 'Lamont's famous kit,' he said. He bent forward to look at the lock and then took a silver key from one of the pockets in the cloth. He moved up to the door, poised the key, and nudged it squarely into the slot. He nodded. When he turned the key, we heard the bolt sliding back into its housing. Tom put the key into his jacket pocket, rolled up the length of fabric, and slid the fabric into a pouch on the inside of his jacket. I vaguely saw the shape of the Glock's handle protruding from a soft, glovelike holster just in front of his right hip.

'Try the penlight,' he said, and both of us pulled from our pockets the narrow, tubular flashlights he had produced just before we left the house. I turned around and pushed up the switch. A six-inch circle of bright light appeared on the brown wall opposite. I moved the light sideways, and the circle swept along the buildings across the alley, widening as it moved toward the other end. 'Good, aren't they?' he said. 'Lot of power, for a little thing.'

'Why would he come back, if he already moved his notes?'

'Dick Mueller. He'll imagine that Mueller will try to outfox him by showing up early, and so he'll show up even earlier.'

'Where would he put the notes?'

'I'm thinking about that,' Tom said, and grasped the bracket and opened the right half of the double doors. 'Shall we?'

I looked over his shoulder. In ten minutes the street lamps would switch on. 'Okay,' I said, and moved past him into the pure darkness of the theater.

As Tom closed the door behind us, I switched on the penlight and ran it over the dusty cement wall to our right and found the single black door in front of us that opened into the main body of the theater. To my left, wide concrete steps led down into the basement. 'Over here,' Tom said. I swung the light toward the door he had just closed and zigzagged it around until I found the interior indentation, painted over with black, that matched the one on the outside. 'Good, hold it there,' Tom said, and relocked the door. I trained the yellow circle of light on him as he unfolded the cloth, inserted the key, and packed the kit away into his jacket again.

'You know, those notes might still be here. Fee might have come over here from Armory Place right after we called and unlocked the chain to make it easier to get in tonight.'

He switched on his light and played it over the door. He held the beam on the doorknob and switched off the penlight as soon as he took the handle. I also turned off mine, and Tom opened the door.

8

After the door closed behind us, Tom placed the tips of his fingers in the small of my back and urged me forward into a dimensionless void. I remembered a long stretch of empty floor between the first row of seats and the back exit; in any case, I knew that all I was stepping toward so cautiously was the aisle; but it was like being blind, and I put my hands out in front of me. 'What?' I said, whispering for no rational reason. Tom nudged me forward again, and I took another two cautious steps and waited. 'Turn around,' Tom whispered back to me. I heard his feet moving quietly on the bare cement of the theater's floor and turned around, less out of obedience than fear that he was going to disappear. I heard the knob turning in the exit door. If he goes out, I thought, so do I. The door swung open an inch or two, and I realized what he was doing – a distinct line of grayish light shone along the edge of the door. He opened the door another few inches, and a column of gray light shone in the darkness. A shaft of the rough cement surface of the cement floor, painted black and lightly traced with dust, opened like an eye in front of the shining column. We would be able to see anyone who came into the theater.

He gently shut the door. Absolute blackness closed in on us again. Two soft footsteps came toward me, and his hand whispered against cloth as it slid into his pocket. There was a sharp *click*! and a round beam of yellow light, startlingly well defined and so physical it seemed solid, cut through the darkness and picked out the last two seats in the first row. 'Tom,' I began, but before I got any further, he had snapped off the penlight, leaving me with the shadow image of the raised seats. The floor moved under my feet like the deck of a boat. Over the shadow-flash image of the chairs, the hot beam of light hung in my eyes like the ghost of a flashbulb, increasing the darkness.

'I know,' Tom said. 'I just wanted to get a general idea.'

'Let's just stand here for a couple of minutes,' I said, and pressed the burning circle in my back against the wall. The floor immediately stopped swaying. Through the jacket, the cool roughness of the wall seeped toward my skin. I remembered the walls of the Beldame Oriental. Red, printed with a raised pattern of random, irregular swirls, they were stony, as abrasive as coral, sometimes sweaty with a chill layer of condensation. I bent my knees to concentrate the pressure on the hooks and ratchets, flattened my palms against the rough stipple of the cement, and waited for details to swim up out of the blank dark wall in front of me. Tom's soft, slow breathing at my side seemed indistinguishable from my own.

A sense of space and dimension began to shape the darkness. I began to be aware that I stood near one corner of a large tilted box that grew smaller as it rose toward the far end. After a time, I could make out before me the raised edge of the stage as a slight shimmer, like rays of heat coming up off a highway. This disappeared as Tom Pasmore moved in front of me and then returned when he moved quietly away up the side of the theater. I heard his footsteps dampen but not disappear as he left the cement apron extending from the first row of seats to the stage and stepped onto the carpeting. The shimmer solidified into the long swelling shape of the stage, and the seats gradually became visible as a dark, solid triangle fanning up and out from a point a few feet from where I stood. Tom's face was a faint, pale blotch up the aisle.

At the far end of the theater was another aisle, I remembered, and the wide space of a central passage, probably mandated by the fire department, divided the rows of seats in half.

I could now just about make out the curved backs of the nearest individual seats, and I had a dim sense of the width of the aisle. Beneath the pale smudge of his face, Tom was a black shape melting in and out of the darkness surrounding him. I followed him up the aisle toward the front of the theater. When we reached the last row, Tom stopped moving and turned around. A metallic glint like a slipperiness in the air marked the panel in the lobby door. Looking down, we could see a great soft darkness over the stage that must have been the curtains.

The gleam of the metal plate disappeared as he put his hand over it, and the door yielded before him in another widening column of shining gray light.

The lobby was filled with hazy illumination from the oval windows set into thick doors opposite leading out to the old ticket booth and the glass doors on Livermore Avenue.

Two chest-high pieces of wooden furniture stood in the place of the old candy counter. Even in the partial light, the lobby seemed smaller than I had remembered and cleaner than I had expected. At its far end, another set of doors with metal hand plates led into the aisle at the other side of the theater. I went up to the furniture where the candy counter had been, bent down to look at a round carving in what I thought was the back of a shelf unit, and saw ornate letters in the midst of the filigree. I took out my penlight and shone it on the letters. INRI. I pointed the light at what looked like a lectern and saw the same pattern. I was standing in front of a portable altar and pulpit.

Tom said, 'Some congregation must use this place as a church on Sundays.'

Tom went toward a door in the wall next to the pulpit. He tried the knob, which jittered but would not otherwise move, unrolled the burglar kit, peered at the keyhole, and worked another key into the slot. When the lock clicked and the door opened, Tom packed away the kit and peered inside. He took out his light, switched it on, and with me behind him went into a stuffy, windowless room about half the size of Tom's kitchen.

'Manager's office,' he said. The penlights picked out a bare desk, a small number of green plastic chairs, and a wheeled rack crowded with shiny blue choir robes. Four cardboard boxes stood lined up in front of the desk. 'Do you suppose?' Tom asked, running his light along the boxes.

I went through the chairs and knelt in front of the two boxes at the center of the desk. The open flaps had been simply laid shut, and I opened those of the first box to see two stacks of thick blue books. 'Hymnals,' I said.

I played my own light along the other boxes while Tom started moving things around behind me. None of the boxes showed anything but ordinary wear, no rips or holes made by busy rats. All four would hold hymnals. I checked them anyhow and found – hymnals. I stood up again and turned around. The rack stuffed with choir robes angled out into the room. Tom's head protruded above the rack, and the circle of light before him shone on a plywood door almost exactly the color of his hair. 'Fee always liked basements, didn't he?' Tom said. 'Let's take a look.'

9

I walked around the rack as Tom opened the door, and trained my penlight just ahead of his. A flight of wooden stairs with a handrail began at the door and led down to a cement floor. I followed Tom down the stairs, playing my light over the big space to our right. Two startled mice scrambled toward the far wall. We descended another three or four steps, and the mice darted into an almost invisible crevice between two cement blocks in the wall on the other side of the basement. Tom's light flashed over an old iron furnace, a yard-square column of bricks, heating pipes, electrical conduits, rusting water pipes, and drooping spiderwebs. 'Cheerful place,' he said.

We reached the bottom of the steps. Tom went straight ahead toward the furnace and the front of the theater, and I walked off to the side, looking for something I had glimpsed while I watched the mice scramble toward the wall. Tom's light wandered toward the center of the basement; mine skimmed over yards of dusty cement. I moved forward in a straight line. Then my beam landed squarely on a wooden carton.

I walked up to it, set down the thermos, and pushed at the edge of the flat top. It moved easily to the side and exposed a section of something square and white. I slid the top all the way off the carton and held the light on what I thought would be reams of paper arranged into neat stacks. A lunatic message gleamed back into the light. Black letters on a white ground spelled out BUYTERVIO. Above that, in another row of letters, was MNUFGJKA. Two other nonsense words filled the top two rows of the carton. 'Buytervio?' I said to myself, and finally realized that the carton contained the letters once used to spell out the movie titles on the marquee.

'Come over here.'

Tom's voice came from a penumbra of light behind the furnace. I picked up the thermos and followed the beam of my own light across the dirty floor to the side of the furnace and then shone it on Tom. 'He was here,' he said. 'Take a look.'

I misheard him to say *He's here*, and, thinking that Fee's corpse lay on the ground beside the gun with which he had killed himself, experienced an involuntary surge of rage, sorrow, grief, and pain, all mingled with something that felt like regret or disappointment. My light swept over a pair of cardboard boxes. Did I want him to live, in spite of everything he had done? Or did I simply want to be in at the end, like Tom Pasmore? Raging at both Fee and myself, I aimed my light at Tom's chest and said, 'I can't find him.'

'I said, he *was* here.' Tom took my hand and aimed the beam of light on the boxes I had overlooked in my search for the corpse.

Their flaps lay open, and one box was tipped onto its side, exposing an empty interior. Ragged holes of various sizes had been chewed into two sides of the box still upright. Tom had tried to prepare me, but as much as a body, the empty boxes were the end of our quest. I said, 'We lost him.'

'Not yet,' Tom said.

'But if he moved the notes to some other safe house, all he has to do now is kill Dick Mueller.' I placed my hand on my forehead, seeing horrible things. 'Oh, God. It might already be too late.'

'Mueller's safe,' came Tom's voice from the darkness beside me. 'I called his house last night. His answering machine said that he was on vacation with his family for

808

the next two weeks. He didn't say where.'

'But what if Fee called him? He'd know . . .' It didn't matter, I saw.

'He still has to come back,' Tom said. 'He knows *somebody's* trying to blackmail him.'

That was right. He had to come back. 'But where did he put those notes?'

'Well, I have an idea about that.' I remembered Tom saying something like this earlier and waited for him to explain. 'It's an obvious last resort,' Tom said. 'In fact, it's been in front of our face all along. It was even in front of his face, but he didn't see it either, until today.'

'Well, what is it?'

'I can't believe you won't see it for yourself,' Tom said. 'So far, you've seen everything else, haven't you? If you still don't know by the time we're done here, I'll tell you.'

'Smug asshole,' I said. We separated again to probe the rest of the theater's basement.

On a hydraulic platform beneath the stage, I found an organ – not the 'mighty Wurlitzer' that would have appeared in a billow of curtains before the start of features in the thirties, but a tough, bluesy little Hammond B-3.

The old dressing rooms on the basement's left side were nothing but barren concrete holes with plywood counters to suggest the twelve-foot mirrors and rings of light bulbs that had once stood along their far walls.

'Well, now we know where everything is,' Tom said.

Back in the office, Tom led me past the glimmering robes and pushed the rack into place. We went back out into the lobby, and he relocked the door. I started toward the entrance we had used on our way out, but Tom said, 'Other side.'

His instincts were better than mine. From the far side of the theater, we would be invisible to anyone entering through the back door, while he – Fee – would be outlined in the column of gray light the instant he came inside. I walked past the altar and pulpit to the padded doors on the far side of the lobby and let us back into the darkness.

10

We moved blindly down the far aisle, touching the backs of the seats for guidance, moving through total blackness, a huge coffin, where every step brought us up against what looked like a solid, unyielding black wall that retreated as we moved forward.

Tom touched my shoulder. We had not yet reached the wide separation between rows in the middle of the theater, but could have been anywhere from the third row to the twentieth. The black wall still stood before me, ready to step back if I stepped forward. I groped for the worn plush of the chair beside me, pushed down the seat, and slid into it. I heard Tom moving into the seat directly in front of me and sensed him turning around. I put out my right hand and felt his arm on the back of the seat. I made out the faint shape of his head and upper body. 'All right?' he asked.

'I usually like to sit closer to the screen,' I said.

'We're probably in for a long wait.'

'What do you want to do when he comes in?'

'If he comes through the exit door, we do what we have to do until he settles down. If he checks the place out with a flashlight, we get out of our seats and crouch down here in the aisle. Or we flatten out under the seats. I don't think he's going to be very thorough, because he'll be confident about being the first one here. The point is to get him comfortable. Once he sits down to wait it out, we split up and come toward him from opposite ends.

Silently, if possible. When we get close, scream your head off. I'll do the same. He won't know where the hell we are, he won't know how many of us there are, and we should have a good chance to take him.'

'What happens after that?'

'Are you thinking about disarming him and taking him to Armory Place? Do you think he'll confess? Or that we'd ever walk out of Armory Place? You know what would happen.'

I said nothing.

'Tim, I don't even believe in the death penalty. But right now, the only alternative is to get out of here and go back home. In a couple of years, maybe ten years, he'll make a mistake and get caught. Is that good enough?'

'No,' I said.

'I've spent about fifteen years working to get innocent men off death row – saving lives. That's what I *believe* in. But this isn't like anything else I know – it's as if we discovered that Ted Bundy was a detective with so many fallbacks and paper trails that he could never be brought to justice in the normal way.'

'I thought you said you weren't interested in justice.'

'Do you want to know how I really see this? I don't think I could say this to anyone else. There aren't many people who would understand it.'

'Of course I want to know,' I said. By now I could dimly make out Tom's face. Absolute seriousness shone out of him, along with something else that made me brace myself for whatever he would say.

'We're going to set him free,' he said.

As a euphemism for execution, the phrase was ludicrous.

'Thanks for sharing that,' I said.

'Remember your own experience. Remember what happened to your sister.'

I saw my sister sailing before me into a realm of utter

mystery and felt Tom's psychic assurance, his depth of understanding, strike me like a tide.

'Who is he now? Is *that* worth saving? That person is a being who has to kill over and over again to satisfy a rage so deep that nothing could ever touch it. But who is he, really?'

'Fee Bandolier,' I said.

'Right. Somewhere, in some part of himself he can't reach, he is a small boy named Fielding Bandolier. That boy passed through hell. You've been obsessed with Fee Bandolier even before you really knew he existed. You almost made him up out of your own history. You've even seen him. Do you know why?'

'Because I identify with him,' I said.

'You see him because you love him,' Tom said. 'You love the child he was, and that child is still present enough to make himself visible to you, and he makes himself visible to your imagination because you love him.'

I remembered the child who came forward out of swirling dark, on his open palm the word that cannot be read or spoken. He was the child of the night, William Damrosch, Fee Bandolier, and myself, all of whom had passed through the filthy hands of Heinz Stenmitz.

'Do you remember telling me about your old nurse, Hattie Bascombe, who said that the world is half night? What she didn't say was that the other half is night, too.'

Too moved to speak, I nodded.

'Now let's get to the important stuff,' Tom said.

'What?'

'Give me that thermos you've been carrying around. I don't want to be asleep when he finally gets here.'

I handed him the thermos, and he poured some of the coffee into its top and drank. When he had finished, he passed the thermos back to me. I didn't think I would ever sleep again.

11

He's psychic, I thought. It was as if Tom Pasmore had seen into my mind. I felt intense gratitude and another, darker emotion combining resentment and fear. Tom had probed into private matters. My early memories, those that had refused to come on command in front of my old house or my family's graves, came flooding into me. One of these, of course, was Heinz Stenmitz. Another, equally powerful, was my sister's last day of life and my brief journey across the border into the territory from which she had never returned. I had never spoken of these moments to Tom – I had just learned of one, and of the other I never spoke, never, not to anyone. Every particle of my consciousness fled from it. That moment could not be held in the mind, because it held terror and ecstasy so great they threatened to tear the body apart. Yet some portion of the self retained and remembered. While knowing nothing of this, Tom Pasmore still knew all about it. My resentment vanished when I realized that he had read a version of it in one of the books I had written with my collaborator; he was smart and perceptive enough to have worked out the rest by himself. He had not probed: he had just told me what he knew. I sat in the dark behind Tom, realizing that what had sounded like sentimental froth made me chime with agreement – I wanted to release Fee Bandolier. I wanted to set him free.

12

I sat in the dark behind Tom Pasmore, wide awake and *loose in time*. Forty years collapsed into a single endless moment in which I was a child watching a movie called *From Dangerous Depths* while a huge blond man who smelled like blood ran his hand over my chest and spoke the unspeakable, I was a soldier in an underground room staring at an altar to the Minotaur, a greenhorn pearl diver unbottoning the shirt of a mutilated dead man named Andrew T. Majors, a shred of infinite being speeding toward an annihilating ecstasy, a wounded animal in St Mary's Hospital, a man with a notebook walking through a city park. I turned around to look six rows back and saw myself kneeling before Heinz Stenmitz, doing what he wanted me to do, what I thought I had to do to stay alive. *You survived*, I said silently, *you survived everything*. His pain and terror were mine, because I had survived them. Because I had survived them, they had educated me; because they were a taste always in my mouth, they had helped to keep me sane in Vietnam. What was unbearable was what had to be borne. Without the consciousness of the unbearable, you put your feet where Fee had placed his, or ended up as unaware as Ralph Ransom. I thought of John, whose life had once seemed so golden to me, peering into the depths of Holy Sepulchre, and of the closed-off place where his readiness for experience had taken him.

I thought for a long time of what had happened to John Ransom.

13

I don't know how long Tom and I sat waiting in the dark theater. After I started thinking about John, I got restless. I stood up to stretch and pace the aisle. Tom never left his seat. He sat without moving for long periods, as if we were at an opera. (Even when I am at the opera, I have trouble sitting still.) After two or three hours in the dark, I could make out most of the stage and the great hanging weight of the curtain, without being able to see individual folds. When I looked back, I could see the shape of the double doors into the lobby. All of the seats more than four or five rows ahead of me congealed into a single object. I got back into my seat and leaned back, thinking about Fee and John and Franklin Bachelor, and after half an hour had to get up and swing my arms and walk down toward the stage and the curtains again. When I got back into my seat and settled down, I heard a noise from the other side of the theater – a creak. 'Tom,' I said.

'Old buildings make noise,' he said.

Half an hour later, the back door rattled. 'What about that?' I asked.

'Uh huh,' he said.

The door rattled again. Both of us were sitting up straight, leaning forward. The door rattled a third time, and then nothing happened for a long time. Tom leaned back. 'I think some kid saw that the chain was unhooked,' he said.

We sat in the dark for another long period. I looked at my watch, but the hands were invisible. I crossed my legs and closed my eyes and was instantly in Saigon, the restaurant not the city, trying to tell Vinh about John

Ransom. He was working on the accounts, and he wasn't interested in John Ransom. 'Write a letter to Maggie,' he said. 'She knows more than you think.' I came awake with a jerk and felt under the seat for the thermos. 'Me, too,' Tom said.

The ceiling ticked. A footstep sounded in the lobby. The ceiling ticked again. Tom sat like a statue. Write a letter to Maggie? I thought, and realized to whom I could write a letter about John Ransom. She was probably a person who shared certain of Maggie's gifts. Time wore on. I yawned. At least an hour passed, second by slow second. Then the alley door rattled again.

'Wait for it,' Tom said.

There was an unendurable silence for a few seconds, and then a key slotted into the keyhole. The sound was as clear as if I stood on the other side of the door. When the door swung open, Tom eased out of his seat and crouched beside it. I did the same. Someone walked into the space between the alley door and the theater exit. The exit door cracked open an inch, and gray light filtered through the crack. It opened wider, and a man stepped into the column of gray light and became a silhouette. He turned to look behind him, exposing his profile in the column of gray light. It was Monroe, and he had a gun in his hand.

14

Monroe stepped forward and let the exit door close behind him. The dark shape of his body moved a few steps alongside the stage. He stopped moving to let his eyes adjust. Tom and I crouched behind the seats, waiting for him either to take a seat or to check to see if his caller had already arrived. Monroe remained standing in the far aisle, listening, hard. Monroe was good – he stood next to the stage for so long that my legs began to cramp. The hot circle below my shoulder blade started to throb.

Monroe relaxed and pulled a police baton from his belt. A beam of light flew from the end of the baton and darted from the middle of the front seats to the rear doors on his side, then to the wall six or seven feet down from John and me.

Monroe walked up the aisle, training the light along the rows of seats. He reached the wide central passage that divided the front seats from the rear and paused, working out if he'd be wasting his time by going farther. Tom noiselessly lowered himself to the floor. I sank to my knees and kept my eyes on Monroe. The detective moved across the divide between the seats and went up another two rows. Then he scanned the light in long sweeps across the seats in front of him. If he walked up another five rows, he'd have to see us, and I held my breath and waited for the cramp in my legs to subside.

Monroe turned around. The beam of light flitted across the wall beside us, traveled over the folds of the curtains, and struck the exit door. Monroe started to move back down the far aisle. I watched him reach the side of the stage, turn around to stab his light in a long pass back over the seats, and then push through the door. I sat down and stretched out my legs. Tom looked up at me and put his finger to his mouth. The alley door opened.

'He's getting away,' I whispered.

Tom shushed me.

The back door opened and closed in a flurry of foot-steps. The exit door swung in. Monroe and a man in a blue running suit came back into the theater. Monroe said, 'Well, I don't think anyone got in.'

'But they unlocked the *chain*,' said the other man.

'Why do you think I called you?'

'It's funny,' said the other man. 'I mean, they take the

chain off, and then they lock the *door*? Only but two other people got the keys.'

'Church people?'

'My deacon has one. And the owner's got one, that's for sure. But he never shows his face – I never even met the man. Did you look at my office?'

'Do you keep any money in there?'

'Money?' The other man chuckled. 'Holy Spirit is just a little storefront church, you know. But I keep the hymnals, choir robes, that kind of thing, in my office.'

'Let's have a look, Reverend,' Monroe said, and they set off up the aisle, the flashlight trained straight ahead of them. I lowered myself to the carpet and heard them pass by on the other end of the long row of seats and open the doors to the lobby.

As soon as they had left the theater, Tom slid into his row and I into mine, scooting along the cool concrete floor. The murmur of voices from the lobby ceased when the two men went into the office. I flattened out on the dusty concrete, my face an inch from a patch of fossilized gum. I could see the bushy outline of Tom's head and the pale blot of his left hand through the seat supports. The lobby doors swung in again.

'It doesn't make sense at *all* to me, officer,' said the reverend. 'But tomorrow, I'm getting the locks changed, and I'm buying a new padlock for that chain.'

I stopped breathing and tried to disappear into the floor. My cheek flattened out against the wad of gum. It felt like dead skin. The two men came down the far aisle. My heart accelerated as they approached my row. Their slow footsteps neared me, passed me, continued down the aisle.

'How did you come to check us in the first place, officer?'

'Some lunatic called me this afternoon, asking me to meet him here this morning.'

'*In* here?' They stopped moving.

'So I thought I ought to come down here, take a look at the place.'

'The Lord thanks you for your diligence, officer.'

The footsteps resumed.

'I'm putting that chain back on the door and getting new locks tomorrow. The Lord doesn't favor fools.'

'Sometimes I wonder about that,' Monroe said.

Their shoes clicked against the concrete beside the stage. The exit door swished open, closed. The door into the alley clanked open. I got to my feet. Tom stood up in front of me. From the alley came the sound of the chain rattling through the brackets. I exhaled and began brushing invisible dust off my clothes.

'That was interesting,' Tom said. 'Monroe turns out to be a good cop. Do you suppose all three of them will come down?'

'I hope the two don't show up together.'

'Which one do you think is Fee?'

I saw Ross McCandless's seamy face and empty eyes leaning toward my hospital bed. 'No hunches,' I said.

'I have one.' Tom stretched out his arms and arched his back. He swatted his jacket and brushed off his knees. Then he walked back to the end of the aisle and sat down in his old seat.

'Which one?'

'You,' he said, and laughed.

15

'What is Fee going to think when he comes back and finds the chain back in place?'

'Oh, that's going to be helpful.' Tom turned around

and placed his arm on the back of his seat. 'He'll think the reverend came here after someone reported an attempted break-in, checked the place out, and locked it up again. When he works that out, he'll be even more confident that he got here first. So he won't be paying as much attention – he'll be careless.'

We settled back down to wait.

16

I drifted into a strained half-sleep. My eyes were open, and I did not dream, but I began hearing voices speaking just above the level of audibility. Someone described seeing a blue-eyed baby cut in half beside a dead fire. A man said that it would catch up with me in a day or two. I could see everything, another said, I saw my dead friend and his team leader standing beneath a giant tree. They told me to go on, go on, go on.

Dark patterns unfolded and moved in the air before me, shifting as the voices rose and fell.

Someone spoke about a rattling chain. The rattle of the chain was important. Couldn't I hear that the chain was rattling?

The voices whisked backward into the psychic vault from which they had come, the darkness stood still, and I sat upright, hearing the chain clanking over the brackets on the alley doors. A great deal of time had passed, an hour at least, perhaps two, while I drifted along the border between sleep and wakefulness. My mouth felt dry and my eyes could not focus.

'Were you asleep?' Tom asked.

'Will you be quiet?' I said.

The tail of the chain struck one of the brackets as it

passed through, making a tinny *clink*!

'Here we go,' Tom said.

We moved out of our seats and listened to the key sliding into the lock. The alley door opened and shut, and a man moved two steps past the alley door. Harsh light flew around the frame, and then shrank to a yellow glimmer visible only at a point about waist-high on the frame. It disappeared as the footsteps ticked away into silence.

Tom and I looked at each other.

'Should we wait for him to come back up?'

'Aren't you curious about what he's doing down there?'

I looked at him.

'I'd like to know what it is.'

'He'd hear us on the stairs.'

'Not if we use the office stairs – the wooden ones. They're so old they're soft. Remember, he's convinced no one else is here.' Tom stood up and began moving quickly and soundlessly up the aisle.

I almost ran into him at the door. He was sitting on the armrest of the last seat, bending over. 'What are you doing?'

'Taking off my shoes.'

I knelt to unlace my Reeboks.

17

We moved out into the lobby and padded past the church equipment to the office door. I whispered something about his being able to hear us unlocking it.

'I can take care of that.' Tom took out the length of ribbed cloth and, after finding the key that fit the office door, pulled out a short length of soft black cloth, about an eighth of an inch wide. With it came a small, narrow metal rod that looked like a toothpick. 'You can only use these once, and sooner or later it fouls up the lock, but do we care?'

He knelt in front of the door, wet the tip of the cloth in his mouth, and patiently worked a small portion into the keyhole. He prodded it into place with the metal toothpick, then nudged the key in beside it. Most of the rest of the cloth moved into the slot along with the lock. When he turned the key, the last of the cloth disappeared. The lock made no sound at all.

Tom motioned for me to squat beside him. He leaned toward me to whisper. 'We're going to have to pick up the rack and set it down again. I'll go through the door first. Count to a hundred, and listen to what's going on down there. If nothing happens, come down. Don't worry about where I am.'

'You want me to sneak up on him?'

'Play it by ear.'

'What if he sees me?'

'Eventually, he has to see you,' Tom said. 'Don't tell him that you made the call, and don't let him see your gun. Give him some stuff about Elvee – say you couldn't stay away, say you were going to call him as soon as you found Fontaine's notes.'

'And what are you going to do?'

'Depends on what he does. Just remember what you know about him.'

What I knew about him?

Without giving me time to ask what he meant, Tom stood up and slid the door toward us and went inside. In utter darkness, we moved side by side toward the rack. My outstretched hands touched smooth fabric, and I felt my way up the robe to the top of the rack. Tom and I worked our way to opposite ends, and he whispered, '*Now*,' so softly that the command nearly vaporized before it reached me. I lifted the pole on my side, and the entire heavy rack went two inches off the floor. The rack moved with me when I stepped sideways, and then continued to move. I took another sideways step. Tom and I gingerly lowered the rack, and its wheels noiselessly met the floor.

I heard his feet whisper around the rack and groped toward the wall and the basement door. Suddenly, what we were doing seemed as absurd as the attempt John Ransom and I had made to capture Paul Fontaine. It was impossible to go downstairs without making noise. I rubbed sweat off my forehead. A few cautious steps took me to the wall, and I reached out for Tom, imagining him easing open the plywood door. My hand touched nothing but empty air. I moved sideways, still reaching out. I took another step. My hand brushed the edge of the door, and I nearly banged it against the wall. I lowered myself back down into a squat, still trying to find Tom. He wasn't there. I leaned forward and poked my head over the top of the staircase. In the very faint illumination provided by a flashlight at the other end of the basement, a dark shape glided away from the bottom of the stairs and disappeared.

I pushed myself slowly upright, moving with exaggerated care to keep my knees from popping, and started counting to one hundred.

18

I wanted to keep going until I got to two hundred, maybe two thousand, but I made myself walk through the opening and set my right foot down on the first step. Tom had been right – the wood was so soft it was almost furry.

I felt the grain through my sock. I grabbed the rail and went down the next two steps without making any noise at all. I padded down another three steps, then another two, and my head finally passed beneath the level of the floor.

Someone was sweeping the beam of a flashlight over the floor behind the furnace. I saw the circle of light leap to the right of the big furnace and then travel slowly along the floor until it disappeared behind it. A few seconds later, it reappeared to the left of the furnace and moved another five or six feet toward the wall of the dressing rooms. Then it skittered over the floor, looping and circling on the cement until it steadied again a few feet further from the furnace and began making another long steady sweep across the floor. Fee was standing behind the furnace and facing in my direction, looking for something. I thought I knew what it was.

I moved slowly down the last five steps. He would not be able to see me even if he moved around the furnace – all he could see was what fell into the beam of his flashlight. I came down onto the cement and began walking carefully toward the place where I remembered seeing the brick pillar. The man with the flashlight backed up and swung the light wildly over the floor between the furnace and the dressing rooms. I stopped moving, and the elongated circle of light swooped over the furnace, throwing the pipes and conduits above it into stark black silhouette, streaked across the wall near the stairs, and came to rest on the floor to the left of the furnace. The man backed up again, and I took a few more quiet steps toward the invisible pillar.

Judging from the direction he'd been moving, Tom must have been hidden in the rear of the basement, probably behind the crate of marquee letters. He would wait until I identified the man with the flashlight before he made his move. Maybe he would wait until Fee said something incriminating. I hoped he wouldn't wait until Fee started shooting.

Another quiet step, then another, took me to the spot where I had seen the pillar. I felt the air in front of me, but not the pillar. I took a third step forward. The beam of light was making big sideways sweeps over the territory to the right of the furnace as Fee began a more systematic search. I moved sideways without bothering to check the air with my hands and bumped right into the pillar. It didn't make any more noise than an auto wreck. The light stopped moving. I pressed up against the side of the pillar, drenched in sweat.

'Who's there?' The voice sounded much calmer than I was.

I felt around for the back of the pillar and stepped behind it, hoping that Tom Pasmore would come forward out of the darkness.

'Who are you?'

I put my hand on the little holster clipped to my belt. The man with the flashlight moved to the left side of the furnace – the beam of light flared across the basement and flattened on the back wall. His footsteps clicked against the cement. Then he stopped moving and turned off his light.

'I'm a police officer,' he said. 'I am armed and prepared to shoot. I want to know who you are and what you're doing here.'

This wasn't right – he wasn't acting guilty. Fee would have switched off his flashlight the instant he realized that someone else was in the basement. He wasn't even protecting himself by moving away.

'Say something.'

In my panic, I couldn't remember the voices of either of the two men who could have been Fee Bandolier. Rough chunks of mortar pushed into my side. Wishing that I was anywhere else but in this basement, I grasped a thick chunk of mortar, broke it off the pillar, and tossed it toward the stairs. The mortar hit the concrete and shattered.

'Oh, come on,' the man said. 'That only works in the movies.'

He took another step, but I could not tell where.

'Let me tell you what's going on,' he said. 'You came here to meet a man who knew all about you – he called a bunch of detectives, me, Monroe, and I don't know who else. Either he called you, too, or you heard people talking about it.' He was moving noiselessly around as he talked, his voice seeming to come from first one side of the furnace, then, in what seemed an impossibly short time, the other. He sounded perfectly calm.

'You know me – you can take a shot at me, but you won't hit me. And then I'll take you down.'

There was a long silence, and then he spoke again, from somewhere off to the right. 'What troubles me about this is, you're not acting like a cop. Who the hell are you?'

I wasn't acting like a cop, and he wasn't acting like Fee Bandolier.

The pillar was still between us. It was a good, sturdy pillar. Not a bullet in the world could go through it. And if he didn't shoot, we were in the basement for the same reason.

'Sergeant Hogan?' I said.

Sudden light flooded over me from somewhere behind my right shoulder, and my shadow loomed against the wall like a giant. My stomach plummeted toward my knees, but no gunshot resounded, neither from the man with the light nor from Tom. I wanted to duck around the pillar, but I made myself turn into the glare.

'I thought we got rid of you, Underhill.' He sounded angry and amused at the same time. 'Are you trying to get yourself killed?'

'You surprised me,' I said.

'It's mutual.' He turned the light off me. I put my hand back on the holster as the beam swept across the floor toward the source of his voice. The circle of the beam diminished as it sped toward him and then flattened out against his chest and jumped up to illuminate Michael Hogan's handsome, weathered face. He blinked under the light, and then turned the flashlight back on me, aiming the beam at my chest, so that I could see. 'What are you doing here?'

'The same as you,' I said. 'I wanted to see if I could find the papers that used to be in those boxes. When I saw that they were gone, I was looking for anything that might have fallen out.'

He sighed, and the beam dropped to the floor. 'How did you know where the papers would be?'

'Just before Paul Fontaine died, he said "Bell." It took me a couple of weeks to understand that he was trying to say Beldame Oriental.'

'You're the lunatic who made the calls?'

'I didn't know anything about that until you told me,' I said. 'What did he say?'

'How did you get in here?'

'John Ransom's father owned a hotel. He has lots of skeleton keys.'

'Then how did you manage to reattach the chain from the inside?'

'I came in the front,' I said. 'About fifteen minutes before you showed up. I didn't think I'd see anyone else in here.'

'You were down here when I came in?'

'That's right.'

'I guess I'm lucky you didn't shoot me.'

'With what?'

'Well, you picked a hell of a night to go exploring.'

'I guess you're not Fielding Bandolier, are you?'

827

The light jumped into my face again, blinding me. I held up my hand to block it. 'Did Ransom come down here with you? Is he somewhere in the theater?'

A jolt of terror went through me like cold electricity. I kept my hand up over my face. 'I'm alone. I don't think John cares anymore.'

'Okay.' The light dropped to my waist, and I lowered my hand. 'I'm sick of the subject of Fielding Bandolier. I don't want to hear anything more about him, from you or anyone else.'

'So you knew about the theater because of the telephone call?'

'Knew what?' He waited, and when I did not answer, he said, 'The caller asked me to meet him here. I thought that was unusual, to put it mildly, so I checked up on the ownership. I gather you've heard of Elvee Holdings.'

'Didn't you get confirmation from Hubbel, the head of Bachelor's old draft board?'

'We never talked to Hubbel. McCandless said he was going to organize that, and then he called it off.'

'McCandless,' I said.

Hogan said nothing. I heard his feet move as he turned around. The oval of light swung away from me and traveled across the floor toward the stairs. 'I don't know why we're standing here in the dark,' he said. 'There's a switch on the wall next to the stairs. Go over there and turn on the lights, will you?'

'I don't think that's a very good idea.'

'Do it.'

He moved the beam to just in front of me and lit my way to the bottom of the stairs. I walked along the moving oval on the floor, wondering where Tom had hidden himself. When I got to the bottom of the stairs, Hogan aimed the light at the switch.

'What if someone else shows up?'

'Who would that be?'

I took a breath. 'Ross McCandless. He's a murderer. And if someone called a bunch of detectives, trying to lure the right one here, then – even if he already moved his papers – he has to come back to kill the person who called him.'

'Turn on the lights,' Hogan said.

I reached for the switch and flipped it up.

19

Bare light bulbs dangling over the bottom of the stairs, near the furnace, somewhere near the crate of letters, and far at the front of the basement, threw out enough light to stab into my eyes. The entire basement came into being around us, larger and dirtier than I had expected. It was brightly lit around the hanging bulbs, shadowy in the corners, but entirely visible. Matted spiderwebs hung from the cords of the light bulbs. Tom Pasmore was nowhere in sight.

In a gray suit and a black T-shirt, Michael Hogan stood about twelve feet away, looking at me dryly. A long black flashlight tilted like a club in his right hand. He moved his thumb and switched it off. 'Now that we can see, let's check out the place where he put the boxes.' Hogan wheeled around and strode past the pillar and the furnace.

I walked across the basement and came around the side of the furnace. Hogan was standing near the boxes, staring down at the cememt floor. Then he noticed my feet. 'What did you do with your shoes?'

'Left them upstairs.'

'Humph. Junior G-man.'

The empty boxes lay on the dusty floor. Hogan scanned the area between the furnace and the wall to our right, then the long stretch of floor between the furnace and the dressing rooms. There were no crumpled pieces of paper. I looked back at the dressing rooms. The door of the first, the one farthest from us, hung slightly ajar.

'You notice something?'

'No,' I said.

'Tell me about McCandless,' he said.

'Some Millhaven policeman has been using a false identity.' Hogan's face hardened with anger, and I took a few steps away. 'I know you think it was Fontaine, *I* thought it was Fontaine, but not anymore.'

'Why is that?'

'That piece of paper I found in the Green Woman was about a woman named Jane Wright. She was killed in May 1977, if those papers are what I think they are. The name of the town was partially destroyed, but it looked like Allentown. So I looked through all the Allentown newspapers for that month, but nobody of that name turned up.'

'You think that proves anything?'

'I found a Jane Wright who had been murdered in a town called Allerton, Ohio, in that same month. When Paul Fontaine was a detective in Allentown.'

'Ah,' Hogan said.

'So it has to be someone else. Someone who used Billy Ritz as an informant and who came to Millhaven in 1979. And there are only three men who have those things in common. You, Monroe, and McCandless.'

'Well, obviously, it isn't me,' he said, 'or you'd already be dead. But why did you rule out Monroe? And how on earth did you find out about Billy Ritz?'

'I kept my ears open. I talked to a lot of people, and some of them knew things.'

'Either you're a born cop or a born pain in the ass,' Hogan said. 'What about Monroe?'

Since I'd already said that I had come inside the theater

only fifteen minutes before he did, I couldn't tell him the truth. 'I stood outside in the alley and watched the door for a long time before I came in. Monroe showed up about twelve, twelve-thirty, something like that, looked at the chain, and left. So it's not him.'

Hogan nodded, swinging the big flashlight, and started walking away from the furnace toward the dressing room side of the basement. 'McCandless comes as kind of a shock.'

'But when you first heard me, you thought I was someone you knew. Someone on the force.'

'Monroe told a lot of people about that crazy phone call. I didn't know any of this stuff you just told me about the place in Ohio. Allerton?'

I nodded.

'I'll fax a picture of McCandless to the Allerton police, and that'll be that. It doesn't matter if he shows up here tonight or not. I'll take care of him. Let's go upstairs so you can get your shoes, and I'll take you to Ransom's, or wherever you're staying.'

'I'm staying at the St Alwyn,' I said, hoping that Tom could hear me, wherever he was. 'I'll walk there.'

'Even better,' Hogan said.

I walked away from him faster than he expected, uncertain why I had not trusted him completely. Why should it be better for me to be staying at a hotel than at John's? I moved toward the stairs, hearing Tom Pasmore telling me to remember what I knew about Fee Bandolier. It seemed that I knew a thousand things about Fee, none of them useful. Hogan came after me, moving slowly. I put my hand on the penlight in my pocket.

I got to the bottom of the stairs and said, 'Would you just stay where you are for a second?'

At the worst, I thought, I'd just look like a fool.

'What?' Hogan stopped moving. He had been reaching toward the button that fastened his suit jacket, and he dropped his hand when he saw me turning to face him.

I slapped the light switch down with my left hand, and with the other turned the bright beam of the penlight on his face. He blinked.

'Lenny Valentine,' I said.

Hogan's face went rigid with shock. Behind him, I saw Tom Pasmore move fast and silently out of the dressing room. I switched off my light and scrambled away from the stairs in the darkness. I had the impression that Tom was still moving.

'We're not going to go through this all over again, are we?' Hogan said. He hadn't moved an inch.

From somewhere near the pillar, Tom's light shot out and outlined his head. Hogan turned to face the light and said, 'Would you mind explaining what you think you're doing, Underhill?' He could not have seen any more than the bright dazzle of the flashlight, but he did not raise his hands.

I reached into my jacket, pulled out the revolver, thumbed the safety, and aimed it at his head.

Hogan smiled. 'What was that name you said?' He tilted his head, still smiling at Tom, and raised his right hand to unbutton the jacket of his suit. I remembered seeing him make the same gesture just before I had surprised him by turning off the light. He would have shot me as soon as I got to the top of the stairs. I realized that I was holding my penlight along the barrel of the revolver, aiming it at Hogan like another gun as if I had been planning my next act all along, and when Hogan's hand reached his jacket button, I switched it on. Tom instantly extinguished his own light.

'Lenny Valentine,' I said.

Hogan had already turned to face into my light, and he was not smiling anymore. A shadow moved into his eyes, and he opened his mouth to say something. The thought of hearing his next words sent a wave of pure revulsion

832

through me. Almost involuntarily, I pulled the trigger and sent a bullet down the bright, hot beam of light.

There was a red flash and a loud, flat crack that the cement walls amplified into an explosion. A black hole appeared just beneath Hogan's hairline, and the light illuminated a bright spatter from the back of his head. Hogan rocked back out of the beam and disappeared. His body hit the floor, and the stench of blood and cordite filled the air. A twist of white spun in the beam of light and disappeared.

'You took a while to make up your mind,' Tom said, shining his light on me. My stiff, outstretched arms were still aiming the revolver at the place where Hogan had been. I let them drop.

I could not remember what I'd seen in Hogan's face.

Tom shone his light downward. Hogan lay sprawled on the cement with most of his weight on his shoulder and hip, his legs bent and his arms flopped on either side. Blood flowed steadily out of the back of his head and pooled beneath his cheek.

I turned away and wobbled toward the wall. I groped around on the cinderblocks until I found the switch. Then I turned on the lights and looked back at him. A narrow line of red trickled out of the hole at his hairline and slanted across his forehead.

Tom came forward, holstering his automatic, and knelt beside Hogan's body. He rolled him onto his back, and Hogan's right arm landed softly in the growing pool of blood. The odor lodged in my stomach like a rotten oyster. Tom thrust his hands into one of the pockets of the gray suit coat. 'What are you doing?' I asked.

'Looking for a key.' He moved to the other side of the body and slid his hand into the other pocket. 'Well, well.' He brought out a small silver key and held it up.

'What's that for?'

'The papers,' he said. 'And now . . .' He put his hand

into the inner pocket of his own jacket and came out with a black marker pen. He uncapped the pen and looked up at me as if daring me to stop him. 'I'm no policeman,' he said. 'I'm not interested in justice, but justice is probably what this is.' He duck-walked a step away from the body, brushed a layer of dust off the cement, and wrote BLUE ROSE in big slanting letters. He spun himself around and looked at me again. 'This time, it really was the detective,' he said. 'Give me that gun.'

I came toward him and handed him the .38. Tom wiped it carefully with his handkerchief and bent over to place it in Hogan's right hand. Then he wrapped the fingers around the handle and poked the index finger through the trigger guard. After that, he raised the front of the suit jacket and pulled Hogan's own .38 out of its holster. He stood up and came toward me, holding out Hogan's gun. 'We'll get rid of this later.'

I slid the revolver into the little wallet clipped to my belt without taking my eyes off Hogan's body.

'We'd better get out of here,' Tom said.

I didn't answer him. I stepped forward and looked down at the face, the open eyes, the slack, empty face.

'You did the right thing,' Tom said.

'I have to make sure,' I said. 'You know what I mean? I have to be sure.'

I knelt beside the body and gathered the material at the waist of the black T-shirt. I pulled the fabric up toward Hogan's neck, but could not see enough. I yanked up the entire shirt until it was bunched under his arms and leaned over to stare at the dead man's chest. It was pale and hairless. Half a dozen circular scars the size of dimes shone in the white skin.

A wave of pure relief went through me like honey, like gold, and the reek of blood suddenly smelled like laughter.

'Good-bye, Fee,' I said, and yanked the shirt back down.

'What was that about, anyhow?' Tom asked behind me.

'The body squad,' I said. 'Old habit.'

I stood up.

Tom looked at me curiously, but did not ask. I switched off the light, and we went up the stairs in the dark.

Less than three minutes later, we were outside in the alley, and five minutes after that, we were back in the Jaguar, driving east.

20

'Hogan reacted to the name.'

'He sure did,' I said.

'And the business about his chest?'

'Bachelor had little round scars on his chest.'

'Ah, I forgot. The punji stick scars. One of those books I have mentioned them.'

'They weren't punji stick scars. Fee had them, too.'

'Ah,' Tom said. 'Yes. Poor Fee.'

I thought: Sail on, Fee, sail away, Fee Bandolier.

21

In the dark of the night, we threw Michael Hogan's revolver into the Millhaven River from the Horatio Street bridge. It was invisible even before it smacked into the water, and then it disappeared from history.

22

The last thing I remembered was the pistol smacking down into the water. I walked out of the garage, having spent all the time between Horatio Street and Eastern Shore Drive with Michael Hogan in the basement of the Beldame Oriental, and went across the top of the drive-way in the dark of the night. The moon had long ago gone down, and there were no stars. The world is half night, and the other half is night, too. I saw his face in the sharp, particular beam of the penlight; I saw the black little hole, smaller than a dime, smaller than a penny, appear like a beauty spot beneath his thinning hair.

He had grown to the age of five a block away from me. Our fathers had worked in the same hotel. Sometimes I must have seen him as I wandered through the neighbor-hood – a little boy sitting on the front steps beside a bed of carefully tended roses.

Tom came up beside me and opened the kitchen door. We went inside, and he flicked a switch, shedding soft light over the old sinks and the white wainscoting and the plain, scarred wooden counter. 'It's a little past three,' Tom said. 'Do you want to go to bed right away?'

'I don't really know,' I said. 'What happens now?' I meant: Whom do we tell? How do we tell?

'What happens now is that I have a drink,' Tom said. 'Do you feel like going straight upstairs?'

Frederick Delius and the stuffed alligator, the Florida Suite. 'I don't think I could go to sleep,' I said.

'Keep me company, then.' He dumped ice cubes in a glass, covered them with malt whiskey, and sipped from the glass, watching me. 'Are you okay?'

'I'm okay,' I said. 'But we can't just let him lie there, can we? For the church people to find?'

'I don't think the church people ever go into the basement. The only thing they use down there is the organ, and they raise that from the stage.'

I poured water into a glass and drank half of it in one long swallow.

'I have some ideas,' Tom said.

'You want people to know, don't you?' I swallowed most of the rest of the water and refilled the glass. My hands and arms seemed to be functioning by themselves.

'I want everybody to know,' Tom said. 'Don't worry, they won't be able to bury it this time.' He took another sip. 'But before we start shouting from the rooftops, I want to get those papers. We need them.'

'Where are they? Hogan's apartment?'

'Come on upstairs with me,' Tom said. 'I want to look at a photograph with you.'

'What photograph?'

He did not answer. I trailed along behind him as he went into the vast, cluttered downstairs room, walked past the couch and the coffee table, and went up the stairs to the second floor, turning on lights as he went.

Inside his office, he walked around the room, switching on the lamps. He sat down at his desk, and I fell into his chesterfield. Then I unclipped the holster and placed it on the glass table before me. Tom had pulled out the top drawer of his desk to remove a familiar-looking manila envelope.

'What I don't understand,' he said, 'is how Hubbel identified Paul Fontaine. Hogan was in that picture, standing right next to Fontaine. So how could Hubbel make a mistake like that?'

'He had lousy eyesight,' I said.

'That bad?'

'He had to put his eyes right up to what he was looking

at. His nose practically touched the paper.'

'So he actually examined the photograph very carefully.' Tom was facing me, leaning forward with the envelope in his hands.

'It looked to me like he did.'

'Let's see if we can solve this one.' He opened the flap and drew the newspaper photograph out of the envelope. Tom set the envelope on his desk and carried the photograph and his drink to the couch and sat beside me. He leaned forward and placed the photograph between us on the table. 'How did he identify Fontaine?'

'He pointed at him.'

'Right at Fontaine?'

'Right at him,' I said. 'Dead bang at Paul Fontaine.'

'Show me.'

I leaned over and looked at the picture of Walter Dragonette's front lawn crowded with uniformed and plainclothes policemen. 'Well,' I said, 'it was right in front of him, for one thing.'

'Move it.'

I slid the photograph before me. 'Then he pointed at Fontaine.'

'Point at him.'

I reached out and planted my finger on Paul Fontaine's face, just as Edward Hubbel had done in Tangent, Ohio. My finger, like Edward Hubbel's, covered his entire face.

'Yes,' Tom said. 'I wondered about that.'

'About what?'

'Look at what you're doing,' Tom said. 'If you put your finger there, who are you pointing at?'

'You know who I'm pointing at,' I said.

Tom leaned, lifted my hand off the photograph, and slid it across the table so that it was directly in front of him. He placed his finger over Fontaine's face exactly as I had. The tip of his finger aimed directly at the next man in the picture, Michael Hogan. 'Whose face am I pointing at?' Tom asked.

I stared down at the photograph. He wasn't pointing at Fontaine, he was obliterating him.

'I bet it wasn't Ross McCandless who canceled the trip to Tangent,' Tom said. 'What do you think?'

'I think – I think I'm an idiot,' I said. 'Maybe a moron. Whichever one is dumber.'

'I would have thought he meant Fontaine, too. Because, like you, I would have *expected* him to identify Fontaine.'

'Yes, but . . .'

'Tim, there isn't any blame.'

'Fontaine must have looked into Elvee Holdings. John and I led Hogan straight to him, and all he wanted to do was get my help.'

'Hogan would have killed Fontaine whether you and John were there or not, and he would have blamed it on random violence. All you did was confirm that another shooter was present that night.'

'Hogan.'

'Sure. You just gave them a nice convenient eyewitness.' He took another swallow of his drink, seeing that he had succeeded in banishing most of my guilt. 'And even if you hadn't seen some indistinct figure, wasn't McCandless intent on making you say that you had? It made everything easier for him.'

'I guess that's right,' I said, 'but I still think I'm going to retire to Florida.'

He smiled at me. 'I'm going to bed, too – I want us to get those papers as soon as possible tomorrow morning. This morning, I mean.'

'Are you going to tell me where they are?'

'You tell me.'

'I don't have the faintest idea,' I said.

'What's the last place left? It's right in front of us.'

'I don't appreciate this,' I said.

'It starts with E,' he said, smiling.

'Erewhon,' I said, and Tom kept smiling. Then I remembered what we had learned when we first began looking into Elvee. 'Oh,' I said. 'Oh.'

'That's right,' Tom said.

'And it was only a couple of blocks from the Beldame Oriental, so he probably moved them around five or six yesterday evening, right after he got off shift.'

'Say it.'

'Expresspost,' I said. 'The mail drop on South Fourth Street.'

'See?' Tom said. 'I told you you knew.'

Shortly afterward, I went upstairs to Frederick Delius and the alligator, undressed, and crawled into bed to get four hours of restless, dream-ridden sleep. I woke up to the smell of toast and the knowledge that the most difficult day I was to have in Millhaven had just begun.

PART SEVENTEEN

John Ransom

1

By eight-thirty the sun was already high over the rooftops of South Fourth Street, and we stepped out of the car's briskly conditioned air into ninety-degree heat that almost instantly plastered my shirt to my sides. Tom Pasmore was wearing one of his Lamont von Heilitz specials, a blue three-piece windowpane check suit that made him look as if he had just arrived from Buckingham Palace. I had on more or less what I'd worn on the airplane, jeans and a black double-breasted jacket over a white button-down shirt, and I looked like the guy who held the horses.

Expressport Mail and Fax was a bright white shopfront with its name painted in drastic red letters above a long window with a view of a clean white counter at which a man with rimless glasses and a red tie stood flipping through a catalogue. The bronze doors of individual mail receptacles lined the walls behind him.

We came through the door, and the man closed the catalogue and placed it on a shelf beneath the counter and looked eagerly from Tom to me and back to Tom. 'Can I do something for you?' he said.

'Yes, thanks,' Tom said. 'I want to pick up the papers that my colleague deposited here for the Elvee Corporation yesterday evening.'

A shadow of uncertainty passed over the clerk's face. 'Your colleague? Mister Belin?'

'That's him,' Tom said. He brought the key out of his pocket and put it on the counter in front of the clerk.

'Well, Mister Belin said he was going to do that himself.' He looked over his shoulder at a rank of the locked boxes. 'We can't give you a refund, or anything like that.'

'That's all right,' Tom said.

'Maybe you should tell me your name, in case he comes back.'

'Casement,' Tom said.

'Well, I guess it'll be all right.' The clerk picked up the key.

'We're grateful for your help,' Tom said.

The clerk turned away and went to the wall to his right, twiddling the key in his fingers. The boxes in the bottom row were the size of the containers used to ship dogs on airplanes. When he had nearly reached the rear of the shop, the clerk knelt down and put the key into a lock.

He looked back up at Tom. 'Look – since you already paid for the week, I can reserve this one for you until the time is up. That way, if you want to use it again, you won't have to pay twice.'

'I'll pass that on to Mister Belin,' Tom said.

The clerk began pulling stacks of paper stuffed into manila folders out of the box.

2

We carried the long cardboard container the clerk had given us up the stairs to the office, Tom in front and me behind him. On the way back, Tom had stopped off at a stationery store and bought six reams of copy paper, four of which were now distributed across the tops of the files, with the other two slipped down beside the files at each end of the box. Halfway up the stairs, the handholds started to rip, and we had to carry the box the rest of the way by holding the bottom.

The box went on the floor beside the copy machine. Tom flipped its square black switch, and the machine hummed and flashed. I picked up one of the fat manila folders and opened it up. Papers of varying sizes and colors filled it, some of them closely filled with single-space typing that ran from edge to edge without margins, other crowded with the handwriting I had first seen in the basement of the Green Woman. I turned to one of the typed pages.

When we left the bar it was one or two in the morning, and she was too drunk to walk straight. I ought to take you in for public intoxication. You ain't a cop now, are you? No, honey, I own one of those big hotels downtown, I already told you that. Which one? The Heartbreak Hotel, I said. I already been there. I probably owe you lots of rent. I know that, honey, we'll take care of that. She giggled. Here's my car. Her black skirt rode up on her thighs when she got in. Skinny thighs, one black and blue thumbprint. We got to the GWT and she said This dump? Don't worry, there's a throne all ready for you downstairs.

I looked up at Tom, who was leafing through another file. 'This is incredible,' I said. 'He described them in such detail. He even put in the dialogue. It's like a book.'

Tom looked a little sickened by whatever he had read. He closed his file. 'They seem to be more or less in order – each murder takes up about twenty pages, from what I see here. How many pages do you think we have, about a thousand?'

'Something like that,' I said, looking down at the stacks.

'At least fifty murders,' Tom said. Both of us looked at the stacks of papers. 'I suppose he let Fontaine solve some of the most colorful ones.'

'Who are you going to send copies to?'

'The FBI. Isobel Archer. The new chief, Harold Green.

Someone at the *Ledger*. Geoffrey Bough?'

'You'll make his day,' I said. 'You're not going to identify yourself, are you?'

'Sure, I'm the worried citizen who found these papers in a garbage can. In fact, I think the worried citizen is about to call Ms Archer right now.'

He went to his desk and dialed a number. I sat down on the couch and listened to his half of the conversation. When I realized that I was still holding the thick file, I put it on the table as if I thought I might catch something from it.

'I'd like to speak to Isobel Archer, please. It has to do with a shooting.

'Yes, I'll hold.

'Miss Archer? I'm glad to be able to speak to you.

'My name? Fletcher Namon.

'Well, yes, it is about a shooting. I didn't know what to do about this, so I thought I'd call you.

'I don't want to get involved with the police, Miss Archer. It's *about* a policeman.

'Well, yes.

'Okay. Last night, this was. I saw a detective, I don't know his name, but I saw him one night on the news, I know he's some kind of detective, and he was going into the old movie theater down on Livermore.

'Late at night.

'No, I couldn't tell you what time. Anyhow, after he got inside, I heard this shot.

'No, I got out of there, fast.

'I'm sure.

'Sure, I'm sure. It was a gunshot.

'Well, I don't know what I expect you to do. I thought that was your business. I gotta go now.

'No. Good-bye.'

He put down the phone and turned to me. 'What do you think?'

'I think she'll be down there with a hacksaw and blowtorch in about five minutes.'

'I do, too.' He took all the pages out of the folder on his lap and tapped their bottom edges against his desk. 'It'll take me two or three hours to copy all this stuff. Do you want to hang around, or is there something else you feel like doing?'

'I guess I should talk to John,' I said.

'Do you want me with you?'

'You're an executive,' I said. 'Flunkies like me do the dirty work.'

3

I walked through the heat down the pretty streets toward John Ransom's house. The Sevens, Omdurman Place, Balaclava Place, Victoria Terrace; brick houses matted with ivy, stone houses with ornate entrances and leaded windows, mansard roofs and pointed gables. Sprinklers whirled, and small boys zipped past on ten-speed bicycles. It looked like a world without secrets or violence, a world in which blood had never been shed. A FOR SALE sign had been staked into the neat lawn in front of Alan Brookner's house.

The white Pontiac stood at the curb across from John's house, in the same place I had found it on my first morning back in town. It was squeezed into a parking place just long enough to accommodate it, and I remembered, as I had last night, a noisy little patriot in shorts charging out of his flag-draped fortress to yell about abuse. I walked across sunny Ely Place and went up to John's front door and rang his bell.

He appeared at the narrow window to the left of the

door and looked out at me with frowning curiosity – the way you'd look at an encyclopedia salesman who had come back after you'd already bought the books. By the time he opened the door, his expression had altered into something more welcoming.

'Tim! What are you doing back here?'

'Something came up,' I said.

'More research? The book going well?'

'Very well. Can I come in for a minute?'

'Well, sure.' He stepped back and let me in. 'When did you get in? Just now?'

'Yesterday afternoon.'

'Well, you shouldn't be staying in a hotel. Check out and come back here, stay as long as you like. I just got some information about houses for sale in Perigord, we could go over it together.'

'I'm not in a hotel,' I said. 'I'm staying with Tom Pasmore.'

'That stuck-up phony.'

John had followed me into the living room. When I sat down on the couch facing the wall of paintings, he said, 'Why don't you make yourself at home?'

'Thanks again for sending me the Vuillard,' I said. He had not rearranged the paintings to compensate for its absence, and the place where it had been looked naked.

He was standing beside the couch, looking down at me, uncertain of my mood or intentions. 'I knew you appreciated it. And like I said, I couldn't have it in my house anymore – it was too much for me.'

'I'm sure it was,' I said.

He gave me the encyclopedia salesman look again and then moved his face into a smile and sat down on the arm of a chair. 'Did you come here just to thank me for the painting?'

'I wanted to tell you some things,' I said.

'Why do I think that sounds ominous?' He hitched his knee up beside him on the fat arm of the chair and kept his smile. John was wearing a dark green polo shirt, faded jeans, and penny loafers without socks. He looked like a stockbroker on a weekend break.

'Before we get into them, I want to hear how Alan's doing.'

'Before we get into these mysterious "things"? Don't you think I'll want to talk to you afterward?'

I reminded myself that John Ransom was pretty smart, after all. 'Not at all,' I said. 'You might want to talk to me night and day.'

'Night and day.' He tucked his foot in close to his thigh. 'Let's try to keep that tone.' He looked up, theatrically. 'Well, Alan. Dear old Alan. I don't suppose you ever saw him when he was out at County.'

'I stopped in for five minutes, on the way to the airport.'

He raised his eyebrows. 'Did you? Well, in that case, you know how bad he was. Since then – really, since I moved him into Golden Manor – he's come a long way. They've been giving him good care, which they damn well better, considering how much the place costs.'

'Does he mind being there?'

John shook his head. 'I think he likes it. He knows he'll be taken care of if anything happens to him. And the women are all crazy about him.'

'Do you visit him often?'

'Maybe once a week. That's about enough for both of us.'

'I suppose that's right,' I said.

He narrowed his eyes and bit on his lower lip. He didn't get it. 'So what did you want to tell me?'

'In a day or two, this whole town is going to go crazy all over again. There'll be another big shakeup in the police department.'

He snapped his fingers and then pointed at me, grinning with delight. 'You bastard, you found those papers. That's it, isn't it?'

'I found the papers,' I said.

'You're right! This town is going to lose its mind. How many people did Fontaine kill, anyway? Do you know?'

'It wasn't Fontaine. It's the man who killed Fontaine.'

His mouth opened, and his mouth twitched in and out of a grin. He was trying to decide if I were serious. 'You can't be trying to tell me that you think Alan –'

He hadn't even been interested enough to ask about the ballistics report. 'Alan didn't shoot Paul Fontaine,' I said. 'Alan shot me. Someone was hiding between the houses across the street. I think he must have had some kind of assault rifle. Alan, you, me – we had nothing to do with it at all. He was already there by the time we got to the house. He was with Fontaine in the ghetto. Maybe he even saw him call me here. He probably followed him to the house.'

'So the guy in Ohio identified the wrong man?'

'No, he identified the right one. I just didn't understand what he was doing.'

John pressed a palm to his cheek and regarded me without speaking for a couple of seconds. 'I don't suppose I have to know the whole story,' he finally said.

'No, it's not important now. And I never saw you today, and you never saw me. Nothing I tell you, nothing you tell me, ever leaves this house. I want you to understand that.'

He nodded, a little puzzled about the notion of his telling me anything, but eager enough to grasp what he thought was the main point. 'Okay. So who was it?'

'Michael Hogan,' I said. 'The person you knew as Franklin Bachelor changed his name to Michael Hogan. Right now, he's lying dead on the floor of the Beldame Oriental with a gun in his hand and the words BLUE ROSE

850

written beside his body. In black marker.'

John took in my words avidly, nodding slowly and appreciatively.

'Isobel Archer is going to wangle her way inside the theater and find his body. A couple of days from now, she and a few other people, including the FBI, will get photocopies of the notes he took on his killings. About half of them are handwritten, and there won't be any doubt that Hogan wrote them.'

'Did you kill him?'

'Look, John,' I said. 'If I killed a detective in Millhaven, I should never tell anyone about it. Right? But I want you to understand that everything we say here is only between us. It'll never leave this room. So the answer is yes. I shot him.'

'Wow.' John was absolutely glowing at me. 'That's amazing – you're fantastic. The whole story is going to come out.'

'I don't think you want that,' I said.

John stared at me, trying to read my thoughts. He slid his leg off the arm of the chair. Whatever he saw in me he didn't like. He had stopped glowing, and now he was trying to look injured and innocent. 'Why wouldn't I want everything to come out?'

'Because you murdered your wife,' I said.

4

'First, you brought her to the St Alwyn and stuck a knife in her, but you didn't quite manage to kill her. So when you heard that she was coming out of the coma, you got into her room and finished her off. And of course, you killed Grant Hoffman, too.'

He slid down off the arm of the chair into the seat. He was stunned. He wanted me to know that he was stunned. 'My God, Tim. You know exactly what happened. You even know *why*. It was you who came up with Bachelor's name. You put the whole thing together.'

'You wanted me to know about Bachelor, didn't you? That's part of the reason you wanted me to come here in the first place. You had no idea he was living here – he was supposed to have come in from out of town after seeing your picture in the paper, killed Hoffman and your wife, and then slipped off into his new identity when things got too hot.'

'This is so absurd, it's crazy,' John said.

'As soon as I got here, you told me you thought Blue Rose was an old soldier. And you had worked out this wonderful story about what happened when you got to Bachelor's camp in Darlac Province. It was a good story, but it left out some important details.'

'I never wanted to talk about that,' he said.

'You made me work it out of you. You kept dropping hints.'

'Hints.' He shook his head sadly.

'Let's talk about what really happened in Darlac Province,' I said.

'Why don't you just rave, and when you're finished raving, why don't you get out of here and leave me alone?'

'You shared an encampment with another Green Beret named Bullock. Bullock and his A team went out one day and never came back. You went out and found their bodies tied to trees and mutilated. Their tongues had been cut out.'

'I *told* you that,' John said.

'You didn't think the VC had killed them. You thought Bachelor had done it. And when you saw Bullock's ghost, you were positive. You were where you thought he was

852

all the time – you were at the point where you could see through the world.'

'That's where I was,' he said. 'But I don't think that you've ever been there.'

'Maybe not, John. But the important thing is that you felt betrayed – and you were right. So you wanted to do what you thought Bachelor would do.'

'You better know what you're talking about,' John said. 'You better not be throwing out guesses.'

'Bachelor had already escaped by the time you got there. So you burned his camp to the ground. Then you systematically killed everyone who had been left behind, all of Bachelor's followers who were too young, too old, or too feeble to go with him. How did you do it? One an hour, one every two hours? At the end, you killed his child – put him on the ground and cut him in half with your bayonet. Then you killed his wife. At the end, you hacked her up and put her in the communal pot and ate some of her flesh. You even cleaned her skull. You were *being* Bachelor, weren't you?'

He glowered at me, working his jaws. I saw that held-down anger surge into his eyes, but this time he did not try to conceal it. 'You don't really have the right to talk about this, you know. It doesn't *belong* to you. It belongs to people like *us*.'

'But I'm not wrong, am I?'

'That's not really relevant,' John said. 'Nothing you say is really relevant.'

'But it isn't wrong,' I said.

John threw up his hands. 'Look, even if all this happened, which no one in the normal world would believe, because they could not even *begin* to comprehend it, it just gives Bachelor more reason to want revenge on *me*.'

'Bachelor never worked that way,' I said. 'He couldn't. You were right about him – he was always across the border, and every human concern but survival was meaningless to him. After Lang Vo, he went through three or four different identities. By the time he spent twelve years calling himself Michael Hogan, all he cared about Franklin Bachelor was that the world should keep thinking he was dead.'

'What you're saying just proves that *he killed my wife*. If you don't see that, I can't even talk to you.'

'He didn't kill her,' I said. 'He beat her up. Or he had Billy Ritz beat her up. It amounts to the same thing.'

'Now I know you're crazy.' John threw back his head and growled at the ceiling. His face was starting to get red. 'I told you. I hit her. It was the end of my marriage.' He lowered his head and looked at me with spurious pity. 'Why in the world would *Billy Ritz* beat up my wife?'

'To slow her down,' I said. 'Or stop her altogether, without killing her.'

'Slow her down. That means something to you.'

'April was writing a letter a week to Armory Place about the Green Woman. Hogan took his victims there. He kept his notes in the basement. He had to stop her.'

'So he killed her,' John said. 'I wish you could hear yourself. You turn everything around into its opposite.'

'You went out for a drive with April the night she admitted seeing Byron Dorian. You'd been planning to kill her for weeks. You had an argument in the car, and you got out and went to the bar down the street. I think you were drinking to get up the courage to finally do it. You thought you'd have to get home by yourself, but when you left the bar, her car was still parked down the street. And when you looked inside it, there she was, unconscious. Probably bleeding. You were very convincing about the shock of seeing the car, but part of your shock was that she was waiting for you to come back.'

He rolled back in the chair and put his hands over his eyes.

'You didn't know who had beaten her up – all you

knew was that it was time to carry out your plan. So you drove behind the St Alwyn, let yourself in the back door, and carried her up the stairs to the second floor, beat her and stabbed her, and wrote BLUE ROSE on the wall. That's where you made a mistake.'

He took his hands off his eyes and let his arms drop.

'You used a blue marker. Hogan's markers were either black or red, the colors used to mark homicides as either open or closed on the Homicide Divison's board. I bet you went into the pharmacy in the old annex and bought the marker that night. When you killed Grant Hoffman, you got it right – you wrote BLUE ROSE with a black marker. You probably bought that one at the pharmacy, too, and threw it away later.'

'Jesus, you don't quit,' John said. 'So after I spend all night by her bedside, I suppose I got up the next morning and ran all the way down Berlin Avenue with a hammer in my hand, miraculously got into her room, killed her, miraculously got out, and then ran all the way back. And I managed to do all that in about fifteen–twenty minutes.'

'Exactly,' I said.

'On foot.'

'You drove,' I said. 'You parked on the street across Berlin Avenue so no one in the hospital would see your car, and then you waited on the lawn until you saw the night workers leave the hospital. The man who owned the property saw you out in front of his house. He could probably even identify you.'

John knitted his fingers together, propped his chin on them, and glared at me.

'You were going to lose everything, and you couldn't take it. So you cooked up this Blue Rose business to make it look as though her death were part of a pattern – you used some kind of story to sucker poor Grant Hoffman into that passage, and you tore him to pieces to make sure he'd never be identified. You're worse than

Hogan – he couldn't help killing, but you murdered two people for the sake of your own comfort.'

'So what do you think you're going to do now?' John was still glaring at me, his chin propped on his joined hands.

'Nothing. I just want you to understand that I know.'

'You think you know. You think you understand.' John glared at me for a moment – his feelings were boiling away within him – and then he pushed himself up out of his chair. He could not sit still any longer. 'That's funny, actually. Very funny.' He took two steps toward the wall of paintings and then slammed his hands together, palm to palm, not as if applauding, but as if trying to give himself pain. 'Because you never understood anything. You have no idea of who I really am. You never did.'

'Maybe not,' I said. 'Not until now, anyhow.'

'You're not even close. You never will be. You know why? Because you have a little mind – a little soul.'

'But you murdered your wife.'

He swung himself around slowly, the contempt in his eyes all mixed up with rage. He couldn't tell the difference anymore. His own bitterness had poisoned him so deeply that he was like a scorpion that had stung itself and kept on stinging. 'Sure. Yeah. If you choose to put it that way.'

He smoldered away for a second, waiting for me to criticize or condemn him – to prove once and for all that I did not understand. When I said nothing, he whirled around again and moved closer to the wall of paintings. For a moment, I thought that he was going to rip one of them off the wall and tear it to shreds in his hands. Instead, he thrust his hands into his pockets, turned away from the paintings, and marched toward the fireplace.

I got a single burning glance. 'Do you know what my life has been like? Can you even begin to imagine my life? Those two people – ' He got to the fireplace and whirled to face me again. His face was stretched tight with the sheer force of his emotions. 'The fabulous Brookners. You know what they did to me? They put me in a box and nailed it shut. They rammed me into a *coffin*. And then they jumped up on the lid, just to make sure I'd never get out. They had a high old time, up on top of my coffin. Do you even begin to imagine that those two people knew anything about *decency*? About *respect*? About *honor*? They turned me into a babysitter.'

'Decency,' I said. 'Respect. Honor.'

'That's right. Am I making sense to you? Do you begin to get the point?'

'In a way,' I said, wondering if he were going to make another rush at me. 'I can see how you'd feel like Alan's babysitter.'

'Oh, first I was April's. In those days, I was just Alan's little flunky. *Later*, I got to be his babysitter, and by then my wonderful wife was jumping into bed with that sleazy *kid*.'

'Which was indecent,' I said. 'Unlike luring your own graduate student into a brick alley and tearing him to pieces.'

John's face darkened, and he stepped forward and kicked at one of the wooden legs of the coffee table. The leg split in half, and the table canted over toward him, spilling books onto the floor. John smiled down at the mess, clearly contemplating giving the books a separate kick of their own, and then changed his mind and moved to the mantelpiece. He gave me a look of utter triumph and utter bitterness, picked up the bronze plaque, raised it over his head, and slammed it down onto the edge of the mantel. A chunk of veiny pink marble dropped to the floor, leaving a ragged, chewed-looking gap in the mantel. Breathing hard, John gripped the plaque and looked around his living room for a target. Finally, he picked out the tall lamp near the entrance, cocked back his right arm, and hurled the plaque at the lamp. It sailed past the lamp and clattered against the wall, where it left a dark smudge and a dent before dropping to the floor.

'Get out of my house.'

'I want to say one more thing, John.'

'I can't wait.' He was still breathing hard, and his eyes looked as if they had stretched and lengthened in his skull.

'No matter what you say, we used to be friends. You had a quality I liked a lot – you took risks because you believed that they might bring you to some absolutely new experience. But you lost the best part of yourself. You betrayed everything and everybody important to you for enough money to buy a completely pointless life. I think you sold yourself out so that you could keep up the kind of life your parents always had, and you have scorn even for them. The funny thing is, there's still enough of the old you left alive to make you drink yourself to death. Or destroy yourself in some quicker, bloodier way.'

He grimaced and looked away, balling his hands. 'It's easy to make judgments when you don't know anything.'

'In your case,' I said, 'there isn't all that much to know.'

He stood hunched into himself like a zoo animal, and I stood up and walked away. The atmosphere in the house was as rank as a bear's cage. I got to the front door and opened it without looking back. I heard him get to his feet and move toward the kitchen and his freezer. I closed the door behind me, shutting John Ransom up in what he had made for himself, and walked out into a sunny world that seemed freshly created.

5

Tom was sitting in front of his computer when I got back to his house, scratching his head and looking back and forth from the screen to a messy pile of newspaper clippings on his desk. Across the room, the copy machine ejected sheet after sheet into five different trays. There was already a foot-high stack of paper in each of the trays. He looked up at me as I leaned into the room. 'So you saw John.' It wasn't a question.

He nodded – he knew all about John Ransom. He had known the first time John came into his house. 'The papers will all be copied in another couple of hours. Will you give me a hand writing the note and wrapping the parcels?'

'Sure,' I said. 'What are you doing now?'

'Messing around with a little murder in Westport, Connecticut.'

'Play on,' I said. 'I have to get some sleep.'

Two hours later, I yawned myself back downstairs and used the office telephone to book my return flight to New York while the last of the sheets pumped out of the copy machine.

Tom swiveled his chair toward me. 'What should we say in the letter that goes along with the papers?'

'As little as possible.'

'Right,' Tom said, and clicked to a fresh screen.

I thought you should see this copy of the bundle of papers I found in the garbage can behind my store yesterday evening. Four other people are also getting copies. The originals are destroyed, as they smelled bad. The man who wrote these pages claims to have killed lots of people. Even

859

worse, he makes it clear that he is a police officer here in town. I hope you can put him away for good. Under the circumstances, I choose to remain anonymous.

'A little fancy,' I said.

'I never claimed to be a writer.' Tom set the machine to print out five copies and then went down to his kitchen and returned with big sheets of butcher's paper and a ball of string. We tied up each of the stacks of copied papers, wrapped them in two sheets of the thick brown paper, and tied them up again. We printed the names and working addresses of Isobel Archer, Chief Harold Green, and Geoffrey Bough on three packages. On the fourth, Tom printed BEHAVIORAL SCIENCE UNIT, FEDERAL BUREAU OF INVESTIGATION, QUANTICO, VIRGINIA.

'What about the fifth one?' I asked.

'That's for you, if you want it. I'd like to keep the originals.'

I printed my own name and address on the final parcel.

Millhaven's central post office looks like an old railroad station, with a fifty-foot ceiling and marble floors and twenty windows in a row like the ticket booths at Grand Central. I took two of the fat parcels up to one of them, and Tom carried two shopping bags with the others to the window beside mine. The man behind the counter asked if I was really sure I wanted to *mail* these monsters. I wanted to mail them. What were they, anyhow? Documents. Did I want the printed matter rate? 'Send them first class,' I said. He hoisted them one by one onto his scale and told me my total was fifty-six dollars and twenty-seven cents. And I was a damn fool, his manner said. When Tom and I left, the clerks were passing long spools of stamps across the wet pads on their counters.

We went back out into the heat. The Jaguar sat at a meter down a long length of marble steps. I asked Tom if he would mind taking me somewhere to see an old friend.

'As long as you introduce me to him,' Tom said.

6

At five o'clock, we were sitting downstairs in the enormous room in front of a television set Tom had wheeled out of the apparent chaos of file cabinets and office furniture. I was holding a glass of cold Ginseng-Up, three bottles of which I had discovered in Tom's refrigerator. I liked Ginseng-Up. You don't often find a drink that tastes like fried dust.

Alan Brookner had gained back nearly all of his weight, he was clean-shaven and dressed in a houndstooth jacket with a rakish ascot, his gold cufflinks were in place, and he'd had a haircut. I introduced him to Tom Pasmore, and he introduced us to Sylvia, Alice, and Flora. Sylvia, Alice, and Flora were widows in their late seventies or early eighties, and they looked as if they'd spent the past forty of those years shuttling between the hairdressing salon, yoga classes, and the spa where they had facials and herbal wraps. Because none of them wanted to leave either of the others alone with Alan, they left together.

'I have to hand it to John,' Alan had said. 'He found a place where I have to work to be lonely.' His voice carried across Golden Manor's vast, carpeted lounge, but none of the white-haired people having tea and cucumber sandwiches in the other chairs turned their heads. They were already used to him.

'It's a beautiful place,' I said.

'Are you kidding? It's gorgeous,' Alan boomed. 'If I'd

861

known about this setup, I would have moved in years ago. I even got Eliza Morgan an administrative job on the staff here – those girls are all jealous of her.' He lowered his voice. 'Eliza and I have lunch together every day.'

'Do you see much of John?'

'He came twice. That's all right. I make him uncomfortable. And he didn't appreciate what I did after I came to my senses, or whatever is still left of my senses. So he doesn't waste time on me, and that's fine. I mean it, it's hunky-dory. John is a little childish sometimes, and he has the rest of his life to think about.'

Tom asked him what he had done.

'Well, after I got acclimated here, I put my finances back in the hands of my lawyer. You have to be a man my age to understand my needs – you might not know this, but John has a tendency to get a little wild, to take risks, and all I want is a good income on my money. So I replaced him as my trustee, and I think he resented that.'

'I think you did the right thing,' I said, and Alan's dark, icy eyes met mine.

Tom excused himself to go to the bathroom.

'I think about John from time to time,' Alan said, lowering his voice again. 'I wonder if he and April would have stayed married. I wonder about who he really *is*.'

I nodded.

'Alan, there will probably be something on the news tonight that relates to April's death. That's all I can say. But it's likely to wind up being a big story.'

'About time,' Alan said.

I sipped my Ginseng-Up. Jimbo took off his glasses and looked out through the screen like Daddy bringing home news about a layoff at the plant. He informed us that a distinguished homicide detective had been found dead this morning in circumstances suggesting that the recent

862

upheavals in the Millhaven police department may not be over. Suicide could not be ruled out. Now to Isobel Archer, with the rest of the story.

Isobel stood up in front of the cordoned-off Beldame Oriental and told us that an anonymous tip about a gunshot had brought her here, to an abandoned theater near the site of the murders of April Ransom and Grant Hoffman, where she had persuaded the Reverend Clarence Edwards, the clergyman who rented the theater for Sunday services of the Congregation of the Holy Spirit, to look inside. In the basement she had discovered the body of Detective Sergeant Michael Hogan, dead of what appeared to be a single gunshot wound to the head. Beside Sergeant Hogan's body had been written the words BLUE ROSE.

What she said next made me want to stand up and cheer.

'This matter is now under intensive investigation by the Millhaven Police Department, but older residents of the city will note the chilling similarities between this scene and the 1950 death of Detective William Damrosch, recently exonerated in the Blue Rose murders of that year. Perhaps this time, forty years will not have to pass before the truth is known.'

Tom turned to me. 'Well, I'll keep you in touch, of course, but I bet you'll be able to read all about it in *The New York Times*.'

'Here's to Isobel,' I said, and we clinked glasses.

Long after the news was over, we went out to dinner at a good Serbian restaurant on the South Side – an unpretentious place with checked tablecloths, low lighting, and friendly, solicitous waiters, all of them brothers and cousins, who knew Tom and took a clear, quiet pride in the wonderful food their fathers and uncles prepared in the kitchen. I ate until I thought I'd burst, and I told Tom about the letter I was going to write. He asked me to send him a copy of the reply, if I ever got one. I promised that I would.

And when we got back to his house, Tom said, 'I know what we should put on,' and got up to pluck from the shelf a new recording of *A Village Romeo and Juliet* conducted by Sir Charles Mackerras. The music took us on the long walk to the Paradise Gardens. *Where the echoes dare to wander, shall we two not dare to go?*

At two o'clock, midday for Tom, we said good night and went to our separate rooms, and before noon the next day, after another long session of cathartic talk, we embraced and said our good-byes at Millhaven airport. Before I went through the metal detector and walked to my gate, I watched him walk easily, almost athletically, away down the long corridor, knowing that there was nowhere he would not dare to go.

PART EIGHTEEN

The Kingdom of Heaven

1

I returned to my life, the life I remembered. I worked on my book, saw my friends, took long walks that filled my notebook, read and listened to lots of music. I wrote and mailed the letter I had been thinking about, never really expecting a reply. I had been gone so short a time that only Maggie Lah had even noticed that I had been away, but Vinh and Michael Poole knew that my old habits, those that spoke of peace and stability, had returned, and that I no longer paced and churned out pages all through the night. Intuitive Maggie said, 'You were in a dark place, and you learned something there.' Yes, I said, that's right. That's just what happened. She put her arms around me before leaving me to my book.

The New York Times brought news of the upheavals in Millhaven. Detective Sergeant Michael Hogan first appeared on page A6, and within two days had moved to A2. The next day, there was another story on A2, and then he landed on the front page and stayed there for a week. Tom Pasmore sent me bundles of the *Ledger*, two or three issues wrapped up in a parcel the size of a pre-Christmas Sunday *Times*, and Geoffrey Bough and a lot of other Millhaven reporters filled in the details my own newspaper left out. Once the extent of Hogan's crimes became known, Ross McCandless and several other police officials retired. Merlin Waterford was forced out of office and replaced by a liberal Democrat of Norwegian stock who had been a Rhodes scholar and had a surprisingly good relationship with the African-American community, largely, I thought, because he had never, ever said anything even faintly stupid.

Some of the less lurid portions of Michael Hogan's diarylike notes were printed in first the *Ledger*, then the *Times*. Then some of what Hannah Belknap would call the gooshier sections were printed. *People*, *Time*, and *Newsweek* all ran long stories about Millhaven and Hogan, Hogan and Walter Dragonette, Hogan and William Damrosch. The FBI announced that Hogan had murdered fifty-three men and women, in Pensacola, Florida, where he had been known as Felix Hart, Allerton, Ohio, where he had been Leonard 'Lenny' Valentine, and Millhaven. There were short, carefully censored stories about his career as Franklin Bachelor.

Demonstrators packed into Armory Place all over again, marches filled Illinois Avenue, photographs of Hogan's victims filled the newspapers and magazines. From the cell where he was waiting for his trial, Walter Dragonette told a reporter that in his experience Detective Sergeant Hogan had always been a gentleman, and it was time for the healing to begin.

After a great deal of legal wrangling, eighteen innocent men were released from the jails where they had been serving life sentences. Two innocent men in Florida had already been executed. All eighteen, along with the families of the two dead men, filed monumental lawsuits against the police departments responsible for the arrests.

In September, a consortium of publishers announced that they were bringing out *The Confessions of Michael Hogan* as a mass-market paperback, profits to go to the families of the victims.

In October I finished the first draft of *The Kingdom of Heaven*, looked around, and noticed that the sun still beat down on the Soho sidewalks, the temperature was still in the high seventies and low eighties, and that the young market traders in the restaurants and coffee shops on the weekends were beginning to look like Jimbo on my last evening in my hometown. Daddy had come home with ominous news about layoffs. Some of the young men in the carefully casual clothes were wearing stubbly three-day beards and chain-smoking unfiltered Camels. I began rewriting and editing *The Kingdom of Heaven*, and by early December, when I finished the book, delivered it to my agent and my publisher, and gave copies to my friends, the temperatures had fallen only as far as the mid-forties.

A week later, I had lunch at Chanterelle with Ann Folger, my editor. No bohemian, Ann is a crisp, empathic blond woman in her mid-thirties, good company and a good editor. She had some useful ideas about improving a few sections of the book, work that I could do in a couple of days.

Happy about our conversation and fonder than ever of Ann Folger, I walked back to my loft and dragged out of the closet where I had hidden it my own copy of *The Confessions of Michael Hogan* – the parcel with my name and address on it that Tom Pasmore had mailed, one window away from me in Millhaven's central post office. It had never been opened. I carried it downstairs and heaved it into the Saigon dumpster. Then I went back upstairs and began work on the final revisions.

2

The next day was Saturday, and December was still pretending to be mid-October. I got up late and put on a jacket to go out for breakfast and a walk before finishing the revisions. Soho doesn't get as relentless about Christmas as midtown Manhattan, but still I saw a few

Santas and glittery trees sprayed with fake snow in shop windows, and the sound system in the cafe where I had an almond croissant and two cups of French Roast coffee was playing a slow-moving baroque ecstasy I eventually recognized as Corelli's Christmas Concerto. And then I realized that I was in the cafe where I'd been just before I saw Allen Stone getting out of his car. That seemed to have happened years, not months, before – I remembered those weeks when I had written twenty pages a night, almost three hundred pages altogether, and found that I was mourning the disappearance of that entranced, magical state. To find it again, if it could be found without the disturbance that had surrounded it, I'd have to write another book.

When I got back to my loft, the telephone started ringing as soon as I pushed the key into the lock. I opened the door and rushed inside, peeling off my jacket as I went. The answering machine picked up before I got to the desk, and I heard Tom Pasmore's voice coming through its speaker. 'Hi, it's me, the Nero Wolfe of Eastern Shore Drive, and I have some mixed news for you, so – '

I picked up. 'I'm here,' I said. 'Hello! What's this mixed news? More amazing developments in Millhaven?'

'Well, we're having a three-day snowstorm. Counting the wind chill factor, it's eighteen below here. How is your book coming along?'

'It's done,' I said. 'Why don't you come here and help me celebrate?'

'Maybe I will. If it ever stops snowing, I could come for the holidays. Do you mean it?'

'Sure,' I said. 'Get out of that icebox and spend a week in sunny New York. I'd love to see you.' I paused, but he did not say anything, and I felt a premonitory chill. 'All the excitement must be over by now, isn't it?'

'Definitely,' Tom said. 'Unless you count Isobel Archer's

big move – she got a network job, and she's moving to New York in a couple of weeks.'

'That can't be the mixed news you called about.'

'No. The mixed news is about John Ransom.'

I waited for it.

Tom said, 'I heard it on the news this morning – I usually listen to the news before I go to bed. John died in a car crash about two o'clock last night. It was the middle of the storm, and he was all alone on the east-west expressway. He rammed right into an abutment. At first they thought it was an accident, a skid or something, but he turned out to have about triple the legal alcohol level in his blood.'

'It could still have been an accident,' I said, seeing John barreling along through the storm in the middle of the night, clamping a three-hundred-dollar bottle of vodka between his thighs. The image was of endless night, almost demonic in its despair.

'Do you really think so?'

'No,' I said. 'I think he killed himself.'

'So do I,' Tom said. 'The poor bastard.'

That would have been the last word on John Ransom, but for a letter that I found in my mailbox, by the sort of ironic coincidence forbidden to fiction but in which the real world revels, late that same afternoon.

To get my mail, I have to leave my loft and go downstairs to the rank of boxes in the entry, one door away from the entrance to Saigon. The mail generally comes around four in the afternoon, and sometimes I get to the boxes before the mailman. Like all writers, I am obsessive about the mail, which brings money, contracts, reviews, royalty statements, letters from fans, and *Publishers Weekly*, where I can check on the relative progress of myself and my myriad colleagues. On the day I heard from Tom, I went down late because I wanted to finish up my revisions, and when I finally got downstairs I saw that the box was stuffed with envelopes. I immediately pitched into the big garbage can we had installed beneath the boxes all envelopes covered with printing, all appeals for funds, all offers to subscribe to esoteric literary journals published by universities. Two were left, one from my foreign agent, the other from some foreign country that liked exotic stamps. My name was hand-printed on the second envelope in clear, rounded letters.

I went back upstairs, sat at my desk, and peered at the stamps on the second envelope. A tiger, a huge fleshy flower, a man in a white robe up to his knees in a brown river. With a small shock, I realized that the letter was from India. I tore open the envelope and removed a single sheet of filmy paper, tinted rose.

Dear Timothy Underhill,
I am late in responding because your letter took an extra time to reach us here. The address you used was rather vague. But as you see, it did arrive! You ask about your friend John Ransom. It is difficult to know what to say. You will understand that I cannot go into details, but I feel that I may inform you that we at the ashram were moved by your friend's plight at the time he came to us. He was suffering. He required our help. Ultimately, however, we were forced to ask him to leave – a painful affair for all concerned. John Ransom was a disruptive influence here. He could not open himself, he could not find his true being, he was lost and blind in an eternal violence. There would have been no question of his being allowed to return. I am sorry to write these things to you about your friend, but I do hope that his spiritual search has after so many years finally brought him peace. Perhaps it has.
Yours sincerely,
Mina

3

Two days after receiving Mina's letter and faxing a copy
to Tom, my revisions delivered to Ann Folger, I walked
past the video store again, the same video store I had
been passing on my walks nearly every day since my
return, and this time, with literally nothing in the world
to do, I remembered that during my period of insomnia I
had seen something in the window that interested me. I
went back and looked over the posters of movie stars.
The movie stars were not very interesting. Maybe I had
just been thinking about *Babette's Feast* again. Then I saw
the announcement about the old noir films and
remembered.

I went into the shop and rented *From Dangerous
Depths*, the movie Fee Bandolier and I had both seen at
the Beldame Oriental, the movie that had seen *us* at the
moment of our greatest vulnerability.

As soon as I got home, I pushed it into the VCR and
turned on the television set. I sat on my couch and
unbuttoned my jacket and watched the advertisements
for other films in the series spool across the screen. The
titles came up, and the movie began. Half an hour later,
jolted, engrossed, I remembered to take off my jacket.

From Dangerous Depths was like a Hitchcock version
of Fritz Lang's *M*, simultaneously roughed up and dom-
esticated for an American audience. I had remembered
nothing of this story; I had blanked it out entirely. But
Fee Bandolier had not blocked it out. Fee had carried the
story with him wherever he went, to Vietnam, to Florida
and Ohio and Millhaven.

A banker played by William Bendix abducted a child

from a playground, carried him into a basement, and slit his throat. Over his corpse, he crooned the dead boy's name. The next day, he went to his bank and charmed his employees, presided over meetings about loans and mortgages. At six o'clock, he went home to his wife, Grace, played by Ida Lupino. An old school friend of the banker's, a detective played by Robert Ryan, came for dinner and wound up talking about a case he found disturbing. The case involved the disappearance of several children. Over dessert, Robert Ryan blurted out his fear that the children had been killed. Didn't they know a certain family? William Bendix and Ida Lupino looked across the table at their friend, their faces dull with anticipatory horror. Yes, they did know the family. Their son, Ryan said, was the last child to have vanished. 'No!' cried Ida Lupino. 'Their only child?' Dinner came to an end. Forty-five minutes later in real time, in movie time three days after the dinner, William Bendix offered a ride home to another small boy and took him into the same basement. After murdering the boy, he lovingly sang the boy's name over his corpse. The next day, Robert Ryan visited the child's parents, who wept as they showed him photographs. The movie ended with Ida Lupino turning away to call Robert Ryan after shooting her husband in the heart.

Tingling, I watched the cast list roll the already known names toward the top of the screen:

Lenny Valentine–Robert Ryan
Franklin Bachelor–William Bendix
Grace Bachelor–Ida Lupino

And then, after the names of various detectives, bank employees, and townspeople, the names of the two murdered boys:

4

I ejected the tape from the VCR and slid the cassette back into its box. I walked three times around my loft, torn between laughter and tears. I thought of Fee Bandolier, a child staring at a movie screen from a seat in the wide central aisle of the Beldame Oriental; probably it had always been Robert Ryan, not Clark Gable, of whom Michael Hogan had reminded me. At last I sat at my desk and dialed Tom Pasmore's telephone number. His answering machine cut in after two rings. At the end of a twenty-four-hour day, Tom had finally gone to bed. I waited through his message and said to the tape, 'This is the John Galsworthy of Grand Street. If you want to learn the only thing you don't already know, call me as soon as you get up.'

I took the tape out of the box and watched it again, thinking of Fee Bandolier, the man I had known and the first Fee, the child Fee, my other self, delivered to me at so many times and in so many places by imagination. There he was, and I was there too, beside him, crying and laughing at the same time, waiting for the telephone to ring.